D1389822

THE LAST
of the
RENSHAI

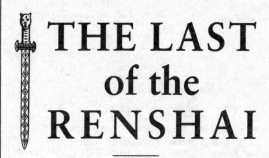

THE LAST
of the
RENSHAI

Mickey Zucker Reichert

MILLENNIUM
An Orion Book
LONDON

First published by DAW books, USA in 1992

First published in Great Britain in 1993 by
Millennium,
An imprint of Orion Books Ltd
Orion House,
5 Upper St Martin's Lane,
London WC2H 9EA

Interior map by Michael Gilbert

A CIP catalogue record for this book is available
from the British Library

ISBN (Csd) 1 85798 107 3
(Ppr) 1 85798 069 7

Millennium
Book Eight

Printed in Great Britain by Clays Ltd, St Ives plc

For Janny Wurts,
who helped make the dream a reality,
and for
The Thomas Jefferson Medical Class of 1985
who waited so patiently,
each believing in his own way

Acknowledgments

I would like to thank the following people for their contributions over nine years:

Sandra Zucker, Gary Reichert, Mimi Panitch, Sue Stone, Pat Lobrutto, Sheila Gilbert, and Ray Feist for recognizing a pearl in an oyster and encouraging me to find it.

To Joel Rosenberg and Barry Longyear for a well-timed slap. Also, Jonathan Matson and Dave Hartlage for their usual, thankless, heroic time and effort.

But not to Dr Mark Fabi, the only man in the world to fight me, sword to nunchaku, on an anatomy table.

In an age of change
When Chaos shatters Odin's ward
And the Cardinal Wizards forsake their vows
A Renshai shall come forward.

Hero of the Great War
He will hold legend and destiny in his hand
And wield them like a sword.
Too late shall he be known unto you:

The Golden Prince of Demons.

Crypts of Kor N'rual

Contents

Contents

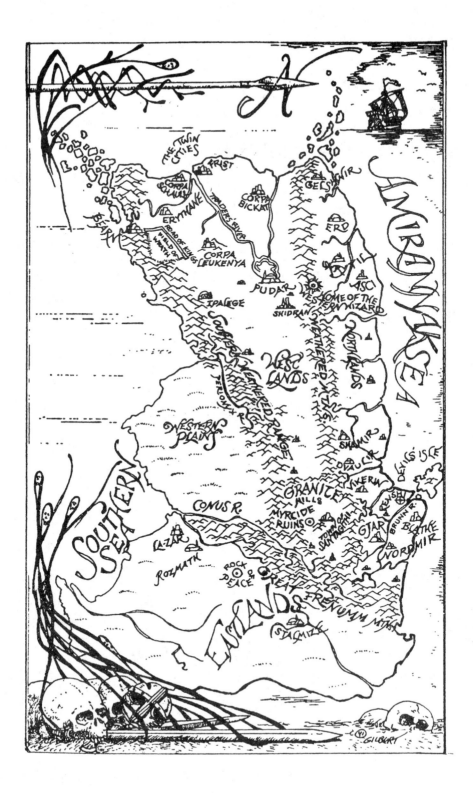

Meeting on the Wizard Isle

Year: 11,194
(Year 23 of the Reign of Buirane)

The Eastern Wizard, Shadimar, did not know how long he had sat with his elbows propped on the table in the Cardinal Wizards' Meeting Room and his bony chin cupped into his slender, wrinkled palms; but his hands had gone numb and long since ceased to register the cottony cascade of his beard between his fingers. The movements or stillness of his three colleagues had grown familiar beyond notice, and the only true mortal in the room, the bard Davrin, sat on the floor in his usual deferential silence, his mandolin cradled in his lap.

For the last seventy years, from the day Shadimar had become one of the four true mages, chronology had lost all meaning for him. At one time, a bird's flight across a meadow seemed to take days while, at another, an infant might come of age between Shadimar's breakfast and lunch. At first, these lapses had terrified him; a mad link in the chain of Eastern Wizards might harm the system that Odin the AllFather had created at the beginning of time and nurtured in the hundreds of centuries that followed. By his law, each of the four Cardinal Wizards selected his time to die in a glorious ceremony that passed his memories, and those of his predecessors, to his chosen successor. Thus, over time, the Wizards became stronger, more knowledgeable, and more powerful.

So far, that system had operated with reasonable precision. The original Wizards had been weak, essentially oracles and prophets. With Odin's guidance, they shaped and studied the world and its forces, found the best or most necessary courses of action, and created prophecies that their stronger successors would need to fulfill. Over eons, those visions had become clearer, and the abilities of the Wizards had grown to allow them to fulfill their own predictions. Now only the oldest and most unclear of the prophecies remained, spouted but little understood by the first Wizards, scrawled on cave walls, passed down in the legends of generations of mortals, or simply funneled through the memories of previous Wizards.

Shadimar remained unmoving, recalling how his near-immortality had muddled his time sense, making him fear that his contribution to the line of Eastern Wizards would be insanity. But, drawing on the memories of his predecessors, he discovered that nearly all of them had experienced a similar period of adjustment. Over the years, as he became more comfortable with his position as Wizard, Shadimar had grown accustomed to the leaps and pauses in time. He had learned to focus instead on the functions of the current Eastern and Western Wizards: to fulfill a handful of prophecies, to keep the mortal populaces believing in the gods and Wizards without violating Odin's laws of noninterference, and spreading the cause of neutrality by mediating between the Northern and Southern Wizards, who championed good and evil respectively.

The Southern Wizard, Carcophan, ceased his pacing and slammed a meaty fist on the tabletop. 'Enough of this waiting. He's not coming back. I say your man has failed the Tasks.'

Startled from his reverie, Shadimar jerked erect in his chair, riveting his steely gaze on the keeper and sower of the world's evil.

In the seat directly across the empty table, Tokar, the Western Wizard, remained still. His gray mane of hair and beard framed creased features and knowing, dark eyes that remained distantly fixed. Only a brief downward twitch of his lips revealed that the oldest of the Cardinal Wizards noticed Carcophan's interruption.

To Shadimar's right, the Northern Sorceress, Trilless, scowled with a revulsion aimed more at her impatient opposite than his sudden, violent gesture. She wore layers of silky white robes that frothed and folded around her slender frame, emphasizing her fair, Northern features and snowy hair. Pale from head to toe, she looked the epitome of the goodness she championed, almost to the point of caricature. Though the wait involved Tokar's apprentice, it was Trilless who answered the Southern Wizard's challenge. 'Be patient, Carcophan.' She cut off the words abruptly, as if to stay a natural urge to address the Evil One with an insult. It would accomplish nothing, except to make her seem the pettier of the two. Odin's laws forbade the Wizards from harming one another, especially on such impartial territory as the Meeting Isle, but the enmity between the Northern and Southern Wizards had grown beyond all proportion. 'I'm more than twice your age, yet I still remember when I underwent the Seven Tasks. The gods never made them easy. Don't begrudge Tokar's apprentice the time he needs to think.'

Shadimar nodded absently at the wisdom in Trilless' words. As intermediaries between the gods and men, it fell to the Wizards to select their apprentices, to choose not only for power and dedication to their god-assigned causes, but for stability and strength of character as well. To aid in the judgment, Odin had designed a series of seven god-mediated tasks to assess the worth and survivability of apprentices. Failure at any one resulted in death. According to Shadimar's predecessors, more than half of those sent to the Tasks did not return, yet Tokar's chosen, Haim, was the first to be tested since Shadimar himself. The Eastern Wizard was not quite certain what to expect, but patience seemed crucial.

Lost in his thoughts, Shadimar did not notice that Carcophan had come up beside him until the Southern Wizard stood only a hand's breadth from Shadimar and spoke into his face.

'And we wouldn't have to sit here in dark ignorance if you had placed the Pica Stone in capable hands.' The Southern Wizard's yellow-green eyes seemed to bore through his companion's gray ones. 'Through it, we could see every move that he makes, hear every syllable.'

Rage suffused Shadimar, the tragedy of Myrcidë still raw enough to incite anger in him. Before the Eastern Wizard had chosen him as successor, he had lived among his people, a reclusive race of priests, oracles, and minor magicians. During his apprenticeship, a Northern tribe of warriors, called Renshai, had rampaged through the Westlands, devastating the Myrcidians and leaving the world with no wizards except the Cardinal four and a handful of charlatans and fakes. He had left the clairsentient Pica Stone in the hands of his people, believing it safe there. The Renshai had plundered the huge sapphire, and it would violate Wizards' vows for Shadimar to take it back by force. He gathered breath to barrage Carcophan for his insensitivity.

Before Shadimar could speak, a presence touched his mind. Though calm and peaceful, it startled him into silence. Only the Wizards could communicate in this fashion, and then only with other Wizards. Yet it was considered disrespectful to the point of assault to enter another's mind without invitation.

Tokar did not probe or search. His voice filled only a tiny, shallow portion of Shadimar's mind. 'Best not to imitate the Evil One's weaknesses. You are above that.' Then the presence disappeared.

Shock shattered Shadimar's anger. Though Tokar had phrased his warning carefully, it still came as a surprise. It made sense for the oldest and wisest of the Wizards to advise the youngest and weakest, especially since the Eastern and Western Wizards shared the burden of balancing good and evil and protecting the peoples of the area known as the Westlands. Yet Tokar, like the Western Wizards before him, was the most powerful and aloof of the four. He had never previously chosen to communicate with Shadimar in this manner. The Eastern Wizard could only guess that the tension of discovering whether his chosen successor had passed the task touched Tokar more than his quiet exterior revealed.

Subdued and forgotten on the floor, Davrin strummed a string of chords on his mandolin, the sound barely audible in the silence that followed Carcophan's accusation. A square-cut shroud of gray-flecked brown hair hid the bard's dark eyes and placid features. He had no purpose in the ceremony except to observe and record like his mother before him and her father before her.

Put off by Shadimar's lack of response, Carcophan whirled toward Trilless, with a suddenness that sent his salt-and-pepper hair whipping into a wild tangle.

The Sorceress remained still, not sparing the Southern Wizard so much as a glance.

Carcophan edged toward her, presumably to agitate. But before he could take a second step, a door that had not existed a moment before opened in the far wall, and Tokar's apprentice appeared through it. Haim's normally rosy Pudarian features looked a waxy yellow. Though only in his mid-twenties, he now had white hairs hanging conspicuously among his dark curls. He seemed to have aged a century since the combined Wizards' magics had sent him to the Tasks earlier that same day. He tottered forward, eyes moist and features shaken.

Shadimar recalled his own success with the Tasks of Wizardry, remembered feeling triumphant, confident, and revitalized at the conclusion, despite the difficulty of the challenge. Scanning the memories of his predecessors, Shadimar found the same remembrance of their own trials. Concerned by Haim's weakness, Shadimar frowned, glancing at his colleagues questioningly.

Tokar and Trilless had raised icy lack of expression to an art form. Reading nothing on their faces, Shadimar turned his attention to the least patient Wizard. He glanced at Carcophan just in time to see the keeper of evil draw a dagger from the folds of his cloak. Carcophan lunged at the returning apprentice.

Haim recoiled with a gasp. Slowed by fatigue, he did not move quickly enough. Carcophan's knife jabbed through his robes at the level of his heart.

Instinctively, Haim clasped his chest, staring at the Southern Wizard in wide-eyed horror. He fell to one knee.

But the knife emerged bloodless, as Shadimar knew it must. There could be no wound. Those who survived the Seven Tasks could not be harmed by any object of Odin's world. Like the Cardinal Wizards, nothing short of the conjured magical creatures called demons or the

Swords of Power could harm Haim; though, until Tokar's passing, Haim could still fall prey to mortal illnesses and old age.

Carcophan returned his knife to its hiding place. Turning on his heel, he calmly strolled to his seat at the farthest end of the table from Trilless, chuckling beneath his breath along the way.

Haim rose with a slow shakiness that caused Shadimar to worry that the youth had survived the attack, only to die of fear. Trilless scowled, but she did not come to the aid of Tokar's apprentice. Any lessons or comforting must come from the Western Wizard.

The room lapsed into uncomfortable silence. Concerned by the weakness and insecurity of the one who would become trained to the position of Western Wizard, Shadimar discarded propriety and extended his mind to touch Tokar's. He hoped to catch a thread of the reason why Tokar had chosen Haim as his successor.

But Shadimar's projection entered only the most superficial corner of Tokar's mind, neatly enclosed by mental defenses he could never hope to defeat, even if he had wanted to enrage his stronger ally.

What is it you wish from me, Shadimar? Tokar kept his thought as patient as his person, yet the undertone rang through clearly. Shadimar's entrance into his mind was an ill-mannered intrusion.

Shadimar kept his answer general, not wanting to speculate too much while linked with Tokar. *I only wondered if there were things I should know about Haim.* He emphasized the pronoun to explain his use of nonverbal communication.

I think not. There was veiled annoyance beneath the response that quickly turned to bland caution. *I know him well enough to see things you do not. Haim is young. I have three or five decades to work on experience and confidence.* The Western Wizard made a subtle, dismissing gesture that bid Shadimar leave his mind.

Shadimar obeyed, not wholly satisfied with the explanation. As he withdrew, he thought he caught a faint feeling of doubt, but he could not be sure whether it came from the Western Wizard or as backlash of his own concerns. Tokar's composure did little to ease Shadimar's mind; tranquility was the Western Wizard's trademark. Should the newest in the line of Wizards prove too weak, the memories of his predecessors might overwhelm him. Of them all, this was especially true of the Western line. For reasons Shadimar could not fathom, Odin had decreed that it would always have the most power, while the Northern and Southern lines should stay equal, and the Eastern should remain the weakest.

Perhaps Tokar wants his successor to be feeble, so that he can overpower Haim from within and remain in control past his time. The thought seemed ludicrous. *Why would he do such a thing when he could simply wait to choose an apprentice and remain in power several more centuries?* Tokar had served as Western Wizard for longer than six hundred years; but according to Shadimar's inherited memories, others had remained in power nearly a millennium. Since each Wizard chose his own time of passing, there was no specific criterion for such a decision. At some point, each Wizard simply found the time right to expire, and only a rare one had lost his life early to demons or to one of the Swords of Power.

The silence grew unreasonably long, even for a meeting of near-mortals. Davrin did not strum, though his lips moved as he composed a song. Haim stood with his head bowed, waiting for his master to speak. Even Carcophan sat in stony quiet.

At length, Tokar broke the hush. 'You have finished the Seven Tasks of Wizardry.'

Shadimar frowned, even his vast patience tried. It seemed non-sensical for the Western Wizard to wait so long to voice a self-evident statement.

'I have,' Haim replied as formally.

'And the eighth task?' Tokar continued.

Now all the Wizards shifted forward to hear the answer, the rustle of robes and cloaks disrupting the stillness.

'There is no eighth task.' Haim parroted the instruction given to him just before the Cardinal Wizards' magic had sent him to face his destiny.

Tokar questioned further. 'But one was offered to you?'

'Yes.' Haim looked at the Wizards uneasily, specifically avoiding Carcophan's piercing, cat-like stare. 'The Keeper of the eighth task offered me a chance at ultimate power, even over the gods. As you advised, I refused it. There is no eighth task.'

Though often quoted among the Cardinal Wizards, the final statement was not wholly true, at least in Shadimar's experience. The decision to refuse or accept the task itself seemed a test of judgment. In the millennia since Odin had created the Tasks of Wizardry, no survivor of the tasks had ever chosen to attempt the eighth one. Shadimar had no way of knowing for certain, but it followed that some of the potential Wizards had tried the task. And it followed equally as naturally that every one who tried it had failed and died. Each Wizard held his or her own theory, but Shadimar believed that Odin had added the eighth task to protect the gods, the world, and the system of Wizardry. Surely, anyone interested in ultimate power could not be trusted to obey the many laws that hemmed in and restricted the Wizards, and he guessed that the simple act of accepting the eighth task meant failing it.

'Did the Keeper say anything more?' Tokar asked.

Every breath and movement became clearly audible as the silence waxed even deeper. Usually the Keeper did nothing more than offer the task. But when he did speak, his words were always of the greatest significance.

'He did,' Haim said. His gaze darted from rapt face to face. Apparently intimidated, he chose to focus on his master's feet as he spoke. 'He said that the age of change would begin during Shadimar's reign.'

Trilless gasped. It was the first time Shadimar had seen the keeper of all goodness lose her composure. Davrin clutched his mandolin so tightly his fingers blanched on the frets. Even Carcophan looked pale and shaken.

An ancient prophecy flashed into Shadimar's mind, words carved on a wall in the Crypts of Kor N'rual by the original Northern Wizard. Committed to writing, this first prophecy had survived the longest, known not only by the Wizards, but by the few adventurous Northmen who happened to explore the cliffs in the wilderness outside what had once been the tribal city of Renshi:

In the age of change
When Chaos shatters Odin's ward
And the Cardinal Wizards forsake their vows
A Renshai shall come forward.

Hero of the Great War
He will hold legend and destiny in his hand
And wield them like a sword.
Too late shall he be known unto you:

The Golden Prince of Demons.

Not all about the prophecy seemed clear, but one part left little doubt in any Wizard's mind. The age of change referred to the *Ragnarok*, the apocalyptic war that would result in the virtual destruction of all life, including the gods. Shadimar shivered. Certainly, against this threat, even Trilless and Carcophan would band together. And Shadimar reminded himself a hundred times in the next second that prophecies did not just occur by destiny; it was the Wizards' job to see them fulfilled.

Only Tokar seemed unaffected by Haim's pronouncement. 'The Keeper said *the* age of change, or *an* age of change?'

Haim shifted from foot to foot, looking like an errant child caught daydreaming during an important lesson. 'Master, I'm almost certain he said *the* age of change. He said that Carcophan would incite the Great War.'

Forgetting his manners, Shadimar interrupted. 'The Keeper mentioned Carcophan by name? And myself?'

Haim glanced as Shadimar. 'Yes, lord.'

'And us?' Tokar regained control of the proceedings with a warning glare at Shadimar. 'Did he say whether you or I would carry out the Western Wizard's portion of the prophecies?'

Haim whipped his attention back to Tokar. 'No, master. He did not mention either of us. Nor the Lady Trilless either.' He inclined his head to indicate the Sorceress. 'In fact, he said nothing more.'

Shadimar grappled with the information. Each Wizard knew his role in the Great War, though some in more detail than others. Parts of the prophecies had been lost; at least one premature death of a Wizard had interrupted both the Eastern and Southern lines, taking with them all previous memories. By piecing together legends and Wizards' writings, Shadimar knew that the Great War would pit evil against neutrality in the bloodiest battle the world had ever seen. Trilless' people, the Northmen, would have little or no involvement. The stories conflicted as to who would triumph.

Long contemplation of the Great War always frightened Shadimar. As the Eastern Wizard, his loyalties lay with the Westlands. Should evil win, nothing would stand between good and evil, and the wars would rage for eternity, or until one or the other triumphed. Yet if neutrality completely defeated evil, there would remain no force to equalize Trilless' good. The weakest of the Wizards cleared his throat. Should such a thing happen, goodness would lose all meaning, and he could not discount the possibility that the loss of symmetry alone would plunge the world into the *Ragnarok*. 'Colleagues, it's certain that nothing positive can come of the Great War. If either side wins, it would disrupt the very balance we were created to uphold.'

Tokar nodded his support without a trace of the passion that had filled Shadimar's words. Trilless said nothing. The matter did not involve her. A brief silence followed, shattered abruptly by Carcophan's laughter. 'Balance?' He laughed again, with malice. 'My Wizard's vows and duties say nothing of balance. But they do say that I must fulfill the prophecies set up for me by Southern Wizards down through eternity.' He rose, anticipation dancing in his yellow-green eyes. 'There will be a Great War, a bloody rampage like nothing your weak mind could imagine. If you choose not to oppose me, I will be disappointed, but it will only make my job that much easier.' Piece spoken, he rose from his chair and stomped out the only exit from the Meeting Room.

Surprised and crushed by the unexpected hostility of Carcophan's opposition, Shadimar said nothing. He had misjudged completely, and he needed time to understand his mistake. It had all seemed so clear to him. *Carcophan's refusal is folly. Surely even the Southern*

Wizard can see the danger. If the Ragnarok *annihilates the world, who will remain to espouse his beloved philosophies of evil?*

Trilless rose. Though slender and graceful, she maintained an aura of great power. 'It pains me to side with the Evil One, but he's right this time. Though he supports the wrong cause, he is as honor bound to Odin as any of us.' She glanced toward the door, obviously reluctant to remain on neutral territory while her opposite wove his evil into mortals unopposed. But the captain of the ship that carried the Wizards to and from the Meeting Isle was one of her own minions. He would not return Carcophan to the world without her presence to balance his. 'It's our duty to the gods to fulfill whatever prophecies our predecessors created. To abandon that duty would mean forsaking our Wizards' vows and would bring the very *Ragnarok* you intended to avoid.' Unwilling to wait any longer, she hurried after Carcophan.

Shadimar went utterly still. His neutral position surely gave him a clearer view of the consequences, and he could see nothing but disaster coming in the wake of the Great War.

Tokar rose, waving his apprentice to his side. 'Shadimar, don't let your fears for the masses make you lose sight of details. We are each honor bound to fulfill our own predecessors' prophecies, but nowhere does it state that we can't thwart one another. Carcophan can no more choose to suppress the War than you can let the high king's heir die. Yet we can oppose the Evil One even as we execute our own roles.' He headed through the door, Haim following in his wake, then turned back to voice a final thought. 'Odin constrained us so that our followers could remain free, heroes and victims of their own mistakes. We can only motivate; the mortals choose their routes and methods and create their own consequences.' He continued into the gloom, his last, soft statement nearly swallowed by position and distance. 'I believe there may be more to this Golden Prince of Demons than any of us knows.'

The Ragnarok *in my lifetime.* Shadimar let his chin sink back into his palms. Davrin played a gentle song of comforting, passed along and perfected across hundreds of generations. Yet today the melody fell on deaf ears. *We can only hope,* Shadimar brooded, *that my reign is infinite.*

Prologue

Year: 11,224
(Year 10 of the Reign of Valar Buiranesson)

Ten-year-old Rache Kallmirsson leapt and kicked and spun, his sword slicing arcs through the deepening dusk. Light flashed like a signal from the blade, as if it gathered the glow of the stars and crescent moon to scatter them from the silver of the steel or the gold of his close-cropped hair. An outsider might have been hard-pressed to differentiate whether Renshai-child or sword initiated each action, but to Rache every movement was his own, precise and directed. Called *Gerlinr*, the Renshai maneuver had a proper sequence of motion and balance; every deviation, no matter how slight, was a mistake that could spell the difference between life and death in combat. Each sweep, trip, or thrust was designed to cut down an enemy who had avoided the previous one, or to finish the opponent who had not blocked quickly enough.

Rache whipped the sword in a sidestroke, seeing nothing but the imagined form of an enemy before him, hearing only the crisp whistle of his blade through air. Like all Renshai, Rache was physically immature for his age, his blue eyes relatively wide, his head, body, and legs proportioned more like a seven-year-old than a boy who had reached double digits. Though honed and finely-balanced, his sword was small, lighter than the weapons the adults used, and the leather-wrapped hilt felt snug and proper in fists scarred from practice. Rache's strokes lacked the power his adult musculature might someday lend them, but it did not matter. The Renshai maneuvers were designed for speed and agility, and Rache had both beyond his years.

Rache sprang into the last sequence, snapped through a wild parry of a fancied enemy attack, then performed the final stroke. He ended in a well-set stance, prepared to cover his mistakes or his enemies' wiles, to defend or attack again. He held the position as if he had hardened to stone, reviewing each purposeful movement, every twitch. *I've mastered* Gerlinr. Self-esteem flooded through Rache, the innocent, shameless pride of a praised child. *Tonight is the night I move to the next class.* He sheathed his sword with reverence. The promotion would make him only the third of the ten children his age to advance to daylight training sessions. He knew a few younger ones had already surpassed him; one girl, scarcely five, had left her peers far behind. But the gods had granted her a rare natural dexterity and competence. Rache's progress pleased him.

Gradually, Rache lowered his concentration to let the remainder of the world in. The familiar scenery of Devil's Island filled his vision: swatches of evergreen woods interrupted by the cleared patches for cottages, cook fires, and sword lessons. Rache practiced too far inland to see the sheer cliffs enclosing the fjords or to hear the ceaseless crash of waves against shore, but he knew those things like the sight and sounds of his own parents. Across the Amirannak Sea, on the northern mainland, the other Northland tribes kept a wary truce with the exiled Renshai they hated.

Rache glanced at the moon through the thickening night, and its position in the sky drove all other thought from his mind. *Modi's wrath, I'm late!* Fear gripped Rache and swelled to self-loathing. He had never arrived late for a sword practice before. He ran, swerving between the towering trunks, shed needles crunching beneath his feet as if in accusation. His lateness went far beyond careless folly, it demonstrated disrespect for his teacher, his *torke*. So many years, Rache had pushed himself, hoping someday to earn the chance to be trained by Colbey Calistinsson, the most skilled sword master of the Renshai and, therefore, the best in the world. Now that dream had become reality, and Rache had proven himself unworthy of the honor.

Colbey! Tears pooled in Rache's eyes. The wind of his run splashed the liquid from his lids, and sweat trickled, salty, on his tongue. He sprinted toward discipline, and he was glad of it. *It's nothing more than I deserve.* An adult thought in a child's mind. For the Renshai, war training began in infancy, and it left no time for youthful play or fantasy. Rache was as much a man as a ten-year-old could be. And though he could not fathom the reason, he knew punishment would absolve his guilt.

Rache second-guessed Colbey's inflicted penalty. *Probably a one-on-one after practice.* The thought made Rache smile. A spar with the master served as a proper punishment for adults, especially those who had experienced combat and knew the importance of maintaining control at all times. Colbey's easy victory made them feel helpless and wretched, reminding them of the Renshai's second worst sin, disrespect for a *torke*, only one step below cowardice. But to Rache the idea seemed as much a treat as a penalty. He held Colbey in too high esteem to revile him as an enemy, even for the duration of the one-on-one. A spar would give Rache the opportunity to watch the beauty of Colbey's perfect dance, the grace of a live, golden flame in flawless harmony with his sword.

Guilt and anticipation blinded Rache to a growing red glow from the southern corner of the town. Even the acrid odor of smoke passed unnoticed. He skidded from the edge of the forest between two aging pines and into the practice clearing. Blurred by wind, tears, and sweat, Rache's gaze bypassed the massed group of flailing student swords, and he ran straight to the leader at the front, gathering breath for apology.

Rache slid to a winded stop. Damp grass mulched beneath his sandal, an agile sidestep all that spared him from a fall. He wiped moisture from his eyes and took a clear look at the *torke*. Instead of Colbey's cruel, gray eyes beneath a fringe of white-tinged golden hair, Rache met a glance as soft and blue as his own. Though blond as all Renshai, this *torke* sported the long braids of the warrior Northmen. Rache knew her as one of the finest sword mistresses on Devil's Island, but she was not Colbey. Rache stared, assailed by a mixture of confusion and unconcealed horror.

She stiffened, outrage etched into her features. 'You're late.'

Rache gaped. Her anger scorched him. He wanted to accord this *torke* all the honor she deserved, but she was not *his torke*. Colbey was beginning his sixth decade, ancient for Renshai, whose love of war rarely brought them through their thirties. *Colbey's sick; he's dying.* The worst possibility rushed to Rache's mind, filled it, and could not be banished. He could conjure no worse fate. Renshai died in glorious battle, their souls taken in honor to Valhalla to serve as Odin's *Einherjar*. Cowards died of illness and withered in Hel. *Colbey is a hero. The consummate hero. Surely he would have stumbled from his deathbed and challenged one of us. We could have given him the death in battle he deserved. And should he win the spar even through fevered delirium, I, for one, would be proud to die on his sword.*

'*Rack*-ee *Kall*-meers-son, defend yourself,' the *torke* demanded, distinctly enunciating every syllable of his name in her annoyance. The students paused in their practice, nudging one another and passing hissed comments. 'You're late, and I want to know why.'

Rache knotted his small, callused hands. He met the *torke*'s stare and tried to explain, but he managed only to gasp out his concern. 'Where's Colbey?' He spoke softly, then louder, almost in accusation, 'Where is Colbey?'

The *torke*'s cheeks went scarlet, and anger spread like a rash across her face. 'Rache, you disgrace your namesake!'

It was the basest insult anyone could hurl at a Renshai. Rache, like most Renshai, was named for a hero who had died in valorous combat, one whose soul would watch over him from Valhalla. It was an honor that had become all the more sacred as peaceful times had prevented the younger Renshai from attaining patrons. Rache recoiled as if slapped, hurt beyond physical pain. He cried, not caring who saw. He tried to sputter out the *torke*'s deserved apology, but concern channeled his thoughts in a single direction. 'Where's Colbey ? Please, just tell me, where's Colbey ?' He became aware of a distant sound, constant, muffled, and metallic. He attributed it to his own heart, though the rhythm seemed erratic.

The entire class had ceased its practice, apparently shocked by the exchange. The *torke*'s fist blanched around the hilt of her sheathed sword. 'Colbey's old enough to take care of himself. As for you, little man, you've delayed this lesson long enough. I believe – '

'Fire !' The cry cut over the *torke*'s tirade.

Rache sifted the speaker from among his classmates. The child stood with a finger jabbed toward the south, and every student turned in the indicated direction. Rache could see a small but angry collage of red, black, and orange flaring from a few thatched rooftops. Wisps of smoke swirled in the spring breeze, lost in the darkness but coloring the moon a sickly gray. The noises Rache had attributed to his heart resolved into the bell of sword-play.

The *torke* stiffened. A strange, unreadable expression crossed her features. 'We're under attack,' she said with unusual calm. 'Go. Go ! Warn your families. No one should be caught unaware.' A light blazed in her eyes, a pure, cruel joy of battle. She whisked her blade free.

As if it were a signal, seven strangers with swords and shields burst from the southern and eastern woods, their blades dripping scarlet rivulets.

The *torke* sprinted past the crowd of youngsters. She sprang for the warriors unhesitatingly, and the nearest students joined her.

Rache paused. It was not fear that held him ; he would not admit such an emotion even to himself. Renshai trained all their lives for death in battle. But the *torke* had told him to warn his family, and his cottage lay to the west. *Mama and Papa. My little sister.* Rache whirled and pounded into the evergreen forest.

The hollow crash of swords chased him between the pines, echoing from the trunks. Someone screamed in pain, 'Modi !' It was the name of a god, the son of the Renshai's patron, and it literally meant 'wrath.' Rache felt blood madness burn through him. It rose like instinct, though it came of intensive training. He had learned not to fight through injury, but because of it. A wounded Renshai became a crazed blur of battle, and his pain-cries spurred his fellows.

Rache's legs ached. The air tasted caustic, and his lungs felt raw and parched. A figure materialized before him. He paused to identify it as a stranger, and the hesitation nearly cost his life. A heavy sword slashed for his head. Rache ducked, drew, and raised his blade to parry. Steel scratched steel. Momentum staggered Rache forward, and his follow-through drew the enemy sword harmlessly over his back. A carefully-timed backswing gashed the enemy's thigh. The man's leg buckled, and he collapsed. Rache continued running without looking back.

The woods seemed to close in on Rache, blotting the meager light of the moon. He sprinted over the paths from memory, racing toward home and the sounds of battle growing louder.

'Modi !' The cry came from ahead, in the voice of Rache's sister. His heart leapt, despite the anguish in the shout. *I'm getting closer. They weren't caught asleep.* Without enough breath for a battle cry, Rache burst from the woods. Moonlight dazzled him, intensified by a myriad reflections off swords and shields. Some of the enemy wore chain shirts that hung to their knees, but the Renshai disdained armor, shields, and bows as cowards' toys. Swords dulled red with blood capered like living things, a fierce chaos of slash and counter. Even the youngest Renshai outmaneuvered the enemy, Northmen each one, but Rache counted four invaders for every friend.

A blade sliced for Rache's chest. He blocked, catching a stroke so powerful, his hands stung with the impact. Ignoring the pain, he bore in. He slammed his foot onto the enemy's, crashed his knee into the groin. The Northman off-balanced. Pressing his advantage, Rache cut for the neck. Before the blow could fall, a hand clapped to Rache's forehead, and strong arms ripped him backward. Rache toppled, scarcely managing to keep hold of his sword. A blade in his new opponent's hand whisked for his face. Rache parried, rolling to his feet. A back-step realigned him, an enemy to either side.

Both sprang at him. Rache lunged, in a feint, for the man who had felled him. The other made a wild attack for Rache's unshielded back. At the last instant, Rache spun and slashed at the one behind. The sword whisked beneath the shield, opening the man's gut. He crumpled as Rache whirled back to his other opponent with a frantic sweep meant only to force the enemy back.

They squared off. Smoke burned Rache's eyes, and he gasped for each hot, dry breath. His chest felt on fire ; his lungs rattled as if filled with blood. Beyond his opponent, there was no sign of his sister. He could see his mother engaged with three Northmen. His father, Kallmir, wove an agile web of steel between himself and his single opponent, driving his Northman to the edge of the woods.

Rache lunged.

Suddenly, Kallmir spun and caught Rache's enemy by the hair. With a single stroke, he decapitated the Northman before placidly returning to his own battle.

Rache pulled his own thwarted thrust, for the moment without an adversary. He turned, scanning the masses for an enemy, when a hand closed over his own. He whirled, sword poised, recognized his mother and held the blow. 'Mama?'

Sweat plastered yellow ringlets to her forehead. Her raised brows and the crinkles in her young face revealed an internal struggle. Her eyes looked as glazed as a becalmed sea, and her taut expression frightened him. 'Rache, come with me.' She dragged at his wrist, drawing him away from the battle.

Rache tripped hesitantly after her. 'Mama?' Her behavior made no sense to him. To run from combat was cowardice. Already, a new wave of Northmen had joined the fray, and a chorus of 'Modi's' rose like echoes in a dozen different voices, each spurring Rache back to the fight. 'Mama!'

Rache's mother shifted her grip from his flesh to the material at the back of his tunic. She yanked, breaking into a trot, hauling an unwilling Rache behind her. 'Rache, come with me. Just come with me.'

Rache staggered.

A moment later, Kallmir drew up, panting, beside them. 'What are you doing?'

No answer. His mother broke into a ragged run, Rache bouncing along with her.

'What the hell are you doing?' Kallmir was shouting now. 'You're setting a bad example. There's a war!'

'I have my reasons,' she snapped back. Her pace quickened.

Rache howled, struggling now. *My mother's gone insane.*

A band of Northmen closed in from the east. Another chased the retreating Renshai, their battle calls frenzied and hungry as wolf howls.

'There *are* no reasons for cowardice!' Kallmir screamed something else Rache could not hear, but his mother's answer came clearly to him.

'The prophecy at Kor N'rual. The Northern Sorceress' prophecy. A Renshai must fight at the Great War.'

'A prophecy!' Kallmir shouted over the roar of flame and the victory cries of pursuing Northmen, growing closer with every step. 'You would damn yourself and my child to Hel for a prophecy that bodes as much evil as good? Let the Wizards handle their own damned prophecies. The West is their concern, not ours. We owe them nothing. Nothing! Every life in the Westlands is not worth the cost of one Renshai soul.' He whirled suddenly, hurling himself onto the growing crowd of Northmen. For several seconds, Rache saw his father's blade skip through the masses, flinging blood. Then Kallmir disappeared beneath the charge without so much as a dying cry. The Northmen's pace scarcely slackened. Shore sounds wafted, soft beneath the shouts and the pounding feet.

'Papa!' Rache bucked against his mother like a madman.

'Rache, no.' She stumbled, and Rache's tunic tore.

He sprang toward the battle, but his mother caught her balance and a fresh grasp. The noise of waves smashing rock sifted beneath the din of swordplay. Rache jarred backward, slipped, and his mother dragged him several steps further. The Northmen closed the gap between them.

'Turn and fight!' Rache flailed. *Death in glory. A place in Valhalla.* Rache had learned his lessons well. 'They're coming closer.' He lunged, pulled up short by his mother's grip, but his sword buried itself in a Northman's gut.

Rache's mother tripped him, heaving him backward. The sword ripped from his fist, sheering off calluses. Something sliced his side, flashing pain across his abdomen. Rache tumbled, and suddenly, there was nothing but air beneath him. The cliff faces of the fjord blurred past. Before he could react, even in panic, he crashed into the depths. Water spewed over him. Darkness pressed him, his consciousness jerking and swaying. He clawed to the surface, feeling the bubbles churned by his fall. The ebb tide dragged at him.

'Modi!' His mother's scream echoed in the cavern. She crashed to a ledge, lying still, awkward and broken.

Stunned by the fall and the battle, Rache made no sound. He swam into the shadow of a cliff face and clung there, his ears full of voices amplified by the towering stone, Northmen's words in the high king's tongue.

'Did someone get the child?'

'Sigurd's blow knocked him off the fjord. Then the woman killed Sigurd.'

A third voice: 'The boy's dead.'

A new man continued the conversation. 'Well, someone get down there and find the body, or it'll cost us. Never saw a Renshai run from swordplay.'

One spat. 'Cowards all. Dead cowards now.'

The voices receded.

The salt of the Amirannak Sea stung Rache's hand and the gash in his side. Ghosts of blood curled into the water. And Rache began to cry.

Rache awakened bruised and battered in every limb, and the pain throughout his entire body made the superficial gash in his side seem trivial. Despite the spring weather, he felt chilled, his clothing soaked through, his skin macerated. He moved, feeling grit and seashell fragments shift beneath him. He opened his eyes and discovered only dark sand; he lay, facedown on the shore. Gradually, memory returned. He recalled swimming, longer, harder, farther than ever before. Disoriented by the darkness, Rache was caught by the mainland tide, tossed repeatedly against the cliffs, fighting at first from strength of will, then only from habit. Dimly, he remembered finding the open beach, hauling himself across the sand like a cripple, and there surrendering to a deeper darkness.

Rache twisted his head. The midday sun glazed into his vision, blinding him. He flicked his lids closed and sank back to the sand. Other memories assailed him then: hungry red flames consuming the only world he knew as home; death screams in wild, savage triumph; the silver clang and beat of swordplay that was deadly, beautiful music to the Renshai. Rache's fists cinched violently around sand, shell shards biting into his palms. Again, he saw his father, silently trampled beneath a mass of flying swords, his mother's shattered form on the cliffs, his sister's death nothing but a pain cry in his memory. Tears rose, washing grit from Rache's eyes, but he fought them down. *My parents died in valorous combat. The brave dead should be glorified, never mourned.* Though Rache believed the tenet, it was not enough to hold grief at bay. Faith stricken, he ground his face into the sand, besieged by a single, unspoken question: *Why did I survive?* But the answer came in a thousand different voices. It was the breath of the wind, the swish of the receding tide, the steady pounding of his own heart: *Because, Rache Kallmirsson, your mother was a coward.*

'No!' Rache shouted at no one, and his words emerged hoarse as a whisper. His hands spasmed, grinding the jagged fragments deeper into flesh. Guilt knotted in his gut, twisting with a pain worse than his strained and hammered muscles, the salt-rimed sword scratch or the bloody tears where calluses had torn loose from the palmar pads below each finger. Little of what had happened made sense to Rache. He had been told a Renshai named Episte was stationed in the high king's city of Nordmir to uncover plots and inform the Renshai of coming attacks. But the Northmen had struck without warning. His mother had mentioned the need to fulfill a prophecy; yet Rache had always thought of prophecies as Wizards' glimpses into a future already predetermined by the Fates, not events mortals must fulfill. And his father's comment, that this prophecy boded as much evil as good, gnawed at Rache. Still, his mother had sold not only her life but her soul for him; and Rache had no choice but to survive. *Maybe, if I can spend my own life bravely enough, the gods may find it possible to forgive her.*

Rache uncurled his fists and rose to his hands and knees. Pain rocked through him. His vision spun, but he held the position, strengthened by another thought. *If Colbey was, in fact, on his deathbed, surely he found an opportunity to die in combat rather than of illness.* Rache staggered to his feet, gritting his teeth against the myriad aches inspired by the movement. Pain, at least, he understood.

Rache had lost his sword at the fjord, his sheath and sandals in the sea. Without the weapon he had carried since infancy, Rache felt naked despite the gashed and tattered tunic and breeks that, though grimed with sand and sour with old water, still covered him adequately enough. The taste of salt made him crave fresh water, and grit grated between his teeth. *Where do I go?* Rache turned his thoughts to his own survival, glad for the excuse to push memory to the background. Details receded, leaving a wake of sorrow.

Cold, alone, empty, Rache considered his next course of action. Obviously, hunger and thirst took precedence. The Renshai skills were few and specialized: swordsmanship, warcraft, medicine to protect the wounded from becoming infected and to heal the sick so they could live long enough to die in battle with dignity. In the warring years, the Renshai had gathered their food from the stores, herds, flocks, and gardens of their victims. In the subsequent twenty years of peace on Devil's Island, they had turned to more mundane means. Rache knew how to hunt and fish, to gather certain roots and berries that graced the evergreen forests on the island. But without a bow, nets, or boats and ignorant of mainland plants, Rache found his knowledge woefully inadequate.

Needing a goal, Rache chose to head for the high king's city. There he might uncover details of the battle; if other Renshai lived, he would need to track them down. There was still the Renshai, Episte, to find, though likely the king had discovered the spy in his castle. That would explain why the older Renshai had not warned his people of the Northmen's attack.

Choosing a destination proved the easiest of Rache's decisions. The history, linguistic, and geography lessons that supplemented Rache's sword practices supplied enough information for him to know the Northmen lived from the Amirannak Sea to the Weathered Mountains, the Great Frenum Mountains to the east and across the continent to the west. The vast majority of the Northern tribes congregated around the Brunn River in the easternmost part of the territory. There were eighteen tribes, each with its own king who swore fealty to the high king in Nordmir. Uncertain on which side of the Brunn his swim had taken him, Rache could only guess the path to Nordmir.

Over the next few days, the quest for food proved consuming enough to keep Rache's thoughts from the past. He appreciated the distraction, though it meant he often slept with his stomach empty and aching or spasming with cramps from some strange plant or berry that turned out to be weakly poisonous or indigestible. Where forest broke to farmland, he stole the rare chicken or fruit and grain stores when he could find them, but the spring plants had barely sprouted, and the fields were barren. Even in the harvest season nature was never kind to the Northlands.

By the seventh day of his journey, grime had replaced the sand on Rache's face and clothing. His tunic hung, too large over jutting ribs, and his breeks bunched on his legs, itchy from dried salt. Rache struggled from the forest for what seemed like the hundredth time. But this time, instead of a young field or a pasture of goats nearly as lean as himself, he discovered a road scarred with wheel ruts and pitted by the passage of hooves and feet. A path this well used could only lead to a major city, likely Nordmir. Rache smiled, then, just as quickly, he frowned. He was uncertain where he had beached, and his geographical knowledge was sketchy at best. The sun had barely started its downward slide, and Rache could see the road ran east and west. Until now, he had traveled south.

Rache rubbed pine needles from his hair, longing for a bath. The sun hurt his pale eyes, making him squint, so he chose to travel east and keep the light at his back for now. Wary, he kept to the edges of the forest, skulking between the trees like an animal. The pungent reek of a campfire touched his nose. Rache froze. So far, he had not seen a single person on his travels, though the farms he passed had been well-tended. Silently, he faded back into the woods, creeping toward the smell. Gradually, the sweet aroma of roasting meat and tubers reached him from beneath the more acrid scent of the fire. Rache's belly groaned hollowly. He had not eaten since morning, and then it had only been a handful of bitter flowers. His previous meal had come more than a day earlier.

Rache turned a curve in the roadway and, suddenly, he caught sight of a wagon parked on the path. Its unharnessed horse grazed the weeds on the roadside. A tent jutted over the cart bed, and fabric whisked against canvas as something moved about inside. Peering out between the tree trunks, Rache spotted the fire in a ditch beyond the horse. Brown potatoes interrupted the checkered pattern of the coals, and a small duck roasted on a spit. Fat dribbled from the meat, hitting the embers with a series of sharp hisses.

Rache knew any Northman who discovered his heritage would kill him on principle, but hunger made him bold. He slunk toward the camp, his gaze darting around the site. He saw no one, and the rustling in the cart continued. The greasy odor of the duck grew stronger, bringing saliva to Rache's mouth, though his jaw felt pinched. Before he could think, he had a stick in his hands, but he hesitated, still two arms' lengths from the fire. *If I take this man's food, then he'll go hungry.* Rache sucked in his cheeks, not wanting to inflict his own misfortune on another. On Devil's Island, he would never have considered stealing food, nor would he have found need; any Renshai would share with his own. But Rache was no longer among Renshai, perhaps never again. Now he knew only enemies who attacked like jackals, in unsporting numbers, unannounced, and at night, and then dared to call the Renshai, the chosen of Thor's wife Sif, cowards.

Anger flared, driving through Rache's guilt. He shuffled the last few steps toward the fire and thrust the stick among the coals. Even then, he could not bring himself to take much. He looped the tip of the stick behind one potato and levered it over the coals. It rolled to the edge of the fire. Another poke, and it spilled free onto the dirt.

A creak from the cart drew Rache's attention. He glanced up in time to see a heavyset, blond man emerge from the tent. His head turned toward the fire.

Rache dropped his stick, darted forward, and seized the potato. It burned his fingers. He nearly dropped it, but squeezed it tighter and ran.

'Hey !' the man called after him. 'Hey !'

Rache bounded over a deadfall, dodged between closely spaced trunks and skidded around a moss-covered boulder. Hearing no sounds of pursuit, he squatted and thrust an end of the potato into his mouth. It singed his palate and tongue, and he tasted coal dust and dirt, but he continued eating. The white of the vegetable crunched, hard and grainy between his teeth, only partially cooked. But it was still the best thing he had eaten in days, and he bolted it. Even so, it scarcely grazed his hunger.

Rache lowered himself to the ground, sitting on layers of shed needles. He stared at his hands, the right with grime caked into the hollows of his sloughed calluses, the left still with horny buttons at the base of each finger but stinging where the potato had burned it. Scabs, abrasions and tears marred the back of his hands and knuckles. He rubbed his face, feeling the sharper cheekbones, his eyes sunken back, and the skin loose beneath his lids. It seemed as if he had touched a stranger's features rather than his own. *So this is what my mother's soul has bought.* Rache hung his head in shame and despair. The wind chilled over him, and rain began, pattering down across the blanketing umbrella of trees as if in mockery. His people, dead in war, killed in the wild blaze of glory they sought. And Rache, who might be the last of the great Renshai, sat wasting in the lands of his enemy, swordless, reduced to petty theft.

The rain intensified to a steady, reviling thrum, exposing Rache to his own ugliness. He had killed his first warrior in the battle; blooded, by Renshai law he was not a child but a man. *A man. A Renshai!* A spark of defiance rose, flared, and grew with the roar of the rain. *I'll go to the high king's city and find out about my people. There, I'll get a sword any way I can. From that time on, I won't go hungry again.* Rache sprang to his feet. *Until then, I have to get food. If that means stealing from Northmen, so be it.*

Rache headed back toward the trader's campsite, first quickly, then more slowly as he spied the thread of smoke winding through the trees. Near the forest's edge, Rache hunched behind a wall of dwarf pine, staring through a gap. The heavyset man now sat on a log before the fire, worrying at a drumstick. The moist air smelled thick and greasy, and each raindrop hissed onto the fire.

Too late. Sick with the aroma of food and the knowledge he would go hungry again tonight, Rache dropped back to his haunches. His movement shook the trunk, showering him with a spray from the branches. Rache sputtered, back-stepping. Then, he caught sight of a flat scrap of tin resting on a log a short distance from the fire. It held part of a breast and wing of the duck and a steaming potato. Rache froze. *Another man? I didn't see one.*

Rache glanced toward the wagon. The horse continued grazing, its red-brown fur darkened with water. Rain pooled into a sag in the canvas roof. Rache neither heard nor saw any sign to suggest the trader traveled with a companion. *Maybe he's out in the woods.* Concerned, Rache whirled, ears tuned for the rattle of brush beneath the rain. Hearing none, he grew bolder. Eyes fixed on the trader who seemed intent on his own supper, Rache crept toward the food.

Rache's soaked and tattered clothing shifted and clung with every movement. He placed his toes carefully on the rain-slicked needles. He could feel his heart pounding in his throat. He was just reaching for the plate amid a rising sense of triumph when the trader glanced up.

Rache shrank back, tensed to run.

The trader did not move. He spoke softly. 'The food is yours. I just want to talk.'

Rache fidgeted uncertainly. He glanced around to make certain the trader was not distracting him from some companion who was preparing to grab Rache from behind. Seeing no one, he looked back. The golden-brown skin of the duck enticed.

'Go ahead, boy,' the heavyset man said. 'You must be hungry.'

Edging forward, Rache seized the wing. It felt warm and oily in his fist, slicked with rain. He took a bite, unable to recall a time when meat tasted so good.

The trader dropped a bone to his own plate, licking each finger. 'Can you cook, boy?'

Rache shook his head, chewing furiously.

'Can you set a camp?'

This was more familiar to Rache. He nodded, taking another bite of the duck. Again, he peeked behind him and saw no one.

'Do you know how to tend a horse?' The trader gestured at the chestnut in the ditch.

Again, Rache nodded. Some of the Renshai war techniques were performed from horseback, and Devil's Island had its share of horses. Rache had heard that those horseback combat maneuvers not invented by Colbey were perfected by him. Late one night, Rache had seen Colbey leaping from beast to beast, his sword a flying blur. One horse had pitched him to the dirt, the first and only time Rache had seen his *torke* fail at anything. Though he had had no reason to believe anyone watched, Colbey had slashed, rolled, and remounted without skipping a beat.

Unaware of Rache's reverie, the trader continued. 'Then I propose a deal. You take care of the camp and the horse. In return, I'll let you ride along with me, give you a place to sleep out of the rain, and feed you as much as you can eat. Is it a deal?'

Rache gnawed the last scrap of meat from the bone, his stomach churning at the food with the same vigor as his mouth. The agreement seemed too good to be true, yet previous experience gave him no reason to mistrust. A small, close-knit tribe, the Renshai did not cheat one of their own, and Rache had had no exposure to mainland trade or diplomacy. Renshai combat training focused on individual skill, not wile or strategy. Still, Rache considered.

'Well?' the trader pressed. Apparently interpreting Rache's hesitation as suspicion, he rose nonthreateningly, raising his hands to demonstrate he held no weapons. 'I didn't have to feed you. If you refuse to help me, I won't do it again, I promise.'

Familiar with the sign language, Rache's eyes naturally drifted to the stranger's hip where no sword hung. He bit into the potato, irrationally afraid the trader might reclaim it. 'Where are you headed?' The thin quaver of Rache's voice surprised him. He had not spoken aloud since the battle.

The trader dumped the bones from his plate. His muddled gray-green gaze swung toward Rache, unreadable. 'Nordmir. The king's city. I've got some trading and selling to do there. I'm a tinsmith.' He made a stiff-fingered gesture of greeting. 'Arvo Ranulfsson of the Gjar.'

Rache returned the salute. 'Rache,' he said and immediately wished he had not. Like most of the Renshai names, 'Rache' was nonspecific among the Northern tribes; but the Renshai's custom of calling newborns after their own dead had limited their pool of names. He left off his sire's name, probing his memory for a distant tribe unlikely to be closely tied or at war with the Gjar. 'I'm Varlian.' Rache held his breath, waiting for Arvo to challenge his claim. But if the trader saw through Rache's lie, he made no sign.

'Very well, Rache.' Arvo spoke in a mid-Northern accent, clipping the final syllable of Rache's name so it sounded more like a breath than a sound. 'I'll take care of the plates, you hitch up the horse, and we'll be on our way.'

Rache gulped down the last morsel of potato, feeling better and more energetic than he had in days. He had never harnessed a horse before, but the system of straps and poles proved easy enough to figure out. Within a few short moments, he had the horse tied in. Glancing up, he discovered Arvo on the driving seat, patting the bench beside him. Rache climbed up beside Arvo, the trader clucked, shaking the driving reins, and the horse started down the roadway.

At first, the strangeness of the territory kept Rache tensed and coiled, and every bounce of the cart's wheels jangled his tightly drawn nerves. As the hours passed, the bump and jounce of the wagon grew familiar. The rhythmical chitter of the rain against the canvas lulled him. Arvo began talking of his travels the instant Rache swung into his seat, and the tinsmith scarcely seemed to stop for breath. As Rache relaxed, he listened. Though Arvo used words as mundane as the lands in which he traded, Rache's ignorance of any place but Devil's Island stimulated his imagination. His mind added the pageantry Arvo's descriptions lacked.

For Rache, the hours went by in dry contentment. Protected from the rain, his belly full, he reveled in the damp odors of evergreen, canvas, and horse. Attention on Arvo's ceaseless droning, Rache let the tragedy of the previous week slip from his mind, reminded of it only once. That evening, over a dinner of jerked lamb, Arvo talked about the son who had once performed the tasks for which he had hired Rache. 'Scarcely thirteen, but as cocksure of his abilities as any child.' Arvo's oddly colored eyes blurred with tears. 'He chose to fight his first battle against Renshai and died on Devil's Island.'

Rache stiffened, as much confused as horrified. He wanted more information, particularly about his people. But even at ten, Rache was dimly wise enough to know Arvo's thoughts focused on his son, not his enemies. Crying for a hero killed in battle made no sense to Rache. 'At least he died in glory.' He spoke the platitude from habit, shocked when it seemed to goad Arvo to further tears.

Arvo's words rattled in his chest. 'When they found his body, he was . . .' Arvo paused, his face lapsing into grieving wrinkles.

Rache waited, certain Arvo's next word would explain his sorrow.

'. . . headless,' Arvo whispered.

Rache cringed, aware, as were all Northern warriors, that the loss of a major body part would bar the soul from Valhalla, no matter how heroic the death. Nearly a century and a half ago, the Renshai's habit of dismembering the dead to shatter morale during border skirmishes had led to their exile and a hundred years of wandering without a country. Rache lowered his head, sharing the father's anguish. Even the understanding that Arvo's son had died, an enemy of the Renshai, could not stay Rache's sadness. 'I'm sorry,' he said. And he meant it.

Arvo recovered quickly. They continued their journey until dusk touched the horizon, then Arvo pulled up the horse, jumped down, and signaled Rache to take care of the beast.

Rache clambered to the ground, raindrops falling coldly on his scalp. Shortly, he had the horse unhitched, hobbled, and cropping calmly at the roadside grass. He returned to the wagon and nearly collided with Arvo, who clutched a coil of thin rope. 'What's this?' Rache asked.

'I'll let you sleep in the wagon where it's dry.' Arvo's voice emerged matter-of-factly, without a trace of apology or discomfort. 'I need to tie your hands while I'm sleeping.'

Rache shied, tripping over the cart pole. He clutched at the wagon to catch his balance. 'Tie me? Why?' This was a matter he'd never considered. The thought of allowing a near-stranger to bind him filled him with dread. Still, he liked Arvo. The tinsmith had given him much in exchange for very little, and Arvo's casual manner made it seem like a routine request.

Arvo stood where he was, not pressing. 'I've got valuables in the back. I can't take a chance on those things disappearing while I'm sleeping.'

Insulted by Arvo's mistrust, Rache defended himself. 'I wouldn't take anything.'

Avro shook the rope, and the loops swung in shallow arcs. 'You already stole from me once. I can't afford to take the chance.'

Rache flattened against the wagon, not wanting to be tied but unable to come up with a suitable compromise. He enjoyed the company and needed the shelter and the food. The horse cart would carry him to the king's city faster and more comfortably than walking, especially since Rache did not even know the route. Still, the thought of sleeping, bound and helpless, broke his flesh into a cold sweat.

Arvo met Rache's stare, gently but unyieldingly. 'If I wanted to hurt you, I could have done so already.'

Rache conceded. He moved toward Arvo, holding his hands out before him, hoping the gesture alone would convince Arvo.

But the tinsmith granted Rache no quarter. He wound the rope around Rache's wrists tight enough that Rache could not separate his hands without the cord biting flesh. Unable to reach the knot with anything but his teeth, he followed Arvo docilely, and spent the night beneath the sheltering canvas amid stacks of tin bowls, plates, tankards, and figurines.

By the third night, the routine had grown familiar. During the day, Rache reveled in the breeze created by the progress of the cart. Birdsong followed them down the roadways, and a small flock trailed the wagon, picking grain seeds from the horse's manure. Arvo continued his monotonous descriptions of the nearby towns. And at night, Rache learned to sleep with his hands bound.

On the fourth morning, Rache awoke to a sudden stripe of sunlight in his face. Arvo's face poked through the gap between the flaps of canvas, looking harder and older than in the past. Rache sat up. Always before, the tinsmith had awakened him just before dawn. Now, sun rays slanted into the wagon, sparking silver glints along the piles of tin. Behind Arvo, Rache saw open sky rather than the towering columns of evergreen he recalled from the previous night. Apparently, the wagon had moved without his knowledge.'Wh-what?' he stammered. 'Where?'

'We're in Nordmir.' Arvo grasped the rope between Rache's hands and helped him from the wagon.

Sunlight glared from rows of thatch-roofed dwellings, momentarily blinding him. To his right, a tall blur seemed to stretch to the sky. Rache blinked until his vision cleared and the structure became clear. Constructed of stone and mortar, it towered to four times his height, taller than any building he had ever seen or imagined. Vines curled and stretched along the surface, making it appear painted in splotches of green and brown. Though simple in shape and unadorned, its size alone robbed Rache of his breath.

'Come on.' Arvo nudged Rache toward the castle.

The touch broke Rache's daze. He shuffled a step forward, noticing that the wagon stood parked just off a hard-packed roadway. Men and women passed, in couples and small groups, seeming to take no notice of the tinsmith and the child, despite the ropes still taut about Rache's wrists. A pair of burly men dressed in long, mail shirts belted at the waists stood guard before the iron-embossed door of the palace. Each clutched a blade on a pole, a weapon unfamiliar to Rache. He stared at the sentries. They reminded him of the soldiers who had attacked Devil's Island, and he felt deeply chilled. 'How did we get here?'

Arvo gave Rache another shove toward the pathway to the castle door. 'Come on.'

Rache staggered, then whirled. He raised his hands to remind the tinsmith of his promise. 'You forgot to untie me.'

Arvo continued to ignore Rache's comments. Catching the Renshai child by both shoulders, Arvo steered him toward the castle.

Suddenly frightened, Rache jerked back, resisting. Caught by surprise, Arvo lost his grip. Rache spun, making a desperate break for freedom. Arvo swore. He shot a foot between Rache's legs, sprawling him. Unable to catch himself without his hands, Rache landed on his face. Pain smashed through his nose. Grit scratched furrows in his skin as he slid half under the wagon. Awkwardly, he twisted to rise. Then Arvo's booted toe thumped into Rache's side, driving air through his clenched teeth.

The attack made no sense to Rache. Howling, he thrashed his legs and whipped his bound hands in a childish frenzy, his combat training forgotten. Catching one flailing leg and avoiding the other, Arvo dragged Rache back into the road, 'Stop it,' he screamed. He kicked Rache in the ribs, then planted a foot on the boy's chest.

Rache gasped, forcing himself to think. Weaponless, hands tied, this was unlike any battle situation for which he had prepared. But the Renshai had constructed their maneuvers by combining the best techniques gleaned from a hundred years of wandering. Rache had never understood the philosophical aspects of Colbey's training. Still, he called the *torke*'s words to mind: 'Wars have been won by numbers, skill, guile, sheer audacity, and even simple luck. But never, *never* by panic. Panic instantly reveals your every weakness to your enemy. The secret of combat is to hide your weaknesses. Whenever possible, bide your time until your enemy's impatience or stupidity causes him to reveal his own weaknesses, then use them against him.' Berating his loss of self-control, Rache went still.

Face flushed with anger, Arvo caught the ropes and hoisted Rache to his feet. The cord chewed into Rache's wrists. 'Modi,' he whispered, spurred rather than cowed by the pain. His bruised ribs ached. He had trusted Arvo Ranulfsson. The betrayal hurt, fueling Rache's hatred. Moments before, he would have risked his life for Arvo; now, the tinsmith had earned a place as Rache's enemy, one step only beneath the high king in Nordmir, who had surely launched the surprise attack against the Renshai.

Arvo shook Rache, his grip tight and careful on the rope, his features twisted into a snarl. 'Listen, Rache,' he said, his voice coarse, his words clipped. 'I've seen too many waifs like you living as thieves and beggars, growing into the vile gutterscum that plagues honest merchants. Be grateful I've saved you from that fate.'

Sorrow, bitterness, and rage crushed down on Rache, but not a twinge of gratitude. Ideas spun through his mind. He wanted to protest, to force Arvo to feel guilty for what he had done. Instead, he bit his lip and said nothing, aware silent obedience would best hide his intentions until he found an opening to act. *Patience*, Rache reminded himself.

Arvo apparently accepted Rache's quiet stillness as acquiescence; his cheeks paled to their normal ivory color and his voice turned friendly. 'Not every boy has a chance to grow up in a king's palace nor to serve his lord so closely.'

Hatred burned in Rache like fire. He clenched his jaw, concentrating on Arvo's every movement, reading him for stereotyped or repeated motions, a tendency to shift one way more frequently than the other. So far he had determined only that Arvo favored his right hand. Like most Renshai, Rache was trained from birth to use both hands equally, at least when engaged in combat.

Arvo continued more slowly, fidgeting as his ire died, perhaps bothered by the intensity of Rache's scrutiny. 'Don't do anything stupid. If the king likes you, your future's enviable. If you whine and scream on his floor, like you did for me, he'd as soon have you killed. And if you embarrass me, my next kick won't be so gentle.' He glared, awaiting an answer.

Rache met the tinsmith's murky stare with mute defiance.

'Come on.' Arvo jerked Rache toward the castle door. Docilely, his blond head low, Rache walked at Arvo's side.

As the pair approached the doorway, one of the guards stepped forward. A grin split his thick features. 'Arvo, how's the trade?'

'Not so good as last spring.' Arvo sounded casual, but his grip on Rache's ropes never lessened. 'Is his majesty expecting me?'

'The king is taking audience in his court today. I'm sure he can fit you in. I'll check.' The guard turned on his heel, opened the door, and disappeared inside, closing it behind him.

Arvo sighed, exchanging smiles with the remaining sentry at the door.

The guard shifted, the chains of his shirt rattling. 'Into a new trade?' He inclined his head toward Rache.

Rache stood, his body a still contrast to his racing thoughts.

Arvo shook his head. 'Just a gift.'

'An unwilling gift.' The guard had obviously seen the struggle that had ensued beside Arvo's wagon.

Arvo shrugged in reply. An awkward silence ensued, broken by the other sentry's return. He held the door open. 'The king will see you now.'

Arvo ushered Rache in. The door slammed shut, and the guard escorted them down a corridor crafted of stone blocks. Some artisan had painted a repeating, boldly lined pattern in smaller squares, simulating tile. Irregularities in the sizes and shapes of stone had forced him to work the design even over the mortaring, making it appear warped and cracked. Wall sconces held unlit torches, and the semidarkness smoothed the rougher edges, adding to the illusion. Niches on either side of the hallway held finely-crafted golden vases of a Western artistry Rache did not recognize. The Renshai had no king; their leader varied depending on the task and convenience. Understanding little of castles, statecraft, and governments, Rache could not know Nordmir's palace was a paltry imitation of the richer citadel of the West's high king in Béarn. To him, the grandeur of Nordmir's castle seemed staggering. It took a conscious effort to keep his attention on his enemies rather than on the furnishings. The stone felt grainy and cold beneath his bare feet.

The corridor ended at a door. The guard signaled Arvo to stop and tapped on the wood with the base of his pole arm. In response, the door swung inward, revealing a chamber. After the dullness of the corridor, the lantern-lit room seemed blinding. Rache squeezed his eyes shut. Arvo dragged him forward, halfway down a narrow, blue-carpeted aisle, before Rache's eyes grew fully accustomed to the lighting.

Ahead, an arched array of three chairs perched on a wooden platform. The one in the center held a portly, stiff-bearded North-man in silken robes trimmed with milky white fur. A jeweled crown balanced on blond braids wound through with leather thongs. He watched Arvo's and Rache's approach, his lids sagging with boredom.

To the king's left sat a younger Northman of lighter build, a sword at his side. His keen, blue eyes measured the approaching pair, his posture anything but careless. On the opposite side, a frail man slumped in his chair. He appeared unlike anyone Rache had ever seen before. Colbey sported a few white hairs at his temples, but Rache had always accepted them as a normal peculiarity, specific to his *torke*. The man at the king's right hand had a headful of hair the color of snow, hacked short. Wrinkles recessed his eyes into pits, and his forehead appeared wrapped in permanent bewildered creases. Brown patches marred the skin of his hands and cheeks, and blue veins wound, thin but visible, through brittle, yellowed flesh. Though feeble-appearing, the man still stared with ferocity through watery eyes.

Despite his plan to reveal nothing of his thoughts, Rache recoiled. Having no experience with age, he assumed the elderly figure was wasting from disease and wondered why the Nordmirians allowed the infected one so near their king. A dozen guards, each with a sword and shield, held at-ease but attentive stances around and before their king. Rache's subconscious registered three sentries with pole arms near the door behind him, including the one who had escorted them to the court. A handful of richly dressed men and women occupied benches on either side of the aisle, though most of the seats lay empty.

Arvo stopped some distance from the closest guards. He knelt respectfully. 'Your majesty.'

Caught by surprise, Rache remained standing, though the cord abraded his already bruised wrists until they bled. He bit off a cry of pain.

Arvo winced as resistance on the rope bit into his fingers, too.

The king frowned but otherwise seemed to take no notice of Rache's disrespect. 'Rise, Arvo Ranulfsson. I presume you've come for your usual trade?'

Arvo stood. He kept his gaze fixed on the royal presence, but stomped on Rache's foot to show his displeasure. 'I have, your majesty. Would our usual terms be agreeable, your majesty?'

Rache worked his smashed toes from under Arvo's boot, trying to keep control of the blind fury inspired by the pain.

'They would,' the king said. 'And what is this you've brought with you?'

Rache loathed being referred to as an object even more than he did Arvo's insistence on calling him 'boy.' He remained still, waiting for Arvo to drop his guard.

Arvo bowed his head. 'Your majesty, I found this homeless child in your woods learning the trade of a thief. Better his neck in your service than stretched by the hangman's noose.'

The king's pale-eyed gaze rolled to Rache, though he still appeared disinterested. 'Very well.' He addressed the next command randomly to his guards. 'Take the boy to the slave quarters.'

One of the guards near the front shifted his shield to a companion and trotted toward Rache. He wore the usual mail shirt; and, as he moved, his sword sheath swayed at his hip. Arvo stepped aside, passing Rache's hands to the guard who caught the rope in a lighter grip than the tinsmith's. Without a word, the guard tugged at Rache's hands, preparing to turn him around to face the back of the courtroom. For an instant, Rache resisted. As the guard increased pressure, Rache spun.

Suddenly, Rache was moving in the same direction as the yank. Surprise drove the guard off-balance, and Rache seized his opening. The side of his foot crashed against the guard's knee, all of his weight behind the blow. The guard staggered with a gasp. His hands fell away from the rope. Rache sprang. He seized the guard's hilt in his bound fists and ripped it from the sheath. The leather felt familiar and proper against his damaged hands. He whirled, whipping the blade in a wild arc to hold off enemies until he could assess their positions.

Screams and shouts rose from the nobles on the benches, and they scuttled to safety. The king's command was lost amid the noise and the clack of swords, armor, and shields as the guards leapt toward Rache. Only one thought came to Rache: to fight his way free or die in the attempt, taking as many of the enemy with him as possible. He lunged randomly at the closest figure, Arvo, swiping high. Rache's sword tore a lethal gash in Arvo's neck before the tinsmith realized he was menaced. Blood splashing, Arvo fell without a sound. The injured guard rolled beneath the benches to safety.

The ropes burned Rache's wrists with every movement. He clutched the hilt in whitened fingers, meeting the first guard with an overhead strike. The guard caught the blow on his shield and riposted. Rache back-stepped and thrust for his abdomen. The guard blocked low, knocking Rache's sword downward, opening his upper defenses. Sword low, hands bound, Rache used the only weapon available. He drove his head into the guard's chest.

An expression of surprise crossed the guard's face; apparently, he did not expect such a maneuver from a child. He staggered a step backward. Rache bore in, whipping his lowered sword upward in a cut that claimed the guard's leg above the knee.

Rache found himself surrounded by guards. He spun from side to side, slashing in a savage frenzy that kept the guards just beyond sword range. His hands ached, making the sword feel lead-weighted. Sweat plastered hair to his forehead and stung his eyes. The wild chaos of his strategy wore quickly. His lungs felt raw, his breaths came in a pant, and he knew he could not delay much longer. The time had come to die in the same bold glory as his people had. With a howl of triumph, Rache singled out a guard at random and plunged toward him.

The guard parried the blow, but before he could answer with a strike of his own, Rache had redirected his attack against another. This time, Rache swung high. His sword slammed against a shield, jarring his arm to the elbow. A movement to his right touched the corner of his vision. Before he could turn, a meaty hand enclosed his wrists, spining him off his feet. He tumbled to his knees, the sword wrenched painfully from his grip. Blindly, Rache kicked, missed. The flat of a sword cracked against his skull. White-hot pain flashed through his head, and his vision disappeared. He sprawled to the floor. His thoughts scrambled, and his eyesight returned as shadowy blurs of movement through a screen of red stars. Boots stabbed his sides from both directions, jolting agony along his ribs. He screamed, struggling to roll free, but something pinned his limbs to the floor.

'That's enough.' Though soft, the command carried, all the more effective because it was not the king who had spoken.

The kicks stopped. The guards went still.

The same voice spoke again. 'Forgive me, your majesty. But he's just a child. Sire, do you really want him beaten to death on the floor of your court?'

The murmurs of the guards made it clear the speaker was out of line, yet the king's quiet acceptance made it equally apparent that he found the dissident valuable enough to accept a little defiance. Gradually, Rache worked his head to the side. The king sat, fingers laced thoughtfully through his beard, his gaze on the sickly-looking elder to his right. 'Very well.' He addressed Rache. 'Boy, you like fighting so much? You're going to get the chance. Let's see how you do against the other slaves who like to fight.'

'Sire?' The elder seemed alarmed by the suggestion. 'You would put this child against a gladiator?'

The king's patience appeared to be waning. 'The child injured my guards and killed a visitor in my court. *I want him dead!*'

The cold of the stone seemed to seep through Rache. Senses muddled, he found the situation difficult to decipher, although he remembered his *torke* once telling him that the term 'gladiator' meant fighter. The words seemed to come from a great distance and thickly, as if through water. It appeared the king wanted Rache to die in combat, while the other man opposed the idea. Though Rache preferred the king's bent, he appreciated the moments of peace the elder had gained him.

'We all want him dead, of course, your majesty.' The aged man persisted. 'But at least get some enjoyment out of it.' He made a grand gesture, his sleeve falling away from a wrinkled, freckled arm. 'Make it a spectacle. If he has to die young, at least let him go out with enough showmanship and style so your people will remember it.'

'I just want him dead.' The king spoke stiffly.

Rache tried to move but managed only to twitch his fingers. He met instant resistance.

The older man's voice dropped so low, Rache had to strain to hear it. 'My lord, would you have your people believe you sanction murdering babies in public fights with gladiators ?'

The king went rigid. His eyes narrowed.

The elder continued quickly. 'If it was entertaining . . .' He trailed off provocatively.

The king's expression softened in consideration. 'What's your idea ?'

The aged man tapped his fingers on his armrest. His gaze passed over the tight ring of guards to focus on Rache. His mouth bent into a cruel, tight-lipped smile. He leaned toward the king, and Rache heard nothing of the whispered exchange that followed.

Rache awakened, curled on a hard-packed earthen floor, unable to recall how he had gotten there. His last memory was of a dozen guards pinning him to the courtroom floor. His head throbbed, making thought difficult ; his ribs and wrists ached. He tasted dirt.

Rache rolled, and the sudden increase in pain jarred a whimper free before he could suppress it. He lay in a cell with three solid walls and a ceiling. Bars formed the fourth wall, looking out over a path. In the distance, a forest loomed, trees swaying in the breeze, leaves and needles rattling a chorus. Twilight dribbled through the branches, making Rache aware he had slept through the night. He could not remember ever sleeping so deeply and wondered if he had been struck. The agony thrumming in the back of his head supported the possibility.

Forcing himself to a sitting position, Rache drew his hands into his lap, intending to assess the damage from the rope. But a glimmer of metal seized his attention. A manacle encircled his left wrist, held in place by a bronze rivet. A short chain trailed from it, hanging free. Blood-crusted gashes from the rope, purple bruises and abraded skin poked from beneath the steel. Aside from the absence of a fetter, the right wrist appeared similar.

Noises came to Rache then, the soft sough of cautious, animalistic movement, creatures stirring around him. The stone walls hid them from his sight, but he guessed they were light sleepers awakened by his rolling. Humans, perhaps, whose lives depended on their instincts and split-second reactions. Fear clutched at Rache, and, finally, he lost control. He sagged to the ground, crying, lonely as death. He was no longer a blooded man of a warrior tribe, just a child lost in a world of enemies.

The sobs came harder, racking Rache's ribs with pain. Grief seared him, and he cursed himself with angry gasps. *The brave dead should be glorified, never mourned.* Words he had known since infancy lost all meaning, smothered beneath a wave of grim sorrow. He gritted his teeth until his pounding head felt as if it might explode. He imagined his little sister, hacked down by Northmen laughing at the slaughter, again saw his father tramped beneath the horde and his mother's shattered corpse dangling like a snarl of gulfweed on the reef. The image sliced deep into his memory, and he vomited with a violence that wrenched his bruised ribs into fiery anguish.

Rache scuttled away, pressing his back into a corner, hard, jamming his spine against it as if it might collapse, trying to drive the sacrilege from his mind. *They're in Valhalla. They've earned their reward and ultimate happiness.* He was supposed to celebrate the dead, but his mind would not allow it. Regret wedged through his defenses, raising doubts about a religion that had served the Renshai and the mainland Northmen for centuries before his birth. He forced himself to forget that the act of cowardice was his mother's, not his own. To live a coward was wretched, but it could be undone by future feats of valor. To die a coward doomed the soul to Hel. Rache buried his face in his palms, feeling ugly, empty, and hollow, scourged by his own sinful thoughts. The edge of the shackle scratched his cheek.

Another sound rose over the restive activity around him. Voices flowed along the path, and two of the king's guardsmen came into view. They wore belted chain shirts over leather breeks. One held a spear. Otherwise, they were unarmed.

Rache worked to a crouch, rubbing the tears from his eyes with grimy fists.

The guards stopped before Rache's cage. Shorter and broader than his companion, the one with the spear examined Rache through the bars. 'He's a boy.'

'I told you that.' The other plucked a ring of keys from his pocket and stabbed one into the lock.

The smaller guard leveled his spear at Rache. 'I thought you meant twelve, thirteen. This one's a child.'

The larger guard grunted a noncommittal reply. He twisted the key, and the lock snapped open.

Rache's heart raced, but he hid fear behind a mask of defiance. He did not move, studying the guards' every movement from habit.

The spearman persisted. 'Why's he got the one manacle on the left? Is he left-handed?'

'Who knows.' The larger guard entered the cage, and the other poked his spear through the doorway. 'It's part of the king's plan to even the fight. They're doing some strange thing with a horse. I'd still put my money on the gladiator.' He glanced toward his companion.

Rache grasped the moment. He sprang for the open door.

The side of the spear crashed into Rache's gut, driving him a step backward. He struggled for breath and balance as the large guard seized the dangling end of the chain, deftly flicked it over Rache's free hand, and pulled it taut. Yanked forward, Rache stumbled and fell to one knee. A thin trickle of air wheezed into his lungs. The guard looped the chain around his wrists a second time.

The maneuver was so fast and well-coordinated, the guards had obviously practiced it repeatedly. The smaller man continued speaking as if nothing had happened. 'I heard the boy did some serious damage in the courtroom.'

The guard in the cage levered the chains so they could not come undone. 'He caught them by surprise. A couple of lucky strikes.' He interrupted himself, his words intended as much to discourage Rache from attempting escape as to inform his companion. 'The boy's condemned to death. If he tries anything, stab him.'

Rache shivered. Gasping, he followed the guard from the cell without comment, the chains gouging into his swollen wrists.

The guards led Rache around the block of cells and across a plain to the castle. Grass pricked and tickled Rache's bare feet, and he concentrated on this less unpleasant sensation, trying to forget his mangled wrists and the shifting pressure of metal against them. Gradually, the ground sloped downward; the back side of the palace was built on lower ground than the front. A huge, iron-embossed door stood ajar, opening into a part of the structure below ground level. The guards brought Rache through it and into a dingy, straw-lined corridor lit only by the sun glare filtering through the gap of the open door.

The hallway ended at another door. Immediately in front of it, a gaunt horse with a heavily muscled rump whipped its tail at flies. The darkness made its bay hide look almost black. A saddle perched on its back, carefully cinched. A man dressed only in a loincloth crouched to the animal's right, facing its hindquarters, his right wrist chained to the saddle. To the left, another chain hung from the pommel. Positioned between the horse and the door, a guard gripped the animal by its halter. A sheathed longsword girded his wrist, and he held two swords in his free hand. Even in the dark and from a distance, Rache could see they were poorly crafted, the blades notched and the sparse light glittering from pocks, dents, and scratches.

'Bring him in,' the guard by the door said.

Rache lost himself to despair. Motion became automatic; the sting of the spear tip sent him forward, stumbling after the guard. He was Renshai, trained to sword skill from childhood. But even Renshai had to break practice for chores, to chop firewood and scour the fishing boats, to hunt and gather food. Gladiators had no demands other than to fight, perhaps to live and drill to fight some more. Rache was only ten years old, far from the peak of his competence. *How can I possibly hope to stand against a gladiator?* Death in combat did not bother Rache; it was a reward. But a death without honor was the ultimate curse, and Rache worried about dying without returning a single stroke, or trampled beneath the horse's hooves.

The guard drew Rache to the beast's left side. Caught in a narrow lane between horse and wall, his escape cut off by a swordsman on one side and a spearman on the other, Rache allowed the unarmed guard to chain him to the saddle by his manacle. The horse's ears flicked flat to its head, and it pawed the ground with a white-stockinged forehoof. Only then did Rache recognize the extent of his advantage that went beyond having his right hand free while the gladiator would be forced to fight left-handed. Everything done with horses was done from the left side, his side, including mounting. He wondered if the king had considered that fact when he chose the positions of the combatants. Confidence buoyed, Rache did not dare to hope too hard. The gladiator's strength, experience, and learned desperation still made him more powerful than Rache. *But it's not over yet.*

The guards exchanged silent signals. Nerves wound to coils, limbs shaking, Rache clung to the saddle's pommel with his left hand, unable to see the gladiator over the back of the horse. The guard near the door shoved the hilt of a sword into Rache's hand, gave the other to the gladiator, then moved aside. The familiar feel of the weapon lulled Rache. Dizziness left him, and the dull throb of his head lost all significance. Colbey's training surfaced mechanically, and, with it, the rules of battle: 'Step on his feet, gouge his eyes, kick him in the groin, bite, pull hair, spit in his face, piss on him, anything that works, do it. The victor is the one left standing at the end of combat. The honor comes not from the method of warfare, but in defeating your enemy with nothing but skill and wits and, perhaps, a sword.'

The door whisked open onto an oval-shaped arena larger than any cottage on Devil's Island. Stone walls rose to three tiers of wooden benches half-filled with curious, Northern faces. The horse stood, rooted, in the doorway. Its ears whipped forward into excited triangles. It bugled out a whinny. Then, apparently spurred from behind, it bolted several steps into the ring.

The sudden movement all but sprawled Rache. He staggered backward as the horse froze again. The gladiator took the first strike, a wild sweep over the animal's saddle. The crowd roared. Rache felt the horse bunch. It swung its hindquarters toward the gladiator. Arching its neck, it kicked out at the man, bucking in a circle to the right. Hand wrenched, Rache threw up his sword arm for balance and chased the horse's revolution from necessity. Tense noise sputtered through the spectators as the battle progressed in a manner they apparently never expected.

The horse threw a kick at the gladiator. He leapt backward to avoid it, jarred to the end of his chain. Balance lost, he toppled. The horse stepped on him, rocking sideways. The gladiator screamed. Upset by the presence beneath its hooves, the horse danced back toward Rache and went still. Slammed suddenly into the horse's side, Rache wrapped both hands around the pommel. As the gladiator unsteadily gained his feet, Rache sprang for the saddle. He hit, belly first, then scrambled astride, grip so tight on the sword its knurling left impressions on his palm.

The gladiator swore. His sword swept for Rache's leg. Not bothering to meet the attack, Rache brought the flat of his blade whistling onto the horse's rump. It sprang forward, the power of its leap throwing Rache backward. For an instant, the certainty of a fall touched Rache's awareness. Desperately, he caught hold of the horse's inky mane, resettling into his seat. The gladiator screamed again, his cry shrill over the roar of the crowd. The horse floundered over the fighter's flailing limbs, then bucked, its momentum flinging Rache from front to back like so much flotsam. Somehow, Rache managed to cling on. Wrapping his chained arm around the beast's neck, he leaned forward and chopped the blade down on the gladiator's wrist. The sword bit flesh once, then again. On the third whack, the gladiator fell, free and limp, to the arena floor, his hand tumbling to the ground beside him.

The horse slowed to a trot circling the ring in savage confusion. Suddenly it spun, racing back toward the lower entrance to the ring. A soft voice cut over the din of the audience and the patter of the horse's hooves. 'This way !' The door swung open, and Rache caught a glimpse of the ancient Northman who had sat at the king's right hand. Then the horse charged through the doorway and down the hall. It shied around the still bodies of the guards lying in the corridor, bumping Rache from side to side, then galloped through the outer door, also, strangely, open.

The grasses of the cleared plain parted for the horse's run. Then the forest loomed in Rache's vision. Hoofbeats pounded behind him. *They're after me!* He leaned forward in the saddle, air washing over him, the horse's mane whipping into his eyes. The pursuit grew louder, closer behind him. Craning his neck, he glanced over his shoulder. Only one horse chased him, a long-legged black with the white-haired elder on its back. Every stride inched closed the gap between them.

Rache's first thought was to outmaneuver the man. But as he raced toward the woods, Rache knew he would need to slow down or risk crashing his panicked mount into the trees. Besides, logic dictated that, should the king have recovered enough from shock to give chase, he would send guards, not an ill and aging adviser.

'Ho! Slow down!' Rache commanded his steed. As if noticing the wall of trunks for the first time, the horse shied. Rache slid, hands clamped rigidly to its neck.

A moment later, the black cut between Rache's mount and the forest. 'This way!' the rider screamed. Not bothering to point, he galloped along the edge of the forest.

Spooked, Rache's horse chased its fellow, oblivious to or unfamiliar with Rache's kneed signals. Without reins, Rache found it impossible to force his will. Instead, he flattened to the beast's pumping neck, fingers entwined in the dark snarl of mane. Ahead of him, the black horse veered into the woods. As Rache's mount came up behind it, he saw it ran on a road lined with pine and aspen. Without a choice, he followed.

The course curled and spun, the white-haired man choosing turns and intersections without hesitation. Aside from worn pits and crevices, the road remained safe for swiftly moving hooves, and the horses did not slow. Wind tore at Rache's grip. The mane bit like wire into his palms. Lofty branches blocked the sun into dappled shadow, and Rache lost all sense of time and direction. He felt as if he had run forever through a never-ending maze of twists and turns before his horse slackened to a canter, then a trot, and finally a walk. Yet the older man still led them on, now picking his way through clutching vines, over sparsely set underbrush and between trunks packed so close Rache had to swing his legs over the saddle to keep from getting pinched between bark and the horse's side.

As the day wore on, Rache's horse protested the long trip with explosive snorts and strings of grunts. And finally, when Rache was considering making some groaning noises of his own, the elder drew his mount to a halt and swung to the ground. Rache paused, watching the white-haired man untack his horse and release it to graze. Rache recognized the opportunity to escape, but exhaustion highlighted curiosity more than fear. Having come this far, Rache found it impossible to completely mistrust the elder now. Someone must have opened the arena doors and killed the guards in the corridor. His companion seemed the only likely possibility. Cautiously, Rache swung from the saddle.

Not wanting to take a chance on the animal bolting with him still chained to it, he quickly uncinched it, removed the saddle, and set it on a fallen log. Grasping a rock, he pounded at the brass rivet of the manacle.

'Let me help.' The old man's voice came from closer than Rache expected.

Alarmed, Rache jumped, drawing his trapped wrist protectively to his chest. He had known the other man was nearby, of course, but he had expected him to make more noise with his approach.

The white-haired man stood within arm's length, offering a key tucked between his fingers. Though unarmed in the king's court, he now wore a sword in a sheath at his left hip. 'Well done . . .'

Rache leapt to his feet, angling his own weapon between them.

Smiling, the stranger tossed the key.

Rache caught it in his manacled hand, without lowering his sword or his defenses. He had trusted once and been betrayed; it would not happen so easily again.

The old man finished speaking as if he had never paused, 'Renshai.'

Rache choked, hating himself for the lapse. He tried to act nonchalant, but his fingers shook as he fitted the key to the lock, and he had to put aside his sword to use both hands. He kept his gaze locked on the other man, prepared to defend himself at the slightest provocation. Not wanting to damn himself with silence, Rache forced a challenge. 'Why do you call me that?'

The white-haired man remained still, his expression solemn. 'Because it's what you are. It's in your stance and your style, your bold rebellion against a king accustomed to unquestioned obedience. The Renshai sword maneuvers are unlike those of any other warrior. The trained eye can spot them in a single stroke. You are Renshai . . .'

The lock clicked. The manacle fell from Rache's aching wrist, and he snatched up his sword again.

'. . . and so am I. My name is Episte.' He offered both hands in greeting, a gesture of peace from fingers empty of weapons.

Many thoughts crashed and tangled in Rache's mind, a muddle of emotions. Rache had neither the time nor inclination to sort. Suspicion tainted the joy of reuniting with one of his people. Episte looked unlike any Renshai he'd ever known, and Rache needed explanations. 'Rache,' he said, stalling.

'Kallmir's son,' Episte finished. 'Yes, the resemblance is there. Though your defiance is more suited to your namesake. Brave warriors both, and your mother, too.'

Though intended as a compliment, the reference to his mother made Rache cringe. His resentment flowed out before he could measure his words. 'You were supposed to warn us of attacks. Many Renshai died without glory.'

'All but you, Rache.' Episte's arms fell to his sides.

Rache felt squeezed, chilled in every part. 'What do you mean?' he demanded. 'They all died? Or they all died without glory?' Simple semantics became the difference between honor and disgrace, a gap that spanned times and worlds, life and death.

Episte sat, his sagging skin and withered features looking monstrous on a wasted human figure. 'Rache, I don't want to bother you with politics. Only know that Northerners and their kings tend to be impulsive, enamored with war and the solutions it brings. Relations between Renshai and their neighbours have been rocky forever. I'm not certain exactly what thought or words inspired the king, but the attack was a sudden decision made without my knowledge. By the time I found out, it was too late.' His eyes rolled toward the sky as if in prayer.

Rache waited, certain Episte had not yet finished.

Episte studied Rache as if to determine whether the child could handle the news.

'I'm blooded,' Rache reminded the elder.

Episte nodded. As a man, Rache had the right to know. 'The king set a bounty, paid against Renshai right ears.' He hesitated as the full effect of his disclosure sank in.

Grief ground in on Rache, suffocating in its intensity, but followed by confusion. He knew loss of a major body part would bar a warrior from Valhalla. 'But is an ear a major body part?'

Rache did not realize he had spoken aloud, so Episte's reply startled him. 'I don't know. Apparently the Northmen doubted, too, and their uncertainty kept them from mutilating their own dead. I counted. Two hundred thirteen ears came into the king's court.' Episte winced at the memory. 'I love my people, Rache. Believe that. And I know every Renshai by name, age, and description. Eight missing, and I dared to hope. Then the other reports came in: four corpses charred beyond salvaging, mostly babies, three bodies lost in the Amirannak Sea. That left only one.'

Struck with too much sorrow at once, Rache went numb. He let the sword sag.

'Probably a miscount, one dead lost in a blanket of bodies. Then you came to Nordmir . . .'

Unable to deal with his grief, Rache turned to anger. 'And you tried to kill me, too, by telling the king to put me against his fighting slave.'

Episte opened his mouth. Suddenly all color drained from his face, and he clutched at his chest.

Rache froze, uncertain what he was seeing, but frightened by the ghastly mask forming over Episte's features.

Episte coughed, the noise a wet rattle. He hesitated several seconds, then he continued as if nothing had happened. 'On the contrary, Rache. I kept him from letting the guards kill you in the court. I talked him into the horse. And I freed you from the arena.'

Rache pressed. 'That horse could just as easily have trampled me as the gladiator.'

'No.' Episte glanced at the grazing bay with a wry smile. 'I picked Raven. As a filly, she got clawed by a bear. Since then, she's had a sore spot on the right, and she always bucks to that side.'

An uncomfortable hush dragged into a long silence. Not wanting to be alone with his sadness, Rache questioned. 'Are you ill?'

'Yes.' Episte sat, his voice soft. 'I'm older than any Renshai before me, and I haven't a lot of years left. Those I have, I give to you. Consider it a gift.' He pointed to a spot beside him on the log, and Rache straddled it. 'We're going south, past the Granite Hills and beyond the Northern king's realm. There are many villages in the Westlands you could serve with your sword; find one that recognizes the value of your skill, though not its source. Even there, be careful to whom you reveal your heritage. The enemies of the Renshai cover the continent, limitless, and most would see you dead. If you choose to marry, make certain the woman is faithful and close-mouthed. By our law, only full-blooded offspring are Renshai, but you'll be the last of our people, so any child of yours is Renshai. If you have no heirs, you may teach the Renshai arts to anyone you trust, but by doing so you subject him to the wrath of our foes. Choose well, Rache.'

Rache absorbed Episte's warning with the same superficial under-standing as he had Colbey's philosophies on war. Thoughts of the future and marriage seemed centuries distant and of no consequence. Right now, Rache had prayers to deliver and souls to mourn. He wanted to commune with gods, to have them answer as they never had before. He had to know, if not with his head then in his heart, whether missing ears and, in one case, cowardice had banned his people from heaven.

Over the next two months, Rache's grief faded to a ragged, bitter hole in his memory. By day, Episte led them on a route characterized by diversionary loops and patterns, and, by night, he sword drilled Rache until the younger Renshai fell into sleeps as deep as the one he'd experienced in the king's gladiator quarters. The constant travel wore on Rache, but Episte's ruses proved effective. If the king's guard pursued, Rache never knew it.

An aged man and a boy seemed easy prey for bandits on the wild streets of the Northern cities, but the rabble were unprepared for Renshai. Though age slowed his reactions, Episte's skill more than compensated, and Rache improved by the day. Episte's gold and the coinage they got for the horses kept them fed, clothed, and bought Rache a finer weapon; when that money ran out, the thieves they were forced to kill supplied them with more.

Episte made Rache a fine *torke*, more patient and understanding than Colbey, if less competent. With time, his movements became stiffer, slower, increasingly less coordinated. Frustration darkened his moist eyes, but he never took it out on Rache. He resorted less to spar and more to description. His chest-clutching episodes increased.

Then, one morning when they were halfway through the Granite Hills, Episte did not awaken. Rache pawed at his *torke*'s neck, finding no pulse, more horrified by a death in peaceful sleep than another man might be at the gruesome results of war. Though he knew Episte could never reach Valhalla, he set the body to pyre with all the dignity of the greatest war hero. Alone again, he cried without guilt; the manner of Episte's death allowed it. Then, leaving one heritage behind, Rache headed south, seeking another.

By midday, Rache descended a pass through the Granite Hills and entered a different sort of forest. Broadleafed giants intermingled with the accustomed evergreens. There was no road, but deer trails wound through the brush, and Rache followed them into an area of younger trees that signaled an end to the woods. Soon the forest broke to a village. Cottages stood in neat rows, packed-earth roads between them. Men and women traversed the lanes, and children chased one another between the homes. The clang of a hammer rose over the shrill shrieks and giggles of the children.

At the farther edge of the town rose a hill capped with larger buildings of stone. Even from a distance, Rache could see that a wall surrounded the estate on the top, although the remainder of the village sported no obvious protections from attack. Boldly, Rache wandered into the town and trotted up the main street toward the raised citadel. Though travel-stained, his tunic and breeks were whole, and his sheath swung in a place of honor at his side.

Women watched Rache from the doorways of cottages or over churns and looms. A crowd of screaming children ran from his path then returned, peering at him from behind stones, fences, and cottages, exchanging whispers and laughter. A man leaned against the door frame of a shop, wiping his hands on a bloodstained apron.

Rache ignored them all, wanting to appear bold and in control though excitement quivered through him. No one stopped him from climbing the hill to the citadel. When he arrived at the top he found the gate standing open, a single, bored guard sitting in the grass of the entryway. The man rose as Rache approached, bulky with mail beneath a uniform of black and silver. A sword girded his waist, and a halberd rested against the stones of the wall. 'What can I do for you, stranger?' He smiled as he spoke, his intonation unnaturally wavering and high-pitched, like a poorly imitated mockery of the singsong Northern speech. The guard used the common trading tongue of the West.

Rache tried to look defiant. 'I have business with your king.'

The guard loosed a snorting laugh. He smiled condescendingly, turning the darkest eyes Rache had ever seen toward him. 'You do, do you now? Hmmm.' He scratched at a brown beard. Rache had never seen hair that color, and he wondered if the man needed a bath. 'That may be a problem, boy. We don't have a king. Will our leader do?'

Rache nodded mutely. This was not going at all as he'd expected.

The guard hollered. 'Halnor!'

'What do you want?' someone called back. As Rache watched, another man came into view, darker even than the first and dressed in a similar uniform.

'This young whip wants to see Santagithi. What do you think?'

Halnor stared at Rache. Then he, too, snorted, and both guards broke into laughter. 'Today? Just after the birth of his first child? I think Santagithi would see the Eastern king. Bring the child in.'

Rache balled his hands into fists, unaccustomed to this type of treatment. No one had ever talked to him before as if he were an imbecile, and the guards' levity enraged him. Still, they were doing as he asked, so it seemed foolish to quibble.

'Come on.' Halnor led Rache into a well-tended grassy courtyard. He headed away from the series of buildings to the north, and the direction confused Rache. He expected to find the leader tending business in his citadel, but Halnor trotted around a garden and toward a cluster of two dozen men seated and sprawled in circles on the grass. The reek of alcohol hovered around them, and their celebratory laughter sounded as sharp as the children's playing had. Halnor threaded through the group as all eyes turned towards him. He stopped before a tall, well-muscled blond in the center of the group.

Rache stared. These men wore no uniforms but shirts and britches and breeks in a variety of colors; their features mixed races. Some, like the blond, had skin nearly as light as the Northmen while others looked as swarthy as Easterners. Hair colors ranged from black to sandy and, though the majority studied Rache with wood-colored eyes, more than one trained a pale gaze on the stranger. Most carried swords.

'Santagithi.' Halnor addressed the blond. 'This child demands to see our king.'

Laughter broke out in the ranks. All other conversation ceased.

Santagithi smiled kindly, ignoring his followers' mirth. He rose, extending a hand. 'Hello, boy. What can I do for you?'

Rache scowled. 'Man,' he corrected.

Again laughter ruffled through the ranks, and, again, Santagithi did not join in. 'Very well. "Man" you are until I know your name. I'm Santagithi.' He examined Rache through mild, gray eyes.

The guards snickered, nudging one another, but Santagithi's frown silenced them. They grew appropriately serious.

Rache took an instant liking to this down to earth leader and an equally instant hatred of his off-duty guards. 'My name is Rache. I'm a soldier. I'd put myself in your service if you will have me.' He fondled the hilt of his sword.

Laughter spread like fire in a dry field. Santagithi grinned but maintained his composure. He raised a hand to quiet the guards. 'Let the *man* speak.'

The guards' laughter angered Rache, and Santagithi's easy-going manner inspired him to challenge. 'I'll take any man among you in spar.'

Now Santagithi did laugh. 'I need spirited men, Rache. Do you have a home? A family?'

Rache shook his head, not explaining further.

'I'll find you a home in town. When you come of age and Nantel has taught you to fight, perhaps you will make a soldier. In the meantime . . .'

Patronized by the one man who seemed worthy of his time, Rache shook with rage. He considered leaving, but anger forced his tongue. 'This Nantel can teach me nothing new. Maybe I can give him lessons.'

One of the younger guards beside Santagithi, a homely man with curly, dark hair and a mustache, flushed scarlet. He leapt to his feet, lips splayed open in sudden outrage. 'Sir, I'd like permission to give this child his first lesson.' Though respectful, his tone was razor-edged, and his hand kneaded his hilt as if to strangle it.

Santagithi frowned, considering all aspects of the challenge. His gaze turned from Nantel to Rache.

Eager to demonstrate his skills, Rache nodded his willingness. His first *torke* had told him the Renshai maneuvers combined and honed the highest techniques of warrior societies throughout the continent, and the Renshai's emphasis on early training conveyed many advantages over outsiders. Though only ten years old, it never occurred to Rache that he might lose.

Santagithi looked back at Nantel. Then, apparently deeming a supervised spar more prudent than a lawless feud, he consented. 'Very well.'

Nantel sprang toward Rache, impulsive as a child, while Rache waited with the patience of an elder.

Santagithi's eyes narrowed in disapproval, and he finished carefully, obviously too familiar with Nantel's temper. 'See to it what you're teaching is sword techniques.'

The guards passed whispered comments, and one laughed out loud. Several exchanged a bottle of wine, tipping it back in turns, while others watched the coming spar with bland curiosity. They had experienced too many contests to waste their off-duty revelry time watching a man train a child.

Nantel drew his sword. Though Rache started the movement later, his blade came free faster, but he did not press his advantage. Instead, he took a defensive posture, waiting for Nantel to make the first attack.

Nantel prodded a backhanded swing toward Rache's chest with the gentle ease of a *torke* with a toddler. Rache could not recall anyone using a sword that slowly since he turned three. He blocked easily, noting as he did that Nantel had committed too far forward, and the tip of the sword sagged at the end of the strike. Surprised by Nantel's sluggishness, Rache did not bother to return the attack. He wondered how much Santagithi's celebration and free-flowing beer had affected Nantel's reflexes.

Nantel swung again, and Rache blocked. On Nantel's third attempt, Rache tired of the tedium. He caught Nantel's blade with an outside block, snapped the sword away, and seized Nantel's sword hand. As the sword spun harmlessly aside, Rache whipped his own blade back toward Nantel's abdomen. Pulled, the cut caressed Nantel's stomach without biting flesh.

Killing stroke. Rache smiled, not bothering to announce his obvious win. The guards snickered.

Nantel's lips clenched to thin, white lines, and muscles bunched in his arms. Suddenly, he planted his palms squarely on Rache's chest and shoved with a violence that sent Rache stumbling backward. 'All right, you little worm!' He plunged at Rache, sword circling high in a feint, then whisking for Rache's knees.

Rache back-stepped and blocked low, meeting the wild force of a blow that could not have been pulled. In his rage, Nantel was fighting for real.

'Nantel! Half speed.' Santagithi's reprimand fell on deaf ears. Nantel's sword became a savage blur, and Rache relied on the instincts hours of daily practice had given him.

Rache counterslashed high. Nantel parried with an outside circle that drove down Rache's sword, then upper cut toward the Renshai's face. Rache sprang back. Reversing the movement the instant his foot touched ground, he thrust toward Nantel's knee. Nantel scarcely batted the attack aside, then returned with an overhead strike aimed for Rache's skull.

Forsvarir. The name of the maneuver came to Rache's mind as fast as he performed it. He blocked high, then spun toward Nantel, steel scraping steel with a high-pitched screech. Reversing his grip, he slapped the flat of his blade across Nantel's knuckles. Nantel's grip gave, and Rache snagged the haft of Nantel's sword as it fell. A sword in each hand, Rache slid back into a defensive position.

Nantel clasped his injured hand, counting digits like a new father with an infant. Accustomed to Renshai spars, where disarmings were routine and it was considered discourteous to let a sparring companion's sword hit the ground, Rache could not know the usual methods of disarming would have severed two or three of Nantel's fingers.

Now every stare fixed on the combatants.

Nantel loosed a rabid howl of anger. His face darkened to purple. 'Give me a weapon!'

'I would,' one guard answered from the mass, 'but he's already got two. Where's he going to hold the third one?'

Mercifully, no one laughed.

'Nantel, calm down.' Santagithi used the composed, firm tone of a man accustomed to instant obedience.

Nantel quivered, hands balling and loosening at his sides.

Santagithi glared, and, for the first time, Rache realized the leader was not yet thirty, younger than many of his guards though a decade older than Nantel. 'Nantel, sit.'

Nantel hesitated, and several of the guards tensed to rise as if to force their commander's decree. Grudgingly, Nantel complied.

Santagithi turned his attention to the Renshai. 'Rache, it's not my policy to send chil – ' He caught himself, '*young* men to war. But if your offer of service still stands, I'd be happy to give you a home among my guards.'

Rache beamed proudly.

Santagithi twisted toward the sulking Nantel. 'Nantel, I want you to show Rache to his quarters.' The crowd seemed to hold its breath as one, but Santagithi continued, oblivious. 'You can put him in your room or with Quantar. Your choice.'

Rache noticed he, too, had stopped breathing. He sucked air through his teeth, trying to understand Santagithi's intentions. If nothing else, it would force the issue.

Nantel's features faded to their natural, bronze hue. He considered aloud. 'Let me understand this. You're giving me permission to share my room with a brazen child who embarrassed me in front of the entire guard force?' Nantel's annoyance emerged as sarcasm. 'If I like, I can hand over half my quarters to a child who can't be older than seven yet who just beat me in a spar, who could have beaten anyone else here even more easily?' He grimaced, staring down his peers in turn, daring anyone to challenge his assertion.

No one did, though whether from deference to Nantel's skill, his rage, or Santagithi's warning gesture, Rache could not tell.

Nantel rose, rambling as he fumed. 'A child who stole the sword from my hands. A child arrogant enough to march up here and challenge the entire guard force. A child who knows more about sword fighting than anyone here. A child who . . .' Nantel broke off, suddenly aware of his own words. '. . . nothing,' he finished softly. He rose, and a smile graced his oddly set features. 'Come on, Rache. Let's go to our room.'

Part 1

The Town of Santagithi

1 Master of Immorality

Year: 11,240
(Year 13 of the Reign of Morhane Buiranesson)

The Southern Wizard, Carcophan, strode through the rough-hewn corridors of the castle in the Eastern royal city of Stalmize. Gray hair dappled with black streaked into a wild mane behind him, uncovering features pinched in an angry grimace. His green-yellow eyes glared with an intensity that sent the guards skittering from his path like crabs, their ruddy brown, lacquered leather armor completing the picture. No one challenged Carcophan, despite his obvious destination of the strategy room where their general-king plotted alone. The legends claimed that the gods had sanctioned Carcophan as the keeper and sower of all the world's corruption; and, though he rarely acknowledged any mortal except King Siderin, it was generally believed the Wizard would joyfully kill anyone who bothered him, no matter how slight the offense.

In truth, Carcophan scarcely noticed the crisp, wary movements of Siderin's sentries; as always, he was concerned with more important matters. In his two centuries as a Wizard, he had seen mortals rise and fall, replaced by new, equally frail generations. The Cardinal Wizards' rite of passage assured that the lines became stronger, more knowledgeable, and thus more powerful over time. But humans simply died, replaced by equally incompetent humans who seemed determined to learn nothing from those who came before them.

The paired sentries before the strategy room door moved silently aside for Carcophan. Without a word or gesture to either of the men, the Wizard twisted the knob and entered, closing the door behind him.

A detailed map of the continent, its edges curled from use, was spread across a simple, wooden table in the center of the room. Light from an overhead lantern bathed the scratched and timeworn parchment. Two dozen chairs surrounded the table, but currently only one was occupied. King Siderin studied terrain he already knew by heart. Hair black as pitch hung over his face like a curtain. Tan and blue silks covered his leather britches and jerkin, tight across a heavily-muscled chest. His broadsword rested on the table beside the map along with his helmet, a finely-crafted piece of battle gear that, when worn, hid all but Siderin's flinty eyes. A row of steel tines ran in a line from the nose piece to the fur at its base. The general-king did not look up as Carcophan entered.

Positive that Siderin had heard his entrance, Carcophan frowned at his champion's disrespect but chose to ignore it. 'I have something to show you.'

Siderin made no reply, continuing to trace one of the marked lines on the map with his finger.

But the near-immortal, too, knew patience. Carcophan waited, unmoving, until Siderin raised his head.

The veil of hair fell away, revealing Siderin's craggy, aristocratic features and irises so dark Carcophan could scarcely differentiate them from the pupils. 'What is it, Wizard?'

Now Carcophan remained silent, a war of wills between two men accustomed to receiving total obedience and respect, one for decades, the other for centuries. The Southern Wizard crossed the room, hooked the chair next to Siderin's with a sandaled foot, and sat. He paused to press wrinkles from his forest green robes.

By the time Carcophan finished settling, Siderin had returned his attention to the map.

Annoyance fluttered through Carcophan, and he reminded himself he had chosen Siderin as his champion not only because of his skill with weapons, but for his leadership, guile, and adherence to the tenets Carcophan upheld. He had not planned on Siderin's arrogance and ungodly patience, but he had tolerated increasing amounts of both for twenty years. This close to the start of the Great War, he could not afford to waste another several decades finding and training another hero.

The Southern Wizards preceding Carcophan had used subtlety and tact as their weapons, gradually insinuating evil, pestilence, and corruption into the followers of the other Wizards. Often, the only difference between good and evil was intent. Since the four Wizards had no way to penetrate the thoughts of mortals, it was easy for the Northern Sorceress to become complacent, to believe that her supposedly humane followers, the Northmen, killed for glory and honor, stole only from need, and that her kings loved and cared for their followers and slaves as they believed best. But Carcophan felt certain many Northmen knew the brutal joy of slaughter for its own sake and theft simply out of greed. Though personally appealing, Carcophan could find nothing virtuous about gladiators forced to kill and die for the pleasure of nobles. Still, Carcophan was not careless enough to believe the guardian of morality had made no gains against his own followers; even King Siderin was not wholly wicked. As the Keeper had decreed, the time had nearly come for a bolder attack than Carcophan's more discreet forebears had dared, the Great War prophesied by the first Southern Wizard, a wholesale massacre that would subjugate the world to Carcophan's champion.

'Look at this.' Carcophan did not wait for Siderin's attention. With an effortless gesture, he cast his magics onto one of the unadorned walls of the strategy room. A picture snapped into vivid focus. Two young man faced off in a cramped room. The one to the left of the picture was slim, of average height, but with a swordsman's definition of sinew. He sported a short disarray of blond hair and held a sword lightly in his right fist. Though the other stood slightly shorter, he weighed easily half again as much, his frame thick with hard-packed muscle. He wore only a loincloth, his exposed chest and abdomen smeared with sweat and dirt. His dark hair hung in a lengthy snarl. He studied the blond through green eyes blazing with hatred, but the weapon in his scarred, abraded hand was a blunt-edged practice sword.

Chains lay piled in a corner behind the blond. On the opposite side of the room, before the only door, another man kept a loaded crossbow leveled at the grimy man's back.

Given the scarcity of Wizards and the constraints Odin's Law placed upon them, Carcophan's spell would have shocked most mortals. But Siderin had become too familiar with sorcery to react with surprise or awe. He did, however, look up. 'What's this? A pair of adolescents in an unfair fight? Of what possible interest could this be to me, Wizard?'

'Adolescents?' Carcophan stared at the image he had conjured, recognizing the danger Siderin could not know. 'I suppose you might consider the gladiator an adolescent.' He indicated the filthy man with the practice sword. 'The other one, the weapon master training him.' He waved vaguely toward the blond. 'That's Rache. He's twenty-six.'

Siderin frowned but did not voice his disbelief.

'He's a guard in a Western village they call the Town of Santagithi, after its leader. Rache's been among them almost sixteen years.' He paused, waiting to see if Siderin would recognize the significance of that number. When he received no reply, he continued. 'He's served as guard captain and weapon master the last eleven.'

Now Siderin pursed his lips, apparently intrigued.

'Watch him closely.' Carcophan indicated the wall where Rache demonstrated a stroke to the coiled and glaring gladiator. The

Wizard added sound to the picture, a tinny thunk as the sharpened sword bumped the blunted one. The gladiator imitated the cut.

Siderin settled back in his chair, staring at Carcophan's conjured window with flat, dark eyes, obedient to his own curiosity rather than the Wizard's command.

'Head up, Garn!' Apparently oblivious to his audience, Rache caught the gladiator's sword on the flat of his own. His glance darted across every sinew of Garn's tensed body, and his scowl revealed his displeasure. 'Head up.' He lunged.

A dexterous sweep of the gladiator's sword redirected the blow.

'Good,' Rache said.

Garn returned a high sweep, and Rache caught it on his sword. The gladiator scuttled backward, but the tip of the sword master's blade nicked his naked side.

'Too slow, Garn!' Rache reprimanded as he danced to the left.

The hollow sound of a knock rose over the swordplay.

Reflexively, Siderin glanced toward the strategy room door.

Not so used to magic as you think you are. Carcophan suppressed a smile, aware the noise had come from the door to Santagithi's training room.

In Carcophan's magical image, Rache used an agile downstroke to trap the gladiator's sword with his own. 'Relax.' He held his position without taking his gaze from Garn. 'Who is it?'

A voice wafted through the door. 'Mitrian's here for you.' The tone turned musical as the unseen man teased. 'Trying to score favors from the general's daughter?'

Garn tensed. His eyes seemed to hollow, as if all rationality fled him, leaving only savage, driving rage and a glint Carcophan identified as envy. For a moment, he felt certain the gladiator would charge Rache, despite the sword master's weapon and the crossbow at his back.

Rache's gaze never left the gladiator. 'I'll be out shortly.' He inclined his head toward the guard with the crossbow, then masterfully yanked the practice sword from Garn's hand. Tossing it aside, he gathered the chains and wound them around Garn's wrists and ankles.

Menaced by the crossbow, Garn submitted docilely, but Carcophan read murder in the slave's rigid crouch. Rache, too, seemed unfooled, aware that only the loaded crossbow shielded him from death.

Garn addressed Rache softly. 'May your soul rot in Hel, *wisule.*' The insult referred to a foul-smelling disease-carrying rodent, one of the few creatures that would abandon its offspring rather than face an enemy.

Rache hesitated, his surprise evident. He lashed a hand across the gladiator's face, but the slap lacked the wild force of a strike performed in anger. Apparently, Rache merely intended to remind the gladiator of his station rather than to hurt him. 'Watch your mouth. This morning you fought like an old woman who had never seen a sword. You'll die quickly in the pit if your tongue doesn't kill you first.'

'Die quickly?' Acid entered Garn's tone. 'Brave words from one who arms me with a stick and himself with a sword. And you dare call yourself a man? Give me an even fight, coward. I'll kill you.'

The crossbowman edged closer, weapon trained steadily on Garn's chest. Rache paused, as if in deep consideration.

Carcophan nodded sagely. Garn had trapped Rache neatly with his own bravado, the same bold audacity that had earned the weapon master his position as captain at the age of fifteen. The Wizard watched with amusement as Rache removed Garn's shackles, returned the dull-edged weapon to the gladiator's hands and, without a word, freed his own longsword.

Garn sprang. Rage tripled the strength of his blows. Rache countered the frenzied onslaught, his expression somber.

Carcophan could almost feel the thoughts spinning as Rache realized the consequences of a decision made out of pride instead of reason. Garn was the stronger of the two. A wild or lucky strike could kill Rache. And if Rache or the bowman killed Garn, it would infuriate Santagithi.

The gladiator rained blows upon his teacher. As Rache retreated, he wove a careful barrier of metal between them. The room rang with the clamor of steel smiting steel, Rache's sword like an anvil beneath Garn's hammering blows.

Rache's back touched the wall, his sword a blur of defense before him. The crossbowman's finger tightened on the trigger. With Rache cornered, Garn did not need a sharpened blade to pummel the life from him.

Rache's sword flashed in offense only once; it licked across Garn's neck.

The gladiator froze abruptly, eyes wide with awe. He clasped his hand to his throat, and blood trickled between his fingers.

Rache's expression did not change, but a light of triumph flickered in his blue eyes. He smacked the weapon from Garn's weakened grasp before the gladiator could recognize the superficiality of what Carcophan could see was simply a well-aimed scratch. 'If I had given you a sharpened weapon, the fair fight you wanted, I would have had to kill you.' With a nod to the crossbowman, who appeared as shocked as Garn, Rache rechained the slave and left the room.

Carcophan dropped the image and turned his attention to the Eastern king. 'What do you think?'

Slowly, Siderin rolled his gaze from the fading magic on the wall to his companion. 'I think you wasted my time watching a single, recklessly arrogant soldier who won't survive long enough to oppose me.'

Carcophan grimaced. He pressed. 'Didn't anything strike you as odd about Rache?'

Siderin shrugged, still patient as always, but not interested in Wizards' games.

Carcophan summed his findings for his champion. 'A Northman living in the West who looks younger than his age. A superior swordsman, even as a child.'

No reaction from Siderin.

Aggravated, Carcophan suggested the solution before fully revealing the problem. 'You have to murder Rache. Before the Great War.'

Siderin whirled toward Carcophan. His fist crashed on the table-top with a force that made his sword and helmet jump, a grim, dark statue come suddenly to life. Still, his swarthy features held no emotion. 'I won't expose myself before I'm ready. You've given me this thing to do, this war, and I've planned it for twenty years. I've waited and I've waited for the time to be just right for it. My time is coming. I'll cause a wholesale slaughter such as this world has never seen. At my order, the continent will run crimson with blood.' He jabbed a finger at his own chest. 'When I'm done, the Westlands will be enthralled to me. My people will no longer have to live in crowded, disease-riddled cities. They will be the masters, and I will be the master of all.' He made a broad gesture to indicate his kingdom. 'You expect me to risk that because of your fears of one little speck of dust of a man you perceive as a threat? You want me to risk everything I've built for one soldier?'

'Yes.' Carcophan gathered breath to explain, but Siderin had not finished his piece.

'Do you understand the lengths I've gone to to keep the West ignorant? I blasphemed the gods! I created an idol-worshipping cult in the West composed of my spies and assassins, priests that I tracked down, bred, and trained. Wizard, I used only albinos so the Westerners wouldn't recognize them as Easterners. Do you know how hard that was? If it weren't for your stupid Wizards' prophecies, the West wouldn't even know I was planning the greatest massacre of all time. As it is, my delay has made them complacent. I won't risk that advantage by making a move too early.'

'Yes,' Carcophan said. 'I know all that. You've done well with the ideas *I've given you.*' Carcophan locked his gaze on Siderin as he delivered the end-all piece of information. 'But Rache is Renshai.'

'Renshai,' Siderin repeated, but his features gave away nothing. 'Renshai?' His dark eyes narrowed to slits. 'You told me all the Renshai were killed fifteen years ago.'

'Sixteen,' Carcophan corrected. 'And so I believed.'

Siderin tried to control his emotions. But now his flared nostrils and the hand wandering unconsciously to the sword on the table betrayed his anger. 'So you believed?' he mocked. 'You believed, Wizard? You're telling me the information you've conveyed as fact is ungrounded speculation? I've based an entire crusade on your flimsy guesses?'

Carcophan's tone went flat as he suppressed his own rising anger. 'Nothing is certain, Siderin. You're a general. You know a tiny detail can destroy the best laid plans.'

'Sheriva damn you to the Pits, Wizard!' Siderin no longer attempted to hide his rage. '*I* convinced Morhane to usurp the Béarnian throne and destroy his brother's line so he wouldn't have to contend with Béarn's armies and her allies. *I* planted the lies that drove the high king in Nordmir to destroy the Renshai. I've seen beyond everything you've ever dreamed. I've taken what you wanted me to do, not one step, but vistas farther than you ever could have planned. I relied on you to do one thing, to gather information, and you fail me like this?'

Carcophan raised his hand in threat but reined his anger before he slammed his champion with lethal spells. 'To gather information? You make it sound like a simple spying mission. That kind of general knowledge doesn't come from men. I consorted with demons, damn it. Demons!'

Siderin blinked, obviously unfamiliar with the term. 'Demons?'

An image writhed in Carcophan's mind, a creature composed of parts that did not seem to fit, as if some warped god had seamed it together from leftover pieces of creation. Each demon took a different form, and, at times, no form at all or a semi-solid conformation of no substance Carcophan could define. 'Demons. Creatures from the world of magic. I had to call it and bind it just right.' Though no coward, the Southern Wizard shivered. The creatures of magic went beyond evil, representing a force unlike anything in the world of men, barely fathomable despite the tens of centuries of information and experience at Carcophan's command. No matter their background, all the races of men had some code of honor they adhered to strictly. Even the decadent Easterners, who would slay a foreigner for the joy of it, would not murder one of their own without just cause. Each clan, tribe, or kingdom fell into its neat square in the order of the world. But the demons obeyed no laws, honored no vows, followed no codes. And many Wizards had paid to gather that small amount of knowledge.

Carcophan glanced at Siderin and realized the general-king was waiting for him to finish the description. 'I had to phrase the question just right and force the demon to give the answer. Demons serve no master. They mislead and lie as much as the bindings allow. Then, I had to pay its price. In blood.' Carcophan did not expound. The demons claimed the lives of a Wizard's followers as its fee, as if to touch the Wizard with cold, demon chaos, if only for the moment. If not completely controlled, the demon could also attack its summoner. And, though Carcophan would never admit the weakness to a mortal, demons were one of the few things that could injure, even kill, the Cardinal Wizards.

Siderin remained relentless. 'So you misphrased your question.'

'Not necessarily,' Carcophan defended himself. 'That particular demon was weak. It may not have known Rache lived. Whatever the case, now that the Great War is imminent, I was thorough enough to check again.' Unconsciously, his hand slid to his upper arm, kneading a healing scar from the demon's claw strike, hidden beneath his sleeve. 'And I *know* Rache is the only living, full-blooded Renshai. There's a mixed tribe in the west, but Renshai law acknowledges only thoroughbred Renshai; and the Wizards' complete version of the prophecy states that the hero of the Great War will be accepted as Renshai by his people. Rache has to be the one. You must kill him as soon as possible.'

Siderin sat in silence for a long time, his open eyes and the ceaseless movement of his forefinger across his lips the only evidence he was awake. At last, he spoke. 'Rache will die in the war like all the others, if his own stupidity doesn't kill him first.'

'No!' Frustration hardened Carcophan's tone. 'You don't understand. Prophecies aren't random. The Wizards' strength and credibility lie in completing their predecessors' oracular visions. It is the Western Wizard's job to see that the prophecy is fulfiled and Rache survives to fulfil *his* destiny.'

'Necessary?' Siderin frowned. 'Then it's hopeless?'

'Not hopeless.' Carcophan gestured with hands tightened into claws by frustration. In the past, his talks with Siderin had concentrated on the war, and it seemed illogical and impossible to impart all the knowledge since the world began in one afternoon. 'Wizards are fallible. They can be thwarted along with their prophecies. If you act, we can still win. If you don't kill Rache, the Western Wizard will go unopposed, and you may lose the Great War. All the plans that you've made, all the plans that I've made, all the plans that the

Southern Wizards before me have made for the last ten thousand years will come to nothing.

Siderin shook his head. 'If you're so powerful, why don't you kill this Renshai? Why should I risk myself?'

Carcophan traced the edge of Siderin's sword, feeling its sharpness, though the blade could not cut him. 'For the same reason the other Wizards can't just kill you. To do so would put me in direct conflict with the Western Wizard. My vows don't allow that. If we killed one another's champions, nothing would ever get done.'

Siderin's fist clenched around his sword hilt as if he feared the Wizard might try to take it from him. 'I don't believe you, Wizard. You're creating monsters out of smoke. The Renshai is too rash to survive. I didn't see any Wizard defending him from that gladiator. Can the Western Wizard raise the dead, then?'

'No,' Carcophan admitted, and Siderin's words stirred doubt. It did seem odd that Tokar had taken no measures to protect Rache. Thinking back, Carcophan could not recall hearing of or from the Western Wizard since Haim had passed the Seven Tasks almost half a century ago. It was not unusual for a Wizard to disappear for years, particularly while training an apprentice. As the current oldest of the Four, Tokar must have reached his time of passing. Yet, it was customary for the new successor to make his advancement known.

Unless something happened during the ceremony. Now Carcophan sucked in his breath. If so, Siderin might take the West nearly unopposed. Most of the prophecies about the War were composed for Carcophan and Tokar to fulfill. Though Shadimar could take over the Western Wizard's duties, it was a well-known fact that the Eastern Wizard was always the weakest of the Four. 'You must kill Rache.'

Siderin's grip blanched. 'Must? I won't be ordered.'

Carcophan closed his hand, equally tightly, across Siderin's blade. 'Don't challenge me. You may believe you're powerful, but you don't know the meaning of power. Power lies in subtlety, not brute strength.'

'Not brute strength?' Siderin ripped his sword from Carcophan's grasp with a suddenness that would have severed every finger if the weapon could have harmed the Wizard. 'How many necks have you broken by subtlety, Wizard? I could crush you like a bug.'

'Go ahead. Try it,' Carcophan sneered. 'Just keep in mind that once I destroy you, everything you've planned will come to naught, at least for you. I'll just find some other body to fill your place, one who will do as I want.'

Siderin slammed the hilt of his sword down on the map with a sound like thunder. 'You can't treat me like this, Wizard. I'm not something that can be cast aside or ordered about. I . . .' He pounded the table again for emphasis. 'I, not you, *I* am going to control the world. *I* am the one who shaped destiny. You merely placed the seed of an idea in my mind. You can't fathom the plans I've made. You can't possibly stretch your imagination to the boundaries of the world I'm going to create. A world that I'm going to create in *my* image.'

Confined by Odin's Law, Carcophan did not dispute. Mortals were pawns, but the world belonged to these pawns. Siderin was his champion, the king on his chessboard, and Carcophan was too large, too distant to take a real position in the game. 'Fine. Do as you wish. The constructs you make to please yourself don't bother me at all. *But you must kill this Renshai!*'

Siderin screamed, 'How dare you order me!'

'How dare I order you?' Siderin's loss of self-control sparked Carcophan to surrender his as well. 'I can order you to do anything. If I wanted you to grovel on this floor, you would. I made you everything you are. I built you block by evil block. When I found you, you were nothing. If it wasn't for me, you'd still be shoveling shit behind your father's donkey cart!' He sprang to his feet, his mind made up. The time had come to destroy his champion, even if it meant another century of planning the Great War. 'You speak of destiny, yet you have no destiny but what I gave you. You're a crop that I planted, nurtured, and grew, and now you turn out to bear poison fruit!'

Siderin drew in a long breath, as if to shout, but all that emerged were great, shuddering peals of laughter.

Carcophan hesitated, some of his rage dispelled by Siderin's mirth. 'Fool, what are you laughing at?'

'Us,' Siderin managed before succumbing to another round of laughter.

'Us?' Curiosity sapped the last of Carcophan's anger. 'What do you mean "us?"'

'Don't you see it, Wizard?' Siderin worked his sword into his sheath. 'We're the same, neither one willing to bow to the other. But because we are the same and I am going to trample the world beneath the feet of *our* army, I will give you this one life.' Siderin smiled, an open-mouthed grin that displayed every tooth. 'I'll organize my assassins and send them today. Within the month, Rache will be dead.'

2 The Weapon Master

Rache left the gladiators' training chamber quivering with strain, self-directed anger, and the understanding that pride and Garn's affront had goaded him to reckless stupidity ... again. *I had everything to lose and nothing to gain.* Rache flung Garn's blunted practice sword into a box by the door containing similar weapons. Metal struck metal with a high-pitched clang. *Egotistical fool,* Rache berated himself, cursing himself for the lesson he had learned as well as taught. Any guard less practiced would have died; and, had Garn triumphed and survived, he would have become uncontrollable. *Why do I let what he thinks bother me?* With a sigh of irritation, he headed down the long corridor that led to the alcove before the outer door.

When Rache had first arrived in the Town of Santagithi, the memory of his capture and battle in Nordmir made the idea of gladiators reprehensible. But, with time and Nantel's encouragement, he discovered that Santagithi's gladiators were not children kidnapped and forced to fight against their will, but savage, scarcely human beasts: barbarians captured in war, the most intractable of criminals, and a few savages bred and raised exclusively to kill. They snarled more than they spoke. When they did talk, it was always to threaten or to brag to the guards and never one another, though their cages sat in a row.

And then there was Garn.

Rache trotted past a cross corridor, his lips twitching into a frown. Vivid as yesterday, he recalled a moment from thirteen years ago, when a pit fighter named Carad lay dying on the sand of the South Corner Arena after winning hundreds of contests. A willing, proud, and capable gladiator, Carad had won the guards' respect and the favors of the woman who had borne him Garn. He had also won his freedom, though he had refused it. The one-on-one wars had become his source of pride; they were all he knew. Yet, in his last moments of life, he had called for the one guard who wanted nothing to do with the gladiator fights, who had agreed to train them only because he could not stand the thought of men dying without the final fulfillment of having given their all to the battle. Rache came, and Rache alone heard Carad's final words: 'With my blood and your training, Garn can be the best. Take care of my son.'

Now, more than a decade later, Rache again heard the gladiator's rattling whisper beneath the rasp of stone against leather, and it haunted him. Though only thirteen years old to Garn's five, Rache had become more of a parent to Garn than the uncaring servant who was his birth mother. Yet the combination of Rache's training and Carad's proud ferocity had created a monster neither of them could have foreseen. Born a free man, Garn had committed himself to a life of pits, whips, and cages with his own viciously wicked temper.

Shame and outrage twisted into a painful braid within Rache, and he deflected his train of thought before the ugly details plagued his mind again. Nothing good could come of dwelling on a tragedy now eight years old. But he could not keep himself from thinking of what Garn had become and what he could have been.

Many of the gladiators liked Rache for the maneuvers he taught that kept them alive in the pit; most of the others at least gave him a grudging respect. But Garn's hatred for the weapon master seemed tangible. For weeks, the gladiator would say nothing, loathing fairly radiating from him. Then he would make a remark designed to goad Rache to violence. And for reasons Rache could not fully explain, he nearly always fell prey to Garn's insults. *He knows exactly how to antagonize me, and he does it again and again. He knows because I handed him the spears, sling stones, and arrows to hurl against me, the knowledge of Northmen's gods and the reality of Valhalla and Hel.* Santagithi's mixed populace worshiped a host of gods, but only Rache followed the Northlands' faith as well as its pantheon. *When Garn's rage takes control, he can't even remember a simple dodge. So how does he always manage to recall things that annoy me?*

Angered anew by the memory of his own carelessness, Rache turned into the smaller armory/storage room to reclaim the short-sword he had left there. Seventeen crossbows hung from pegs on the walls above a carton of quarrels. The other walls held gladiators' weapons: swords, fighting gauntlets, knives, clubs, and pole arms in sharpened and practice varieties. The actual armory in Santagithi's citadel held more finely crafted and balanced weapons, as well as mail and shields. Rache shunned the armor, too indoctrinated with the Renshai ways to consider it anything but cowardly. Like most of Santagithi's soldiers, he preferred swords, but Rache had learned the techniques of the other weapons in order to instruct guards and gladiators. Discovering his shortsword in the corner where he had left it, Rache affixed it to the right side of his belt, opposite his longsword, and returned to the main hall.

Rache spotted Mitrian sitting on the bench near the exit. Though not quite sixteen, she had inherited her father's broad-boned frame. Already, her hands and feet had grown nearly as large as Rache's. She wore her shoulder-length, chestnut hair tied into a ponytail, revealing her father's spacious, pale eyes and her mother's oval face and fragile features. Though unusual, the combination was appealing. Beyond her, the heavy main door was propped open, revealing brilliant blue sky and gray buildings etched against forest.

Mitrian rose as she noticed Rache and raised a woven basket. 'Ready?' As he drew closer, her smile of welcome faded. 'Rache, are you well?'

'I'm fine,' Rache replied brusquely, taking Mitrian's arm. Apparently the girl could see the tremor of his overworked muscles, and it infuriated him. 'Let's eat by the stream.' He yanked her toward the door.

Sensing Rache's discomfort, Mitrian did not question further but accompanied him to the doorway. They had nearly escaped into the sunlight when Jakot's voice reached them from a distant corridor. 'Rache?'

When a man least wants company, it is most apt to find him. Rache measured the distance to the door, wondering if he could slip through before the guard turned the corner. Then, aware it would look bad to avoid his duties in front of his leader's daughter, he turned to face the sizeable, sandy-haired guard who hurried from an opposite hallway.

Jakot stopped, still some distance from Rache. 'How about a spar?'

Rache smiled despite his mood, glad to see the guard interested in an unscheduled practice. 'Sure. I've got a gladiator to train after lunch, but I'll meet you by the guardhouse first.'

Jakot nodded his thanks and returned the way he had come.

Quickly, Rache and Mitrian slipped through the doorway into the comforting heat of the midday sun. Warmed, Rache's sinews uncoiled; and, as thoughts of Garn faded, peacefulness settled over Rache. The sky stretched, cloudless, over the familiar buildings of Santagithi's estate, and the tiny but concealing patch of forest enclosed between the walls beckoned. He headed toward it.

But before Rache and Mitrian had taken a dozen paces, Nantel's voice stopped them. 'Rache?'

The sword master gave Mitrian an apologetic glance. Though not averse to seeming busy in the presence of Santagithi's daughter, the interruptions were becoming annoying. He stepped around to face the captain of archers. 'Nantel?'

'Sorry to disturb you.' Nantel's mischievous olive-brown eyes revealed that he was not at all sorry. 'There's a new guard, one of the village boys. Will you train him?'

'When?'

'Tomorrow morning.' Though he addressed Rache, Nantel's gaze swept to Mitrian who shifted impatiently from one leg to the other.

Rache considered his already overly busy schedule. 'I'm training gladiators this evening. Tonight I'm on guard duty. You snore like a bear, but even I sleep sometimes.'

Nantel sighed heavily, as if Rache had placed all the burdens of the world on his shoulders. 'Then I'll have to train him.'

Rache winked. 'Eh,' he teased. 'The boy'll be deprived of the master, but you're almost as good.'

Nantel raised his thick eyebrows questioningly. 'Almost?'

Rache laughed. He turned with Mitrian and headed toward the woods. Suddenly, he spun, flinging his shortsword. Nantel had no chance to react before the blade buried itself in the doorjamb, nearly touching his knee. 'Almost,' Rache confirmed. He returned his attention to Mitrian, too busy laughing to notice the envious stare Nantel awarded his back.

Rache and Mitrian entered the forest, brushing between the trees in silence. Rache's friendly rivalry with Nantel had become local legend. He smiled at the realization that he had won this time, knowing Nantel would pay him back, tenfold and shortly, with some ingenious prank. His exchange with his roommate had dispelled the last of his annoyance, and he reveled in the sounds of the forest. Red squirrels scolded and skipped across the boughs. A fox slipped from brush to rock to tree, visible only as a pair of curious, amber eyes and lingering musk. Mayapples quivered in the thin, spring breeze, and poison ivy trembled in silent warning.

Rache knew Mitrian remained quiet in deference to his thoughts. She was a beautiful woman, he decided, despite or because of her solid but slim figure and natural grace. Though she bore no resemblance to the baby sister Rache had lost, she had come to replace the child in his mind. Still, his relationship with Mitrian remained a mystery to the other guards and citizens. Nantel spent countless hours trying to wheedle the secret from him. Santagithi used a direct approach. Rache satisfied them both with vague answers that did little to quell the rumors. *Let them think a romantic interest exists between us,* he mused. It kept them from discovering the truth that would open him to punishment and scorn. Against all custom and propriety, Mitrian was Rache's student.

They sat in a circle of elms by the bank of a winding stream. Mitrian passed Rache a piece of roasted rabbit and a handful of scarlet fruit. She spoke softly, with the subdued catch in her voice the captain had come to associate with trouble. 'Rache ?'

Rache stiffened, becoming inordinately engrossed in his food, certain Mitrian would ask an awkward favor or a question Santagithi considered improper for a woman. Three years ago, in this same tone, she had begged him to teach her to wield a sword.

'Rache ?' Mitrian repeated. When he still hesitated to respond, she continued. 'I heard the gladiators fighting last night. Tell me about it.'

Jarred suddenly back to the near-disaster in the training room, Rache scowled. Among Renshai, if he had suggested women should be protected from warcraft, death, and battle, they would have laughed him down. Fifty women with drawn swords would have taught him the error of his ways, but sixteen years among Santagithi's people had touched him with their customs, if not with a true understanding of them. Unlike Rache, who had seen ailing Renshai attacked and slaughtered by their own people so as not to die a coward's death, Santagithi protected Mitrian from images of blood and death.

Removed from the gore, Mitrian treated swordplay like a sport or a dance, a lithe choreography of steel and man. Even as an infant on the lawn, her eyes had followed the moving, silver glimmers, as fascinated as a crow by things that shine. Since childhood, she had spent much of her free time watching Rache practice katas or train and instruct the guards. Though young and unlearned about weapons, she had recognized the differences between Rache's style and the techniques he taught, picking out the strange, precise Renshai maneuvers he used in spar but never demonstrated. Her sharp notice and zeal had awakened memories of his mother. Rache set aside his meal, aware Mitrian would persist until he answered. 'What do you want to know ?'

Unaware of Rache's reverie, Mitrian squeezed a pit from a cherry. 'I want to know about yesterday's fights.'

Rache trailed his fingers in the cool stream waters as he sifted through the memory, trying to think of a way to tell Mitrian of the grisly contests without disgusting her. He never cared much for watching them, though he oversaw the battles to make certain nothing untoward happened and to discover the successes and failures of his training. 'Well, your father lost quite a bit of gold up until the last match.'

'That was Garn. Wasn't it ?'

Rache scowled, forced back to the topic he had worked so hard to forget. He understood and sympathized with Mitrian's interest. As a child, Garn had lived as a servant in her father's citadel and, at Rache's request, she had drawn the gladiator's young son into her circle of friends, a mixed group of merchants and ranking soldiers' offspring.

Thoughts of those children triggered the memory Rache had suppressed earlier, and it returned too quickly for him to evade it again. He recalled how damp, afternoon fog had swirled over the town of Santagithi, shrouding a frothing mob of citizens near the southern border. Their shouts knifed through the usual quiet peacefulness, sending Rache scurrying to the scene, though he was off-duty. Just beyond the crowd, Santagithi screamed orders lost beneath the hubbub; eight-year-old Mitrian clung, sobbing, to his legs, hindering his every movement. The handful of guards in attendance wove and darted, apparently trying to obey commands they could not quite hear and thwarted by the sheer numbers of the crowd. It seemed to Rache as if the entire village had massed.

Rache remembered how he had drawn up directly at Santagithi's side. As always, the town leader watched with an admirable composure that soothed the nearest citizens. Only a faint scarlet flush to his cheeks revealed his anger. He was gaining control of his people far too slowly to please him, and the distraction of a terrified daughter did not help his cause.

'What's going on?' Though Rache shouted, he was uncertain whether his general could hear him.

Either Santagithi understood or he guessed the obvious question. 'It's Garn . . .'

The general's remaining words were lost beneath the clamor, but Rache had heard enough. Jerking free his sword, he slashed at a section of the crowd with a wordless battle cry that drew every eye. Years of teaching had made him a master at anticipating the dodges and strikes of even the most erratic beginners, and he knew as much from instinct as sight how to pull or redirect his strikes. The citizens scrambled, screaming, from his path, little knowing that at no time were they ever truly in danger.

Rache remembered using the opening his maneuver gained him to shove to the center of the disturbance. There, a child's corpse lay on the grass, several of its limbs broken, its clothing torn, and its face a bloated mass of bruises. Rache recognized the boy as a merchant's son; a few steps away, the father nursed a wrist swollen to twice its normal size. There could be no question who had done the slaying. Garn rolled, kicked, and bit, half pinned beneath three adults who lunged in whenever he swung for one, then retreated whenever he shifted his attack. Hemmed in by the crowd, the goldsmith's daughter and a guardsman's son cowered back from the struggle.

Rache sheathed his sword, plunging unhesitatingly into the fray. He caught the butcher by his thick shoulders and spun the larger man into the crowd. The butcher crashed into a goading mob of cattlemen. Three fell, flailing, taking the butcher down with them. Heedless, Rache ducked between Garn and his other two attackers, realizing only then that one of the men held a knife. Rache made a grab for the weapon.

Garn's wild kick caught Rache in the shin. Driven off his timing, Rache felt the blade skim across his forearm, opening the sleeve and the skin. *Modi!* The Renshai's pain cry came naturally to his mind. Though he had learned not to shout the name aloud, the battle wrath it inspired was less easily suppressed. Rage bucked against his control. He slammed the dagger from the man's hand with enough force to break its wielder's thumb. The movement threw a thin arc of Rache's blood across the closest spectators, and they shrank back in revulsion. With a shriek of pain, the man skittered beyond Rache's reach. Garn's third attacker withdrew, ending the need for another confrontation.

Though only eleven, Garn already sported his father's thick, compact musculature, nearly as broad as he was tall. He crouched in the defensive posture that Rache had taught him, and his green eyes held the madness of a hungry jaguar. Yet Rache saw details that others surely missed: the trace of rigidity that fear added to Garn's stance, the upward twitch at the corner of his mouth that betrayed joy and relief at having found an ally against the enraged mob. Caught between a temper as indomitable as a volcano and a childish need for a parent's comforting, Garn froze.

The level of noise had diminished, and Rache sought soothing words to pacify the wild creature that was not quite Garn. But before he could speak, a condemnation cut clearly over the crowd, picked up and carried by what seemed like all two thousand of Santagithi's citizens. 'Kill him! Kill the child murderer!'

Now, in the forest clearing with Mitrian, Rache cringed from the memory of what came next. He had reached for Garn, but the boy had sprung away. As the crowd pressed in again, Rache knew he had little choice but to subdue Garn before the mob slaughtered him. Drawing his sword, he whipped the flat for Garn's head.

As he spun to face the crowd, Garn saw the blow too late. For an instant, his gaze met Rache's, and the captain thought he saw an expression he had never known before or since, a self-righteous pain of betrayal so innocent that only a child could suffer it. Then the sword struck a clouting blow that had seemed to vibrate through

Rache's hands to his shoulders. And he knew a hatred nearly as pure as Garn's pain, against himself for what he had done, against the crowd for a savagery every bit as revolting as Garn's own, and against Garn for misusing Rache's teachings and taking a young man's life.

Garn collapsed without a cry. And Rache shielded Carad's son with his own sword and body.

So familiar, the memory compressed to an instant. Still, Rache had hesitated long enough that Mitrian repeated her question.

'Garn was the winner of the last pit fight. Right?'

'Garn. Yes.' Rache rubbed his aching forearms with a frown, his past and present thoughts of Garn equally disturbing. 'Mitrian, I'm sorry. I really don't want to talk about gladiators.' *Especially that one.*

'All right.' Mitrian did not press. 'Then let's talk about swords. Will I have a lesson tonight?'

Though well beyond hearing range of the other guards, Rache grimaced. 'I'm on duty on the south side. I can't teach, but you can practice in the clearing near the arena.' Consumed by irritation, Rache left his meal half-finished. 'I have to get back to work. Remember? I promised Jakot a spar.'

Mitrian quietly replaced the basket, but her eyes betrayed excitement. Her obsession with action never seemed to dull.

'Want me to walk you back?'

'No,' Mitrian said. 'I want to sit here for a while. I'll see you tonight.'

'Right.' Rache rose and headed back toward Santagithi's estate. His discussion with Mitrian, though brief, had displaced thoughts of work for a time, but now all the day's burdens rushed back. Due to three impromptu spars initiated by guards, Rache had fallen behind in his duties and would have skipped eating if he had not already promised Mitrian. Even so, Garn's challenge had whittled away at one end of Rache's lunchtime, and Jakot's lesson had forced him to cut the meal short.

At the edge of the forest, Rache shaded his eyes from the sun's glare, hurrying in the direction of the guardhouse. He had scarcely reached the familiar portal when a darkly bearded guard accosted him. 'Hey Rach!'

Rache chuckled at the laziness of a culture that insisted on shortening even his simple, two syllable name.

'How about a match before you get back to work?'

Rache stemmed the tide of oaths that burned on his tongue. Usually, he enjoyed his job, and he did not want his temper to discourage the guard. 'I promised to spar Jakot after lunch. Since he's not here yet, I suppose I can take you first.'

The two men found an open space and began their contest. Rache bested his opponent with every stroke. After he had twice sent his bearded companion to his knees, the sword master called a halt to the match. 'You place too much weight on your leading foot,' Rache explained as he sheathed his sword. 'You commit yourself to each lunge and leave too little time to prepare for the next.'

'Thank you,' the guard muttered glumly as he trotted toward the guardhouse.

Rache turned to face Jakot.

That evening, Rache staggered against the door to the quarters he shared with Nantel. After Garn's sledgehammer blows and an afternoon spent sparring with students, Rache could scarcely lift his hands to the door's handle. The wooden panel yielded, more to his will than to strength, to expose the brightly lit room. Nantel roasted a piece of salt pork on an iron spit in the fireplace. Beyond him, the bedroom beckoned, a keg of ale outside it, but Rache collapsed into one of the two chairs at the table. Shoving aside plates and mugs, he buried his face in his arms.

'Rache, my friend,' Nantel called cheerily. 'What a beautiful day. I hope tomorrow's just like it.'

With effort, Rache raised his head. Nantel's gaiety irked him. 'I hope the end of your tongue catches on the spit with the pork, you swine.'

Nantel turned. 'I hope I'm wrong,' he said, too innocently. 'But it sounds like you had a bad day.'

Rache replaced his face on his arm, too dazed to realize Nantel was baiting him. 'The worst. And it's not over yet.' He groaned. 'I hate guard duty.'

'Aah,' Nantel asserted in a singsong. 'A chance to breathe the cool night air, enjoy the stars, and march the borders of this splendid town. One of the more pleasant duties of a soldier.'

'Fine.' Nantel's levity compounded Rache's misery. 'You do it. So far this day I taught that dog, Garn, a lesson, trained six other gladiators, and sparred with fourteen fools who scarcely know which end of the sword to hold. Then I crawl home to listen to the ramblings of an idiot who can find no other pleasure than standing in the woods at night getting bitten by blackflies.' He leaned on his elbow and regarded Nantel from the corner of one eye. 'I believe I deserve a drink.'

Seizing one of the two mugs at random, the guard captain rose and strode to the keg. He filled it and faced Nantel. 'In all my years of teaching, I've never had so many men attack me with such vigor. If I'd inspired this enthusiasm when I first became captain, Santagithi would now rule the world.' He downed the drink in a single, hasty gulp.

'My friend.' Nantel stood. 'That enthusiasm has touched even me. I'm sure you have enough energy to teach one you so inspire. We've got time for one more spar before we eat.'

Rache glared. 'Forget it. You want a favor, go ask your brothers. I'm sure the asses in the stable have more energy than I do.'

Nantel ignored the insult. 'One spar is a small price to pay for a chance to avoid the blackflies.'

Rache glanced up, some of his lost vitality returning in a rush. 'If you take my place as sentry, I'll spar with you.' He added quickly, 'Once.'

'Agreed.' Nantel drew his sword and headed out through the door into the field before the guardhouse. Sunset touched yellow wildflowers amid weeds mulched by the feet of practicing guards. To the west, the rugged silhouettes of the Granite Hills rose distantly above the forest beyond the wall surrounding Santagithi's citadel.

Rache followed more slowly. Irked by Nantel's obvious ardor, he did not think to question why his companion chose this particular evening for a match. He yawned, anticipating a moment of talk before the contest, a chance to prepare. So the blinding ferocity of Nantel's attack made Rache catch his breath. Nantel hacked for Rache's side. Rache dodged, overtaxed muscles flashing complaint. The blunt edge of his sword slapped Nantel's knuckles. The archer captain dropped his weapon.

'Done.' Rache turned, his arms aching.

Nantel cursed and retrieved his sword. 'Not ... done ... yet, Rache !' He lunged for Rache's back.

Rache spun. Again, the unsharpened side of his blade struck Nantel's bruised hands. For the second time, Rache disarmed Nantel.

Nantel snatched up his weapon. 'You won't escape this easily.' He tensed, but as quickly as Nantel regained his sword, Rache chopped it from his grip. Nantel dove for his hilt.

'Enough ! You win !' Rache hurled his sword at Nantel's feet and swore violently. 'We sparred three times. After tonight, you owe me two more nights with the blackflies.'

Nantel laughed. 'A small price to pay,' he muttered to himself as Rache stalked sullenly inside their quarters and fell into his seat before the table. He leaned on his elbows, scowling, as Nantel merrily finished preparing the meal. In no mood to consider his own thoughts, Nantel's mumblings and whistling interested Rache far less. He scarcely tasted the pork and ale Nantel served, though he downed prodigious quantities.

'Pass the salt please.' A friendly smile graced Nantel's twisted features.

When Rache raised his arm, pain danced along it. He could feel every muscle fiber and followed every over-used tendon to its source. 'Go to the ocean, and sift your own damned salt.'

Nantel chuckled. He reached across the table and slid the small bowl of salt toward his plate. 'Rache,' he said in the same congenial tone. 'I'm afraid you'll have to prepare the next few meals for yourself. I'll be forced to eat with Santagithi and his family.'

'What are you babbling about, idiot?' demanded Rache, in too much discomfort to guard his tongue. 'You're barely fit to dine with Santagithi's dogs.'

A grin decorated Nantel's face. 'True, but I earned a seat at his table. I defeated his "unbeatable" captain.'

Understanding struck Rache with vivid clarity. 'You what?' He leaped to his feet, jarring the wobbly table. Mugs toppled and rolled, splashing Nantel before hitting the floor with a tinny clang. 'You . . .' The string of expletives that followed was harsh even to Nantel's ears.

The archer laughed, though ale stained and dripped from his jerkin.

Rache thundered into the bedroom and out the opposite doorway. His head pounded with anger. As he tramped through the corridors, he saw nothing but his goal, the main chamber where he knew he would find Santagithi chastising his guards for last night's card game. Ignoring the doors into the other quarters, he burst into the meeting room. 'I want you to know about that spawn of a lizard turd you call captain of archers!'

Two dozen off-duty guards looked up from the array of chairs, chests and tables. Santagithi whirled, his voice unusually calm for a general addressed in this manner by a subordinate. 'There is only one "spawn of a lizard turd" among my guards. I presume you mean Nantel.'

Abashed silence erupted into laughter. Rache noticed his roommate had slipped into the room behind him and joined the mirth, and, if his arms were any less swollen, Rache would have throttled Nantel.

'He's just mad because I won the week of good food,' boasted Nantel.

Rache quivered with rage. He jabbed an accusing finger at Santagithi. 'What sort of reward did you offer these men to assault me?' Rache rarely allowed his emotions free rein, but this day had been a long string of outrages. 'And just tell me. Did you offer it to the gladiators, too?'

Santagithi smiled tolerantly. He placed a heavy hand on Rache's shoulder. 'I only thought of it this morning. I hoped it would encourage the guards to practice if I offered a week at my table to the man who bested you. I was going to tell you before guard duty tonight.'

'Do you know how Nantel won that spar?' Fatigue began to replace Rache's ire. 'He let the others wear me down.' His broad gesture included every man in the room. 'Then he just kept pestering me until I gave him the match so he'd leave me alone.'

Santagithi frowned and all amusement left his features. As his stormy eyes riveted upon Nantel, Rache reveled in his minor victory. He doubted Santagithi would punish Nantel, but he enjoyed watching the archer shift nervously from foot to foot.

'Is that true?' Santagithi addressed Nantel.

The archer swallowed and glanced about, seeking aid and not just sympathy in his companions' eyes. 'Well, sort of.'

Santagithi nodded. 'Make it two weeks at my table, then. This town needs strategists as well as swordsmen.' He gave Nantel a hearty slap across the back.

Rache stared, rage fading beneath the wild chorus of guards' laughter. Finally, realizing Nantel had won this time, Rache joined his companions' merriment until another thought wiped the grin from his face and reawakened his exhaustion. He had promised to meet Mitrian on duty that night. Fate had chosen him as its victim again, and Rache would attend his detail. But Nantel still owed him three nights on watch. If Rache had a choice in it, he would schedule those nights consecutively and in the rain.

As the light through Mitrian's window faded, bathing the room in blackness, she slipped from her bed, fully clothed in a worn, comfortable dress. She groped beneath the bed frame for the candle and striker she kept secreted there. The dull thud of a guard's footsteps outside reassured her. He would be at the far end of his watch when she crept from the house.

The scattered glow from Mitrian's candle scarcely pierced the darkness, but it would reveal objects in her path. If she stumbled and awakened her parents, she would lose the sword training more than three years of stealth had earned. She stuffed her feet into her sandals, opened her bedroom door, entered the corridor, and closed the door behind her. Padding silently through the halls, she passed the kitchen and dining chambers and paused before the brass door to Santagithi's armory. There was little of interest on the route. A practical man, Santagithi shunned unnecessary finery.

Mitrian freed the keys from her pocket, all senses focused beyond the door. Once she had interrupted a practicing guard. She had managed to escape before he recognized her, and she suspected he had not given chase because he had no more right to enter the armory at night than she did. Mitrian inserted the key, turned it, and pushed. The door swung open.

The polished faces of a dozen ornamental shields reflected her candle, scattering weak highlights that widened her view. The stately assemblage of Santagithi's armory contrasted with the simplicity of his furnishings. Mitrian strode unhesitatingly to the weapons and lifted a broadsword from its perch. Her elbow brushed a scimitar, a fine work of tempered steel with a grip encrusted with rubies. Longing filled her. *When I get my own sword, it'll look like this one.* She had asked Rache to train her to wield it many times, but he insisted she learn the double-edged weapons first. Mitrian paused, grinning. *But Rache's not teaching me tonight.* She returned the broadsword, but still she wavered. The scimitar belonged to one of the villagers. If she damaged it, she could not replace it. She stroked the sheath longingly, envisioning it as her own. *There'll be no target for my blade. I can't hurt it.* Convinced by her rationalization, she buckled the scimitar to her belt.

Exiting, Mitrian closed and locked the door behind her and walked the last short hallway to the outer door. Once through it, she extinguished the candle and pocketed it. The sliver of moon became her guide as she followed the border of the woods, watching the wall to the east and picturing the town beyond it unfurling beneath her father's estate. So familiar, her mind drew the image clearly as a map. Neat rows of cottages stood like proud soldiers, the landscape graced by fluffy, silver sheep. During the daylight hours, the blacksmith's hammer rang ceaselessly upon his anvil while his son, Listar, pumped the bellows.

Mitrian smiled as she padded south, past the slave training quarters and the individual cells of the gladiators. She knew Listar awaited her sixteenth birthday impatiently. In a few weeks, when she came of age, he would court her, nearly unopposed. Of the five boys who had been Mitrian's closest friends, he alone remained. Garn had slaughtered Mukesh and was enslaved for the crime. Trapped too near the violence, Helvor had withdrawn into a quivering, teary adult more often drunk than sober, and the last boy had lost his life in a hunting accident.

Listar was a hard-working, amiable man, and his features were not unbecoming. His pale eyes complemented sand-colored curls.

Though not fat, his softly-rounded body contrasted sharply with the thickness of arms trained to master the hammer. Mitrian enjoyed his company at times, but found him dull. Unlike Rache, Listar had no tales of war with which to amuse her. He had not traveled to distant lands like Nantel. And, although his sex gave him the privilege to join Santagithi's occasional forays, Listar chose to remain safely in the village as if shunning the weapon training Mitrian had won only with luck and effort.

As Mitrian rounded the guardhouse, she turned from her path. Farther south, she recognized the huddled mass of the South Corner Arena, the stone wall that encircled it obscured by trees and brush. Near it, someone moved.

Mitrian melted into the shadows and waited for moonlight to reveal the other. Soon, Rache's confident stride became unmistakable. His golden hair rivaled the moon. Mitrian's memory completed the figure: hard blue eyes, a boyishly handsome face, and the lithe musculature of a warrior. She watched him appreciatively. Usually, he stood and moved casually, oblivious to the fact that he could have almost any woman in Santagithi's town. But, with a sword in his hand, nature could not match his beauty or skill. He seemed to age more slowly than other men, too, as if the gods recognized his attractiveness and wanted to preserve it like some rare specimen. Still, the qualities that made Rache so desirable kept him unattainable. The love this master lavished upon his sword equaled that of most men for their families. The one time Mitrian had gathered the nerve to question Rache about his social life, he had muttered something indecipherable about never passing a brutal heritage and time, then quickly changed the subject.

Rache hesitated, as if he sensed Mitrian's presence.

Mitrian stepped into view. Instantly, the captain slid his sword from its sheath and crouched, from habit rather than alarm. His gaze swept across her to rest on the curved scabbard at her hip. He scowled but did not verbalize his displeasure. 'Let me know when you leave.' He handed her an unlit lantern.

'Thanks.' Mitrian accepted the lantern and slipped into the woods, veering around trees that shivered in the night wind. The rustle of their leaves and the song of crickets melted into a sweet duet. Mitrian found her path by rote. In a clearing just beyond the edge of the forest, Rache had taught her some of the finer points of swordsmanship.

Mitrian lit the lantern and placed it on a high rock. Its beam drew shadows of objects in the clearing, but the pristine beauty of forest darkness went unnoticed as Mitrian began movements so delicate and precise they commanded all her attention. Her feet skimmed lightly over the grass and seemed barely to touch ground. The graceful glides of the scimitar in her hand blended with the forest setting as if Mitrian was some woodland creature performing a rite with origins beyond creation. Each technique followed naturally from the last. She never lost the rhythm of her dance.

Mitrian had just completed a right feint with a sudden upstroke when a double glare of crimson reflected from the brush. *Eyes? But animal eyes glow amber not red.* Mitrian froze in position, sword raised more from coincidence than threat. Her heart raced.

Suddenly, the eyes disappeared, without any accompanying noise of breaking branches or rustling leaves. The creature still lurked in the brush, invisible now that the lantern no longer illuminated its eyes.

Time dragged. Mitrian held her defensive pose, a duplicate of Rache's earlier crouch. Her arms ached from remaining in an unnatural position too long. Sweat trickled down her forehead and into her eyes. Then came the momentary crackle of movement, and the beast departed as quietly as it had come.

Mitrian wiped her brow and lowered her sword, quivering from what she hoped was strain but knew was alarm. Those eyes had seemed hostile, dangerous. *Nonsense.* Mitrian dismissed fear no more reasonable than a child's terror of darkness. *A skunk probably. Or a fox. There's no way to judge intent by the reflection of light from eyes.* Despite her brave thoughts, the glaring crimson points seemed burned into her memory, making it impossible to concentrate on practice. She sheathed the scimitar and hastened home, pausing only to wave to Rache.

3 Garn's Revenge

Garn stood, glaring between the bars of his cage in the southern corner of Santagithi's estate. Rust and pits in the steel dug into his shoulder, and his arms throbbed from overexertion. He clutched a walnut-sized, jeweled trinket he had stolen from the sentry's pocket. Alert as always, he knew without looking that the gladiator to his right curled in wary sleep while the one to his left hunched, still but awake, on the floor of his cell. For now, they did not concern him. He kept his gaze locked on the pair of guards headed toward him, still too distant to identify.

Garn growled deep in his throat, lowering his head until his shaggy, bronze hair fell into his eyes. He dropped to a crouch as the guards drew near enough to recognize. *Rache and Nantel.* Garn watched the golden-haired sword master through narrowed eyes, thrown into a familiar maelstrom of loathing that washed his vision red. Eight years of living like an animal had fanned the sparks of his hatred into a raging bonfire he could scarcely contain. *It was Rache who trained me to respond to threat with violence, who pounded war tenets into me until they became instinct. Then, when I followed them, he turned against me to side with a spoiled bully who planned to force himself on Mitrian.*

The new train of thought further fueled Garn's rage. Mukesh had been the leader of the group, a loud-mouthed, only child who would never have let the gladiator's son join their play if not for Mitrian's insistence. Still, when she was not there, Mukesh stole every opportunity to call Garn 'slave brat' and to remind Garn how poetic the names Mukesh and Mitrian sounded together. Garn tightened his hands into fists, feeling the trinket bite into his palm. Years later, he could still hear Mukesh's taunt verbatim: 'Mitrian needs a strong man, one who can bend her to his will. One way or another, I'm going to do a kindness to her.' He thrust his narrow pelvis, in case Garn had missed the obvious euphemism. 'And when I'm done, she'll beg for more.'

Garn continued to stare at the guards through vision blurred by rage and anguish. *Mukesh never got Mitrian, but I never won her either – because the man I trusted sold me into slavery to take her for himself.* The image of Rache and Mitrian together thrust him to the brink of the same blind, uncontrollable madness that had goaded him to continue battering Mukesh's body long after death.

For the sake of his sanity, Garn refocused his attention on Nantel. The sight of the quick-tempered archer captain rasied a less biting malice. Yesterday, during feeding, he had dropped his defenses to steal the trinket he now clutched from the guard distributing food. During his lapse, Garn's right-hand neighbor had stolen his dinner.

Garn recalled how he had spun, managing to grab the thief's hand as it disappeared. Dragging the other gladiator toward him, he had grasped the man's neck in both hands. He remembered the feel of his fingers twining around the cords of the throat, the other slave fighting, first with trained deliberateness, then in wild, gasping panic. *I had him.* Garn's hands curled and twitched at the memory. *Until Nantel came.* Garn snarled, recalling how Nantel had jabbed and pounded him with a staff until he released the other man, then whipped him through the bars. Garn's stomach still churned from a day without food, and the beating made every movement painful. *Damned archer coward didn't even have the courage to come into the cage to hit me.* Garn clenched his fingers so tightly, the grimy, jagged nails cut into his palm, and the metal frame of the trinket gouged creases into his flesh. Maddened to a frenzy that left no thought for the consequences, Garn drew back and hurled the jewel at Rache's head.

As the missile left Garn's hand, Nantel glanced over. Before he could shout a warning, the trinket crashed against Rache's ear, staggering him. Hesitating only long enough to make certain his friend had not been badly injured, Nantel raced toward Garn.

Panic seized the gladiator. An attack against a guard demanded punishment, and Nantel would certainly deal it. *What have I done?* Garn's throat dried to raw misery. 'No!' His plea emerged as a dull croak that went unheeded.

Nantel paused at the training quarters to gather a whip and chains. Then, sword drawn, he wrenched open Garn's cell.

Garn leapt backward. His head struck the wall, harder than he expected. Dazed by the impact, he could not dodge. The flat of Nantel's sword crashed against his skull, knocking his awareness to the fuzzy quality of a dream. Garn staggered. He thrust out an arm for balance and felt it yanked painfully against the other. Familiar chains secured his wrist and ankles. Garn howled. He lunged blindly, but steel cracked against his ear and jarred him to his knees. Cold fingers yanked him to his feet, jerked him from the cage and pinned his chest against his cell door. Garn clasped the bars and fought to regain numbed senses.

The sting of the whip across Garn's back jolted him to alertness, the taste of bile bitter in his mouth. Every lash shocked pain through his body, sharpening his wits with hatred. But Garn remained flaccid as a doll against the bars and hoped Nantel would tire of battering a semiconscious slave.

Garn screamed once in anguish, and Rache's voice chorused with his, far closer than he'd expected. 'Nantel! Watch out!' Rache lunged in, hauling Nantel away from a threat Garn could not yet see. The beating stopped abruptly.

The gladiator in the next cage hurled a rock that Rache barely dodged. Though dizzied, Garn tapped his hatred for strength. He sprang. His chain-wrapped fists hammered Rache's back, and he and the guard captain tumbled to the ground together. Rache lay limp beneath him. Garn bellowed in triumph as he plunged steel-weighted hands to shatter Rache's skull. Then his own head exploded into blackness.

As Garn awoke, the whip cuts' sting and the cold, hard floor felt reassuringly familiar. Although conscious, he did not move, and his eyes remained closed. The other gladiators would certainly notice the subtle change in his breathing pattern and know he had awakened, but the guards would not. Their survival did not depend on their perceptiveness. Usually.

After years in the pit, Garn knew a good blow when he gave or received it, and the one he gave Rache should have been fatal. A single thought ran repeatedly through his mind: *I killed Rache. I killed Rache! I wish I'd got Nantel, too, but I killed Rache!*

Garn heard the creak of cart wheels and focused on the sound. After killing a guard, alertness became even more necessary for survival. A short while later, he heard the rattle of wooden bowls and the familiar plop of meat falling into them. These sounds continued for some time, followed by the grating of wood across stone as the bowls slid into the cages. Since the guards only served meat as the evening meal, he knew it would soon become dark. Then, he must escape. After killing Rache, he had even less of a future here. His only option was to escape or die in the attempt, though the unknown seemed even more frightening than forced battles and the guards' whips. Garn remained still.

Later, the guards collected the bowls as the last rays of sunset left Garn's eye-closed world totally dark. The smaller man in the cage to Garn's left settled down with his back pressed against the bars separating him from Garn. There was a reason for his neighbor's choice of resting place. Whether he meant well or ill did not matter. As long as Garn remained awake, the man was no threat.

Garn heard the guard pace past his cell three times before the smaller man whispered, 'Rache's bad, but alive.' Then he scuttled to the center of his cage.

No! Now Garn did not care whether the guards knew he lay awake. Frustration flowed, scalding within him. Until Rache recovered or died, they would watch him too closely for escape. *Gods! Don't take this one triumph away from me.* Over and over, Garn drove his fist into the cold stone floor until blood ran. The knuckle next to his thumb bulged oddly, and agony shot through his hand. Garn concentrated on the pain as the familiar sensation lulled him to sleep. He slept the sleep of the innocent.

That night, Mitrian's father did not come home for dinner. Instead, Nantel arrived at the house and announced that Santagithi had business with his guards and would not return until morning. Mitrian squirmed with curiosity. Her father rarely missed one of her mother's meals. Only a matter of grave importance could detain Santagithi, perhaps one substantial enough to keep Rache from her promised lesson as well.

Mitrian found waiting for her mother to extinguish the candles in her parents' bedchamber nearly unbearable. She rested only until her mother had time to enter the pre-sleep haze that dulls the senses. Then Mitrian sneaked from her bedroom, took a broadsword from the armory, and slipped into night's concealing darkness. She stole south, along the forest's edge, hearing a steady, unidentifiable rhythm above the song of the crickets. As she crept nearer to the guardhouse, the noise resolved into the bells and rattles of the medicine man. *Someone's sick.* Judging from her father's absence, it was someone important. Icy fear touched Mitrian, but she forced it away. It made no sense to speculate; she felt certain her mind would invoke the worst possibilities in her ignorance.

Mitrian fumbled through the brush and into the clearing of the southern woods, certain whatever concerned her father had detained Rache as well. An opening in the foliage admitted a beam of moonlight for which she felt grateful. Usually Rache brought the lantern. Drawing the broadsword, she angled it until its steel reflected the full moon. She raised her head regally and imagined herself upon a snow-maned stallion, riding into battle at Rache's side, her movements as smooth and graceful as his.

Still haunted by the memory of the eyes in the clearing as well as Rache's absence, Mitrian slid angrily into her practice. The more she mulled over the presence of the medicine man, the faster she drove herself to force the distraction from her mind. She labored over a complex maneuver Rache had taught her. Mitrian had never learned the word 'Renshai,' nor would she have understood its meaning. She knew only that many of Rache's recent feints were incredibly difficult to master.

A breeze toyed with Mitrian's sweat-dampened hair. She sheathed her sword, discovered she was trembling, and wondered whether to blame the cooling night air or anxiety. Rache had never missed a promised practice before. Though uncertain whether his loyalty was toward her or the sword craft, Mitrian knew the pattern had been ingrained in him in his childhood by a teacher he once described as 'hard as flint and half as human.'

Mitrian headed home. As she rounded the guardhouse, the chitter of rattles and the high, clear chime of bells sang a warning. Cold sweat dampened her skin, clammier than the perspiration induced by exertion. Her feet grew leaden. She knew she could not sleep until she assured herself that her father, Nantel, and Rache were well.

The shuffle of approaching footsteps sounded unusually loud to Mitrian. She pressed against the stone wall of the guardhouse and listened to a brief exchange between passing sentries.

'. . . gladiator's strong as a bear.'

'Rache's not stirred yet, poor . . .'

Numb as death, Mitrian did not hear the men part. Grief tightened her throat and nearly paralyzed her body. She unhooked the sword from her belt and allowed it to fall to the ground. With a flicker of hope, she paced, stiff-legged, along the wall and pounded on the guardhouse door.

Nantel opened the panel, eyes wide with surprise. 'Mitrian? What are you doing . . . ?'

Mitrian pushed past before Nantel could finish. She raced down the hall to the main chamber. The tools of the medicine man had fallen silent. Tense whispers mingled eerily from beyond the closed door. Opening it, she stepped inside; the stillness compounded her fear. Rache lay on a wooden table, swaddled in a woolen blanket, his hair the color of the straw on which his head lolled. His face was so pale it appeared carved.

'No,' Mitrian said in disbelief. She reached for his face, but a callused hand seized her wrist.

Mitrian whirled, noticing the circle of guards for the first time. She stared into her father's eyes. His face looked haggard. 'You shouldn't have come. Rache wouldn't want you to see him this way.' Santagithi nudged Mitrian to a corner. 'Stay quiet and out of his sight.'

Rache's eyelids fluttered, and his head wobbled.

A lump grew in Mitrian's throat. The scene had the terrifying, unreal quality of a nightmare. Surely someone had painted Rache's features on a frail and dying stranger.

'What?' Rache's childlike tone seemed to come from a great distance.

The guards settled into an uncomfortable silence. Santagithi controlled his words with obvious effort. 'How do you feel?'

Rache's voice rasped like sea against stone. 'Why did you tie me up?'

At a nod from Santagithi, one of the guards loosened the blankets. Mitrian stared at Rache, his weakness awakening pity and outrage. *What could have done this to Rache?*

What little color remained in Rache's face drained away. His mouth fell open, but his words never came.

Questioning murmurs swept from a dozen throats.

Rache thrashed his head wildly. 'Get out!' he managed to scream. 'Everyone leave me alone!' His next breath was an anguished sob.

Mitrian's heart hammered against her ribs. No one moved.

'Go!' Rache's voice trembled. 'Go, please. Go.'

'Go.' Santagithi's softer, calmer voice echoed Rache's.

As the men trooped obediently through the portal, Mitrian hung back. She met her father's warning glance with pleading eyes, but he shook his head, granting no quarter.

Miserably, Mitrian trailed the others from the room until only Santagithi remained.

The closing click of the door released a flood of tears from Rache's eyes. He had always hoped death would take him with a violent separation of spirit and flesh, his life consumed by flailing steel. This could not be real. He lay there, completely paralyzed.

Maximum effort of Rache's neck and eye muscles assured him that his limbs remained intact, but the knowledge gave him scant comfort. The loss of a major body part would have barred him from Valhalla, but to reach the haven of dead warriors, he still must find death in battle. Affixed or not, a limp arm could not wield a sword; useless legs could never carry him to war. He had lost all means of entering Valhalla, the glories of death stripped away as fully as the pleasures of life. Trapped in a limbo of pain and despair, Rache fought madness.

'Rache?' Santagithi prodded gently.

Frustration and grief channeled into rage. 'I hate you.' Rache's words emerged too choked to sting. 'A friend would never have let me awaken.'

'I don't understand.'

'I can't move.' Tears hot as fresh blood coursed down Rache's cheeks. Self-pity closed over him. 'Don't let me lie here like a sword without a soldier. Kill me.'

Santagithi's features framed concern and confusion. 'Rache, I can't – '

'Kill me.' Rache's mind narrowed to these two words. He gritted his teeth until his vision hazed to dancing pinpoints of light.

'Listen to me, Rache,' Santagithi started firmly.

'Damn you, kill me !' Rache clenched his eyes, his face streaked with tears he could not wipe away. 'Don't make me beg.'

'Rache !' Santagithi's command left no place for interruption. He reached for his captain. '*You will listen.*'

Rache could scarcely feel his leader's hands upon his shoulders. His tear-blurred gaze met eyes nearly as cold as his own. 'Or what, Santagithi ?' Rache's voice seemed to drip with venom. 'You'll have me walk extra guard duty ? I've served you faithfully for sixteen years. Why should I listen to an old dotard who won't honor my one request ?' Rache's attention fixed on the scabbard at Santagithi's hip. Beyond reason, he hoped his leader would retaliate with action rather than words.

'Rache . . .'

Rache raved. 'Should I listen to a man who leads farmers to war ? My people razed a thousand Western towns like yours, and we had half the numbers. We . . .' He broke off in horror. He had spent so many years hiding his heritage only to reveal it in one burst of hopeless anger. Surely Santagithi knew the gory history of the Renshai. Rache's face fell into a grimace. *What does it matter now ? Will my million enemies travel long distance to kill a dying man ?*

'Rache.' Santagithi seized upon his sword master's silence. 'I've seen men in your condition recover in days. Days, Rache.' Santagithi's features contained the hungry look of a falcon. 'If you've finished insulting your companions and wallowing in self-pity, you might try recalling them also.'

Sanity slowly replaced Rache's wrath. Men who survived the initial spinal shock of a back injury sometimes did recover surprisingly quickly. Rache attempted speech. The world spun. His ethereal grip on consciousness failed, and he dropped into oblivion.

Delirium stripped Rache of years, driving him back into memories he had hidden behind elaborate defenses. Ghosts returned, veiling him with remembrances that ranged from gleeful to terrifying : his sister's laughter, his father's ululating battle cry, and old Episte's stoic misery during the days when he sacrificed his soul to train the last Renshai. It forced scarcely remembered images of a child a few years younger than Rache, a huge, dark boy, silent with misery, brought by the Eastern Wizard to live in Santagithi's guardhouse three years before Garn became Rache's charge. Other things assailed Rache, too, dream devils that disabled him, then conjured enemy sword strokes he no longer had the prowess to dodge.

Thoughts of Garn came, too. A thousand times, Rache's fevered mind replayed the crippling blow, each time driving him deeper into the same black rage Garn felt for him, a loathing that chased Rache into his rare moments of lucidity. And Rache relived a time he would rather have forgotten, a foolish age when he had still dared to care about the child that Garn had been:

At eighteen, Rache had scarcely entered his early adolescence. Yet lack of chest and facial hair and a hand's length of difference in height could not keep Rache from questioning his leader he usually trusted and obeyed unconditionally. 'Sir, if Garn says he was protecting Mitrian, I believe him.' The words fell just short of a challenge. Mukesh's father had played on the sympathies of the masses, and Garn's savage thoroughness had seen to it that no one would take his word at the expense of a mutilated child's honor. 'Doesn't rescuing your daughter gain him anything?'

'Yes.' Santagithi skirted the issue of Garn's credibility, speaking with his usual gentle insight. He grasped Rache's hand like a father. 'It gains him a life as a gladiator instead of execution.'

Rache lowered his head. He believed in his leader's judgement. Yet this seemed wrong.

Reading Rache's hesitation, Santagithi explained further, his tone soothing yet firm. He was wholly in control. 'Rache, I'm not punishing Garn for protecting Mitrian.' Wisely, he avoided the uncertainty of the statement, accepting Rache's viewpoint as if it were fact. 'The boy's motives are of no significance. I can't have a free citizen who explodes into killing frenzies, especially a man as strong as Garn. You saw what he did to that boy and how he fought off the adults as well. He's only eleven. Imagine the destruction he could wreak at your age.'

'I'll watch him,' Rache promised. 'I'll keep him out of trouble.'

'No.' Santagithi left no room for concession. 'You're my guard captain, damn it. I need you for more important things than playing nanny. And I won't be forced into the position of sentencing you for Garn's violence.'

Rache fidgeted, staring at his feet. This time he knew Santagithi was right. Already, the more vengeful and vocal of Santagithi's citizens clamored for Rache's neck as well as Garn's; many of them attributed Rache's youth, battle wrath, and skill to evil magic and Garn's tantrums to his exposure to this unnatural Northman. Still,

Carad's plea ached at Rache, and he could not shake the burden of responsibility.

Santagithi sighed, torn between his loyalty to his people and to his captain. 'Of everyone, I would have thought you could understand the best. The pit gives Garn the opportunity to die in the glory of combat rather than dangling from the end of rope. As strong as he is, he might live for years or decades. His father did.'

Rache cringed, remembering his own short time in the pit, and quoting his *torke* from deeply ingrained habit. 'There is no honor in fighting another man's battles.'

'Given a choice between execution and the gladiator pit . . . ?'

Rache finished the sentence without meeting his leader's gaze '. . . I would choose death.'

'But you're not the one being punished.' Santagithi squeezed Rache's hand until the young Renshai met his gaze. 'To him, following in Carad's footsteps is an honor. Garn believes his father was a hero . . .'

A hero. A hero . . . The concept swirled through Rache's dream-erratic thoughts, nudging his mind in another direction. Frenzied wolf howls, death screams, and Renshai pain cries assaulted him. Female hands secured him again, his mother pitching him into the Amirannak Sea, her voice loud in his ears, speaking words she had never said: 'Though I place the burden of a nation upon you, do not hate me. My weakness was cowardice; you must not make the same mistake. Rache, whatever happens, you can do nothing wrong if you die a hero.'

'Mama!' Rache blundered into consciousness, the screams he heard his own.

A face lined with concern stared down at him, a rounded, female visage he did not immediately recognize. Her hands reached for his neck.

Instinctively, Rache caught the woman's hands, and his movement startled them both.

'Rache?' the woman said. 'Rache?'

Now, Rache recognized Emerald, a village woman infatuated with him since childhood. Once, he had cared for her, too. Six years ago, they had made love in the woods in adolescent passion. Afterward, the memory of Episte's warning had frightened him, reminding him of the danger into which his heritage would place Emerald and their offspring. She was soft and gentle, full of love, not at all the type of woman he could expose to a legacy of vengeance and death. Afraid to become too close, he had run from her without explanation, at first blaming his work for keeping him from spending time with her, later offering no excuses at all. Because he could never reveal his true reasons, she could only interpret his actions as cruelty. Yet she was here.

'Emerald.' Rache tested his limbs and found his arms weak and his legs still uncontrollable. But he breathed easily and had improved tremendously since awakening in the guardhouse. Suddenly, Rache realized he had no way to measure the time that had passed during his fevered nightmares. 'What day is this?'

Emerald knelt at the bedside and caressed Rache's damp forehead. 'One since you ate. Three since Santagithi moved you from the guardhouse. Which do you remember?'

'Neither.' Rache stared at the thatched ceiling of the unfamiliar cottage. The dreams had drained him of emotion, but his mother's words made him patient.

'Who is Eh-*piss*-tay?' Emerald rested one hand on Rache's blanketed chest and gazed into his face questioningly.

'Episte?' Rache restored the northern inflection. He met her dark eyes and plain features with concern. 'A childhood friend. Where did you hear that name?'

'You cried it out several times. He must have been important to you.'

Rache edged toward panic, afraid for the long-buried memories his ramblings might have uncovered. 'What did I say?'

Emerald sat on the edge of Rache's bed. 'Mostly things I didn't understand. I think you used the Northern tongue.' She blushed. 'What little you said in our language, I wouldn't repeat. And as you woke, you called me "Mama."'

Rache noticed the shadows beneath Emerald's eyes and the worried creases at her chin and forehead. Her vigil had been prolonged and loyal, and she had never seemed so beautiful to him. 'Would I do this to my mama?' Rache gathered Emerald in his arms with a strength only recently gained. His kiss met eager lips. Emerald responded at first tentatively, then with bold relish. She pressed against him, awakening white hot passion. Suddenly, the fear of an heir disappeared beneath wild desire and the wish, the *need* to know whether he could still function as a man.

Rache's hands traced Emerald's breasts and came to rest upon the ribbon that laced her dress. He tried to untie it, failed, and tried again. His fingers lacked their usual coordination. With great difficulty, he completed this task and wandered to the strays. The first three exhausted him. Rache's arms fell to the bed, and he trembled with frustration. *I was a fool.* Tears distorted his view, and the rustle of Emerald's skirts taunted him. He lacked the mental will to face her and the physical strength to turn away.

Emerald removed her clothes and slipped beneath the blankets. The warmth of her body aroused Rache again. He had never known Emerald to act forward, yet her hands remained steady as she caressed the fine, blond hair that covered his chest and followed its path along his abdomen.

'Emerald.' Rache attempted a protest, but Emerald's mouth smothered his and set him to a giddy height of passion. He could not move, but Emerald insured he did not need to. When her hands found his loins, she laughed gleefully. Her discovery restored some of Rache's confidence. She climbed onto him gracefully, patient with his awkwardness. Her gentle motions gathered his wits then scattered them in a rush of exuberance. He felt her stiffen before he lost consciousness again.

When Rache awakened, he found Emerald curled in a chair by the bed, her head resting on his chest. He freed his arm from beneath the coverlet and touched the rumpled skirts covering her knee.

Startled, Emerald sat up, her features haunted and hollowed.

Rache savored his newly recovered clarity of mind, free at last from the delirium caused by his injury. His legs remained beyond his command, but Rache suspected he could sit up with some effort. He set to the task courageously, grateful Emerald did not try to help him, even when his ungainly attempt disloged items she had placed for his needs and comfort. Gradually, Rache forced his body to obey him until, panting with exertion, he was sitting up, victorious and yet annoyed at the satisfaction such a simple act inspired.

Emerald replaced the blanket across Rache's shoulders. 'This is your cottage,' she said, anticipating his question and breaking what had nearly become an awkward silence. 'Santagithi moved your things from the guardhouse until you recover.'

Rache forced bitterness aside. The guardhouse was no haven for cripples, even ones recovering quickly. 'Were you one of my "things"?'

Emerald's cheeks tinted scarlet. 'I promised to tend you. I've fed you and cleaned you and undertaken all the other matters too trivial for men.'

Despite sixteen years in a town with strict differences between the genders, Rache found the description strange. He wondered if Emerald's 'trivial' duties included sex. Guilt assailed him. He knew Emerald's tasks included attending to the bodily functions he could not control. She had sacrificed her time and her pride, even after he had brushed her away. Emerald's kindness and practicality more than offset her plain appearance. Many men would have married her, and Rache wondered why she willingly gave her love to one so undeserving.

Emerald misinterpreted Rache's silence. 'Rache, I'm not greedy.' Her long lashes hid the longing in her deep brown eyes. 'You're the best man this town's ever had, and I don't want anyone else. I promise I'll be content with whatever you can spare me: an occasional smile, a few warm nights. I ask nothing more and give undying love in return.'

Emerald's words hurt. Rache gathered her to him, and her tears on his chest seemed to burn like acid. He had scarcely emerged from a world of shadow, and nothing seemed real but the woman he held. She had become a light in his tragic life, but even now, he could not forget the heritage he dared not thrust upon her. *The burden is my own, and the line will end with me.* He struggled to find words to comfort Emerald yet still hold her distant.

A knock on the door rescued Rache from the need. 'Just a moment,' he called.

Emerald rose, dabbed at her face and smoothed her skirts. 'Come in.'

A sweet-smelling gust of air entered with Santagithi and Nantel. Both wore wooden smiles. Nantel dropped into a chair by the table. The mail bulging beneath his leather jerkin revealed that he belonged on duty. Santagithi took a place at Emerald's side. 'You're doing well.' He added smugly, 'As I predicted.'

Rache nodded. 'By the efforts of two women. Emerald and Nature.'

'Sure,' Nantel added. 'It has nothing to do with your iron will. You're too damned annoying to stay hurt long.'

Rache marveled at how easily protected men spoke of will. In the North where food scarcely existed, a baby spent its first night outdoors, so only those strong enough to earn what they consumed would survive. Rache had been born in winter. 'Within a week, I'll spar the entire guard force at the same time.' He grinned insolently. 'I'll win, too. I'm sure the guards have withered without your "unbeatable sword master."'

'And the gladiators,' Nantel started, then broke off, adding a ripe oath for his careless insensitivity.

Rache went taut and sweat gleamed on his forehead. Otherwise, he showed no sign of the loathing that flared within him. Heedful only of his own recovery and Emerald's care, Rache had avoided thinking about its cause. At length, he asked the obvious question. 'What have you done with Garn?' It needed to be asked, though Rache knew it put Santagithi in a precarious position. Anything short of execution would belittle Rache's life, though the captain also recognized the value of a good gladiator. And Garn was one of the best.

Santagithi cleared his throat. 'He awaits whatever punishment you mete.'

Neat. Rache smiled, impressed, as always, by Santagithi's diplomacy. Ideas tumbled across one another, memories of the ghastly vengeance that charged hatred against the Renshai. As much from hazy recall of the receiving end of chains as to spare Emerald from harsh words, Rache answered gently. 'Life and death in the pit is punishment enough.' He added beneath his breath, 'At least until I'm well enough to inflict worse by my own hand.'

Someone rapped at the door. Rache sighed complacently. 'As soon as I wake up, the vultures flock to feed on me.' He laughed alone.

'It's Mitrian.' Santagithi's voice held a note of apology. 'She wants to talk with you privately, and I promised I'd ask you.'

'Sure,' Rache replied eagerly.

His companions exchanged knowing glances. Emerald lowered her head.

Too late, Rache realized their discomfort stemmed from the belief that he and Mitrian shared more than friendship. 'I'm always happy to talk with your child,' he added, emphasizing the last word for Emerald's benefit.

'Anything else we can do for you?' Santagithi asked.

Rache considered. His gaze swept the room, alighting upon his sword propped in a far corner. 'Pass me my sword. I think I miss it more than my legs.'

Nantel and Emerald retreated through the doorway as Mitrian entered. Santagithi retrieved the sword and handed it to Rache. His other hand clasped Rache's wrist. 'I've forgotten all you said in anger.' Without awaiting a reply, he turned and trailed the others.

Rache watched Santagithi leave with admiration. The general knew ways to comfort as well as command, and Rache understood why Santagithi's people had chosen him as leader. He listened for the sound of the closing door before turning his attention to Mitrian.

The girl stood tensely, obviously impatient to speak but deferring to Rache's acknowledgment first.

'What is it?' Rache coaxed.

Smiling, Mitrian blurted out her news. 'That last sequence you taught? I've mastered it.'

Gerlinr. The thought came to Rache's mind, though he had never named it for Mitrian. He recalled his own excitement when he had learned the aesthetic technique at ten. Now, he grinned with her and passed her his sword. 'Show me,' he said.

4 Memories in Oilcloth

Shadimar was the first to realize Rache would never walk again. The Eastern Wizard brooded in silence at his makeshift table, a block of wood resting on four boulders of equal size. Fire danced in the hearth, a warm contrast to the lash of rain amid the ruins that served as his home. The downpour came of no normal storm, but of a magical tempest wound through with lightning and the ceaseless hammer of thunder, a grim show to ward away intruders. The wolf, Secodon, lay at his feet, whining softly at his master's consternation.

Shadimar patted Secodon, but the gesture did little to comfort the wolf who, the Wizard knew, could read his master's mood as easily as his actions. Shadimar was agitated for the second time in the century he had served as Eastern Wizard.

Where is Tokar? Sixteen years was an eye blink in the cosmos to the Wizards; decades of seclusion usually meant little to them. But Carcophan's sudden silence convinced Shadimar that the Southern Wizard was plotting the final stages of the Great War. Siderin's armies would leave the East any day, and the Westlands needed to make their own preparations during the months in which the Eastern general-king marched toward the battle plains.

Already, Shadimar had fulfilled his share of prophecies; he had raised and protected the only surviving child of the defeated high king in Béarn. His remaining task associated with the Great War was to rouse the armies in his small territory when the time came. But the responsibilities of the Western Wizard included mustering a Renshai to the war, rallying the remainder of the Westlands, including the larger, civilized cities, and uniting the Béarnian prince with the Renshai who would help him regain his throne if the West won the Great War. And, as far as Shadimar could tell, Tokar had done none of these things.

Shadimar rose, pacing from the warmer half of the room near the hearth to the cooler area by the door. In the last decade, he had sent Tokar three notes via the Wizards' messenger, a falcon called Swiftwing. The Western Wizard had acknowledged none of them, and Shadimar was forced to contemplate the possibility that, though weakest and youngest of the Wizards, he acted alone.

Alone. Shadimar shivered at a concept that went far beyond the obvious. That prophecies could be thwarted was certain, the consequences less so. At the least, the Westlands would fall subjugated to a general-king who would as soon kill them all as waste time and money feeding them. And how would the loss of a Wizard, even one who did not champion a specific cause, affect the already tenuous balance of the world? Shadimar considered, but his thoughts kept returning to one question: *How could we have lost the most powerful of the Wizards without so much as a cry of distress?*

Only three things could harm the Cardinal Wizards: demons, the ceremony of passage, and the Swords of Power, three great blades of which only two had been forged. The swords lay, untouched, on the plain of magic. It was the other two possibilities that concerned Shadimar. Over the millennia, only a few of the strongest and bravest Wizards had dared to consult demons; of the current four, only Carcophan had done so. Immediately after the destruction of the Renshai, the Southern Wizard had mocked the others, saying the demons had told him that no Renshai had survived. Shadimar had come upon Rache by accident. At that time, he had sent one of the unacknowledged notes to Tokar. But, by then, it might already have been too late. *Maybe Tokar bound a demon of his own. Maybe...* Shadimar tried to suppress the thought, but it came too fast to discard... *the demon killed him.*

Shadimar cringed at the thought. The wolf whined, its concern tangible. *Or perhaps he chose his time of passing, and something went wrong. Perhaps his apprentice proved too weak or someone interfered.* Having reached the door, Shadimar turned and started back toward the fire. He dredged up memories from his predecessors. Though rare, he found three instances where Wizards had died before their time, one Southern and two Eastern. The Southern Wizard had been run through by the White Sword of Power. Demons had taken each of the Eastern Wizards. Near their times of passing, the Southern Wizard and the first of the Eastern Wizards had each had a trained and tested apprentice who took his place. In the most recent case, no Wizard was close to his time of passing, so there had been no apprentice. Luckily, the remaining Wizards had swiftly found a woman capable of handling the power and near-immortality. They had sent her through the Seven Tasks of Wizardry and established her that day.

Near the hearth, Shadimar spun about again. As part of the Wizards' vows of Odin, they must always keep their number at four. If Shadimar could prove the Western Wizard had died without a successor, the Southern and Northern Wizards would have to help him replace Tokar. But until Shadimar could gather enough evidence to verify his theory, he had no right to call a Wizards' meeting. And this near the war, he had only three choices: gather evidence, during which time he left the Westlands unprotected against Siderin's attack; assume the Western Wizard was alive and working on his prophecies; or presume the worst and try to fulfill the Western Wizard's tasks himself.

The final realization brought Shadimar's thoughts full circle to Rache. *The freedom of the Westlands lies in the hands of a hopeless cripple.* Shadimar sat, drawing his fingers through his white beard and across his too-sharp chin. *There must be another way.* He considered the prophecy, aware the hero of the Great War must meet the Renshai's definition of one of their own. *Carcophan's demon was wrong about Rache. Perhaps there was another survivor.* Shadimar frowned, aware the only way to know for certain required him to summon another demon at great peril to his own life. *I can't afford to risk myself now that I'm burdened with the tasks of two Wizards.* Still, something squirmed at the edges of his consciousness. Shadimar tried to conceptualize his discomfort, but the image remained, frustratingly just beyond his grasp. *Something about the Renshai meeting the definition of his own people.*

Shadimar rose and headed for the door, the wolf padding silently behind him. Opening the panel, he trotted through the awkward, piled granite of the ruins of the city of Myrcidë, once the home of his people before the banished Renshai had ravaged it like so many others in the Westlands. Shadimar no longer held a grudge. Those Renshai who had caused the slaughter had passed away, along with everyone Shadimar had known in the mortal years before he had become the Eastern Wizard, and Shadimar was not the type to loathe children for the sins of their parents.

Striding past several doors, Shadimar and Secodon passed through the entrance to his library. Unlike most of his crude, handmade furniture, he had lavished attention on the sturdy shelves lining every wall of this room, crammed full with texts. He went directly to the upper section of the eastern wall. The second shelf contained information and historical texts written by the Eastern Wizards, some of the entries in Shadimar's own hand. The Wizard's mind contained the memories of his predecessors, accompanied by their misconceptions, gaps in recall, and mistakes, and he was handicapped by his own limited ability to sort through the information.

Shadimar scanned the stack. Selecting the volume entitled *Human Societies and Their Codes of Honor,* Shadimar pulled it free, leaned its back against the edge of the shelf and opened it to the page on

Renshai. Familiar with the history and general rules of behavior, he skimmed them, settling at length on the passage that interested him:

'The convention of accepting only full-bred Renshai as members of the tribe at first seems incongruous to a people whose pride stems from valor not bloodline. In truth, certain characteristics have already become ingrained, and inbreeding may weaken the tribe enough to prove their downfall.'

Not a likely problem anymore, Shadimar could not help adding, aware he would need to update the material. For now, he continued reading:

'But the decision makes more sense when viewed in the context of the "Western Renshai." As the Renshai made their way back to the Northlands from which they had been banished nearly a hundred years earlier, two male members of the tribe, Sjare and Menglir, chose to marry women in the Westlands and remain there. These men were treated by the Renshai as exiles of the exiles, and at first were condemned to death. Finally, it was decided they could stay so long as they agreed that the Renshai's special, hard-won battle techniques would never be taught to their offspring. That compromise reached, it was committed to law that only full-bred Renshai could be considered Renshai and, thus, had the right to learn the now legendary Renshai maneuvers.

'In this light, it could be said that what makes a Renshai truly Renshai is not bloodline, but the privilege of learning the battle skills. Viewed in this fashion, the Renshai's decision not to accept the "Western Renshai" as their own makes sense. If they had, distance would have separated them from a piece of their tribe that would have been unrecognizable, darker of features and different of culture, and circumstance and their love of battle could pit them against one another in time. By refusing the "Western Renshai" the knowledge of their superior battle techniques, they never had to concern themselves with decimating one another in battle.

'This particular theory of battle skills, not blood, making a Renshai is borne out by the laws concerning the last Renshai. Should a time come when the tribe contains only one member, or any number of a single gender, any and all heirs could learn the battle techniques, no matter how mixed their blood. Additionally, if there were no heirs, the last Renshai could teach the maneuvers to an outsider who would then continue the line. These conditions support . . .'

Shadimar closed the book with his finger still marking the page. The last sentence had jarred loose the idea at the corner of his mind. *Therefore, anyone to whom Rache has taught Renshai maneuvers is technically Renshai. And there is one person.* Shadimar frowned, slipping his digit from the book. He returned the volume to its place, leaving it slightly forward to remind him to make revisions. A teen-aged girl who knew nothing of war and collected battle techniques the way others hoarded baubles seemed little better than a crippled sword master when it came to pinning the hopes of a nation upon her. And other things bothered Shadimar. Again, he recalled the inscription in the Crypts of Kor N'rual, a prophecy forecast by an ancient Northern Wizard for a future Western Wizard to fulfill:

'. . . Hero of the Great War
He will hold legend and destiny in his hand . . .'

The distinct reference to a man made Shadimar question his theory. It had become convention to use the male pronoun for groups of mixed gender, but individuals were usually referred to by their proper sex. *Unless the Northern Wizard didn't know the gender and simply assumed. Besides, anyone can make a mistake, and the prophecies usually turn out differently than their letter would imply.* Shadimar considered. If correct, his theory granted slim possibility to what had become a hopeless situation. *Carcophan, and, therefore, Siderin, won't expect a woman. It's not over yet.*

Shadimar stepped back from the shelves. Nimbly, Secodon leapt aside, saving his paw from his master's boot. *But how am I going to get this sheltered girl to take the burdens of a world upon her, not to mention instill the heritage of the Renshai in her?* The thought seemed madness. Heroism could not be thrust upon a person; it had to be taken willingly, as if by the person's own design. *As a Wizard, it's my job to direct, not to manipulate. It's man's world, not the gods' or the Wizards'. Mitrian must take this responsibility on her own or not at all. I can only guide her.*

Thoughts scattered and mingled in Shadimar's mind. He stood, frozen like the whole and fragmented statues in his courtyard for longer than he knew. The wolf left for meals and returned twice before Shadimar finished molding his plan. Then, possessed of a way and a means, Shadimar awaited his opportunity.

Mar Lon, son of Davrin, sat cross-legged on the floor of Mizahai's Tavern in the Eastern city of Rozmath, singing 'The Tale of Sheriva' to the accompaniment of his *lonriset*. Dedicated to the Easterners' god, the song had been written by a forefather of Mar Lon. Its range spanned three and a half octaves, assuring that no one but the current bard and his heir could properly manage it; and the compact, ten-stringed *lonriset*, crafted by Mar Lon's great grandmother, held a richer, more mellow tone than the best made lute or mandolin.

As always, patrons packed Mizahai's Tavern, a shifting mass of swarthy men spending the day's coppers on beer. The reek of unwashed flesh ruined the intricate patterns of Mar Lon's breathing, spoiling the fine, delicate timbre of the music, but the Easterners did not seem to notice. Those nearest listened with joyful intentness. The buzz of conversation started just beyond the area of his audience and gained volume only with distance.

'. . . and when the foeman's god lay dead at Sheriva's feet,
'the Favored One created the world from its parts.
'The four moons :
'an eye, a shuddering lip, a clipped nail crescent, and a gullet dark,
'each takes its turn in the sky Sheriva made . . .'

Mar Lon sang on, pleased by the swaying, pious circle surrounding him because he had brought peace to his listeners in a time of approaching war. As the bard Davrin's heir, Mar Lon knew that the Easterners' god was no more real than the pantheon of his own Western people, that only the Northerners and a few of the mixed cultures of the Westlands worshiped the true gods. Yet the Easterners followed their mythology, and their leaders, with a dedication and fanatical honor few could match. To argue against centuries of deeply set belief would gain Mar Lon nothing but violence. And if the gods, Wizards, and centuries of previous bards had chosen not to interfere in the Easterners' religion, who was he to belittle it?

Mar Lon launched into the most difficult bars of 'The Tale of Sheriva.' The music vacillated between major chords and diminished minor sevenths. Notes jumped sixteenths, and Mar Lon met them with the perfect pitch passed from bard to eldest child for millennia. Now, all corners of the common room quieted, and the spectators listened in spellbound silence. Still young in the ways of the bards, Mar Lon drew pleasure from their intensity and pride from performances that had not yet grown routine. It was still his father's job to guard the high king in Béarn, which left Mar Lon both free and obligated to travel and learn to understand the many cultures of the world. Without that knowledge, his lyrics and music would lack the emotional overtones of pieces like the one he performed now.

As Mar Lon slipped back into a part of the song that required less concentration, he considered the people of the East. Like the Northmen, they mistrusted outsiders. But unlike their good cousins in the North, they crammed into cities that sprawled ever further into the farm fields and forests, until nearly every tree had become a stump and the crops, though healthy, were not plentiful enough to feed them and all their livestock. Mar Lon considered his own Westlands, the expansive forest teeming with wildlife and the checkerboard of farm towns and fields that spanned from just west of the Granite Hills nearly to the great trading city of Pudar.

Beautiful scenery. An abundance of food. No wonder the Eastern army has had its eyes and swords turned westward for centuries.

Mar Lon played the last note, then lowered his *lonriset* to hearty applause. A gaunt serving girl wove through the listeners and handed Mar Lon a mug of ale, on the house. Needing a break, he set the instrument down beside him and sipped at the bitter, watery brew. As conversation once again picked up, the barroom filled with a wild hubbub that sounded unusually discordant in the wake of Mar Lon's talent.

The bard had harbored doubts about visiting the Eastlands. It seemed recklessly insane, almost certainly fatal, to visit towns devoted to Carcophan's evil. Yet Mar Lon had found himself intrigued by the peoples east of the Great Frenum Mountains. Big-boned, dark-haired, and bronzed, they closely resembled the people of the most southern parts the Westlands, particularly the Béarnides and especially the Béarnian line of high kings. *Or rather*, Mar Lon reminded himself as he took a swig of his drink, *the kings resemble the Easterners.*

Davrin's history lessons had taught Mar Lon that the line of kings contained a heavy dose of Eastern blood. In fact, creation legends often started with the Westlands as a vast, empty vista. According to these stories, disgruntled Northmen and Easterners had come to this new land and interbred. And there was some truth to the story. No doubt the Westerners were a mongrelized race, though they did exist as a people even before the rare Northern and Eastern stragglers came to live among them.

A shadow fell over Mar Lon. He glanced up at a broad, heavily-featured stranger who dropped to a crouch in front of him. The man reeked of sweat and beer. 'Play "The Aristiri's Lament,"' he demanded. He thrust his wide-fingered hand into his pocket, emerging with an Eastern silver, and tossed the coin toward Mar Lon. It struck the floor near the bard's left knee, bouncing into the hollow between his folded legs.

Ignoring the coin, Mar Lon studied the man before him. The Rozmathian's brusque manner and lack of amenities fit the Eastern culture, a strange contrast to the Northmen's cold politeness toward outsiders. Mar Lon took another sip of beer, weighing the length of his pause to maintain his dignity without inciting the Rozmathian to violence. Then he set aside his drink, wiped his hands the length of his breeks, took his *lonriset* in hand, and plucked out the chiming introduction of 'The Aristiri's Lament.'

The Easterner squatted, listening at first in stony, expressionless silence. When the melody began, his eyes drifted shut as he sacrificed vision to concentrate on sound, and the corners of his mouth twitched upward in appreciation.

The compliment fueled Mar Lon's pride. It did not matter that the man before him followed the ways of evil, or that the Wizard's prophecies foretold that he and his people might one day slaughter the Westland races who were Mar Lon's relatives and neighbors. For now, they were two men communicating through song the thoughts and emotions they could never share in words. *The next bard. I am the luckiest man alive.*

Yet the song told otherwise. The stranger had chosen to hear the story of Mar Lon's first bardic ancestor. And, though Mar Lon had found nothing but joy in his birth-right, the legend reminded him that Odin had intended the duties of bards as a curse upon his line. 'The Aristiri's Lament' was only one of seven versions in the Eastern tongue. It spoke of gods the Easterners found pagan, and the translated rhyme scheme did not work as well as Mar Lon would have liked. Still, the Easterners seemed to enjoy the tune and the fable:

Jahiran was born on a warm Western day.
The babe looked at his father, and then he did say:
'Father, why is the way of the world the way?
Why does the hen, not the rooster, lay,
While our men, not our women, enter the fray?
And why do the gods rule us all?

Jahiran turned ten on a spring day so cold,
And vowed to know all by the time he grew old.
That night he read every use for mined gold
Why the wisule *is timid, the* aristiri *bold.*
But he understood naught of laws Wizards uphold,
And why the gods rule us all.

When Jahiran turned twenty, he had to know why
The stars took the patterns they did in the sky.
Why aristiri *hawks sing as well as fly,*
Why the fox slinks from brush to rock on the sly,
The messages hidden in a baby's cry,
And why the gods rule us all.

At thirty, he knocked on the West Sorceress' door
Said, 'Natalia, please,' and he knelt to implore.
'There's a fire inside me that burns to my core
It feeds not on air, but on knowledge and lore.
I will die if some power won't help me learn more.
And I must know why gods rule us all.

Natalia fixed him with an ancient's knowing eye.
'You cannot learn all, and you shouldn't even try.
There is danger in knowledge,' and her look went wry.
'Understanding cost even the AllFather an eye.'
But the pain on his face almost made her cry,
Though she knew why the gods rule us all.

So Natalia, she gave him aristiri's shape,
And he saw things that men and gods usually drape:
Saw the passion of love and the violence of rape,
Saw upstanding men fall prey to wine's grape,
Saw Thor coit with a mortal, and that made him gape,
But he still knew not why the gods reign over all.

The first bard learned much of the gods and their rule,
But facts don't bring wisdom unto a fool.
Jahiran used singing hawk form as a tool,
And he crooned to Thor's wife of his tryst by a pool.
Though Jahiran's purpose was stupid, not cruel,
Thor showed him why gods rule us all.

Odin stepped in before Jahiran was flayed.
'I realize your need, but this can't go unpaid.'
Then the One-Eyed god grasped the hawk by its head
And cut out half its tongue with a razor sharp blade.
Then, where once perched a hawk, now a wounded man lay
Who wished he knew less of the gods.

Then Odin spoke, and his voice it did ring,
'You can no longer speak, but you can still sing,
And your fingers will keep the grace of hawk's wings;
They will dance across any instrument's strings.
Yet your quest to know all will continue to sting.
Mortal life is too short to know gods.

Mar Lon let the last notes fade, hearing the near and distant conversations drop with them, as if the patrons needed to catch the final vibrations regardless of whether they had listened to the body of the song. He put the *lonriset* aside, cradling his drink again, the gesture ridiculously casual in the tranquil wake of his music.

The Rozmathian opened his eyes, flopped to a sitting position beside Mar Lon, and gestured to a serving girl for a beer.

For Jahiran's descendants, the curse took a less brutal form. Though it was still their job to study other cultures and chronicle the world's history, the subsequent bards kept their tongues. Only a vow bound them from revealing any of the information they gathered, except in song.

The Easterner grinned, displaying a serrated row of crooked, yellow teeth. 'I like the bawdy part. And I like where the guy's tongue gets sliced out.' He made an abrupt cutting motion, then laughed. 'I'm Trinthka.'

'Mar Lon.' The bard smiled, amused by the man's honest simplicity.

The Easterner flicked his gaze across Mar Lon, as if truly noticing him for the first time. His grin wilted. 'Marlon?' He slurred the syllables together. 'What kind of weird name's that?'

'An old family name.' Mar Lon took a careful swallow, aware he had addressed the shallow specifics but not the true intentions behind the man's question. The bard's dark hair and eyes fit well with the locals, but his fairer skin betrayed his Western heritage. Now that he had spoken in other than song, he guessed his accent also became clear. 'My family's not really from anywhere. That's why they call us wandering minstrels.' It was not quite true. Upon his father's death, Mar Lon would find a permanent position as the Béarnian king's personal guard, but he saw no reason to cultivate hostility from a man so close to giving him an inside glimpse of Eastern motivations.

The Easterner made a noncommittal noise.

Mar Lon waited. Westerners had never been welcome in the Eastlands, and it was within the law for Easterners to kill strangers with little or no provocation. In the last fifty years, as the time for war approached, the Easterners had placed guards at the only pass through the Great Frenum Mountains. Anyone who traveled from the West to the East required special permission. If denied, he was executed on the spot. Mar Lon had gotten his authorization directly from Carcophan.

The serving girl wove through the crowd. She handed the Easterner a drink, then disappeared back into the tavern's depths.

Her interruption dispelled the tension. Apparently concluding that Mar Lon's overt presence in a public tavern made him a safe confidant, the Easterner remained beside him. 'You also a soldier, minstrel?'

'No. You?'

'No.' The Easterner took a hearty swig of his beer. 'My brothers and I pulled sticks to see who got to train in Stalmize and who had to stay and tend the crops.' A frown scored his thick features. 'I lost.'

Mar Lon nodded, presuming from the Easterner's choice of words that 'lost' meant staying home. The attitude surprised the bard. In the North, men clamored to become soldiers, both to spare their brothers and to die in glorious combat. The latter meant that their souls went to Valhalla to serve the gods and help defend them from enemies during the *Ragnarok*. But the Easterners had no apocalyptic legends, and their god had a superiority and omnipotence that did not require them to serve him after death. 'You would prefer to go to war?'

'Of course.' The Easterner drained his mug while Mar Lon's was still half-full. He scowled, studying the dregs as if disbelieving that nothing remained. He made a brisk gesture at the serving girl. 'At least to get called up for training. If we don't go to war, I'd still get paid, and I'd get respected for doing nothing. If we do go to war, I'd get to butcher infidels.' He glared at Mar Lon with a cold-blooded gleam in his brown eyes, as if to challenge the bard to dispute. 'We are Sheriva's Elite, yet the infidels have all the land's rewards.' He waved vaguely Westward, either ignorant of or blithely dismissing the fact that the East once had soil as fertile as the Westlands before overtilling, constant planting of the most valuable crops without rotation, and indolence had ruined it. They had lost their forests by burning them to provide land for their cities or to clear the ground for mining of the abundant gems and minerals beneath the earth. 'Sheriva promised us that a day would come when his people owned the world, and the infidel inferiors became our chattel. I will be a part of that. I want to hear them beg for mercy, then deliver them, piece by bloody piece, to Sheriva's hell. I want to feel their wenches struggle helplessly beneath me and know the agony of their screams. I want my share of gold and land and slaves.'

Though familiar with Carcophan and his tenets, Mar Lon could not suppress a shiver of horror and disgust. 'But your people will die, too. Your cousins, your brothers, perhaps yourself.'

'Ah!' the Easterner's eyes fairly danced with triumph. 'But then I would die in Sheriva's cause, following his Chosen general, and the god will reward me with wealth and slaves and women in the afterlife.'

Mar Lon nodded, intrigued that he appeared to have found the essence of the Eastern culture so easily, though Carcophan's motivations had always seemed obvious. *Self-interest, maliciousness, greed.* Yet the Easterners had learned to work in concert in a way even the Northmen, with their eternal border skirmishes, never completely had. *Whatever their weaknesses, they have as much law-restricted order and honor as any culture. They are, in their own strange, evil way, as predictable as Trilless' Northmen.* It seemed odd to Mar Lon that his own people, the Westerners, had proven the most difficult for him to understand. Like his forefathers, Mar

Lon believed that, unlike the Wizards, no man could be fully wicked or pure. But the impartial Westerners spanned a vast continuum of intentions and behavior.

The Easterner lapsed into religious rhetoric, praising Sheriva and his Chosen general/king/disciple, Siderin. Familiar with the litany, Mar Lon let his thoughts wander. And the answer hit him so hard and suddenly, it took all his self-control to keep from shouting in triumph. *Education and cooperation. If the Westerners could share their techniques for preserving the soil and the forests, if they could open trade – food for crafts and gems – if they could learn to understand and respect, if not believe, one another's religions, then the Easterners would no longer need to attack.*

Youthful idealism held Mar Lon briefly spellbound, before reality intruded and his view widened to the larger picture. *The system of the Cardinal Wizards, and thus of their followers, was never geared for collaboration.* Truth struck him a staggering blow, and he dared to question a god-created process accepted by his ancestors for millennia. Indeed, the Wizards' vows forced them to work in concert on certain matters, but only in those situations necessary to keep their system working. And though Mar Lon knew it was sacrilege, he could not help wondering if Odin's choice of method for balancing forces had been a mistake. *The great Powers in constant opposition. In the long run, it will lead to the* Ragnarok *and, thus, to the gods' own predestined downfall.*

Mar Lon shoved the thought aside. *Judging Odin. I've gone beyond blasphemy into madness.* And the humility allowed another idea to come to the forefront. *Eleven thousand years ago, when the AllFather banished the nether, we probably needed a strict, stiff system of law and balance. And it's worked this far. Who am I to question?* Yet, Mar Lon could not wholly keep his doubts in check. After all, if his father's brooding ballads told the story, Mar Lon would be the last bard ever on a world shortly doomed to destruction.

Mar Lon set aside his drink, balanced his *lonriset*, and strummed a sad, slow melody written by Davrin.

Rache awakened with a vague discomfort that had grown familiar in the two weeks since his injury. Resignedly, he sighed and steeled himself for his morning ritual. Careful not to disturb Emerald, he forced his legs painfully over the side of the bed. Each night, Emerald would leave two chairs at his bedside. With mounting anxiety, he wrapped a hand about the back of each.

The sinews of Rache's neck tightened, and his stomach drew into a tense knot. As he lifted his body from the bed, his arms trembled.

He tried to focus his attention on his upper limbs and forget the persistent weakness of his legs. Hope had died days ago; habit alone motivated him to continue this empty charade. He lowered his feet to the floor. They buckled, quivering, and rage flared at reality too strong to deny. From the day Nantel's hopeful glances became pitying stares and Santagithi presented Rache with a chair onto which he had affixed four, wooden wheels, Rache knew he would not walk again. He forced away anger, despair and memories of his past prowess and hurled himself violently into the wheeled seat.

Emerald stirred, the ease of her movement underscoring Rache's limitations.

'Good morning,' he said with none of the kindness the amenity implied.

'Good morning.' Emerald rose and pushed the chairs from the bed routinely.

Rache's resolve grew as weak as his legs. Emerald's greetings flowed past him, unheard. The discomforting sympathy of strangers, friends insisting they understood his frustrations, and condescending platitudes voiced in the streets had driven Rache nearly to deafness. Mechanically, he donned his tunic and sword belt while Emerald pushed past the table and built a fire in the hearth.

The breeks lay like limp snakes in Rache's fist. He studied his legs. All attempts to move them failed. The shriveling muscles occasionally twitched despite his efforts to hold them steady. Disgusted, he pulled the linen over his feet and remembered how Santagithi's chair had changed him from a groveling lizard who dragged himself along the floor to a broken man forced to rely on others for his transport.

A frenzied pounding on the door dispelled Rache's bitter musings. Emerald turned, rose from the fire, and walked to the door. Throwing the bolt, she wrenched open the panel.

Mitrian burst into the room. Her hair hung in an uncombed mane. Her eyes seemed wild as a frightened deer's. She ran to Rache's side and plucked desperately at his sleeve.

Years of training hid Rache's anxiety behind a mask of cold purpose. 'What's wrong?'

Mitrian paced frantically. 'My father! He needs your help.' A strange catch in her voice confused Rache; but when she clutched the back of his chair and rolled him out the door, he did not resist.

'What happened?' asked Rache, wondering what could demand his attention over that of someone closer and more mobile. His heart raced.

Unable or unwilling to answer, Mitrian pushed Rache through a patch of grass and wild flowers scarred by numerous passes of his chair. The chestnut mare Mitrian had ridden down from her father's estate grazed placidly before the cabin. As the front set of wheels touched the road, Mitrian glanced up the weed-swarmed hill to the citadel and slumped across the back of Rache's chair. 'It's no use.' She spoke despairingly. 'I can't push you all the way up there.'

Sweat slicked Rache's palms and trickled along his spine. He searched his mind for a solution but discovered only failure. Awash in desperation and self-pity, Rache fondled his sword hilt. Violence had usually dispelled his tension in the past, originating as it always had on the battlefield. Now Rache sat still and let disbelief overtake him.

'I have an idea.' Mitrian pushed Rache's chair to the side of her horse. 'Climb on.'

'What?' Rache's mouth fell open.

'On the horse.' She nudged him. 'Get on! Please.'

Rache paused, blaming panic for her ludicrous suggestion. 'I can't climb. And even if I could, I'd fall off.'

'By the gods, Rache!' Mitrian pranced a hysterical half-circle around him. 'Hurry! He'll die!'

Mitrian's terror mobilized Rache. *I have to try.* He wrapped his left hand in the horse's mane. His right groped across its neck, his face and chest pressed to the animal's side. The odor of horse and fresh hay filled his nostrils. As he tensed his arms and pulled, the sweat of his exertions mingled with the thin oils of the animal's coat. Gradually, with each new grip, Rache edged toward the saddle. The strength of his arms surprised him. His legs ached without reason. Wild with concern, Rache did not notice that the stirrups were tearing rents in his tunic and skin. Finally, his chest touched the seat of the saddle and, with great difficulty, he arranged his legs across it.

Lightly, Mitrian vaulted up behind him.

At Rache's urging, the mare lurched into a trot. Rache slid, swore and tangled his fingers in its coarse mane. The rise and fall of the animal's paces jolted him like a poorly-secured sack of flour. *Maybe I need to get tied to the saddle like cargo.* Angrily, he cast aside this self-deprecating digression for the more pressing matter of Santagithi's health.

The ride smoothed as it progressed, and Rache gained control with rein, voice, and the modest power remaining in his thighs. 'What happened to your father?' he called over the clamor of shod hooves on cobble.

'Rache, my father is fine. I lied so you'd try to ride. I knew you could, but you wouldn't listen.'

Rache hesitated, unable to recall Mitrian telling him anything. In the past few days, he had not heard much at all.

'Rache, you're riding!' Mitrian laughed exuberantly.

I am riding! Rache's spirit soared from contented realization to excitement. The world broke through the barriers his mind had built for protection. Like an old, forgotten friend, the sun smiled upon the clean stones of the road. A breeze tickled Rache's nose with the herbal aromas of his neighbors' morning teas. Mitrian became the most beautiful woman in the world, the horse the finest of its breed.

Rache reveled in the potential of his discovery. On horseback, he could travel where he chose without need of someone to carry him or to direct his chair. His thoughts exploded like a flock of birds when a rock lands in their midst, then channeled in a single direction. *From a horse, I can fight.* Rache howled with delight. He slid off-balance, rolled from the horse, and crashed to the cobbles.

Pain shot along Rache's shoulder. He bit his tongue with enough force to draw blood. The horse shied, neck low, staring at Rache as if he had done something stupid beyond the animal's comprehension. But the fall did not dispel Rache's glee. He scrutinized deserted streets bordered by copses of goldenrod, sweet pea, and Queen Anne's lace. Chips of quartz glimmered among the dull, gray cobbles, and a weed-swathed boulder lay on the roadside. Rache had passed the stone, without notice, on his infrequent jaunts into the town or on his way to a foray. Now it became the focus of his attention. Serpentlike, he wriggled toward it.

Sharp stones abraded Rache's abdomen. He ignored the pain and continued dragging himself toward the rock. He heard hoofbeats behind him as Mitrian followed on the horse. His hand clasped the jagged edge of the rock when he heard the thump of her dismount. Her fingers closed about his shoulder. 'Are you hurt?'

'No.' Rache shook her loose impatiently and slowly pulled himself up the rock. 'And thank you. I'll finish the ride.'

Mitrian beamed. 'Let me help you.'

Rache could not fathom the anger that rose in him at Mitrian's suggestion. 'No!' He turned on her. 'I won't have your help on the battlefield.' He heaved himself to the boulder's peak and reached for the horse.

'Battlefield?'

Ignoring Mitrian, Rache found remounting easier than his initial attempt. He settled into the saddle. Earlier, he had compared himself to a flour sack needing to be tied to the saddle. Now, risen again to manhood, he could benefit from the same security as the sack. 'Mitrian, lend me your sandal straps.'

Though obviously taken aback by Rache's suggestion, Mitrian removed her footwear without question and stood, barefoot, in the street. Removing the rawhide bindings, she gave them to Rache along with the horse's reins.

As Rache wove the leather around his legs and the saddle, insecurity and doubt descended on him. Perhaps the straps would not hold him, or he could not control his horse without his legs. Some forgotten detail might leave him vulnerable in battle. Rache knew, for his sanity, he must overcome his fears before his feet touched the earth again. And he knew a way.

'Keep the horse.' Mitrian rested a hand on Rache's calf. 'Get acquainted.' Hesitantly, she stopped speaking, as if she wanted to continue but had decided otherwise.

'Thank you again.' Rache slapped the mare into a trot along the cobbles and up the main path to Santagithi's citadel.

The guard at the gate waved Rache past, mouth gaping in surprise.

Rache scarcely noticed. Engrossed in the rolling rhythm of the horse beneath him, he compared the motion of his memories. As he reined toward the archery range, he found the bumps of a trot painful and the smooth rock of a canter reassuringly familiar.

So welcome a short time ago, the sun now wrung sweat from Rache. His thoughts raced to the cycle of the mare's hooves, and he leaned forward to whisper in its ear. 'You're my legs now, girl. Let's see what you can do.'

The horse raised its muzzle to the sky, whinnying at some sound Rache did not hear. He slapped it to a gallop. Soon, several figures at the archery range became distinguishable. The musty, loam smell of the stumps they used as targets signaled a new beginning to Rache. He reined his steed to a halt at Nantel's side.

The archer captin lowered his bow, his arrow shafts decorated with the familiar black and silver rings of Santagithi's crest, catching the light. He examined the chestnut with a smile. 'Very nice.'

Rache said nothing.

Nantel circled, as if studying the beast from all sides. 'Very nice indeed, Rache. Good to see you. Do you want to shoot?' He offered his bow.

Rache ignored Nantel's question. His voice rang with regained power. 'No. I came to call you out.'

Nantel glared. 'I won't let any man ridicule you, Rache. Not even you.' He rested one end of his bow on the grass.

Rache continued as if he had not heard. 'Mounted. On the practice field. Unless you're afraid a cripple might beat you in spar.' He wheeled his mount and reined it, at a canter, toward the field.

Rache realized how much more than life or death rested on the outcome of this spar. The thought frightened him. If he could still best Nantel, Rache knew he would again lead Santagithi's guards into the wars, raids, and forays that had for so long been his only pleasures. If he lost, he surrendered his soul to the half-dead goddess,

Hel, and existed until his death as Emerald's helpless toy. But, by the time Rache drew rein upon the small practice field near the South Corner Arena, his heart beat with the same calm cadence he felt prior to battle.

The sky grew as doubtfully gray as Rache's thoughts. He drew his sword, and the haft heated to his grip. The sword took his spirit along with his warmth. It seemed to gain a life of its own, given by its wielder. Deliberately, Rache began an intricate kata. As the sword danced about his steed, he thought of the link between himself and the steel as that between mother and child, although he was uncertain which was the child. *It's still there.*

The rhythmical pounding of Nantel's approaching mount shattered the reunion. Rache sat patiently as Nantel swept toward him, sword circling his head like some ghastly, silver halo. As the distance narrowed, Nantel aimed a high stroke for Rache's head. Suddenly, Nantel's face pinched in horror. Rache knew Nantel doubted he could still avoid the deadly strokes.

Rache imagined Nantel cursing himself for his friend's demise. Perhaps he even believed Rache's challenge an attempted suicide. The sword master spurred his chestnut. Nantel's blade fell on empty air. Rache swung. His riposte drove the heavy links of Nantel's mail into his jerkin.

The two men pulled their horses about, Rache pleased with himself, Nantel obviously unamused. Rache swelled with the new vitality that pulsed through him. It seemed odd that a piece of steel slightly longer than a man's arm could so quickly restore life, though it took life with equal fervor.

On the second pass, Nantel did not charge with the fevered bravado that caused the first blood shed by many a young warrior to be his own. The gap closed gradually. Each man kept his sword arm toward the other. Rache caught Nantel's strokes on the blade or crosspiece of his sword, content to parry all the assaults and let Nantel collapse from exhaustion.

After a time, Nantel disengaged, wheeled his horse, and galloped for Rache. When the horses met muzzle to muzzle, Nantel viciously kicked his mount and yanked its head to Rache's unprotected side. Too late, Rache realized his mistake. Both horses lunged, and the flat of Nantel's sword smacked the flank of Rache's enraged chestnut.

Rache cursed himself as he fought to control his steed. In a real battle, with his horse not as fresh or himself slightly less lucky, that blow could have killed him. The straps that held him in place limited his movement so he could not fight men on each side. He would have little chance in war, surrounded by enemies. Rache's eyes went cold as he approached Nantel.

In his anguish, Rache became a whirling blur of fury. No longer content to parry blows, he lunged avidly for Nantel's head. The archer captain reeled. Rache changed his maneuver to a wicked slap that bruised Nantel's knee. Pain and surprise threw Nantel off balance and bared his cinch. Rache's next stroke hacked nearly through the fabric. His sword battered the horse's flank, sending it surging with sufficient power to burst the few remaining strands securing Nantel's seat. Nantel and saddle pin-wheeled. The archer sprawled, gasping in the grass.

Both horses galloped off; Rache left an aching Nantel on the ground. Surely, the archer captain expected laughter, but Rache's rage left no place for mirth. His ride home seemed as one through the raw, red gullet of a demon. He remembered none of it, not the cobbled streets, not the ripe, yellow sun that burned away the clouds as if to taunt him, and not Emerald's concerned face as she eased him from the saddle.

Once inside his cottage, Rache pulled himself along the floor. He groped beneath the worn, wooden frame of his bed until his hands closed on a coarse box he knew nearly as well as its contents. Amongst a poniard, buckler, and gem-studded belt lay a tied bundle of oilcloth, nearly black with age. The cloth was part of a cloak he had worn as a boy. Its contents had made him a man. He untied the packet with trembling fingers and loosed the hilt, crosspiece, and a few shards from the sword Episte had bought for him. The blade had been broken when struck while its tip was still embedded in a dying foe. Rache wallowed in the irony of a sword and its master both broken by nonentities, one by a nameless thief, the other by a slave.

Sun flooded the brown, lifeless room where Rache lay, draped across his bed, a swatch of oilcloth across his knees and a shattered piece of metal in his hand. Engrossed in his past, he did not notice when Emerald opened the door and quietly left him to the mercy of this other mistress who now shared his bed. He could not see the tears in her eyes.

A sturdy knock at Rache's door ushered in nightfall as a cock's call heralds the morning. Whether the crow beckons the coming day or mourns the ended night matters only to a man who hears and cares. Rache noticed nothing.

Nantel's hand upon Rache's shoulder scarcely roused him from a world of fragmented hopes and dreams. When Rache spoke, his proud voice shriveled to an impotent shadow of its former self.

'Nantel, don't come to gloat over me. Though you bested me in combat today, I don't want to hear you mock a foolish cripple.'

'Rache?' Nantel hesitated in disbelief. 'You left me sitting in a field and forced me to walk almost a league to get home. My friend, I didn't win that little duel.' A twisted smile formed on Nantel's face. ' A pretty sight I must have seemed. A large dolt in chain sitting in the dirt, staring at the rump of a horse.' Nantel's mouth framed a wry laugh, but Rache saw no humour in the scene.

The two companions stared at one another; neither knew what to say or do. Rache fondled the hilt of his shattered sword.

'Gods!' Nantel cursed. 'Anyone can fall prey to bad luck. When I spurred my horse . . .'

The hilt in Rache's fist struck the headboard. The blow sent pieces of his broken blade tumbling to the floor. Regathering his composure, Rache turned away from his friend to stare into the fireplace where the embers dwindled as swiftly as his hopes. He delivered his words more like a prayer than conversation. 'Nantel, though your sword never touched me, you bested me today. You saw I could defend only one side of my horse and knew I couldn't turn quickly enough to meet a blow from my left. Your attack vanquished me. In a battle, you would have felled my horse and left me trapped to kill however you wished.'

The light guttered and sank. Rache watched Nantel struggle for words and suddenly recalled the time the archer had sought to question a haggard priest who was beseeching the Westlands' faceless god of winter to allow spring to return. Then, the controlled power in the speaker's words had struck Nantel dumb. Rache tried to match his tone with the memory. 'While I still have the strength and courage, I must seek my death. Many enemies would like nothing more than to force one of my people to wander the frozen wastes of Hel.' Rache did not explain further. Nantel had lived with Rache long enough to know there was something strange and secretive about his past. 'I have fought many battles within my soul today, and I have only one more left before I look upon the gates of Valhalla. Tomorrow, I leave for my last battle against the cowards of the North.' A tear formed in Rache's eye as he tore his gaze from the dull, red coals and cast it upon the green gem that adorned the hilt of his broken sword.

Slowly, the glow and heat of the embers faded before the growing fires in Nantel's eyes. 'You selfish bastard! Perhaps you deserve to wander Hel. At least you should remember you will not die alone.'

'Surely, I will take many men with me,' started Rache. 'But when has it become a sin to slay enemies on a battlefield and die in glory?'

'The lives that damn you will be those of women and children . . .' Nantel paused.

Thoughts raced through Rache's mind, dim racial memories of the crimes of his forefathers, tales of slaughter that had lulled him to sleep as a baby and the grisly stories told to him by those who could not guess his heritage. He had given Nantel clues, the greatest one today, but not enough, he had thought, to know.

This thought was redirected by the end of Nantel's speech '. . . and perhaps even mine. If you leave, may all of this town who die in the following raids and the coming Great War rest heavily upon your soul.'

'You can't place this burden on me!' screamed Rache. 'No one man decides the fate of a city.' He choked on the words, his mind thick with the memory of a mother selling her spirit for her son's life and a prophecy. *A prophecy that will save the Westlands. A prophecy that damns its own hero as a prince of demons. A prophecy that bodes as much evil as good.* Anger alone allowed Rache to complete his tirade. 'For lying to me, may you be the one who walks the frozen ground of Hel, *barefoot* for eternity!'

Nantel's voice gained the restrained power Rache's lost. 'Our strength doesn't lie in numbers. You know it lies in the skill of the few men we have, the skill you've placed there. If you leave, you might just as well take the guards with you. They'll do us little good once they forget how to wield a sword.'

Resolution ebbed from Rache. What little remained was born of hatred and vengeance, and even these became hollow thoughts. When Garn had struck Rache, he robbed the sword master of life. No longer could Rache smell the mingled sweat and blood nor see life with the crystal detail revealed to him in battle. But it was this town, Mitrian, Emerald, Nantel, and the others who cared for him that barred him from Valhalla. Although he had no wish for martyrdom, he made himself one vow: *If it costs a prophecy, my mother's spirit, and the last Renshai soul to teach a group of helpless fools to use swords, they'll become damned good swordsmen. These things will not be cheaply bought.*

Rache watched Nantel shuffle past his iron-bound door and gaze into the heavens. If the archer captain sought guidance from the Faceless One, his expression told Rache that he received no answer.

5 Storm Master of the East

In Rache's cottage, removed from the townsfolk and the certainty of their disapproving glares, Mitrian's sword sang a dirge as it swept the air around her. Engaged in an unusually punishing practice, she felt sweat-matted hair sting her eyes and laughed at the thought that she could double for a fountain in the town square.

Mitrian's lapse drew bitter words from Rache, who lay on his bed watching her critically. 'I don't know where your mind went, girl, but if you give no more attention to your sword than this, your body might as well go with it.'

Mitrian stared, confused. Her mistakes had never angered Rache before. Often he corrected, chided, even belittled her, but now the malice in his voice struck her speechless. In the past, Rache had never mentioned it when she surpassed his guards; his pleasure always shone in his eyes. Now, they held only the same pale fire that smoldered whenever he mentioned Garn.

Rache explained. 'When you place your weight on your right foot, you have to delay pulling your blade across in front of you. If you wait, your opponent will strike your blade and add momentum when you bring it across his thigh. Again, girl. Again.'

Mitrian's lithe body swayed opposite her sword, dancing to the same rhythm as the blade. For the course of the kata, her weariness abated and three years of Rache's instruction merged flawlessly. She felt certain her performance would please Odin himself. She tore into the last sequence, then held her stance expectantly.

Rache never gave praise freely. Occasionally, in spar, he would shout 'fine' or 'good,' and Mitrian would grow warm with pride. Now Mitrian waited, believing neither new nor arcane words could describe the fluid grace and power of her last series of movements.

Rache simply stared through her vacantly. 'We're done for the day.'

'Done?' Sweat trickled into Mitrian's eyes. She lowered her sword. Though accustomed to Rache withholding compliments, she dared not believe her demonstration had left him unaffected. 'Done?' she repeated. *Done, indeed. This practice has lasted far too long; and, in Rache's frame of mind, it should never have begun.*

'Yes, done,' Rache said. 'You've had enough sword training for one day.'

'Agreed.' Mitrian continued, determined to collect the reward she felt she had earned, if not in praise then in payment. 'You may now teach me to shoot a bow.' She braced herself for an argument. They could hide sword practices from her father, but archery needed to be performed on an open range. It was dangerous, but Mitrian felt certain Santagithi would approve almost anything that drew Rache from his depression and his cottage. Of course, she could not use that particular explanation on Rache.

'Your father,' Rache reminded predictably.

'Does it matter?' Mitrian drew breath for a long, well-rehearsed justification.

But, in his apathy, Rache seemed satisfied with the single question. 'I suppose not.' He sighed, his voice a defeated monotone. 'Find Nantel. I'll meet you on the range.'

Eager, yet disappointed by the ease of her victory, Mitrian returned Rache's sword and sped from his cottage in search of the archers' captain.

When Mitrian and Nantel rode toward the target range, they found Rache sitting on a weathered stump. Their horses did not disturb the human addition to the stump; the sword master seemed oblivious to everything, as soulless as the wood beneath him. His chestnut mare grazed nearby.

Dismounting, Nantel unpacked two bows and quivers of arrows. Mitrian swung down, and the two released their mounts to graze with Rache's. Nantel explained archery to Mitrian while Rache sat in silence. The archer demonstrated nocking point, draw length, release, aiming, and stance in detail. After the delicate Renshai strokes, archery sounded easy to Mitrian. Gradually, her initial excitement ebbed, and her mind wandered to the western world of Nantel's other stories. It took a great deal of effort to focus on his continuous drone. She fixed her eyes on him attentively, though from their corners she watched Rache waiting motionlessly.

'Here. You try.' Nantel offered Mitrian a longbow noticeably thinner than his own. Her enthusiasm returned as she seized the bow. She nocked an arrow, trying to remember Nantel's instructions. Nantel passed the other bow and quiver to Rache.

Rache accepted Nantel's offering. He loosed silver shafts at the waist-high stumps that served as targets.

'No!' Nantel covered his eyes in exaggerated anguish. 'Release the string smoothly, Mitrian. And leaning forward won't help your shot.'

Mitrian made many mistakes, as if the birds whose feathers fletched her shafts took control and landed them at random in the field. Yet failure only fueled her determination. She recalled the struggle for her abilities with a sword and was willing to repeat all her efforts for this new skill, if necessary. She had convinced Nantel to teach her only under the pretext of helping Rache, and, once her father found out, she might not get another lesson.

Beside Mitrian, Rache scarcely moved. He never seemed to recognize whether his shafts struck home. His fine, white features appeared chiseled in ivory, and his arms motioned as mechanically as Mitrian's water clock. Only his disordered, yellow hair and cold eyes reflected any life, and that as savage as his Northern blood.

When the last arrow was spent, Mitrian and Nantel crossed the field to retrieve them. The girl roamed through the clearing, seeking fletches or a crest that would disclose a hidden arrow while Nantel plucked Rache's shots from the stump. Mitrian consoled herself by recalling Rache's stories of undefeatable swordsmen who shunned bows as cowards' weapons. Still, Rache's talent with weapons seemed boundless, and his arrows alighted with surprising accuracy. She decided that once she learned to find the target, she would surpass him. Every extra moment she found, she would spend practicing in the woodland clearing.

As Nantel and Mitrian returned, quivers nearly full, the archer detailed Mitrian's flaws. 'Let the bow lie in your hand. You don't have to crush it. And when you release, let the string slide from your fingers. Don't pluck it like a harp. Also, when you draw, anchor your hand at the corner of your mouth . . .' The rest went unheard. Mitrian wished Nantel was as easy to understand as Rache.

After a few more flights, Mitrian no longer needed to scour the field for uncooperative lengths of feathered wood. Gradually, her arrows discovered their target. Nantel beamed, obviously crediting her improvement to his expert instruction. Though intrigued by her growing talent, Mitrian studied Rache's melancholia with concern. She listened raptly as Nantel turned his attention from her and addressed the sword master.

'Rache, have you found time to shoot? I thought you spent all your time honing our swordsmen.'

Rache sat in silence. Mitrian thought he would not reply, but, at length, he spoke with hate-tinged anger. 'Nantel, don't babble. You know I haven't drawn a bow since our last hunt.'

Undaunted, Nantel continued. 'Then explain to me how you're

grouping your shots in an area the size of my palm. Rache, you have talent.'

Mitrian set aside her arrows and tried to imagine the strange ideas taking form behind Rache's blank mask. Momentarily, guarded hope flared in his eyes. 'I haven't shot for nearly a month. And I don't have the use of my legs anymore. Nantel, you're lying to make me feel better, aren't you?'

Unable to look at the longing in Rache's face, Mitrian turned away. She guessed at his thoughts. Armed with a bow, he could join the forays as an archer. Apparently, he found a coward's weapon better than none at all.

Thoughtfully, Nantel ran a finger along the edge of his mustache. 'Perhaps you shoot better now not in spite of your legs but because of them. I used to scold you for shifting your weight like a swordsman. Now you have to sit steady.'

Mitrian nocked an arrow and loosed it at the stump. She could not possibly know the turn of Rache's thoughts to the arrows that wrought carnage on his people before the foe came within range of the Renshai's swords.

Nantel spoke softly. 'Rache, Santagithi mentioned a foray.'

Rache stared at the ground, and Mitrian cursed Nantel's insensitivity. In the past, Rache was the first to know of her father's raids.

Nantel sat on the stump beside Rache. He spoke so low, Mitrian strained to hear. 'I have things to do here. Someone has to command the archers in battle. I would be honored if it was you, Rache.'

Slowly, Rache raised his gaze to the bow in his grip. Mitrian thought she saw tears in his eyes.

Four days later, Santagithi rallied his people before the meeting tree. Though any of his citizens could attend these gatherings, few of the women bothered to take part in the governmental decisions of the town. Curiosity drew Mitrian to the large oak stump that served as her father's dais.

Santagithi faced a crowd of nearly two hundred men. Their dress and demeanor covered a broad spectrum. His guards, noticeably in the foreground, wore lacquered leather jerkins studded with black, iron rings, shields slung across their backs, and swords at their waists. Some of the off-duty guards also wore mail. Mitrian nodded in tacit understanding. *My father's men know him well.*

The blacksmith and his son, Listar, stood in leather aprons black with sweat and grease. Merchants huddled in robes of silk and velvet over tunics of fur. Jeweled or tooled belts were fastened about their waists, and shoes of as fine a cloth as their robes covered their feet.

'Friends!' Santagithi shouted. 'We have assembled . . .' His voice died beneath the clamor of the guards' swords crashing against their shields. It seemed to Mitrian they must have practiced all morning to unsling their shields so fast.

Santagithi's scowl, though false, silenced them. 'My friends,' he began again. 'Too long we have sat in our huts. The arm must be worked to stay strong. The one that rests becomes withered and soft. We have rested too long. In three days, we ride against Strinia, not for gold, although we will find it, but for a strong arm and a fierce heart.'

Again, clamor arose from the guards. The merchants shifted uneasily from silk-covered foot to silk-covered foot. The blacksmith showed no emotion, although a light flashed in Listar's eyes and then disappeared. He would not go.

The crowd dispersed as Santagithi stepped down from the oak stump to view the men who had chosen to stay for the battle plans: his guards and a few of the cattlemen and farmers. Not many, but all capable hands with a sword. And then there was Rache. The strange combination of chair and wheels sat motionless as Rache glanced from face to face. Everywhere, Mitrian saw the same stupid look of incredulity, everywhere except on the face of Nantel. Santagithi, too, recovered quickly, but the rest remained gaping.

'I'm coming,' Rache said.

Startled visages alternated looks of horror and disbelief. No one moved, as if some warped artist had carved statues to replace them. Mitrian's hands balled to fists.

Santagithi gripped Rache's shoulder. 'You're always welcome next to me in battle. Of course you'll go.'

The ease with which their leader accepted Rache's presence obviously unsettled the guards. Whispers passed through the crowd. 'Our leader must be daft . . . why does he want Rache dead . . . what can he hope to do in battle?'

Nantel's gruff baritone rose above the speculations of his peers. 'Quiet, you bunch of cackling hens! You sound like women pounding clothes in a stream. I fought Rache since he lost the use of his legs, and he won. None of you can beat me. He would make fools of all of you. Santagithi knows the best men in this town. If you wish to grumble into your beards about his choice, go to the stream and pound clothes!'

This once, Mitrian found Nantel's temper welcome. The archer burst through the crowd, pushing men from his path.

Santagithi took the back of Rache's chair and followed in Nantel's wake.

*

The morning the men left on the foray, Mitrian sat on her bed, examining her collection of gems. They slid through her fingers and fell to her bed covers in a multicolored stream. Rubies, emeralds, topaz, and tiny, flawed diamonds clicked together, each a memento from one of her father's raids. When the last stone dropped from Mitrian's palm, she pressed her hands to the bedspread. Gems rolled into the depressions her fingers made in the coverlet. She paid them no heed, her attention straying to the largest member of her collection, an oval-cut, blue stone lying on a shelf near her window.

Mitrian referred to the stone as a sapphire, though it was unlike any other gem that bore the name. Each facet seemed smoother than a salt grain, cut and shaped with a perfection far exceeding the technique and skill of the jewelers in Santagithi's town. It sported the rich color of berries with cream, and its radiance remained long after the sun failed and night blanketed the sleeping village.

The sapphire had been a special gift from Santagithi the first time he had led a foray on Mitrian's birthday, and she knew it had cost him a large portion of his take from the war spoils. Since then, he had missed her birthday many times, though he never forgot it. He would return from battle with a unique bauble and spend at least one of the following days telling the stories she loved. Still, by tradition, a birthday was a time to be spent with family. Now, on the occasion of Mitrian's coming of age, she wished her father were home.

Mitrian's mother understood her disappointment. She served her daughter's favorite breakfast and amused her with romantic tales that would have made Santagithi blush. As a treat, she was packing a lunch for Mitrian to share with Listar while Mitrian played with gems and memories in her room.

Mitrian scooped the glittering pile of gems up in her cupped hands and poured them into their pouch. She hung the collection on a bedpost, rested her chin in her hands, and tried to decide which stories to beg from her father's repertoire upon his return. Certainly, she would ask details of the foray. His raiding tales sang the praises of his soldiers' glories, in which Rache always played the most important role. But this time, Mitrian knew the sword master turned archer believed more than the honor of a single battle was at stake.

After sating her curiosity and capturing her father's memories of his latest escapade, Mitrian decided she would question him about the world beyond their village. It was his favorite story, and Mitrian never tired of hearing it. He would always begin by describing the Eastlands, a place of deceit and hatred cut off from their Western world by an impassable barrier of peaks known as the Great Frenum Mountains. For as long as Mitrian could remember, there had been rumors the dark-skinned Easterners would ride through the southern trails to the Western Plains. Led by a demon, they would war against the Westerners until either the heroes of the West or the decadents of the East triumphed and claimed both lands.

Mitrian shuddered at the memory of Eastlands so evil the Western cartographers trailed their maps into black obscurity beyond the Great Mountains. She turned her thoughts to the neighbors who shared their Western world. To the south lay smaller towns like their own with which Santagithi traded or waged war, depending on the proclivities of the chieftains. Northward, blond reavers amused themselves throughout the frigid winters by warring amongst themselves with the same savage honor Rache displayed in battle.

Mitrian most enjoyed the descriptions of the civilized cities to the west. In Santagithi's youth, his people had lived among the prosperous western towns, until a band of exiled Northmen ravaged many of the cities for food, treasures, and love of violence. Santagithi's city had fallen, though not without valiant resistance, and the survivors had relocated farther east. Unlike men more prone to despair, Mitrian's father held no grudge against the Golden-haired Devils who had wreaked havoc on the Westlands. He believed in the superiority of might. In their new home, his strength of character and wisdom as a tactician unanimously earned him the position of leader.

On the bed, Mitrian rolled to her stomach. Effortlessly, her mind shifted from her father's historical explanations to Nantel's vivid descriptions of the modern West. For several months each year, the archer captain journeyed to the market town of Pudar with gladiators and other goods which he traded for exotic foods, spices, and weapons of extraordinary design.

Her mother's voice interrupted Mitrian's musings. 'Mitrian, Listar's worked hard all day. He must be hungry.'

Mitrian stood, yawned, and grinned at her mother's flagrant hint. At a trot, she traversed the long, plain corridor to the kitchen where, with a smile of welcome, her mother handed her a basket. The aroma of stew rose in thin wisps of steam.

'Thank you.' Mitrian accepted the packed lunch, then pushed through the door and trotted down the vine-covered hill to the town below. The basket slapped against her thigh as she headed toward the blacksmith's cottage. The regular rhythm of wicker against cloth focused her thoughts on her continuing archery lessons with Nantel. She had made progress since her first experience and now spent more time tearing arrows from wood than soil. Before Santagithi had left for the foray, he had accepted her new pursuit with little more than a frown of disapproval, a circumstance Mitrian attributed to the kind support of Rache and Nantel. But Mitrian knew her father would never accept her knowledge of swordcraft. Men used bows for competitions and hunts, but to Santagithi's mind, the only purpose of a blade was for killing men.

Mitrian arrived at the main road and slowed to a walk. The metallic thump of Listar's hammer grew louder. The crackle of weeds in the wind reminded her of the southern clearing where she practiced sword techniques. Last evening, a rustling in the brush had interrupted her session as had the red eyes a few weeks earlier. As Mitrian sat, cross-legged, behind Listar's anvil, she decided to tell Rache about the animal in the clearing when he returned.

Engrossed in his work, Listar apparently did not notice Mitrian's arrival. She studied his soot-streaked, blond curls and the stocky set of his body. His arms bulged as he swung his hammer in tight arcs. As he brushed sweat and hair from his eyes, his gaze fell on Mitrian. He smiled.

Mitrian grinned back, but her thoughts followed Rache. She imagined the enemies of her town fleeing before his feathered shafts, and her mind conjured images of silver turrets stretching toward the sky.

Listar tossed a strip of steel to the sand pile. He wiped his brow, smearing ash across his face. Turning, he strode to Mitrian, took her hand, and recoiled as if from fire. 'I'm sorry, Mitri. I got soot on your sleeve. Let me go wash.' Listar jogged in the direction of the fountain.

Mitrian opened her basket, removed a checkered blanket, and spread it on the grass near the anvil. She knew she would probably marry Listar someday, and this thought awakened a strange sorrow. Listar cared deeply for her. Honest, tender, and sincere, he would make a fine husband. But Mitrian could not love him. *I wonder what sort of man I do want. Maybe one like my father, a strategist, a leader loved by his people and feared by his enemies.* Listar could become aggressive at times, but he lacked the wild war passion that drove Santagithi and Rache to battle. Even as the idea came into Mitrian's mind, she pitied Emerald. Rache was beautiful and more heroic than any man she knew, but he could belong to no one.

Listar returned, sitting so close to Mitrian she could smell the clean perspiration of hard labor. She passed him a bowl of stew and a spoon. 'What did you make?'

'Barrel hoops.' Listar spooned warm stew into his mouth. His friendly, blue eyes met Mitrian's.

'That sounds . . .' Mitrian struggled for words, not wanting to damn with faint interest.

'. . .boring.' Listar spared her the need. 'It's not one of my favorite projects.' He set aside the spoon and rubbed Mitrian's arm with affection.

A sudden breeze draped strands of matted hair across Listar's brow. A plan entered Mitrian's mind so naturally, it seemed as if some power had placed it there. Her voice assumed the strained quality Rache had learned to mistrust. 'I wonder what my father will bring me from the foray.' She glanced at Listar, sidelong.

Listar chewed slowly, attention on Mitrian.

Mitrian fondled his leather pant leg absently. 'He always brings me a special present for my birthday. And Rache . . .' She let her words trail, feeling necessarily cruel.

At the mention of the sword master's name, Listar's face pinched. Despite Rache's living arrangements with Emerald, Mitrian's visits to Rache's cottage were no secret to the townsfolk, though only she and her mentor knew the meetings were actually sword lessons. Surely, Mitrian's crass reference, rumors, and Listar's own insecurity bit deeply. When Mitrian did not continue, he spoke. 'Rache?' The name emerged as a choked whisper.

Fidgeting, Listar waited while Mitrian took a mouthful of stew, chewed leisurely, and swallowed. 'Rache always brings me something nice, too.'

'Does he!' Listar's voice rumbled with challenge. 'Well, my gift's better.' He leaped to his feet so abruptly, he nearly spilled his stew. 'Because I'll get you anything you want. Name it.'

Mitrian teased. 'A country.'

The color drained from Listar's face. Then, noticing her smile, he chuckled in relief, sat down on the blanket again, and retrieved his stew. 'What would you want with a country? Your father already leads one.'

Carefully, Mitrian set her spoon in her bowl and spoke in the most sincere tone she could muster. 'Fine, then. Make me a sword.'

Despite her attempt to radiate candor, Listar laughed. 'Stop kidding. What would you do with a sword?'

'The same thing anyone else would do with it.' Annoyance hardened Mitrian's sarcasm. 'Butter bread. Listar, you asked me to name anything. I want a sword, a longsword with a good, split leather grip.'

Mitrian's knowledge of weapons held Listar momentarily speechless. 'You're serious,' he stated the obvious. 'I don't understand.' He awaited an explanation.

Mitrian offered none. She shrugged.

Listar took Mitrian's hand and stared past his anvil to the stout workhorse tethered to his father's cabin. 'If you really want a sword, I'll make one that rivals the weapon of the god of steel.' He closed his fingers about hers. 'I'll start on it tomorrow and have it done before the warriors get back from the foray. When I finish the rough work, you can choose the type and pattern of jewels in the hilt.' He added, emotion trailing back into his words. 'Perhaps then you'll tell me what, by the gods, you plan to do with the thing.' He raised one eyebrow.

Mitrian avoided the question, excitement enveloping her in waves.

With a sigh, Listar finished his stew, kissed Mitrian lightly on the cheek, and resumed his work.

Mitrian remained in the grass, her thoughts triumphant and distant.

Excitement kept Mitrian from sleep that night. Anticipation formed a vivid picture of the sword that would become hers by Listar's efforts. Soon, she would own a weapon as bright and new as her mastery of its craft. Pride of ownership thrilled through her, and she reveled in the fantasies awakened by its intensity. She pictured herself in a soft black jerkin, whirling with the grace of a dancer while her sword carved perfect arcs, grim silver highlights flashing from its steel.

Mitrian's thoughts shifted. She imagined herself on a white stallion. Beside her, Rache controlled his eager mare with light tugs at its rein. From memories of guards' stories, Mitrian created a background of the Western Plains. She stared across a vast flatland, sparsely populated with coarse grasses and twisted, broad-leafed trees. Far to the south, rock and clay gave way to ocean sand, and surf soughed as softly as a man's last breath. North and eastward, peaks rose to the sky, many times higher than the hills surrounding Santagithi's town. As Mitrian watched, a dark-skinned army swarmed through the eastern passes.

Rache tensed. Mitrian's hand fell to a hilt crafted to her hand. Her fingers curled across leather flattened and smoothed by the familiarity of her fist. It would fit no other grip as well; the sword would serve Mitrian and no other master. This realization sent a fresh wave of excitement through her, pulling her from her reverie. But with some effort, she reestablished the continuity of the dream.

An ashen horde of Eastern soldiers poured down the cliff face. As they neared, Mitrian concentrated on the leader, a huge man as broad as Garn and as tall as Santagithi. Then she recalled that the guards named him a demon. *What does a demon look like?* wondered Mitrian, and her mental image faded as she pondered the question. She pictured Nantel's homely visage, twisted in anger by the antics of his archers. She lengthened the nose, added protruding canine teeth and goatlike horns, then colored the image olive-green.

The effect was stunningly hideous. Mitrian gave her creation the body of an obese man covered with the keeled, dark scales of a viper and positioned it directly before Rache and herself.

The creature hissed. 'Who dares stand before the army of the Eastlands?'

Rache's reply rang with power. 'We are emissaries from the West come to demonstrate our skill. I am Captain Rache . . .'

The demon paled.

'. . . and this is Lady Mitrian, Mistress of the Gleaming Blade.' Rache gave a signal.

Mitrian leapt from her mount and launched into a kata that combined all of Rache's teachings. She began with simple blocks and strikes performed with a dexterity that would awe any man with knowledge of swordcraft. Her maneuvers grew more complex. The sun reflecting from the polished steel of her sword danced like a silver flame about techniques marred only by the imperfection of Mitrian's understanding of their intricacies. Her mind added perfection her body could never match. The grace of her dance drew Mitrian closer to sleep. As she completed her final sequence, a technique she had seen no man but Rache perform, the demon stared, transfixed.

'You've stopped us for now,' said the Eastern general humbly. 'But it is not for a Northman and a girl to divert destiny. We will return with a way around your skill . . .'

Mitrian's imagings lulled her into sleep. A discomforting chill swept through her, like the tingle of thawing fingers after a day in the snow. She rode her mare, trotting across fire-cleared meadow she somehow knew as the area west of her town. She welcomed the warm wind across her face. The sun gleamed in a sky bright as the sapphire that was the pride of her collection. As Mitrian reveled in the beauty of the scene, she reined her mount over the crest of a low hill. In the vale below her lay the ruins of a town. Huge pillars leaned horribly, like the uneven teeth in a shattered skull she had seen as a child.

Suddenly, clouds darkened the horizon. The caress of the spring breeze became the cold slap of a gale. Mitrian kicked her horse to a canter as water poured from the sky. The tempest whipped her hair into her eyes. Rain lashed her cheeks. Fear welled inside her, as sudden and cruel as the storm. She hunched against her mount's neck and steered toward the valley, hoping the walls of the hill might dampen nature's frenzy, and the ruins might protect her from the rain. Mitrian kept the wind in her face to maintain her course. Realization seeped into her mind. She could not remember starting this journey nor her purpose for being on the fire-cleared wastes west of home. But recognition of her dream state did little to ease growing panic. For now, the storm seemed more real than her bed.

The rain pitched with redoubled fury. A wolf howled. The horse bolted in terror. Mitrian's heart pounded while she calmed her reeling steed. Rain drowned her screamed commands. She pulled the hood of her cloak down to protect her face and buried her hands in her mare's wet mane. She clung, hoping the horse could find shelter.

The mare slogged onward. Moisture penetrated Mitrian's last layer of dry clothes, and she fought to drag herself from nightmare. The horse lurched abruptly. Mitrian threw out an arm for balance, and her fingers scraped stone. She tossed hair from her eyes and confronted two headless statues guarding the entrance to the long-dead city she had viewed from the hilltop. Her horse sprinted inside.

High granite walls and arches crowded the inner streets, providing protection from the rain. Vines obscured the sides of buildings and made statues appear to have sprouted hair. Ripe blueberries hung from the foliage. Relieved for this rude shelter, Mitrian slowed her mare to a walk.

After a short distance, the street opened to a courtyard that held a statue of a mounted warrior. Along its walls, multicolored birds waged ravenous war on the berries. Their song thrilled Mitrian despite the strange surroundings of her dream. She followed the birds as they winged down a road on the far side of the square.

Fear faded, and despair replaced it. Mitrian felt her wet jerkin peel away from her skin with every movement. She passed through streets and alleyways to a vast, roofed hall. Here she dismounted, tugging angrily at clinging undergarments. Engrossed in her discomfort, she did not notice the robed figure at the farthest corner of the room. 'Mitrian, your journey is finished. Accept my hospitality.' The voice echoed between pillars with a power that quailed her.

Mitrian whirled, and her grip on the bridle went lax. Before her stood an old man, tall and thin as a fence rail. On another man, the narrow frame might have appeared frail. But it seemed more as if this man found bulk unnecessary for strength and so discarded it. The sight stirred the memory of a childhood story, but it did not surface to conscious thought. Mitrian stared as her mind filled with questions she could not bring her mouth to verbalize. 'I – I'm sorry,' she stammered. 'Is this your city?'

The man laughed, the sound like the peel of a bell. 'I don't own the ruins, but they are my home. My name is Shadimar. Your people know me as the Eastern Wizard.'

Mitrian gasped. 'Eastern?'

Shadimar made a reassuring gesture. 'By name, not affiliation.' From any other person, the words would have sounded stilted, but they fit the image of this elder. 'The Western Wizard and I protect the Westland peoples, your people. Come, Mitrian. I've called you here for a reason. Is it true you will soon own a sword?' As he finished speaking, a wolf slunk from a passage behind the Wizard and settled beneath his outstretched palm.

'Yes,' Mitrian replied as she absorbed the remainder of his words. 'You called me here? How do you know my name?' Boldness swiftly replaced surprise as she recalled part of Rache's tale. The guard captain had spoken of a childhood exploration soon after his arrival in Santagithi's Town that had led him to inadvertently trespass on a Wizard's lands. In payment, the Wizard had forced Rache to share his quarters with a gentle, foreign child, a punishment that had seemed more like a gift. Vaguely, she recalled mention of a wolf. All else muddled into a single description: 'He looked old as the earth, but seemed kindly.'

'I have dealt with Rache and your father. Little escapes me.' Shadimar turned toward the passage from which the wolf had appeared. 'Leave your horse. She'll be tended.' He pushed past the open door and strode down the corridor, the wolf at his heels.

'Tended?' Mitrian repeated, still dazed. The ceaseless echo of rain on the roof made the ruins seem comfortable. *I suppose she won't stray.* Mechanically, she removed the saddle and bridle, wondering why Shadimar both intimidated and intrigued her. *And why isn't my horse scared of his wolf?*

Shadimar offered no answer, but he poked his head through the portal. 'Time's growing short, Mitrian. I offer the adventures you seek and a spell for your sword. If you accept my bargain, neither the sword's edge nor its sheen will dull. Come. At least see what I offer.' His head disappeared from the doorway, and his footfalls retreated down the corridor.

Excitement and fear warred in Mitrian. Though her parents had taught her that magic was no more real than Rache's myths of elves, she did not doubt Shadimar's abilities. Even the absurd seems plausible in dream. Mitrian shied from the grisly face that held the door's ring and followed Shadimar through a corridor dimly illuminated by evenly spaced, brass lanterns. Rainwater ran from her hair and clothes, trailing droplets on the stone floor. She could find nothing dry on which to wipe her sweating palms.

Although Mitrian saw less finery here than in Santagithi's citadel, she found the crumbling simplicity engrossing. Bronze-bound oak doors interrupted the time-worn walls at regular intervals, and Shadimar opened one of these. He gestured Mitrian through it.

Mitrian pushed past Shadimar and his wolf. Her jerkin brushed a damp spot onto the satin of the Wizard's robe. The room beyond seemed confining after the spacious entry hall. A copper brazier held rectangular blocks issuing a steady orange flame. Two chairs stood before a fireplace filled with a larger stack of the glowing bricks. Shadimar sat in one of the chairs, and the wolf settled at his feet. Mitrian took the seat beside him. Already, the warmth of the room was drying her clothes.

In these well-lit quarters, Mitrian examined her host. He appeared older than any man she had ever seen, yet vitality radiated from him, everywhere except from his eyes. They reminded her of ancient stone. 'Why would you magic a sword for me?' Despite Mitrian's anxiety, her question emerged calmly.

A frown parted Shadimar's beard. 'I mentioned a bargain, not a favor. Understand, I will extract payment for the only magic sword of the Eastern, Western and faerie worlds.' He leaned forward, and his eyes went cold. The wolf shifted uneasily. 'Magic comes of Chaos, unpredictable even in a Wizard's control. This sword will grant responsibilities as well as abilities. It will offer a culture of warrior men and women, a heritage of blood and glory dedicated to the battle goddess, Sif.'

Mitrian plucked key phrases from the Wizard's speech. *Payment, Chaos, responsibilities, blood.* She studied the beast at Shadimar's feet. *If I run, will the wolf chase me?*

Shadimar continued, seemingly oblivious to Mitrian's distress. 'It will become your destiny to return an heir to his throne, to fight in the Great War against the East, to . . .'

Excitement fluttered Mitrian's heart. 'War,' she whispered. Dream flowed into dream. Mitrian imagined castle spires on the horizon, her arm linked with a young prince as beautiful as Rache. 'You promise adventure?'

'No!' The Wizard's shout shattered Mitrian's reverie. 'I guarantee only a sword *worthy* of adventure. It won't come to you. You must create it.' His thick, white brows beetled beneath a creased forehead. 'For you, Mitrian, finding adventure would require an act of defiance.'

The thought of Santagithi's wrath made Mitrian shudder.

Shadimar loosed a derisive laugh, apparently guessing her thoughts. His voice went strangely cold. 'A would-be adventurer afraid of her own father?' He sneered. 'Forgive me. I've chosen wrongly. I withdraw my offer.'

Shadimar's tone infuriated Mitrian. She leapt to her feet. Her hand fell to her belt, though she wore no weapon. 'You can't just retract it! The offer's been made.' The realization that Shadimar could indeed refuse to work his magic drained Mitrian's anger. She sat down again, sulking. 'Where will you find another with my sword mastery and knowledge ?' Consumed by rage, Mitrian did not realize how easily the Wizard played her.

Shadimar smiled. 'Your potential abilities cannot be easily matched. But knowledge ? Really. What does a girl understand of war ?'

Mitrian reined in annoyance with effort. 'I don't see what my sex has to do with it. You said this Sif was goddess of warrior men and *women*,' she reminded him icily. 'Nantel and Rache have told me . . .'

The Wizard interrupted, his face wrinkled. 'Half truths. To spare you from the gore, they focused on the glories of victory, the beauty of swordcraft, and your father's strategic wisdom. Men die . . .'

Mitrian knotted her hands in her lap. 'Don't you think I know that !'

'Fine. If you don't fear war, take these.' His hand dipped into his pocket, then flicked outward. Two tiny amber gems bounced at Mitrian's feet. 'If we transact this deal, these must become the eyes of a wolf on your sword hilt. Now, with my help, they can serve as a window to a battle in which you have a stake. And so does the demon of the gems.'

Mitrian closed her fist around the gems. The Wizard uttered three short words, each harsh as cliff stone. The walls of the ruins faded to the consistency of frosted glass. The patter of rain became the clash of distant steel, and the scene unfolded to a pine forest near the barbaric town of Strinia. The woods were dark, yet through the matted interlace of branches, Mitrian recognized Santagithi's archers. Their horses stood in no formation, demeanors relaxed and unhurried. Rache waited before them. Though alert, his eyes lacked the fire of interest. His hair hung in a golden veil.

Mitrian received another's thoughts as clearly as the image. At first, she believed they were Rache's because they fit him nearly perfectly. Yet there was an alien quality as though relayed by a stranger, apparently, the so-called 'demon of the gems.' Through him, she learned that the Strinian town lacked fortifications, and Santagithi had no need for bowmen or crippled swordsmen. The source of the thoughts believed Rache had chosen his current position for the fragrance of the pines and the sounds of the battle. Yet each clash of steel awakened a wild war passion that quickly broke to despair. Soon the pine scent became familiar enough to allow the musty aroma of humus through it. The chatter of squirrels was displaced by the pounding of hoofbeats. Before Rache could shout a warning, large figures in beast skins burst through the forest.

Swords leapt for the archers; copper blades washed red. Half the archers fell dead before they could draw weapons. A few released arrows that dropped some of the ambushers as they howled war cries. *Gods!* Mitrian flinched as guards' eyes glazed. But Rache's projected presence within her warmed to command. He shouted orders that seemed senseless to her and surely were lost beneath the battle din. But the archers obeyed, weaving into a tight formation.

Through Rache's eyes, Mitrian watched the forest depths blur as every movement of man or beast sprang to vivid clarity. Like a war machine, his mind assessed every flaw, pattern, and strength of each man. He noticed an archer cut off from the rest.

Mitrian knew the archer. Called Ancar, he often practiced at the range with Nantel, Rache, and herself. His wife was a few years older than Mitrian, had been a playmate in her youth. Before the foray, Ancar had carried his baby son to the range and patiently explained archery amid the good-natured gibes of his peers. Rache alone had not smiled at the spectacle. Now Ancar wore a mask of desperation, having already exceeded his best efforts at defense.

All the information Rache and the demon had gathered was stored in pockets of consciousness for instant retrieval. Mitrian's mind exploded to a vast plain of red. Battle madness welled to enveloping euphoria, pleasure like nothing she had ever experienced. Rache brought the flat of his sword across the rump of his mount. It lunged forward.

The forest rang with sound as Ancar fought with borrowed strength. He blocked a strike to his head, whipped his blade around, and buried it in an attacker's skull. The barbarian's death throes wrenched the sword from Ancar's grip.

'No !' With his free hand, Rache drew a second sword to throw to Ancar as skin-clad riders closed on them from all sides. A hilt in each fist, Rache set to his own defense. Swords flashed around him. He deflected every blow, then used the force of one to redirect his own blade through the neck of an attacker.

A cry of fierce joy sprang from Rache's throat. While defending all sides, he had not found time to question his abilities. His mind did not need to answer, his body did. His swords moved with such speed they seemed invisible and unstoppable. He easily sliced through hide armor, spilling entrails over the coarse hair covering his opponent's torso.

In the distance a great horn sounded. One attacker hesitated. With a quick thrust, Rache pierced the barbarian's chest. The man fell with scarlet froth on his lips as Rache's last opponent reined toward the sound of the horn. Suddenly, Rache's head and, apparently, his attention returned to Ancar's plight; he galloped to the position where he had last seen the archer. Barely able to cling to his horse, Ancar bled from scores of wounds. The worst laid his scalp open and oozed a yellowish liquid. Rache pulled the dying man to his saddle, cradled him in his arms, and returned to his men.

The forest was littered with bodies. Of the original seventeen archers, five remained. Mitrian realized the horn blast had summoned the barbarian warriors back to their town. Had it not, none of the archers would have survived the ambush. The stench of blood and death obscured the perfume of pine and humus. Rache lowered Ancar's body to the ground.

If Mitrian could believe the demon of the gems, peace settled over Rache, quickly displaced by a rush of joy inspired by his triumph over his handicap. But Mitrian's sorrow lingered, forcing her to contemplate the eternity that would continue after the deaths of these men, *and her own as well*. Rache's faith in the afterlife of Valhalla shielded him from Mitrian's turmoil, but she envisioned each corpse as the spirit that once inhabited it, a priceless life lost to the stroke of a sword. She recalled the lamentations of widows and fatherless children, a grief she never shared because Santagithi always returned. *And what of Ancar's child? Will he become a warrior bound to avenge his father, or will he disdain war? Will love for his father's valor become hatred for abandoning his son?*

Mitrian tried to consider a grown child who had lost his father to battle, but her mind drew a blank. Then she thought of Rache. His presence seemed to enter her consciousness with his name, his happiness so incongruous with the deaths around him that it pained Mitrian. With a sharp intake of breath, she dropped the gems from her fist. Instantly, the forest faded. She clung to her final thought, and it kindled a memory.

Mitrian pictured herself beside the stream crossing the forest near Santagithi's citadel. She was five years old. On the far bank, Rache tossed pebbles into the water, breaking its placid surface in widening rings. Though nearly of age, Rache appeared a child. And while he should have been exuberant over his recent promotion to captain, bitterness tinged his words. 'My mother fought with a skill Santagithi's guards can only envy. My family was slain by enemies of our own race who served in other days as allies. My baby sister would be your age.' Rache did not address Mitrian. His blue eyes strayed past her to another figure on the bank. The image blurred as Mitrian attempted to form a mental picture of the boy at Rache's side, a stranger she had long ago forgotten. His name escaped her. She recalled only that his large size and persistent silences had frightened her.

Shadimar's voice sheared the last, wispy bindings of his spell. 'He is the prince of the high kingdom, Béarn.'

'Who?' Mitrian stammered, unwilling to believe the Wizard could influence her memories as well as create her dreams.

Shadimar clenched his lips in a slight smile. 'The child who frightened you, though he would no more harm you than Listar or Nantel would. He alone survived his uncle's spree of murder. Someday, you may restore him to his throne.'

Mitrian replied in a voice devoid of confidence. 'Restore him? I don't even remember what he looked like. How?'

'No matter. He's changed since childhood, and so have you, Mitrian. When the time comes, you will know him, just as you will join the Great War, just as you will kill a friend . . .'

'Kill a friend?' Mitrian repeated, stunned.

The Eastern Wizard replied evenly. 'Yes, Mitrian. Kill a friend.'

Mitrian jumped to her feet with a violence that toppled her chair. 'Stop!'

The wolf crouched. The Wizard shied away from Mitrian, obviously startled for the first time since they'd met.

'Stop!' Mitrian screamed again. 'I don't want to hear any more. Let me live my life, not have it displayed like a rich man's feast. Don't talk about destiny. Right or wrong, I'll believe my life is a consequence of chance and the things I've done.' She turned away. 'If you know so much about the future, why do you live alone in shabby ruins?'

Shadimar remained silent for a moment, as if he recognized her harsh words came from uncertainty rather than cruelty. His stone gray eyes softened. He rose, and his hand dropped to Mitrian's shoulder. 'Mitrian, there are many things you can't understand. But this time you're right. I have talked too much for the excitement of fulfilling prophecies. The magic I offer will add to your sword skill, give you a new perspective and a heritage, nothing more. The other events I spoke of will occur only by your decision. If my advice can make your choice simpler, remember that allies and enemies can change.' He let his arm fall to his side and sat down. 'And now, your time has come. Will you accept my magic in exchange for an item of far less value?'

Mitrian whispered, fearing to ask. 'Which is?'

Shadimar's smile returned. 'The Pica Stone, a sapphire in your possession, worth no more to you than the gems I offer in trade. To me, it is everything. It belonged to my people before the Northmen's raids that killed them. Many hands have held it before yours. Many eyes have admired its beauty. May I have it back?' Doubt settled across the aged features and made him seem far less formidable.

Mitrian sat, overwhelmed by conflicting emotions. She bent and reclaimed the amber gems from the floor. 'I'll bring it tomorrow.'

The wolf emitted a strange, laughing whine.

'No need,' said Shadimar. 'I can get it.'

6 The Demon in the Gems

Mitrian awakened with a start. Pale pink dawn light filtered through her bedroom window, washing over the shelf and sparkling from the brass fittings of her clothing chest. *A dream. It was all a dream.* She lay still, sorting reality from fantasy. The excursion to the ruins of Myrcidë seemed to meld and tangle with the events of the previous day, and Mitrian was having difficulty carving the two apart. *It was so vivid.*

Golden reflections danced on the door, wound through with shifting line-shadows as wind ruffled the pattern of the trees outside her window. *Yellow, not blue.* Mitrian stiffened, certain what she would find. Her gaze swept from the door across the room to the chest along the wall to the shelf beneath the window centered on the wall and to the left of her headboard. Sure enough, the sapphire was gone. In its place sat the two gems Shadimar had given her in the ruins.

It was real. Mitrian sank back to the bed. *Now what do I do?* Shadimar had seemed kindly, but why should an enemy trying to influence her seem otherwise? *He is the Eastern Wizard. Easterners are enemies of the West.* Yet Mitrian's own logic defeated her. *If he wanted to trap me, why would he admit such a thing? Had he claimed to be the Western Wizard, I would never have caught the lie. He could even have just used his name.* Now Mitrian frowned. Yesterday, she would have denied the existence of Wizards; now, having dreamed of one, she lay in her bed hypothesizing more. Shadimar had claimed to be a friend, a protector of the Westlands' peoples, yet, at times, he seemed to be manipulating or hiding facts. And he said things Mitrian did not like. *He claimed I'd kill a friend.* Mitrian chewed her lower lip, wondering which friend the Wizard meant. The train of thought made her feel morbid. *Does it matter? If I knew, would I weigh that friend's life against the price of a sword and adventure?*

Disturbed by the direction of her thoughts, Mitrian consoled herself with another. *Shadimar amended, saying the killing of a friend might not happen. I'll just need to be careful.* Still, many things confused and excited her. *The Wizard claimed to have had dealings with Rache and my father. When they return, I'll have to ask some guarded questions about the Wizard and the child Shadimar called a prince.* Mitrian sat up with a smile, aware Santagithi had become accustomed to her begging odd stories, Rache to questions she dared not ask her father. And Mitrian recalled one thing more. *Shadimar said his magic would only provide a sword worthy of adventure. The simple crafting of the weapon won't cause anything without the act of defiance he mentioned.*

Mitrian climbed out of bed, crossed her room, and reached for the yellow gems. She paused, hand outstretched and not quite touching the stones, recalling the images of battle that had swum through her mind in the Wizard's ruins. Mitrian had not seen Rache so exuberant since his accident, yet his joy had seemed cruel, horrifyingly misplaced amid the mangled corpses of his companions. He had often spoken of the glory and honor of vanquishing foes or of the raw courage of those killed in the fray, but Mitrian's glimpse of battle had shown her only crude, desperate strokes, painful wounds, and gory deaths. Mitrian stood, frozen, and Shadimar's mocking voice seemed to fill her mind: 'What does a girl understand of war?'

Angered anew by Shadimar's scorn, Mitrian seized the gems. They pressed into the skin of her palm, but the war scenes did not recur. *What did I expect? Shadimar's not here to guide their magic.* Mitrian clutched more tightly, now more curious than afraid. The picture of Rache and his archers engaged in battle had looked dramatic enough, the knowledge of Rache's senses had added reality to the image, but his strategy, war passion, and excitement had touched her with far more strength and depth. It had seemed more as if the emotions had radiated from a nearer source, the so-called 'demon of the gems,' though the mood had fit Rache's actions perfectly. *As if the 'demon' knew Rache.* Mitrian considered, recalling that the Eastern general had also been named a demon. *How? And what exactly is a 'demon?'* Mitrian had heard the term used as everything from a friendly gibe to any phenomenon men could not explain.

A presence curled through Mitrian's thoughts, then eased in so gently she scarcely noticed it. Until the visions came. A man lay, shivering beneath a rumpled pile of blankets. Though young, skin sagged around his features revealing gaunt cheeks and pale, hollowed eyes. Greasy, blond hair hung, sweat-plastered to his forehead. A cough rattled, wet and suffocating, in his chest, though it cleared none of the fluid from his lungs. A sense of desperation radiated from the figure, a certainty of death, a weakness, and a fear.

Drawn into the image, Mitrian did not think to recoil from it. As she watched, another stranger flitted into the picture, a white-haired man appearing more ancient than Shadimar, yet with all the vitality the dying blond lacked. The bedridden one wheezed. 'Wizard, I've helped you. Is there nothing you can do for me?' He used a Northern tongue Mitrian did not know; she did not question how she understood him.

'Nothing,' the Wizard said, though whether in repetition or as a reply, Mitrian could not tell.

'I'm not asking for life,' the blond managed. 'Just an honorable death, a chance at Valhalla. Please . . .'

His voice trailed off, and several moments passed in silence until he could continue. 'Just enough strength to stand.' The rest came to Mitrian as a thought. *Just enough to stagger out the door and attack one of the other Renshai. If I challenge, they'll give me the death in battle I desire.*

The Wizard did not move. 'It's too late,' he said.

The blond struggled in his final moments. Coldness seeped into him, and he shivered so hard, his entire body convulsed. His vision disappeared. *Hel's ice. Hel's darkness.* 'Please,' he gasped. 'Please, you owe me. I can't go to Hel. Not now. Can you do something?' It was a plea. Numbness spiraled through the dying man's mind, and Mitrian felt herself surrendering, too. *So easy to give in. So hard to fight.*

'Yes.' The Wizard sat on the edge of the bed, though the Renshai could not feel his presence. 'There is something I can do. But it's only a substitute for dying, only another tomb. Time to muse, too long. It will keep you from Hel for now, but it will not stop you thinking of it.'

I'll take it. The blond did not speak aloud, but the Wizard seemed to understand. He drew a gem from his pocket, a yellow sapphire or a topaz. A few guttural words, these beyond Mitrian's comprehension, and the scene exploded to yellow. Mitrian shielded her eyes, forgetting the image came from inside her, and fire snapped through her mind's eye, the flaming gold of the stone. A crack echoed, the terminal sound of a tree before it falls, then the image reformed. The body lay still, its spirit stripped away. The topaz had broken into the two perfect pieces that now sat, squeezed into the creases of Mitrian's hand. The presence faded from Mitrian's mind.

Mitrian opened her fingers, staring at the gems cradled in her palm, too confused to be afraid. *These stones hold a human soul by magic? Is that what a demon is? Or was that just the term Shadimar used because he had no other way to describe it?* The possibilities sent Mitrian's mind whirling. *Am I awake even now?* Speculation seemed futile, so she discarded it. *The question is, dare I contain someone's soul in the hilt of a sword?* The answer came so quickly, Mitrian wondered whether she or the 'demon' in the gems initiated it. *Vicarious glory. A chance for a warrior to fight again, if only in another's hands. A Northern warrior. No wonder he knows Rache so well.*

Having made the decision to craft the sword, Mitrian let ideas swirl through her mind as she dressed. The prospect seemed impossible and immense. One day, a simple townswoman with an interest in swordcraft, the next acquaintance to a Wizard and a demon. Over one night, the world had changed, yet Mitrian felt no different. She drew solace from her sameness. Whatever the Wizard offered, he had apparently kept his promise to let her make her own decisions and determine her own life.

Mitrian stepped into the corridor and headed toward the outer door. As she passed the kitchen, she could hear her mother humming and the sounds of dishes rattling. Mitrian hesitated, the domesticity so real, so comforting, yet so wrong for her. She tried to imagine herself preparing meals for Listar, but the vision would not come. Instead, her mind crafted pictures of swords capering in moonlight, wolf howls, and the bittersweet triumph of war. Keeping the gems clamped against her fingers, she headed out into the deepening dawn.

Mitrian ran past the wall and down the hill from Santagithi's citadel, ignoring the tendrils that grasped at her sandals and the red flowers hanging from the vines. Mind still mired in the events of last night's dream-journey, she traversed the familiar streets from habit. Pulling up before the blacksmith's cottage, she found Listar and his father preparing the anvil and forges for the day's work.

When Mitrian arrived, Listar looked up. He passed a brief exchange with his father that Mitrian could not hear, then trotted over and drew her beyond earshot of the blacksmith. 'Mitrian, what are you doing here so early?'

'I have something for you.' Mitrian held out the pair of amber gems. 'I'd like you to make the hilt of my sword as a wolf and use these for eyes.'

Listar frowned. He glanced over his shoulder as if to ascertain his father was not eavesdropping. 'You're still serious about that?'

Now it was Mitrian who frowned. 'I thought we'd already determined that. Do I have to convince you again?'

'No, of course not.' Despite his negative answer, Listar's tone suggested he needed persuading. 'I was just thinking I have to give my father a reason why I'm spending a week working on a sword without pay.'

'Can't you just tell him you're making me a birthday present?'

Mitrian imagined her mother's help and enthusiasm on any project she might choose to make for Listar.

'A sword for my girlfriend's birthday? My father'll think I've gone insane.'

'Don't tell him what you're making,' Mitrian suggested practically. 'Just say it's a special project.'

Listar fell silent.

'I can pay,' Mitrian added, frightened by the prospect that the sword might never exist despite her decision. It was one thing for her to choose not to defy her father, another to never have the opportunity.

'Pay?' Listar paled. 'I wouldn't hear of it. It's just . . .' He sighed. 'Mitrian, please. Why can't you tell me why you want a sword?'

Mitrian hesitated, aware Listar had the right to know, yet not daring to take a chance her father might find out about Rache's teachings. The last thing she wanted to do was lie, but she saw no way around it. If she gave him no explanation, Listar might put the clues together: her time with Rache, the sword. She slid closer until her shoulder touched Listar's chest. 'I just want something you've made. Something beautiful to stare at and remember the effort you made to craft it, just for me.' Mitrian held her breath, afraid to think she could deceive him so easily.

But Listar believed because he wanted to. He flushed, obviously embarrassed by her attention and over forcing her to reveal such a fine and noble cause. He accepted the gems Mitrian thrust into his palm. Finally, he managed to speak. 'All right. But I'm not sure I want to explain that to your father. The last thing I want to do is anger Santagithi. Would you mind if we kept this project a secret?'

Few things could have pleased Mitrian more. She brought her excitement under control before replying. 'That's fine, Listar. Thanks.'

'I love you,' Listar said.

'I love you, too.' Mitrian replied from rote, wishing she could mean the sentiment as seriously as her request.

Though Mar Lon carried the history of the world in a hundred generations of song, it was his own insight in a shabby Eastern tavern that plagued him. He composed half a dozen ballads in as many days. Each braided chords, single string harmonies, and voice into complex, cooperative melodies designed to emphasize the beauty that could be achieved by the unity of disparate sounds. Each told a story of enemies working in concert. He sang of the wild rampage of the Renshai as they passed through the Westlands on their way home from a hundred years of banishment, and how much better the many and varied Westland peoples fared when they finally learned to league against the reavers. He pieced together tales of the Cardinal Wizards, choosing those few instances where Odin's laws allowed them to work toward a common goal. He created fables of two godlike rivals stranded on a hostile world that forced them to act together to survive, wolf packs that used group tricks and traps to surround their prey, and a jaguar and a songbird who pooled their knowledge and divergent experiences to form a peaceful coalition that aided all animals and humans as well.

The beauty of Mar Lon's music held the Easterners spellbound. They set aside mugs of watered beer and handfuls of stringy poultry to listen. They laughed at the animals' antics and dismissed the tales of Wizards, who most believed were only myths. And they applauded the grisly stories of the Renshai's spree of slaughter across the Westlands, the world of their infidel enemies. The perfectly interwoven triads, arpeggios, and harmonics had drawn them together in a cause, the cause of defeating and enslaving the peoples of the West.

And on the seventh day, the song that Mar Lon wrote rivaled his father's for desperation and despair.

For nearly a week, Listar's hammer rose and fell on the most intricate weapon he would ever craft. When he finished, Mitrian clutched the hilt in shaking hands, warm with the pride of ownership. Had it been a crude piece of bronze, she would have felt as awed for possessing it. But this sword was a masterpiece.

Its overlarge pommel took the shape of a wolf's head with the promised amber eyes. In battle, it would not easily slip from hands slick with sweat or blood. Listar had etched square designs in a neat row over both sides of the blade, making it shimmer with alternating areas of dark and light. The edge looked keener than any weapon in Santagithi's armory. It held Mitrian entranced. Listar glowed with pride and seemed reluctant to surrender the fruit of his efforts, even to the woman he loved. Thanking him, Mitrian ran home and sat in her room, studying it for most of the morning.

At length, Mitrian sheathed the blade and slid it between her headboard and the wall. But almost as soon as she did, she was possessed of an urge to stare at it again. And so it went into the afternoon. Mitrian performed her few chores and, whenever chance took her into her room or she found a free moment, she would examine the blade again, test its balance, reacquaint her hand with the grip. Each time, she would memorize it; but on the next inspection it seemed just as strange, new, and beautiful.

During one of Mitrian's staring sessions, her mother's voice wafted to her from down the corridor. 'Mitrian?'

Startled, Mitrian nearly dropped the weapon from her lap, catching it and sheathing it with a quick, guilty motion. 'Mother?'

'Nantel's here. He said one of the townswomen spotted the war party and asked if you want to greet your father.'

Mitrian slipped the sword back into its hiding place. Although her mother had phrased her words as a choice, Mitrian knew her mother wanted her to go. Santagithi's wife had long ago resigned herself to the realization that her husband might not return from a foray, no matter how trivial it seemed. It would not look good for the general's wife to stand in a frenzied huddle with the others nor to break down in front of his people. So she sent Mitrian instead.

Aware of Nantel's concern for his archers and Rache's mental state and curious as to the accuracy of her dream, Mitrian would not have missed this homecoming for anything. 'I'll be right there.'

'Hurry, dear. Don't keep Nantel waiting. He's got your horse all saddled and ready.'

Mitrian laughed. *Nantel knows me. Maybe I have been spending too much time at the archery range.* Leaving her room, she closed the door behind her and trotted to the outer door. Her mother held the heavy panel open, supported with her back. She glanced up as Mitrian approached, cutting off exchanged amenities with Nantel, who stood clutching the reins of Mitrian's mare and of a rangy bay gelding. Her mother smiled, but Mitrian read concern in the aging features. Mitrian wanted to reassure her, but she knew better. The Eastern Wizard had shown her no images of Santagithi and his swordsmen. Until the war party arrived, there was no way to know whether Santagithi would return alive.

Nantel swung up into his saddle. 'Good afternoon, lady.'

Mitrian giggled, springing into her seat with Nantel's power and far more grace. He had started calling her 'lady' the day she came of age, and Mitrian had not yet gotten accustomed to it. 'Let's go.' She kicked her mare into a trot through the gateway, slowed to a walk to descend the vine-swarmed hill, then picked up to a canter through the streets of the village.

Apparently, the news of the men's return had spread quickly. The streets were filled with men, women, and children scurrying toward the eastern border of the town. Many were the wives of combatants, but others came, too, out of concern for friends or from curiosity. By the time Mitrian and Nantel tethered their mounts and joined the anxious throng at the outskirts, the lead horses of the war party had come near enough to recognize. At their head rode Santagithi, identifiable by his familiar iron breastplate. The retreating rays of sun colored his armor the somber hue of dying embers. Relief filled

Mitrian at the sight of him, though he held his head low and, even from a distance, his expression looked grim.

A child in front of Mitrian bounced excitedly. So close, the boy's cry was decipherable amid the hubbub. 'They're here ! They're here !'

'Is that a wagon ?' a leather clad figure asked Nantel, and Mitrian recognized him as a guard who had remained behind. 'Did they take a wagon ?'

Nantel shook his head. 'Hopefully, they needed it for treasure.'

'Or wounded,' the other guard muttered.

Nantel glared. But before he could speak, a tearful woman beside him hissed. 'Quiet ! I won't have you wishing tragedy upon my husband and the others.'

The rest of the conversation disappeared beneath the mingled din of the crowd. Mitrian peered over the child. She knew Rache wore only a jerkin of sable leather, as always refusing the chain mail Santagithi gave his officers because, he said, it hampered his sword-craft and took some of the glory from battle. As the war party closed the gap, Mitrian discovered Rache near the back. Most of the men appeared wearied and glum, their heads sagging, their clothes stained. Many horses carried no riders, and the ranks were greatly whittled.

Rache alone seemed the piece that jarred. He carried his blond head high and with great dignity in his bearing. A smile creased his lips, and his cheeks fairly glowed. He still wore a sword at each hip, the bow and quiver slung across his back. The crowd broke into relieved or grieving huddles as all the men came into view. Bitter howls cut over conversation, more than Mitrian could ever recall. One woman raced toward the war party, as if she could only believe her husband's death by examining the survivors up close.

Mitrian half-heard more than one whispered comment about Rache's callousness, but she understood. For the others, death was an unfortunate consequence of war. For Rache, it was the goal, to triumph and triumph again until a superior opponent took his life in a wild blaze of glory. If he was the one killed, he would want the others to feel as happy as he did now, to celebrate and honor his death, not mourn it. Mitrian knew that but others did not, and they judged him from their own narrow definition of morality. Mitrian backed away from the crowd, and Rache pulled up his horse beside her. His blue eyes sparkled, and he laughed.

They walked together, Rache mounted, Mitrian on foot toward Rache's cottage. Excited by the prospect of showing Rache her sword and asking the many questions her dream-visit to the Eastern Wizard had raised, Mitrian waited only until her voice could not be easily heard by the townspeople. 'Practice tonight ?'

Rache threaded through the throng, so glad he did not even cringe at her public request. 'Mitrian, the battle went well for me, but I'm exhausted. Tomorrow, I promise we'll have the best practice yet.'

Mitrian's heart beat a joyous cadence, buoyed by Rache's mood. She felt certain the demon in the gems had revealed true details of the battle, and she could hardly wait to show the new sword to Rache. 'Deal.'

Rache drew rein before his cottage. There, Emerald met them. She helped Rache from the saddle and onto his chair, then hurled herself into his arms, dark eyes glaring at Mitrian.

Rache gave Emerald a reassuring hug, but returned his attention to Mitrian. 'Can you take my horse back to the stable?'

Mitrian nodded. Centered on Rache, she scarcely noticed the milling crowd. She headed toward the animal.

'Wait.' Rache gestured her to him, apparently oblivious to Emerald's discomfort. Mitrian felt certain he did not intend to be cruel. 'I have something for you.' He offered the bow and quiver. 'I won't be needing these anymore. I thought you might want them.'

Mitrian's jaw sagged. She turned the shocked gesture into an open-mouthed grin. 'Thank you,' she breathed, not daring to believe her luck. First the sword and now her own bow. She reached for it.

Before she could take it, a meaty hand clamped over the top of the bow and wrenched it from Rache's grip.

Emerald sprang to her feet with a tight-lipped scream. Rache stiffened, dropping the quiver. Silver and black fletched arrows spilled to the ground. Mitrian whirled to face Santagithi. His pale features wrung into a tight grimace, and his eyes went dark as flint. He hurled the bow to the ground, whipped free his sword, and slammed it down on the shaft. The wood snapped.

Santagithi jabbed his sword back into its sheath. 'Rache, I don't want you giving my daughter any more presents. Do you understand that?'

Mitrian had never seen her father so angry. She stared, too shocked to speak.

Rache looked away. His handicap made it impossible for him to leave with dignity or even under his own power. The first joy Mitrian had seen in Rache for a long time drained away. 'Yes, sir,' he mumbled. He addressed his next words to Emerald. 'Take me inside.'

With an apologetic glance at Santagithi, Emerald spun Rache's chair and wheeled him into the cottage.

Rache's humiliation touched Mitrian deeply, rousing her to rage. 'Why did you do that to him?' she screamed, her voice rising an octave.

Respectfully, the crowd dispersed to leave father and daughter alone, but Mitrian did not notice. Her hands shook at her sides, and she could not have stemmed her question had she wanted to do so.

Santagithi frowned, waiting until Emerald closed the cottage door before replying. 'Weapons from a war do not make appropriate gifts for a young lady.'

Mitrian could not believe what she was hearing. 'You didn't mind me using a bow before.'

'I thought your interest then was helping Rache. I see now it was otherwise. I was wrong the entire time.'

Mitrian tried to consider what might have happened on the foray to make her father so unreasonable. She knew many men had died and he felt responsible, but she could not fathom what relation that had to Rache. 'What do you mean?'

Finally, Santagithi turned his attention to his daughter. His glare chilled her. 'For one thing, young lady, I mean you're not allowed on the archery range. For another thing, you're not going to back talk me anymore today. Go home.' He stabbed a finger at the citadel.

Enraged, Mitrian did not consider punishment. Few things seemed worse than denying her Nantel's lessons and her time spent with the archers. 'I will not go back home! Quit commanding me. I'm your daughter, not one of your soldiers!'

Santagithi's jaw clamped tight. A pulse pounded at his temple, and Mitrian could hear the sound of his teeth scraping before he opened them to speak. 'I never lost this many men in a foray before in my life. All the rough jokes, all the gutter humor, all the low-life practical jokes my men play on one another while they're on the range or in the barracks is what forms them into a unit. Little things like those are why the men are willing to fight and die for one another. Then, they're not just acquaintances, but brothers. You've been at the range. The men have changed. You haven't noticed it because you don't know what they were like before. But they have. During this foray, they were a lot more quiet and a lot more restrained. And I've never lost this many before.'

Taken aback by the ferocity and candor of her father's explanation, Mitrian found no reply.

'It's not your fault, I know it's not,' Santagithi said quickly. 'But these men trust me. I'm not willing to take the chance that your presence has softened them. If you won't accept it for your own good, then think of it as for the good of my men. You're not allowed on the range. Now back to the house with you.' He added with an authority too firm to resist, 'Now, Mitrian!'

Mitrian went.

*

Mitrian lay on her bed, her door shut and the sword between her hands when a fist pounded on the keep's front door. Usually, the sound would not have carried this far, but the visitor had struck the wood with brutal force. Curious, Mitrian sheathed and hid her sword, crept to her door and opened it a crack.

Rache's voice wafted clearly to her. 'I want to talk to Santagithi.'

Apparently, the guard, Jakot, was in the citadel and had answered the knock, because his gruff bass replied. 'Santagithi's busy right now. Is there anything I can help you with ?'

Rache's voice rose in bitter anger that scarcely passed for sarcasm. 'You'll excuse me if I don't get down and walk in to talk to Santagithi. Damn it, Jakot. Bring him here !'

A short silence ensued as Jakot considered whose wrath he feared more, his captain's or his general's. 'All right,' he said at length, though whether in answer to Rache's tone or some threatening gesture, Mitrian did not know. 'I'll talk to him.' She heard the sound of Jakot's footsteps sweep past. A cross draft whipped through Mitrian's window, and she knew Jakot had left the front door open for Rache. She remained still, tucking her hair behind her ears to make listening easier.

Rache's horse snorted twice. Otherwise, Mitrian would not have known whether he was still waiting.

Soon, Santagithi's heavy bootfalls clomped down the passageway, and he approached Rache alone. 'You know the procedure, Rache. What's the idea of yelling at Jakot ?'

Rache's question rang equally loud. 'What's the idea of you yelling at me in front of a crowd ?'

'Let's talk in private.'

Mitrian felt a sudden gust as the door swept closed, then the air stilled. *Damn!* She wanted to hear the explanation as much as Rache, perhaps more, and the fact that it was a personal matter made no difference. She felt certain it involved her, and she might be able to help. *Unless he's mad because many of the archers died under Rache's command.* Mitrian frowned, doubtful. *If Father didn't completely trust Rache's abilities as a commander, he would never have made him captain.* Mitrian considered slipping from her room, out the front door and following, but she knew one of the few things worse than spying was getting caught at it. She hesitated in indecision.

Santagithi's voice came faintly through her window, alternately discernible and muffled beyond comprehension. '. . . you know . . . that's about . . . been around . . . long enough to know . . .'

They're talking by the side of the house. Excitement shivered through Mitrian, and she bounded across the room. As she approached the window, she crept forward more cautiously. Rache was shouting, and his words came to her distinctly. 'Maybe I'm just stupid, but I *don't* understand. You always allowed me to be a friend to your daughter before. You used to trust me. Now, all of a sudden, because some crazed animal of a slave hit me across the back of the neck and I can't walk, I'm not allowed to see her. Am I not good enough anymore? I'm no longer whole enough to be a brother to her?'

A hush seemed to follow, and it took Mitrian a moment to realize her father was speaking. After Rache, he sounded unnaturally quiet. Cautiously, she edged her head into view. She saw a grassy field studded with trees and laced over a background of forest. She could not spot Rache or Santagithi and knew they stood by the side of the house. She pushed aside the shelf before the window. She could squeeze through, but climbing back inside would prove difficult; and, just by sticking her head through the opening, she could hear even Santagithi without difficulty. '. . . You know that's not it.'

'Then what is?' Rache demanded.

Santagithi's voice rose to the same volume as Rache's. 'You're standing here yelling at me? I should be yelling at you. My daughter's of age now. When have you ever given me a straight answer about her?'

Mitrian held her breath. Rache did not answer, but Santagithi did not seem to need one.

The general continued. 'When, Rache? You never have. I've asked you your intentions. Now you say you're like a brother to her. Brothers don't spend that much time off alone with a sister. Then you not only bring her back presents, you bring her ones unbefitting her sex and her station. How am I supposed to read that? At first, I was worried about you taking advantage of my daughter. Now I'm worried about you making my daughter into my son.'

Mitrian bit her lip until it hurt, trying to staunch the guilt. She knew it was her fault, goading Rache to train her with a sword and later with a bow. She had always known Rache might pay the consequences, but it had proven easier to pretend it would never happen than to give up the opportunity.

This time, Rache had a reply. 'You may want a pretty flower that just sits there, but you don't have one. Mitrian is every bit your daughter. Why did we go on this last raid? We didn't need food. We didn't need money. You just couldn't bear to sit anymore.' He added quickly, apparently not wanting to make the wrong point or to appear judgmental, 'And that's the way it should be. If you don't go out looking for death, you never find life. Mitrian's the same way as you. She has to go out and search. There's a whole world out there that you, as her father, have always given her tantalizing glimpses of with your stories. All the things you've seen, all the things you've done. Finally, she gets old enough to experience her own piece of the world, and you tell her she can't. You don't tease your dogs that cruelly.'

Mitrian held her breath, awed by Rache's insight. At first, she had believed he taught her swordcraft because she had manipulated him into it. Later he seemed to get a personal pleasure from watching her in action. It reminded him of something or someone distant. Now she realized he knew her a lot better than she suspected. Yet she understood him, too. She waited, certain her father must feel equally impressed by Rache's points.

'Fine,' Santagithi said coolly. 'Perhaps you're right.'

Mitrian laced her fingers, grinning, scarcely daring to believe it might work out.

But the remainder of Santagithi's reply struck. like granite. 'I very well may have been making a mistake for the last ten years. But I'm no fool. That mistake has ended. No more stories from me. And nothing from you. Nothing, Rache. I don't want you seeing her anymore.'

'No,' Mitrian whispered. Tears welled in her eyes, and she missed Rache's answer, if there was one.

'I have eyes and ears throughout this village,' Santagithi said firmly. 'Any leader does. I know you've been sneaking off to see my daughter. That belies everything you said about being like a brother. Mitrian is my daughter. I won't have her hurt, even by someone I consider a friend.'

Rache's tone went dangerously flat. 'That's not what's been going on.'

Mitrian felt as if she had been ripped in half. Part of her wanted Rache to keep the secret, truly believed that if he said nothing, things could continue the way they had. Another side knew Rache had to protect himself from Santagithi's anger and wished he would place the blame on her, where it belonged. If for no other reason, Santagithi would be less harsh on his daughter than on a soldier.

'I've gotten enough different accounts.' Now Santagithi had lost control. 'All of them can't be liars, and only one needs to be telling the truth. If you were anyone else, I would kill you out of hand. It's going to stop. And it's going to stop now. I won't kill you, but I will throw you out of this village. I'll give you a horse and whatever you own. And I better never see you again.'

The world fragmented around Mitrian. Nothing existed but the two voices around the corner and the shards of a shattered dream.

'You're overreacting,' Rache said.

The simple phrase helped Mitrian bring things back into perspective. *It's not over yet.*

'I am not,' Santagithi screamed. 'Mitrian is my own daughter, my only child. She stands to inherit a lot of things. She's all my hope for the future. Like it or not, I'm going to die, no matter how strong I am. And she's what of mine is going to continue. There are very few people in this world who would trifle with me. Fewer still had better trifle with my daughter.'

Now Mitrian found it was Rache she was straining to hear. 'But that's not why I'm seeing her.'

Mitrian held her breath, her chest clenched into knots.

'Fine,' Santagithi said. 'Then you explain it.'

'I'm teaching her something.'

Lack of air made Mitrian dizzy, and she forced herself to inhale. *This is it.* She fondled the bedpost, glancing to the location of the sword, irrationally afraid. Even if Rache and her father came to blows, either could defend without her help. *And whose side would I take?*

'Rache, what you might be "teaching her" is exactly what bothers me.'

Rache did not mince words. 'I've been teaching her to use a sword.'

This is it. Mitrian cringed, awaiting the explosion.

But Santagithi's voice emerged too calmly. 'You've been teaching her to use a sword.' He repeated, as if trying to make sense of the words: 'You've been teaching her to use a sword. *A sword?*' A thud sounded as Santagithi struck something, perhaps the wall of the house. 'You've been teaching my daughter to use a sword! You stupid, pigheaded, overly aggressive, Northie bastard! How dare you! Are you insane?'

Silence. Mitrian had a sudden fear her father might have hit Rache; the Renshai's lack of reply spoke louder than words.

'Are you willing to marry my daughter today?'

'No,' Rache admitted.

Santagithi regained his composure, though a sharp edge still tinged his explanation. 'A very important part of what Mitrian's going to become and what's going to happen to this town depends on how and who my daughter marries. Men do not want to marry other men. You make my daughter unweddable. After what you've taught her, any man who does marry her is not going to be interested in her, they're going to be interested in her dowry. Mitrian deserves better than that. I'm not going to let you take it from her.'

Mitrian waited, aware Rache's view of a woman's place differed from that of the rest of the village, and she wondered if he could even understand her father's concern.

Rache spoke evenly. 'First, Mitrian is not a man. Anyone who believes she is a man is completely blind . . . and stupid, too. Second, your daughter is a strong woman. Any man who isn't tougher than her and able to, at least, compete with her on an equal level doesn't deserve her and couldn't handle her anyway.'

Despite the danger of the situation, Mitrian could not help but smile at the compliment.

'That's not your decision to make.'

'Fine. If and when this town is attacked, if you want Mitrian to be stuck here, helpless, to be used at the whim of the enemy, that *is* your decision. If she was my daughter, I'd rather she could fight, to have a chance to die with some semblance of honor and dignity.'

'Fathers are not normally concerned with the way their daughters die,' Santagithi roared. 'They're concerned with the way their daughters live. You're taking a possibility, a remote possibility, and putting it at the forefront in this conversation. I'm talking about what is going to happen. Rache, you've got a different background than the people of this town.' Santagithi started out diplomatically, but his tone and his words rapidly degenerated to thinly veiled bigotry. 'That may be the way you were raised. That may be what you believe. But we're different here. Normal people don't think that way. If we were in your culture, you'd be right. But we're not. And you're not.' Apparently, the words did not achieve the desired effect, because Santagithi tried another tack. 'Rache, I'm not asking that you agree with me. A soldier doesn't have to agree with his *commander*. But he does have to follow orders. You're not seeing Mitrian again. Is that clear?'

Mitrian strained for Rache's reply. So much of her happiness and her future rested on it.

'Completely,' Rache said. 'Yes.' He nodded, as if in afterthought. 'Sir.' The rhythm of hoofbeats echoed between the stone of house and wall, then receded into silence.

Mitrian withdrew from the window and flopped down on her bed. She felt drained and empty. In one day, she had lost all those things most important to her: the stories, the sword and bow lessons and, perhaps worst of all, Rache's company and the beauty of his movements as he demonstrated a sequence. *It's over.* But she couldn't give up so easily. *I can't let it happen. I won't let him take it away from me.* Yet Mitrian saw no way around her father's decree.

An act of defiance. The phrase came to Mitrian in Shadimar's voice. *Was this the act the Wizard meant? That I should defy my father and continue to see Rache?* Mitrian curled into a fetal position on the covers. It's one thing to defy my father, another to put Rache's life in danger. If we're caught, my father will banish Rache; he's never been one for empty threats. A worse thought displaced the one before. *When Shadimar said I'd kill a friend, did he mean Rache?* Terror ground through her. She recalled the image of Rache lying, pale and still, on a pallet in the guardhouse and the seconds of pure panic that had held her when she thought he might be dead. *Not Rache. Please not Rache. No adventure is worth the price of Rache's life.* As an abstract, nameless idea, the death of a friend seemed tolerable or, at least, distant. Given a face, it drove her nearly to madness.

An act of defiance. Mitrian coiled tighter. Though she had not yet eaten dinner, she cried herself to sleep.

7 Foes and Friends

Mitrian sprawled in her bed, staring at a ceiling blurred to a gray smear by tears that came and went in head-pounding intervals. Moonlight filtered through the window to the opposite wall, forming dappled patterns she had learned to associate with midnight. Sleep came only in spurts.

No stories. No sword or bow lessons. No Rache. The loss made her feel hollow, stripped of all the things she loved, and she gritted her teeth until her jaw trembled and self-pity transformed to rage. *I won't stop seeing Rache. My father can't stop me. No one can.* She catapulted out of bed so suddenly that dizziness swam down on her. Catching the headboard, she waited until the swirling lights passed and her balance returned. The lapse only fueled her anger. *Rache means too much to me. And I mean too much to him.* She pictured the sword master as she had seen him so many times, practicing sword figures for hours that passed, for her, like so many moments. His blade cut arcs as swift and silver as lightning. Even sweat-soaked and disheveled, his face, figure, and grace defined the West's standard for male beauty.

I need to talk to Rache. We'll find a way past my father's unreasonable demand. Without bothering to change, Mitrian belted her sword over her sleeping gown and hastily bound her sandals to her feet. She glanced toward the window. The shelf beneath it still lay askew, where she had shoved it aside to hear the conversation between Rache and Santagithi. Its contents were scattered across the floor, aside from the pouch of collected gems which, she guessed, must have slid beneath the bed. A late summer breeze carried the first cool touch of autumn, nudging the curtains so that they alternately flared open and spiraled closed. *And, if we can't find a way around my father, we'll run away together.* The thought brought a smile, and the tears subsided. She pictured herself riding at Rache's side, her sword skill nearly matching his since he no longer needed to train anyone but her.

An act of defiance. Mitrian considered the words, but she received no support, no confirmation that she had found the feat to which the Eastern Wizard had referred. Nor did she need it. For now, her father's treatment of Rache infuriated her, and the need for Rache's lessons and company drove her to act without full consideration of the consequences. With long-practiced stealth, she crept from the citadel to find Rache.

Darkness settled over the Town of Santagithi, broken only by the watery lines the moon drew over roads so familiar to Mitrian that she knew every rut and stone. She kept to the shadowed edges, not wanting to be seen, especially carrying a sword. Rows of cottages stood like identical dark lumps, yet memory filled in the details she could not see: the miller's grinders, the stonecutter's yard full of blocks and statues, and the blacksmith's forge.

Behind Mitrian, something rustled.

She whirled, going utterly still, using her ears to scan the darkness her vision could not. The repetitive trill of night insects and her own breathing filled her hearing, nothing else. An uncomfortable sensation of false memory settled over her, as if she had lived this moment before. She shivered, exploring rather than shying from its strangeness, and discovered the cause. She felt as if someone was spying on her, and the idea of being seen without seeing raised the same vulnerable uneasiness that had frightened her the night she had seen the red eyes in the practice clearing.

Far to the left, an explosive grunt broke over the insect noises.

Mitrian drew in a sharp breath, her body going rigid so suddenly that pain shocked through her. Slowly, her mind identified the source of the sound as the aging workhorse that belonged to Listar's father. *Of course. So that's all I heard.* Mitrian used humor to force herself to relax. *Mitrian, the great shield mistress, died in fright because a horse snorted.* She shoved aside the apparent misperception that the first sound had come from behind her.

More at ease, Mitrian headed along the roadway again. Soon she picked Rache's home from a huddled group of dwellings and tapped on the door.

After a long pause, the panel edged open. Emerald peered at Mitrian through the crack. Folds from her pillow had left creases on her cheek, and her hair hung in a disordered tangle. Though glazed with sleep, her eyes betrayed a hostility her concerned greeting did not match. 'Mitrian? Is something wrong?'

'I have to talk to Rache.' Mitrian frowned. In her haste, she had forgotten Emerald.

The woman's gaze fell to the sword at Mitrian's hip, and her eyes widened in surprised question. Her lips pursed, and the annoyance now spread to encompass her expression. 'Rache just came home from a battle. And he had a bad evening.' She glared at Mitrian, as if holding her accountable. 'He's asleep.'

The last was a blatant lie. Mitrian knew just glancing at Rache could awaken him. If Emerald had heard the knock, surely the sword master had also. The rage Mitrian knew for her father now channeled against the woman who stood between her and the man for whom she had decided to risk so much. 'Wake him.'

'Not without a good reason.' At last, Emerald's tone matched her mood. She started to close the door.

But Emerald's belligerence only incited Mitrian. She slammed her shoulder into the panel so hard it knocked Emerald back a step. The door swung fully open, crashing against the wall. 'My good reason is this. If you don't move aside and let me talk to Rache, I'm going to cut your arms off and feed them to you.'

Emerald paled, hastily retreating.

Rache's voice sounded from the darkness in the direction of the bed, booming with an anger of his own. 'Mitrian, that's enough! Emerald, it's all right. Let her in.'

Mitrian skirted Emerald, finding her way through the darkened cottage by memory. Most of the furniture lay shoved against the walls to accommodate Rache's chair, and the wide open space held little clutter. She whirled back to face the older woman. 'I need to talk to Rache. In private.'

Night hid Emerald's expression, but her stance held the deadly stiffness of a wolf protecting cubs.

Rache sounded tired. 'Emerald, please. This *won't* take long.' His enunciation made it clear the last sentence was intended for Mitrian. Flint scraped steel. Sparks flared then settled to a steady flame on a candle's wick. The circle of light illuminated Rache's fair features and stormy eyes. He sat in the bed, his back propped against the headboard, his legs and abdomen covered by a light blanket. He set the candle in a holder on the bedside table.

Emerald backed outside, flinging the door closed with a force just short of rude.

The click of its latching sent Mitrian scurrying to Rache's side. A lump formed in her throat; her words seemed to tumble and garble around it. 'I know what my father said to you tonight and . . .'

Rache interrupted. 'How do you know that?'

It was the last response Mitrian expected. 'I heard him. I was listening.'

Rache drew the edge of the coverlet over his chest, pinning it in place with one hand. 'Mitrian, that was personal. You had no business listening.'

'Personal? It was about *me*!' Mitrian started to justify her eavesdropping. Then, realizing it was indefensible, she redirected the conversation back to the pertinent. 'Rache, that's not the issue. My father wants to keep us apart.'

'It's no longer just a matter of what he wants. He's given me a direct order. Mitrian, if you heard what your father said, then you know that your coming here puts me in danger.'

Rache's bitterness scrambled the ideas that had seemed so obvious to Mitrian moments before. 'I . . . we . . .'

'*Why are you here?*'

Rache's question shocked Mitrian, but the malice in his voice struck her even more. She slammed her fist to the table so hard the candle jumped, and only Rache's swift steadying grab kept it from falling. 'You know damned well why I'm here! I'm here because we can't let him do that. We can't let him destroy everything we've worked so long and hard for.'

Rache looked away. 'It's over, Mitrian.'

'Over? Over!' Mitrian's voice became a squeal. 'No, Rache. It's not over. It's *not* over. It can't be over. You know how much your training means to me.' Mitrian's rage left no room for modesty. 'And I know I'm your best student.'

'*Were* my best student. Damn it, Mitrian, I don't like it any more than you do. But Santagithi made his decision, and he gave his orders.'

Mitrian gaped, torn between anguish and outrage. Her hand fell naturally to her sword hilt. 'And that's it? You're just going to give up now?'

'This has nothing to do with giving up.' Rache's cold blue eyes seemed to bore through Mitrian, and his voice betrayed no emotion. 'Santagithi is my general, my leader, and the wisest man I've ever met. And you're his daughter. If he says I can't see you, then I can't see you. Mitrian, you're going to have to leave. Before you get me into trouble.'

Mitrian was seized by a sudden urge to hit something. Her fingers tightened over the haft. 'Since when does Captain Rache cower from a little trouble? Are you telling me you're sacred to stand up to my father?'

'It's not a matter of fear, Mitrian. It's a matter of loyalty.'

'Loyalty to whom?' Mitrian screamed. The pattern of the sword hilt gouged her palm. 'My father means more to you than I do?'

'I didn't say that.' Rache spoke with a casual softness that cut Mitrian to the heart, especially when he did not directly deny the accusation. 'I've followed your father for sixteen years. I don't always agree with him, but I've never seen him make a bad decision – not at home and not on the battlefield. I'm his guard captain.

You're his daughter. If he can't trust us, Mitrian, who does that leave? And if we don't obey him, why should anyone else? If this town lost Santagithi, it would become as poor, weak, and barbaric as most of our neighbors.'

Mitrian scowled, saying nothing.

'When I came to this town, I was an annoyingly cocky, little orphan. A foreigner, by Odin. Worse, a Northman. Your father would have been within his rights to execute me or to just hurl me into the gladiator pit. Hel, he could have simply stood back while I antagonized his entire guard force into hacking me to pieces.' Rache met Mitrian's gaze. 'I owe Santagithi my life, my position, and most of all, my allegiance.'

Mitrian felt her face grow hot. Pressure throbbed behind her eyes, and she bit her cheeks. Rache's loyalty to his general was obvious. She needed to understand his feelings and loyalty toward her. 'But this time, my father is wrong!'

'I'm not so sure anymore.'

'What?' The word slipped out before Mitrian could think. She dared not say anything more or she would certainly burst into tears.

'Look at what my training has done to you, Mitrian.' Rache closed his eyes, leaning back with an anguish that obviously went beyond his words.

This time, Mitrian could not hold her tongue. 'What are you talking about?' The tears seemed to explode from her eyes, and her voice emerged in a hysterical shriek. 'It made me competent to face a threat.' Angrily, she used her free hand to brush tears from her cheeks. 'It made me happy. It made me feel . . .' Mitrian broke off, unable to say that Rache's teaching had made her feel special, as if she had a rapport with the emotionally reclusive sword captain that no one else could understand. Now it had become obvious that he had always meant more to her than she did to him. *I was as foolish as Emerald.*

Rache's eyes whipped open, and he caught Mitrian's sword arm so suddenly that she did not even think to pull away. 'It turned you into something unfit for this village. Mitrian, you barged into a friend's cottage in the middle of the night, knowing your presence alone might get him banished or executed. You threatened an innocent towns-woman with dismemberment.' He gestured at the door through which Emerald had exited. 'And you're clutching that sword tight enough to shatter it. What were you planning to do with it? We both know that, outside of spar, you don't draw a weapon unless you're prepared to kill. Were you going to try to kill me, Mitrian?'

At the moment, the idea seemed morbidly welcome. Mitrian

jerked her hand from the hilt and Rache's hold, staring at the creases the knurling left in her palm. She opened her mouth to defend herself, tried to find the words to make him understand how much he and his lessons had meant to her.

Rache spoke with infuriating calmness. 'Mitrian, it's cold outside. Emerald needs warmth and sleep. And you have to leave now.'

The arguments Mitrian had prepared collapsed into a jumble of words she no longer had the rationality to string into proper sequence. Her hands gripped and opened like gaping fish. She wanted to run outside and warn Emerald how foolishly she was acting, to tell the older woman she could no more own Rache than Listar would ever have Mitrian. She needed Rache to know how hard she had tried to reach him. *And I thought he understood me, too. It was all an ugly lie.* She felt on fire, and only one thing managed to emerge from the boil of words, tears, and emotions. 'I hate you!' she screamed. Crying coarsened her voice, lending frenzied credence to the accusation. 'You don't care, and you never did! I hate you, and I hate my father!' Whirling, she ran out into the night.

Rache's voice chased her. 'Mitrian, wait . . .'

Mitrian paid him no heed. She blundered through the darkness, wanting to go somewhere, anywhere that fathers did not crush their daughters' dreams and heroes did not become enemies overnight. She ran at random, but her legs carried her naturally toward the citadel that had been her home since birth.

At the bottom of the hill, her destination came to conscious understanding, and she hurled herself to the dirt. Her sobs sounded loud in the stillness of the sleeping village; she did not care. *There's nothing left for me here. The Wizard promised me adventure, and I'm going to find it. With or without Rache.* Images of the golden sword master drove her to more tears, until she was crying so hard she could no longer think. The noises of the night beasts disappeared, and her vision dimmed to black.

Strong arms enfolded Mitrian then, and a soothing voice whispered in her ear, 'It's all right, Mitrian. You'll be all right. I love you.'

Beyond caring, Mitrian went limp in the embrace, burying her face against a chest as hard as stone. She wanted to believe that it was Rache who had come after her, yet he could never have transported himself this quickly. And the arms that gathered her held a power that made Listar feel weak and Rache seem insubstantial. Despite his strength, he clutched her with the same exaggerated gentleness as her father's hounds did when they pretended to bite her in play. He rocked her cautiously, as if afraid he might accidentally crush her.

Gradually, Mitrian's tears diminished, and curiosity cut through hatred and rage. She tried to catch a grip on her benefactor's back, but her hands slipped from taut muscles, and her fingers closed only over damp and tattered leather. Still, that gave her the support she needed to pull away far enough to see his face.

Alert, green eyes stared back at her, looking too time-worn for a face only a few years older than her own. Bronze hair fell to shoulders clothed in bucksin that had blackened with age. The features seemed vaguely familiar, but his wary crouch seemed even more so, and she guessed his movements would be crisp and confident simply by the way he held himself. She knew every person in the village, especially the other teenagers. It made no sense for a man to appear familiar but unidentifiable. Still, it seemed rude to ask his name; he clearly knew hers.

'I have to run. And quickly. You'll come with me?' he said softly but aloud this time, his words more plea than question. His voice jarred the final piece into place.

Garn. Mitrian jerked free of his embrace, not yet able to deal with another wild squall of feelings and ideas. She could not help but recall the child with whom she had wrestled as a toddler on the kitchen tiles. Though two and half years older and ten times stronger, he had always let her win, performing comical flips and rolls in response to her most feeble attacks. Yet her mind also conjured images of Garn hammering Mukesh into gory oblivion and far beyond. Rache and Nantel had told her that Garn was no longer the sweet child she had known. He had turned into a bitter, savage man, poisoned by an anger that drove him to kill people and, eventually, to cripple Rache. Still, he had held her with a warmth and gentleness Listar could not match. And when she needed consolation, he was the one who had been here for her.

The last thought grated at Mitrian. 'How did you know? How could you possible know?'

Despite the vagueness of the question, Garn apparently understood, because he addressed her concern exactly. 'The guards talk freely around the gladiators. I heard the rumors about you and . . .' He paused, then pronounced the name with an emphasis that reeked of disgust and aversion '. . . Rache. Tonight, the stories changed.'

Mitrian felt a new wave of tears rising, and she banished them with rage.

Her lapse, though brief, did not go unnoticed. Smoothly, Garn reached for her arms, and she did not pull away. Hands rough as tree bark closed over hers. 'Sometimes, when things got too horrible, when the guards' whips left me bleeding on the cold, wet stone of my cage, I'd remember when you used to talk me into playing family. And I'd pretend those were real memories, that you and I were married and . . .' He pulled her closer. 'I always loved you, Mitrian. You know that.'

Mitrian met Garn's gaze. His words haunted her, raising images of the boy she had loved as a brother and a friend, who had played father to the rag doll her mother had made, who had helped her steal cookies from the pantry. And she saw something else, a deeper emotion she could not explain. Beneath Garn's pain and uncertainty, she found the same tender protectiveness her father displayed when he studied her, believing she slept, or the look Listar beamed at her whenever she claimed she loved him.

Mitrian had to know. 'Why did you kill Mukesh?'

Garn stared. 'Wasn't it obvious?'

'Not to me.' Mitrian blocked out the images she had run through a thousand times then packed away years ago.

'I . . . he . . .' Garn seemed flustered. 'He told me he was going to force himself on you. I couldn't tell anyone. Who would have believed a slave's child over a merchant's? And I hoped it was just talk. Then, when he grabbed your . . . your . . .' His face flushed, and he patted his own chest rather than say the word '. . . and he got that ugly look on his face . . .' His voice faltered, and words failed him.

Mitrian's gaze fell naturally to her breasts. Having recently turned sixteen, she had only come to grips with her sexuality in the last few years. Her memories of the childhood incident had centered on Garn's violence. At eight, she remembered being confused by some of Mukesh's actions and words, but she had no experience to think of them as anything except innocent play, especially since his advance had been aborted before any clothing was removed. Now, thinking back, she remembered how Mukesh had rubbed himself against her. And he had planted both hands on her chest. 'Gods.'

'I didn't mean to kill him,' Garn went on. 'I lost control.' His tone changed abruptly, and his eyes turned cold as steel. 'And *that* was *his* fault.'

The last statement did not seem to fit. 'Mukesh's?'

Garn's jaw set, and he released Mitrian. 'Rache's.'

The change in Garn's manner chilled Mitrian. She back-stepped. 'What do you mean?'

Garn cleared his throat, then did a poor imitation of Rache's Northern singsong: 'If a situation demands that you draw a weapon, then it demands that you kill.' Garn quivered with a rage that foiled his impersonation. 'Whenever you get an enemy at a disadvantage, you don't gloat. You don't talk. You kill.' He dropped the accent. 'He drove his savagery into me as if it were a gift. Then, when I naturally followed his rules he turned against me.' The pink blush of embarrassment gave way to scarlet outrage. 'He blathers about dying with honor and dignity, yet he turned me over to a frothing pack of wolves. He knew exactly why I did what I did. Yet at the trial, he never said a word in my defense.'

Mitrian nodded. Huddled in the back of her father's court with her mother, she had watched Rache sitting motionless in the back corner, his expression so blank it seemed as if the features had fallen from his face. And when the sentence was pronounced, Rache had risen and left the room in silence.

Though Garn had imitated Rache's voice badly, his words perfectly matched the Northman's teachings. Sparked to the memory of Rache's words in his cottage, Mitrian knew now more than ever that she could not stand to remain in this town another moment: 'Look at what my training has done to you . . . It turned you into something unfit for this village.' *Unfit. Like Garn.*

A wolf howled, a long low melody in the distance, reminding Mitrian of the Eastern Wizard and his pet. A number of questions still plagued her, not the least of which was how Garn came to be free. Yet for now, none of that mattered. 'Yes,' she said, though a full conversation had passed since he had posed the question. 'I will come with you.' *Defiantly. And gladly.*

Hoofbeats. The noise pounded through Rache's dream. He drew breath to command the archers into a fighting unit and sprang to protect them from the endless stream of Strinian barbarians spewing from among the trees. The sudden tightening of his body awakened him, his heart pounding. Swiftly, he reoriented to his cottage, the thatched roof barely visible in a thin stream of moonlight through the window, Emerald's deep, regular breathing beside him. And still, he heard the hoofbeats.

Hoofbeats? Rache sat up, dumping the thin coverlet onto Emerald. Still dressed only in the worn, battle britches in which he had fallen asleep, before and after Mitrian's interruption, he rolled from the mattress to the floor and belted on his sword. Aside from the blacksmith's workhorse, all of the town's steeds were stabled on Santagithi's estate, close to the guards and defensible in case of attack. There could be only three explanations for a horse galloping through town in the middle of the night: an emergency on the hill, something had frightened the blacksmith's horse, or an intruder. Rache wriggled to his front door, hating all of the possibilities. Nudging the panel open, he peered outside.

Starlight trickled through an overcast sky. Chips of quartz glimmered from the cobbles, drawing spots and lines in the granite. The cottages lay, still and silent, on either side of the street, but Rache could hear the regular, four-beat hammer of the hoof falls beneath the hum of insects. He cocked his head toward the citadel, and a distant movement caught his vision, coming toward him quickly. Then, abruptly, it was on him, a horse whisking past in the darkness, its neck outstretched and its mane flying. A lean but large-boned figure hunched over its neck, dressed in a woman's sleeping gown. *Mitrian?* Rache sucked in his breath. Behind her, astride the saddle, a man clutched the reins in one hand, steadying the woman with the other. Though coordinated, he was at the same time awkward, like a trained athlete attempting a new sport for the first time.

Rache knew the man the way a rabbit knows the shadow of a hawk. *Garn.* He caught the door frame, hauling himself to his knees, willing his useless legs to walk. But the shriveling muscles defied him, and the effort only gouged slivers of wood into his palms. *I have to stop him. I have to find a horse.* He dropped to his belly, slithering through the portal.

The animal and its riders disappeared into the darkness beyond the cottages, headed east. The hoofbeats faded, and the cries of the insects seemed to fold over the sound. Rache's face felt hot with frustration. *Why didn't I have Garn executed while I had the chance? Idiot!* He cursed himself. *I knew the guards couldn't handle him. Who did he kill to get free? And what has he done to Mitrian?*

Rache slithered across the cobbles, dragging himself toward the blacksmith's cottage. *Why didn't I chase after Mitrian? And why didn't I have Garn killed?* The stones twisted and jammed his fingers, and dirt abraded his chest and arms. His mind rose to answer his questions. The first came easily. Mitrian had needed time alone, and Rache had no way to guess that Garn had broken free. Then, as so many times in the past, memory threw back a vision of Garn's father gasping out his dying plea. Rache shook his head to dispel the image. *I made Garn; and, evil as he is, I couldn't stand to destroy what I created.*

Rache's arms ached from their pounding on the cobbles and soreness from the previous day. Even after years of sword work, he thought little of a practice or a foray in which he did not push himself hard enough to feel stiff the following morning. He crept off the road and onto the dry, stabbing grass of the blacksmith's yard. *I tried so hard to instill temperance as well as swordcraft. Instead, I taught Garn to murder and to hate. I built a monster, a killing machine without a conscience. And now, because of my stupid vanity and mercy, Garn has Mitrian.*

Rache found the thickly muscled workhorse hobbled beside the blacksmith's cottage. Cursing his slowness, he edged toward the animal. The horse swished its tail in wide arcs and stomped flies from its legs. Rache avoided the hooves, each the size of both his fists together. The hobbles were scarcely visible beneath the feathered fetlocks of its hind legs. Rache used the stone blocks that composed the cottage and the beast's long mane to drag his body toward the hollow of its back. His arms throbbed and shook, his legs hindering his every movement. Gradually, he draped his chest and abdomen across the animal's spine and arranged himself into a riding position.

The workhorse tolerated Rache's scrambling docilely, though it did raise its head to stare at him. Now, he paused to consider. The sooner he gave chase, the more likely he would catch Garn. Rache shook his head. Unarmed and unsecured on a horse without tack and unaccustomed to running, he had little chance of overtaking Garn. *Santagithi has the right and the need to know.* Another thought came to Rache, more disturbing. *After last night, if Mitrian and I both disappear, Santagithi's certain to believe we ran off together. He'll have the entire guard force after me.* He smacked the horse's rump.

The animal shuffled forward, tripped on the hobbles and rocked for balance. Nearly thrown, Rache cursed, grabbing a tighter hold on the mane. Freeing his sword, he slammed the flat across the horse's haunches. This time, it reared and lunged. The hobbles snapped, and it lumbered into a canter. Repeatedly, Rache slapped the blade across the beast's neck, urging it to greater speeds. The horse lurched into a gallop, Rache guiding it toward the hill with shouted commands, prods, and smacks with the sword. Soon, it raced up the path to Santagithi's citadel.

No one stopped Rache at the gate. A glance showed him the sentry sprawled facedown amid the vines. *Dead,* Rache assumed, not taking the time and effort to check. *He would never expect an attack from behind. Probably didn't even see Garn's blow coming.* The horse slowed to a walk, and Rache guided it around the stable and toward Santagithi's home. The building looked cold and sterile in the darkness. 'Ho!' Rache called before the door, and the horse went still. A faint moan rose from the ground. Something moved near the workhorse's hind legs and it danced aside, nearly unseating Rache again. Regaining his balance, Rache looked down in time to watch a sentry named Bromdun sit up in the grass.

'What happened?' the on-duty guard asked, straggling unsteadily to his feet. Apparently realizing Rache could not possibly have the answer, Bromdun explained. 'I thought I saw movement, then something hit me.'

Guilt stabbed Rache. He felt responsible for every death and injury Garn might have caused. 'Bromdun, listen closely. Go inside and get

Santagithi. Tell him it's an emergency. Then I want you to go to the south and check Garn's cage. After that, wake up Nantel and tell him to get over here immediately. Do you have all that ?'

Bromdun snapped to attention, hand clamped over the side of his head. 'What's going on ?'

'No questions !' Rache roared. 'Do it !'

Wincing, Bromdun scurried through the portal.

Rache gritted his teeth until his jaw ached. *My fault. I let Garn live. My enemy, my fault.* He sheathed his sword.

Shortly, Bromdun and Santagithi burst through the door. Santagithi wore only a wrinkled, crooked pair of breeks, obviously pulled on hurriedly. He clutched a naked broadsword in his fist. Bromdun hesitated.

Rache made a sharp gesture toward the south, and Bromdun ran off. Santagithi waited. 'Rache, what's the emergency ?'

'Is Mitrian in her room ?'

Santagithi's expression did not change, but his pitch rose, revealing concern. 'Of course she's in her room. Where else would she be ?'

'Could you look, please, sir ?'

Santagithi fidgeted, torn between complying and questioning further. 'Rache, if you know something important, you'd better tell me.'

Rache wound the horse's mane between his fingers, annoyed by wasted time. 'I think I do, but before I say it, I have to be certain.'

Santagithi opened his mouth as if to press for more. Instead, he whirled on his heel and stomped back into the citadel.

The moments that passed felt like hours. Sensing Rache's discomfort, the horse danced beneath him, its every quiver clear to him with no saddle to dull the movements. At length, Rache heard running footsteps headed toward them from the guardhouse.

'She's gone,' Santagithi said unnecessarily. The expression of alarm on his features told it all. 'Where is she ?' His tone became threatening. 'Where is my daughter ?'

Though Rache addressed Santagithi, his head swiveled toward the south. Three figures emerged from the darkness. 'Clinging to the neck of a horse. Forced, I'm certain. I saw a man riding from town with her.'

Santagithi went rigid. 'A man ?' he shouted. 'What man, Rache ?'

Bromdun's breathless voice emerged from the shadows. 'You're right, Rache. Garn's missing. How did you know ?' He pulled up in front of Santagithi, Nantel and Jakot close behind him.

Santagithi stared at Rache, his pale eyes unnaturally wide.

Rache nodded sadly.

'Kadrak !' Santagithi blasphemed the Western god of war. He

glanced about quickly, as if seeking something to strike, then turned his rage on Bromdun instead. 'Who's on duty on the south side ?'

'Monsamer, sir.'

'Find him !' Santagithi bellowed, his voice like a whip crack. 'If he isn't dead, I want to know why.'

Bromdun rushed to obey. As he disappeared, Santagithi rounded on Nantel. 'Get a unit together. We're going after Garn and Mitrian.' Then, to Jakot, 'Go ! Get my horse ready. Now !' Jakot whirled and raced toward the stable, Santagithi striding after him.

Finally, the pieces fell together for Nantel. Surprise made him hesitate. Rache wheeled his horse and drew it up beside Santagithi. Reaching down, he grasped his commander's shoulder. 'No,' he said quietly, but with authority.

Nantel froze in horror.

Santagithi spun toward Rache, wearing a mask of outrage. 'What did you say ?'

'No,' Rache repeated. Then, realizing he had become insubordinate, he added. 'No disrespect, Santagithi. Mitrian is your daughter. I can't expect you to think clearly in a situation like this, but I have to let you know when concern clouds your judgment.'

Santagithi quivered with anger, and Nantel took an involuntary step back. The general glared. 'Rache, this doesn't involve you.' He ripped from Rache's grip, stomping toward the stable.

Again, Rache edged his horse forward and seized Santagithi's shoulder. 'Listen to me, damn it ! You're making a mistake.'

Santagithi stopped dead, not bothering to turn. Rache could feel the general's muscles, balled and twitching beneath his hand. 'Rache, I'm warning you. This isn't your problem. I told you, you don't have anything to do with Mitrian anymore. Go back to your cottage, right now !' Again, he shook off Rache's hand and tromped toward the stable. Jakot had long since disappeared from sight.

Rache had never disobeyed a direct order from Santagithi before. Spurred by certainty and desperation, he drove the horse directly in front of his leader.

Nantel gasped.

Santagithi barely drew up in time to keep from crashing into the animal's side. Even in the darkness, Rache could see that his leader's face had turned crimson, and the fist on his sword hilt had blanched. 'Rache, this is treason ! Get out of my way before I decide to execute you myself.' He slammed the pommel against the horse's flank.

The animal skittered forward, clearing a path for Santagithi. Prepared, Rache kept his balance. With effort, he brought the horse's head around in front of Santagithi again.

Santagithi did not squander time with words. With a cry of

outrage, he swung his sword at Rache's chest. In a single movement, Rache drew and parried the cut. Santagithi looped his sword, gathering momentum for a second attack. As his sword reversed direction, Rache slammed his blade against Santagithi's hilt, a finger's breadth from the general's hand. Santagithi's sword crashed to the ground at the horse's feet.

Santagithi went still, his expression and stance a study in rage. It was the first time Rache and Santagithi had crossed blades, even in spar. Apparently, like Rache, Santagithi had always assumed himself the better swordsman.

Rache kept his sword leveled defensively, seizing on his general's silence. 'Damn it, Santagithi, forget about Mitrian. We're talking about Garn. Garn!' He spat the name as if it were the coarsest profanity. 'I'm the only man you have who can handle Garn.'

Santagithi stared with the coldest expression Rache had ever seen. He spoke through clenched teeth. 'Enough people can kill *anybody*.'

Rache recognized the threat directed as much at him as Garn. He did not want to further anger Santagithi, if possible, but he saw no other way to make his points. 'If you send an army after Garn, he'll panic and kill Mitrian.'

'If he hasn't already done so in the time I've wasted on you!'

Rache cringed, dismissing the possibility out of necessity. 'If Garn wanted to kill Mitrian, he could have done so while I found and mounted the horse. I think he's using her as a hostage to get safely out of town. Garn doesn't know where he's going. The way the mountains and passes sit, I'd bet everything I own he'll go north. I know Northmen. If you send an armed party into their territory, like it or not, you'll start a war you haven't enough men to win.' He studied Santagithi. 'I'm the only soldier who speaks their tongue.'

The general remained rigid, but he did appear to be listening. 'What are you suggesting?'

'Send me,' Rache said. 'Alone.'

'Are you crazy?' Santagithi screamed. 'Send one cripple after my strongest gladiator? My daughter's life is at stake.'

Nantel caught Santagithi's arm warningly, but the general threw him off.

Santagithi's words stung, but Rache knew they stemmed from anger not cruelty. 'Garn won't see one man as a threat. Crippled or not, I am the only single man you have who can handle Garn. I know Garn's mind like no one else does, and I think he respects me a little. I know he doesn't respect anyone else.' Rache held his breath, not quite able to understand why so much seemed to rest on Santagithi's decision. He knew he felt responsible for Garn, but the reasons went deeper than he could comprehend. Garn had stolen

Rache's glory and his manhood, his belief in himself as a person, and, somehow, defeating Garn would prove him the better of the two and restore the self-respect Garn's blow had cost. Until then, he would always be the man broken by the slave. A warrior defeated but not killed and, therefore, a coward.

Santagithi snatched up his sword from the ground. He examined Rache as if to decide through which vital organ to thrust his blade. At length, he spoke. 'Take my horse. But if you don't come back with my daughter . . .' He jabbed the sword toward Rache, murder in his eyes '. . . don't come back.'

Joy filled Rache, tempered by the seriousness of Santagithi's threat. He whacked the workhorse's flank, and it galloped off toward the stable.

Santagithi stared after the retreating guard. His fists tensed and loosened spasmodically, his guts felt as though tied in knots, and rage bunched, a tense lump filling his throat. The sword remained in his rigid grip.

Behind him, Nantel cleared his throat. 'You did the right thing, sir.'

Santagithi watched the rump of the workhorse disappear into a cloud of swirling dust kicked up by its hind legs. He spoke without turning. 'You really believe that, don't you?'

Nantel made no reply.

Santagithi faced his archer captain, trying to extract the man's thoughts by the grim expression on his homely features. 'You may speak freely, Nantel. Of all people, I trust your opinion.'

Nantel's muddy gaze met Santagithi's. The mood was too somber for him to grin, so only a flicker in his eyes revealed he appreciated or acknowledged the compliment. 'You're the best strategist I know, perhaps the best in the world.' The seriousness of Nantel's tone convinced Santagithi the archer's words were not simply an exchange of praise. 'Rache may not care much for the formalities of rank, but he respects you. He's never questioned your judgement before. When someone I trust takes exception to one plan in sixteen years, I have to believe he has reason. Mitrian *is* your daughter.' He paused, as if awaiting an answer, though the statement did not require one.

'Yes,' Santagithi said, fighting the blind fury that threatened to overwhelm him again. 'Mitrian is my daughter.'

'What if Garn had taken one of the village girls? Would you have organized an army then?'

'I don't know,' Santagithi admitted. The pound of hoofbeats caused him to look away. His long-legged roan gelding galloped toward the town. Astride it, Rache looked small, young and frail, an injured, golden child. Living under the constant threat of war had taught Santagithi not to question circumstance, only to react to it. His choice had been made, the action taken. Now there was nothing to do but wait. Yet, for the first time in his life, he was doubting and mulling over his own decision.

'Do you trust Rache ?' Nantel's question snapped like a challenge.

Santagithi grimaced, but the weapon sagged in his grip.

'The Northie taught my daughter to use a sword !'

Nantel remained composed. 'That's not what I asked.'

Santagithi returned his attention to the archer. 'He's an arrogant, insubordinate bastard !'

Nantel remained relentless. 'That's still not what I asked. Do you trust Rache ?'

Santagithi did not care for Nantel's tone. He reined his rage long enough to think. 'With anything but my daughter.'

Nantel's mustache twitched. 'Rache taught Mitrian to use a sword because he saw her as a sister. He meant well. You may not trust him with your daughter socially, but would you trust him with her life ?'

'Are you defending what he did ?' Santagithi's tone went bitter as he forgot he had bid Nantel to speak his mind.

Nantel shook his head briskly, whipping his short, brown locks around his face. 'Not defending. Let's just say, I understand why he did it.'

Santagithi fell silent. Annoyance tempered his concern for his daughter and his decision.

Apparently accepting Santagithi's hush as encouragement, Nantel explained. 'Recall, I taught Mitrian, too.' A tight-lipped smile formed like a crooked gash. 'She hooked me with the claim she wanted to help Rache. Once on the range, she had me. She was just so damned eager.' His gaze drifted to the bottom of the hill as the hoofbeats receded into nothingness. 'The guards view their lessons as a necessary duty. Mitrian acted like archery was the greatest experience of her life. She's got her mother's natural grace.' Nantel looked back, adding quickly, 'And yours, too, sir, of course. She listens and learns from her mistakes. I can't begin to describe how good it makes a teacher feel to find a student that loves the sport, actually hears and understands the instruction and visibly improves with every lesson.'

Santagithi frowned. The idea of his beautiful daughter drenched in dirt and gore sickened him.

Apparently missing the warning, Nantel continued. 'And Rache said she was the same way with sword. He said she was *good*. Have you ever heard Rache call anyone good ?'

Santagithi stiffened. He had, but only applied to some enemy chieftain slaughtering men like sheep. 'Stop it!' His words emerged as a command. 'I don't want to hear any more.'

But once started Nantel's tirades became difficult to staunch. 'Sir, you asked my opinion, and I'm giving it. Everything Rache said makes sense to me. One man is a challenge; an army is a threat. We can hope that Garn has retained a tiny spark of humanity, enough to remember the friendship he once had with Mitrian.' Nantel's tone clearly implied that his experience with Garn made the thought unlikely. 'But I have to be honest. If Garn feels threatened, I truly believe he won't hesitate to kill her. On the other hand, he may be willing to compete with Rache. I've seen Rache train Garn, and I'm confident Garn would welcome the chance to prove he's the better swordsman.' He shrugged. 'Luckily, he isn't.'

Santagithi pursed his lips so severely, his chin puckered. 'Nantel, I appreciate your loyalty, but you seem to have forgotten something. *I* don't like it any more than you do, but Rache is a cripple.'

Nantel's face went as red as it did when he chastised the guards. 'A cripple who is still the best soldier we have. If I thought it would make me as capable as Rache, I'd beg the gods to cripple me, too. Your entire army should be so crippled.'

'Stop!' Unconsciously, Santagithi rubbed his sword hand, the memory of Rache's casual disarming aching within him. He tried to sort all the information from the emotions swirling through his mind. One of his strengths as general had arisen from acting logically rather than intuitively. The loss of his daughter addled him as nothing else ever had. 'For now, I'll concede Rache may still be capable of handling Garn.' Doubt filled his voice, and he felt certain Nantel knew that point had not been fully laid to rest. 'There's the possibility Rache may not find Garn.'

Nantel shrugged. 'Rache can follow a trail as well as anyone.'

Santagithi continued as if Nantel had not interrupted. 'And Rache is the last man I'd send anywhere as a diplomat.' *He's disrespectful, not good at dealing with people and far too quick to resort to violence.*

Santagithi's implication seemed to confuse Nantel. 'We're talking about the Northlands, here, vast tribes of honorable savages just like Rache. Who would know the Northlands better than Rache?'

Though unable to admit it even to himself, Santagithi appreciated the turn of the topic away from Mitrian and Garn. 'Doesn't it strike you as odd that, as close as we live to the Northlands, Rache's never gone back even to visit? When you make your yearly excursion to the West, you never have trouble gathering men to go. In fact, I've had to intervene to keep enough men here to protect the town.'

Nantel hesitated, obviously hiding some piece of information. 'That's not the same thing. Many of the men who go with me were born here. The trading town of Pudar is loud and interesting. Every time I go, I find things I've never seen before, and you haven't tasted beer until you've had a fresh mug in *The Dun Stag*. The Northlands are a cold wasteland full of warriors.'

Santagithi pressed, fully aware Nantel knew something he chose not to tell. 'Nevertheless, as seriously as Rache embraces the tenets of the Northmen, he seems awfully accepting, not to mention free, with racial slurs against them. You were the one who told me he planned to attack the entire Northlands in a fit of despair. He called them cowards. As far as I can tell, that's the basest insult Rache uses.'

Nantel avoided Santagithi's gaze. 'What are you thinking?'

'Rache doesn't visit his home. He has some hatred against his own people. The way I put that together, he's an exile. Maybe a criminal, a thief who'll be executed if he returns.'

Nantel loosed a snorting laugh through his nose.

'What's so funny?' Santagithi demanded.

'I was just picturing Rache stealing.' He laughed aloud. 'Instead of skulking around dark alleys, Rache would choose and approach the strongest warriors from the front in broad daylight. Then he'd battle to the death, enjoying the fight so much he'd forget to take their coppers. And,' Nantel chuckled again, 'Rache was a child when he came here. Who would recognize him now?'

'All right,' Santagithi said, seizing on Nantel's mood. 'How do you put it together?' The disappearance of his daughter faded to a nagging worry at the edge of his consciousness.

Nantel's mirth disappeared. His eyes rolled upward, the whites making his coarse features appear even more ugly. He seemed to come to a decision. 'Do you remember when the Wizard came, claiming Rache had trespassed on his property?'

Santagithi nodded at the distant memory, but Nantel's certainty bothered him. 'You believed Shadimar was a Wizard?'

'You didn't?' Nantel sounded incredulous.

Santagithi shrugged. To say he was not easily taken in would imply that Nantel was, so he chose silence.

'Shadimar appeared without getting past the gate guard accompanied by a wolf that obeyed him better than any dog. He knew everyone by name. He gave Rache a child to guard, never bothering to ask if you minded, and you didn't question. Before he left, he told you, no *commanded* you, to watch over the boy because he was important. And, though he never said it, you and I both knew he meant Rache, not the child he brought.'

Santagithi stared, able to pass off most of the events as carelessness or coincidence. But Nantel's last line floored him. *Kadrak's sword, how could Nantel know what I was thinking?* He recovered quickly. 'What does Shadimar have to do with Rache's background?' He intended to discover why the archer had raised this forgotten issue now, but Nantel misinterpreted the question.

'I don't know,' Nantel said. 'But Rache used to tell the Wizard's boy things he wouldn't say even to me. I'm not sure why. The boy was so quiet, I think maybe Rache felt obligated to do the talking.'

The Wizard's child had only stayed a few years, and Santagithi had paid him little attention. Unable even to recall the boy's name, Santagithi latched onto the important part of Nantel's speech. 'You overheard Rache talking to the child?'

'On occasion, yes.' Nantel plucked nervously at his tunic.

'Things I should know about Rache?' Santagithi pressed.

Nantel made a throwaway gesture. 'If you overheard something I said in confidence, would you tell anyone?'

'No.' Santagithi understood Nantel's point, but concern superseded it. 'But if you know something that may affect my daughter, I order you to tell me. If you force me to, I'll beat the information out of you.' Santagithi's hands knuckled into fists, the threat far from idle. Larger and heavily muscled, Santagithi could beat any of his men in a fistfight, despite his age. Until a few moments ago, he would have believed he was the best with a sword as well. He had never had to prove himself. Always before, Santagithi's men had respected him too much to act against him.

'It's not that.' Nantel's gaze fixed on Santagithi's hands. 'I think I know why Rache doesn't care much for certain Northmen. Are you aware he almost wound up a gladiator?'

Santagithi's eyebrows shot up, surprised despite himself. 'Rache?'

'I heard Rache tell the Wizard's boy that the high king in Nordmir captured him and tried to keep him as a gladiator.'

Incredulous, Santagithi shook his head. He would have passed it off as a child's fantasy except he recalled Rache's early reluctance to involve himself with the pit fights. 'That would have been the stupidest thing anyone ever did.' Nantel nodded agreement, but Santagithi felt obligated to continue. 'Sure he would have won, but imagine wasting the life of a soldier that loyal and capable.' Unbidden, Santagithi's mind envisioned the possibility, though it seemed not unlike considering Mitrian as a beef cow. 'Gods! Could you picture trying to control Rache? Every time a guard tried to chain him, the guard would be taking his life in his hands. Every lesson would turn into a war; could you imagine the competence and caution of the trainer? In the pit, you'd have to put him against two or three opponents.'

'Sir?' Nantel interrupted.

Lost in the reverie, Santagithi replied vaguely. 'Hmmm?'

'You just described Garn perfectly. Rache knows and understands. Do you still think he can't handle Garn?'

Trapped neatly, Santagithi wrenched back to the problem at hand, now able to see it more calmly. An idea formed, and he ignored Nantel's question. 'When were you planning to leave for Pudar?'

Nantel stared suspiciously. They both already knew the answer, but Nantel obediently gave it. 'Three months, sir.'

'The plan's been changed. I want you to gather your men and leave in the morning.'

'Sir?' Nantel started, then stopped. 'Sir?' he began again, but still did not finish.

Santagithi glared. 'Nantel, I told you to speak freely.'

'Very well.' Nantel stared at his feet. 'Rache isn't stupid. He'll know you sent us to help him. He'll know you don't trust him, and that'll hurt him more than anything Garn could do to him.'

'My daughter,' Santagithi reminded. He grasped the simplest solution. 'Stay behind him. Help him only if he needs it, but this isn't a game. If you get a chance to rescue Mitrian, take it. Rache will just have to understand.'

Nantel twisted the hairs of his mustache, saying nothing.

'Do you have something to say?' Santagithi kept his tone level. He had always taken great care to keep his men's friendship without sacrificing their respect. In the last day, he had failed in a way he never had before, and it pained him. He would have found Nantel's loyalty to Rache touching had it taken the form of resistance to anyone but himself.

'Only this.' Nantel met Santagithi's gaze, fire in his dark eyes. 'A soldier doesn't have to agree with his commander, only follow his orders faithfully.' He whirled.

Struck by the similarity between Nantel's words and the ones he had shouted at Rache the previous night, Santagithi wondered if he was being mocked.

Nantel's retreating back gave him no answer.

8 The Chase

Dawn light reddened the towering peaks of the Granite Hills, making them appear capped in blood instead of snow. Though smaller and less stately than the Weathered Mountains stretching to the west or the impassable Great Frenum range to the east, the Granite Hills were still formidable enough to limit Rache to their natural passes. His surefooted roan gelding picked its way without complaint, one ear flicked back for Rache's commands. Until now, Garn had left an easily followed trail, shunning the fire-cleared plains to the west and the south for the concealing forests of the northeast. As Rache had suspected, Garn apparently had heard enough geography to know he could not travel far to the east, and he had soon veered northward.

At first, Rache had found the pursuit almost too easy. Hasty and unfamiliar with travel, Garn left a wake of muddy hoofprints, broken branches, and scattered leaves that a child could trace. As the flat land rose gradually to slopes, the forest became sparser. Garn's horse left fewer marks in the hard surface of stone. Unable to easily mount and dismount, or to lead his mount on foot, Rache was forced to guess his route. At times, he rode long distances in uncertainty, but he always discovered a travel marker to reassure him he had second-guessed Garn accurately.

As Rache descended the Granite Hills into the Northlands he had not seen for sixteen years, doubts pressed in upon him. In his hurry, he would have galloped from Santagithi's Town without any supplies except the swords at either hip. Jakot had prevailed on Rache to bring torches and a tinderbox; those had served well in the denser areas of forest where the moonlight did not penetrate. Jakot had also pressed a full waterskin and a pair of straps on Rache. But when the dark-haired guard ran off for food, changes of clothing, and chains to handle Garn if necessary, Rache had bound his legs to the saddle and ridden off without waiting. In the forays, supplies had not been Rache's concern, and he had never learned to worry about them. Now, without the circle of hills to protect him from the howling, Northern winds, he shivered in his battle britches and wished he had at least worn a shirt.

The roan's hooves clattered over the rocky cleft of the final hill. Below Rache, a short stretch of forest melted into a huddled town he knew belonged to the tribe of Vikerin. He hesitated, his mind jangling with concerns. Likely, Garn would have veered off here and headed west, avoiding human company, but a hunting party or patrol might have spotted the gladiator and might be able to give Rache word on whether he still carried Mitrian.

The last thought plagued Rache. Garn could not have broken free at a worse time, and the coincidence seemed all but impossible. Obviously, he had come upon Mitrian wherever she had gone to think about and control her temper. *She probably chose the clearing near the South Corner where I taught her, never guessing it would put her right in the wolf's path.* Anguish touched Rache. He knew Mitrian had carried a sword. Surely, she had fought; she might have beaten Garn if skill was all that mattered. But the gladiator had strength and experience to use against her, and he had learned to move as quietly as the animal he had become. Rache shook his head, hating the current direction of his thoughts.

In the Renshai culture, sword training began from the day a toddler could walk and his short, thick fist could grip a hilt. He became an adult the moment his sword took an enemy life. The concepts of childhood and play made little sense to Rache, and Mitrian's adolescent outburst even less. He could understand her need. Had someone tried to deny his lessons from the greatest of all sword masters, Colbey Calistinsson, Rache would have done everything to see that he again became worthy of those lessons. Until he did, he would find another *torke* or drill himself with *svergelse*, sword figures practiced alone. But Rache would sooner hurl himself on an enemy's spear than shout hurtful words at or show any disrespect for his *torke*.

Weariness dulled Rache's movements and clotted his mind. The possibility of losing time to sleep bothered him, but Garn, too, would need rest. *It'll do me little good to catch Garn if I'm too tired to fight him.* He recalled how the gladiator had squashed opponents in the pit, the hammer blows that had driven Rache on the practice floor and how, still chained, the tremendous arms had crippled him with a single strike. Anger lent Rache a second wind. Santagithi's threat faded beneath thoughts of a far more dangerous enemy. Exile from the town Rache loved paled beneath the exile from glory Garn's escape promised. Rache understood Santagithi's concern was necessarily for Mitrian; Rache worried for her, too, and would see her home. But his battle could not end there. Every woman Garn hurt, every free man he killed, every sin or crime he committed must be assessed against Rache's soul. *Garn was my responsibility.*

Rache reined his horse into the woods and toward the town, aware he would be closely watched by scouts or sentries. Evergreen needles rattled from the leather of his britches and added to the myriad of scratches over his arms and ribs. The aroma of pine raised ancient memories, forcing a new concern to the forefront. A long time had passed since he had cause to use the Northland tongue or that of the Renshai tribe. He would need to speak cautiously and not confuse the two. If the Northmen recognized him for what he was, his danger became far greater than facing Garn, weaponless, in the pit. Also, like it or not, Rache represented the Town of Santagithi. The right words could gain Santagithi a valuable ally; the wrong ones could incite a war. Against Vikerin alone, the odds might prove even, but the Vikerians might be able to coax neighboring tribes onto their side while Santagithi's town had no strong allies on which to call.

By the time these thoughts ran through Rache's mind, the forest opened to reveal the southern boundary of a wheat field and a road winding into the town. From the hilltop, Rache had seen no guards. Now, eight warriors clad in chain stood at the border, glaring at him. Three carried halberds, and they all wore swords at their hips. Beyond them, Rache could see dwellings of rock chinked with mud and moss. Surrounded by a granite wall, a single, larger building rose from the center of the village. One of the soldiers addressed Rache in the language of the North. 'Who are you, stranger? And what do you want in Vikerin?'

Rache drew up his horse a respectful distance from the guards. 'I'm from a town to the south.' Rache waved vaguely over his roan's rump. 'My name is Rache.'

The Vikerians exchanged glances and whispered comments, though Rache had not yet stated his purpose. Uncertain why his name should inspire a response, Rache froze. *Do they remember me from the escape in the high king's court?* He frowned, doubting the possibility. *None of these men should have been in Nordmir, and I was a child then. Only Arvo knew my name, and I killed him.* Other ideas flashed through his mind. *My name is one the Renshai used; but at the time of my birth other tribes used it as well.* Now Rache fretted. *I haven't kept up with the conventions of the North. Perhaps they abolished all Renshai names. My heritage does make me seem younger than I am.* His thoughts raced, and he fingered the hilts of his swords. The idea of fighting eight enemies at once usually would have excited him, but now he had a higher purpose to fulfill, a responsibility to Santagithi, Mitrian, and a world upon which he dared not loose Garn.

The same soldier who had spoken before addressed Rache again. '*Captain* Rache? From the Town of Santagithi?'

The melodious Northern tongue caused the guard to shift the accent of Santagithi's name from the second to the first syllable, and the 'i's' acquired the long 'e' sound.

Under other circumstances, Rache might have found the verbal mangling humorous. For now, he was too surprised. 'You know me?'

Again the men exchanged looks. 'We know *of* you,' the halberdier said.

Rache waited, hoping the man would continue and reveal the reason.

But the halberdier took a different direction with his questioning. 'Which tribe are you from, Rache?'

They know. Rache felt suddenly strangled. In battle, he always reacted quickly and without need for thought. But he had little practice with conversational parrying. In the last sixteen years, he had had no need to recall the names and locations of Northern tribes. Suddenly, his mind emptied of all but Renshai. 'Excuse me?' he delayed.

'Which tribe?' the man repeated, watching Rache's reaction curiously. 'There's a lot of tribes who would like to claim blood with the Northern hero of the Westlands.'

Rache stared, speechless. *Do they know about the prophecy?* He shook his head, settling yellow hair nearly as tangled as Garn's. *If they did, they would also know I'm Renshai, and they would kill me.* Afraid to say something incriminating, Rache would have preferred to remain silent. But seven pairs of eyes watched him expectantly in the shadows of the pines. 'Hero?' Rache tried. 'I don't understand.'

A different halberdier spoke this time. 'I've met some of your men at the tavern in Pudar. The way they talk, you've vanquished armies by yourself. They say you spar their best three at a time, best them, then tell each one his mistakes.' The other Vikerians nodded agreement.

Rache snuffed a sigh of relief. 'They exaggerate.' The latter description was true, but Rache felt it better not to encourage the stories. A common legend stated that one Renshai possessed the skill of three soldiers, and he could not afford to provoke supposition. Besides, any admission of skill would encourage Northmen to challenge, and Rache could not spare the time for duels or spars.

'My men are loyal, and they're not used to Northern enthusiasm. I'm just a soldier.'

'And Odin is just a god,' one man said. The others laughed. 'I once saw Nantel fight. I believe he'd know a good swordsman, and he claims you're the best.'

Rache could think of nothing to say that would neither sound immodest nor insult Nantel. He had known the city of Pudar served as a trading route for citizens of all types, even the occasional Easterner, but he did not know Nantel had befriended Northmen. He imagined it was a loose affiliation, soldiers bragging in a foreign tavern then forgetting the incident on the return trip. Even so, Rache's men must have lauded him well. Attempting diplomacy, Rache turned the compliment back on the Vikerians. 'The best means little without a time and place. If Nantel had grown up among Northmen, he might not be so easily impressed by me.'

Rache changed the subject before the others could reply. 'I'm in a hurry. I was sent after an escaped slave who abducted Santagithi's daughter. Last I saw, he was riding a red-brown horse with dark points. Have you seen him ?' Rache did not bother with a description. The Vikerians would have noticed passing strangers. Both Mitrian's and Garn's dark hair and Western features would have singled them out in the Northlands.

The Vikerian guards exchanged negative glances and shrugs. The halberdier who had done most of the talking gestured Rache forward. 'My name is Riodhr. None of us has seen them, but King Tenja would know better. I'm certain he would want to meet you, Captain.'

Rache frowned at the delay. He had no wish to offend a tribal king, but the idea of letting Garn escape pained him even more.

Apparently noting Rache's consternation, Riodhr continued. 'It won't take long. While you talk and rest, we can get you a fresh horse and supplies.' He eyed Rache's bare chest with concern. 'Either Santagithi's Town is a lot farther south than I thought, or you left in a terrible rush.' Stepping forward, he reached hesitantly and non-threateningly for the bridle of Rache's horse, watching for a reaction. When he received no challenge from Rache, Riodhr seized the leather, heading toward the village. 'If King Tenja likes you, he may send out some scouts to help you locate this slave and princess.' He gave Rache a meaningful look. 'Captain, three men came asking about you just yesterday. Our king knows the details. I think you should hear them, too.'

Intrigued, Rache allowed his horse to be led, knowing all of Riodhr's suggestions made sense. Rache needed sleep and rations, but he could not fathom why men would have come seeking him, especially in the Northlands where he had not set foot since childhood. Since Riodhr had not specified the nationality of those men, Rache could not begin to guess their purpose.

Riodhr released Rache's horse long enough to make several broad gestures. The Vikerians separated. Three remained to guard the borders of the town, another two ran ahead, presumably to make arrangements, and the remaining two walked near Rache's horse as Riodhr led it down the road into Vikerin. Despite the late summer season, angry winds whined against them, and Rache knew the weather was sharper farther North. Though brown, the height of the grasses edging the pathway told Rache of a successful harvest in a land of bleak, unreliable weather. Cottages lined the road. Smoke drifted from the chimneys as the inhabitants cooked breakfast, fighting a morning chill that would grow far crueler with winter.

Riodhr stopped before a wrought gate of silver metal that led to the larger building Rache had seen from the woods. In front of it, a pair of sentries regarded him with unbridled curiosity. Beside them, gaunt sheep grazed at stubble in a paddock. Riodhr left Rache's side to speak with his fellows in voices too low for Rache to decipher.

The Renshai yawned. Hunger growled through his gut, and his head felt heavy.

Riodhr returned. 'King Tenja is eager to share breakfast with you. If you'll dismount here, these men will tend your horse.' He indicated the guards.

Rache's gaze fell to the straps lashing his legs to the saddle. 'I'd be honored to meet your king, but I can't dismount.' Bitterness welled for the first time since he had realized he could still fight. The familiar reserve that ebbed through him in times of duress reassured him, and his tiredness receded. 'I'm crippled.' His own words brought home the gravity of a situation he could no longer blame entirely on Garn. When Rache chose to cross the Granite Hills, he knew the manner of men who dwelt beyond them and his own limitations.

Riodhr's eyes widened, and he gaped at Rache's legs. The guards' gazes, too, riveted on the disabled limbs.

Rache waited, hating their stares. He considered wheeling his horse and galloping from town. But Riodhr still clutched the bridle of the horse, and Rache doubted the Vikerians would take well to a legendary stranger trampling one of their military leaders. *I need supplies, rest, and as many allies as possible. And who, by Sif, would be searching for me?* Rache made a polite noise in his throat.

Guilty, Riodhr jumped to attention. Apparently angered by his lapse, he rounded on his men. 'Don't stand there,' he snapped. 'Get a cart for the captain and tell the king we're on our way.'

The gate sentries remained in place. The two who had accompanied Rache and Riodhr tore their gazes from Rache's battle-stained britches and trotted into the castle.

A stilted hush followed their disappearance. Riodhr squirmed, obviously wanting to speak but not knowing what to say. 'I'm sorry,' he tried at length.

Rache unbound his legs, wondering whether the Vikerian meant his words as an apology for his stare or as a condolence. Uncertain, Rache did not know how to reply, and the silence grew even more awkward.

After what seemed like hours but was only a few moments, one of the guards returned, towing a small cart constructed for bringing goods into the castle. At Riodhr's gesture, the three guards lifted Rache from his mount and eased him into the cart. Riodhr grabbed the front and steered, apparently preferring to turn his back on Rache in his embarrassment.

The bottom of the cart sloped downward, and Rache's buttocks slid into the hollow. Forced into an undignified position, he rearranged his legs into a more natural angle, feeling like a roasted pheasant being escorted to the king's table. Riodhr rolled Rache through an antechamber painted with mosaics, past a sitting room, and into a meeting area with a crumbling fireplace. Colored to seem metal, wooden doors stood propped open between the rooms, and flickering candles sat in sconces or on tables. After Santagithi's simplicity, the furnishings seemed gaudy, a mockery of the richer, civilized countries in the far west. Riodhr brought Rache to a set of double doors. The creak of the ancient wheels grated against Rache's raw nerves.

The guard accompanying Riodhr opened both doors, and Riodhr pulled Rache's cart through them. The three guards who had preceded Riodhr and Rache stepped out of the way to let the cart inside the dining room. Behind an age-darkened table surrounded by chairs, three men eyed a meager feast. In the center, King Tenja wore gray-tinged blond braids that fell about a thick neck. Well-set eyes and cruel lips gave him an air of stern command. An expertly tailored suit of fur-trimmed silk draped a physique trained to war. Riodhr bowed. 'Your majesty, King Tenja,' he said both as respectful greeting and introduction.

Though glad his handicap exempted him from bowing to a Northman, Rache lowered his head politely.

Riodhr introduced the other men. 'Alvis, adviser to the king.' He gestured toward a thin, pale Northman clad in wolf skins and sitting to the king's left. 'And the warrior, Eldir.'

To the king's right, the massive, ugly Eldir did not acknowledge the introduction. He regarded Rache with dead, blue eyes and an aloof indifference. Despite the promise of a friendly meal, he wore a sword at his hip and a sword-bladed pole arm rested against the wall by his right hand. Suddenly, Rache appreciated that Riodhr had not forced him to relinquish his own weapons before entering the king's presence. The guards remained at attention.

The king addressed Rache first. 'Well met, Captain.' He indicated a place across the table, the only empty seat with a plate before it.

Riodhr rolled Rache's cart to the table, and the guards shifted closer. Quick as a cat, Rache grasped the chair back and hoisted himself into it before the guards could reach to help him.

A strange smile played over King Tenja's lips. He dismissed the guards with a wave but addressed Riodhr before the commander could slip through the door. 'Let the Slayer know Rache's here.'

The Slayer? Ice seemed to wash Rache's skin into gooseflesh. He glanced up quickly, but only Eldir met his stare, the warrior's expression hard, unchanging, and unreadable.

'Yes, sire.' Riodhr slipped from the room after his men and closed the door behind him.

King Tenja met Rache's gaze. His voice remained friendly, and he answered the Renshai's discomfort with eyes crinkled in curiosity. 'I know you're in a hurry, Captain, so I won't keep you long.' As he spoke, Alvis quietly ladled food onto the king's plate. 'We'll keep this meal quick and informal, and I'll refrain from asking some of the many questions I have for the heroic Northman of the Westlands.'

Alvis filled Rache's plate next. The aroma of wheat meal, meat, and bread made Rache's mouth water and increased the protestations of his empty stomach. 'I appreciate that, sir.' Instantly recognizing his mistake, he corrected it. 'Sire.' The difference was cultural. Aside from the Renshai, the leader of every Northern tribe was called 'king' no matter how few his followers. Santagithi had always preferred the title leader to king and his name to either.

Alvis frowned, but the king seemed to take Rache's error in stride. 'Just one question before we exchange necessary information. Rache, which is your tribe?'

This time the question did not catch Rache completely off his guard. Knowing a casual answer would prove less suspicious than a mysterious explanation, Rache responded carefully. 'My mother was Ascai, my father Varlian. They courted when the two were at peace and escaped south when they turned to war.' Unless the king pressed for names and dates, it seemed a safe assumption. The status between tribes changed continually. The Vikerians' persistent interest in his tribe bothered Rache, but he knew it was probably an innocent request. Heritage was important to Northmen, and sire's name and tribe usually came with the first introduction. Still, he could not shake the memory of the king's reference to a slayer. *He said slayer, not executioner. Maybe I misheard him. He seems friendly enough otherwise.*

Alvis and Eldir served themselves. Though hungry, Rache waited for the king to take the first bite.

King Tenja poised his fork above his meal. 'While we eat, a room is being prepared for you to rest as long or as little as you want. Food and water are being gathered as well as clothing. Is there anything else you need?'

Rache already felt indebted. 'No, sir-ire.' He caught himself in the middle of the word. 'You've been more than generous, your majesty.'

The king smiled, amused by Rache's verbal clumsiness. He started eating, and the others followed his lead. From the first bite, the wheat meal soothed Rache's empty gut, and he had to concentrate on eating at a polite pace.

'Your horse?' the king asked.

The words reminded Rache he had taken the mount Jakot saddled for Santagithi. 'Sire, it's my leader's favorite. If you could let me have a fresh one, Santagithi would like this one back. I brought no money, but I'm certain Santagithi would pay for any horse you give me and for whatever trouble returning his might cost.'

The king swallowed.

'. . . Sire,' Rache ended quickly, wondering if he had said too much without tacking on the title somewhere.

'We can arrange that,' King Tenja said agreeably. A brief silence followed, broken only by the clatter of forks on plates. Rache took several more bites before Tenja continued. 'Captain, I think you should know about a trio of visitors I had a few days ago.'

Rache nodded as he chewed. Concern over the king's words and formality had usurped curiosity. He had nearly forgotten the men Riodhr had alluded to in the town. 'Your majesty?' Rache encouraged.

'They came from the west on horseback, three men fully armed, grim-faced, and quiet. The sentries who met them at the boundary thought they were Northmen, though they were heavily dressed for men accustomed to Northern summers and they spoke the Western Trading tongue with an accent. And they claimed no tribe.'

Rache loosed a noise of befuddled interest. Northmen tended to be fiercely loyal to their tribes and xenophobic. The Vikerians' fascination with Rache demonstrated the rarity of Northmen living south of the Granite Hills. It made little sense for men of enough

Northern blood that the Vikerian guards accepted them as Northmen to come from the West.

The king regarded Rache curiously. Then, apparently convinced Rache's vocalization came of confusion rather than recognition, he continued. 'They asked how to find you and your town. Thinking they were Northmen, my men told them. But when my men questioned them, the strangers grew belligerent. After a time, they rode off spouting something about you being Renshai . . .'

Rache's muscles hardened to painful knots.

'. . . and us not recognizing the real enemies in our midst.' King Tenja stopped, studying Rache's rigid form. He chuckled at the captain's discomfort, mercifully misinterpreting it. 'That was my reaction, too. Obviously they're enemies of yours, willing to lie to turn countries against you. What can you tell me of them ?'

Though he had swallowed the food in his mouth, Rache pretended to chew until his vocal cords relaxed enough to let him speak at his normal octave. 'Nothing,' he admitted, hoping his fear did not make it sound as if he was hiding information. In his uneasiness, he forgot to use titles of respect. 'The only enemies I know of are the usual ones a soldier gains in war. But I've never fought Northmen.' It was a lie, but Rache could not fathom why any Northman would hunt him sixteen years after his last battle in the North.

The king finished the food on his plate and set aside his fork. 'The more I think of the story my men told, the less I believe the strangers were Northmen. Their skin was milk white, fairer even than any of my people. They wore strange robes of black and gold and, where the robes didn't cover, their flesh appeared wrinkled as a sea captain's. Though young, they all had thin, sparse hair, almost brittle. From what my men said, two were blond, like us, the third had hair as white as an elder. Does this sound more familiar ?'

From politeness, Rache considered, though the description sparked no memories, near or distant. 'No, sire,' he said. 'Though I wish it did. I like to know my enemies.' *Especially ones who might know what I am.* The possibility sent him into a cold sweat. Though not finished, Rache pushed his plate aside. He forced the proper amenities. 'Thank you for the warning. The meal was excellent, sire. I'm grateful for that, too.'

'But tired,' the king finished for him. 'I understand.' Reaching up, he knocked on the panel behind him.

I've wasted too much time already. I can't let Garn get too far ahead. Rache's mind felt fuzzed from exhaustion, dulling the threat of an unknown enemy. *Garn has to sleep, too.* 'Thank you, sire. Yes. Please don't let me rest long, though.'

'I understand,' the king said. Apparently, the guards had informed him of Rache's mission.

Shortly, a servant appeared from a door beyond Rache's vision. The man bowed to his king.

King Tenja pointed to the cart by Rache's seat. 'Please take our guest to his room. Give him whatever he needs.'

Rache scuttled back into the cart as gracefully as his handicap allowed, and the servant wheeled him through the door from which he had emerged, through a library, down a short corridor and into a bedchamber that consisted only of an alcove and a pallet. Rache crawled into bed without removing his sword belt.

The servant covered Rache with a blanket of fur. 'If you need anything, lord, tap on the wall behind you. Someone will come.'

The 'lord' made Rache uncomfortable. Even his followers called him by his name rather than his military title. 'Thank you.' On a whim, he added, 'Sir.'

Flushing at the unexpected title, the servant slipped from the room. The door clicked closed.

Doubts converged on Rache now, but he shuffled them aside. There would be plenty of time to worry about a trio of white enemies while he rode. For now, sleep took precedence.

Rache jolted awake with a suddenness that could only have come from an unexpected noise or presence. Without opening his eyes, he edged his hand toward his hilt beneath the coverlet.

'You've no need of the sword.' The male voice sounded uncomfortably close and held a trace of menace.

Not reassured, Rache seized the hilt and sat up. He met a pair of crisp blue eyes above a hawklike nose. The face was middle-aged and unfamiliar, framed by blond braids. A broadsword dangled in a sheath at his hip. 'Who are you?' Rache demanded.

A slight smile played over the man's lips; he seemed amused but not insulted or surprised by Rache's caution. 'My name is Kirin. The Vikerians call me Valr.' He studied Rache with a predator's intensity.

'Valr,' Rache repeated. *Slayer. So this is who King Tenja meant.* Still uncertain of the Northman's intentions and unable to know whether Kirin had earned his nickname, Rache worded his reply in an ambiguous manner. 'A title worthy of a warrior.'

Again Valr Kirin smiled, but his features never lost their dangerous severity. 'And one you might deserve too, Rache. Your soldiers boast of you often. Any captain whose men forget he's crippled must have great skill. A cripple whose king will entrust his daughter's life to him and him alone ...' Kirin lowered his head in admiration. 'I stand in the presence of a legend.'

Twice, Valr Kirin had made mention of Rache's disability, yet he had done so with a matter-of-factness that stung less than Riodhr's anxious staring. Rache released his hilt and threw aside the bear pelt covering him. 'I have to leave as soon as possible.' He had awakened abruptly enough to shake the burden sleep leaves even after a long rest. He had arrived in Vikerin at dawn, and he guessed it might now be midday.

Valr Kirin reached into the cart at Rache's bedside, pulled out a clean, wool shirt, and passed it to the Renshai. 'A fresh horse, equipped and stocked, awaits you. I'll escort you outside.'

The coarse weave of the shirt scratched Rache's hands, but he donned it without complaint. It would serve him well when night brought dropping temperatures and ice-grained winds. 'Thank you.' Rache glanced at the cart, not liking the idea of leaving himself defenseless as he maneuvered himself inside it nor of putting himself in Kirin's hands. The Slayer seemed gracious enough, but Rache could not shake the memory of awakening suddenly in the Northman's presence.

Kirin shifted toward Rache, apparently misinterpreting hesitation as a plea of help.

Rache skittered into the cart before Valr Kirin could raise a hand. To Rache, a battle sprawled in a cart seemed preferable to accepting physical aid.

Kirin's features twisted into a strange expression, another smile hardened by ferocity. He opened the door. Gripping the cart by its drawing tongue, he maneuvered it back the way Rache had come. 'It seems unfair that a man with a disability should have to battle not only his confidence, his injury, and his enemies, but his friends as well.'

Rache flushed, scarcely noticing the painted walls, the fireplaces, or the doors Kirin opened in a series. The words struck home. 'How do you know so much about crippled soldiers?'

Valr Kirin rolled the cart into the antechamber. Again he left Rache and stood before doors, this time the ones to the outside. But instead of opening them, Kirin turned to face the Renshai. 'My brother, Peusen, lost an arm in battle . . .' The Slayer made a cutting motion at the level of his right elbow '. . . but continued to fight.'

Peusen's injury went far beyond Rache's crippling. Having lost a major body part, he could never reach Valhalla, no matter how bravely he fought. Rache cringed at the thought of living with that knowledge. If Peusen had been Renshai, his friends would have seen to it that he never left the battle alive, even if it meant cutting him down themselves. But Rache knew other Northmen might react differently. 'I'm sorry,' he said sincerely.

Valr Kirin slammed a fist against the outer doors. The panel held firm against the blow, but the sound echoed through the ante-chamber. 'Before his injury, Peusen was an officer in the high king's army, and a good one, too. Suddenly, the same men who trusted him with their safety, their very souls, the lives of their wives and children . . .' He trailed off, his face now contorted in anger. 'Suddenly, those same men didn't trust him to lace his own damned shirt !'

The doors rattled open, pulled ajar by guards on the outside who had apparently misinterpreted Kirin's blow as a signal.

'Piss,' Kirin added. 'Men are stupid.' He seized the tongue of Rache's cart and worked it roughly through the door frame. Wood scratched wood, shearing a line of paint from the cart.

Rache suffered the manhandling of his cart in silence, but curiosity goaded him to press his host further. 'What happened to your brother ?' The cart bounced across the courtyard beneath a gray sky and air tinged with the clean odor of coming rain. Shortly, Rache noticed a well-proportioned, dark brown chestnut tied to the gate. *My horse*, he guessed.

'I tried to help.' Valr Kirin fondled his sword hilt, then, becoming aware of his own violent but unconscious gesture, he added quickly, 'I talked to the men. My meddling only made Peusen feel more helpless.' Kirin drew the cart up to the horse's left side. Dropping the bars, he circled the animal, still talking. 'People tend to believe a crippled man loses his hearing, too. Or maybe they don't feel a cripple is man enough to matter.' Kirin unbuckled the horse's cinch, tugged it tighter, and fitted it back into place. He tossed the leather straps Rache had used to tie his legs.

Rache caught the bindings, tucked them into his belt and waited for Kirin to finish.

'Driven to the edge of madness, Peusen left Nordmir. He claimed he would find every handicapped, injured, aging, or exiled soldier and forge them into the deadliest fighting unit in the world.' Valr Kirin returned to the cart side. 'Then he'd find the bloodiest, damned war this world has ever seen and humble the fools who drove his men away.'

Rache caught the stirrup, and clambered up the side flap, using the saddle crest for support. 'Interesting.' He considered as he fought his way into the saddle. 'Noble, even, in a way. Did he succeed ?'

Behind Rache, Valr Kirin made some gesture the Renshai could not see. 'I don't know. He went years ago, and I haven't heard anything since. If nothing else, he must have left the Northlands.'

Rache settled into his seat and plucked the straps from his belt. Behind him, a canvas bundle held the supplies the Vikerians had packed for him. The waterskin he had brought from Santagithi's Town was tied on top of it, refilled. 'He must have gone West, then.' He glanced at Kirin, who nodded.

'And died there.'

Rache wound the strap around his right leg, lips bunching into a frown. 'Now who's underestimating your brother?'

Valr Kirin froze, obviously catching the full effect of Rache's words. 'Well spoken, Captain.'

Tying off the right leg, Rache started on his left. 'Doubtless, he's preparing whatever men he found for the Great War between the Eastlands and Westlands.' Rache's mind filled with doubts. *How many crippled soldiers can there be, and how would anyone go about mustering them?* He imagined an entire troop of twisted, gouty, gasping soldiers and flinched at the picture. His revulsion raised guilt. *Here I am having the exact reaction that disgusts me when it's trained on my defect.* 'I believe King Tenja will be sending someone to return Santagithi's horse. Do you speak the Western Trading tongue?'

Kirin moved the cart away from the horse. 'Yes.'

'If you want to see Peusen again, befriend Santagithi. I'm certain he'd be glad to have you among his soldiers at the Great War.' Realizing he had forgotten to untie the horse before mounting, Rache sighed. The idea of wasting time climbing down and back up again rankled, especially without the extra altitude of the cart. 'I've never known a northern warrior who didn't leap at a chance to go to war.'

Valr Kirin stood, deep in thought. 'You know Northmen. Quick to war for honor and glory, but less so for some other race's problems. The Great War doesn't involve the North.'

Rache shrugged, eager to be on his way before Garn put too much distance between them. He felt certain Garn could only have followed the Northern edge of the Granite Hills westward. Possibly, he was following passes in the mountains which would slow him.

'I'm not a Vikerian.' Valr Kirin seemed oblivious to Rache's haste. 'I'm Nordmirian, a lieutenant in the high king's army.' He glanced behind him, then spoke in a conspiratorial whisper. 'Vikerians are as tough and brave as weasels and almost as smart. King Tenja requested a strategist from the high king. I needed to get away from the men who mistrusted Peusen, so I was sent.' Casually, Kirin worked at the knot that held the horse's bridle to the gate.

Relieved, Rache listened, impressed by the Slayer's titles. Lieutenant placed Kirin only one step below his king in the strongest army of the Northlands.

'I was sent to organize a band of fools, and I can't forsake that duty.' Kirin considered aloud. 'But maybe I can make an alliance between your king and Tenja. Then the entire tribe could go to the Great War.' The hitch came free. Kirin looped the reins over the horse's ears.

Rache accepted the reins with a smile. *Perhaps I'm a better diplomat than I thought.* 'Thank you.'

With a nod to a soldier stationed outside the gate, Valr Kirin wrenched open the metal doors for Rache. But he remained standing between the horse and freedom. The clouds bunched tightly, obscuring the sun. 'Rache,' the Slayer said. 'I believe all Northmen are brothers. If we could stop these stupid skirmishes between tribes, the North would become an unbeatable power. I'm sorry minor offenses drove your parents from the North and left you without a home. If the tales of you are true, Captain, I would be proud to claim you as kin.'

'Thank you,' Rache said again, wondering who had sung his praises to Valr Kirin.

Kirin rested a hand on Rache's leg, though the sword master could not feel the touch. 'Friend, can we join hands as blood? Should your path lead you back to the North, you have a brother among the tribe of Nordmir.'

Rache stared. He could think of no higher commendation. 'I would be honored.'

Rain pelted the Northmen as they reached for one another. When their fingers met, the Slayer spoke. 'I would have welcomed your sword beside me in the tainted battle that saw the end of the devils known as Renshai.'

Rache's blood ran cold as the viselike grip of Valr Kirin closed about his hand. A flash of lightning split the heavens, accompanied by a boom of thunder so loud it seemed to crack the heavens.

'A sign!' cried Valr Kirin. 'Thor the Thunderer sanctions this union.'

Rache found a different message, not from Thor, but from his golden-haired wife who was goddess of Renshai.

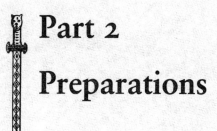

Part 2
Preparations

9 An Act of Defiance

Night drifted by in a gray blur of passing stone, and Mitrian ceased to notice the front of the saddle grinding into her spine at the end of every beat. The regular motion of the horse, Garn's close warmth, and the clap of hooves on stone became familiar. His lengthy silences seemed stranger, but she appreciated the time they gave her to think. She considered her father's casual cruelty, the single order that had stolen all that seemed important in her life, leaving no possibility for compromise. The memory raised an anger so hot even night's chill could not dispel it. She relived her conversation with Rache, and her mind added an animosity to the sword master's tone that went far beyond strangled frustration and exhaustion. *He claimed to be like a brother. I believed I understood him well. Yet what did I really know about him? What did anyone ever really know about Rache?*

Morning sunlight glazed the Granite Hills to a vast vista of ruddy crags and shadowed hollows. To Mitrian, the distant peaks had always symbolized adventure and ultimate freedom. The reality of cold, dull stone, the stomp and roll of the horse beneath her, and the autumn wind cutting beneath her sleeping gown stole all romance from the image. She pictured Santagithi just awakening from sleep. Soon he would discover Mitrian missing. He would realize how much he had taken from his daughter, and he would regret the hurt he had inflicted upon her. A self-satisfied grin rose, then wilted into a frown as Mitrian's thoughts turned to Rache. *Will he feel guilty, too? Or will he be relieved that he no longer has to worry about me getting in the way of obedience to his general?*

The day wore on as the horse meandered through the passes. Occasionally, it slid on a loose stone or tripped into a crevice, rocking off-balance with a suddenness that made Mitrian gasp. But it always reestablished a pace an experienced rider would have considered reckless on mountainous terrain. Time exhausted Mitrian's rage, and more immediate concerns replaced it. As midday flowed into afternoon, her stomach pinched and groaned, and her throat felt parched. Lack of sleep made her thoughts fuzzy, and her thighs ached from clutching the horse. Lightning split the sky, and thunder boomed as if in a heavenly battle. Then the rain gusted down, pelting her with droplets as sharp and cold as ice.

Discomfort sparked irritability. Mitrian alternately resented and appreciated the lack of social training that kept Garn silent far longer than courtesy demanded. Her thoughts turned to him, turbulent with doubt. Rache's description of gladiators came clearly to the forefront of memory: 'Wolves in man form. Unpredictable killers who need no cause or reason but the joy of slaughter.' Yet she could not banish the memory of Garn's naive embarrassment when he found himself unable to say the word 'breasts,' the soft uncertainty of his features, his wild, childlike eyes. She recalled his motions, too, graceful, confident, never wasted. *Animal? Maybe. But not a wolf.* Mitrian considered. Once, Nantel had brought a cat from Pudar. She had watched it glide silently through shadows and shrubbery, leaping to rocks and windowsills at a full run. Even when it fell short, it managed to make the mistake seem intentional, never losing its agile dignity. Garn's lithe commitment to every action reminded her of that cat, but Rache's even more so.

Water plastered Mitrian's hair to her cheeks. The rain soaked through the light fabric of her gown, chilling her skin to bumps. As Mitrian became completely wet, the rain ceased to bother her, and her discomfort stemmed from the icy wind blowing across damp flesh.

And still they rode on.

As evening lengthened, the storm darkened the sky early, though the rain eased to a trickle. The horse stumbled more frequently, slowing to a halting walk. Finally, it balked at moving forward at all. Garn's kick sent it into a rear. Mitrian caught a handful of mane, clinging as the world seemed to surge beneath her and momentum hurled her backward. The saddle horn bit into her spine. Garn shifted his weight too late. The horse's abrupt movement dumped him to the rocks.

Mitrian seized the opportunity. The instant the bay's hooves touched ground, she leapt to the rocks beside Garn, catching the bridle, though she doubted the horse would run. The landing shocked pain through knees held far too long in one position.

Garn reached around Mitrian for the reins, standing so close she could feel the touch of his body, through wet leather that now reeked of sweat. 'We need to keep moving. The guards will catch us.'

Mitrian turned to face Garn. Water wound down his bronze locks, and he wore a frenzied expression. Still, he offered her a smile.

Mitrian shook her head, as unwilling as the horse to take another step. 'We have to rest, and we have to eat. A head start will do us little good if you work the horse to death and we have to continue on foot.'

Garn's smile faded. The lost look reappeared on his young features, lending them a handsome, harmless innocence. 'I didn't know.'

How could he know? Mitrian could not help picturing herself locked behind bars day after day as her life stretched into years, her only reprieve the time spent fighting and learning weapon craft. Prying open the buckles, she stripped off the saddle and bridle, setting them down among the stones. The horse wandered a few steps. Its head drooped with exhaustion, and it nuzzled the rocks in search of grass and water.

'Will it be all right?' Garn asked with sincere concern.

'I think so,' Mitrian replied, wishing she had considered the horse's welfare sooner. *I hope so.* Accustomed to trusting Rache's and Nantel's judgment, she had simply assumed Garn's competence. And self-righteous indignation had left room for little else. 'But we'll have to find some grass and let it graze a long time tomorrow.' She rubbed her hands along arms speckled with gooseflesh. 'For now, I don't think she'll go far.'

Garn watched the mare.

'I'll gather as many dry twigs as I can find for a fire.' She glanced through the dark, frowning at the sparsely forested hills. 'Why don't you ready whatever rations you brought. Oh, and dry clothes would be a blessing.'

The pained expression forming on Garn's face alarmed Mitrian. When he offered no explanation, she put the clues together. 'No rations?' she guessed.

Garn said nothing.

'And no dry clothes.'

Garn lowered his head.

Mitrian made a noise of annoyance and frustration. 'No destination. No supplies. Kadrak! What were you thinking?'

A flame flickered through Garn's eyes. 'I was thinking about freedom. I was thinking that I no longer had to kill.' He tensed, muscles bunching into knots. 'I've been hungry before. And wet.' There was a gauntness about his features that lent credence to his words, and Mitrian knew from his touch that little of his huge frame was fat.

Aching muscles, fatigue, cold, and hunger made Mitrian curt. 'No bow, no streams, no hunting skills. Who needs to worry about guards? We'll die of starvation long before anyone could find us.'

'I'd rather die in the wilderness than in the pit. I'm free.'

'Yes,' Mitrian snapped. 'And, frankly, I'm tired of hearing it. If you hated your life so much, why didn't you just refuse to fight?'

Garn's fists tensed at his sides, the movement rippling through his forearms. But his voice was controlled. 'I did.' He peeled off his sodden tunic, placing it neatly beneath an overhang. 'This is my reward for refusing to fight.' He thrust an arm toward Mitrian.

The sudden motion sent Mitrian skittering backward. Gradually, she realized Garn had intended it for demonstration, not violence. For the first time in nearly a decade, she took a close look at the man with whom she had run away. Scars marred the perfect sweep of sharply defined musculature. Narrow, pink flaws marked blade cuts, the largest ones hatched with suture lines. Mitrian had seen similar blemishes on the guards; one had a flattened nose and dense bands of healed tissue across his face. But she had never seen so many scars on one man, nor grouped in close, parallel lines. Mitrian had grown up surrounded by her father's guards, the biggest, strongest, most savage men in the village. Yet, somehow, Garn's conformation and power went beyond her understanding. Though no older than Listar, Garn already sported a tangle of chest hair, each of his arms as thick as both of Rache's together.

Apparently attributing Mitrian's interest to the scars, Garn explained. 'Whip cuts.'

Mitrian started, embarrassed to be caught staring at his body.

'I was lucky. One gladiator met his cousin in the pit. He refused to fight.' Garn's eyes narrowed to slits. 'Nantel shot him.'

'No!' Mitrian looked away. The anger at her father and Rache did not extent to Nantel, and she loved her people too much to believe Garn's accusations. 'Nantel wouldn't do that. You're lying. No one forces the gladiators to kill. It's what they do.'

Garn waved his hand in a gesture of frustrated dismissal. 'Believe whatever you want. What difference can it make to me now? I'm free.'

Mitrian scowled. Santagithi's words to Rache still hounded her, compounded by Rache's apparent decision to ruin her life rather than stand up to her father. Cold, wet, and irritable from the ride, Mitrian needed to vent her frustration against someone. And Garn was the only possible target. 'I've heard stories. I know the gladiators scream in triumph after a kill and brag about it to the guards.'

Garn remained calm. 'Have you heard that I do those things?'

Mitrian considered. 'No,' she admitted. 'But – '

Garn interrupted. 'And I've heard the guards boasting about all the men they killed in battle.'

'That's different.'

'Yes,' Garn agreed. 'And the difference is that they choose to kill.

They force men like me to do it for their entertainment. Which is more brutal ?'

'It's ...' Mitrian sputtered. 'I ...' Realizing she did not know how to answer him, she went silent. She stared out over the peaks. Coming night and the overcast sky turned them into a strange, dark sea of points and crags. The rain had stopped. Cold evening wind washed over her soaked sleeping gown, and she shivered. Suddenly, she felt glad for Garn's company, and the idea of antagonizing him seemed folly. *Hasn't my family done enough harm to him ?* The urge seized her to defend Santagithi. She recalled the gathering before the meeting tree, when he had sent only those men who volunteered to war. But the image of Santagithi snatching the bow from Rache's hand replaced the initial memory. And with it came a feeling, foreign but pleasant, and the whisper of a Wizard's words: 'For you, Mitrian, finding adventure would require an act of defiance.' This time the memory was accompanied by the inexplicable certainty that she neared that act.

Garn said nothing, apparently seeing no need.

Mitrian had thought leaving home with Garn had been the answer to the Wizard's reference, but the encouragement that now flooded her mind told otherwise. Freed from social conventions by Garn's ignorance of them, she focused internally, trying to decipher Shadimar's intention. *What could the act of defiance be ? And what does it have to do with Garn?* She glanced at him again. The lengthy snarl of hair seemed out of place, a lion's mane surrounding simple features that were almost attractive, in a more savage, less classical way than Rache's.

Garn lowered his head, an abashed child. 'I'm sorry I didn't bring food. I didn't know it would be hard to find. I didn't really think. I just wanted to be free. And I wanted you.' He stared at Mitrian with an intensity she found disarming yet flattering.

Mitrian chided herself for letting a childhood ordeal destroy her friendship and a man's life. *In all the times I sneaked out to practice near the South Corner, I never once let Garn tell his side of the story.* Mitrian remembered how she had watched the gladiators shift restlessly in their cages. Night and distance had blurred them to hulking shapes, yet she had often wondered which was Garn. Still, she carried the memory of Garn's wild killer's eyes in a child's face, his repeatedly pounding at a companion with the power and impersonal coldness of the blacksmith's hammer on steel. And she had accepted the guards' word that Garn had become as much an animal as the other gladiators. *A life like that could make anyone into an animal.* Now she looked at him with new insight. *Except maybe Garn. There's something special, something different about Garn.*

Garn turned, headed for the saddle and bridle.

Garn's movement reminded Mitrian that she still had not started on the camp. 'I'll get that wood now. In the morning, I'll show you how to get food and water.' The words came more easily than the solution. She guessed they might find some berries but, for more substantial rations and clothing, they would need to find a town and buy what they needed. *And I didn't even bring money. Kadrak! What was I thinking?*

Mitrian assessed what little gear they carried. She had her own weapon, and Garn also wore a sword, apparently taken from a guard. She hoped but doubted the bulge in his left hip pocket was flint and steel. Other than the horse's tack and their current clothing, they had nothing. *We'd better hope we didn't ride that mare too hard. She may be all we have to barter for food.* Mitrian unfastened her sword, laying it beside Garn's tunic. She felt safer with the weapon at her hip, but for now the fire took precedence. She might need to range far for wood, and she could carry more sticks unburdened. 'Watch this for me, please.'

No longer familiar with conversational patterns, Garn did not question. He simply waited in silence for Mitrian to continue, accepting her leadership without objection.

Free man or not, he's used to following orders. Still, for an instant, Mitrian feared she had made a mistake. Pride of ownership turned to jealous possessiveness. Surely Garn could see the gems and craftsmanship of the hilt. He need only draw it to realize how superior it was to any weapon he had ever held. And if he chose to take it from her, she could do little to stop him.

Mitrian forced her concern aside. Garn truly seemed to care for her. And his upbringing did not prepare him for deceit and treachery. When the guards wanted something of him, they demanded it; and he submitted or died. His only other contact with men was in the pit, and there the conflict was always straightforward: kill or be killed. 'I'll be back.' She trotted off into the night.

The search for dry kindling sent Mitrian in broad circles, but she returned with an armload and a deer antler she found lying in a crevice. Starting the fire proved more difficult. Without flint, she was forced to use a bow and drill while Garn watched with rapt curiosity. But, once begun, the fire burned brilliantly, drying the moister twigs and logs Mitrian set nearby for later use. Garn slept with his back propped against the cliffs. Mitrian chose a spot on the opposite side of the fire. Clipping her sword back to her belt, she placed it near her right hand, the weapon's presence reassuring. She used the horse's saddle for a pillow.

Irregularities in the surface of granite gouged Mitrian's back. Her sandals proved scant protection on the crags, and her feet throbbed from stepping on stones and branches in the darkness. Her lower spine ached, and her muscles felt sore from a day hunched over a running steed. Her stomach gnawed at its own lining. Amid a chorus of pain, sleep would not come. She flopped from side to side without relief. Finally, unable to sleep and needing to inflict the same misery on another, she found the hole in Garn's defense. 'You say you don't like to kill and that you killed Mukesh to protect me. But you would have killed Rache out of hand.'

Garn did not move or tense. He gave no indication of awakening, yet his distinct reply made it clear he did not sleep. 'Yes.' The same sibilant tone that Rache used when speaking of Garn now entered the escaped gladiator's voice. 'I would have killed Rache. I still would.'

'I thought you hated killing.'

'I hated being forced to kill,' Garn clarified. 'When the cause is right, killing can be good and necessary. Haven't you ever hated anyone enough to kill him?'

At the moment, Mitrian considered several people she would like to slap unconscious, not the least of which was Rache. But the thought of actually raising a weapon against Santagithi or Rache or even Emerald sobered her. 'Of course not.'

Unaware of Mitrian's thoughts, Garn responded to her words. 'Perhaps that's because your father protected you, and the guards did your killing for you.'

The accusation angered Mitrian. She gathered breath to reply when the whisk of brush caught her attention. Three human figures appeared, skulking just beyond the edges of the firelight.

Garn rose to a crouch, grip tight on his sword hilt. Mitrian groped for her own weapon, never taking her eyes from the trio.

One stranger spoke, sneering. 'Well, look what we have here. Two children alone in the hills.'

'Do you think we should help them?' the second asked in the same mocking tone.

'Oh look,' the first and largest of the three said, his hand casual on his own hilt. 'The girl has a sword. Maybe we shouldn't attack.'

The one who had not yet spoken piped in. 'Don't worry about her. We'll take care of him, then stab her with something friendlier.'

Mitrian could not suppress a whimper. Her chest seemed to squeeze closed around her pounding heart. All of her training had made her certain she would respond to threat with skill. But she knew only fear.

Garn stood, revealing the huge physique that had impressed Mitrian. For the first time, the strangers hesitated. Then one chimed in. 'No worry. A man that big'll be slow.'

Garn's serious tone made a sharp contrast to the sarcasm of the strangers. 'Go away. If you're not gone by the time I draw my sword, I'll kill all of you.'

The largest of the three, apparently the leader, stepped into the light. His nose and cheek merged into an indistinguishable mass of scar tissue. Three days of black stubble covered his chin. 'Oh fear.' He clutched his chest in a grandiose gesture. 'Oh fear. Should we run ?'

Garn drew and sprang. His sword whipped for the leader's head. The stranger blocked, sword ringing against Garn's. Before Mitrian could think to draw her own weapon, Garn reversed the stroke, driving his blade into the other's neck. Blood geysered from the wound, splashing Mitrian, and the stranger sank, lifeless, to the ground.

The odor of blood made Mitrian gag.

Garn lunged for the others who were not caught as unaware as their leader. Swords rasped from sheaths, their blades almost invisible in the darkness. Garn met the first with a block. He used his superior strength to shove through the joined swords and plant a foot behind the stranger's heel. The man sprawled, rolling. The other dodged behind Garn.

'Behind you !' Mitrian shouted.

Too late, Garn whirled. The stranger's blade raked a gash across Garn's shoulder blade. As Garn turned, the other thrust for a kill. Garn caught the jab with an outside block. Again, he used strength to bully through the stranger's guard and smash his elbow into the man's chin. The stranger sank to one knee. Garn slammed his sword down on the man, slicing open his abdomen. Bowel spilled out, filling the air with its stench. The man screamed, high-pitched and frenzied. Mitrian turned away, but not in time. Her stomach was empty, but she heaved dry again and again, until the pain in her gut vanquished all her other aches.

Garn's threat seemed unimportant. 'You're not getting away.' Footsteps clattered over the stone, then faded beneath the shrieks of the gut-slashed man.

Gradually, Mitrian suppressed her nausea. She clambered to her feet, forcing herself to breathe through her mouth, certain the odor would send her back into uncontrollable spasms. *Shadimar was right. I can't handle war.* The thought brought hot, angry tears to her eyes. She belted her sword to her waist with shaking fingers, aware the last of the bandits could still kill Garn and return. *I won't be here for him to rape.* Mitrian hid behind a crevice watching to see who, if anyone, came back to camp.

The screams of the injured man dropped to moans, then stilled as life drained from him. Mitrian clung to the rock, deeply chilled, helplessly watching the fire dwindle to ash. The battle replayed through her mind repeatedly. It had gone fast; she had not even found the chance to assess the techniques or pluck individual sequences from the swordplay. But neither had she thought to try. The first scream echoed through her head, the first splash of blood mesmerizing her. She remembered the warm droplets pelting her cheek and rubbed at the site as if to take off the skin beneath it. *I'll get used to this. All soldiers do.* Mitrian glanced at the dark blur of the sword at her hip, feeling more like a frightened girl than a warrior.

No food, no water, and only my own unskilled hand to protect me from bandits. Mitrian frowned, aware it was not lack of ability, but lack of experience that had made her react the way she had. Still, the result was the same. *I'll starve or die at sword point, if the cold doesn't get me first. Gods! Garn has to come back. I don't want to be alone.*

As if in answer to Mitrian's unspoken prayer, Garn's form emerged from the shadows of the cliffs. Hefting the gut-slashed bandit's corpse, he dragged it from the camp. A moment later, he returned. 'Mitrian?' he tried softly. 'Mitrian?'

Relief flooded Mitrian. She bounded to Garn's side, wrapping her arms around him, his body real and solid against hers. She let the tears flow where they would.

At first Garn tensed, surprised. Then his hands cinched tight around Mitrian, pulling her closer. His fingers stroked Mitrian's hair with the understandable awkwardness of an adolescent male with little exposure to women.

For some time, they clung to one another, the warmth of Garn's body protecting Mitrian from the chill. Gradually, other sensations came to her. Their closeness felt pleasant and right, as if condoned by some higher being. The powerful ridges of his muscles felt pleasant to her touch, and his arousal intrigued her. She glanced up into his face, and he wore the same insecure, vulnerable expression that had surprised her in the past. Despite the scars, he looked attractive and, though she knew it was wrong, she hoped he would kiss her. For all the times she had hugged Listar, it had simply felt like two people invading one another's private space. With Garn, she felt something different, more positive and stronger.

Garn hesitated, apparently fighting his own, less civilized instincts and unsure what to do next. Only then, Mitrian noticed her left hand, clamped to Garn's back, was wet. She examined it. Blood smeared her palm and fingers. At once, Mitrian thought it was her own and back-stepped with a gasp. Then she recalled the slash Garn had taken in the battle. 'You're hurt.' She released him, stung with guilt. Alone and without supplies, Garn would have nothing to fear from bandits. *They wanted me.* Mitrian shuddered at the thought, feeling responsible for Garn's pain.

'I've known worse.' Garn loosed his hold with obvious reluctance.

Mitrian circled him. Blood stained his back, mostly dark and clotted. The sword cut ran across his shoulder blade to his spine, and muscle tissue gaped from the edges. Mitrian cringed in sympathy. She had seen similar wounds on guards and had, at times, tended them. 'This needs sewing. Come with me.' She headed back to the ashes of the fire, Garn following.

Tearing loose a corner of her sleeping gown, Mitrian used it to clean the wound. She clamped the damp fabric tight to his skin to staunch the bleeding. The depth of the cut required her to hold it for the time it took her to think rationally, and she realized the mistake she might have made. No one could forgive her cuddling with a gladiator, not her father, not Listar, not Rache. In her current frame of mind, a thought that usually would have repulsed now enticed. *And who would ever know?* She stared at Garn, enjoying the sight of him, again knowing an attraction she had felt for no other man but Rache. *Garn saved my life. I owe him.* Mitrian frowned. aware she was rationalizing. *Stupid,* she chided herself. *I'll do it willingly or not at all.*

Mitrian's mother had often told her sex without love was an ugly, shameful thing. Yet Mitrian found it impossible to consider the pleasure of Garn's body against hers anything but good. Here in the wilderness, no one could ever discover anything they did. Several times, out in the woods near Santagithi's Town, Listar had reassured Mitrian that there was no risk with the first intimate contact. She had turned down the blacksmith's son for other reasons, glad now that she still had her virginity to share with Garn if things went that far. She never thought to doubt Listar's reassurance. Her parents had been married ten years before her mother conceived, and no pregnancy since Mitrian had come to term.

Removing the cloth, Mitrian turned and pawed beneath the woodpile for the stag's antler she had found while gathering kindling. Seizing it, she returned to Garn. 'Do you have a knife?' She held out her hand.

Garn rose. He retrieved a dagger from his hip pocket, handed it to Mitrian and sat, cross-legged, his back to her.

Mitrian whittled a needle from the horn. She carved the point as sharp as possible and notched the other end. Ordinarily, she would have used a heated wire to make an eye, but lacking that, the crude indentations would have to do. Catching the bottom edge of her sleeping gown, she carefully unwound the hem. Threading the needle, she set to work on the gash in Garn's back. 'Normally I'd let you have a few mugs of ale before I did this.' She brushed aside his tangle of hair.

Garn shrugged, as if to imply he had done this many times without so much as a taste of alcohol. He did not flinch.

Mitrian felt a closeness with Garn that she had not known since childhood. To draw his attention from the pain, she asked some of the questions that plagued her. 'So how did you get free?' She pulled a loop tight.

Garn answered indirectly. 'I was thinking about how you said a lot of the gladiators take pride in their kills.'

'Mmm?' Mitrian encouraged, wondering where the conversation was leading.

'I think maybe everyone needs to believe he's good at something. There's not much to a gladiator's life: sleep, eat, train, and kill. They . . .' Garn paused, and Mitrian imagined he was smiling at the fact that he no longer needed to use the term 'we.' '. . . can't even make friends with one another for fear of facing off in the pit. There's few things more dangerous than hesitation or too much thought in battle and few things worse than having to kill or be killed by a friend.'

The sentiment struck dangerously close to Shadimar's warning. Mitrian jabbed the needle too deep and had to remove it, costing Garn an extra stitch.

Garn seemed oblivious. 'Anyway, when killing's all a man has, it becomes his source of pride. All his other needs are taken care of. If he can tolerate fools commanding him and learns to like the killing, it might not be such a bad life for some.'

Garn's insight astounded Mitrian. 'But not a good life for you.'

'No,' Garn said emphatically. 'I don't enjoy killing; I did it from necessity. I had to amuse myself in other ways. So I listened and learned as much as I could. And,' he admitted without shame, 'I stole things. A trinket, here. Perhaps a snack or a scarf. Once, I got the keys.'

Mitrian tightened her fifteenth suture. 'You've been free before.'

'Yes,' Garn admitted. 'A few times I watched you dancing in the woods.'

The use of the term 'dancing' to describe her swordcraft annoyed Mitrian, but before she could correct Garn, he fidgeted like a child waiting for his turn to speak.

'You looked so beautiful, so graceful. Just like I remembered.' The back of Garn's neck flushed, and Mitrian guessed his face had turned the same color. 'The guards would talk about the girls they met in the cities out West. I used to imagine I was free, and you were my woman. I never saw you clearly in the dark, though.' He added nervously, 'I'd forgotten how pretty you are.'

Now Mitrian was blushing, glad Garn could not see her. The words sounded incongruous from this huge killer who, since the age of eleven, had learned about women only from a group of foul-mouthed soldiers. Yet lack of contact with women apparently had prompted Garn to create an overly romanticized image of her. Quickly, she finished the last few stitches. Embarrassed by the compliments, she changed the subject. 'If you had the keys, how come you waited so long to escape?'

'I don't know,' Garn admitted.

But, having heard Garn speak, Mitrian believed she did. His talk of security added the final piece to the puzzle. The guards had beaten and threatened Garn, but they fed him as well. She imagined a familiar situation, no matter how bad, might seem easier to face than the unknown. Already, Garn had gotten himself deep into strange territory without rations or the tools and knowledge to hunt. Any guards who might be chasing him held the advantage of maps, horses, supplies, and the ability to deal with townsfolk. When they found him, they would have no choice but to punish him severely as a deterrent to the other gladiators, perhaps they would even kill him. *I can't let that happen.* 'But what finally gave you the courage to leave last night?'

'Finding out that you and Rache weren't . . .' Garn trailed off, obviously flustered.

'Lovers,' Mitrian finished the sentence naturally, suddenly intensely enthralled with the man beside her. She knew without the need to question that sleeping with Garn was the Eastern Wizard's act of defiance. And for the moment, the knowledge that it would upset Santagithi and Rache only made it more alluring. Mitrian tied off the final knot. 'All done.'

Garn turned, but he guiltily evaded her stare. 'I'd better admit something. I stole from you, too.'

Surprised, Mitrian considered, open-mouthed. She had noticed nothing missing. 'When did you take it?'

'I was by your room, trying to find a way to talk to you. I found this by the window.' Rising, Garn took the knife from where Mitrian had set it on the ground. He replaced it in his buckskins and exchanged it for the pouch of gems Mitrian kept on her shelf.

Joy swept through Mitrian at the sight of valuables that could be used as barter. 'Perfect.'

Garn tossed the pouch onto his tunic, staring at Mitrian as if she had gone mad before his eyes.

'Don't you see? If we go up into the Northlands tomorrow, we can find a town and buy food and water. Even fresh horses and tack and clothes . . .' Mitrian laughed with delight.

Garn nodded uncertainly, apparently not wholly certain where the pouch of gems fit in to all this, but willing to take Mitrian's word for it. He trotted to Mitrian's side and sat. Tentatively, he trailed his fingers along her arm.

Desire spiraled through Mitrian from that single touch. Smiling, she caressed the bunched muscle of his thigh. A glance told her she had excited him, too. She met his gaze, and found a hunted look in his green eyes, as if he feared he was doing something sinful. His uncertainty stirred her, too. She started to pull away. Then his arms enwrapped her, drawing her against him. His lips found hers, and nothing had ever felt more right to Mitrian. He levered her down gently among the scattered rocks, and she gave herself willingly.

10 Crests of Blue and Gold

That night, Mitrian dreamed of Rache proudly perched on a white stallion that stood rooted like a statue. Beside him, Mitrian's little chestnut mare waited docilely, saddled and bridled but without a rider. The sword master remained as unmoving as his horse, his gaze on some distant threat she could not see. Wind howled between dunes as craggy and barren as the Granite Hills, flinging sand in a wild spray that made vision all but impossible. Yet still Rache stared.

Mitrian tried to locate herself in the image, at first finding nothing. She tried to guess where she must stand by the images she saw and the perspective from which she saw them; but the dream state let her know and see all, and the view seemed too wide for normal sight. Then, gradually, the picture settled. She found herself behind Rache and his mount, clutching her sword in a fist turned fiery red from the cold. 'Rache,' she said.

He did not turn.

'Rache,' Mitrian repeated, louder.

Still no response.

Rache raised a hand to shield his eyes, continuing to look out among the dunes. Clearly, he had not heard Mitrian, and that struck terror through her. She had all but shouted and, despite the wind, she could hear his every breath and heartbeat.

'Rache?' Mitrian circled him, placing herself directly in his line of vision. His bright blue eyes seemed vibrant, fixed beyond the dunes, yet surely he could see her.

If he did, he gave no sign. His hands rested on the hilts of his swords, his forearms crossed. His features held the serious expression that her father always wore in the war god's temple.

'Rache, damn it, talk to me.' The cold cut through Mitrian, bringing with it a fear as primal and incomprehensible as thoughts of death. She could not remember why they had come there, nor how she came to be on the ground. She knew only that it had some connection with a battle.

Rache said nothing. Though Mitrian had to be in his line of sight, he seemed to stare right through her.

Panic spiraled through her. She wanted and needed him to hold her, and terror made her desperate. She rushed to his side, catching his leg near the stirrup. 'Rache, come on. Don't do this. Please.' She pulled. His leg fell free, dangling like a rag doll's limb. Mitrian withdrew with a gasp.

For the first time Rache turned his gaze in Mitrian's direction, but he looked at his leg, not at her.

'Rache, please stop. You're scaring me.'

If Rache heard, he gave no sign. Leaning over the horse's side, he reached for his leg.

'Stop it !' Mitrian screamed, as incensed by his rebuffs as she had been the night she fled her home. 'Stop !' She reached for him as he moved.

Rache seized his ankle and the stirrup. He did not flinch from nor dodge Mitrian's lunge. Her hands closed over his wrists.

For a moment, he seemed oblivious even to her touch. Then he tried to move laterally and met the resistance of her hold. Surprise crossed his features.

Having finally gained Rache's attention, Mitrian jerked him toward her. She had meant only to force him to listen, but her abrupt pull unhorsed him. Awkwardly, he pinwheeled, sprawling to the sand. The horse shied, then broke into a gallop, the stirrups flapping emptily against its ribs.

Rache moved with a dazed clumsiness that seemed too uncharacteristic, yet, in her dream state, Mitrian believed. 'Rache.' She knelt at his side, catching movement at the edge of her vision. She jerked her head toward the dunes just in time to see an army headed toward them, sunlight sparkling from breastplates and buckles. She screamed.

Mitrian jerked suddenly awake, her heart pounding. The first thing she noticed was the cold and the high-pitched whistle of wind between stones. A heavy arm lay draped across her abdomen. As she stiffened, it tightened reassuringly around her.

Mitrian lay still, trying to get her bearings. She lay on stone. Though cliffs shielded her on three sides, wind funneled through chasms in the rock, chilling her. To her left, she could still feel the warmth of the dwindling coals from the campfire. *Campfire.* Mitrian relaxed slightly. *So it was only a dream.* Relief flooded her at the realization that she had not flung Rache from his horse and left him, helpless, at the feet of the Eastern army.

Still, other things could not be so easily dismissed. Mitrian placed her hand over the arm that held her, feeling the muscles, tense and strong, beneath her touch. There could be no doubt who that arm belonged to, yet she dared not believe that the events of the last two nights were real. *I slept with Garn. I gave myself to the slave who crippled Rache.* The thought revolted her, and self-loathing pounded her until she curled into a ball to escape it.

Sensing her distress, yet not knowing its source, Garn tightened his hold.

Mitrian felt safe in his arms. She recalled how gently Garn had handled their lovemaking, so unlike the raging murderer the guards described. Her mother had warned her that it would hurt the first time, and it had. She had cried out once in pain; he had apologized so profusely and sincerely that she had felt sorry for the outburst. And, later, it had become the most wonderful and exciting night of her life.

Garn's not a slave anymore. And he never should have become one. The thought soothed, but it could not erase the reality of the physical and emotional agony Garn had inflicted on Rache. The rage of the previous evening had finally run its course. *Fleeing from home was wrong, a childish reaction not a solution to the problem. I love my father. And I love Rache. Even if they both made* stupid *decisions.* She considered the town, the people, and places she had forgotten in the wanton blur of anger. *Retreat is the coward's way. I'm going to stand up to my father.*

Filled with new resolve, Mitrian uncoiled and stretched out over the rocks. To her left, the coals of the fire warmed her nearly as much as Garn's presence to her right. *I want Garn, and I want adventure. But we're ill-prepared to face the elements, let alone a war.* The darkened sky and high position of the moon told her she still had several hours left to sleep. But this revelation could not wait for morning. 'Garn,' she said aloud. 'Are you awake?'

Garn did not reply in words, but he squeezed her hearteningly.

'We're going home.'

Garn went utterly still.

Mitrian flipped over to face him. His green eyes lay open, flat and dangerous in the silence. 'Did you hear me?'

'I heard you.'

'And?'

'I heard you.'

'What do you think?'

'I think,' Garn said slowly, 'I think that hunger has driven you mad. And it saddens me.'

Mitrian frowned, doubting Garn's assessment, though plainly fatigue had affected her clarity of mind. Still, she felt more lucid now than at any time since she had allowed rage to cloud her judgment. 'No, you don't understand.' Excitement urged her on. 'We'll go back home. I'll explain to my father what really happened with Mukesh, that it was all a mistake, and how much you mean to me now. Then they'll let you free and . . .'

'No !' Garn sprang to a crouch, dumping Mitrian to the stone.

Mitrian scrambled to her feet. The coiled violence in Garn's stance alarmed her.

'Santagithi would kill me.'

'No, he wouldn't do that,' Mitrian insisted. 'Not if I explained.'

'Especially if you explained.' Shadows draped Garn's face making it look lean and hungry. 'They'd think I forced you to say those things. And if they found out what we did last night, they'd dismember me with dull knives.'

The image horrified Mitrian. 'That's just stupid. That won't happen.'

'It won't,' Garn agreed. 'Because I won't go back.' He finished so softly Mitrian had to strain to hear him '. . . yet.'

The afterthought suggested that Garn would eventually return to the Town of Santagithi. While it should have raised Mitrian's hopes, his strange, savage expression frightened her instead. 'So you *are* planning to go back ?'

Garn tossed logs on the fire, then hefted a stick as thick as his forearm, passing it from hand to hand. 'Eventually.' He sounded unsure. 'Maybe. I don't know. There's a score that still needs settling.'

Horror strangled Mitrian. 'You're not going to try to hurt my father ?'

'No,' Garn said, to her relief. 'Santagithi is not the one.' His fingers clamped down over the stick. 'And I love you too much to hurt your father.'

'Then who ?'

Garn said nothing. The back and forth movement of the branch quickened. 'It's personal.'

'Who ?' Mitrian pressed, knowing in her heart that it was Rache, yet needing to hear the name from Garn.

Garn changed the subject with awkward abruptness. 'You're not going back.' For an instant, his words seemed a threat, then he softened them with a question. 'Are you ?'

The Garn that Mitrian had known last night, the man whose naive tenderness she had enjoyed seemed to have disappeared, replaced by the gladiator about whom she had heard so many tales of directed, mechanical killing. She turned away. 'I have debts to handle, too. My dreams are telling me I left things undone, and I said evil things to someone who means too much to me to leave that way. I ran away in a infantile tantrum. My home and my people mean everything to me.'

Garn looked stricken. The stick sagged in his hand. 'And I mean nothing.'

'That's not right.' Mitrian took a hesitant step toward Garn. 'If I don't love you yet, and I'm not sure I don't, then I could. Soon.' The sentiment did not emerge well, but she felt certain Garn would understand. 'I asked you to come back with me.'

'Mitrian, you know I can't. If Santagithi didn't kill me, one of his guards would. Or Mukesh's father.' Garn went rigid, the stick clamped in both hands, his eyes cold. 'Worse, I'd probably kill them. Then it would all start again. If anyone so much as showed me a whip . . .' His voice trailed into a growl. The log bowed in his grip.

'I *have* to go back.' Mitrian wanted to believe Garn was wrong, but she could not banish the images of Santagithi smashing the bow Rache had given her and the cruelty of his words to his captain. *If my father would exile Rache for spending too much time with me, what would he do to Garn?* She tried to rationalize, reminding herself that her father would not have interfered had Rache agreed to marry her. But much as she wanted to return and to exonerate Garn, she knew her father would never let them wed.

'So you're going back ? You're going to just leave me after all we shared ?'

Mitrian lowered her head, the answer obvious. 'I'll stay with you long enough to get supplies and find an escort to take me home so I don't have to worry about bandits.' The memory of the attack pushed its way into her mind, and she brushed it aside for more urgent matters. 'When I get there, I'll tell my father not to send guards after you. You won't have to fear for your life anymore. Eventually, we'll find each other again. I'm sure of it.' Mitrian felt far less certain than her words implied. Having lived all her life in the Town of Santagithi, just the Granite Hills seemed endless. And Nantel and Santagithi had told stories of vast farmlands and huge cities beyond the mountains.

Garn froze, anguish etched across his features. As much as their lovemaking meant to Mitrian, it had obviously meant far more to him. Suddenly, he came to life. He slammed the log against a rock outcropping with a force that shattered the wood. The broken end skittered harmlessly into the darkness, but chips of flying bark stung Mitrian.

Garn whirled, charging off into the night. He moved without a noise, and darkness swallowed him before Mitrian could think to follow.

Alone, Mitrian shivered, tears tracing cold lines along her cheeks.

Uncertain what to do next, she curled up beside the fire and once again, cried herself to sleep.

The strains of Mar Lon's song wound through Mizahai's Tavern, weaving between the patrons in a musical tapestry of peaceful coexistence and harmony. Over time, he had added serenity to his message of unity, and he had changed his repertoire to less subtle stories of enemies laying aside their weapons to live and work as neighbors. Limited by a language with no single word for 'peace' and a dozen for 'war,' it had taken Mar Lon weeks to compose the finest piece of his experience. Now, at his first performance of it, he concentrated with a grim solemnity that left little room for observation of his audience. And threads of his own despair wound through the music, adding a deeply personal sincerity to its message.

The last sequence rang from Mar Lon's *lonriset*, the concluding note quivering across the string, leaving a crisp, perfect echo that did not sharpen or flatten so much as a quarter tone. Mar Lon stilled it to silence with a finger, reveling in the quiet stillness of an audience enraptured by his talent. For the first time in weeks, joy tempered Mar Lon's depression. He pictured the radiant notions of peace taking form behind the wall of blank faces, culminating in a vast brotherhood that would span from the Southern to the Amirannak Seas.

Gradually, expression returned to the Eastern features. A man at the next table raised a full mug of beer. 'Beautiful.'

Mar Lon smiled.

'*Very* beautiful,' another said.

Joy thrilled through Mar Lon. *I reached them. Finally, I reached them.* If not for the gravity of his lesson, he would have laughed aloud.

Then a third voice cut through the growing buzz of returning conversation. 'Play "The Bastard Tinker of LaZar!"'

Cries of approval flashed through the crowd, then blended into a dull roar of consensus.

Mar Lon's grin wilted. *A drinking song. They want a damned drinking song.* Excitement died, snuffed in an instant. Alone at a corner table, he let his *lonriset* sag into his lap, his fingers feeling too weak and clumsy to play. Sorrow returned, trebling in an instant. He recalled his father's performances, the sweet, solid grief trembling from every word and sound, every nuance of instrument and voice driving his listeners to tears. The staunchest atheist left his shows believing in gods and Wizards, if only for the moment. *If only I could share that skill. If only I could show them the virtue of universal peace.* For the first time in his life, Mar Lon hated the curse that Odin had inflicted upon the line of bards. *Given the right to speak outright, I could convince them.* Folding his arms on the tabletop, he lowered his head to the crook of one elbow.

Snorts of disappointment wafted to Mar Lon, as if from a great distance. These coalesced into a goading, clapping chant that he did not try to decipher. As the patrons bored of prodding an unmoving bard, their collective shouts died to a few disparaging remarks amid a humming undercurrent of conversation. Mar Lon thought he heard at least one murderous threat before his mind shut out all but his own thoughts.

Mitrian awakened alone, cradled between two jutting formations of rock, her sleeping gown dried into clinging creases. She sat up amid the rustle of cloth. Her sword hilt had left a painful impression in her side, as had her pouch of gems laced beside the sheath. The horse stood near its bridle and saddle, head sagging, leaves hanging from its whiskered lips. Dressed in his buckskins, Garn crouched before a small glade, his sword drawn.

Though relieved by Garn's presence, his caution alarmed Mitrian. She stood, rearranging her belt into a more comfortable position. 'What is it?'

Garn raised a hand for silence. Slowly, he shifted his weight, examining all sides of the brush. Apparently finding nothing, he advanced. Now Mitrian could hear the rattle of brush as something moved in front of Garn. He took a wary step back, and the thing went quiet.

What is it? This time Mitrian kept the question to herself, certain Garn had no answer.

Garn crashed into the weeds, and the stems closed around him. Mitrian held her breath, now fully awake. She edged forward, wanting to back Garn but uncertain what to expect. The glade parted again, and Garn emerged, dragging a deer onto the rocks.

The horse shied, snorting its displeasure. Mitrian stared. It was still late summer; starvation could not have started culling the deer population yet. Picking her way over the rocks, she knelt beside the carcass. Tentatively, she touched its side. It felt warm beneath her hand. Fleas parted trails through the gray-brown fur, having not yet abandoned it for a living host. 'It's fresh,' she said, not daring to believe their luck. *Maybe it died of illness.* The animal appeared relatively healthy, a well-fleshed doe with sharp, dark eyes only just starting to glaze. *More likely a man or beast injured it, and it staggered here to die.*

Garn hesitated, apparently trying to make sense of Mitrian's announcement. 'You mean we can eat it?'

'Yes.' Mitrian laughed with joy. Hunger had settled into a constant dull ache, but the thought of food made her stomach growl anew. 'You skin it, and I'll make the fire.'

Garn looked doubtfully at the deer. He drew his dagger; but, from that point, he appeared lost.

Mitrian turned her back, not wanting to admit she knew nothing of preparing deer. In Santagithi's Town, the hunters and some of the off-duty guards would shoot the game, skin it, and haul the carcass to the butcher to dress. By the time Mitrian's mother received her family's share, it came as a glistening, nearly bloodless packet of muscle.

When Mitrian did not offer any suggestions, Garn set to work with his dagger, mutilating a pelt that might have made a warm suit or blanket. Mitrian used the bow and drill to light the twigs and logs she had gathered the previous night. Dry, the kindling caught more easily, and she finished while Garn was still struggling to separate fur from muscle. Blood covered the hair on his arms, speckled his face, and stained his already grimy clothing.

Trying to forget the rumbling in her gut, Mitrian concentrated on other matters. The battle against the bandits filled her memory. *I froze.* She lowered her head, humiliated by the realization. *The best student of the greatest sword master I've ever known; and when the time to fight came, I reacted like a panicked townswoman. I left Garn to defend me, one man against three. And it's my fault he got wounded.* She thought of the wild chaos of battle, of Garn's sword flying in all directions. The main body of the conflict had passed in less than fifteen heartbeats, but that seemed time enough for Mitrian to have done something. *If I'm going to find adventure like the Wizard promised, if I'm going to war at Rache's side, I've got to get past this fear of killing.*

Unconsciously, Mitrian kneaded the wolf's head hilt of her sword. *Do I really want to become a heartless killer?* She considered Garn, his sensitive innocence one moment, followed by a rage so intemperate it drove him to smash fire logs with his bare hands. She thought, too, of Rache, so crazed in battle, yet so beautiful and quietly dedicated in peaceful times. *It's like two different people, a war-Rache and an everyday-Rache. I need to find a war-Mitrian. I need to cross that fine line between knowing the techniques and using them to kill.* Rache had always taught her not to pull her strokes in spar, to treat him instead as a real enemy. He claimed that if he could not counter anything a young student tried, he deserved to die. *Maybe if I just keep practicing, the swordcraft will become so routine I'll use it without hesitating.*

An answer seeped into Mitrian's consciousness, a grim certainty that her solution was not enough. *Mitrian, what you seek does not come from skill but from inside yourself.* Mitrian startled at the foreign concept, her hand falling from the yellow gems in her hilt. The presence faded from her mind, its strangeness lingering. Mitrian knew the idea must have emanated from the demon in the gems. She doubted Shadimar had tried to harm her with this magical sword, but she could not shake the feeling that there was something awful about this once human creature trapped in topaz, not so much evil as unholy. Still, she had chosen to accept the Eastern Wizard's gift. With that responsibility came a trust, and the demon's lesson intrigued her. Again, she clamped her fingers to the hilt.

The change will come when you accept your own death as inevitable, when you come to seek it as a reward. Death in glory! A place in Valhalla! A savage wave of pride suffused Mitrian, wholly foreign. *The joy does not come from the killing, it comes of testing your skills against a worthy opponent and proving yourself the better. The more capable the enemy, the more honorable the fight, and the more deserving the opponent of the death you deal him. Those meriting life will seek death in battle. The others, like the bandits, you kill because their lives have no value to mourn.*

Mitrian tried to mull over the demon's points, her thoughts muddled, mixed inseparably with his. *Once you've learned to look upon death as a goal, every battle takes you one step closer. Death screams become music, the clash of steel applause. The odor of blood and death is perfume, the slash and counterslash art, a perfect, final dance.* Something struck Mitrian as wrong, dishonorable, beyond yet still beneath the laws of all humanity, but the demon carried her like a new bride across the threshold of its madness. She launched into a kata, unmarred by days without practice. She tried to concentrate on her choices, but her thoughts tumbled as swiftly as the blade. Visions of strange men and women filled her head, a Westland town set upon by golden-haired reavers as merciless as starved wolves. Flailing swords flashed, trailing a wake of corpses.

Trying to rip free of the demon's images, Mitrian changed her grip, envisioning Rache and leaping into his favorite maneuver. Immediately, she formed a picture of the sword master upon a white charger, a sword in each fist and his face a blank mask of concentration. He spurred his mount toward a wall of attackers, mouth splitting into a grin. The mental picture came to Mitrian so vividly that she recoiled from it. Then a wild yearning seized her. Death, blood, and glory no longer repulsed, they enticed. Her mind buzzed with growing excitement. Suddenly, her inner control snapped, and the sword's power overwhelmed her with battle madness.

When Mitrian regained her senses, she stood panting on the crags, the soles of her sandals slashed and torn by loose stones. Her heart hammered. She felt certain she had executed a dozen maneuvers, though she remembered none of them. Afraid she might lose control again, she swiftly sheathed the weapon. *Why? Why would Shadimar give me a weapon that does this to me?* Assaulted by fear, anger, and frustration, Mitrian wanted to scream. The dangers of a weapon that could twist her thoughts were obvious, its subtleties less so. Now free of the grip, she fell back into her normal pattern of thought, still Mitrian in every way.

Mitrian tried to remember all Shadimar had promised about the sword: 'The magic I offer will add to your sword skill, give you a new perspective and a heritage, nothing more.' A demon that could lecture her on war and death, that could infuse battle rage like euphoria seemed like much more to Mitrian. 'This sword will grant responsibilities as well as abilities. It will offer a culture of warrior men and women, a heritage of blood and glory dedicated to the battle goddess, Sif.' Mitrian considered. So far the demon had acted within Shadimar's description. Its views on battle fit clearly within a warrior heritage, a heritage the demon had once referred to as Renshai. *It can help me breach that wall between practice and reality.* Still, Mitrian could not forget Shadimar's other warning. 'Magic comes of Chaos, unpredictable even in a Wizard's control.' *Does Shadimar know this demon can infiltrate my very thoughts?* In no position to ask, Mitrian shook her head. *For now, it's the only weapon I have. There is much this demon can teach me. So long as I can release the hilt, the decisions are mine. I'm in no danger.*

A stranger's voice interrupted Mitrian's deliberation. 'Thank you for skinning my deer.' He used the common trading tongue with a Western accent.

Mitrian whirled. Garn sprang to his feet, dumping the carcass to the stone. A small, thin man stood just beyond Garn's sword reach. He wore a tattered, brown cloak over a woolen shirt and pants of forest green. Short, brilliantly red hair covered his head, dirty and standing nearly on end in places. He clutched a longbow of yew, an arrow notched against its string. A quiver of matching shafts lay slung across his shoulder.

'*Your* deer!' Garn grasped his sword hilt. 'I spent the morning skinning it.'

The man rubbed his knee with the base of his bow. 'I thanked you.'

Garn tensed. The little man back-stepped, raising the bow.

Afraid for Garn, Mitrian intervened. 'Wait. Let's talk.' She looked from Garn, his sword arm rigid, to the archer whose dark eyes studied Garn as if seeking a bull's-eye. Uncertain what to say, Mitrian blurted, 'Are you sure this is your deer?'

The little stranger smiled. 'Quite certain, lady. I can see it from here. A perfect shot.' The last sentence was obviously for Garn's benefit, as if to warn him the archer's aim was unerring even at a distance and at a moving target. 'On the left between neck and shoulder. A hardy beast to have traveled this far before falling.'

Garn's stare never left the stranger. Reluctantly, Mitrian pulled her gaze from the men to examine the deer. Even as close as she stood, it took her a moment to find the entry wound. Brushing aside clinging tatters of pelt, she dug out a piece of arrow shaft chased with three rings. She rubbed off blood with her fingers to reveal the crest colors: one royal blue and the others gold, a perfect match to the one on the hunter's string. Mitrian's hopes fell. 'He's right. It's his kill.'

Garn seemed unimpressed. 'Go away. I cleaned it. I'll eat it.'

The hunter plucked at his string. Garn bunched, whipping his sword from its sheath. Mitrian spoke hurriedly. 'Surely, there's enough meat for all of us.' She glanced from Garn to the stranger and back.

Still coiled, Garn nodded.

The redhead lowered his bow. 'Deal,' he said. 'I'll be back in a moment. I left my missy in the scrub.' He disappeared as silently as he had come.

Mitrian tossed more sticks on the fire. Garn tore the last clumps of fur from the deer, gaze straying repeatedly to the glade into which the hunter had disappeared.

Shortly, the stranger returned, leading a long-eared, horselike creature with a pack strapped to its back. He looped the lead rope around a crag near Garn's stolen mare, and the animals sniffed noses, nostrils widely flared. Turning his back on the creature, the archer faced Garn and Mitrian, still carrying the bow and quiver. 'My name's Arduwyn.' He looked down at the mutilated carcass and winced. 'Who are you that never learned the proper way to skin a deer?'

'Garn.' The ex-gladiator seemed unmiffed, not recognizing the comment as an insult.

'I'm Mitrian.' Mitrian turned the conversation back to Arduwyn. 'What's an archer doing alone in barren hills?'

'Hunter,' Arduwyn corrected. 'Or woodsman.' He waved Garn away from the kill, knelt and drew an ivory-handled skinning knife shorter and thicker-bladed than Garn's, its tip a dull semicircle. Arduwyn did not carry a sword on his person, though Mitrian could see the curved tip of a scimitar roped against his animal's pack.

'Archer implies soldier. I don't make my living killing men.' He glanced up. 'Though I'm quite capable of it,' he added quickly, apparently for Garn's benefit. Removing his cloak and shirt to reveal a ribby, almost hairless chest, he set to work gutting and butchering the deer.

The reek of deer innards and blood radiating from Garn made Mitrian wish he had thought to remove his shirt as well. *Soon enough, we'll buy new clothes.* Suddenly, she realized Arduwyn had never answered her question. She rephrased it. 'All right then. What's a *hunter* doing alone in these barren hills?'

Arduwyn hacked and pried at the deer with a skill that could only come from long years of practice. Yet his face twisted in concentration, an expression Mitrian attributed to her question. He looked from Garn to Mitrian thoughtfully, as if trying to decide whether they could be trusted. At length, he replied, 'I stopped for a few supplies at one of the small villages at the foot of the hills.' He gestured westward. 'There, I received a letter written in the trading language. Because of the poor quality of the handwriting and a series of smudges, neither I nor anyone in the village could read it. They told me there was a larger town on the other side of the hills.' He gestured eastward. 'Many of its citizens read, and the trading tongue is their native language, so I thought they might do better with it.'

Aware Arduwyn was headed toward the Town of Santagithi, Mitrian sucked in her breath. The possibility of an escort home intrigued her, but small, scrawny Arduwyn hardly seemed much protection against bandits. *Besides, I promised I'd get Garn supplies before leaving him,* she rationalized, not daring to admit she would sorely miss him. *And I need supplies of my own.* She glanced toward Garn and saw his hand creeping toward his sword hilt. With alarm, she realized his concern. Anyone in the Town of Santagithi would recognize Arduwyn's descriptions of Garn and herself, and the use of their real names could only add proof to his story.

Arduwyn swept the deer's innards into a pile, oblivious to Garn's threat.

Quickly, Mitrian caught Garn's sword hand and clasped it between both of her own. 'Perhaps I can save you the trip. I read the trading tongue.'

Arduwyn studied Mitrian. A doubtful frown creased his face, easing into a thoughtful smile.

Garn gently freed his fingers from Mitrian's grip. To her relief, he did not reach for his weapon again but awaited Arduwyn's reply.

'It can't hurt to try,' Mitrian encouraged.

'No, I don't suppose it could.' Arduwyn did not sound convinced by his own words. 'Certainly no more dangerous than having the message read in a town.' He spoke more to himself than to Mitrian. Finally, he came to a decision. 'Thank you. I'd appreciate your help. I've never had anyone send me a message before, and I can't imagine why anyone would want to. Naturally, I keep thinking of all the worst possibilities.'

'Naturally,' Mitrian agreed, trying to soothe. If Arduwyn refused her and headed for the Town of Santagithi, Garn would have to try to stop the flame-haired hunter. *Garn said he hated killing, but his freedom is too important to risk. He barely knows how to keep up a normal conversation, let alone talk a stranger out of going to my father's town.* Mitrian harbored little doubt. *No matter his good intentions, Garn is still trained to handle his problems with violence. If Arduwyn insists on going to the town, Garn will kill him. Killing in battle is one thing. I can't be a party to murder.*

Arduwyn continued speaking, apparently unaware of Mitrian's concerns. 'All I ask is that you read the entire message aloud, no matter what it says, that you give me a chance to tell my side, and that, regardless of the contents, we'll still share dinner.'

Garn relaxed.

Mitrian suppressed a smile at Arduwyn's fears. *What could be worse than being an escaped gladiator?* 'Agreed,' she said. Then, using the hunter's expression, 'Deal. Let's get some meat on the fire, and I'll read while it's cooking.'

Arduwyn carved out the venison tenderloins, heart, and liver. Then he had Garn help him construct a spit and set the meat to roast. That settled, Arduwyn washed his hands and arms in one of the larger puddles, pulled his shirt and cloak back on, and trotted to his pack animal.

Garn looked up from the fire. 'What is that thing?' He pointed at the pack beast.

Arduwyn removed the pack and scimitar from his animal's back, pausing to assess the direction of Garn's question. 'Who, Stubby girl?' He patted the thick, gray flank. 'She's a donkey.'

Garn glanced at Mitrian, who shrugged. She had never seen its like before either.

Arduwyn rummaged through the pack. 'She's like a rotten-tempered pony with half the brains and twice as stubborn.' He removed a folded scrap of parchment from the pack and closed the flap. 'But she's an old friend.' He carried the note to Mitrian, frowning at the gory, foul-smelling pile of deer guts as he passed.

Guessing at his thoughts, Mitrian reached for the message. 'We'll clean up later. Let's take care of this first.'

Reluctantly, Arduwyn surrendered the message.

Mitrian opened it. Neat rows of lettering filled her vision, the only smudges from dirty fingerprints in the margins. *Arduwyn said something about poor handwriting and smearing.* Mitrian started to contradict him but closed her mouth before the words came out. *I've seen it before, men too proud to admit they can't read.* Santagithi required his traders and officers to learn to read at least the common trading tongue, and he encouraged his other citizens to learn as well. Any guard hoping for promotion made the effort. Those unable to understand the complexities of written language often tried to hide their ignorance behind elaborate lies. *No need to embarrass Arduwyn.*

Arduwyn fidgeted at Mitrian's delay.

Clearing her throat, Mitrian read aloud:

Dear Arduwyn:

I know how much the forests mean to you and how they call you with a passion no woman can match. I always knew you would leave us but always expected you would say 'good-bye.' We've been friends too long for me to hold such an offense against you. I forgive you. For Bel, it's not so easy. She misses your stories, and, I suspect, the company you were to her those days you didn't hunt. Rusha keeps asking about her Uncle 'dune.

I hope this letter finds you well, if it finds you at all. Things are not so good for me. I've just discovered I have the Trembles. I'm still getting around, and I should be able to continue working for the next few months or years. Eventually, we all know it will kill me. I have no family to take in Bel, and hers lives so far away. I apologize for laying such a burden on you, but I can think of no one else I would trust with the lives and future of my family. If you can find the time, please come back. I'd like to see you one more time before I die.

Mitrian could not make out the signature. 'It's signed by someone whose name begins with K.' She glanced up at Arduwyn.

Tears blurred the hunter's dark eyes, and he turned away.

Garn flipped the meat, the brief sizzle and plop loud in a suddenly uncomfortable silence.

Arduwyn's sobs disarmed Mitrian. She had never seen a man cry openly before. Her townsfolk would look upon it as a sign of weakness. She imagined he was mourning the health of his dying friend, but, ignorant of the hunter's past, she felt uncertain how to comfort him. She knelt beside him. 'This person who wrote the letter. She was an old friend?'

'He. Kantar is a he.' Arduwyn avoided Mitrian's gaze, hands clenched over his face. 'We grew up together.'

'I understand,' Mitrian said. She started to rise, believing Arduwyn might prefer being alone with his sorrow.

But Arduwyn caught Mitrian's forearm and tugged her back down beside him. He met her gaze directly, his eyes soft and brown, bewildered as a yearling lamb's. 'I need to talk to someone. May I?'

Mitrian nodded, shocked that Arduwyn would choose to confide in a stranger.

'Kantar has a wife, Bel, and three children.' Arduwyn looked away. 'The one he mentioned, Rusha, she's the youngest. I lived with them in Pudar for a time.'

Mitrian patted Arduwyn's hand encouragingly. By the fire, Garn appeared annoyed by their closeness, but he simply listened, saying nothing.

'Bel is plump, dark-haired, strong. Not pretty by some standards, but attractive in other ways.' Arduwyn kicked at a rock outcropping, still evading Mitrian's eyes. 'She was Kantar's wife. I wanted to like her, so I made every effort to get to know her.' He fell silent.

'And?' Mitrian prompted.

'And,' Arduwyn finished, 'I liked her. I liked her a lot.' He raised his head as if to meet Mitrian's eyes at last, but his gaze rolled beyond her to the fire. 'And she liked me.'

Understanding seeped slowly into Mitrian's brain. 'You slept with her,' she guessed, not wanting to drag out the conversation any longer than necessary.

'Firfan, yes.' Arduwyn blasphemed a god unfamiliar to Mitrian, and he seemed more serene for having confessed the sin. 'Bel's a wonderful woman, and I couldn't trust myself not to do it again. But Kantar's wife . . .' He choked on the words. 'I had to leave.'

Now Arduwyn met and held Mitrian's gaze, his expression pleading.

Mitrian knew he wanted advice, but she did not feel qualified to give it. She had heard enough town gossip to know the unmarried men and women often risked sex; Listar's attempts brought the idea vividly home. Occasionally, an unexpected pregnancy preceded marriage, surrounded by whispered condemnations of the mother or speculations about the father. Mitrian had even learned to accept that the guards who accompanied Nantel to the west often cheated on their wives. But she doubted any man would forgive his friend sleeping with his woman. The only instance she could recall had resulted in one guard challenging and killing the other.

To Garn, the answer was simple. He spoke with confidence, as if he had the only solution and it was obvious. 'You take care of your responsibilities. That woman needs you, and that man deserves to see his friend one more time. You owe him that courtesy. Then . . .'

A snarl entered Garn's voice '. . . you never lie with another man's woman again.'

Arduwyn sagged, but Garn pursued, relentless.

'Having a woman is a privilege not every man has. There's no excuse for mistreating her. If you think you're worthy of Bel, marry her and leave the other women alone. If you're not, let a better man have her.' Piece finished, Garn returned to the fire.

Mitrian stared, more surprised by Garn's words than by Arduwyn's abashed silence. She knew his romantic ideals came from living in a cage, deprived of the simple luxuries most men looked upon as rights. Since their argument the previous night, Garn had not mentioned her decision to return home. Yet his tirade made it clear that it pained him. Unnerved, Mitrian returned her attention to Arduwyn. 'Did that help?'

Arduwyn did not address Mitrian's question directly but his words were as much answer as statement. He took the parchment from Mitrian and crumpled it in his fist. 'I'm going back to Pudar.'

Pudar. Arduwyn's words gave Mitrian an idea. *As much as I need an escort home, Garn could use someone to help him adjust to freedom and the Westlands.* She glanced over Arduwyn's frail frame doubtfully. *He'll be more useful to Garn as a guide than to me as a bodyguard.* 'Pudar? What a coincidence. That's where Garn's headed.'

Garn jerked up his head, obviously displeased with Mitrian's assertion.

Undaunted, Mitrian continued, phrasing her request to try to please both men. 'Garn doesn't speak the Western tongue, and he's never been out of our city before. He could use a guide to lead him as far west as possible, especially one who knows how to gather food and find water.'

Garn's face crinkled in thought, and Arduwyn's expression became wary. 'I'm used to traveling alone,' the hunter asserted. 'Fast and quietly in the woods. I'm not interested.'

Mitrian frowned, gathering her thoughts. After manipulating Rache into sword lessons, Nantel into training her with a bow, and Listar into forging a sword, she had developed a certain confidence in her ability to persuade. Arduwyn's caution and familiarity with the West and his quick and winning confidences seemed too useful to discard without a fight. She glanced at the pile of deer innards, nose bunching in disgust, and the sight gave her an idea. 'Garn, your clothes are already dirty. Would you mind throwing this stuff somewhere so we don't have to smell it while we're eating?'

Garn nodded good-naturedly, gathered the guts, and headed into the glade.

Arduwyn was not so easily fooled. A tolerant smile formed on his features. The moment Garn stepped beyond earshot, he spoke. 'What did you want to talk about?'

Time limited, Mitrian did not mince words. Opening the pouch of gems that Garn had stolen from her room, she plucked out the largest gem from the remaining collection, a fist-sized garnet, its grainy surface casting ruddy reflections on her palm.

Arduwyn's lips parted. He pursed them quickly, but not before revealing his interest in her proposition.

'I can pay,' Mitrian said unnecessarily. 'In advance.' She offered the stone.

Arduwyn's fingers headed for it instinctively. He stopped before touching it, and his hand retreated. He smiled at some private thought. 'Why would you pay me to travel with Garn?'

Mitrian wriggled her fingers, bobbling the garnet enticingly. 'Does it matter?'

'Yes.' Arduwyn looked off in the direction Garn had taken. 'Very much. For all the gem's worth, my life is worth more.' He twisted back, pointing at the garnet. 'How many enemies would this buy me?'

Mitrian closed her fist over the garnet. 'None necessarily.' She sighed. Arduwyn deserved as much of the truth as she could give him. *He was honest with us, sharing his embarrassing secret. I've come too far to give up now.* Another thought made her draw in her breath. *Besides, I might have just gotten him interested enough to continue on to the town and see how much my father would pay to lead the guards to Garn.* 'Look, the truth is that Garn's been sheltered. He's never left home. He's never had to get his own food or water. He only knows one language. He's never had to bargain or deal much with people.' Measuring her words carefully, Mitrian did not notice she had described herself nearly as well as Garn.

Arduwyn made an impatient gesture. 'Garn was a slave, wasn't he?'

Mitrian gaped, too stunned to care that her expression gave away the truth. 'How could you possibly know that?'

Arduwyn combed down a spiky, red lock with his fingers. 'I've taught myself to notice things. Those scars on Garn's wrists looked like chain marks to me.' He shrugged. 'Mind you, that doesn't bother me. Most of the cities I consider worth living in don't have slavery. Pudar is one, and it's a good place to get lost in, too. The people are too used to strangers to question.' He glanced at Mitrian. Then, apparently realizing his words had completely disarmed her, he continued. 'What I need to know is who Garn's enemies are, how strong, and if they caught us, would they spare me. For that much money, I can understand a certain amount of danger. But my death's going to have to cost you more, and I'd kill myself before I'd let anyone lock me in a cage.'

As adamant as Arduwyn sounded, Mitrian almost expected him to end his statement with 'again.' For now, she let the matter rest and tried to address all the concerns he had raised. 'First, I'm not certain anyone is chasing Garn, though it wouldn't surprise me. Once I get home, I can call off the pursuit. Second, even if they caught up with Garn, no one would try to make you into a slave.' The image of the skinny, little archer as a gladiator was so humorous, Mitrian barely suppressed a laugh. 'If a fight started and you didn't attack, I don't believe anyone would hurt you. Third, I've seen Garn in the woods. He can move as quietly as an animal. I don't think he'll hamper you. Fourth, I'm willing to pay you vast sums of money. What more do you need?' Again, she offered the garnet.

This time, Arduwyn scooped the gemstone from Mitrian's hand and placed it in his pocket. 'All right. I suppose Garn's presence ought to keep me safe from muggers in the towns. I like being alone, but sometimes it's nice to have someone to talk with, too.' His words seemed more for convincing himself than explaining to Mitrian.

A smile of excitement touched Mitrian's features. Finally, everything seemed to have fallen into place. *Garn's in good hands. We're no longer hungry. I have my special sword, and I've performed Shadimar's act of defiance.* With the other concerns settled, Mitrian wondered how the Wizard's magic would work. *Will my father have changed his mind about women and swords?* Mitrian shook her head, unable to picture the possibility. *Perhaps the war will threaten our town, and we'll need every sword arm, no matter how untried their skills.*

Sudden fear gripped Mitrian. Her mind created images she could not shake. She pictured cruel, dark soldiers swarming upon her friends and family, the Easterners' sword skills crude but as deadly as the Strinian barbarians she had seen by Shadimar's magic. The men of her village sprang to the attack, some with nothing but the tools of their trades: Listar swung his father's hammer, his strokes frantic, the butcher hacked a bloodstained cleaver in strong but wild arcs, the farmers used only their picks and hoes. Women's screams and wolf howls echoed down the streets Mitrian had known from childhood. Again, she saw the bandit Garn had disemboweled writhing on the stone, but her mind gave him Rache's familiar features. *Not Rache. Please, gods, not Rache.* Terror ground through her. Gritting her teeth, she forced her thoughts from the illusion. *Maybe my father's right. War is not for women.* As the visual imagery faded, Mitrian calmed, and the idea ached within her. *War is not a pleasure; it's a necessity. I know how to fight, and I know how to do it well. It's my responsibility to help my town and the Westlands in any way I can, no matter the cost.*

Apparently realizing their conversation was finished, Arduwyn slipped away to tend to dinner. Mitrian scarcely noticed. Her life had turned upside down just in the days since Shadimar gave her 'the only magic sword of the Eastern, Western, and faerie worlds.' *I've come of age. I've seen war and death.* Though both frightening and beautiful, Mitrian's night with Garn seemed to pale in comparison, a grand passage into womanhood dwarfed by larger concerns. *And why did the Wizard choose me to wield the sword?* At first, she had accepted the reason that Shadimar had traded it for the sapphire he had named the Pica Stone. *But he came into my room and took it without awakening me. Why buy it from me when he could so easily steal it?* Mitrian sighed, doubting she would ever discover the truth. One thing seemed certain; she had no choice anymore but to trust the Wizard's words. *Somehow, I'm going to war. For the sake of my life and those of my friends, I can't be afraid to kill.* For now, she put aside the threat of Shadimar's prediction that she would kill a friend, the image too vast and appalling to contemplate.

Arduwyn's call cut through Mitrian's musings. 'Time to eat.'

Mitrian turned, still haunted by her thoughts. She headed back toward the fire.

Mar Lon did not know how long he sat in his chair in the Rozmathian tavern, but the arm beneath his head had gone past pain to numbness; his body had ceased to register the presence of the *lonriset* in his lap. Slowly, he raised his head. The tavern crowd had thinned. Sunlight no longer streamed through the windows. Only scattered candles lit the room, but even those looked painfully bright after hours of self-inflicted blindness. Sensation returned to Mar Lon's arm in a rush of pins and needles that made him grunt. He gritted his teeth, waiting for the ache to subside and coherent thought to return.

Gradually, the pain faded to a fuzzy throbbing, and Mar Lon noticed he had company for the first time. An elderly man sat in the chair directly across from the bard. His hair had turned gray, masking its original color. Creases marred what might once have been a handsome face, and skin sagged around his cheekbones. Deeply etched crow's-feet made the eyes seem squinted and sunken. He reclined in his seat, his gaze squarely on Mar Lon, occasionally pausing to sip from a mug.

'Hello.' Mar Lon straightened, surprised by the company.

In reply, the other nodded.

'I'm Mar Lon,' the bard said, hoping to elicit the same courtesy from the stranger.

The elder obliged. 'Tyrle.'

Accustomed to playing with words, Mar Lon considered the spelling. The stranger gave it the Eastern pronunciation. 'Tie-*ar*-lay,' though it did not seem like any Eastern name Mar Lon had heard. In the North, it would have meant 'present from the god Tyr' and been articulated as '*Teer*-li,' with the last syllable scarcely audible.

'Tyrle, pleased to meet you.' In Mar Lon's Western accent, it came out more like '*Tur*-lee.' The oddity of the name clued him to take a closer look at the stranger. In the dimness of the tavern, Tyrle's eyes seemed nearly invisible, but Mar Lon caught a faint glimmer of watery paleness. Obviously, this man was, at most, half-bred Eastern.

Tyrle set down his mug. 'Do you really believe you can overcome generations of prejudice and breeding? Surely you don't believe one young man can stop a war.'

Mar Lon shifted position, sending the lonriset into a dangerous slide toward the floor. He caught it against his knees, hauling it safely back into his lap. 'I have to try.' Resolve returned with the verbal challenge. 'If I can only find the right words, the right tune, I can get them to see that we can accomplish the same goals with trade and cooperation. Imagine a world fully at peace.' He made a grand gesture, buoyed by the picture his own words conjured. 'No more hunger. No more wars.'

Tyrle seemed unimpressed. 'It's good that you've chosen to do some traveling, Mar Lon.' He gave the name its proper, Western pronunciation. 'Neither geography nor the laws of either culture encourage intermingling of our races. But you have much to learn about people.'

Mar Lon balanced the lonriset beside his chair, his feelings mixed. He felt certain he could learn much from Tyrle. Westerners who visited the Eastland even once were rare enough. Aside from Renshai, Mar Lon had never heard of a Northman setting foot in the East, let alone living there; yet Tyrle's name and blue eyes gave the bard pause. Still, Mar Lon could not help feeling insulted by Tyrle's slight against his knowledge. 'We all have the same needs: food, shelter, and loved ones.'

'Basic needs, perhaps. But that's too simplified. So long as men can think, they will always have the need to believe in causes and higher purposes.'

'I don't see your point.'

'It's very easy really.' Tyrle took another sip of beer. 'Unlike animals, men can understand and, thus, fear death. It's a cruel burden inflicted by Sheriva or Ruaidhri or Odin or nature or whatever theology you believe in. The result is, each man has this irresistible need to leave his mark on the world, to prove that he lived and that he did not die in vain.' He drained the mug. 'The only way to do that is to dedicate your life to a cause, whether it's religion, tribe, country, family, self, *or peace*, and to believe that cause takes precedence over all other causes.' Tyrle set the mug down, wiping his mouth with the back of his sleeve. 'Then, to give your cause meaning, you have to believe all other causes are inferior, along with the people who champion them.'

'That's not right.' Mar Lon's experiences told him that at least part of Tyrle's explanation was true. Imbued with evil, the Easterners seemed self-dedicated to a man, and the Northerners had an unshakable devotion to tribe and family. 'We could all learn to respect one another's causes, even if we don't believe in them ourselves.'

'Maybe,' Tyrle said, though the partial agreement sounded grudging and the words that followed denied the possibility. '*If* there wasn't this driving need for each man to believe that his cause is *the* cause. And to prove it. The slave needs to believe that he is the fastest and strongest worker, that he is secretly smarter than his captors, or that his god or gods will come and crush those of his oppressors. The kings in Stalmize, Nordmir, and Béarn each believes himself the one and only, true, divinely-appointed ruler.' His voice became a whiny parody. 'My god is bigger than your gods. My family deserves more food than your family. This finger's breadth of land should belong to me.'

Tyrle struck closer to home. 'Do you truly believe that you have some sort of new idea? Do you have the arrogance to think you're the first person who ever considered unity and peace? There's not a man nor, I'd venture to guess, a woman who hasn't had the same idea in his or her youth. Peace. Only with time and observation, they come to learn that the differences between people become more, not less, defined. It's not enough to understand one another. To achieve peace, you'd first have to overcome each man's need to prove his cause's superiority. I don't think that's possible.'

'Of course, it's possible.' Tyrle's opposition fueled Mar Lon's fervor. 'All it would take is for people like you to stop thinking it's impossible. And well worth the effort if it means every man would put aside his weapons. We could focus on the things we have in common, to learn about each other's causes.'

Tyrle laughed. 'You're singing to the wrong crowd, minstrel.'

Mar Lon knew he was overstepping his boundaries as a bard by slipping from the role of listener to teacher, but he could not let Tyrle's misconceptions go unchallenged. 'World peace, Tyrle! How could anyone possibly believe this would be a bad thing ? How could any intelligent person be against it ?'

'It's not a matter of being for or against peace.' Tyrle rolled the empty mug from hand to hand. 'Clearly, war isn't necessarily good or evil. And neither is peace. If so, the Easterners would be constantly at war and the Northerners constantly at peace. War brings change and the need to rethink causes. Strategy spurs creative thought and invention. To some, it brings profit.' Tyrle cupped both hands around his mug. 'Think about it. If war was evil, the Easterners would have enslaved the Northerners by force. The peaceful North-erners would never rise against their captors. The Northmen slaves to the Easterners' causes.' Tyrle spread his arms to indicate a grand solution. 'Ultimate peace.'

The image made Mar Lon shiver. 'That would be evil.'

'Exactly.' Tyrle let his hands fall to the table. '*Evil* ultimate peace. What a concept.'

Mar Lon looked up. His musical talent had always gained him awe, thanks, and respect. He had little experience with being mocked. Yet the elder's words brought home other circumstances he had never thought to doubt before his arrival in the Eastlands. Once before, he had questioned Odin's system of balance and the oppo-sition of the Wizards. This time, he looked at it from the perspective of the men beneath its rule. *Pure evil and pure good may have meaning to the gods and Wizards but not to mortals.* Mar Lon had never met the Southern Wizard, Carcophan, but stories led him to wonder if even the champion of evil were wholly evil himself. *After all, the Wizards begin as mortals.*

Still, Mar Lon clung to his hopes for peace. 'I appreciate all you've taught me. You understand that I have to try, and I hope you'll help me. Try believing in peace. See what happens.'

Tyrle rose, smiling. 'Mar Lon, you've chosen your cause. I'm not sure it fits you, and I fear it will destroy you. But I wish you all the luck in the world.' He headed for the door.

Mar Lon raised his *lonriset* and, amid the noises of revelry, began to compose a new song.

11 Golden-Haired Demon

As the day dragged into late morning, Mitrian sympathized with Garn's impatience to move onward. Unwilling to waste a commodity as valuable as meat or to let a forest creature die in vain, Arduwyn insisted on the full day it would take to jerk the meat. Mitrian brought the men to a compromise that pleased neither. Garn waited while Arduwyn peppered and packed the venison for the trip, and the horse grazed the scraggly vegetation of the glade.

Mitrian, Garn, and Arduwyn headed off before midday, the archer leading his donkey, grumbling about spoilage, Garn guiding the horse through the mountain passes and sulking over wasted time. Mitrian ignored both men, usually walking between them, sitting on the horse's back when the terrain grew too uncomfortable for her sandaled feet.

By evening, they reached the Northern boundary of the Granite Hills. The sun hovered above the western horizon, its beam radiating over a cluster of thatch-roofed buildings. Though this town sported no wall, the huddled arrangement of dwellings appeared defensible, and distant dots that were people walked the streets.

Arduwyn stopped at the top of the last rise, looking down over the Northern town. 'Exactly what supplies do you need?'

Mitrian rattled through the list she had constructed in her mind as they traveled. 'Food that will keep and something to hold it. Water. Clothing.' She swept a hand over her sleeping gown and tattered sandals, then gestured at Garn's secondhand buckskins, crinkling her nose at the mixed odors of sweat and deer guts. 'Fresh horses.'

'One horse,' Arduwyn corrected. 'For you. Traveling the forests is a lot quieter and easier on foot.'

Garn glared at Arduwyn, opening his mouth as if to protest.

The hunter finished forcefully. 'Especially if we're being pursued by others on horseback.'

Garn closed his mouth, obviously surprised by Arduwyn's knowledge of possible pursuit and willing to listen to the hunter's explanation.

'There are places horses can't maneuver but we can. Between the trunks we'll need to move at a walk anyway. Why leave any more evidence than necessary?'

Garn looked at Mitrian who nodded her agreement. Deferring to his companions' judgment, Garn turned his attention back to the town.

Arduwyn folded his donkey's ear, scratching absently behind it with his other hand. 'I'll get the supplies, but I work alone.'

'Work alone?' Mitrian regarded Arduwyn curiously. 'What does that mean?'

Arduwyn eyed the town intently, as if measuring its defenses and plotting war strategy. 'I've stood on both sides of a selling table, and I pride myself on getting the best of a bargain in either case. Just the presence of a woman can double the prices.'

'Really?' The statement floored Mitrian. In Santagithi's Town, it seemed exactly the opposite, particularly with the spice seller who always had a special deal when her mother came to his shop. *Of course, I've never had to bargain.* She recalled Nantel's stories of Pudar's rapid-fire haggling and how a slick-tongued salesman could sell him junk he did not want for more money than he could purchase it for back home. Other times, the men boasted of deals they had put together by double-teaming the merchants. In Santagithi's Town, the prices were set fairly and generally paid without a struggle. For the cooper to slight the blacksmith meant being treated in kind when the time came to buy barrel hoops or a new knife.

'Really,' Arduwyn confirmed. He released Stubby's ear, still staring out over the town. 'I wouldn't mind having Garn along, for protection at least, but I'd rather I was alone than that you were.'

Mitrian nodded in agreement. Not yet ready to confess her feelings for Garn, she had convinced herself that the danger of bandits and other unseen perils in the Granite Hills was the major reason she had waited for a horse and supplies before heading home. *Maybe I can hire an escort while we're in a town.* 'So you want us to wait here?'

'No.' Reluctantly, Arduwyn pulled his gaze from the town to confront Mitrian. 'I'd rather you waited in town, so I can find you if I need money or get into trouble. A village this small probably won't have an inn, but they may have a meeting house or a tavern.'

'Money?' Mitrian reached for the pouch of gems in her pocket. 'Of course, I'll give you money. I don't expect you to pay for our supplies.'

Arduwyn frowned, brushing away her offer. 'We can settle up later. I do better when I'm limited by what I have in my pocket. If I don't have it, I can't spend it.' He patted the packet of deer meat strapped to his donkey's back. 'Between the venison and trading your horse, I think I may manage to buy everything we need.' He considered aloud. 'I don't speak much Northern, which may work against me, but I don't imagine they see a lot of fresh meat this close to the mountains.' He considered. 'I don't suppose either of you speaks the Northern tongue ?'

Mitrian shook her head.

'You take Stubs. I'll take the horse.' Arduwyn traded lead lines with Garn. 'Let's go.' He started down the final crest, dislodging a line of stones with his first step.

Garn and Mitrian followed.

'Have you ever been in the Northlands before ?' Arduwyn called over his shoulder.

'No.' Mitrian answered for them both.

'Well, watch yourselves. They like to fight, and they don't care much for strangers.'

Mitrian looked up quickly, not liking the sound of Arduwyn's description, but he added, apparently to put them at ease, 'So long as you're polite and don't let their stares or whispers bother you, there shouldn't be a problem.'

Shortly, the three arrived at the border of the town. Arduwyn motioned them toward the main thoroughfare. 'Look for something well-lit with people going in and out. It may not look like much.' Without awaiting a reply, he disappeared down a side road.

Alone with Garn on foreign streets, Mitrian was suddenly gripped by doubt. *I just gave money and my horse to a stranger I met this morning. What's to stop Arduwyn from disappearing now that he's gotten rid of us ?* As soon as the thought surfaced, Mitrian realized it was paranoia. *If he wanted to cheat us, why didn't he take the money I offered ? And why would he leave us his beast ?* Mitrian examined Stubs, who was standing obediently behind Garn. The woman had no idea what a donkey should look like, but this one seemed healthy. Its thick gray fur appeared clean, its dark eyes deep and clear. *My instincts for people are usually good, and they tell me to trust Arduwyn.* Mitrian started down the roadway, past rows of darkened, mud-chinked cottages.

Few people roamed the streets, but the ones who did stared, nudging one another and passing comments Mitrian could not hear. Garn tensed at her side, his head swiveling like a trapped animal's. Tiring of searching at random, Mitrian approached a woman staring from the door of a cottage.

As Mitrian neared, the woman closed the door to a slit and peered out suspiciously.

Mitrian stopped just close enough so the woman could hear her without her having to shout. 'Please, could you tell me where to find a tavern or a meeting hall?'

The woman opened the door far enough to make a throwaway gesture. She said nothing.

Uncertain of the meaning, Mitrian tried again. 'An inn?'

The woman repeated the gesture, this time accompanied by a short burst of speech in a singsong language.

She doesn't understand me. Mitrian considered the best way to overcome the communication gap. *Signals.* She curled her fingers as if around a mug, then tipped it to her mouth and pretended to drink.

The woman's lips twitched, but the smile never formed. She pointed farther down the road, raising three fingers, apparently to indicate how many dwellings Mitrian would need to pass. Retracting her hand, she nudged the door back to a crack, watching.

Mitrian waved her thanks and returned to Garn. 'We're headed the right way.'

Garn nodded, having seen most of the conversation from the street. As they walked along the roadway, he seemed as edgy as the Northern woman. Obviously, he had never set foot in a tavern before, and Mitrian thought it wise not to admit that she had never done so either. *No need to upset him any more than he already is.*

Garn and Mitrian passed two darkened cottages. As they rounded the second, they came upon a building in the same simple style, but slightly larger than the family dwellings. Light flickered, warped through thick glass windows. Smoke curled from the chimney. As they watched, the door banged open, and two men exited, speaking in loud tones. One staggered, and neither seemed to notice Mitrian, Garn, and Stubs standing silently in the shadows. Noise escaped the building in an unfathomable roar. Then the door swept shut, cutting off the sound as abruptly as a knife. As the Northmen wandered away, Mitrian and Garn found themselves alone in the street.

'That's it?' Garn asked.

Mitrian guessed it was. 'Yes,' she said, disappointed by the tavern's appearance. The guards' stories of drunken levity, good ale, and wild companions had caused her to imagine something more glamorous than a shack. At least the tavern in Santagithi's Town had shuttered windows, fresh red paint, and a sign that identified it. 'Let's go.' *Maybe the inside will look more impressive.* She frowned, doubting the possibility, and headed for the door. Garn paused to tie the donkey's lead to a corner post.

Mitrian pulled open the door, momentarily blinded by all the lanterns and candles. Conversation rumbled, stilled to a hush, then resumed at a lower level. Mitrian did not bother to sift individual voices from the hubbub. They all spoke the Northern tongue.

Gradually, the room came into clear focus, as dingy inside as out. Nothing graced the chinked log walls. Benches lined the walls, barrels before them serving as tables. In the middle of the room, three regular tables stood with odd numbers of unmatched chairs around them. Currently, six Northmen sat around the central table, their leathers and homespun rimed with dirt and sweat, their faces red from the sun. Mitrian counted a total of nine more Northmen on the benches, sitting in groups of three. Directly across from the entrance, a door opened into the back room. A sinewy man dressed in red and brown leaned in the archway between the rooms, apparently the proprietor. Despite their obvious status as farmers and peasants, every man in the room had the raw-boned frame of a warrior, a curly yellow or reddish beard, and a sword at his hip.

Mitrian shuffled forward, convinced of Arduwyn's warning that Northmen loved to fight. In Santagithi's Town, aside from Rache, few of the off-duty guards and none of the civilians carried weapons. Not wanting to appear as inexperienced with taverns as she was, she forced herself not to gawk. The Northmen did not succeed as well as she. Some stared with obvious hostility in their hard, blue eyes. Others acted more furtive, studying Garn and Mitrian when they thought they went unobserved, then glancing away quickly when the couple's faces turned toward them.

Disconcerted by the Northmen's attention, Mitrian sat self-consciously on a bench near the doorway, avoiding their stares. Garn quickly joined her. He seemed less bothered by the gawking, returning the Northmen's regard glare for glare. He kept his right hand looped across his sword belt.

As Mitrian took her seat, the proprietor wandered over. He spoke in the Northern tongue.

Mitrian imitated the gesture the woman had used in the doorway to indicate she did not understand. 'I'm sorry,' she said slowly and distinctly, as if this would make him suddenly able to communicate with her. 'We don't speak the Northern language. Does anyone know the Western Trading tongue?' She addressed the proprietor, but her gaze traveled over every man in the tavern.

Every Northman looked away.

The proprietor hesitated, as if in consideration.

His expression confused Mitrian. *If he didn't understand me, he would have shrugged me off.* It seemed more as if he spoke the language but was trying to decide whether to admit that fact to Mitrian.

At length, the man nodded. 'I speak it,' he confessed, his accent so thick and musical, it took Mitrian several seconds to realize she understood him.

Mitrian tried to act casual, like she frequented taverns on a daily basis. 'Food?'

'Today it's goose.'

'Fine,' Mitrian said. 'And ale for us both.' She had never tasted anything stronger than watered wine, but the guards' description of ale made it sound like a mixture of fresh honey and nectar, and her own glimpses of the foaming, golden drink intrigued her.

'Pay in advance.' The proprietor held out his hand. 'Six mynten.'

It never occurred to Mitrian that the proprietor's insistence on immediate payment was anything but normal, so the insult was lost on her. 'I have no local coin.' She pulled the pouch of gems from her pocket, rummaged through, and selected a tiny ruby. She offered it. 'Will this do?'

The proprietor's nostrils flared, and the corners of his mouth curved upward. 'Very well. Yes.' He snatched the ruby and flicked it into his pocket. 'I'll be back with the food.' He turned and whisked back toward the kitchen.

The proprietor's acceptance must have satisfied his patrons. They returned to their food and drinks, their voices rising to their previous vigorous volume.

Garn remained silent. He took Mitrian's right hand in his left, obviously satisfied by her presence and not needing conversation.

Mitrian sighed raggedly and managed a smile. *This may work yet.*

The proprietor returned with a pair of crudely crafted tin mugs and set them on the barrel before Garn and Mitrian. 'The food will be along later.'

'Thank you.' Mitrian watched the proprietor retreat back through the doorway before turning her attention to the ale. White froth bubbled atop a viscous drink the color of clean straw.

Garn waited for Mitrian to take the first sip, apparently expecting her to give him clues to the proper way to drink it. Uncertain herself, Mitrian took a tentative sip. Winding up with only a tasteless mouthful of foam, she took a deeper gulp. The ale was thick, almost syrupy, raw and bitter. Mitrian gagged, covering it with a cough, then forced an even expression. Garn clutched his own mug, his features pinched, revealing the revulsion Mitrian fought to hide.

'Takes getting used to?' Garn suggested.

Mitrian nodded, thinking that after some of the meals the gladiators received, any drink that could distress Garn must be evil-tasting indeed.

Before Mitrian could reply with words, the outer door twitched open, and another Northman stepped into the tavern. Though just shy of average size for the men of Santagithi's Town, the newcomer seemed small, dwarfed by the meatier, local patrons. A fur-trimmed cloak covered stained leathers which had once been crisp and expensively tailored. A sword girded his left hip. Unlike the others, this Northman was clean-shaven and wore his hair cropped shorter than style should have allowed. White flecked his golden hair, and the creases in his face seemed to come more from age than hardship.

As before, all talk ceased, then resumed as whispers accompanied by sidelong glances. Mitrian felt a pang of pity. She could understand the patrons' speculations about herself and Garn, odd-looking strangers with another culture and language. But the Northmen's mistrust of one of their own seemed cruel. She imagined the stranger's discomfort, an aging soldier no longer confident of his abilities yet knowing he might have to prove himself to more than a dozen warriors.

Leaning toward Garn, Mitrian whispered her observations, forgetting for the moment that she was adding to the unwelcome atmosphere of the tavern.

But if the stranger knew the uneasiness Mitrian projected on him, he gave no sign. He seemed almost too casual, oblivious to the comments and actions of his peers. Removing his cloak, he tossed it across the back of a chair and sat, alone, at one of the tables.

Just as Mitrian wondered if the newcomer was deaf and blind, the proprietor approached him, saying something rapidly in Northern. His voice rose at the end in friendly inquiry.

The stranger looked up. 'Renshai,' he said.

Mitrian stiffened in surprise, certain she had misheard. Just as the members of an unfamiliar race can seem identical, the words of the Northman's musical language sounded the same in general timbre and pronunciation.

The proprietor laughed, and a chuckle swept through the ranks of his patrons. He addressed the stranger again.

In reply, the newcomer simply shrugged. When he did speak, his voice remained calm. He pointed toward a barrel with one finger, apparently ordering food and drink.

The proprietor's demeanor stiffened, and he looked down his nose at the aging newcomer. They exchanged a few more words before the proprietor held out his hand for money as he had done with Mitrian.

Every eye in the tavern watched expectantly as the older man drew out a fistful of copper coins, handed one to the proprietor and dropped the rest back into his pocket.

Though apparently only partially satisfied, the proprietor swept across the common room and into the kitchen.

Garn took a smaller sip of his ale. 'What do you think that was about?'

'I'm not sure,' Mitrian admitted. 'I guess he's from a different part of the North, maybe from a town that's not on friendly terms with this one.' Mitrian could not help siding with the stranger. He seemed so unsuspecting, as if he didn't realize he was the topic of conversation or the piece that jarred. 'It hardly seems fair, though, that this one fading soldier should have to take the blame for his entire village.'

'Tribe,' Garn corrected, his fingers wrapped around his mug. 'How old do you think he is?'

Mitrian studied the stranger's sturdy, coarsening features. Though no scars marred the man's face, he wore the serious, predatory expression of an experienced soldier. Despite the obvious white among his golden locks, his frame still looked hard, sinewy instead of sagging. So far, all his actions had seemed slow and careless, so she had not had a chance to assess him in her usual way, by agility of movement. But something about him gave the appearance of great age, and only several seconds of staring enabled Mitrian to figure out its source. Occasionally, his lips moved or his head twitched, seemingly in response to nothing, as if he carried on an internal conversation. The only other people she had known with this mannerism were ancient townsfolk who had grown senile or warriors who had taken too many blows to the head. She responded to Garn's question as if no time had passed. 'He's about forty, I guess.' Spoken aloud, it didn't sound ancient, though the stranger was still the oldest in the tavern by a decade. Only then, Mitrian considered Garn's original comment. Tearing her eyes from the stranger, she examined Garn curiously. 'You said "tribe." How did you know Northmen live in tribes?'

Garn's expression remained deeply sober. 'I told you, I spent a lot of time listening. I paid specific attention to details about my enemies.'

Garn's intention became instantly clear to Mitrian. There was only one Northman Garn could have considered his enemy. *Rache.* The realization ignited a frightening thought. *When Shadimar said I might kill a friend, did he mean I would do so directly? Maybe my decision to help Garn was the mistake. What if Garn and Rache meet in the future, and Garn kills Rache?* A shiver ran through Mitrian. Her hand struck her mug, and only a quick, steadying grab saved it from a spill. She tried to steer her mind away from such ideas, but not before she dared to wonder. *Could Garn beat Rache in a fair fight?* Rache certainly possessed more skill, but Mitrian had seen Garn bull through ability with strength. *And Rache can't use his legs.*

The reappearance of the bartender with a drink for the strange

Northman helped pull Mitrian from her uncomfortable thoughts. Logic intervened. *I can't judge everything I do by the possibility that it might cause someone else to harm a friend in the distant future. What my father did to Garn was wrong.* Mitrian studied the gladiator beside her. Though he lacked Rache's pale beauty, Garn's rugged features and bright green eyes held a mysterious handsomeness all their own. *I care deeply for Garn. And once I've gotten him far enough away, there's no reason to expect he and Rache will ever meet again.* The thought brought a strange sorrow.

As Mitrian laid her fears to rest, the atmosphere in the Northern tavern seemed to grow equally peaceful. The proprietor returned to his kitchen. The lone Northman took a pull at his drink then set it down, his gaze roving to the half-dozen locals at the table in the center of the common room. As Mitrian followed the man's focus of attention, one of the Northmen at the table beckoned the stranger with a crooked finger.

Ignore them. Mitrian tried to send a mental message to the stranger, certain nothing good could come of a direct confrontation. *You'll get yourself in trouble you can't handle.*

But the stranger accepted the invitation good-naturedly. Nudging aside his drink, he trotted over to the group of Northmen, his profile toward Garn and Mitrian.

The Northman who had signaled spun his chair to face the stranger. He said something in the Northern tongue, his words indecipherable, but his tone crisp with warning. Again, Mitrian thought she heard the term 'Renshai.'

The stranger remained unruffled. Nothing about him indicated he saw any danger in the situation. His gaze fixed on the speaker. He seemed oblivious to the Northman's five companions who had leaned toward the conversation, coiled and restless, the other nine locals on the benches, and Mitrian and Garn. His reply emerged composed and gentle.

Despite the caution of the stranger's delivery, his words inflamed the locals. The speaker stood, towering a full head taller than the older stranger. The locals tensed. Some hands clenched into fists. Others fell to sword hilts.

Mitrian measured the distance to the door. *This is none of our business. Best to leave before a fight breaks out.* She turned to say as much to Garn, but the ex-gladiator was gone. Too late, she saw him striding directly to the center of the conflict. The warning died in her throat. *The noble idiot. Now all three of us are going to die.*

Garn was halfway to the table before he spoke. 'You ugly, sniveling bunch of cowards! Leave him alone. Any girl could win a fight against a helpless old man.'

Mitrian cringed, realizing that, whatever else the guards had taught Garn, they had given him a volatile repertoire of insults. She was not certain he realized he had offended the stranger at least as much as the locals. She rose more hesitantly, hoping the Northmen could not understand Garn and that she could avert the battle before it started.

The older man wore a bemused smile.

One of the other Northmen at the table sprang to his feet. He shouted in the Western Trading tongue, 'Who the hell are you?' He examined Garn with the withering disdain of a farmer offered a sickly, shriveled pig. '*What* the hell are you? How come your hair's so dark? Someone shit on your head?'

Mitrian found the comment too stupid for contempt, but it enraged Garn. He crouched, growling deep in his throat.

Oddly, it was the aging stranger who brushed Garn's anger aside. 'Thank you for your stunning defense, but this isn't your fight.'

Garn seemed to take the words as a challenge. 'Not my fight? There's six of them. And that one just insulted me.' He jabbed a finger toward the Northman before him.

The old man shrugged, never losing the composure Mitrian had begun to believe was a permanent facade. 'Fine. You take the one who insulted you. I'll take the rest.'

If Mitrian had felt less concerned for Garn, she would have laughed. Quickly, she trotted to the table and seized Garn's arm. She spoke soothingly. 'There's no reason to fight here. Why doesn't everybody sit down, share a drink. I'll buy a round . . .'

One of the seated Northmen snickered. 'What's the matter, boy? Your wife afraid you'll get beat up?'

The local who had insulted Garn added, 'After we cut you and the old man into pieces, we'll drag her out in the woods and rape her till she screams for mercy.'

The bandits' attack still strong in her memory, Mitrian clamped her jaw shut. Her hand fell naturally to her hilt. Immediately, red rage suffused her, alien yet stronger than any emotion of her own. The Northman's laughter mocked her, as challenging as war drums. Before she could think, the demon had control. She whipped her sword from its sheath and slashed it across the Northman's belly. A scream tore the air. The man pitched to his knees, clutching at the intestines leaking from the wound. Completing the Renshai maneuver, Mitrian slammed her blade down on the injured man's head. He went taut, voice snapping off in mid-scream, and crashed to the floor, convulsing.

In a half-second that passed like an eternity, Mitrian realized what had happened. Garn stood, stunned. Then, as one, every sword rasped from its sheath, except one. A smile crawled over the stranger's features, and he did not draw.

'The bitch killed Thorwald !' One of the Northmen on the benches sprang at Mitrian. He spoke in the Northern tongue, but she did not stop to consider how she understood him. She tensed to meet the attack. But before it came, the unarmed stranger stepped quietly between them.

The attacker's sword hammered for the stranger's head. The older Northman moved with a speed that belied his age. His slapped the blade aside with his bare hand, grabbed the attacker's sword wrist in his other and used the local's own momentum to haul him off-balance. Committed forward, the attacker staggered. The older man ripped his grip backward, fingers grinding into pressure points. A second later, the older man held the sword, slicing it across the attacker's throat. The Northman clutched his neck, blood splashing between his fingers. He started to crumple, but the older man shoved him over backward, callously clearing the way for his next attack. The stranger crouched, clutching his opponent's sword, his own weapon still in its sheath.

To Mitrian, the old man's maneuver would have been too fast, audacious, and competent for belief, but the demon's battle madness and euphoria sent her to a dizzying height of excitement. *Renshai!* The demon identified his own at once. And, though accustomed to skill beyond most men's imaginings, the ability of the old man impressed even the demon in the Wizard's gems.

'Renshai !' This time, the cry issued from one of the Northmen, and the others echoed it like a battle chant.

Suddenly, Mitrian was forgotten as every man in the tavern converged on the aging stranger. The old Northman used a reverse grip to draw his own sword from his left hip with the hand on the same side. He blocked the first attack with his captured sword, thrusting his own beneath the other's guard and up under his rib cage. Even as other blades stabbed toward him, the older man flipped his grip to forehand. He flicked a double jab at another Northman. The local blocked the attack to his face, but the second sword pierced his abdomen. Without pausing to see whether his blow had landed, the Renshai spun, catching a Northman's blade in a cross block. Half a heartbeat later, he spun his right sword from the block and buried the other in his opponent's face. Three men lay dead before Mitrian had a moment to realize she was menaced, too. Others sprang for Garn.

One of the locals from the benches screamed down on Mitrian, apparently preferring her challenge to that of the man reaping his companions like weeds. The Northman's sword plummeted. Mitrian caught his blade on her own, and the force nearly drove her to her knees. Laughter rumbled above the bell of swordplay, the demon's joy escaping Mitrian's throat. Another numbing blow pounded Mitrian's blade. Rache's training had not prepared her for the actuality of combat, but the demon knew what to do. He shouted maneuvers she should try, but the names he spouted in Renshai held no meaning for her. She gained nothing from him but the battle madness that let her defend without thought and attack without conscience.

The Northman kept his strikes big and looping, relying on his superior strength to herd Mitrian backward. She met each attempt with a block or parry. The blows crashed against her sword, hard enough to make her arms ache. Her spine touched mud-chinked wood, pressing the sweaty sleeping gown against her back. She strove to create an opening and saw nothing but flashing steel. The demon's presence screamed a maneuver that echoed through her mind, but she could not understand him. The Northman's sword raced for her head.

Mitrian brought up her sword, but the blades never touched. She used the movement as a diversion, then ducked beneath his raised arms. Pivoting free, she cut at his side. The Northman blocked, redirecting the strike up and outward, a high maneuver. Instantly, Mitrian changed levels and slashed at his legs. It was the first low cut of the combat, and it caught her opponent off-guard. He leapt backward, but not before Mitrian's blade nipped across his shins.

The Northman crouched, his stance gone cautious. He had realized he was no longer facing an uncertain girl, but a woman finally coming to understand her combat training. Mitrian went on the offensive. She swept for his chest. He countered, stepping into her attack. The swords locked, the combatants close, and the man pressed. His superior weight and strength drove Mitrian backward, and a sudden shove slammed her into the wall. Breath surged from her lungs. Her consciousness quivered. Her legs went rubbery, and the demon's inspired blood lust turned fuzzy. The Northman raised his blade for a high stroke intended to split her.

Mitrian's head buzzed, the demon's anger stinging. As the Northman drew up his arms, she sprang in and underneath him. Too close, his sword tore harmlessly through the air where Mitrian had stood. She spun off behind him, whisking her sword back and across his thigh. Tendon severed, the muscle curled into a ball beneath his breeks. The Northman crashed to the floor. Rolling, he swung for Mitrian, but she stomped on his blade, pinning it to the floor.

'Kill him,' the demon hissed.

Mitrian felt like she was emerging from the depth of nightmare.

'Kill the enemy !' the demon said again, its voice in her mind filled with frustration. 'Don't hesitate too long.'

The edges of Mitrian's thoughts tinged to red. She struggled against the demon's command, needing to prove her free will to herself. She kept her gaze locked on the man before her, aware a glimpse of the carnage in the tavern would snap whatever control she still had. Apparently, the demon could infiltrate her mind ; it had filled her with images, battle madness, and had tried to delineate strategies. But it could not dominate the sword or her physical person. *Whatever killing I performed, I did by my own hand.* She shivered, sobered by the thought.

And your own skill, the demon added, though Mitrian did not share its pride.

'Mercy,' the man on the floor gasped. Sword disabled and unable to walk, he was nearly helpless.

Another voice joined the conversation. 'Show him the same mercy he and his people showed the women and children of our village.'

Engrossed with her own problems, Mitrian had almost forgotten she was not alone. She glanced toward the voice. The aging Renshai leaned against one of the barrels, casually sipping his ale as if oblivious to the scarlet splashes streaking the walls and floors and the powerful odor of fresh death. Across the room, Garn was engaged in a wild fistfight with the last of the Northmen. Bodies lay scattered across the floor, some of them in grotesque, folded positions.

A wave of sickness passed through Mitrian. She gagged, and the demon seized on her lapse. Hatred flared through her and, before she could think, she jabbed the point of her sword up and under the Northman's chin. His eyes closed, and he sagged.

Dropping her sword, Mitrian sank to the floor beside him. The intensity of demon-inspired killing rage sapped her of strength. As adrenaline ebbed, so did all emotion. Her limbs felt floppy. The realization of what she had done brought tears to her eyes. The mingled odors of blood, death, alcohol, and urine made her stomach lurch. She vomited until her gut emptied and her throat burned. The memory of the impact of her sword against flesh remained, a ghostly impression stamped into the muscles of her hand. She could feel it hovering, a tangible brand, imprinted for eternity. *I killed a man. Two men.*

Yet Mitrian dared not forget that was what she had wanted. *It's good, right?* She needed someone, something to confirm the question, yet her sword lay embedded in a dead Northman, and her own mind could not endorse what she saw as evil. And it seemed that the demon could only communicate when she made contact with the gems. She reached for the hilt but stopped short. *It made me crazy. It made me instigate a fight. Do I really want to touch it?*

The aging Renshai seemed to read Mitrian's thoughts. 'I instigated that fight, not you. You simply took the first life.'

Shocked by the man's insight and near duplication of her thoughts, Mitrian studied him again. His features appeared hard but handsome, framed by glimmering, golden hair, flecked with white. His blue-gray eyes chilled her. He no longer wore the helpless, innocent expression, though whether because he had lost it or whether, having seen him in action, Mitrian could no longer believe in it, she did not know. *Of course he acted calm and careless. He never perceived fifteen Northern warriors as a threat.* The idea seemed madness. *This man, this* Renshai *makes Rache's skill look paltry.* Mitrian's mind blanked. Had she not seen it with her own eyes, she could never have conceived of such a thing. She looked away. Needing something to center her concentration on, she counted bodies.

Panting, Garn drew up to the Renshai's side, his previously torn and fouled buckskins now even more so. 'Good fighting,' he said, the understatement so vast it sounded ridiculous.

'You, too. You've raised dirty fighting to an art form.' The Northman smiled to show he meant no offense. 'I've seen a lot, but this is the first time I've seen a man break an opponent's face with his forehead.'

Mitrian cringed, not daring to let her mind form the image. 'I only count fifteen bodies, including the proprietor. Someone's missing, probably gone for help. We'd better leave.'

The Northman tore a rag from a corpse's homespun and handed it to Mitrian. 'Here. Clean your sword.'

Mitrian accepted the cloth, glancing reluctantly at her sword. *Dare I touch it?* She knew she had to make a decision now. *Wield it and let it control my mind or use a normal sword and take the chance I'll freeze in combat.* Mitrian frowned. *My death can serve no one. For now, the sword and I need one another. Later, perhaps, I'll give it back to Shadimar.* Obediently, she hefted the weapon and cleaned the length of the blade. Beneath the layer of grime, the steel still shone, its edge honed and without a single notch or flaw. Disgustedly, she flung the dirty rag away.

The stranger said something in a language Mitrian did not understand.

At first, Mitrian thought the aging man was talking to himself, but the demon intervened. 'He said, "Well met, friend," in Renshai.'

Mitrian looked up.

'Tell him thank you.' The demon supplied the syllables for

Mitrian. But when she tried to imitate them, they sounded heavily accented and choppy.

The Northman laughed, returning to the trading tongue. 'I don't know whether to curse or love your teacher. You've not learned our language, and your swordcraft is far from adequate. But apparently even the Western Wizard can make mistakes: I'm not the last Renshai.' He clasped Mitrian's forearm in a gesture of greeting. 'My name is Colbey Calistinsson. We have a lot to discuss.'

Mitrian nodded, unable to think clearly through the maelstrom of questions that filled the void left in her mind by confusion and dispersing excitement. *Yes*, she thought. *More, I believe, than either of us realizes.*

The trio headed for the door.

12 White Assassins

A crazed swordsman who claimed to be Renshai and a pair of dark-haired foreigners. The description ran through Rache's mind until it became an obsession, a wheel of thought spinning with each landing of his horse's hooves. Sandwiched between the Granite Hills and the Northern forests, the road remained generally passable, even at a gallop. Pine trees and barren crags whisked past. The wind struck coldly against Rache's face, and anxiety drew that chill deep into his marrow. *They cut down a dozen warrior Northmen in as many heartbeats. A massacre. One survivor, a coward who ran.*

Rache tried to shake the memory of the Dvaulirian scout jabbering the news as he passed on his route to warn Vikerin. But the more Rache tried to focus on other things, the stronger his fixation grew, until it pushed all other thought from his mind. The scenery passed unheeded. Even Rache's usual natural alertness was dulled by the intensity of his concentration. *A couple of dark-haired strangers, male and female. And the descriptions fit Garn and Mitrian perfectly.* Rache frowned, forced to accept the fact that Mitrian seemed to be traveling free, willingly staying with Garn. *Maybe she's scared and clinging to the only man she has.* Yet that did not fit with what he had heard, that the two had banded together to kill. *Something's wrong here. I'm missing some piece of information that can fit this all together.*

Not daring to contemplate too long, Rache turned his thoughts to the Northman who had claimed Renshai kindred. *Obviously, he's lying. I'm the last Renshai. Episte confirmed that with an ear count.* Still, Rache could not discard the idea. According to the survivor from the tribal town of Dvaulir, a middle-aged Northman had bare-handedly disarmed a soldier and killed him with his own weapon, then murdered several more in the space of time it took the others to react. *Renshai.* Rache shook his head. *Even accounting for exaggeration, what else could he be?* More than a decade had elapsed since Rache had allowed his thoughts to dwell on a past he could not change. He dug deep into his memory for Episte's words: 'Eight Renshai missing, and I dared to hope. Then the other reports came in: four corpses charred beyond salvaging, mostly babies, three bodies lost in the Amirannak Sea. That left only one.' *Episte believed that one was me. All these years I never thought to question. Yet I was one of the bodies the Northmen counted as lost in the Amirannak!*

Understanding struck Rache as hard as a physical blow. Lost in his thoughts, he missed seeing the movement off to his left, the swipe of a sword at his horse's forelegs.

Rache felt the crash of impact; the blade bit deep into his horse's legs. The animal tumbled. Tied to the saddle, Rache was flipped with it. The horse landed on its side, Rache's left leg crushed beneath it, the pain racking through his shoulder and hip all but incapacitating. The horse thrashed, unable to gather its shattered front legs. Suddenly, two armed men rushed Rache, each white as bleached bone.

'Modi!' Rache gasped from habit. One sword lay trapped beneath him, its hilt gouging his waist. With a reversed grip, he managed to whip the other free with the hand on the same side.

The first attacker cut for Rache's face. Awkwardly, Rache blocked, jerking his head aside. *Desperate positions call for desperate measures.* Quick as a striking snake, he grabbed the man's leg in his left hand. He jerked, flinging the albino over his head. Rache slashed for the man as he sailed past and crashed into the horse's flailing hind legs. From the resistance, Rache knew his blade had met flesh, but he did not pause to check. Instead, he swung in a blind frenzy to back off his other opponent. The assassin sprang beyond sword range.

Now the man who had ambushed Rache approached from the direction of the horse's legs.

So there's three of them. Rache ignored the newcomer. *He can't get past my mount.* Rache hated letting his horse suffer, but the animal's panicked kicking was all that protected his legs. *Don't die on me now.*

Cautiously, the albino extracted his companion from the buffeting hind legs, assessing the situation with a single word in a language Rache did not speak.

Dead, Rache hoped. *Unconscious, at least, or he'd be screaming.*

While the albinos dragged their injured companion aside, Rache slashed free the strap that held his right leg. The increased mobility allowed him to draw his second sword. But before he could maneuver the sword's tip beneath the horse that pinned him, the assassins attacked, one from the front, the other from the back. Leading with their swords, they jabbed at Rache, careful to let only their blades fall within his reach. A sword in each fist, Rache rolled back and forth, parrying each stroke in a wild frenzy of movement, always keeping as much sword contact as possible. *Got to do something. Can't keep this up all day.* Rache's arm was already growing tired from fighting gravity in a sideways position, and each movement brought a new wave of pain from his leg. He was forced to strike twice as many blows as either opponent, all of them committed, fast, and frenzied.

I have to change the odds. Rache tensed. As the assassin in front of him stabbed, he waited until the lunge was almost completed before executing a parry that guided his enemy's blade to the dirt. Instead of blocking the other assassin's stroke, Rache dodged, smacking his second sword onto the grounded blade. The weapon jarred from the albino's grip. As Rache whipped around to counter the assassin behind him, he hurled the sword in his right fist. The sword hurtled, spearing through the albino's guts. The man crumpled, screaming.

Twisting back, Rache seized the grounded sword.

Weaponless, the remaining assassin backpedaled beyond Rache's reach.

Rache followed the man with his eyes, aware the last of the three would not underestimate him. The albino muttered a few words in his strange, guttural language; though spoken at normal volume, the sound muted to a whisper beneath the shrieks of his dying companion. Gently, the uninjured assassin hauled away his friend. The screams faded to moans and howls, then disappeared in the forest.

Alone, Rache used the tip of one sword to hack at the dirt beneath his writhing horse. Slowly, the earth yielded. But before Rache could chip away a path to his trapped leg, the albino returned, holding his companions' swords and a handful of rocks.

'What do you want from me?' Rache used the common trading tongue, the most widely spoken second language of the continent.

'I want you dead!' The assassin hurled a sword at Rache.

Having just used the maneuver himself, Rache was prepared. Easily, he parried the weapon in midair, smacking it to the ground in front of him. He retrieved it, aware he might find use for an extra weapon.

'I want you cut into pieces and fed to the ravens.' The albino pitched a rock at Rache's head, then another.

Rache batted each aside with his sword.

'It no longer matters that I was hired to kill you. You murdered my friends, and you're going to die.' Another two rocks sailed for Rache in rapid succession.

Rache knocked them aside. He doubted pointing out that the

assassins had attacked him, not the other way, would gain him any reprieve, so he did not bother to raise the issue. Usually, he frowned on chatting during combat but this wait and parry technique was slower than crossing swords. 'Hired to kill me ? Why ?'

The assassin made no reply. The remaining rocks spilled from his grip, and a warped smile crossed his features. Turning, he headed for the woods.

Ideas tumbled through Rache's mind. *What's he going for now? Reinforcements? More things to throw at me?* Reversing one of his swords, Rache set back to work burrowing beneath his horse. As its life's blood trickled into the dirt, the animal's fight became weaker, its kicks less furious. Rache did not delude himself. For all his sword skill, pinned and crippled, it would only take one boulder to crush him, one bow and a handful of arrows to finish him from a distance.

As the ground loosened, Rache managed to get the edge of his sword against the strap holding his leg to the saddle. Slicing it, he inched free. Movement splashed pain through his back and hips. He bit off a cry, unable to contain the grunt that followed. For an instant, the agony paralyzed him. *Pain is anger. Battle rage.* Gritting his teeth, Rache chose speed over dignity. *Modi!* Instead of a controlled crawl, he rolled toward the forest edge, pain flashing white sparks through his mind.

Rache had spun only halfway to the first trees on the edge of the woods when hoofbeats pounded through his ears. Hope rose, but it was guarded. *A friend? Another assassin?* Rache twisted for a better look, aware a Northern stranger might be just as apt to rob and finish him as to help him. He caught sight of the albino's features over the head of a huge, chestnut stallion.

Rache froze, aware he would need to judge his timing well. The odds seemed hopeless, but it never occurred to him to surrender. *The only cowardice in battle is dying without giving my enemy the best fight I can.* He forced the assassin's threat of dismemberment from his mind. *If I'm condemned to Hel, it won't be because I died a coward.*

The horse galloped toward Rache. Snide, confident, the assassin did not even bother to draw his weapon. The steel-shod hooves should serve well enough.

As the horse bore down upon him, Rache rolled, slashing. The albino ripped his mount aside, narrowly evading Rache's sword stroke. Wiser for the near disaster, he wheeled the beast for another pass.

Rache twisted, bulling through the pain. *Tree. I need a tree. The horse can't gallop through a tree.* Awkwardly, he half-rolled, half-slithered behind a pine, working into a sitting position as the assassin laughed.

'Yah, cripple !' The albino made the word sound like the basest insult. 'You'll tire before the horse does. The more trouble you give me, the more pieces I'll cut you into when this is over.' He awaited a reply.

Rache did not give one, unwilling to waste energy exchanging taunts.

Viciously, the assassin kicked his mount into a gallop. The horse whipped by Rache; this time its legs passed beyond sword range. The assassin's blade cut for Rache. The Renshai dodged. But before he could resettle himself, the horse made a pass from the opposite direction on the other side of the tree. This time Rache barely dragged himself aside in time. The horse whirled for another attack.

Rache tensed. But the assassin dismounted, casting about the ground as if in search of something. Rache flattened his back against the trunk, tucking his legs to the side. He watched intently as the albino hefted a boulder nearly the size of his head and carefully remounted with it. The horse surged toward Rache. As the gap between them closed, the assassin bowled the rock at Rache.

Rache dodged, too late. The stone caught him square in the chest as the horse raced past. Breath dashed from his lungs. Ribs snapped and impact sprawled him over backward. He screamed, the sound distant. Ringing obliterated the assassin's cry of triumph. Darkness pressed in from all sides. Strength drained from Rache in a rush, and the swords fell from his grip. Only one spark ignited through Rache's fading thoughts. *To lose consciousness is certain death.* Desperation strengthened his resolve. He clawed through the curtain that sapped his senses. Vision returned, slowly, waveringly, then the world came into blinding focus. A charging brown blur bore down on him.

Clutching the tree, Rache hauled himself to his knees. 'Modi !' he forced himself to scream aloud. But his reserves were already overdrawn, and the rush of battle madness scarcely powered an urgent lunge for the stirrup. Rache's fingers closed on leather and fabric, a piece of the saddle in his left hand, the assassin's pants leg in his right.

Surprised and frightened by the abrupt weight imbalance, the horse jerked to a stop and stiffened. Wildly, it back-stepped, throwing its head up. Tossed off-balance, the assassin tried to counter. Rache seized the moment. Using the strength of arms trained to serve as legs, he climbed the stirrup. Releasing his grip on the assassin's pants, he caught the man's belt and yanked. The man tumbled from his seat. An instant later, Rache let go of the saddle and dove on top of the fallen enemy.

Rache pinned the assassin's sword wrist with his left hand, then drove his right into the man's nose. Reversing the strike, he ripped his nails through the pale blue eyes.

The assassin screamed, hands clutching at his face. Finding a knife in the white man's belt, Rache drew, stabbing beneath the ribs and into the diaphragm: once, twice, three times. The screams died to breathless moans. Then the pain Rache had forced aside crushed in on him. Darkness hammered him, unyielding, and Rache scarcely managed to roll off the assassin before he lost consciousness.

Rache awakened in the gray wash of twilight and with a suddenness that stabbed pain through his entire body. Moaning, he rolled to his stomach and immediately wished he had not. The movement intensified the aches and throbbing, shooting a line of white hot agony along his spine. Each breath jabbed into his lungs. He moaned again.

Gradually, the pain settled into patterns. The dull throb of his left hip and shoulder seemed to come from abrasions. The back pain, though sharp, radiated off-center. *Torn muscles.* From the double stab of pain that accompanied every inhalation, he guessed two ribs had snapped. And bruises covered his body. Blood smeared his hands, little or none of it his own. *Nothing fatal.*

Having assessed his injuries, Rache turned his attention to his surroundings. The assassin's corpse sprawled within reach and the dark lump that was Rache's horse lay, unmoving, a few lengths beyond the body. Rache's swords sat beside the pine tree at the edge of the forest, the tip of one resting on the hilt of the other. The assassin's horse grazed by the roadside, its leg threaded through its own dangling reins.

Rache would have liked to have secured the horse, but the need to limit his movements and conserve strength sent him first to the assassin. He raised the knife, pressing his fingers to the dead man's neck. No pulse met his touch. Cleaning the blade on the albino's shirt, Rache slipped the knife into his own belt and rifled the dead man's pocket. *Someone hired him. Maybe I can find out who.* His search yielded only a handful of silvers, a mixture of Western and local coinage, and a crudely carved ivory figurine, vaguely man-shaped but lacking ears or hair and with a long, beaklike nose. Rache pocketed what he found, hoping but skeptical that the statuette might serve as a clue. *Professionals.* About this, he harbored no doubt. *Intelligent, careful plotting, working in threes, and revealing nothing, even when my death seemed a certainty.* Leaving the assassin, Rache crawled toward the dead horse. *I could hardly expect them to carry a contract with their employer's name. But why would anyone want me dead badly enough to hire assassins?*

No answer came to Rache as he drew up to his horse and levered his supplies from its back. Looping the strap across his shoulder, he wriggled painfully toward his swords. The only recent enemies he could recall making were on the battlefield where hatreds were short-lived and rarely personal. *And Garn, of course.* The idea made Rache smile, despite his discomfort. *Even if Garn could have managed the complexities of hiring assassins, he would never have had the time or opportunity. And if Mitrian is, in fact, with him freely and willingly, she would never have let him.* Arriving at the pine tree, Rache jabbed the swords into his sheaths. He headed for the horse. His thoughts seemed to have gone full circle, leaving him tangling with the problems that had so obsessed him as to make him carelessly fall into the assassins' well-set trap.

But this time, Rache forced his considerations onto the closer danger. *Who were these assassins?* Though not well-traveled, Rache had gained a reasonable grasp of racial differences from living in Santagithi's Town where the people came of diverse heritages. He could understand why the Vikerians had mistaken the assassins for Northmen; their fair, almost milky skin, pale eyes and blond hair fit no other racial group so well. But their sun-damaged cheeks suggested they came from a land of warmer weather, their hands seemed smaller and more delicate than the usually beefy-fisted Northmen. Their features were thicker, their noses shorter and broader. Aside from coloring, they seemed more suited to the far West or the East, or perhaps even as far south as Erythane.

Rache reached the horse. It was grazing placidly, having managed to extract its leg from the reins. Without help, heaving the pack to its back and scrambling up to its saddle seemed impossible. He recalled how the beast had panicked when it felt his weight on only one side, but he also remembered that it had frozen rather than bolted. Seizing the reins, he tugged. Unaccustomed to receiving commands from the ground, the animal balked at first. Then, gradually, it allowed itself to be led into the forest, placing its hooves carefully so as not to trample Rache's trailing legs. Hemmed in by trees, the animal pranced nervously but did not buck or run as Rache clambered up the side flaps and maneuvered himself and the pack into the saddle. He soon had the supplies secured. Trusting his own shifts of balance and the remaining strength in his thighs to keep him in place, Rache slapped the horse into a canter toward the tribal town of Dvaulir.

The delay bore down heavily on Rache's soul. *So close. I almost had Mitrian and Garn. Now they could be anywhere.* He realized something more. The survivor from the tavern had run before the battle was finished. *A dozen down, still some to go. Maybe Garn or the Northman claiming to be Renshai was killed. Or Mitrian.* Rache's heart skipped a beat, and his lips worried into a frown. None of the possibilities pleased him. *Of course, saving Mitrian's life takes precedence, but Garn is mine. To let anyone else kill him would be a tragedy.*

As the mountains flashed past, Rache turned his thoughts to the mysterious Northman. *If he is, in fact, Renshai, I should know him.* He considered the description the survivor had given. *About forty years old.* Mentally Rache added fifteen years to account for the Renshai's racial feature of appearing younger. *In his fifties? Possibly sixties.* Rache's frown deepened. The Renshai's recklessness and joy of battle invariably killed them by early adulthood. Aside from Episte, who had been rumored to be a hundred and, to Rache's childish assessment had seemed every day his age, the oldest Renshai Rache had known was his master, Colbey, then in his late forties. Excitement suffused Rache as the math worked itself out in his mind. *Late forties. Sixteen years later. It can't be. Of all of my people, Colbey was the one most certainly dead.*

Rache forced his mind back in time, contemplating events he had long ago tucked away in a pocket of consciousness he had vowed never to disturb. The tragedy on Devil's Island had come back to him in flashes too quick to deny and in dream, but never with the detail he called up now. As a boy, he had felt so certain of Colbey's demise that his adult self never thought to question. Now he remembered that his vision of Colbey on his deathbed came of childish delusion, not fact. Of all the Renshai, Colbey had always been the most audacious. He knew war and nothing else, no responsibilities but those of improving his battle craft and passing the knowledge to his students. In his younger, peaceful days, he would often leave Devil's Island, using an assumed identity to join distant tribal skirmishes or pirating raids. *It was far more likely that he set off on some personal adventure and completely missed the assault on Devil's Island.*

Still, Colbey's sudden and secretive departure did not seem to fit all the facts. Suspecting he did not have all the information necessary to draw an accurate conclusion, Rache turned his thoughts to Colbey. An image of his childhood hero filled his mind. In spar, the older man's every movement seemed crisp perfection; he could assess an opponent's repertoire in a single stroke. *Another chance to be trained by the greatest swordsman this world has seen?* Rache laughed, afraid to believe his luck. Then his responsibilities shifted to the forefront, and the smile died. *I should return home. I need to let Santagithi know Mitrian is in no danger. If she remembered even one of the Renshai maneuvers I taught her, Colbey will accept her as one of us. With Colbey's protection, Garn can't hurt her, and neither could half the armies of the West all gathered together.* Still, the memory of Santagithi's last command weighed heavily on him: 'If you don't return with my daughter, don't return at all.' *Surely, Colbey will bring Mitrian home. He'll want to reunite the Renshai as fully as possible, and Mitrian has no reason to guess I'm anywhere but in her father's town.*

Rache rode on, knowing he needed more information before making secure conclusions. Even the most skilled and agile warrior in the world could fall prey to bad luck, superior numbers, or a well-placed arrow. And, if pressed to his own defense, Colbey could not protect Mitrian, nor would he necessarily try.

Rache's arrival in Dvaulir forced him to set aside his thoughts. The incident in the tavern had put the town on alert. Three hard-faced soldiers armed with swords and spears met Rache at the border. 'Who are you, stranger?' The guard emphasized the last word, giving it the same distasteful pronunciation the assassin had used on 'cripple.' 'And what do you want here?'

Understanding the Dvaulirians' caution, Rache took no offense. 'My name is Rache.' The survivor's ride to inform the Vikerians of the events in the tavern suggested the two tribes were allies, at least for now. 'I'm coming from Vikerin. I'm a blood brother to their Nordmirian captain, Valr Kirin.'

The guards' expressions softened, but they remained rigid and at attention.

'Did the enemies who attacked your tavern escape?'

The guard who had spoken nodded curtly. 'Yes.'

'Do you have men to spare for the chase?'

'No.' One of the others answered forcefully, as if awaiting the question. 'Not this close to harvest.'

Rache guessed the unspoken part of the Dvaulirian's assertion. The loss of fifteen warriors would sorely weaken a tribe as small as the Dvaulir. In the North, where allies and enemies changed almost as frequently as the seasons, further weakening the village by sending more fighting men in pursuit would be madness. Rache could almost picture the leaders of neighboring tribes drawing straws to see who would get the privilege of attacking Dvaulir while its soldiers rode after a Renshai. 'I'd appreciate anything you can tell me about what direction they might have gone in or which pathways to try or to avoid.' Rache felt the Dvaulirians deserved an explanation. 'You see, the dark-haired man is an escaped slave and . . .'

The guard cut in with a brisk gesture of his spear. 'A gladiator. Yes, we know all that.'

The remainder of the description died in Rache's throat. *Did one of the Vikerians ride off ahead to tell them about me?* He shook his head, believing King Tenja would have had the courtesy to inform him. 'Who told you?'

'A group of Westerners came by soon after the murderers left. We spoke with their leader. He told us everything.'

Confusion rode Rache and a sense of discomfort, the source of which he dared not consider too carefully. Aware of the dangers of an invalid conclusion, he questioned further. 'Could you describe this leader?'

The guard studied Rache, as if trying to read the intent behind the inquiry. Then, apparently deciding to trust a Northener over a foreigner, he responded. 'Dark, curly hair, muddy eyes, strange features. He had a mustache but no beard.' He seemed amused by the combination.

Nantel. Horror rose first. *The fool will get all his men killed.* He could imagine Nantel attacking Garn, and Colbey slicing down Santagithi's guards in twos and threes, believing them enemies. Then outrage quivered in Rache's chest, flaring to wild anger. His face went hot, his features tightened, and he felt certain his cheeks had flamed to red. 'Thank you,' he said through gritted teeth. Savagely, he jerked his horse's head around, not wanting to subject the Dvaulirians to rage that was not their due. The animal wheeled with a startled snort, almost unseating him. The near-fall only fueled Rache's rage. *Santagithi sent Nantel!* Quickly, Rache reined into the mountains, out of the Northmen's sight, but not before his thighs clamped the horse so tightly, the little feeling left in his legs disappeared, the reins bit into the hollows of his knuckles, and his nails gouged into his palms.

Santagithi sent Nantel. Nantel! After sixteen years, this is the trust I get. Rache threw back his head, howling his frustration, hearing the echoes reverberate from the cliff faces. 'Damn you!' He screamed the words so loud, they burned his throat, his broken ribs stabbing his lungs. Pain only enraged him further. 'May all the gods damn you to Hel!' Seared by his general's treachery, he wanted to mean the words, but he could not. Too much affection had grown between Rache and his adopted home to degenerate into hatred in an instant, too much devotion to the town, too much love for its folk and respect for its leader. *So now the truth comes out. Let's all pity the poor, helpless cripple. Gods, Santagithi. Of all people, I thought you understood. But now I see it was all a lie, a game to you. Humor the dumb, pathetic invalid, then stab him in the back.*

Rache slammed a fist onto his knee, the force enough to overcome the strength in his thigh. Grip lost, his leg dangled for the instant it took to reestablish the hold. Another howl twisted from Rache's lips. In his fury, he wanted to leap down from the horse, draw his sword, and chop his nearly useless legs into pieces. Or to turn back and challenge the entire town of Dvaulir, slashing in blind fury until they hacked him down. But Rache maintained enough of a hold on reality to recognize the foolishness of either plan, aware he would need to regain control of his battlelike frenzy before he could make intelligent decisions. It came to him suddenly that he was utterly, fully alone.

Gradually, uncontrolled rage eased to a hurt that seemed to penetrate Rache. Santagithi's betrayal wounded him more deeply than any physical injury, an aching scar in an ego that had thrived on a loyalty so fierce he had pledged not just his life but his soul to the cause of Santagithi's Town. *And this is the faith I get in return.* Rache realized how useless a soldier he would make to a general who could not put trust in his abilities. *I'm of no further use to Santagithi, ever, but for myself I will do this thing: I will kill Garn. I will return Mitrian, and then . . .*

Rache's original thought was to find a glorious way to die, but it faded nearly as swiftly as it rose, and no thought replaced it. Eventually, he realized where his commitment lay. *I have to find Colbey. He won't treat me differently because of my legs.* Beneath Colbey's quiet perfection beat a heart devoid of mercy, a man so cruel at times that he shocked even the other Renshai, a race known for rampant slaughter and demoralizing opponents in war. *Colbey knows there's no quarter in battle. You fight your best or you die. My enemies won't pity me.* He thought back to his fight with the assassins, the many aches that followed him from that confrontation still a shrill reminder of their using his handicap against him. *And Colbey won't pity me either.*

The idea soothed. All anger drained from him, leaving only the throbbing of his many wounds and the deeper pain of Santagithi's mistrust.

Rache rode onward.

13 The Golden-Haired Devils from the North

Colbey could remember to the day when the madness had struck him. Called to the westernmost peaks of the Weathered Mountains by the Western Wizard, Tokar, Colbey had answered the summons quietly and without formality. Centuries ago, the Renshai had promised to supply their best warrior when Tokar deemed the time had come; and as fiercely loyal as the Renshai were to war and Valhalla, they held their vows equally sacred.

Tokar had indicated no need for urgency. Colbey recalled dawdling in his travels through Westlands he had not seen since his childhood when he'd roved in the midst of a wild band of conquerors. It took him a year to reach the mountain cave that served as Tokar's home. Only then did he discover that the Northmen had decimated Devil's Island and, according to Tokar, every Renshai but Colbey had died.

Now, as Colbey rushed through the mountain passes with Garn, Mitrian, and Arduwyn, grief pressed him again at the memory. *Dead. All of them dead.* At one time, Colbey had used the remembrance to inspire himself to fits of rage, but too many years had passed for the words to sting any longer. He glanced at Mitrian. *Tokar named me as the only survivor, and I never questioned. But there has to be at least one more.* Colbey picked his way over the ledges, more agile than any of his younger companions. He studied Mitrian, aware she could not have more than half Northern blood, and he doubted she bore that much. *She's not bred of Renshai which means whoever taught her also believed he or she was the last of our line.*

Colbey never knew whether the horror of his people's deaths had opened him to the insanity or whether to attribute it to the shock of interfering with a Wizard's ceremony no mortal should have seen. The memory came easily, terrifyingly vivid, his only wholly clear thought in the last decade and a half. He recalled a lush valley deep in the Weathered Mountains. The sky stretching between the peaks held the colors of a rainbow. Streaks of pale light threaded through the clouds like lightning. Tokar stood, sick and frail, racked with an illness he would not let Colbey treat with herbs. Despite that, the Wizard's aura was one of utter tranquillity.

Colbey recalled another man called Haim, aged by mortal years, yet a child compared with the centuries-old Wizard to whom he was apprenticed. Haim sat on a nearby rock, wringing his hands, as Tokar chanted words Colbey could not understand, though the voice sounded deep and rhythmical, almost sacred. The Wizard raised his left hand and a dark globe winked to life before him. It writhed like a living thing, contorting to a figure Colbey recognized as Managarmr, the wolf destined to extinguish the sun with the blood of men at the gods' final battle. Colbey never understood how he knew which wolf the Wizard's image represented. His gaze fixed on Tokar's right arm where a silver sphere appeared beside the image in black. This fashioned more slowly into the likeness of Baldur, most beautiful of the Northern gods.

Colbey remembered how the images had faded, fusing to a ball of grayness that floated upward, disappearing among the clouds. As it joined the glaring colors of the sky, streaks of crimson slid from the heavens to assume the shape of fiery men. Colbey caught his breath at a painful rush of memory. Without thinking, he had sprung to pull Tokar from the path of creatures he would never have believed real until that moment.

'Colbey, no!' Again the words rang in Colbey's ears. He had never known who shouted the warning, but it came too late. He seized the Wizard's shoulder, and pain seared his hand, shocking through his body in a wild explosion of agony. Now, hurrying through the passes of the Granite Hills, Colbey stiffened at the memory. In his life, he had felt the edge of many weapons: sword, spear, arrow, whip. Axes had sliced him to the bone. Yet, he would gladly have reexperienced any or all over what had come with that touch. Always before he had fought through pain, maddened to a frenzy by it. But this time, the seconds to oblivion had dragged like hours. And with it came the madness.

Colbey's next five years had passed in a druglike stupor. In his moments of lucidity, Colbey recalled setting the bodies of Tokar and his apprentice to pyre and deciding repeatedly to attack every tribe in the Northlands until one cut him down, to die before the insanity overtook him completely. But always the madness enveloped him, stunning him with voices of men and women who existed only in his mind and with concepts he could not quite grasp. Always, Colbey wound up back at the Western Wizard's cave, awakening amidst a wild chorus of birdsong and uncertain how he had gotten there.

Only then had Colbey gained the strength to battle his affliction with the same savagery he used in war. Unaccustomed to fighting with anything but his sword, Colbey needed time to master the technique. His will rose, smothering the strangers' commands, grappling them into his control, driving and pounding them from his consciousness. And, gradually, Colbey was winning that battle. One by one, the voices had disappeared, shattered into the same oblivion they inflicted upon Colbey.

Yet Colbey still suffered the aftereffects of his psychosis. A single voice still whispered courses of action he should take, ones that often went against his intentions; its compulsion was strong, sometimes overpowering. At times, he discovered a stray thought that seemed to come from people around him. At first, he had dismissed them as part of the madness. But whenever he spoke the captured thought aloud, he found the same stunned look of incredulity, one that told him he had caught the other's thread of thought verbatim. And sometimes he knew things he should not with a certainty that could not be disputed.

It was one of the latter situations that bothered Colbey now. Inextricably, something drew him south and westward toward the farm towns that dotted the flatter lands of the West. And since none of his companions complained, Colbey gave in to the compulsion. The direction of their travel made no other difference to the Renshai. He had more important matters on his mind than to struggle against an internal force that sent him along a logical, reasonable course.

For some time, Colbey and his new companions traveled in silence. Garn seemed perfectly willing to race through the passes without conversation or a specific destination, as if this was his normal mode of travel. Mitrian appeared dazed by what could only have been her first kill. Of them all, only Arduwyn glanced about nervously as if he wanted to ask questions but did not dare.

As the sun sank deeper toward the western horizon, the smallest man in the group finally gathered the courage to speak. 'Is it likely we're being chased?'

Uncertain, Colbey gave no reply.

Mitrian or Garn must have given Arduwyn a nonverbal affirmation, because he passed his donkey's reins to Mitrian and continued, 'I'll double back and see what I can find. If I see anyone, I'll try to get to you first with a warning. At the least, I can erase some of our tracks. When it gets dark, camp. I'll catch up to you.' He slipped into a hillside glade before anyone bothered to answer.

Colbey, Mitrian, and Garn pushed on until the sun disappeared, leaving a star-studded sky and a pale crescent of moon. 'Camp?' Colbey suggested, and the others nodded raggedly. 'Garn, why don't you pick out some rations from the supplies Arduwyn brought.' He indicated the pack strapped to the donkey's back. 'Mitrian, we need to talk.' Colbey patted a rock outcropping, sat, and waited for Mitrian to approach.

Hesitantly, Mitrian came over, but she chose to stand before Colbey rather than sit beside him.

Mitrian's caution amused Colbey. The idea of harming her seemed ludicrous, but, had he chosen to attack anyway, a kill would take a single stroke. 'I am Renshai.'

Mitrian nodded without meeting Colbey's gaze.

From Mitrian's reaction, Colbey knew that her knowledge of her adopted heritage was less than that of most strangers. Garn rummaged through the pack, apparently unimpressed and even more ignorant about Renshai than Mitrian. 'Do you understand what that means?'

Mitrian fidgeted, apparently grappling with her thoughts. 'It's a warrior tribe from the North that follows the goddess, Sif. I know a few of its tenets.'

Colbey noted the use of the term 'know' rather than 'understand' or 'follow.' He drew a knee to his chest, watching Mitrian for clues to her mood. 'Are you aware that you, too, are Renshai?'

Colbey's words seemed to break through Mitrian's trance. She stiffened. Her hand fell lightly to her sword hilt as if seeking solace from the touch rather than preparing to attack or defend. 'No,' she said. Then, apparently realizing she had answered only the superficial aspect of the question, she qualified. 'I mean, I'm not Renshai. There's no question about my parentage or my parents' parentage.' She paused, considering. 'My father has some Northern blood, but not a lot.'

Most of the Westerners who had some Northern blood were descended from Renshai conquerors, but Colbey saw no reason to point this out. Bloodline was of no consequence. 'What makes a Renshai is not kinship, but a single-minded devotion to swordcraft. Whoever taught you those war maneuvers made you one of us as surely as if he was your father.'

Mitrian cocked her head, as if listening to someone else besides Colbey. For a moment, both Renshai seemed to share another kinship, one of imagined voices and madness. Then the woman turned her attention back to Colbey. 'That's absurd.'

'That's not absurd, it's truth. When you learned the sword techniques, you learned one of the two most important aspects that bond us as a tribe.' Colbey kept the second to himself, not believing Mitrian was yet prepared to accept the Renshai's savage, glorious eagerness to die in battle, usually by early adulthood. 'You also acquired all of the Renshai enemies, enemies that span the world. Sixteen years ago, the other Northmen nearly exterminated our tribe. Merely identifying us as Renshai was considered ample reason for cold-blooded murder.' Colbey sneered at the thought that the Northmen had not found the slaughter simple. *Surely, they lost three or four warriors for every Renshai.* Images rose to Colbey's mind, women hacking huge fur- and chain-protected Northmen to their deaths, weaponless toddlers biting attackers, distracting the Northmen while their Renshai parents seized the openings to slice off enemy heads. 'The way I see it, if you have the same sword skill and the same enemies, you're the same tribe.'

Mitrian opened her mouth to speak, but Colbey interrupted, not wanting to deal with insignificant questions when so much of importance needed to be said. 'Tell me the name of the Renshai who taught you.'

Mitrian backed away, her face crinkled in suspicion. 'You told me everyone hates Renshai. Now you're asking for names. How do I know you're really not one of his enemies?'

Garn extracted a few handfuls of carefully wrapped traveling rations, set them aside and started relacing the pack. Earlier, he had seemed to ignore the conversation, but now he tensed.

Colbey kept his gaze between them, in a position where he could assess both of his new companions. 'Good, I'm glad you're starting to think. With all the enemies you now have, you can't afford to trust strangers.' He focused in on Mitrian. 'No Northman would claim to be Renshai if he wasn't, especially in a crowded tavern. You saw the result.'

Mitrian chewed her lip, hand still light on her sword hilt. Again, she seemed to be listening to voices other than Colbey's. At least partially satisfied by Colbey's claim, she answered hesitantly, 'His name is Rache.'

Garn lowered his head. Bronze-colored hair fell into his face, obscuring his expression, but the low growl he loosed made visual impressions unnecessary.

Colbey remembered a ten-year-old, eager as all Renshai and average in ability. The picture that formed in Colbey's mind was not of a child but of the adult that child had become. Though Colbey had not seen Rache in sixteen years, the image came easily: a handsome face framed by soft, blond hair, a slim but well-defined frame and the Renshai's combination of natural and learned agility. The younger Renshai lay still on the rocks, his limbs limp and his blue eyes glazed.

Horror stole over Colbey. Nonspecific as the warning seemed, Colbey read it accurately: *If Rache and I meet again, he will die.* Understanding accompanied the vision, but details did not. Colbey could not imagine killing one of his own, especially one far more suited to recreating the tribe. *Younger and certainly capable of fathering children, unlike me.* Even in his youth, Colbey had found himself unable to impregnate a woman, though not from lack of trying. *If Mitrian is to survive the coming war, I have to complete her training. Then, I have no choice but to die in battle before Rache and I can meet.*

The decision came easily, the means less so. Renshai believed each battle brought them one step closer to Valhalla. But, for Colbey, the opposite seemed to be true. Every battle honed war skills that already made the next most capable warrior seem a child, brought him one leap closer to perfection. From infancy, Colbey had striven to become the best swordsman in existence. But the reality of success had placed him in a situation he could never hope to win. To lose his life in anything but daring combat would condemn him to Hel's ice, but no opponent could stand long against Colbey's competence. He seemed fated to die damned by age and illness, incapable of finding the death in battle he had sought since birth. And to give anything short of his best in war would doom him as surely as withering in a sickbed.

Suddenly realizing Mitrian and Garn were staring at him, Colbey wrenched free of his thoughts. Annoyed at being caught with his mind wandering, Colbey did not choose his words with proper care. 'Rache did a poor job of training you, girl. You learned enough to be recognized by your enemies but not enough to stand against them.'

Mitrian's face reddened, and she sprang to Rache's defense. 'Rache's the best warrior I've ever known! He taught my father's guards, and he did a damned fine job. It's not Rache's fault my father wouldn't let him – '

Colbey interrupted. 'I'm not blaming Rache. I only had the opportunity to teach him until he was ten years old. But think about this: If you learn everything I can teach you and everything I should have taught Rache, when I die, you'll become the best swordsman in the world.' He paused a moment to let his words sink in, then struck the final blow. 'And you'll need that skill and every bit of Garn's strength to protect your son.'

Mitrian's expression had become increasingly one of startlement, beginning with Colbey's claim to have trained Rache. But it was the last word that sent her jaw sagging. 'Son?' she managed at last. 'What son? I don't have a son. I'm not going to have a son for a long time.'

The word 'son' had slipped out, inspired by the final voice haunting Colbey. He had not meant to speak it, but now that he had, there was no longer any doubt. 'I'm not sure how I know, but you're carrying a son right now. The "long time" you mentioned is measured in months.'

'But that's impossible.' Despite the certainty of her statement, Mitrian clenched her hands in agitation. 'I've only once . . . I mean, we just . . .'

'You did enough.' Colbey stated fact without considering its effect on Mitrian and Garn. To Colbey, the child symbolized a new beginning for a tribe he had believed lost, and he found it difficult to temper his joy with the realization that his companions might not share it.

Apparently believing he had missed something that would seem obvious to men accustomed to pregnant women, Garn stared at Mitrian.

Mitrian still seemed to be in shock. She did not even blink.

Always before, Colbey had read minds by accident, an occasional strong thought radiating to him when he bothered to wonder what another was thinking. Now Colbey recognized Mitrian's mixture of confusion and abject terror. She seemed certain the entire world had collapsed around her. Just the image of what Colbey claimed as truth sent her thoughts into chaotic flight: she had ruined her bloodline, she could never find a husband, the news would kill her mother and drive her father into a fit of violent rage. Threaded between these ideas ran a single observation that made no sense to Colbey: an act of defiance.

Colbey tried to soothe. 'There's nothing wrong with what you've done. Garn's blood can bring strength into the tribe.'

Garn relaxed, his lips bowing into a pleasant smile. Blindly, Mitrian sat, not bothering to choose a comfortable spot. Colbey could almost feel Mitrian's thoughts spinning, then channeling in a single direction. Her expression changed from panicked to careful. Fixing her gaze on Colbey, she started to speak. 'You almost – '

Colbey's madness did not fail him. He interrupted, aware completing her thought word for word would convince her more than anything else he might say. ' – had me believing you told the truth. I only met Garn a couple of days ago. Even if I was carrying a child, how could you possibly know about it?'

Mitrian's jaws clamped shut so quickly, her teeth clicked together. 'How did you . . . ? How could you . . . ?'

'Know what you were going to say?' Colbey shrugged. 'I don't know. But I did. And I also know you're carrying Garn's son.'

Tears filled Mitrian's eyes, and she slumped to the stone, no longer able to pass off Colbey's words as the ramblings of senility. Setting aside the food, Garn approached, crouched beside her, and placed an arm around her trembling shoulders. Before he could speak,

Mitrian screamed, 'Leave me alone !' Leaping to her feet, she dodged Garn's grip. 'Just leave me the hell alone !'

Again, Garn reached for her. Mitrian lashed a hand across his cheek ; the slap rang out. Garn went perfectly still, shock etched across his features. 'Mitrian ?'

Whirling, she ran into the woods.

'Mitrian ?' Garn started after her, but Colbey caught his arm.

'Let her go.'

Restrained, Garn stopped without a struggle. His words emerged softly, aimed at Mitrian and tinged with anguish, but Colbey heard them clearly. 'Do all your people hit ?' Garn tensed, as if to pull free of Colbey's grasp. Then, apparently deferring to the older man's judgment, he turned to face the Renshai instead. 'I'm not good enough for her.' It was as much question as statement.

'You are.' Colbey reassured Garn. 'She just doesn't know it yet. Give her some time alone to think.'

Garn rubbed at his cheek, obviously more pained by the fact that Mitrian had struck him than by the blow itself. He glanced in the direction she had gone.

No longer facing Garn directly, Colbey smiled wryly. He suppressed a laugh, amused by a savage fighter who could give dirty technique lessons to Renshai but seemed innocent as a child regarding affairs of the heart. 'She'll be back. In the meantime, let's get the food ready.'

'No need.' Arduwyn's voice preceded him from the woods.

Unsettled by the realization that Arduwyn had approached without his knowledge, Colbey frowned, his mood soured.

Oblivious to Colbey's annoyance, the flame-haired archer stepped into the makeshift camp. His bow lay, draped across one shoulder. The quiver swung from his back, and he carried three hares in his fists. 'We've got fresh meat tonight.' He dumped the rabbits beneath a low overhang, unslung the bow and quiver, and sat on the ledge. 'If there's any pursuit, it's way behind us. I erased a good part of our trail. But curiosity is killing me. What the hell happened back there ?' Drawing his skinning knife, he used it to gesture vaguely northward.

Colbey wandered off to gather kindling while Garn explained the incident in the tavern, using as few words as necessary and leaving Arduwyn to guess many of the details. By the time Colbey returned with enough wood to build a fire, Arduwyn had skinned one of the rabbits and was working on gutting it with his knife. 'But I still don't understand,' the little hunter said with the exasperation that comes of having asked the same question too many times. 'What did you do or say that started the fight in the first place ?'

Garn sighed, obviously trying to find the answer that would satisfy Arduwyn.

Colbey rummaged through his pocket for a block of flint. 'I simply told them the truth. That I'm Renshai.'

Arduwyn slit his hand with the knife. He scrambled backward with a cry of pain, his own blood mingling freely with that of the hare.

Arduwyn's reaction seemed far more normal to Colbey than Garn's or Mitrian's had.

Apparently unwilling to drop the knife, Arduwyn did not try to stem the flow of blood. 'That's not funny.'

Colbey tossed the flint to the ground beside his piled wood. 'It wasn't intended to be funny.'

'But I'd heard the Golden-Haired Devils were all dead.'

'You heard wrong.' Unlike with Mitrian, Colbey saw no reason to waste time convincing Arduwyn of truth. Flipping his dagger to his hand, he set to work sparking a fire. When the shavings flared to red life, he glanced toward the place where Arduwyn had sat. But the little hunter had disappeared, and only Garn met his gaze quizzically. Colbey laughed. Once the world discovered Renshai still lived, the difficulties one archer could cause would be insignificant. Colbey returned his attention to dinner.

Mitrian curled on a boulder, her legs tucked to her chest, and her tears soaking through the fabric covering her knees. Leaves and needles from the trees overhead speckled the coarsening linen of her sleeping gown. Despite her large-boned, sturdy frame, she felt small ; despite her friends, alone in a world that seemed to have grown impossibly large. *A baby.* Mitrian buried her face against her knees. *Garn's baby.* Terror shivered through her, tinged with anger and self-pity. *Why did I do something so stupid?*

In spite of the thought, Mitrian could not shake the feeling that her night with Garn had been beautiful, yet the consequences seemed anything but. *I can't go home. What man would have me while I'm carrying a gladiator's baby? A gladiator, by Kadrak's sword. And not just a gladiator, the one who crippled Rache.* Self-loathing twined with her other emotions. *How could I do that to Rache? How could I do that to myself?* Guilt wrenched a fresh volley of tears from her eyes. *What am I going to do?*

Mitrian shoved aside the frenzied tangle of emotion that disrupted logical thought. *Maybe the baby won't survive the pregnancy.* In an era when fewer than half of all pregnancies came to term and fewer still survived to adulthood, the thought seemed sensible. Yet Colbey's certainty that she would bear a son made the possibility of the pregnancy failing unlikely. *If I accept that Colbey can predict a pregnancy days after conception, how can I doubt I will bear a son?* Her belief in the revelations of an aging Northern soldier who muttered to himself seemed insanity. But, in that respect, Colbey reminded her of Shadimar: both men stated as facts things they could not possibly know. And Mitrian believed. But there the comparison ended. Though aging, Colbey lacked the Wizard's timelessness, and the Renshai's power stemmed from sword skill rather than magic and mystery. Where Shadimar seemed aloof, above the problems of the mundane world in the same manner as the gods, it seemed more as if Colbey caused those problems, holding anyone who could not kill him in contempt.

Somewhat calmer, Mitrian considered her options. *If I return home carrying Garn's baby, not only will no man have me, they'll scorn me. My mother would live in shame. My father ...* Mitrian could not put the concept into words, but she felt certain the relationship between Santagithi and his guards would change. At the least, he would hunt Garn down like an animal; Garn had convinced her that her father would never believe the baby came of anything but rape. *And the baby? Would they kill my baby?* She hugged her legs tighter protectively, unable to feel anything but love for the son she carried.

What if I don't identify the father? The answer came quickly. *They'll try to figure it out.* Mitrian considered where the blame would fall. *They might think Garn raped me.* A worse thought came to mind. *Or they might condemn Rache. After the rumors our sword lessons caused, who would believe either of us?* Recalling Santagithi's threats the previous evening, Mitrian harbored no doubt Rache would pay and dearly for her indiscretion. She imagined him driven from the town, Nantel and the others restraining her father from shooting down the horse and stabbing Rache where he lay, crippled and helpless, on the ground. Mitrian quivered, not daring to risk Rache with her silence. Only one other option came to mind. *I could seduce Listar. Then he and the others would believe the child his. But I'd have to marry Listar.* Though the idea seemed preferable to letting Rache take the blame, Mitrian hated it. *If I had to, I could live with it. But there has to be another way.*

Suddenly, Mitrian remembered the decision was not wholly her own. Garn's last words had struck deep, chasing her between the trees: 'Do all your people hit?' It seemed ludicrous for a trained killer to ask such a thing, yet the simplicity and innocence of the question burrowed deep into her conscience. *My father hit him, the guards beat him, and now his childhood friend, the one he's fantasized as his wife, the woman carrying his son, just struck him without a reason.* Sympathy for Garn displaced the remainder of her thoughts, and Mitrian felt shamed by her selfishness. *I'm so busy worrying about what my people will think of me, I've forgotten about Garn. I think I do love him. And it's his baby, too.* The realization opened a whole new set of problems. But before Mitrian could consider them, Arduwyn drew up beside her.

The little hunter looked raw with concern, glancing behind him as if he expected pursuers to burst from between the trees at any moment.

Alarmed, Mitrian sat up straighter, letting her feet drop to the ground below her stone seat. 'Are you being followed?'

Arduwyn shook his head, but a darting glance behind him took all reassurance from the gesture. Blood striped his fingers, and he kept the heel of one hand clamped against the palm of the other.

'What's the matter?' Mitrian pressed, glad for the disruption but aware she needed to settle her own problem before returning to Garn and Colbey. Another thought struck her. 'And how did you find me?'

The latter question amused Arduwyn. He smiled, and his manner relaxed somewhat. 'I trailed a wounded deer for two days from the western forests and through the Granite Hills. Did you think you would be harder to find?' He noticed the tear lines on Mitrian's face, and his grin disappeared. 'You know, don't you?'

Mitrian hesitated, uncertain as to which revelation Arduwyn referred.

Before she could ask, Arduwyn clarified. 'You know the Northman claims to be Renshai.'

'Yes.' Mitrian thought that was the least of her problems.

Arduwyn stared. 'Renshai,' he repeated, as if certain she had not heard him the first time. 'You know, Golden-Haired Devils from the North.'

Mitrian was tired of what had started to seem like a game. She knew Colbey's revelations about her future required a great deal of thought, but, for now, the baby seemed all-consuming. 'Look, Arduwyn, I have more important things to worry about than which tribe Colbey comes from.'

Arduwyn blinked twice in rapid succession. He seemed to be looking through Mitrian. 'You don't know what Renshai are, do you?'

'Of course I do.' Now Mitrian was annoyed. 'They're a warlike tribe of Northmen.'

Arduwyn accepted her description with the same lofty disbelief as Colbey. 'Correct. But rather in the same way as saying King Siderin of the Eastlands is a not too friendly fellow. I assume you have some idea of what Northmen are like?'

Mitrian nodded.

'Well, the Renshai were exiled from the Northlands for being too violent. Can you imagine being considered too violent by Northmen?'

Mitrian frowned. She recalled Santagithi's citizens whispering about Rache's callousness in matters of war, but such complaints never came from trained warriors, such as the guards. The idea intrigued her; obviously, there were things she did not know about the Renshai as a people. She doubted the Northmen would exile a tribe simply for being capable swordsmen. 'No,' she admitted. 'What did the Renshai do?'

Discussing his concerns with Mitrian seemed to dispel some of Arduwyn's discomfort. He rested a foot on the rock Mitrian used as a chair. 'They were constantly at war with other tribes. They demoralized the warriors. They hacked apart the dead. That last, apparently, is considered the vilest thing one Northman can do to another. I consider it disrespectful. To Northmen, it's much worse.'

'Why?' Mitrian asked. Then, realizing the question could refer to anything Arduwyn had said, she specified. 'Why would the Renshai cut apart the dead?'

'Northmen believe a corpse has to be intact to reach their Yonderworld. Can you think of a better way to destroy enemy morale than to bar them from the pleasures of the afterlife?' Arduwyn shivered. 'As to why the Golden-Haired Devils directly disobeyed Northern law to desecrate their neighbors, it makes no sense. Since the beginning of time, every race has had its code of honor. I may not agree with the laws, particularly those of the East, but I've never heard of any group or citizen violating the tenets of its culture.' He added rapidly, 'Except the Devils. Some say they were touched by magic.' He shrugged, looking more uncomfortable, if that was possible. 'Other things about them fit that notion.'

If I'm going to be considered Renshai, I may as well hear all the horrible details from a knowledgeable outsider. 'Go on,' Mitrian encouraged. 'Tell me more about the Renshai.'

Arduwyn shrugged. 'The rest is legend. Supposedly, after becoming outcasts, they wandered for a century or so. Where they thought they could learn new warcraft, they tarried. Elsewhere, they slaughtered their way across the continent. Few were spared. It is said that their sword skill comes from blending the best methods of the world: Northern ferocity, Eastern quickness and stealth, and the Westerner's mental discipline. Or else it's magic.'

Arduwyn turned, sitting on the edge of the stone, his back to

Mitrian. 'I don't know how much is truth, but I do know the Renshai have their weaknesses. Their techniques center on sword-play, so they have little skill with other weapons. Some say they ravaged the West, leaving their trail of destruction and death, simply because they couldn't get their own food and supplies by hunting. Their war tactics are based on speed and skill; armor hampers them, so they leave themselves mostly unprotected.'

That explains Rache's refusal of the officers' chain mail he was due. Mitrian felt certain there was more to Renshai avoiding armor than Arduwyn's description explained. A strange but strong sense of honor and the desire to die in battle came to the front of Mitrian's thoughts.

Arduwyn continued, 'Then there're the stories that sound more farfetched, but are grounded in truths I don't understand. They say the Golden-Haired Devils used dark magic to summon demons to torment the souls of those they killed and that they drank the blood of the dead to stay forever young.'

Recalling her first impression of Colbey as a senile soldier, Mitrian laughed. 'At least we know that last idea is untrue.'

Arduwyn twisted far enough to meet Mitrian's gaze. He wore a grimace, obviously displeased by her amusement. 'I used to think the claims of dark sorcery were nonsense, too. But survivors old enough to remember the Renshai's rampage claim the Golden-Haired Devils never aged. They also recall a town mostly filled with mages at the southern edge of the Granite Hills.'

Shadimar's ruins. Mitrian stiffened as the pieces fell together. *And the Golden-Haired Devils are surely the ones who ravaged the Western town where my father and our people used to live.* Mitrian dismissed the idea, unable to carry a hatred for events that had occurred decades before her birth. *If my father can forgive them, so can I. And maybe now I'll find out Shadimar's connection to Renshai and my sword.* She noticed Arduwyn was staring curiously at her and knew she would need to encourage him to go on. 'What happened to the mages?'

Arduwyn hesitated, as if to press Mitrian for her thoughts. Instead, he shrugged in resignation and continued his description. 'The town was called Myrcidë; its people were reclusive. Supposedly, their powers ran in the bloodline, and they didn't want to dilute it with us inferiors. Or maybe its source was a secret they didn't wish to share. In any case, everyone believed the mages would destroy the Golden-Haired Devils, but Myrcidë fell as quickly as the other Western villages.' Arduwyn stroked his chin thoughtfully. 'In Myr-cidë, the sun shone through the night. When it rained, any mage who wanted to remained dry. It's a miracle and a sin that anyone should destroy such a people, and a feat that, in most people's opinion, could only be achieved by sorcery.'

Thoughts bunched in Mitrian's mind, too many to address at once. Her concern for the child she carried became lost in a snarl of questions and ideas. As horrible as Arduwyn made the Renshai sound, Mitrian could not forget the aura of beauty, agility, and honor that had always surrounded Rache. Certainly, he seemed younger than he should, but she felt sure that if he drank the blood of the dead she would have heard rumors. And while some attributed his skill to sorcery, Mitrian knew enough of the Renshai maneuvers and Rache's dedication to them to realize his abilities came of knowledge and constant, hard practice. But Mitrian's understanding of Rache did not extend to Shadimar, and the Wizard's decision to help revive the Northmen who had destroyed his village seemed inexplicable.

Arduwyn drove his point home. 'Mitrian, to befriend a Renshai is simply dangerous. To travel with one is insane. In many towns and villages, they put men to death merely for speaking their name.'

Mitrian had become so intent on gleaning information, it never occurred to her that she was hiding an important fact from Arduwyn. Aware he would find out soon enough and better from her than Colbey, she felt obliged to explain. 'Arduwyn, I'm Renshai too.' The words sounded strange from her own lips.

Arduwyn sprang to his feet with a cry that mixed amazement with pain. 'How could you . . . ? Why did you let me say . . . ?' Unable to finish a sentence, he whirled and ran into the woods.

'Ardy ?' Mitrian rose, wishing she had phrased her disclosure more gently. To try to follow and explain would be folly ; he could move through the woods far more quietly and quickly than she. She tried to put herself in Arduwyn's position. *How would I feel if I just spent the evening calling his heritage savage and evil, and he waited until I finished before telling me where he's from?* Mitrian winced at the thought. It did not matter that she had only known Arduwyn a little over a day. She liked him. *Friends don't treat friends that way. Somehow I've got to let him know I didn't mean any harm. There's no way I can find him. I'll just have to hope he comes back.*

An image flashed through Mitrian's mind, of Arduwyn running ahead to warn the farm villages and larger towns that dotted the Westlands so they could meet the Renshai with warriors. With no means to stop him, she put the idea from her mind. The conversation with Arduwyn had focused her thoughts enough to clarify the issue and her options. *I had placed all my hopes and beliefs on the act of defiance Shadimar mentioned. The act itself was simple, surrendering to one of the most natural and beautiful urges of mankind. The point of decision is now, and the difficulty comes from making a choice not only for myself but for my son.* Mitrian sat again. As far as her friendship with Arduwyn, she could only wait for him to make the next move and apologize profusely when he did. For now, she needed to concentrate on her child while the issues remained vivid in her mind.

Only two of the options make sense. I either return home and credit the baby to Listar or I stay with Garn and Colbey. The Renshai's teachings beckoned, nearly as strongly as her love of home and family. Her relationship with Garn and his right to see his own baby further skewed the decision, but Mitrian banished these biases to consider the welfare of the coming baby. *A quiet life as the blacksmith's son or the wild, ruthless glory of the Renshai.* It was the sort of choice the boy should make for himself, but Mitrian knew the decision needed to be made long before his birth. She took scant comfort from the fact that every man and woman is born to some life-style and heritage, never of their own choosing. *I don't want my child to die young.* The choice should have been easy, but Mitrian could not shake Rache's words to her father outside her window: 'You may want a pretty flower that just sits there, but you don't have one. Mitrian is every bit your daughter . . . If you don't go out looking for death, you never find life.' *Chances are a child of Garn and myself won't be content to sit at home working a bellows and crafting barrel hoops. Can I deny him the chance to become the best trained swordsman in the world as the price for his mother's love?*

Mitrian curled her legs to her chest. Life used to seem so simple when the most difficult decision she needed to make was how to coerce her father's sword master and archery captain into teaching her their skills. *If I'm going to consider inflicting a Northern heritage upon my child, I won't do it in ignorance.* Seeking answers, Mitrian seized the hilt of her sword. She felt nothing, but she knew the demon was there, hovering, waiting for a chance at battle.

Mitrian concentrated on putting her questions into words. 'How much of what Arduwyn told me is truth?'

The demon's presence swelled through Mitrian's mind, as if to read the impressions left by Arduwyn's words. *Most of it*, the demon admitted, a trace of pride leaking through the contact. *Renshai have no magic, and the only human blood I tasted was my own after a blow to the face. The rest seems apt enough, taken from a Western-er's point of view. Renshai tend to mature slowly. It's just a racial feature, like blond hair and fair skin. We all die young in battle, and, by custom, we name newborns for warriors who recently found Valhalla. Put together, I could see where the Westerners might think we never age. It's so easy to blame the unknown on demons, so much simpler to explain skill by magic than by superior effort and dedication.*

The demon's use of present tense, as if the Renshai still lived and ruled by violence intrigued Mitrian. She wanted to ask about demons, but she stuck with the more important issues. 'And the claims that the Renshai are merciless, cruel, and lacking honor? That's all true?'

Anger blazed through Mitrian's mind, its source wholly alien. *So easy,* the demon said, apparently to himself because he continued in a different vein. *Men, Mitrian, by nature are creatures of Law. The Renshai have an honor stronger than that of any people I have met, just different. What makes honor virtuous is sticking to its tenets while your enemies defy them. A man who dies fighting with his ethics and principles intact dies in glory. To expect your enemies to follow the same code of honor defiles that honor, reducing it to a set of arbitrary rules.*

The demon paused, allowing Mitrian time to absorb his words before continuing. *True, the Renshai grant no quarter in combat; a brave warrior worthy of Valhalla would never beg for mercy. It is true we demoralized Northmen by hacking apart their corpses and sending them to Hel, taking all glory from their battles; but a courageous opponent who proved worthy of the fight was always left intact. Renshai honor comes from battling with nothing but our bodies and our swords. Biting, kicking, spitting all fit within the tenets of that honor. We announce ourselves when we attack, and we rely on nothing but our own skill. We never ask our opponents to fight without armor or only with swords. Nor do we complain when their cowards kill us from a distance with arrows or their scouts quietly stab us, unannounced and from behind. Honor, Mitrian, is relative. All manner of men, from the most righteous Northman to the most decadent Easterner follows a code of his people. Odin saw to that when he banished Magic and its creatures, its demons, to another world.*

Mitrian could not help targeting the demon's last revelation. 'So magic is . . .?' She trailed off, allowing him to finish her sentence.

Formless, chaotic. Lacking honor, as you said.

'And demons?'

Creatures from the world of Magic. Apparently catching Mitrian's train of thought, the demon clarified. *I'm not a demon in the true sense. I was a man once, a Renshai whose name died with me since I can never find Valhalla. But I only exist because of magic, so I suppose I'm a demon in that sense.*

Mitrian recalled the description of the Eastern king who was destined to begin the Great War.

The demon answered before Mitrian could put her inquiry into words. *My knowledge is limited to what I knew before the Wizard placed my soul in the gems, the information I've gleaned about magic, and what the Wizards have told me about the Renshai. But the chances that this general is a demon are so remote as to be impossible. Demons are too unpredictable, too ephemeral to unite or lead themselves or men. Even the Cardinal Wizards can scarcely control demons for more than short periods of time.*

Realizing the topic had deviated from her decision, Mitrian released the hilt. The demon's presence disappeared, leaving her to her own thoughts. There was still much she did not understand, but one thing seemed certain. *I'm going to make an informed choice. Before I subject my child to it, I'm going to undergo Colbey's training myself. At the least, the old Renshai can prepare me for the battle Shadimar promised. At the worst, I can refuse the training for my son.* Strengthened by her decision, Mitrian sprang down from the rock and headed for life as a Golden-Haired Devil.

14 Mountain Man

A dark line of clouds rolled over the moon, bringing the threat of rain and compressing the camp to the thick ball of illumination supplied by the campfire. Mitrian emerged from the woods to find Colbey and Garn arranging hare meat on the flames. Both men looked up at her approach.

A pained look crossed Garn's face, and he stood. 'I'll get more wood.' Turning away from Mitrian, he trotted to a glade on the opposite side of the crags and disappeared into the gloom.

Mitrian winced, aware she would need to win back Garn's trust. But, for now, she had another matter to attend to. She fixed Colbey with the hardest stare she could muster. 'Fine. Teach me.'

Colbey rose. No expression touched his features but his blue-gray eyes mirrored a cruelty beyond anything she had known. Despite Mitrian's attempt at ferocity, it was she who looked away as the Northman spoke. 'I want you to understand something. Rache and I will certainly have different methods of teaching.'

Recalling Rache's descriptions of his teacher, Mitrian nodded. The words 'brutal,' 'uncompromising,' and 'intimidating' came to mind along with the phrase 'hard as flint and half as human.' But Mitrian also remembered that Rache always maintained a deep respect for his teacher and spoke of him in a tone of reverence. *Could Colbey really be the same man?*

If Colbey read Mitrian's thoughts, he gave no indication. 'Doubtless, Rache was easier than I will be. He taught you simpler maneuvers, and he didn't have the time constraints of a growing baby and a coming war. This is going to be the most frustrating, difficult, annoying thing you've ever done in your life. And that's the way it should be.'

Again, Mitrian nodded. She kneaded her sword hilt, but the demon seemed as interested in Colbey's words as she was.

The clouds bunched tighter, hemming in the firelight. A light drizzle fell, each droplet a cold touch on Mitrian's face. 'For tonight, I need to get to know you and your repertoire,' Colbey said, reaching for her weapon. 'Let me see your sword.'

Assailed with doubts, Mitrian hesitated, hand looped over the crossguard. *Will Colbey recognize the magic? The demon? Does its power go against the same Renshai honor that causes them . . . us . . . to shun armor, defeating enemies with nothing but individual skill?* Bereft of alternatives, Mitrian drew and surrendered her sword. *Shadimar did claim it as the only magic sword currently in existence. How could Colbey know? But then, how could Colbey have known about the baby?*

Rain pattered on the steel while Colbey studied the blade, glancing along the sharpened edges, testing the balance by its feel in his hands.

Mitrian held her breath.

Colbey returned the weapon. 'Very nice.' Turning, he chose a position within the circle of firelight devoid of rock outcroppings or ledges. He kicked aside a few loose stones to open a practice area confined by cliffs. 'Show me what you know.' He faced Mitrian, drawing his sword.

Mitrian chose her favorite disarming maneuver, *Gerlinr*, the one she had mastered in Rache's cottage. She lunged for Colbey, whipping her sword at his abdomen. Colbey blocked. Reversing her grip, Mitrian looped her blade in an outside sweep, then cut up for Colbey's fingers. Colbey dodged. His free hand licked out, catching Mitrian's hilt below her hand. He pivoted, continuing her stroke, and wrenched the hilt from her grip. Completing the spin, he brought his own sword into a defensive position, slashing hers high. Mitrian leapt backward, too late. Her blade in Colbey's fist whisked over her head, raising the hairs in the breeze of its passage.

Smiling, Colbey returned Mitrian's sword, obviously pleased, though Mitrian could not understand the cause. *He took that sword from me like a branch from an infant.* Apparently, he had seen potential in what she hoped was her skill but suspected was her audacity at choosing a disarming maneuver against a swordsman of his skill.

Colbey did not reveal his reasons. 'Try again,' he said.

This time, Mitrian sacrificed flashiness for practicality. She sprang, executing an overhand strike. Colbey blocked with his crossguard, smacking her blade to the left. Before she could think to stop him, he had his grip behind hers on the wolf's head hilt. Again, he flicked her sword from her hand into his own. A weapon in each fist, he crouched, held the position momentarily, then tossed back Mitrian's sword. 'Again,' was all he said.

Mitrian caught her hilt, her manner now wholly cautious. She circled, always moving, seeking an opening. Colbey stood still, casual and relaxed, though his gaze followed her every motion. He seemed bored, and his lapse sparked rage in her. Mitrian felt slow and cumbersome, like a possum attacking a lynx. *I'll have him this time. I just need patience.*

Suddenly, Colbey's sword flipped upward. Mitrian raised her sword instinctively to block. Colbey's blade spun back down. Its flat tapped her thigh. 'Don't just stand there.' Colbey's voice emerged as an angry roar. 'The first rule of fighting: You always attack! The best defense is to have your opponent bleeding on the ground. Then you're safe. You never stand there. You *always* attack!'

Enraged, Mitrian thrust for Colbey before he finished speaking. He blocked to the outside and caught her sword arm at the wrist. A pivot step brought him close enough so his shoulder touched hers. He spun, dragging her into a circle that drove her, facedown, into the stone. Mitrian dropped the sword, rolled and scrambled to her feet, weaponless once more.

Colbey finished his speech without missing a beat. 'If you don't know how to use the sword, if you make mistakes, you can learn. But I can't teach boldness. If you're too much of a coward to strike, I can't help you.'

The practice continued as the rain drove down. Repeatedly, Mitrian attacked; and, each time, Colbey either left her dumbfounded or lying on the ground with him holding both swords, never disarming her the same way twice. At length, he called a halt to the exercise. 'Fine, I think you've learned your lesson about taking a sword away from an opponent. Now, we'll just spar for a bit.'

Mitrian bit her lip, not allowing herself to show the concern raised by Colbey's suggestion. So far, he had simply defended and still made her look like a child. How could she hope to stand against a mixture of offense and block?

But, having imparted one important lesson, Colbey seemed content to exchange a series of strikes, assessing Mitrian's skills at various heights and angles. At times, he thrust his blade along her side or beneath her armpit, slapped her with its flat or whisked it over her head to demonstrate breaches in her defense. Rain soaked Mitrian, plastering her hair to her forehead. Then she found an opportunity for a wild overhead stroke. Her blade slammed toward Colbey's head. Instead of blocking with his usual agility, he went still, completely opening his defenses.

Horrified, Mitrian pulled the blow, her blade hovering a hand's breadth over his head.

Colbey's pale cheeks flushed scarlet. His crosspiece crashed onto Mitrian's blade hard enough to drive her hilt into her hand, loosening her grip. Colbey seized her sword in his free hand, tore it from her hold, and hurled it at her feet. 'If you're not going to use the sword the way it was meant to be used, let it lie in the dirt until somebody picks it up who's willing to use it! You never pull a blow! If this had been a real fight, you should have split me to the chin.' He indicated the path of the blade through his head. 'Every time you draw that sword, it's a real fight. If that's as seriously as you're going to take my teaching, to Hel with you! Go back to your god-damned town. We don't need another Renshai to die.'

Colbey's tirade astounded Mitrian. 'But,' she gasped, 'but I didn't want to hit you. How can you teach me if you're dead?'

Colbey threw up his arms in annoyance. 'You didn't commit to any of your blows. Do you think I'm dumb enough to open my head to a cut I know is going to fall?' He jabbed his sword into its sheath. 'So not only do you think I'm old, you think I'm stupid. I saw you weren't finishing any of your blows. I knew your sword would stop. I even knew *where* it would stop.'

From around a fringe of wet hair, Mitrian stared at her sword on the ground.

'At first, you don't attack. Whenever you do swing, you don't put enough effort into the blows to cut through one of those rabbits.' He indicated the fire, protected from the rain by an overhang. Mitrian followed his gesture naturally, and noticed that Garn had returned and was sitting on a nearby rock, listening intently. 'Rache might have taught you some things. But there's one thing he didn't teach you, and that's how to use the damned sword. To hit, you have to swing. You're not giving haircuts. You're trying to kill people. Think about what would have happened in that bar if you had pulled your blows.' Shaking his head in disgust, Colbey started toward the fire. He tossed one last warning over his shoulder. 'If you ever do that again, I'm going to take your sword away, break it, and give you a stick instead.'

Tears welled in Mitrian's eyes. Soaked, tired, and humiliated, she crossed the clearing and took the seat beside Garn, leaving Colbey to tend the hares.

Garn seemed to take no notice of Mitrian. His gaze remained fixed on Colbey in silent wonder.

Guilt tightened in Mitrian's chest. Her night with Garn seemed like an eternity ago; so much had happened in the last few days. In her life, she had met only two men she knew she could grow to love: Rache and Garn. Yet since she and Garn had made love, she had dismissed him as less than human in much the same way as her father and his guards had done. *I know how special, how different Garn is. Yet when the time came to think of permanence and eternity, I barely considered him fit to raise his own child.* The thoughts came easily to Mitrian's mind, but the lingering discomfort of Colbey's chastisement kept words at bay. Unable to verbalize her apology, Mitrian draped an arm across Garn's shoulders and snuggled closer. He had changed into the tunic and britches Arduwyn had purchased in Dvaulir. Garn smelled pleasantly of evergreens and clean, wet leather, and he felt warm againt her despite the rain-soaked fabric.

For some time, Mitrian and Garn sat together in a quiet broken only by the sizzle of droplets on flame and the crackle of twigs as Colbey shifted the rabbits in the fire. Finally, Garn spoke. 'You know, he's right.'

Expecting something soothing and romantic, Mitrian found Garn's words nonsensical. She met his gaze. 'What are you talking about? Who's right?'

'Colbey's right. You shouldn't have pulled your strokes. Any of them.'

Mitrian let her hand slide down Garn's back to the ground. 'But it was just a spar.'

Garn shrugged. 'Colbey killed nine warriors, starting bare-handed, and he wants to be your teacher. You couldn't hurt him in his sleep.' Despite Garn's bold denial of a life of violence, his tone betrayed a tinge of jealousy. 'If he's really your teacher and you kill him, fine. He wasn't such a good teacher then, was he?'

Mitrian threw up her hands in dismay. She could understand Garn's attitude; he would have considered destroying his teacher a triumph. But his words sounded like cold savagery, and she wanted him to grasp her more cultivated viewpoint. 'I like Colbey. I want him to become a friend as well as a teacher. I don't want to hurt him.'

'Hurt him?' Garn's features went slack, revealing no emotion. The corners of his mouth twitched, but he drew Mitrian against him before the smile formed. She felt him quiver rhythmically against her in quiet laughter.

Rain lashed Arduwyn between twisted scrub pines and locust, the droplets pelting the leaves like drumbeats. The raggedly sparse mountain forest gave the little hunter scant shelter from the storm, and the paucity of trees made him feel open and naked. Usually, he preferred facing his strongest emotions alone; but this time his seclusion brought no solace. Water trickled coldly beneath his cloak and shirt. His heart felt heavy, and he was uncertain exactly who or what he missed.

Stubs. Arduwyn tried to place the blame for his discomfort on having left his donkey with Renshai. But his hatred would not rise against the Golden-Haired Devils who had ravaged the Westlands, and his people, decades before his birth. As much as he tried to deny his attraction, he had found a certain charm in Garn's strange combination of brutality and naiveté. Mitrian's forthrightness and her concern for an escaped slave who, if nothing else, understood survival was touching, and she displayed an innocence that in some ways eclipsed Garn's own. *Sheltered*, Arduwyn decided. *Each in a different way.* And then there was Colbey.

Arduwyn shivered. Confident, competent, and merciless, the Northman typified nearly every story of Renshai the hunter had ever heard. Yet Arduwyn also felt oddly, almost irresistibly drawn to Colbey, like a moth to flame. Unlike the insect, Arduwyn pondered his lethal fascination, wading through his own awe and fear to discover a dangerous charisma he could only attribute to magic. Only Colbey's whitening hair and creased features did not fit the tales of Renshai remaining forever young, yet age did not hamper him. Colbey moved with more agility and grace than a warrior in his prime.

Clouds blotted out the moon and stars. The rain pounded harder, a constant musical assault upon the leaves and stone. Arduwyn hunched deeper into the folds of his cloak, scanning the cliff face for an overhang or cave that might provide protection. The crags of the Granite Hills seemed like an endless shadow. Arduwyn sighed and kept moving, his mother's words churning through his mind to the rhythm of the rain: 'There comes a time when everyone needs friends. You have to learn to be nicer to people.' She had spoken the words to Arduwyn since early childhood, meaning well, suffixing each repetition with suggestions to make him a better, more likable person. Her advice had its benefits and its price. Arduwyn had learned to give people what they wanted and to tell them what they wished to hear. It had made him a salesman of considerable skill, the type of man to whom people took an instant liking. But in the long run, it always came down to the same thing: Arduwyn preferred the forests to human company. And in the characteristic way of humans, rather than believe Arduwyn loved the woodlands more, his friends would always assume he loved them less.

Arduwyn clambered along a narrow ledge of stone, avoiding an open meadow for the shielding bulk of a hill. Oddly, his desire for solitude and the forest came from a father who placed family and country above both. A successful hunter and exemplary bowman, Arduwyn's father had taught his oldest son the wonders of archery and the Erythanian forests, showing him the natural formations of stone and tree and the simple logic of its animals. It was not enough to demonstrate deer paths and tracks, he indicated the locations of drinking holes, briar beds, fields and vegetation that led the animals to choose their route. The father opened a world few men understood; the son took the teachings one step further. He learned to move silently through brush, how wolves selected their quarry from a herd, and why the doe charged off, leaving her scentless fawn utterly still and unguarded. And Arduwyn's single-minded dedication turned him into a far better archer than his father.

Now Arduwyn cringed, hating the memories that followed. Unconsciously, he slid an arrow from his quiver, running a finger along the faded crest. He recalled when a lone buck had come to the forests of Erythane, its fur white as a hen's egg. For two years, Arduwyn had followed it, fascinated by its choices, seeing himself in the way it remained alone, without challenging the structure of the herds. Then someone else had seen the animal, and the king of Erythane decided its pelt would bring him luck. Arduwyn and others had tried to argue that the buck was a gift from the gods, a symbol of fortune that should be left alive and free, but to no avail. For the previous eight years, the high king, Morhane, who had overthrown his brother, Valar, in neighbouring Béarn, had stifled the Erythanian ruler's power. In some twisted manner, the Erythanian king saw the permanence of that deer on his courtroom wall as a symbol of his own mastery, a demonstration of the small amount of control King Morhane had left him over his own country.

Rivulets trickled down Arduwyn's forehead, trailing wet strands of copper-colored hair. He pressed against the rocky hillside, his search for shelter more intense. He recalled how the king had offered a generous reward that sent hunters of all abilities streaming into the Erythanian forests. Arduwyn had avoided most of them, springing traps that posed a danger to men or those that might maim creatures without holding them. He found deer injured by wild shots that had crawled away to die. These he finished, bringing the meat and fur home to feed and clothe his multitude of siblings. The white deer changed its haunts and pathways, and it remained at liberty.

Failure only fueled the Erythanian king's desire for the white buck. He had gathered the finest archers, hounds, and horses for a hunt. Arduwyn was among those called to a challenge and reward he could not resist, even if the king had given him a choice.

Now in rain-soaked hills far east of his birth home, Arduwyn remembered how the hunters had quibbled over dogs and horses while he spent his days, as always, in the forest. He had freed the instincts men bury, traipsing the forest like a wild thing. Gradually, he found the buck again. Its natural movements and haunts became his. As the days passed, he learned. When the time of the hunt came, Arduwyn did not ride among the other archers. Instead, he chose a likely site and listened to the distant baying of the pack, knowing he waited in the path of the fleeing animal. He kept an arrow nocked to the string of his bow.

The deer had not disappointed Arduwyn. Before the morning sun shifted westward, the buck bounded toward him, its snowy coat speckled with mud. A frothing hound panted at its heels, and Arduwyn could see the mounted hunters still some distance behind. The deer tensed as it sensed Arduwyn's presence. It halted abruptly, so close Arduwyn could have touched its trembling forelegs. In the instant before the hound sprang for its flank, its eyes met Arduwyn's. Russet and soft, they seemed almost human. Before he could think, Arduwyn aimed and shot. The arrow flew straight, piercing the hound's eye. The dog collapsed in a bloodless heap, and the buck disappeared into the forest, never to be seen in Erythane again.

Arduwyn veered around a jagged outcropping, mind filled with the memory of a panicked run home, aware the other hunters had witnessed his act of treason. The king's guards had come, demanding his head, and, fortunately, they had taken the rest of Arduwyn with it. Though quiet, his three days in the gray dampness of the dungeons nearly drove him mad for one last glimpse of the sun and trees, but it only made him certain of the appropriateness of his actions. He had spared the deer a similar fate or worse.

The ugliness of the purgings in Béarn had left the Erythanian king with a softer sense of justice. Rather than claiming Arduwyn's life, the king chose to banish him, allowing the hunter to take one item of value. He had selected his donkey, Stubs, and never regretted the decision. The animal worked willingly, never betraying him or haranguing him over the time he spent in the woods. She was simply Stubs.

And I left her in the hands of Renshai. Arduwyn sighed, aware his thoughts had come full circle. *Renshai.* He shook his head, splashing water over his face. The claim seemed ludicrous. The Renshai had left the West forty years ago, and the Northmen were rumored to have destroyed the tribe more than a decade and a half ago. Still, there seemed little doubt Colbey was exactly what he claimed to be. *But Mitrian?* Arduwyn considered her dark hair, Western features and speech patterns doubtfully. *Is this some sort of new cause, a group that uses the Renshai name to inspire fear?* He thought of the cult that had sprung up in the last decade near Pudar at Corpa Leukenya. Its priests had seemed to come from nowhere, albinos with guttural accents who worshiped a god with a man's body and a bird's head. Their alienness had created a sense of danger that drew Pudar's rebellious youths until the temple held more Westerners than albinos. *Is this Renshai claim the same thing? A crazed but charismatic Northman recruiting outsiders to revive the Renshai tenets of violence?*

Arduwyn frowned at his own conclusion. Mitrian seemed too kind and peaceful to join an organization solely for the purpose of wreaking havoc on innocents. If Colbey's intention was to start such an organization, it seemed far more logical to enlist Garn. One thing seemed certain. *I have to return. I won't abandon Stubs out of fear.* Reaching into his pocket, he fished out Mitrian's garnet. *I've never cheated anyone out of money, and I'm not going to get a reputation for it now. I either have to keep my promise or return Mitrian's gem.* And though slower to admit it to himself, Arduwyn felt drawn to a couple he already considered his friends and a Northman who fascinated as well as frightened him.

Arduwyn thought of families like his own scattered throughout the Westlands, the host of children who would die if Colbey followed the violent way of his people. *I need to warn the Westlands. Don't I?*

Even as the conclusion arose and Arduwyn accepted the responsibility, he spotted the dark mouth of a cave against the cliff face to his left. Relieved for even this rude shelter, he stepped inside.

The rain disappeared to a rattle on the outer stone. Warmer air swirled through the confines, an unexpected luxury whose source Arduwyn did not try to guess. The air smelled of damp and moss. Beneath it, he caught a whiff of stale smoke, but attributed the odor to his own clothing. Shivering, he shed bow and quiver, then spread his cloak to dry. A glimpse of movement from deeper in the cave caught his eye.

Startled, Arduwyn snatched up his bow, deftly fitting an arrow to the string. A shadow lumbered toward him on two legs, its indistinct outline revealing a furry torso and a dark mane. *A bear?* Arduwyn hesitated, uncertain, training the arrow on the beast's neck. 'Don't move,' he shouted, hoping his voice might frighten it.

The creature went still, though whether because of Arduwyn's words or coincidence he could not guess. As his eyes adjusted to almost total darkness, details became visible. He faced the largest man he had ever seen. The tangled mane and coarse hair covering the stranger's face were the man's own. The remainder of his fur he had gotten from animals. He took another step toward the cave entrance.

Arduwyn stepped back, catching his heel on his discarded cloak. He stumbled, fought for balance, then fell to his knees. The arrow slipped from his fingers, clattering on the stone floor. Hastily, he retrieved it, fitting its notch back to the string as he scrambled to his feet.

The bearlike man's laughter rumbled through the cave. Apparently, he judged Arduwyn's competence by his most recent display.

Arduwyn flushed, lowering his bow, though he kept the arrow trapped on its rest with a finger. He had heard of barbarian tribes living in the forests further south but had never come upon any. He knew some of those tribes were violent toward strangers, but this lone man seemed harmless enough. 'Hello,' he said in the Western trading tongue. 'I'm called Arduwyn.'

The black-haired man did not answer, nor did his actions reflect any understanding. He made a benign gesture that seemed to indicate Arduwyn should follow, then turned and headed around a bend in the cave.

Arduwyn considered. The huge stranger's laughter had sounded amiable. Now aware the cave was occupied, Arduwyn realized the smoke he smelled came from a campfire deeper inside. Its warmth beckoned. He glanced over his shoulder toward the entrance where the rain hammered stone. *I can always run.* Turning back, he found the stranger had disappeared around the corner. Cautiously, Arduwyn returned the arrow to its quiver, draped the bow over his shoulder and shuffled forward.

When Arduwyn turned the corner, he discovered the man sitting on piled skins before the fire. A woven basket lay beside the stranger's thick knees. Behind him, a chipped, steel-bladed ax stood propped against the back wall.

'Hello,' Arduwyn tried again.

In response, the huge stranger proffered the basket. Purple juice stained the intertwined boughs, and berries nearly filled it. Some berries lay broken open to reveal meat lighter than their skins.

Is he deaf and mute? Arduwyn accepted a fistful of berries out of politeness. But when he popped them into his mouth, the rich mixture of sweet and sour fruit reminded him he had not eaten since breakfast. *Perhaps he's just deaf or mute.* Arduwyn frowned at his assumption. The stranger lacked the mannerisms Arduwyn associated with hearing loss; he did not focus on Arduwyn's lips to determine when he spoke or to try to interpret the words. Neither did the stranger exaggerate his gestures. *Apparently, he lives alone. Maybe he just never learned the proper social conventions.*

The huge man seized a handful of berries and crammed them into his own mouth. Arduwyn watched him chew, looking for evidence of awkwardness, something to indicate the stranger had an abnormality of his tongue or palate. But the bearlike man ate with a casual ease, despite a trickle of purple juice that twined through his beard. He offered the basket to Arduwyn again.

'Thank you.' Arduwyn accepted more berries. *A language prob-*

lem? He sifted through his knowledge as the huge man continued eating. Raised on the Western tongue spoken in the towns west and south of Pudar, Arduwyn also knew the trading tongue fluently and enough Northern to impress the few Northmen who had come by the stands he had helped work in Pudar. People east of the Great Frenum Mountains had a language of their own, but few Westlanders knew any of its words. The stranger did not look swarthy enough to be a misplaced Easterner. Arduwyn ate thoughtfully, one or two berries at a time. Aside from the possibility that this silent mountain man was a barbarian with only a tribal language, Arduwyn knew the stranger most likely spoke the trading tongue.

Clearing his throat, Arduwyn met the stranger's large, dark eyes. 'Can you understand me?'

A grin split the black beard covering the man's face. He nodded once.

A breakthrough. Arduwyn continued on the same tack. 'You can.'

No reply. The dark-haired man munched another handful of berries.

Frustrated, Arduwyn considered. So far, the stranger had reacted only to a direct question. 'Can you speak?'

The man nodded again.

Arduwyn awaited the natural verbal response that should follow. When none came, he smiled, studying his companion. Despite his size, the hermit seemed harmless. Huge eyes sat, widely-spaced, across a broad, straight nose. A pink glow fanned chubby cheeks. He kept his hands clasped shyly in his lap, his legs tucked beneath him. *All right. Let's try a query that can't take a yes or no answer.* 'What's your name?' Realizing that would only require one word, Arduwyn added, 'And why do you live alone in a cave?'

'Me Sterrane,' the man announced proudly. 'And this home.'

The gigantic man's childish voice and manner nearly made Arduwyn laugh. He bit his cheeks, and several moments passed before he found enough control to speak. Even then, he only managed to say, 'Very nice, Sterrane.'

Sterrane grabbed his ankles and rocked in place, looking even more infantile.

The warmth of the fire slowly penetrated Arduwyn's soaked shirt and britches. Its comfort made him feel sleepy, and Sterrane's gentle manner threw him further off his guard. The mystery of a hermit in the mountains had drawn Arduwyn's attention from his troubles. He accepted the challenge of initiating a conversation, hoping for a longer respite from the discomfort that had haunted him since Colbey announced his tribe. *And this feeble-minded innocent deserves to know he has Renshai near his door.* 'Pleased to meet you, Sterrane. You might want to stay in your home, your cave, a few days.'

Sterrane said nothing, but he went still and looked at Arduwyn quizzically.

'There's a Northman out there who may cause some trouble. I don't know that he'd hurt you, but better to stay out of his way.'

'Northman?' Sterrane repeated.

Arduwyn leaned closer conspiratorially. 'He claims to be Renshai.'

'Renshai.' Sterrane lumbered to his feet. 'Renshai? Where?'

Arduwyn pointed vaguely northward. 'Camped at the forest's edge.'

'Renshai.' Sterrane snatched up his ax and ran half-way to the mouth of the cave before Arduwyn realized he had moved.

Terror ground through Arduwyn, and he realized his mistake. *Firfan's bow! The idiot is going to challenge Colbey by himself.* He sprang to his feet, chasing after Sterrane, pausing only to gather his cloak from the jagged floor. 'Wait. Wait, Sterrane! You can't go . . .'

Sterrane disappeared into the rain and darkness, and Arduwyn stumbled after him. *Colbey will hack Sterrane apart.* Thoughts tumbled over one another. *What if Sterrane goes into some blind rage and kills Mitrian?* Arduwyn skidded through the cave mouth, listening for some sign of passage. But Sterrane's shy awkwardness seemed to have vanished. Despite night's blackness obscuring the crags, he moved swiftly and nearly in silence. Arduwyn caught a glimpse of a hand as Sterrane headed northward. He followed, mostly from memory of his route.

Mitrian lied to me. She supports Renshai, even claims to be one. Why do I care what happens to her? He whipped his cloak over his shoulders, clutching it tight against the rain. Mitrian's garnet lay, a smooth bulge in Arduwyn's pocket. It inspired a sense of responsibility he could not shake, and the realization that he liked this woman he scarcely knew bothered as well as pleased him. *I can't let Sterrane hurt Mitrian. And I can't be responsible for sending a stranger, more boy than man, to his death.* Arduwyn quickened his pace.

But Sterrane glided like a shadow through the darkness, his long strides outdistancing Arduwyn. Soon, even the watery glimmer of moonlight on the ax head disappeared, and Arduwyn found himself wholly alone. *I don't believe this. What have I done?* As his eyes readjusted to the gloom, he quickened his pace, striding across the stone ledges he had fled across only a short time earlier. Thoughts tumbled through his mind. *How much damage can one or two Renshai cause?* The image of Colbey formed in Arduwyn's mind, a lethal fascination, a single wolf in a world of sheep. *But whatever else Colbey is, he's not a rampant killer. It's been sixteen years since word of Renshai has reached me, and a swordsman of his talent does not go unnoticed. If I'm still alive, it's only because he wanted me that way.* Arduwyn burst into the sparse woodlands, only slightly more secure amidst the familiarity of trees and brush. *I need to know Colbey's intentions before I panic the Westlands. And I have to get Stubs.*

Recalling that he had given Sterrane no real directions, Arduwyn gained ground by cutting through the scrub. He no longer heard even faint sounds of the hermit's passage. *Still might get there ahead of him. Maybe I can prevent a fight.* Responsibility turned the berries sour in Arduwyn's gut. His mother's training had made him touchy in social situations, given him an urgent need to be liked and an intuitive feel for other's moods. But his overwhelming love for the forests had ruined every friendship he ever made, save one. And that one he had betrayed when he slept with Kantar's wife.

Memory flared to guilt, but a glimpse of the pale flush of a campfire through fog dispelled Arduwyn's train of thought. As he pushed closer, he discovered three shapeless blurs seated near the flames and the larger shadows of horse and donkey some distance away. *Three people. Thank Firfan, holy god of huntsmen, Sterrane hasn't arrived yet.*

Even as the thought came to Arduwyn, Sterrane's fur-clad figure burst from the woods. Swearing, Arduwyn raced for the camp, nearly at the border before he realized Sterrane had his ax slung across his shoulder in a peaceful, carrying position. Of the three around the fire, only Colbey rose to meet the stranger. Stepping back into the brush, Arduwyn unslung his bow, watching and waiting.

'You Renshai ?' Sterrane said in his childlike, prattling manner.

Unable to see the Renshai's eyes, Arduwyn could not tell how Colbey was reacting to the new arrival. His head did not move, and his stance remained casual, his hands still at his sides. Near the fire, Mitrian and Garn regarded Sterrane and Colbey, their exchanged glances revealing curiosity.

Arduwyn slipped closer in silence.

'I am,' Colbey admitted easily.

Arduwyn's hand clenched on his bow's rest.

'Me Sterrane.' The hermit made a broad gesture of greeting. 'Me go with you.'

Shocked, Arduwyn nearly missed the slight stiffening of Colbey's demeanor that revealed he was as surprised as his companions by Sterrane's sudden appearance and strange demand. Several moments passed in a silence broken only by the swish of rain-wet leaves in wind and the water's hiss against the flames. Colbey stroked his chin with a finger as he contemplated a statement that seemed illogical to Arduwyn. Apparently finding the answer within himself, Colbey nodded. 'Very well, Sterrane. Welcome.' He twisted toward Mitrian and Garn. 'Give Sterrane that rabbit we saved for Arduwyn. There's something I need to do.' Without further explanation, Colbey headed into the woods.

Arduwyn hesitated long enough to see Garn reaching to honor Colbey's request and Mitrian looking rapidly from Colbey to Sterrane, as if seeking some deep meaning in their brief exchange. Arduwyn suspected she echoed his thought. *Why would Colbey allow an armed stranger to join his companions without a single question or warning? And what reason could Sterrane have for doing such a thing?* By the time Arduwyn turned to follow Colbey, the Renshai was nowhere to be seen.

Damn! Arduwyn whirled, aware Colbey could not have gotten far. Using his usual combination of speed and stealth, he brushed through the trees, as always attuned to the rustle of movement. *No matter his grace and skill, Colbey can't walk more quietly than a fox.*

A sound to Arduwyn's left startled him. He shied as Colbey swung around a tree directly into his path. The Renshai's black tunic and red breeks made a rosy contrast to eyes as stark and hard as grains of ice. A slight smile played across his features, revealing personal triumph. 'Arduwyn. I thought I'd find you behind anyone who knows what I am.' No emotion accompanied the words.

Arduwyn back-pedaled, beyond sword range. From habit, he traced Colbey's route from the camp, discovering it went nearly straight. Apparently, Colbey had stood motionless behind the tree, waiting for Arduwyn to find him. Recognizing the simplicity of Colbey's plan eased the hunter's mind and made him bolder. 'I want my donkey.'

'Take it,' Colbey shrugged. 'It's yours. Why would I keep it from you?' The Renshai's gaze drifted to the bow in Arduwyn's hand, and he frowned disdainfully. ' But I do want to know why you're leaving.'

Arduwyn's victory seemed almost too easy, and the answer too obvious to speak aloud. 'You're Renshai.'

Colbey remained silent, as if waiting for further explanation. When none came, he nodded in understanding. 'I see. You're a racist.'

'What?' The question was startled from Arduwyn. 'No.' Words failed him, and he stammered. 'That's insane.'

'Is it?'

Arduwyn regained his powers of speech. 'The Golden-Haired Devils weren't a race. They were a band of mass murderers.'

'Oh.' Colbey accepted the news as if hearing it for the first time. 'I see.' He looked pensive. 'And you've seen me murder? Have you seen me commit any crime at all?'

'No,' Arduwyn admitted reluctantly. He kept his gaze on the Renshai's hands, alert for any hostile gesture. He would not be caught off-guard by conversation. 'But Garn told me you killed nine Northmen.'

Colbey leaned casually against the tree. 'Did he also tell you he and Mitrian killed?'

'In self-defense, yes.'

'And mine was other than self-defense? I didn't even draw my sword until I was attacked.'

'You killed nine men.'

'So, because I'm competent, I should let nine Northmen kill me?'

'You instigated the fight.'

'Only by being Renshai. I was perfectly polite. They were just racists, too.'

Annoyed anew at the insult, Arduwyn raised his voice nearly to a shout. 'Damn it. It's not racism to have proven enemies.' Seeing the trap he had neatly walked into, Arduwyn groaned.

Colbey delivered the coup de grace. 'But we've already determined I've done nothing to make you see me as an enemy.' He smiled. 'Besides, I was there. Of all the Westlands people, the Renshai respected and befriended the high king, Valar, in Béarn. The king's city and its sister, your own Erythane, were spared our attack.'

Though startled by Colbey's knowledge of his birth home, Arduwyn tussled with the anger and frustration of his exile; he pined for the Erythanian forests he knew and loved more than any person and could never see again. 'I don't have loyalties to Erythane or her allies.' *How could Colbey possibly know where I'm from?*

Colbey plucked at a loose curl of bark, addressing Arduwyn's unspoken question rather than the one he had expressed aloud. 'Once the Béarnides and Erythanians had nothing to fear from Renshai, they found an understanding for our culture and our honor. The King of Béarn even came to worship our gods, and . . .'

'That king is gone,' Arduwyn reminded. 'His direct line purged.' But even he realized Valar had been a far kinder ruler than the brother who had murdered and replaced him.

Colbey continued as if Arduwyn had never interrupted '. . . unlike our women, who respected our line too much to bring foreign blood into the tribe, our men would leave their seed behind. The Erythanian women were particularly attracted to our few redheads. Like it or not, Arduwyn, your grandfather was probably Renshai.'

Arduwyn smoothed his spiky, copper-colored locks self-consciously. The image jarred too much to fit into his well-ordered vision of reality. 'If he was, my grandmother was raped.' *All the more reason to hate Renshai.*

Colbey rolled his eyes, as if to suggest that the assertion fell too far beneath his dignity to grace it with a reply. 'Renshai don't rape allies. Why would he have needed to when so many Erythanian women were willing? If you're too narrow-minded to consider the truth, take your donkey and go. I won't stop you.' He stiffened dangerously, and his tone became menacing. 'But if I catch you telling anyone that we're Renshai, I'll hunt you down and kill you.'

Renshai justice was cruel but seldom swiftly finished. Arduwyn shivered. He wished Colbey's threat could rouse him to anger, but he felt only a cold dread. He avoided Colbey's stare. 'It sounds to me as if you want me to stay with you. Why? Is it because of this Renshai blood I might carry?'

'No.' The corners of Colbey's mouth twitched, and he fought back a laugh. 'Bloodline is insignificant. You can never be Renshai, and, without a truly odd set of circumstances, neither can your line.' This time, a grim smile slipped past Colbey's defenses. 'You were traveling with Mitrian and Garn before I met them, and they allowed you. I have to assume you all did so for a reason. I came to train Mitrian, not to interfere with her choice of friends.' Colbey straightened so that his weight no longer rested against the tree. All amusement left him.

'There's more,' Arduwyn pressed.

'There's more,' Colbey agreed. 'You know the stories that the Renshai ravaged the West simply because they didn't know how to hunt for food?'

Arduwyn nodded.

'Lies,' Colbey said. 'The Renshai ravaged the West because they love war.'

Arduwyn stared, surprised by the strange turn the conversation had taken. 'Oh, well, thanks. Now I feel much better about them.'

Colbey raised his hand to indicate he had not finished. 'Some Renshai do know how to hunt. But I'm not one of them. I don't think Garn can either. Sterrane doesn't have a bow or spear. And, even if Mitrian can hunt, and I doubt she's had much practice, she won't have the time.'

Arduwyn kicked at a granite outcropping, gaze fixed on Colbey. 'So you want me along to feed a gang of enemies.'

'Not at all. I don't care whether you come along or not. I have enough knowledge of plants and medicines to barter food for healing. I've done it before. But I may be too busy teaching Mitrian to take the time. Or the West may have a healthy year. If it comes to starving or killing, I'll gladly choose the latter. If nothing else, war is only an extension of Mitrian's sword practices.' Colbey shrugged, as if he had said the most natural thing in the world. 'Think of yourself as Renshai insurance for the West. I won't attack unless provoked.'

Arduwyn considered. 'I have your word on that?'

Colbey hesitated long enough to assure Arduwyn he took his vows seriously. 'Fair enough. You have my word. So long as we have the basic necessities and no one tries to harm us, I won't be violent.'

Arduwyn pressed his advantage. 'And you won't tell anyone you're Renshai.'

Now Colbey grinned. 'You drive a hard bargain, archer.'

'Hunter,' Arduwyn corrected. 'And?'

'I won't tell anyone we're Renshai,' Colbey added. 'So, you'll join us?'

The image of Bel came to Arduwyn's mind, her simple dress baggy over plumply rounded curves. Behind her, he saw Kantar's handsome features and winning smile. He tried to picture his best friend in a sickbed, but the image would not come. 'I don't know. I have to get to Pudar.'

Colbey's brows raised, as if to question Arduwyn's reasons for wasting his time with promises. 'I should think Garn and a pair of Renshai should be able to escort you safely to the Trading City.'

Arduwyn met Colbey's severe, blue-gray eyes. 'You'd change your course for me?'

Colbey laughed. 'What course? I can train Mitrian anywhere. I had an overwhelming feeling we should stay in the Granite Hills for a time. For whatever reason, that premonition has gone. For my own purposes, I'd like to go to the Western Wizard's cave. Pudar is on the way.'

What reason could a Renshai have for seeing the guardian of the Westlands? Arduwyn's eyes narrowed, but he did not challenge Colbey's intentions aloud.

'Of course, we're going to travel slowly. I'll take as many hours a day as I can for practice. I'd like to reach Pudar in about eight months, just in time for Mitrian to have the baby.'

Arduwyn pondered the words. Kantar's illness was fatal but slow, and Arduwyn could use the time to sort through his own tangle of emotions. An excuse for delay seemed like a godsend, but Colbey's plan confused him. 'All right. But wouldn't it make more sense to stay in one place for seven months and spend the first or last traveling?'

'Not exactly.' Colbey's gaze probed the trees between their position and the camp, though surely he could see nothing through the darkness. 'I need to hire you for something else.'

Arduwyn waited, uncertain whether to encourage.

'We *are* being followed. Or will be.' Colbey interrupted himself in explanation and defense. 'Don't ask me how I know. I just do.' He continued in his normal tone. 'He's a young Northman called Rache. I want you to see to it he doesn't catch up to us.'

'No !' Arduwyn backed away, his hand falling to his bow. 'I told you, I'm a hunter not an archer. I'll kill men if I have to, but I can't be hired to do it.'

'Kill Rache ?' Colbey looked genuinely startled. 'I doubt you could.' His gaze rolled to the bow in Arduwyn's grip. 'At least, not in a fair fight.'

The insinuation that a bow could not be used in an honest fight made Arduwyn glower.

Colbey did not address Arduwyn's annoyance. 'I'd sooner have you kill *me*. I'd just like you to keep track of Rache's location, to give me plenty of warning so we can move on before he finds us.'

It seemed a strange request. 'Why ?' Arduwyn asked suspiciously.

'You're just going to have to trust me.' Apparently realizing the unlikeliness of his suggestion, Colbey explained further. 'Even I don't understand the details, but I know a lot of things I shouldn't. For Rache's sake, he can't find us. And you mustn't let Garn and Mitrian know about Rache following us. Garn would hunt him down. Mitrian would insist we let him catch us. Don't tell Sterrane either. I doubt he could keep a secret.'

Aware Colbey either could not or would not explain further, Arduwyn followed the turn of the conversation. 'And Sterrane ? Why did you accept his presence so easily ?'

'I'm not sure,' Colbey admitted. 'He asked, and it just felt right. Besides, Mitrian's training will change her. A lot. Swordcraft, killing, and Renshai philosphy always do. Usually, the amount of teaching I'm going to give her in eight months occurs over the same number of years, along with the social and moral training that comes with experience. With enough dedication, my teachings can be compressed; experience can't. Mitrian's going to need all the gentle, compassionate examples she can get. For whatever reason Sterrane wants to join us, he can fulfill that purpose.'

Colbey did not mention that Arduwyn could do the same and better; the hunter's experiences were accompanied by a social grace Sterrane could not possibly possess. Again, Arduwyn studied Colbey. Arduwyn still felt an odd combination of awe and terror in the Renshai's presence. He suspected Colbey knew more than he admitted, and the Erythanian felt certain Colbey hid much about his motivations. But other things seemed undeniable. *The West is safer with someone who can move quickly and silently watching this Renshai. I can't stop Colbey training Mitrian, but I can see to it his cruelty is balanced by reason.* 'Agreed. I'll come and do these things for you.'

A tight smile formed on Colbey's face. 'Good. Perhaps we can get you over your racism problem, too.' Turning, he headed back to the camp.

'Arrogant bastard,' Arduwyn mumbled to himself.

Colbey's answering laugh rumbled among the trees.

Mar Lon Davrinsson perched on a stone warmed by the late summer sun. In Mizahai's Tavern, the constant reek of alcohol had worn on him, a stifling, endlessly unyielding reminder of his failings. He had sought the solace of fresh air and sunshine on a poorly maintained road that ran between Rozmath and the royal city of Stalmize. The ribbon of pathway wound through dirty towns and muddy farm fields pale from erosion. And Mar Lon had found a quiet sanctuary on which to compose and perfect his newest efforts, an immovably large rock on the road's boundary. The *lonriset* lay in a crevice, supported by a rounded ridge of granite.

A figure appeared in the distance. Mar Lon raked a twig from his straight, brown hair, watching the stranger from the corner of his eyes. He had little to fear from the main body of Eastern citizenry. From a quick glance, most would dismiss him as one of their own. And since his presence had required permission from the same king whom the citizens worshiped as Sheriva's chosen one, Mar Lon doubted anyone would challenge him. Still, he did not fully let down his guard.

Soon, the Easterner became clearly visible as a boy in his early to mid teens. He dragged a dilapidated cart partially filled with stones plucked from the harvested field. A scraggle of coal black hair fell across his forehead, sweat soaked into a clump. His small eyes, equally dark, studied Mar Lon quizzically, and he stopped several arms' lengths from the boulder. 'Hello,' he said, the greeting more curious than polite.

'Hello,' Mar Lon returned. He reached for his *lonriset* and began tuning the strings by ear, more interested in trying his new song than in chatting with a stranger.

The boy waited in silence until Mar Lon adjusted the string of highest pitch and balanced the *lonriset* across one raised thigh. 'Play me a song?' Though the request lacked the Northern or Western amenities, the soft question in the boy's tone lent it a courtesy Mar Lon had not heard since entering the Eastlands.

'What do you want to hear?' Mar Lon sighed, awaiting the request for a bawdy or violent tune, promising himself that, this once, he would not let it bother him. The morning breeze felt too pleasant, the sunlight too welcome.

'Play something gentle and sweet. Something peaceful.'

Mar Lon gaped, replaying the boy's words in his head, certain he had misheard. He had tried for so long to create such an audience, without success. It seemed impossible that now it would come to him. 'Something peaceful?'

The Easterner nodded. He dropped the wagon's handle, taking a seat on the piled stones. 'My name's Abrith. I'm thirteen, and I'm going off to Stalmize in a few months to train for the war. Before I go, I want to hear some peaceful stuff. Do you know some?'

Excitement tingled through Mar Lon. Without replying, he launched into the most complicated melody he had written in the past month. The harmonies glided off the strings in smooth tones as perfect as crystals, and his voice found each note with a flawless precision nature could not match. Every combination begged for peace and promised tranquility.

Abrith's eyes drifted closed. A placid smile softened features prematurely wrinkled by the sun.

The joyful expression seemed contagious. Mar Lon's heart soared, and, here on a boulder in a field, he sang with a beauty none of his previous performances could match.

When the song concluded, Abrith opened his eyes. 'Beautiful,' he said. 'Perfect.' Then, apparently unable to leave the topic long enough to find other words, he repeated. 'Perfectly beautiful.'

Volumes of ideas seemed to converge on Mar Lon at once. Still, he remained silent, afraid to say anything for fear of losing the only support he had yet found in the Eastlands.

Abrith hummed quietly, mimicking the melody line in an imitation so poor it made Mar Lon wince. The Easterner looked up deferentially, as if to ask a favor he knew would be denied. 'Could you sing it again? I want to try to get the words right so I can do it for my friends. They'd love it.'

Mar Lon clamped the *lonriset* between his knees, holding the neck lightly in both hands. His heart pounded. 'Can you bring your friends here? I can play that song and several others for them.'

Abrith's eyes widened, aghast. 'You'd do that?' Then, apparently thinking he had miscommunicated, he clarified. 'My friends are all about my age. We don't got no money to pay you.' He rose, grasping the wagon's tow.

Mar Lon laughed for the first time in weeks. All the money in the Eastlands could not buy the elation born of a message of peace successfully taught nor the price that an appreciative audience could grant him. 'No money is expected or necessary. Please, gather your friends. It would be the greatest pleasure of my life to play for them.' The vitality that seemed to course through Mar Lon drove aside weeks of despair. And Mar Lon knew he meant every word.

15 Becoming Renshai

Farming villages and fields dotted the woodlands west of the Granite Hills and south of the Weathered Mountains, random as seeds scattered by the wind. Mitrian, Garn, Colbey, Arduwyn, and Sterrane spent their nights in inns or rented cottages, their route an unpredictable series of loops and zigzags through towns otherwise conspicuously devoid of weapons and warriors.

For Mitrian, the weeks went by in a whirlwind of flashing steel. Every day, Colbey worked her to exhaustion, pausing only for lessons on Renshai language, history and philosphy, often over a meal prepared by Arduwyn or Sterrane, then pressed her to exhaustion again. Early on, nausea from the pregnancy and Mitrian's low level of conditioning limited her practices. Then the demon would flood her mind with blood lust, driving her nearly as hard as Colbey, filling in details of the past and philosophical gaps when her mind wandered or her endurance failed.

As weeks spilled into months, Mitrian's stamina increased. Her broad-boned frame, always slender, became firm as well. The demon settled into the steel, quivering with eager interest as Colbey's sword maneuvers grew more complicated and Mitrian laboriously mastered them.

Rache Kallmirsson drew rein in a wheat field just outside the farm town of Shidran. His horse slowed to a walk, its hooves digging rents in soil riddled with the mounds of animal burrows. With every few steps, the weakened ground collapsed into tunnels. The horse stumbled, jogging Rache and reawakening the pain of his most recent battle. Eight times in as many months he had been attacked by mixed groups of white-skinned strangers and ardent Western youngsters who followed the albinos like adoring worshipers. Time and again, Rache had patiently turned the teens' impetuousness against them. Not one returned alive to warn his companions or suggest strategy for the next assault; those Rache pressed for information invariably killed themselves or forced his hand against them. He learned only that they exalted a nameless, white god, half-bird and half-man.

Though Rache had won the battles, he seemed certain to lose the war. A chorus of bruises, strains, and gashes always accompanied him. The bony calluses of healing rib and collarbone breaks became familiar. His back ached, and he learned to protect his lower legs, because slashes there healed frustratingly slowly and seemed more prone to infection. A feeling of being watched harried him daily. He learned to sleep like an animal, always at the edge of alertness; the slightest sound awakened him, tense and ready for action.

Rache crossed the border of Shidran's village proper. Between jagged rows of cottages, four muddy children rolled stones across a packed-earth road. Seeing no other people, Rache approached.

Glancing up from his labor, one boy spotted Rache and stared at the tattered, golden-haired warrior from beneath a fringe of dark bangs. Prompted by their companion, the others looked up as well. Long stringy hair swung from every head. One wore her patched and faded homespun as a skirt, cuing Rache that he faced three boys and a girl. In the other towns, he had met adults first, usually in the form of farmers tending crops. But in the manner of his tribe, Rache greeted the children like people rather than infants. 'Hello.'

The boys exchanged glances, and the smallest slipped behind the other two. The girl answered. 'Hallo.' She added guilelessly, 'You a Nort'man?'

Rache smiled tolerantly. 'I am. I'm looking for another Northman, an older man. He's traveling with a burly young man and a woman. They have swords.' From experience, Rache had learned to focus his description on Colbey and the weaponry. Northmen were rare throughout the Westlands and swords every bit as scarce in the farm towns. 'Are they here?'

The two larger boys spoke between themselves rather than directly to Rache. 'He's talkin' 'bout Cull-bay 'n' Garnd.'

'An' Garnd's wife.' Skinny and freckle-faced, the other puffed out his cheeks, looped his arms out in front of him, and clamped his hands.

His male companions giggled at the image.

The girl glared. 'They's had a great, big idiot an' a li'l redhead hunner with 'ems, too.'

Rache nodded. A scrawny, red-haired archer and a hairy, dim-witted man who spent most of their time in the forests but came and went, supplying Colbey, Garn, and Mitrian with food corroborated earlier descriptions by the townsfolk. But this was the first time Rache had heard anyone refer to Mitrian as Garn's wife or imply that she was fat. The former rankled, but the latter prickled the edges of his consciousness with dread. Rache hesitated, hating his need to know. 'What did you mean by that gesture about the woman?'

Addressed directly, the skinny boy flushed, the color highlighting his freckles.

The girl answered for him. 'Nothin' bad. She uz pretty an' all.' She twirled a loop of greasy hair as if in envy of Mitrian's thick, dark locks. 'But the way she dressed in britches an' carried on with a sword, I'da thought she uz a man 'ceptin' she uz real pregnant.'

Pregnant. Surely Mitrian's condition had been clear to the various townsfolk months earlier, but no adult had been crass enough to mention it to Rache. *Mitrian pregnant. A baby. GARN's baby.* Numbing realization seeped through Rache. *Mitrian is carrying Garn's baby. Why? How?* No matter how Rache examined the situation, it made no sense to him. *If Garn raped her, why would she travel willingly with him? But to sleep with him on purpose would defy her life, her father, and everything she's known or cared for.* Rache's own thoughts brought an answer. *I warned Santagithi he had reined his strong-willed daughter in too far.* No satisfaction accompanied the observation, only raw grief and revulsion. To strike back against her father's tyranny by running off with a man was simply foolish; to choose Garn was a cruelty beyond words, a bitter, vindictive decision aimed, not against the man who had shackled her sense of adventure, but the one who had tried to set it free.

Rache recalled the love he had lavished upon Mitrian. He had devoted his time to her as he had to no one else but his swords, teaching her secrets serious warriors would sell their souls to know. He had consoled her from her days of dirty diapers to her years of spurned love. But the sibling kinship Rache thought they had shared seemed a lie, one more betrayal in a long string that had started with her father. Sickened, Rache lowered his head, feeling as battered and broken as an ancient toy kicked aside for a newer, shinier trinket. He struggled against the knowledge that followed naturally. *By law, Mitrian's child is Renshai. So many years I isolated myself to prevent an heir, and now Garn's child will be Renshai.*

Loathing tore through Rache, the wound to his spirit deeper than the gashes and bruises left by his battles with cultists. He ground his teeth until his jaw ached. The pain seemed appropriate, fitting punishment for the evil his joy at watching Mitrian perform sword work had caused. *It was all a game to me, a chance to view the beauty of the Renshai's perfect maneuvers without inflicting the heritage upon anyone.* For a moment, Rache's intellect rose to his defense. *Mitrian begged for those lessons. How could I know she would be drawn from her father's town or discover Colbey?* But

Rache granted himself no quarter. *I saddled Mitrian with the cruelest, most hated legacy in the world, and I created Garn to live among Renshai. His presence alone will rob the tribe of our ancient honor.* Rache concentrated on his myriad injuries, hoping physical pain would divert the anguish of his thoughts.

The girl cleared her throat. 'They left yesterday. Headed west.'

Rache had expected nothing else. For eight months it had gone the same way. No matter how many times he lost and found their strange and jagged trail, Colbey and the others eluded him by a day, a week, sometimes only an hour. Always before, Rache had convinced himself that Garn was somehow leading his companions, keeping them continually one jump ahead, teasing Rache like a dog with a piece of meat. But now, in the depths of this new despair, Rache realized what his subconscious had known all along: *It's not Garn avoiding me, it's Colbey.* It was a cruel blow. *And there can only be one reason why Colbey would shun the only other Renshai.* Guilt slammed Rache. He clutched at the reins, blind to the children's stares. *Colbey knows I survived the assault on Devil's Island. And he can't face, shouldn't have to face, the fact that the greatest swordsman in the world trained a coward.*

A wild conglomeration of self-hatred, frustration, and rage suffused Rache now, and he screamed his denial to a friendly spring sky that seemed to mock him. He yanked on the rein, ripping the horse's head suddenly to the right. The beast half-reared, then spun on its hind legs, leaping into a frenzied gallop for the town border. The children scattered, caught in the swirling dust kicked up by its passage.

Rache gave the horse its head, and it sprinted between sprouting rows of wheat, floundering as the thin-walled burrows collapsed beneath its drumming hooves. The world whipped past Rache in a maddeningly cheerful wash of budding plants and golden sun. The horse pranced, rocking in low, playful bucks at the joy of near freedom and pleasant weather. Rache didn't care if the horse's antics aggravated his injuries, didn't bother to brace himself for the jolts of missteps amid the burrows, almost wished he could slip from his mount's back and be trampled beneath its flying hooves. The two worlds he had known, his heritage of birth and the one he had adopted at Episte's urgings, had forsaken him. Only one thing remained for Rache to live for, that for which his mother had paid with her soul. And Rache now knew the mistake she had made. *The prophecy was never for me. The Golden Prince of Demons is and was always Colbey. My mother damned her soul in vain, and I live cursed by the same fate.*

Like his people, it had never been Rache's way to surrender. His iron will had brought him through battles other men would have forsaken before they started. He had weathered sword strokes and infections. With enviable patience, he had transformed Santagithi's guards from a ragged band of semicompetent braggarts to a force as capable as the larger armies of the Western cities. The things that had driven Rache's life, his friendships, Renshai honor, the price of his mother's soul, had all been stolen from him at once. Nothing remained but the promise of revenge against Garn, and Rache's love and respect for Mitrian might steal that last from him as well.

Gradually, the fields broke to forest. The horse's pace slackened to a walk, and Rache guided it through the tangled web of woodlands. Apparently no longer needed, no longer even wanted, his every reason for existence had disappeared and nothing remained but to end his miserable life. He drew his dagger from a pocket of his leathers. Calmly, his mind traced the route of knife to heart, the careful maneuvering that might admit sharpened steel between the ribs. Clutching the reins in his opposite hand, he probed the lean, hard muscles of his chest, defining the bony ridges and gaps. Yet Rache held the knife. He did not fear the weapon or death; he had waited eagerly and too long for the killing stroke that would send him to Valhalla. But suicide was a coward's way that would bar him from the haven for dead warriors as completely as death on a sickbed.

Again, Rache knew the certainty of being watched. He reined his horse in a clearing beneath towering deciduous trees that blotted out the sun with a cloak of spring leaves. That strangers would intrude upon his misery enraged Rache. The constant pursuit that had haunted him for eight months fueled his anger. Nothing could compare with the chance to die battling enemies, and Rache knew his disdain for his own life would only add to his battle skill. Without need to defend, he could concentrate all his efforts on attack, spilling enemy lives as well as his own. Excited by the opportunity to solve all his problems at once, Rache listened, trying to locate the others and afraid he had imagined them.

Rache froze, sifting sound from the brooding stillness of the forest. A breeze ruffled the leaves overhead. He followed the path of their noise. Beneath the steady rattle, a branch snapped. Smiling, Rache wheeled his horse to meet the sharper sound. 'Come out!' he shouted.

No answer.

'Come out!' Rache called, louder. His horse dropped its head, snuffling for greenery amidst the rotting pulp of drying leaves. 'Sniveling pack of cowards. You want me? Come get me! I'll cut you into pieces for the ravens. And your ugly bird-headed god as well.'

Still no response. The sound did not recur.

Frustrated, Rache traded the dagger for one of his swords. He wrenched up the horse's head, forcing it a few steps nearer to the border of the clearing. 'Who are you men who slink like curs, afraid to face one crippled soldier? I'll kill you all. The more the better. This world needs fewer cowards.'

This time, a man stepped from the foliage, backlit by a stripe of sunlight through the younger trees. Strawberry blond braids framed a weathered, predatory face some fifteen years older than Rache's. Though light, his skin bore the natural pallor of a Northman rather than the strange, ivory hue of the Leukenyan priests. He kept his left side toward Rache, twisted just far enough so Rache could glimpse the sword on his right hip. Something about the man's appearance struck Rache as odd. At first, he attributed the feeling to the reversed location of the sword belt. But Rache had learned to fight with both hands or either, without preference. Two of Santagithi's guards were left-handed, and Rache had sparred with them as frequently as any other. He had also drilled Mitrian far harder on left-handed techniques than right to overcome her long-standing bias.

The stranger spoke in the Northern tongue and with the gruff singsong of the far North. 'Well met.' He added, as if in afterthought, 'Rache.'

Confusion displaced most of Rache's rage. He had expected a pack of crazed cultists or perhaps a spy hired by Garn or Colbey to keep Rache at bay. A Northman in the Westlands seemed odd enough, but to find one trailing him and with knowledge of his name went beyond all possibility.

A ghost of a smile touched the Northman's features and disappeared so quickly that Rache was uncertain he had seen it at all. 'My name is Peusen Raskogsson. Of Nordmir.'

The name struck a spark of memory. Rache recalled having heard it before in the same dialect and nearly the identical voice, that of the dangerous-looking lieutenant whose men called him Slayer. *Peusen. Valr Kirin's brother.* Now that Rache had placed the kinship, the resemblance seemed uncanny. Peusen looked the older of the two by about a decade, yet there was nothing soft about the Northman. Despite his friendly greeting, Peusen held a defensive crouch, his left thumb hooked, not quite casually, on his sword belt. Coarser white hairs wound through the red-gold of his braids, curled through his bangs and colored his sideburns silver. And, now that Rache had taken a closer look, he recognized what had struck him as peculiar about Peusen. His right arm ended at the elbow. He

carried the defect so nonchalantly and easily that it had escaped
Rache's notice on first inspection.

When Rache still did not speak, Peusen began his explanation. 'I
apologize for trailing you, though I hope I wasn't quite as loud as a
whole *pack* of sniveling cowards.' He smiled at the jest.

Rache made no reply. Recalling Valr Kirin's talk of Peusen's bold
promise to unite an army of cripples and outcasts, Rache had a good
idea why Peusen had come. As confusion dispersed, wrath and
despair seeped back into Rache's consciousness with anger
uppermost.

In the face of Rache's hostile silence, Peusen's grin wilted. 'My
scouts located you in one of the farm towns a few months ago.' He
gestured eastward. 'It took time for the message to get to me, more
time for others to track you and then for me to find you. I only
caught up with you today.'

Vultures, Rache thought. But still, he had to admit Peusen seemed
to have organized an impressive network of spies.

'Let me explain what I stand for, Rache – ' He paused, waiting for
Rache to fill in his surname and tribe.

The conversation had gone far enough for Rache. Without bothering to try to recall the lies he had told to satisfy the Vikerian king
of his heritage, he jabbed his sword back into its sheath. 'Save your
breath, Raskogsson. I know exactly what you stand for, and I'm not
interested.'

'You're not?' Peusen sounded more matter-of-fact than surprised.
'I'm not.'

'Then perhaps you don't know what I stand for after all. Let me
explain.'

'I'll free you from the effort.' Wanting to be alone, Rache
channeled his anger against the Northman. 'I know who you are.
I'm blood brother to Kirin.'

Peusen's brows rose in interest, but he did not interrupt.

'You're mustering an army of disabled soldiers to try to show up
those who maligned you.' In his rage, Rache did not mince his
words. 'I won't have any part of your bitterness. And I won't be a
member of a ragged band of cripples. I'd gladly die before I'd fall
that low.'

Peusen took the insults in stride; apparently, he had heard them
all before. 'Is that what Kirin told you?'

Guilt touched Rache. Though his doubts had come clearly through
his words, Valr Kirin had shown far more support of his injured
brother than Rache's explanation conveyed. Not wishing to create a
blood feud, he clarified. 'Just the basic plan. The judgements are my
own.'

'Good. I expected more from Kirin. And, Rache, I expected a lot more from you.' Peusen held his fighting stance as if it were the most natural position in the world. 'Do you really think a commander from the army of the high king of the North would accept anything short of competence? I don't demand any less of my current troops than I did my underlings in the king's army. I can't afford to. My soldiers aren't crippled, Rache, because they choose not to be crippled by birth defects or injuries, banishment or criminal charges against them. History makes no difference to me. I don't care whether a man lost his leg in war or if a whorehouse wench chopped it off out of spite. I don't ask if those charged with crimes are guilty or innocent. It doesn't matter. If he can fight with a Northman's skill and commitment or can be trained to, he's in. Otherwise, he's welcome to stay on as a cook, a smith, a tailor.'

Rache shook his head, unable to banish the image of a town teeming with limping, leering, disfigured men. It brought to mind his childhood visions of Hel, inspired by his mother's stories of the realm for those who died from cowardice, illness, or with body parts missing. 'I just don't think cloistering these men is the answer. They need to learn how to get along in the world as it is, not how to hide from it.'

'Exactly.' Peusen fairly crowed in triumph. 'Think, Rache. What's a soldier banished from a homeland he loves supposed to do? Join an enemy's army? What can a warrior injured in battle do when his higher ups say he can't fight because he might get hurt? Or worse, he can't be trusted with his companions' lives any longer.' Peusen's face reddened in anger. 'Damn it, Rache, it's not perfect. But it's an alternative to never fighting again, to ridicule, or the permanent sanctity offered by that dagger you nearly used on yourself.'

Rache scowled, annoyed at how easily Peusen had guessed his intent.

'All my efforts are temporary. But when the Easterners come to the Western Plains, I'm going to be there at the head of the boldest, most capable army of the Westlands. War makes for strange new alliances. Once my men are proven, every general will be clamoring to take their soldiers back from me. If my men wish to leave, they're free to go. I'll *help* them go. And, I'll be there for the others.'

Rache considered. He had no choice but to admire Peusen Raskogsson's dedication, but he could not picture himself among a unit of outcasts. 'I see the good in what you say. I even thank you for the opportunity. It's just not for me.'

'Very well.' Peusen's voice remained level, but his hand clamped to his sword hilt. 'Pleased to have met you. Now I have to kill you.'

Peusen's statements seemed so incongruous, it took Rache several moments to convince himself he had heard correctly. 'What?'

Peusen crouched, scissor-stepping toward Rache's mount. 'If word of my men gets out, every town in the West will come looking for its missing thieves and murderers. I have to keep you quiet, and the only sure way is to kill you.'

Rache reined his mount backward. 'This is insane.' Uncertain whether to draw his sword or laugh, he tried to reason with the circling general. 'I can't fight you. I – '

Peusen interrupted. 'You're what? Too much of a coward? Afraid you'll be slaughtered by an aging cripple?' He lunged for Rache's leg.

Rache wheeled his horse, catching the stroke on his sword. His half-hearted riposte met a gracefully competent parry. 'I admire what you're doing. Your men need you. Don't throw away your life to make a point to me.'

Peusen's answer was a wild flurry of attack. Forced to defend, Rache quieted, meeting each stroke and returning two for every one. Years of teaching warriors had trained him in assessing the skills of his opponents. Had Rache been anything but Renshai, Peusen's ability would have astounded him. Strong and fast, the Northman's blows seemed committed, yet he recovered every miss, prepared for each of Rache's ripostes, despite their speed. And Peusen fended the attacks to his injured side twice as ably as those to his left.

Rache abandoned speech, hard-pressed in spite of the advantage of his Renshai heritage and training. Sadness crowded him, too, the same that came whenever he discovered a competent enemy with whom he would rather swap techniques and war stories than sword blows. Peusen slashed for Rache's abdomen, opening his own head to Rache's next stroke. Rache's blade whipped for the breach. At the last moment, impulse drove him to turn the sword to its flat. Steel crashed against Peusen's temple, the collision thrumming through Rache's hands. The Northman crumpled to the dirt. His sword rolled from his limp hand.

Rache reined his horse as close to Peusen's sword as possible. Clutching the saddle, he maneuvered himself along the horse's side until he caught a grip on the hilt, then clambered slowly and painfully back into his seat. Turning, he discovered Peusen rolling dizzily to his knees. The Northman rose as Rache drew up to him, a sword in each of the Renshai's fists.

Peusen rubbed at his scalp, and his hand came away smeared with blood. 'Why didn't you kill me?'

Rache opened his mouth to answer, but Peusen spoke first.

'The truth, Rache.'

Rache snorted, disgusted with the whole affair. 'You want me to say I felt sorry for you?'

Peusen's cheeks purpled. He doubled his fist, prepared to battle even without a weapon.

'But,' Rache amended, 'I don't feel sorry for you at all. You're crazy, and I don't kill lunatics.'

Peusen smiled.

'You're also a damned good warrior. Your men need you, and, if your men are half as competent as you, the West needs them. But I'm a better swordsman than you.' Rache spoke fact without a trace of pride. 'Your sword at my side in war would be useful. Your death at my hands would only be a waste.'

Peusen's face returned to its normal color. 'Then you'll join us?'

'No.' Rache tossed back Peusen's sword, and the Northman caught the hilt. 'I'm sorry. I've gotten past my own limitations, and I have to find my own causes. I just don't think I need your support.'

'Support?' Peusen shook his head, genuinely surprised. 'You did misunderstand me. I'm not trying to steal Santagithi's captain. I've heard what you did for his army, and I just hoped you would help me train my men.' Peusen looked pensive. 'If you're no longer in Santagithi's command, you're welcome to join us. You would, of course, start as my highest officer.'

Rache frowned, his current thoughts of Santagithi and his men unpleasant. He wondered if Peusen was humoring him by putting him in a different category from his other misfits. But the expression on Peusen's face seemed sincere. Rache's mind drifted to the past, the years among his own people, the massacre that took all lives but two, and Colbey's rejection. He thought of the time, effort, and caring that had gone into whipping Santagithi's men into a small but able fighting force known throughout the Westlands and the kinship that had goaded him to train Mitrian. Other things came with the memories: Garn's taunts and the blow that had crippled Rache, his mother's soul sold for a prophecy, Mitrian's kidnapping and her apparent decision to marry Garn rather than return to the people who loved her. So many things still to be done, though Rache's reasons for achieving them had disappeared. The realization prompted a question. 'Why are you doing all of this? Why are you training yourself and your men when you know you can't ever . . .' Rache trailed off, recognizing the tactlessness of his query before he completed it.

'. . . go to Valhalla?' Peusen finished.

Rache stared at his horse's mane.

Peusen laughed. 'Leave it to a Northman to remind me of that indecency.'

'I'm sorry,' Rache started, but Peusen waved him silent.

'Don't you think I've agonized about it? There's nothing you could say so nasty that I didn't already think it. At first, the idea haunted me. I mean, why do anything when even if I'm killed in the bloodiest, most glorious conflict ever, the best I could achieve is a coward's death?' Peusen glanced into the sky, as if to challenge deities. 'Then it occurred to me. What if our ancestors were wrong? Why should the gods punish a loyal follower for a stroke of bad luck that has nothing to do with cowardice? What if loss of a body part *doesn't really bar a brave warrior from Valhalla?*'

Horrified, Rache could not keep from interrupting. 'What!' He dared not contemplate Peusen's ramblings further. Like laws, the tenets of religion simply were. To challenge the deep-seated beliefs about dismemberment dooming a man to Hel brought all other truths into question as well. Worse, it meant that the Renshai had been banished and, ultimately, obliterated for a misconception. Rache shut that thought from his mind with a suddenness that added volume to his voice. 'That's sacrilege!'

Peusen shrugged. 'Maybe. But if it is sacrilege, what risk am I taking to challenge? I'm already damned to Hel.' He raised the stump of his hand. 'And, anyway, what kind of honor comes from fighting only to avoid Hel or for the rewards of Valhalla? Now, I'm free. I can believe our priests are wrong and that, even lacking, I can reach Valhalla. Or I can keep the old faith and fight only for my own honor and my own pride.'

Rache winced. The words made his own thoughts of suicide seem all the more petty and selfish. *Peusen is right about the honor. No matter what the others think, I have causes. Whatever the price, I'm going to see to it that Santagithi's army doesn't forget the skills I've taught. I will avenge myself on Garn, and Colbey will know he trained no cowards. Whatever the true nature of the prophecy, my mother's soul will, at least, buy my presence at the Great War, even if it means leaguing with cripples.* History had taught him that, despite its diverse cultures, the West had a strong faith in leadership and could band quickly and cooperatively in times of war. He studied Peusen in the shadows of the clearing. 'All right. I'll help.' He clarified quickly, 'But I have other things to do, too, so I'll need your permission to come and go at will without some crazed Northman threatening my life every time I do.'

'Granted,' Peusen said. He resheathed his sword, trying to look nonchalant. But he could not completely hide his smile.

Mar Lon Davrinsson trotted over the sun-baked roadway toward the boulder from which he had first played for Abrith. Now called the Rock of Peace, it had become a symbol of stability and dedication for Mar Lon's band of peace champions, as well as their meeting place. Over the months, their ranks had swelled to the hundreds, a growing flock of young men who followed the bard like a father and chanted his songs like prayers. At times, the intensity of their devotion frightened Mar Lon, but he could see nothing harmful about sanctioning peace, whatever form this service took. *Once they've spread the cause, once the Easterners and Westerners learn to live in harmony, my followers will have no more need of me. For now, if my person and my songs give them a figurehead, I have little choice but to let them fawn.*

Mar Lon clutched the *lonriset* to his chest, quickening his pace. The first, furled sprouts of the growing season poked from the soil in neat rows on either side of the roadway. The perfume of damp earth and new growth made Mar Lon giddy with joy. Spring always brought pleasant memories, breaking the long, cold depression of winter. This year the renewal portion of nature's cycle seemed to mean far more, boding strength to a small band of peacemakers whose numbers grew with each passing day. He reveled in the warmth of the sun, realizing as he did that its position in the sky meant he was late. He would be the last to arrive. Yet even this did not dampen his spirits. His followers never seemed to mind. In fact, he had found that on those occasions when he came too soon, several of the youngsters would go out of their way to come even earlier the following day in order to be there to greet his arrival.

An *aristiri* hawk sang a trilling melody, and a mimic bird copied the sound, its voice rasping and its notes a half tone flat. Mar Lon smiled, reminded of an old saying: When the *aristiri* finds his voice and loses his appetite, look for a woman.' Mar Lon always loved the changes spring brought to the animals. Woolly winter coats gave way to silky smoothness, the fur in crisp, bright colors not yet bleached by a year of sunlight. And the first birds' mating songs put their winter croaks and shrills to shame. The need for constant hunting kept the *aristiri* hawks silent through the winter. Then, each spring, their voices exploded forth in patterns too beautiful for memory to fully contain.

Yet even as Mar Lon reveled in the music of one of the few mortal creatures more talented than himself, something struck apprehension through him. Buoyed by the events of the last few months and the coming of spring, it took him several seconds to recognize the source of his discomfort. *As close as I am to the Rock of Peace, I shouldn't hear aristiri. A large, noisy mass of people should scare the shy hawks away.* And, as the thought rose, Mar Lon realized he had also drawn close enough that he should be able to hear the rumble of his followers' conversations, if not specific words.

Concern quickened Mar Lon's pace. He raced around curves in the roadway, the silence becoming more ominous as the stone came into sight. Even from a distance, he could see that only a single person awaited him, perched upon the Rock of Peace. The other sat in silent stillness, his form obscured by distance. Mar Lon halted in his tracks. A dozen possibilities drove through his mind in half as many seconds, from the concern that he had come late enough for his followers to go searching for him to the nightmarelike terror that some horrible accident had befallen them all. *Surely the one remaining will have the answers.* Mar Lon broke into a desperate run, clutching the *lonriset* to his abdomen.

As Mar Lon drew closer, details became more apparent. The mysterious person on the rock was tall, lean, and broad-shouldered, a grown man. At first, Mar Lon thought he looked upon a blond, and the pale hair seemed out of place near the Eastern town of Rozmath. But as he came closer, he saw that the shoulder-length locks were a dappled gray. He wore a silk tunic and breeks of an ancient style and cut. Yet, somehow, they made him look regal. Beside him, a cloth bag lay balanced on the stone. As Mar Lon approached, the man rose and called a greeting. 'Ah, Davrin. You're late.'

Breathless, Mar Lon pulled up a polite distance from the stranger. 'Mar Lon,' he gasped. 'Davrin . . . is . . . my . . . father.'

'Yes, of course.' The man fixed a pair of catlike yellow eyes on the bard. 'After a few centuries, you all seem the same. Surely, you were named for your great great great grandfather Martenil and your great grandmother Lonriya.' His hands fell idly to the cloth parcel, outlining a vaguely round object in its depths.

Mar Lon saw no need to discuss his history, so he used his turn to speak to try to catch his breath instead. The stranger's words made it clear he was a Cardinal Wizard, and Davrin's descriptions clinched the identification. Though Carcophan had sanctioned Mar Lon's stay in the East, the bard's heir had never met any Wizard face-to-face. Fear kept his pulse rapid, making it twice as hard to recover his wind.

'I hear you've been stirring up trouble.'

'No.' Mar Lon sucked in a deep breath. 'Not trouble.' Another breath. 'I've been stirring . . .' He cursed his struggling lungs; they took all force and sincerity from his words '. . . peace.'

Carcophan smiled, taking a perverse pleasure in Mar Lon's broken speech. Clearly, it made his own gentle calm seem all the more powerful. 'In this case, the two are the same.'

Mar Lon said nothing, grasping the few seconds his silence gained him to normalize his breathing. Now, his lungs felt raw, and he guessed he would be coughing intermittently for some time.

Carcophan seized on Mar Lon's hush. 'No defense, Mar Lon? Too bad. It seems such a pity to end the line of bards without so much as a whimper.'

'End?' Mar Lon suppressed a cough, and the effort coarsened his voice and brought tears to his eyes. 'What do you mean end?' Finished, he surrendered to the coughing fit.

Carcophan waited impassively for the paroxysm to finish, then laughed. His long, delicate fingers slid to the surface of the stone. 'You tried to foil a prophecy older than all the current Wizards together, one to which I and many before me dedicated our existences.' He glared at Mar Lon, his yellow-green eyes unsettling. His expression indicated that all of Mar Lon's dedication and effort had accomplished little. Yet Carcophan's very presence contradicted this. 'I don't like that.'

Mar Lon coughed again, then swallowed to wet his throat. His thoughts scattered in a thousand different directions, and he felt uncertain of his best approach. It seemed wise to remain deferential, yet the Wizard's arrogance and the missing youngsters drove him to question. And the knowledge gathered by his ancestors and passed on in song did not fail him. 'Your threats may frighten the ignorant, Carcophan, but they won't work on me. I know the Wizards are bound by more laws than any mortal. Odin forbade you from directly killing any of us.'

Carcophan leaned against the Rock of Peace. His touch seemed to defile the artifact. 'I need only carry you to my champion. I'm certain King Siderin would do the deed gladly.'

Mar Lon did not bother to argue the point. Clearly, Carcophan could have already done this thing, yet he had chosen only to talk. 'What have you done with the peacemakers?' He indicated the area around the stone where he should have found the youngsters.

'Me?' Carcophan followed Mar Lon's gesture with his gaze. 'I did nothing with them. They were called up to prepare for war. The law states that, when the king calls, they must go. They went. What else did you expect?'

Mar Lon lapsed into another coughing fit. In truth, he had not expected them to be mustered so suddenly nor en masse. The Eastern and Western lands had been preparing for war for so long it had become meaningless habit. He had expected decades or a lifetime to organize and recruit. By the time his bardic duties called him away, he had hoped to have established a chain of leadership, with actual speakers, perhaps under Abrith. Limited by his family curse, he had not managed to address details. His tone became accusatory. 'You got them all called up at once. Didn't you?'

Carcophan adopted the wide-eyed innocence of one unjustly accused. 'In fact, no. The war is imminent. The army just happened to pass by here, and Siderin took every able-bodied man he could find. Where were *you* that you missed this?'

Mar Lon flushed. Thrilled by spring, he had found one of the Eastlands' rare, surviving pieces of forest and fallen asleep on a bed of leaves, the smell of newborn greenery soothing in his nostrils.

'And besides, isn't this what you wanted?'

Mar Lon stared, certain he must have misunderstood the question. 'My cause is peace. Why would I want my followers in war?'

'Your cause is peace?' Carcophan seemed genuinely surprised.

'Did you hear otherwise?' Mar Lon was equally shocked.

'I had attributed to you some of the cleverness of your ancestors. I thought you had set out to accomplish exactly what you managed to do.'

'Which is?' Mar Lon went rigid, not wholly certain he wanted to know.

'You weakened a faction of the Eastern army, albeit a small one.' Carcophan drummed his fingers against his parcel. 'Your so-called peacemakers have dedicated their attention to things other than winning the war. Distracted, they will surely be the first to die.'

'No!' Mar Lon shouted, the force of the effort sending him into another bout of coughing. The faces of his followers paraded through his mind, eager children not yet burdened by the world.

Carcophan waited until Mar Lon's coughing settled to a volume that did not require him to shout to make himself heard. 'That's why I came to see you, and that's why I'm upset. I don't like seeing my followers die because of some foolish devotion to the cause of an angry, young man.' Carcophan considered. 'Of course, you weren't subtle. Siderin knows about the lapse in his ranks, so I'm certain he'll put your men among the early shock troops. At least that may spare some of my more valuable followers.'

Tears burned in Mar Lon's eyes. 'You can't do that!'

'I'm not doing anything. As you seem to know well, all I can do is advise. I don't make the decisions for any mortal; the army is Siderin's concern.'

Panic drove Mar Lon to a desperate resolve. 'Then I'll go to Siderin!'

'A wise decision. One you should have made months ago.'

'What do you mean?'

'It is easy to preach to those who already agree with you, and easier still to close your ears to things you don't want to know. You united the few ineffectual pawns who already wanted peace. But, Mar Lon, to effect change in a world of order, a world from which Odin banished all dishonor, you have to prove your cause to those with enough power to rewrite the laws. Anything less is a waste of your time. And, in this case, a waste of innocent lives.'

Thoughts and emotions hammered at Mar Lon until his head ached from the need to separate them. Grief overpowered all else, and he could not avoid the pain of guilt, the belief that he had goaded his followers to a cause that would seal their deaths. 'I'll appeal to Siderin then.'

'It's too late.'

'It's never too late for peace.'

Carcophan rolled his parcel from hand to hand on the surface of the Rock of Peace. 'For you, Mar Lon, it's too late. Your father is dead. You're the bard now. By highest law, you must immediately return to Béarn to guard the king.'

The revelation, on top of Mar Lon's other concerns, drove him to an emotional numbness. For several moments, he could not speak. He recalled his father's strong baritone that had brought joy to so many, the gentle manner and agile fingers of the man who had fed him, loved him, and taught him to play. He tried to imagine a world without Davrin's quiet reassurances, without the near-magic of his music or the beauty of his voice. Béarn seemed dark, cold, and empty. Tears filled Mar Lon's eyes, and his vision blurred to watery outlines.

Carcophan waited in silence for Mar Lon to speak.

Tears coursed down Mar Lon's cheeks. 'My father dead? How?'

Carcophan leaned across the stone to face the bard more directly. 'Siderin's messengers paid King Morhane in Béarn to keep the kingdom and its allies out of the war. Davrin made the mistake of playing Western songs of patriotism, trying to convince the king to refuse the alliance.' He grinned. 'I'm afraid your father met with an accident.'

'A purposeful "accident" at the hands of Siderin's assassins, no doubt.' Crying gruffened Mar Lon's voice, making his shouted accusation sound like a childish tantrum.

Carcophan shrugged in reply. 'I thought you'd be glad to go home. After all, Béarn will be at peace; Siderin's gold has seen to that. And note well, Mar Lon. Your own father sanctioned war.'

'My father sanctioned self-defense.'

Again Carcophan shrugged. 'Same thing. If the West chose not to fight, there would be no war as surely as if the Eastlands never attacked.'

There was a logic to Carcophan's claim that Mar Lon could not help but consider. He pictured the fertile West as a wasteland, raped and ravaged by Easterners unable to see past their own self-interest to the futures of their children. He realized that his quest for peace, his driving need to share the light of his knowledge, had made him forget that his mission in the Eastlands was to learn. He had seen much and spoken to many, yet he had missed so much more. He had seen few women and those only working the fields, swaddled in rags that hid even their faces, as if broken and ashamed of their lot.

Once Mar Lon had offered to help a teenage girl with a heavy jug. She had run, a look of terror on her face, water sloshing over her dress with every step. In a land where rape was not only legal but encouraged, where infants were slaughtered on whim, and where minor violations of law meant maiming or death, Mar Lon could understand her reaction. He recalled a song written by his great grandmother about a strong-willed Eastern woman who rebelled against the oppression. Each battle gained her a worse punishment until she had lost both arms, both legs, and her tongue to Eastern justice. Even then, undaunted, she had goaded the other women by drawing pictures and words in the dirt with her nose. It was a dirty, ugly song, one which had brought Mar Lon nightmares as a child. Yet, when correctly performed, the intricate interlacing of harmonies and the perfect choice of every word conveyed a message of encouragement that goaded people to stand up for their causes, no matter the consequences, as well as to expose the Eastern women's lot.

Mar Lon closed his eyes, pained by circumstances that went way beyond his personal loss. The Western women who did not submit to the Easterners would die a cruel and painful death. The Western men would become beasts, forced to ravish the fields their grand-fathers had farmed and nurtured through the centuries. The Western peoples had united before, in times of disease, famine, and war, yet always with the high kingdom in Béarn as their leader. Mar Lon believed that, without Béarn, the Westlands would simply fall, wretched victims crushed by a vicious enemy. Yet the other option, that of war, seemed equally contemptible to Mar Lon. *War is always wrong.* The bard brought his thoughts full circle and back to the conversation. 'If the West does not defend, it will only make it easier for the Eastlands to destroy them.'

'The sooner it's done, the fewer lives lost.'

'If Siderin doesn't attack, there're *no* lives lost.'

'Lives lost isn't Siderin's concern. It's yours.'

'It's everyone's concern!' Mar Lon screamed. 'Am I the only person in the world who believes in the sanctity of life?'

Carcophan threw up his hands, then let them fall back to the stone. 'Mar Lon, don't be a fool. The more of my followers who remain alive, the stronger my cause. If it makes you deal with the situation better, remember that Odin himself gave my predecessors the prophecy to start this war. The AllFather created this world. Surely you sanction his decisions.'

'I don't know anymore.' Mar Lon believed he had confined his doubts to his thoughts, but the horrified look on the Southern Wizard's ancient features told otherwise.

'You would challenge the gods?' Carcophan laughed, the sound rich, almost musical, with evil. 'Then there's no need for me to end the line of bards. Odin will do it for me.'

Mar Lon made a routine gesture of divine supplication. But, turned toward the topic that had bothered him for so long, he opened the tide of his concerns. And once freed, the flow could not be swiftly stopped. 'It's not the gods I challenge, it's a system based on Wizards and absolutes they created which no longer seems to work.' He called upon the teachings of his forefathers. 'A long time ago, when the Eastern mortals rigidly followed evil, the Northern mortals never strayed from good, and the Westerners actively followed neutrality, it made sense. But I have to believe the boundaries between good and evil have blurred when war and peace become equally neutral concepts. Maybe it's time for change.'

'You arrogant little nothing!' Carcophan's fists clenched around his package, his knuckles blanched. 'Do you profess to know more than the gods? Do you believe that your meager twenty-five years can gain you the wisdom of Odin's hundreds of centuries?'

'Certainly not.' Mar Lon made a longer, brisker religious gesture of apology. He had no wish to offend the gods, but the bards could speak this freely only to the Cardinal Wizards, and Mar Lon had a point he felt a desperate, driving need to make. If it bothered the Evil One, so much the better. 'All I know could fit comfortably on Odin's eyelash. But, in nature, it's the shortest lived animals, not the longest, who first see the need for change and adapt the most quickly to that need. We beat the insects from our crops, they learn to fly. We trap them with nets, and they learn to burrow beneath the ground. We poison them and, within a month, they hatch a new generation that thrives on our poison. Yet as man whittled its numbers, it took the *aristiri* decades to become timid and then many more to learn to find one another in the mating season with song.'

Carcophan's expression became as serious and still as a mask carved into stone. 'Ah, great master of the world's wisdom, thank you for sharing the knowledge your tiny fraction of mortal life has gained you.' His tone mocked with a perfect, sneering singsong that could only come from centuries of practice. 'Now let me share some information that I've gleaned in my own time and from the lengthy reigns of my predecessors. Listen closely, bard. This comes of my dealings with demons. In that, my line and myself have far more experience than any other Cardinal Wizard, so I may be the only one who has come upon this information.'

Despite his sorrow and growing hatred for the Wizard, Mar Lon felt his pulse quicken with excitement. The quest for knowledge still ran like fire in his family's veins.

'I believe,' Carcophan said, 'that the *Ragnarok* will not come as a result of evil or the clash between evil and good. All my followers together do not have the power to repel one god, even should I want such a thing to happen. I believe, Mar Lon, that only one force in existence has the power to destroy gods as well as men.' Carcophan paused dramatically.

'Which is ?' Mar Lon prodded.

'Magic. Demons. Chaos. Whatever you choose to call it. The stuff Odin banished. Its threat is the reason why the gods constrain the world's only Wizards with rules. But, every once in a while, a tendril of Chaos escapes. And it can drive a man to drop all semblance of honor, to defy the inviolate laws of his culture. When that happens, it must be stopped.' He raised the cloth parcel.

Mar Lon considered, uncertain where to run with these new thoughts. Chaos rarely appeared in any of his history lessons. It seemed to gain mention only in Northern stories of the world's creation, as the force that kept the universe formless until Odin cast it out to pave the way for shape, order, and law.

Carcophan's features remained grim, but all sarcasm left him. 'Mar Lon, you have to believe that the gods have reason for all they do. Every man and Wizard has his role in this world. My die, and even yours, was cast long before that of any mortal. For you to do anything but return to Béarn and guard the king would open your person to whatever tiny hold Chaos might have in our world. You could become the trigger for the bloodiest, ugliest war in eternity, unless a Wizards' champion killed you first. If you force my hand, I can guarantee slow agony.' He spoke in a low monotone, all the more brutal for its tonelessness. 'It's not your destiny to fight in the Great War nor, apparently, to champion peace. No doubt you'll find a cause for that energy. Might I suggest the king of Béarn ? It is your lot, an honest one paved by centuries of forefathers.'

Mar Lon lowered his head. The idea of serving King Morhane, a heartless despot who had murdered his own brother for the throne, offended him. Yet he also knew that if the West won the war, the prophecies claimed that the Western Wizard and a Renshai would bring the old king's heir back to power. *I can't stop the war, and I have no wish to be a part of it. At least, I can have a hand in returning the king.* Still, the idea of abandoning his quest for peace rankled. Mar Lon mulled over his options, while grief and uncertainty fogged his usual clarity.

The Southern Wizard seemed to read Mar Lon's mind even though the bard knew the Cardinal Wizards had no power to intrude on men's thoughts. 'Lest you doubt the sincerity of my threat.' He opened the bag he had cradled on the stone since before Mar Lon's arrival. 'One of your so-called peacemakers tried to stand against the orders of his king. Chaos-touched he was, and so he died.' Carcophan grasped the lower corners of the bag and shook its contents to the Rock of Peace. A severed head rolled free, the blood clotted and the skin shriveled. Abrith's boyish features were too familiar to Mar Lon.

'Gods,' Mar Lon whispered. He tried to say more, but the words would not come. His train of thought disappeared, leaving an endless, black void which only grief could fill. His muscles failed him. The *lonriset* toppled to the ground, and he crumpled into a heap beside it, feeling frameless, as if his bones had fallen to powder in an instant. Again, the tears came, hot with a sorrow that spanned not only the loss of father, friends, and beloved children, but the lives stolen in this and every war, the lands forced to absorb the blood of men, women, and children.

By the time Mar Lon thought to move, the sun had burned his neck and arms. Resolve coursed through him. Too many men floundered through life, trying to find a way to leave their mark upon the world. Rarely did the gods give any man a specific purpose in life, especially one as important as protecting the high king. And even more rarely did they grant a talent that could affect men as deeply as the bard's music. Mar Lon rose, dusted grime from his tunic, and picked up his instrument. Never again would he let despair conquer him. There were too many heroes deserving of ballads who would die in the coming war. There were too many soon-to-be widows and orphans who would need the comfort of lullabies to sleep or the release that accompanied humorous ditties. Many would seek hymns to restore their faith in whatever gods they worshiped. And Mar Lon would continue to compose his songs of peace, his contribution to the line of bards. He would pass them to his firstborn who would pass them to his firstborn as the line continued. And, maybe, the generations raised on those songs would learn from them. And Mar Lon's great great grandchildren might live in the peace he had helped to gain them.

Buoyed by his thoughts, Mar Lon headed toward the Weathered Mountains, the Westlands, and Béarn, grimly aware, thanks to

Carcophan's candor, that the Eastern army and the Great War would beat him home.

Lying on the straw mattress of a borrowed bed, Garn stared across Mitrian's shoulder and through the window of their rented cottage. Stars spotted the darkness, paled by the watery light of a full moon. He snuggled against her, enjoying the warmth of her naked back against his chest. His hand, looped over her side, caressed the smooth bulge of her abdomen. The rippling movements of the baby made him smile. *My baby. My son.* His grin broadened. *Born a free man.* He relished the thought of the night of passion Mitrian had promised him, despite her condition, after weeks of an abstinence caused by fatigue from Colbey's practices. He pulled Mitrian closer. *I love her so much.* His affection for Mitrian had gradually changed from the shy passion and rabid adoration of a young crush to a more mature devotion that grew stronger with the fetus.

Garn's joy belied the bitterness the day had brought. Simply being free had been enough to keep him happy in the earlier months spent amid the Westland's farm towns. He had learned to accept that Colbey would not allow anyone but Mitrian to attend his teaching sessions. Arduwyn stayed with the group only for brief periods of time; usually his appearance meant a feast or a sudden move to another town. From the hunter's whispered exchanges with Colbey, Garn suspected a method or reason for the diversions, but it was not his way to question. So long as the system kept away pursuit, Garn did not need details.

Sterrane spent most of his time with Arduwyn, hunting or talking about woodland topics that Garn knew nothing about. The only difference between Arduwyn's and Sterrane's patterns was that the larger man returned each night to clean and prepare the meals. Farmers' talk of crops, sheep, and weather bored Garn, so he spent most of his time alone.

Accustomed to taking life as it came, without brooding over the future, Garn found himself with nothing to do or ponder most of the time. At least as a gladiator he had had his daily practices, his feuds with guards, and his need to defend his food from his neighbors. The consideration of returning to life as property enraged him, but he had no tasks to pull his mind from such thoughts. Endless peace and peasants' tedium wore on him. Frustration and the need to banish thoughts that plagued him fueled every minor annoyance into a flaming, uncontrollable rage. He would vent his anger against cottages, furniture, and trees, using his sword or his fists. Once, he had struck a farmer who had sold him a firm, wickedly sour persimmon. The man had fallen, groveling at Garn's feet, promising him not only his coin back but as many ripe persimmons as he could carry.

Garn winced at the memory, vividly recalling the terror etched across the farmer's features. Now, as then, he cursed Rache for teaching him to react to pain with anger, to hit and kill without thought. The Renshai's name burned in his mind, accompanied by a terrifying thought. *What if I hurt Mitrian or my baby?* He clutched her tighter, the idea aching within him. *I have to learn to control this rage.* Understanding followed naturally, a connection Garn could not explain except to say it felt right. *I have to kill Rache. Once I do, my temper will be mastered.*

The matter settled for the moment, Garn turned his attention back to Mitrian. The thought of the night of lovemaking she had promised coupled with the soft warmth of her buttocks against his loins brought him to erection. He slid his hand to her breast, tense with the chance to turn an evening of brooding into a night of excitement he had awaited for weeks. He kissed the back of her neck.

A guttural sound escaped Mitrian's lips.

Garn froze, at first trying to decipher what she must have said, denying the truth of Mitrian's snore. For an instant, Garn considered continuing anyway, but the idea of defiling the woman he loved turned lust to disappointment that flared to rage. He sprang from the bed and snatched up his sword belt from the bedpost. Without bothering to dress, he stormed through the door and out into the night, buckling on the belt as he went.

Spring breezes caressed Garn's skin into gooseflesh, but he didn't notice. At first, he had no idea where to go. Then anger overtook reason, and he stomped a straight path to Colbey's cottage. He slammed his fist against the door; it shuddered beneath the blow. 'Out here, Northman. Now!' He pounded again. 'Out now, or I'll shatter this door and kill you where you lie.'

'Garn?' The panel muffled Colbey's reply. 'What are you doing?'

Garn's head buzzed, and his stomach twisted in anger. 'Open the damned door, old man!' Drawing his sword, he hammered the hilt against the oak door.

From within the cottage, the latch clacked.

Garn adjusted his grip on the sword.

The door edged ajar.

Garn leapt and swung blindly. His weight flung the door fully open. It struck the wall and rebounded into Colbey's side. Garn's sword met Colbey's, and the clang of steel on steel echoed through the confines of the cottage. 'What are you doing alone with my wife? What are you doing that she no longer has the strength or need to lie with me?'

Hot with jealous rage, Garn did not await an answer. He hammered at Colbey. Every blow met Colbey's blade or crosspiece. Where the same strokes had once driven Rache backward on the practice floor, Colbey lost no ground at all. Grimly, he stood in the doorway, catching the impacts effortlessly, waiting for Garn to tire.

Soon, the force of his own strokes wore on Garn. Each blow sent pain burning along his forearms, while Colbey just blocked, patient as a cat. Moonlight glimmered over stern features, striped with the shadows of Garn's movement, and cold, blue-gray eyes that missed little.

Garn halted, panting.

'Done?' Colbey asked, brows arched.

Garn raised his sword for another attack. Rage flared and sputtered. He pulled the blow in mid-swing, not from lack of strength, but lack of motivation. The fury that had driven him drained away, and nothing replaced it. Lowering his sword, Garn nodded.

'Wait here.' Fearlessly, Colbey turned his back, though Garn had not yet sheathed his weapon. The Renshai returned to the darkened depths of his cottage. 'I think we need to talk.'

Garn watched the blood return to his whitened fingers, feeling foolish, wondering if Colbey gleaned any amusement from a naked fool who dared to cross weapons with the best swordsman alive. Now angry with himself, he jabbed the sword into its sheath.

Colbey emerged from the cottage carrying a flaming brand in his left hand, a canvas package tucked beneath the armpit on the same side. Without a word, he strode toward the forest.

Curious, Garn followed. The Renshai slipped between the trees with little sound; Garn crashed like an army in comparison. Slowed by a deadfall, he lost sight of Colbey. Rushing to catch up, he discovered Colbey seated at the base of an elm, the torch wedged between its roots. As Garn approached, Colbey tossed the pack at the younger man's feet.

Kneeling, Garn spread the canvas, revealing four steel horseshoes. He studied them, watching crimson shadows from the fire dance along the polished surfaces. He saw nothing special about these horseshoes other than that they were too clean and straight to have ever been hammered to a hoof. Since Colbey and his companions had descended from the Granite Hills eight months earlier, they had let the horse go barefoot. Seeing no reason or purpose for the shoes, Garn looked to Colbey for an explanation.

'Which is stronger? You or steel?'

Garn stared, confused by Colbey's question. 'What do you mean?'

Colbey motioned for Garn to pass one of the horseshoes. 'A

simple, straightforward question, I believe. Are you stronger than steel?'

Obediently, Garn plucked out one of the horseshoes. He clutched it, testing the unyielding surface against the calluses of his hand. 'No,' he said. 'Steel is stronger.'

Colbey nodded. He looped a finger around the horseshoe and tugged it from Garn's grasp. 'Correct.' His gaze held Garn's as his hands explored the steel. 'But had you given the other answer, you would also have been correct and better for it. A man is as strong as he allows himself to be, and no more.' Colbey positioned his hands on either end of the horseshoe. Wind drew a finger of flame toward the older man, who shifted his attention to the object in his fists. 'Garn, it would violate the laws and honor of my people to teach you the skills I'm teaching Mitrian and will teach to your son. Do you understand that?'

'Not really,' Garn admitted. Until Colbey had raised the issue, Garn had never recognized the envy he harbored for the confidence and skill Mitrian was acquiring. He had attributed his anger to the vast quantities of Mitrian's time that Colbey monopolized, but the Renshai had seen beyond the obvious to Garn's fascination with and desire for the abilities with a sword that so few possessed.

'Rache trained you, too. Didn't he?'

Just the mention of Rache's name sent a white line of anger searing through Garn. 'Yes.'

Colbey watched Garn's reactions with interest, his hands still clamped to the horseshoe. 'Rache, not I, decided who would become Renshai by what he chose to teach. I can understand why he picked Mitrian; she has natural grace and a keen eye for movement. Were the decision mine, I would have had difficulty choosing between you. Can I guess you and Rache didn't get along?'

Garn felt his control slipping. He fought rage with humor. 'That would be the world's largest understatement.'

Colbey showed no expression.

Thinking it safer to change the subject, Garn questioned. 'How could I be stronger than steel?'

Now, Colbey smiled. 'Garn, let me pay you for the time I've stolen from you and Mitrian. I discovered this thing myself. It's not one of the secrets of the Renshai, so I'm free to pass it to whomever I will. But I have to warn you. No one I've taught it to has mastered it.' He examined Garn's forearms. 'You already have the advantage of strength. I'll give you the key, but it's up to you to practice and to find your own potential.'

Garn suppressed a smile, amused by Colbey's solemnity.

Apparently oblivious, Colbey continued, 'The secret to power is to find the weak point. If you see no weak point . . .' He closed his eyes '. . . create one.' As he spoke the final syllable, Colbey snapped his hands apart. The horseshoe broke into two equal pieces.

Garn stared, slack-jawed, unable to think of anything to do or say.

Colbey rose, dropping the broken steel at Garn's feet. 'I'm an old man, more than three times your age. At this, Garn, you can surpass me.' He stepped from the circle of torchlight.

For some time Garn stared, unmoving, at the halves of the horseshoe. He listened for the sounds of crackling leaves and breaking twigs that would signify Colbey's departure. He heard only the whistle of wind through trees; he did not experience the wary prickle that would warn him if someone watched from the brush. Colbey had gone in silence.

Garn's fingers closed about the shards of steel, and he raised them to his face. He scrutinized the break. Each piece was as thick as two of his fingers together, without hollows or flaws. He pocketed them.

'Scarce forty, if that,' Garn muttered sullenly. 'That's not quite twice my age.' Even the flecks of silver in Colbey's hair could not convince him otherwise. *An old man might best me with a sword, but at this I cannot lose.* He pawed a fresh horseshoe from the pack. Settling between the roots of the elm, he worked his hands along the steel until he found the most natural position. Drawing a deep breath, he squeezed his lids shut. He released the air in a grunt of effort, throwing all his bodily strength into this single action. Opening his eyes, he held the horseshoe to the torch's glow. He had not even bent it.

Annoyance threatened to become fury. Garn braced himself for a second attempt, and a third. At the finish of each, he grew weaker and the steel stronger. Garn funneled his mind and body to the task as the torch flickered lower. His struggle sheered the calluses from his fingerpads. Ruts in the steel gashed his flesh, but pain and blood did not deter him. The need to prove himself became an obsession and, as such, it became inexorably linked to the single other project that haunted and frustrated him. *A day will come when I master steel and my temper. And that day, Rache, I will destroy you as well.* Garn prepared for another attempt.

The fire died as the torch burned to nothingness.

16 Pudar

Perched upon a crag in the Great Frenum Mountains, the Southern Wizard, Carcophan, studied the proud ranks of the Eastern army as it snaked along the eastern base of the range. At the head of his cavalry, King Siderin rode a heavily muscled, dun stallion. The general's breastplate gleamed, so well forged it seemed a part of him; the tines jutting from his helmet and bucklers made him appear more like a demon than a man. His broadsword girded his waist, a darkly spiked horseman's flail was slung from a hook on the saddlebow, and a whip jutted from his grip. Siderin's top officers, Harrsha and Narisen, rode at either hand, each in command of a phalanx of twenty-five hundred men. They, too, wore iron breastplates and helmets, but they lacked their general's regal bearing.

Siderin's other three first officers herded the infantry in a tight formation, their unadorned helmets easily visible amidst waves of swarthy features and red-brown lacquered leather armor. Carcophan identified two dozen brigade leaders by their darker uniforms and leather helmets with blue plumes. The brigade leaders relayed their commanders' orders, holding the formation in a perfect lock, their men accustomed to instant obedience though the journey to the southern passes of the Great Frenum Mountains would take another three months.

Carcophan smiled. Evil's day had nearly come, and Siderin seemed equal to the task. The general's scouts brought pleasing news. The clannish Northmen seemed certain to refuse aid to the Westlands during the Great War. In exchange for gold, King Morhane had agreed to keep the armies under his direct command neutral, blithely unaware Siderin would claim Béarn's kingdom at the war's end. Siderin's patience had left the Western generals and kings complacent. Most had expected the war a decade or more earlier, and they had lost faith in Wizards' prophecies. Without the Western Wizard's influence, the central cities near Pudar had civilized themselves into decadence. Only Santagithi had kept his soldiers honed with skirmishes against neighboring towns and barbarians too isolated to understand prophecies or band together in war. But Santagithi's Town was too small to concern Carcophan. Except for one soldier.

Rache. Carcophan scowled, joy swept away by that single name. *The last Renshai. The only one left to fulfill the Western Wizard's prophecy.* Carcophan's last vision of Rache seeped back into his mind, the captain's usually functionally short, blond hair swept into wild tangles, his breeks and jerkin tattered, blood- and travel-stained, his once proud head low in despair. No doubt, the Renshai's indifference to his appearance paralleled his loss of interest in life. *A Wizard's champion crippled, physically and emotionally. How?* Only three explanations came to Carcophan's mind. *Either Tokar is dead, his successor is weak, or he's staying in the background trying to make me believe he's gone, hoping Siderin and I will become smug and make mistakes.*

As the sun touched the highest peaks of the Great Mountains, the soldiers broke into units, busily preparing their camps for the night.

Carcophan dismissed his final thought as madness. *Even the eldest Wizard could not be that patient or subtle.* Among the Cardinal Four, Carcophan was considered a rebel; two and a half centuries as a Wizard had taught him only a modicum of forbearance and lost him none of the exuberance that drove him to prefer brute force and instant solutions over finesse. He could not keep himself from the thought of the quick and simple fix, one killing spell that would remove the prophesied obstacle to his champion's victory. Yet, as all the Cardinal Wizards, Carcophan held his Wizard's vows more sacred than even the cause of evil that Odin had assigned him. To lose the Great War simply meant revising his strategies, perhaps training another champion for himself or his successor; to forsake the Wizard's vows fashioned by the gods, he believed, foretold the world's destruction.

Carcophan waited, ignoring the Eastern soldiers' quiet efficiency, instead watching the sun evolve from yellow to orange to red, its dusk washing the crags with rainbows. His assigned task was finished; he had trained and guided Siderin. From the day the Eastern army left the royal city of Stalmize, Carcophan's vows bound him to step aside and let the mortals fulfill their own destinies. He had no assigned role in the war itself, and he preferred it that way. Before his initiation to Wizardry, he had once been a soldier of moderate skill, and Carcophan knew the joy of slaughter might drive him to take a direct hand in the battle, the ultimate violation of his vows. He could only hope he had chosen his champion well and instilled an immorality in Siderin's followers that time would not undermine.

As the sun slid behind the mountains like a droplet of blood, the odor of cooking meat and tubers perfumed the air. With a sigh of regret, Carcophan transported himself for his last talk with his champion.

Without fanfare, Carcophan materialized at Siderin's campsite. The general-king sat on a log before the fire, his tent at his back and his top officers clustered around him. The suddenness of Carcophan's appearance sent Harrsha and Narisen lurching to their feet. Their swords whipped free with admirable speed, but, immune to the blades' danger, Carcophan paid their wielders no heed. Only a slight stiffening of Siderin's frame revealed Carcophan's entrance had startled him, and he gained his composure instantly. His helmet, whip, and chain flail lay at his feet. Sweat and the previous weight of the helmet plastered coal-dark hair to his face. Yet, even disheveled, Siderin's imperial features made him look dangerous and wholly in command. Patient as always, he waited for Carcophan to speak first.

In no mood for the usual spar for dominance, Carcophan sprang directly to his point. 'We need to talk.'

Siderin said nothing, but his dark gaze rolled from one officer to the other. As one, Narisen and Harrsha bowed respectfully, then retreated beyond the edges of the campfire. Still silent, King Siderin regarded Carcophan. The general's dark gaze met Carcophan's cat-yellow one, locked in a perfect stalemate.

'I thought you were going to kill Rache.' Carcophan did not sit, preferring a position of superiority to his champion.

Siderin did not move. 'I commanded this thing.'

'And?'

'And I thought my assassins had killed him.'

'He killed your assassins.'

Siderin frowned. 'He's crippled.'

'A crippled Renshai is still a Renshai.'

Siderin's features tightened into a scowl, but he did not look away. 'He's reckless, overconfident, and lame. He'll die in the war.'

Carcophan's grimace matched his champion's, and he continued to stare. 'If you couldn't kill him before the war, what makes you so sure you can do it when you have soldiers on both sides distracting you?'

Siderin rose, using the movement as an excuse to break the gaze-lock. He met the Southern Wizard's question with one equally snide. 'If you find this task so important, why did you wait eight months to tell me my assassins had failed?'

Carcophan relished his tiny triumph of will. 'I'm a Wizard, not your nanny. Eight months to me is the time between sunset and midnight. I have other, more important duties than worrying about whether your scouts are doing their jobs.' Even as he spoke the words, Carcophan realized how unfair they were. Likely, the delay did not come of shirking, but of good intention and geographical difficulties. News between the East and West traveled slowly, if at all, and the sending of messages might lose the Eastern army the surprise it required for certain victory. No doubt, the cultists had either witheld information, hoping to correct their mistake before reporting back to Siderin, or lost their messenger en route.

Siderin drew his sword into his lap, tracing the shiny tapering near the edge with a finger. 'The Leukenyans were trained as priests and spies, not soldiers. Those few well skilled in assassination may have underestimated Rache. But I won't. And I'll see to it my warriors don't either.' He waved at the masses of campsites surrounding his own, nearly ten thousand men in all.

Carcophan frowned, unsatisfied. So far, the Western Wizard had taken no hand in fulfilling his own prophecy or opposing Carcophan's plans. Yet the Southern Wizard dared not simply ignore the fact that, despite all likelihood, Rache still lived. 'Rache may be able to best even your skill.'

Siderin snorted. 'I doubt it.' He balanced the sword on his thighs but kept his hands on its grip as he brazenly met Carcophan's stare again. 'If you're so concerned, do something. Surely, a Wizard could find a magical object to more than equal the odds between me and a legless Renshai. If, as you claim, the Southern Wizards have plotted this war for millennia, I should think you would want to help.'

Though phrased as a statement, Siderin's request came through clearly. Magical powders, gems, and weapons were the realm of quackery; the Cardinal Wizards used magic in the form of spells, rarely daring to endow items with power. Even in its simplest form, magic was savagely unpredictable, the stuff of demons. To infuse it into an inanimate object always cost the Wizard dearly in strength, pain, and power. Once created, the piece rarely worked within the intentions and control of the Wizard. Except for the Swords of Power.

Carcophan plucked at his chin, again trapped into a course of action he had considered and rejected several times before. At the beginning of time, after Odin had created the Wizards, he gave the Northern and Southern Wizards the knowledge to magic one Power Sword apiece and the Eastern and Western Wizards to craft one Sword between them. It was not until after Ristoril the White and Morshoch the Black were fashioned and in the hands of their respective good and evil champions that the Western Wizard uncovered and announced his prophecy:

'A Sword of Gray, a Sword of White,
A Sword of Black and chill as night.
Each one forged, its craftsman a mage;
The three blades together shall close the age.
When their oath of peace the Wizards forsake,
Their own destruction they undertake
Only these Swords, their craftsmen can slay.
Each Sword shall be blooded the same rueful day.
When that fateful time comes, the Wolf's Age has begun:
Hati swallows the moon, and Skoll tears up the sun.'

Translated and appropriately embellished, the prophecy indicated that when all three swords existed in the world of men, wielded simultaneously by Wizards' champions, the destruction of the world, including men, the Wizards, and all but a handful of the gods would ensue. For the sake of safety, the White and Black Swords had been banished to the Chaos-world of demons. In the past, Southern and Northern Wizards had recalled their weapons for various champions; with the Gray Sword still not forged, the danger seemed minimal. But with the Westlands menaced, the Eastern and Western Wizards might believe their situation desperate enough to craft the sword that would be called Harval.

Even so, Carcophan knew the danger was limited. Currently unmenaced, the Northern Sorceress, Trilless, had no reason to call for the White Sword. Still, there was no way for Carcophan to be certain. Their purposes at odds, the Wizards did not socialize; even the Eastern and Western Wizards, who shared the burden of keeping morality balanced, worked mostly independently. The Wizards could read one another's minds, but such an intrusion without an invitation went against all propriety as well as their vows.

Carcophan studied his champion in the eerie, flickering shadows cast by the campfire. Siderin's craggy features revealed nothing, not even curiosity at Carcophan's delay. The king's flat, dark eyes watched him without a sparkle, like one of the reptiles that were Carcophan's minions in the same way land creatures bonded with the Eastern Wizard, birds with the Western Wizard, and sea creatures followed Trilless. *The Swords of Power can injure and kill even the Cardinal Wizards. Siderin is difficult enough to control. To put such a weapon in his hands would be foolish.*

Accustomed to Carcophan's manner, Siderin lapsed into his own thoughts, eyes distant and chin cupped in his hands.

As he had so many times before, Carcophan discarded the idea of retrieving Morshoch for Siderin. Seeking a substitute, he pressed a hand into his pocket, and his fingers brushed a vial he had nearly forgotten. 'I do have something that might help.' He retrieved the object. Warm from his body heat, the rounded surface fit easily into the curvature of his fingers. Opening his hand, he displayed the vial.

Siderin's glance came up slowly. He regarded the vial but made no move to take it. 'What's this?'

'Poison.' Carcophan rested a foot on Siderin's log seat. 'Extracted from the most deadly serpent in existence, a colorful ribbon from the forests on the northern part of the Western Plains. A few drops in the blood is all it would take.'

Siderin's lips twitched into a crooked frown.

Carcophan guessed Siderin's thoughts. Poisoned weapons could prove as dangerous to a general's own troops as the enemy's; accidental spills, vials crushed during battle, and wild sweeps that nicked the wielder or his companions could result in more casualties for Siderin than the enemy. And the time spent picking even the abundant mushrooms that dotted Eastern fields would offset any advantage their toxin could give his soldiers in battle. But this was a single container in the general's own possession. 'It's effective, but slow and excruciatingly painful. It destroys the body not the mind.'

Siderin's lopsided expression turned into a grin. He pinched the vial between his thumb and forefinger, but Carcophan closed his hand around the base before Siderin pulled it free.

'Be careful with it. It's deadly but not magical. It doesn't know Renshai blood from anyone else's. Use it wisely.' Carcophan released his hold.

The vial seemed to disappear into Siderin's powerful fist. 'I'll take care of Rache.'

Carcophan nodded agreement. His time to leave had come, but he hesitated, aware this might be his last chance to speak with his champion before the end of the war. There was nothing left to say. A thousand times, Wizard and man had traced the route around the Great Frenum Mountains to the sandy wasteland of the Western Plains and through the passes of the Southern Weathered chain. With any luck at all, they would hit the Trading City of Pudar by surprise, while the Eastern army was at its strongest. Without the Western Wizard to warn and muster a defense, the battle would take place at the city gates of Pudar. Once the largest city of the West fell, the remainder of the Westlands would put up little resistance.

Still, the significance of prophecies struck too hard for Carcophan to banish his concerns about the last full-blooded Renshai. 'Poison or not, it would still be better to destroy Rache before the war.' Almost as soon as he spoke the words, Carcophan realized his mistake. To antagonize his general just before taking his leave might not be prudent.

But perhaps mellowed by the thought of launching the war, Siderin took Carcophan's advice in stride. 'Didn't you say some time ago that Rache was committed to rescuing some girl?'

'Santagithi's daughter, Mitrian. Yes.' Carcophan did not follow the sudden turn in the conversation.

'So if she was menaced, Rache would be obligated to rescue her, even if it meant missing the war or placing himself in an enemy's temple.'

'I suppose so.'

Siderin's grin broadened. 'I'll take care of Rache,' he repeated with such conviction that Carcophan lost all doubt about Siderin's commitment.

'Yes,' the Wizard said. 'I believe you will.'

The human scurry and bustle perpetually surrounding Pudar in daylight came into view long before the stone walls and bronze gates that had become so familiar to Arduwyn. At the edge of the forest, he drew his donkey to a stop, waiting for his companions to catch up, not wanting to take the final step from the safety of the trees to the field between it and the city gates. The urge to see Bel again was strong; the necessities and emotions that might accompany that meeting frightened him. *What if Bel told Kantar about our affair, and he's spending his last months in misery? What if the sight of me sends him into a rage ... or kills him? What if Bel never wants to see me again?*

Arduwyn shivered as his companions drew up beside him. He knew he could handle Kantar. The two men had been friends too long and gone through too much together for Kantar not to forgive. Emotional ties and depth of feeling only slightly curbed Arduwyn's verbal agility. But Bel was another matter. During the last eight months spent hunting and tracking Rache through the woodlands, Arduwyn had mourned his best friend's imminent death and slowly came to terms with it. Yet, in the same way he used the forest sojourn as time to meditate over Kantar, he had used its distractions to avoid the topic of Bel. For reasons Arduwyn could not explain, her reaction to him meant more than anything else ever had. He had traveled all the way across the Westlands to arrive at Pudar. Now, a few dozen strides from the gates, he stood at the edge of the woodlands, unable to take those final steps.

Apparently recognizing Arduwyn's need for hesitation, Colbey turned the focus of the party to himself. 'This is where I leave.' He gestured vaguely northward, toward the pointed, gray blur of the Weathered Mountains.

'I need you,' Mitrian said. Her tone implied she had already lost the argument but felt the need for one last, half-hearted protest.

Colbey placed a callused hand on Mitrian's shoulder. 'I've taught you all you need to know. The rest comes from practice and experience. If anything, you should be harder on yourself than I was on you.'

Though fixed on his own dilemma, Arduwyn winced at Colbey's words. He had caught glimpses of the Renshai's practices now and again. Colbey's methods included a relentless demand for perfection and humility rarely tempered by praise. Arduwyn recalled his own lessons on bow shooting and forest lore. Gentle in tone and manner, his father had shaped Arduwyn's personality and abilities with compassion. *I can't compare Mitrian's sword skills to my knowledge of longbow, but I do know few hunters could best me. It might do well for Mitrian to stay away from Colbey for a while.*

Mitrian lowered her head, and Arduwyn could tell something more important than Colbey's departure bothered her.

'Pudar is the securest city in the Westlands, probably in the world. It's a fine place to bear and raise a child.' Arduwyn tried to comfort her, but Mitrian's demeanor scarcely changed. The little redhead knew his reassurance had missed the mark. Before he could guess what matter besides the baby might be bothering Mitrian, Colbey addressed what could only have been her thoughts.

'You already made your choices, Mitrian. There's nothing left but to live with the consequences, good and bad. The world's not as big as it seems. Likely, you'll see the people and places you miss again, but it can't ever be the same. Nor should it.'

Mitrian said nothing, but her stricken look made it clear that Colbey's words had hit far closer to the problem. Sterrane kept his gaze locked on the activity near the city walls. Garn frowned, as if trying to make sense of Colbey's explanation, certain he would not care for the meaning once he discovered it.

Colbey removed his hand from Mitrian's shoulder and accepted the horse's lead from Garn. 'The Great War has almost become a cliché, but powers are shifting. I have a feeling it's closer than any of us realizes.' He twisted the end of the rope around the saddle, controlling the horse by the side of its bridle. 'War will bring all of us back together.' He addressed Mitrian, but his stare turned to Arduwyn. 'United against a common enemy and death, the changes in your life and the differences between people may not seem so large.'

A shiver traversed Arduwyn. In the wake of Colbey's warning, his concerns about Bel seemed insignificant.

Colbey sprang into his place in the saddle without using a stirrup. 'If not sooner, I'll return in a year or so to start the boy's training.'

Colbey's promise slipped by Arduwyn as he relived the Renshai's perfect mounting in his mind. No doubt Colbey had dedicated a staggering amount of time to horsemanship as well as to his sword work. The awe that always gripped Arduwyn in Colbey's presence strengthened. He watched as the horse broke into a trot, then a gallop, the Renshai's gold and silver hair visible long after crags and distance obliterated other details.

Gone. Arduwyn knew Colbey's departure should fill him with joy, but he could not shake a deep, hollow feeling of loss. Though as unpredictable and dangerous as a mother grizzly, Colbey's presence had seemed too grand for his absence to go unnoticed. *Colbey said he was bound for the Western Wizard's cave. Why?* Arduwyn shook his head, unable to imagine the power of the old Renshai and that of the timeless Wizard in one location. Until eight months ago, Arduwyn would have believed anything a Renshai did would be solely for the sake of violence. Colbey's quiet travel through the Western farm towns had convinced Arduwyn otherwise; Colbey had kept his promise not to reveal himself as Renshai to anyone and had even made some friends along the way. If the Cardinal Wizards really held the amount of power and immortality legend granted them, the Western Wizard was unquestionably the stronger of the two. But Arduwyn also knew the lore of the Wizards was older than that of the Renshai, and so was even more prone to building exaggeration. These days few common men believed in the Wizards and their prophecies as anything but ancient myth. Yet nearly everyone had lost a parent or grandparent to the Renshai's invasion.

Arduwyn had little tolerance for the quacks and magicians who lined their Pudarian stands with cure-alls, powders, and potions, but he believed in the Cardinal Wizards with the same stoic faith as he believed in the gods. He had felt less certain of the Great War. With the passage of time, the prediction of an immense conflict between the Eastlands and Westlands had become a fixture, more like a mother's story than true future history. Undoubtedly, Colbey's assurance of the War's imminence was his reason for addressing the Western Wizard. But the Renshai's certainty also served to reestablish Arduwyn's belief in the Great War because he could not discard any notion Colbey clung to so staunchly. It gave Arduwyn a cause that made every other in his life seem trivial. What difference did his love for Bel make if the Easterners held them both as slaves? What good were forests desecrated by the fires of war or the casual cruelty of the Easterners' evil?

Pictures paraded through Arduwyn's imagination: woodlands

hacked and burned away to make room for bawdy houses and bars while the established Western towns crumbled into ruin; his brothers crawling beneath the Easterners' whips, crying for freedom with their final, gasping breaths; his sisters raped until, all youth and beauty stripped from them, they lived out their years cleansing Easterners' filth.

The images drove a shiver through Arduwyn. Recognizing his concern, if not its cause, Sterrane seized the hunter's arm in a huge, gentle hand.

Grounded back in reality, Arduwyn gripped Stubs' halter tighter and took that final step from the forest to the open field. No longer veiled by overhanging leaves, sunlight blinded Arduwyn. He shielded his eyes with an arm looped across his forehead, jarring loose Sterrane's hold in the process. They crossed the plowed earth without conversation as the noise outside the city gates rose from a distant buzz to a roar. Cottages dotted the grounds, farmers' dwellings built near their fields for convenience and close to the city for protection. Children with parents too poor to afford a stand in the market hawked fruits, vegetables, and handmade crafts outside granite walls striped with shadows. Individuals and groups pleaded their various causes to the citizens and visitors as they came and went through the open bronze double gates. A sentry stood before each panel, watching the clamor through half-closed eyes. A third threaded through the masses, occasionally breaking groups apart when a salesman raised his voice in anger or a beggar became too aggressive in his appeals.

Apparently unused to the flurry of a trading city, Mitrian and Garn drifted, trancelike, toward the gates. Sterrane, too, seemed too far out of his element. His head swiveled as he tried to take in everything at once. Arduwyn knew the big man's unworldly antics would attract every seller and panhandler in the area like a beacon, but he did not trouble himself about his large and quiet companion. Soon enough, the predators would discover that Sterrane carried no money and would leave him in peace. More familiar with the inescapable corruption that accompanied the benefits of city living, Arduwyn had remembered to tuck away the garnet and the coinage he had acquired selling the extra meat from his hunts. Though the topic had never been broached, Arduwyn felt that some of the money belonged to his hunting partner, Sterrane. But, for now, Arduwyn felt safer holding it.

Arduwyn wove through the crowds, glad most people stepped aside for his donkey. With time, Garn's features had lapsed into grim concentration. Every accidental touch sent him glaring in the direction of the passerby. Sweat gleamed on his forehead, and

Arduwyn felt it safest to get Garn inside the city gates where the road traffic would, at least, follow logical patterns. The Pudarian government generally let men settle their differences between themselves. But if Garn flew into one of his wild rages directly in front of the guardsmen, Arduwyn knew courts would be invoked and justice would tend to side against the outsider.

Less than half a dozen paces from the gates, Arduwyn pushed past a pair of albinos in white robes and feathered headbands who shoved an ivory statuette into his face. *Leukenyan priests.* Arduwyn's disgust for the idol-worshiping cult caused him to strike aside the offering with more force than necessary. Other religious organizations accosted citizens outside the the Pudarian walls, but they, at least, subscribed to established Western gods like Cathan and Kadrak, twin goddess and god of War, Itu, goddess of knowledge and truth, and Ruaidhri, the leader of the pantheon, long-standing and harmless churches that kept their followers within the walls of Pudar. *If Colbey was right about the Great War, those rebellious youths seeking causes will find one far better than what this cult can offer.*

At the gate, Arduwyn turned to check the progress of his companions. Mitrian came up directly behind him, tense with curiosity. Garn stood to his right, his crouched posture and slitted eyes betraying a discomfort that could quickly turn to violence. Fortunately, the citizens seemed to read the same menacing uneasiness; they were giving Garn a wide berth. Arduwyn located Sterrane some distance behind, his dark head towering over a surrounding circle of four albino and three Western Leukenyans.

Terror ripped through Arduwyn. Without explanation, he jammed the donkey's lead rope into Mitrian's hand and sprang to Sterrane's aid. Momentarily forgetting the slightness of his stature, he elbowed through the press of cultists to Sterrane's side. He spoke loudly, 'Come on, Sterrane. Mom's waiting.' Taking Sterrane's arm, Arduwyn started back the way he had come.

But the circle had closed behind him. This time, the priests were not caught so unaware. Seven glares met Arduwyn, four watery blue, two brown, and one gray-green.

'Mom?' Sterrane questioned, apparently oblivious to the growing conflict. 'Who Mom?'

Arduwyn glared at the men blocking his path, his forced defiance covering fear. He did not have the skill to fight through seven Leukenyans, especially not with his scimitar strapped to Stubs' back. Sterrane did not seem to recognize the danger. To involve Mitrian and Garn might mean sparking Garn's temper, and a mass slaughter so near the city gates would outrage the guards and Pudarian citizens. He spoke mildly, but with an undertone of threat. 'Move aside. We need to leave.'

The largest of the albinos used a soft tone that made Arduwyn's seem inappropriately gruff in comparison. His accent was unlike anything Arduwyn had ever heard. 'We were talking with your . . .' He smiled, obviously seeing through Arduwyn's ploy. The suggestion that this scrawny redhead and his towering, swarthy companion shared a bloodline seemed absurd '. . . friend. We would like to continue our discussion. Thank you for your concern, but your intrusion was unnecessary.'

Trapped and desperate to end the confrontation without violence, Arduwyn tried again. 'We don't want to make trouble. Just move aside and everything will be all right.'

Sunlight glared from the robes, sheening across each feather. The Leukenyans' white garb seemed to mock purity. The leader's modulated voice did not change, dignified and condescending. He spoke as if to a man too dim to recognize the holiness of his presence. 'Sterrane is old enough to make his own decisions. He has agreed to join us . . .' He lingered over the phrase '. . . for dinner tonight.'

Rage tore through Arduwyn, liberally sprinkled with surprise. As a salesman, he had taken advantage of people's emotions and loyalties, but never their ignorance. To cheat the feeble-minded was simply cruel, and his hatred of the Leukenyans' cause only strengthened his anger. Sterrane tensed beneath Arduwyn's grip. The hunter looked beyond the leader to see Mitrian, Garn, and Stubs trotting toward them, and was relieved to see Mitrian had talked Garn into holding the donkey's lead. At best, it would distract Garn; at worst, it would keep his hands full. 'Sterrane is too good and innocent to know what you are. But I'm not, and I'm going to see to it he knows what you stand for before you drag him off to fill his mind with lies. He already has a cause; he doesn't need your false god.' He gritted his teeth, no longer feigning calm. 'Stand aside or you'll regret it.'

One of the young Western followers sprang forward, apparently enraged by Arduwyn's challenge. 'Fool! Infidel! God damns your evil kind for all eternity. Your soul . . .'

The leader's face crinkled in annoyance. Curtly, he waved his follower to silence and addressed Sterrane. 'I can understand your friend's concern that you would dine with strangers.' He made a gesture of benign regret and tipped his head as if to suggest that he and Sterrane shared some secret the others could not comprehend. 'But I assure you, he's creating evil where it doesn't exist. We only want to share a good meal and some friendly conversation. How can there be any harm in that?'

Aware the priest had just cleverly passed the initiative to Sterrane,

Arduwyn twisted to face his companion. 'No.' He hated to treat his friend like a child, but the comparison fit. He knew that if the white priest talked Sterrane into a meal at Corpa Leukenya, they would sway and sweet talk him to their cause. *Sterrane won't stand a chance, and we'll never see him again.* 'We need to talk. These men aren't going anywhere for a while. If, when we're finished, you still want to eat with them, I won't stand in your way.'

Sterrane opened his mouth. Before he could speak, Mitrian interrupted from behind the leading priest. 'Sterrane, Arduwyn, are these men bothering you?'

All eyes went suddenly to Mitrian. The leader turned to face her, and Arduwyn followed the albino's stare by the movements of his head. First, he met Mitrian's gaze, then his eyes roved to her sword belt and her bulging abdomen before settling on Garn. The ex-gladiator crouched, his free fist tactlessly tight around his hilt.

Arduwyn balanced frustration and anger against the need to keep the peace. For Garn's sake, he kept his voice composed and his words diplomatic. 'No, thank you. Everything's under control. These men were just about to stand aside and let us leave. Right, men?'

Grudgingly, the leader stepped aside, but his tone made it clear the conflict was unfinished. 'Thank you for your time.'

Not wanting to waste a moment, Arduwyn tightened his grip on Sterrane's arm and steered the larger man toward the gate. Mitrian and Garn followed curiously, leading the donkey. 'What happened?' Mitrian asked.

'Nothing much.' The realization of violence narrowly averted made Arduwyn sarcastic. 'Sterrane nearly sold his soul to an idol-worshiping cult, that's all.' Loosing Sterrane, Arduwyn accepted Stubs' lead rope from Garn. He nudged Sterrane. 'Did you really agree to have dinner with those freaks?'

Sterrane's fur-clad shoulders rose and fell. 'They ask. Me hungry.'

Frustrated by his companion's simple logic, Arduwyn rubbed a hand across his face from forehead to chin, peering at the gate sentries through his fingers. The pair gave the group warning scowls, apparently due to the incident with the Leukenyans, but the leather-clad guards did not speak nor delay the party's entrance into the city.

'Not nice refuse invite.'

'Who told you that?' Now on the main road, Arduwyn fell into the familiar comfort of the trading city. He chose the route to *The Hungry Lion*, avoiding the gaudier, rowdier *Dun Stag* that most outsiders chose because of its decor and famous beer. This close to the entrance, market stands, carts, and shops crowded the walkways along a wide, cobbled street designed for merchants' and dignitaries' wagons. Mixed crowds of men and women clogged the roadway, purchasing food for the evening meal or luxuries before leaving the city, though the natives knew the prices tended to rise the closer a stand's location was to the gates. Conversations blended into a buzzing maelstrom, occasionally pierced by a salesman's promise, 'Veg-e-tables ! Fre-esh fi-ish !'

'Friend told me.'

Caught up in the familiar bustle and glitter of Pudar, Arduwyn had forgotten the conversation. 'What ?'

'Friend told me,' Sterrane repeated dutifully. 'Not nice refuse invite.'

Arduwyn led his companions onto a well-traveled side road and, from there, toward the quieter living areas of the locals in the northwest quarter. 'Your friend was wrong, Sterrane. At least in regard to Pudar,' Arduwyn continued, walking backwards to address all of his companions now. 'Cities this big aren't like other places in the West. Most of the people are good and honest, but it only takes a few bad ones to rob you of everything you are and own. From now on, I suggest you remember three rules.' He bent back his index finger with his other hand. 'Number one, everybody wants your money. Don't give it to them unless they give you something of equal or greater value that you need or want.' He added more gently, 'If you're uncertain, ask me.' He uncurled his middle finger beside the first. 'Number two, any stranger who claims to be your friend can't possibly be your friend.' He spread his ring finger, pinning his little finger with his thumb. 'Number three, a stranger who wants to touch you is up to nothing good. Avoid him.'

Arduwyn started to face front, then turned back for one more warning. He met Garn's gaze directly. 'Oh, and no violence.'

Garn stared back without replying, but he seemed to expect an explanation.

'It's against the law.' It was an overstatement. Pudar's response to violence depended upon the cause of the dispute, the status of the participants, and the extent of destruction to lives and property ; but it seemed safer and kinder to encourage Garn to consider consequence before action.

Garn continued to watch Arduwyn. 'You're trying to say I shouldn't do it.'

That being obvious, Arduwyn was caught off-guard. 'Right.' Then, realizing Garn might not have experience with laws, Arduwyn explained. 'If you break the law, you get punished by the government leaders, in this case King Gasir and his underlings. Beating, imprisonment, mutilation, banishment, death, depending on the offense.' He added with a smile, 'The usual stuff.'

Garn said nothing.

Thinking the matter was finished, Arduwyn turned.

Garn caught the hunter's arm, drawing up beside him to talk. 'You mean if someone hits me or insults Mitrian or steals everything we have, I'm not supposed to do anything about it?'

'Not exactly.' Arduwyn grinned again at Garn's naiveté, for Mitrian's benefit, but she was too caught up with gawking at the dense architecture and steady wash of traffic. 'There're provisions for things like that, Garn. I'm just saying to try talking before you try hitting.' Suddenly recognizing the potential offense of directing such a statement at one companion, Arduwyn turned his attention fully on Garn's response.

Garn's expression revealed more distress than resentment. 'How long are we staying here?'

The question drew the attention of all of Garn's companions. Arduwyn frowned. They had spent the last eight and a half months with Pudar as their goal. The idea of eventually going elsewhere had never occurred to him. 'At least until the baby's born. After that, you'll have to decide whether you like this city enough to live here.' It occurred to Arduwyn that if they remained in one place too long, Rache would certainly find them. Colbey had expressly stated that the danger he foresaw for Rache would come about only if the two Northmen met, but other, more indirect statements suggested that a confrontation between Rache and Garn might also prove fatal. Relieved of his spying duties, Arduwyn hoped that whatever the problem between Rache and Garn, it would work itself out in time.

Arduwyn watched Garn's expression, gradually realizing a deeper concern lay beneath the one the ex-gladiator had expressed. When Garn's features did not knit further, Arduwyn guessed his friend was not facing the same struggle the hunter had so many times in the past: to stay or to yield to the lure of travel and forest. That Garn would dislike a town simply because it curtailed violence seemed ludicrous. He always acted suitably repentant when his temper flared beyond his control and seemed otherwise to loathe harming anyone.

Arduwyn studied Garn's silently disgruntled form, trying to guess his thoughts from his meager knowledge of the larger man's past. *Once a slave, now a free man with a volatile temper.* Combined with the realization that Garn apparently had a limited knowledge of laws, the answer came easily. *It's not violence he's defending, it's his right to use his own judgment. He's so focused on freedom he sees rules as a serious restriction.* 'I don't know if this'll help, Garn, but every town and every culture has laws, even the decadent Easterners. You can't avoid them. It's one of the concessions you have to make for the conveniences that come with interacting with other people.'

The crowds thinned to couples and small groups as Arduwyn and his friends drew deeper into the inhabited portions of Pudar.

Encouraged by Garn's change of expression from annoyed to pensive, Arduwyn continued, 'The rules are all logical, the kinds of things anyone with principles would obey anyway. Crowd control mostly. If everyone in the city just started going after what he wanted, a few young, strong men would own everything. This way, the government has a recourse against the tiny handful of people without basic morality. So long as you consider the consequences your actions might have on other people before you do anything violent or extreme, you shouldn't get into any trouble with the law.'

Laws seemed such a fundamental idea, Arduwyn felt strange defending them. But he also knew that laws and witnessed vows were a relatively recent development in human history. His grand-father used to tell stories, heard from his own grandfather, about a time when any man's word was as strong as the laws of nature.

The Hungry Lion's familiar sign came into view, its words a chipped yellow beneath a comical figure of the king of beasts clutching his stomach, a pained expression on his whiskered face. Pulled from his thoughts, Arduwyn pointed. 'You still hungry, Sterrane?'

Sterrane nodded briskly, drawing his hands to his belly until he held nearly the same pose as the caricature on the sign.

The others laughed.

Arduwyn looped his donkey's lead rope across a horizontal post before the tavern. Tugging his scimitar free of his gear, he belted it around his waist. He removed the packs from the animal's back and passed them around for his companions to carry, giving Mitrian's things to Garn. Though most contained only clothing and the last of their rations, Arduwyn saw no reason to tempt thieves. Once all the packs were shouldered, Arduwyn headed for the door, gripped the handle, and pulled.

The heavy oak and iron door opened to reveal beer-stained tables in three rows of two. A chest-high bar concealed shelves of crockery and the cooking pit. Several patrons gathered for drinks or the evening meal, in singles, groups, and families including children. Smoke from the fire twined over the heads of those nearest the bar, rich with the aroma of bread and vegetables in a heavy meat sauce that Arduwyn had grown to love during his previous stays in Pudar. 'We picked a good night.' Arduwyn held the door wide for his friends to enter. 'The proprietor makes an excellent stew.'

Sterrane, Garn, and Mitrian filed inside. Arduwyn closed the door behind them. Turning to follow, he nearly collided with Sterrane who was still standing just inside the doorway. Amused by his companions' ignorance of protocol that Arduwyn had deemed normal from childhood, he pointed to an empty table. 'Let's sit, hmmm ?'

Most accustomed to social customs, Mitrian obeyed first, and the two men followed her example. Except for a few surreptitious glances, the other patrons seemed to take no notice of the newcomers. The locals had long ago become used to people of a variety of sizes and races; even the conspicuous weaponry did not seem to bother them, though no one else in *The Hungry Lion* carried so much as a copper sword.

Arduwyn waited until the others were seated before accepting a chair across from Sterrane that left his back to the strangers but gave him a good view of the door and a sideways look at the bar. From the corner of his eye, he caught a glimpse of a serving girl with a pitcher heading in their direction.

The cook fire smoke filled the room with a mist that, combined with the dizzyingly strong aroma of alcohol and the not-quite decipherable conversations, gave the tavern a homey, peaceful quality. Arduwyn slouched in his chair and closed his eyes. He loved the forests when spring brought them to life or when the air was sharp with the bite of winter, and the way the horizon always teased him over the next hill. But even chasing adventure could, in its own way, become tiresome. Security, permanence, and the warmth of friends and fire had an allure of their own, different but nonetheless special.

The clink of mugs caused Arduwyn to open his eyes. The serving girl leaned over Sterrane, clutching the pitcher in one hand as she groped through the pockets of her apron with the other. For an instant, their gazes met. Arduwyn recognized Bel at once. Her soulful dark eyes had hollowed more deeply into their sockets, and she was leaner than he liked or remembered. Yet still, her round cheeks and full lips attracted him every bit as much as before he had abandoned her and Kantar. *Without saying good-bye.* Arduwyn winced at the memory. For the first time in years, he sat, speechless. His mind and mouth would not work, so he had no choice but to trust his heart. And it told him he still loved this woman who was his best friend's wife.

Bel startled backward with a strangled noise. Mead sloshed over the pitcher's lip, drenching Sterrane. The big man moved aside with surprising speed and grace as mead plastered his hair to his forehead and dripped into his beard.

Arduwyn wanted to laugh but could not do that any more than he could speak.

Bel's expression changed from startlement to pleasure.

Arduwyn grinned. His mind began to function again, and he rose to sweep Bel into an embrace. He managed only a single word, but that seemed enough. 'Bel.'

Bel's smile disappeared. Her eyes went cold. 'It's not my table.' Whirling on her heel, she stomped back toward the bar, leaving Arduwyn staring, gape-mouthed, at her retreating back.

17 Sterrane the Bear

'Bel?' Sick with grief, Arduwyn started after the fleeing woman. Every patron in *The Hungry Lion* turned to stare, from the families at the surrounding tables to loners and couples at the bar.

Sterrane's mead-sticky hand clamped on Arduwyn's arm, stopping him. 'She not want talk you.'

Arduwyn watched Bel disappear behind the bar, irritated by his companion's interference. 'Damn it, Sterrane.' He shook free of the huge man's grip. 'You can't possibly understand.'

Sterrane jutted his lower lip, looking hurt.

Mitrian answered for him. 'No, but I can. You come in here after a year, catch her wholly by surprise, then expect her to throw herself into your arms? She cares for you. That's obvious. Just give her a chance to calm down.'

Arduwyn frowned, unconvinced, but he recognized the need to collect his composure. *Sterrane can't know anything about relationships, but Mitrian does. And she had to have a better understanding of women than I do.* Reluctantly, he sat, but his gaze tracked Bel as she cornered the other serving girl, a teenager with straight, dark hair that swirled to her waist. An animated discussion followed; Bel's arms waved wildly throughout it, then she ended with a jerk of her thumb over her shoulder toward Arduwyn's table. The younger girl stopped to gather four mugs into one hand and a pitcher in the other before heading in the indicated direction.

Arduwyn paid the newcomer no heed; his attention remained fixed on Bel. He watched her stack and brace five bowls of stew in her arms and head toward one of the other tables without giving Arduwyn so much as a sideways glance. Still, a stiffness in her gait betrayed that she was rattled, and the uppermost bowl teetered dangerously.

Arduwyn held his breath, fighting the natural urge to dash over and help Bel. By the time he arrived, it would be too late, one way or the other.

Bel adjusted her balance expertly. For an instant, the bowl hovered. Suddenly, it toppled, dragging over two others beneath it.

Hot stew sloshed over a middle-aged man, who was eating with his wife and two children. The bowl rolled, clattering across their table. A mug of mead crashed to the floor, ringing. Belatedly, the man sprang backward. His chair bashed into Bel, jarring the last bowls from her grip. She juggled them as she fell, but managed only to send one into a back spin that splashed its contents over her. Patrons at nearby tables scattered awkwardly out of the way while the stew-splattered man swore violently in the Western tongue. Apologizing profusely, Bel gathered the bowls.

Caught up in the drama unfolding behind him, Arduwyn did not realize the younger serving girl had addressed him until Garn elbowed him in the ribs. More startled than pained, Arduwyn whirled back to his companions. Four mugs rested on the table, one before him and each of his companions. Mitrian's and Garn's lay empty. Sterrane's held some of the same brew that Bel had spilled on his head. The girl waited at Arduwyn's right, the pitcher in her hand poised tentatively over his mug. 'Mead?'

The word did not register. 'Huhn?' Slowly, Arduwyn pulled his senses back to reality. 'Sure. Yes. Thank you.'

The serving girl poured, biting her cheeks to keep from laughing.

Realizing he was babbling, Arduwyn said to Garn and Mitrian, 'Aren't you having any?'

The pair exchanged looks of revulsion. Mitrian replied, 'Neither of us cared much for it at that tavern in the Northlands. We're having wine.'

Arduwyn glanced back toward Bel. The nearest tables had been edged away from the yellow-brown mess splattered across the floorboards. The patrons had returned to their meals, aside from the stew-stained, family man who was walking back to the bar with the stout, blond proprietor of *The Hungry Lion,* presumably to wash. Bel knelt, scrubbing at the spilled stew with a rag. It pained Arduwyn to watch Bel mopping someone else's floor, but he knew an offer of help would only make things worse. For now, she seemed in no danger, so he forced his attention fully on his companions.

Raised in a city where sewage tainted the drinking water, Arduwyn had grown up on beer, ale, and wine, plain or liberally mixed with water. He knew that adults who tried beer for the first time often found it vile, but he also knew Mitrian and Garn would either need to acquire a taste for it or frequently go thirsty.

The serving girl had just turned to leave. Adruwyn touched her arm. 'Why don't you pour them each a mug at my expense. Bring the wine, too, just in case.'

The girl turned, looking askance at Garn.

Arduwyn explained. 'Don't judge all beer by Northern brew.

Northman's beer is as harsh as its soldiers. Beer of any kind takes some getting used to, but it's worth it. You'll like mead. It's honey-based.'

Garn peered at Arduwyn, skepticism plainly etched on his face. 'Trust me.'

Garn nodded his acceptance, and the server poured mugs of mead for him and Mitrian.

Not wanting to further discomfort Bel by staring, Arduwyn promised himself to take three full swallows before twisting his head to watch her again. Attempting an air of calm detachment, he curled his hand about his mug and drew it to his mouth for the first sip.

'Where do we go after here?' Mitrian asked, gazing uncertainly at the drink the serving girl had poured.

Arduwyn swallowed without tasting the mead, his thoughts still distant. 'An inn. We'll need a place to stay until we can find more permanent shelter. If we're in Pudar longer than a couple weeks, it'll be cheaper to buy a cottage, especially at market place prices.' Forgetting his vow, Arduwyn sneaked a peek at the floor where he had last seen Bel working. Bel and the spilled stew had vanished.

Alarmed, Arduwyn glanced around the tavern until he found Bel near the bar, engaged in a conversation with the proprietor. The man's jowly face was pinched, covered with clusters of blood vessels that curled from central cores like spiders. Shortly, Bel wandered off to tend a patron, and the proprietor headed toward Arduwyn and his companions. Cued to trouble by the proprietor's flushed cheeks and stomping, directed walk, Arduwyn set aside his mug and waited.

The proprietor came up beside Arduwyn, the blond's tall, broad figure dwarfing the scrawny archer. He jabbed a sausage-sized finger at Arduwyn's chest. 'You're going to have to leave. You're . . .' He broke off, apparently noticing Sterrane's gigantic bulk and Garn's shorter but distinctly defined musculature for the first time. The proprietor's tone changed from belligerent to polite efficiency. '. . . upsetting one of my serving girls, making it difficult for her to do her job. Whatever you've eaten so far is on the house, but you're going to have to go.'

A frown creased Sterrane's features, and he looked wistfully at the mug from which he had taken only a single sip. He pouted, a crinkled expression that Arduwyn realized might look menacing to a man unfamiliar with Sterrane's gentle manner. 'Me hungry. Not want to.'

Garn glared, prepared to press the issue.

Arduwyn played diplomat. He spoke soothingly, though the proprietor kept his attention on Garn and Sterrane. 'I didn't come to upset Bel. I'm not going to hurt her. I just want to talk.' Reaching into his pocket, he extracted a fistful of coins and pressed them unobtrusively toward the proprietor's hand. 'If I can talk her into leaving with me, could you do without her for the evening ?'

The proprietor glanced down to Arduwyn's hand. Identifying the offering as a generous mix of silver and copper, he accepted the coins. 'Fine. So long as she goes willingly, she's yours.'

'Thank you.' Arduwyn reveled in his minor victory. 'Please. Send her over.'

The proprietor hesitated, as if to suggest Arduwyn should coax Bel back to the table himself. Then, realizing the value of keeping the matter private rather than encouraging Arduwyn to chase Bel around the tavern, he nodded, turned, and headed back to the bar.

Bel met the proprietor near the cook fire. Arduwyn watched their soft exchange, too distant to catch a single word. Suddenly, Bel looked over.

Feeling stupid to be caught gawking, Arduwyn glanced quickly back down at the table. He heard Bel's gentle step on the floorboards.

Bel drew up beside Arduwyn. 'Carlithel said you refused to leave until I told you to go.' The anger in Bel's dark eyes seemed to burn through him. 'Fine. This is from me, Arduwyn. Get the hell out of here.' She spun on her heel.

Caught off-guard by Carlithel's lie and Bel's hostility, Arduwyn stammered, 'W-wait ! Bel, please. Can't we talk ? Please ?'

Bel froze. She did not meet Arduwyn's gaze, but she did not leave either. 'There's nothing to talk about.'

'Bel, please.' Arduwyn was pleading now. 'I don't understand. At least let me know why you're mad. Let's go someplace private where you can hit me if you want to. I just can't deal with this without talking.'

'Go someplace ? Go someplace !' Bel fumed. 'You want me to just drop everything and go someplace ?'

Every head in the tavern jerked toward her.

Not wanting to make a scene, Bel lowered her voice, but the malice remained. She snorted. 'Same Arduwyn. Don't you see that's exactly the problem ? You act like it's fine to just up and leave anything at any time. Well, I have a job, the best I've had, and I'm not going to lose it to run off and talk. Especially with you.'

Arduwyn's salesman mentality thrilled that Bel had chosen an argument he could counter. He smiled. As long as she kept talking and listening, he still had a chance to win back her love. 'I didn't forget the importance of your job. Carlithel agreed to give you the evening off.'

Bel opened her mouth, but no words came out. Arduwyn's statement obviously caught her unprepared, and he could almost see the rage draining from her as surprise replaced it. Suddenly, she stiffened again. Her eyes narrowed, and she virtually hissed her reply. 'I don't care what Carlithel agreed to. I have three children to feed, not to mention the pay I'll get docked for that incident.' She made a wild motion toward the location where she had spilled the stew. 'I can't afford to lose my tips.'

Bel had walked right into Arduwyn's grasp, and he knew it. His grin broadened. He slipped his fingers into his pocket, tightened them over the garnet and pulled it free triumphantly. 'Will this cover tips?'

Shock etched deeply across Bel's features. Her hand drifted toward the gem, then stopped, hovering.

Arduwyn watched in silence, glad his friends had contributed nothing to a conversation in which only he and Bel had a stake. He hated to force her to sort need from pride, but he saw no other way. He could deal with that matter later. Unless she agreed to talk privately with him, he had no chance at all to mend a relationship he now knew he desperately needed. It made little sense to him. Not since his banishment had taken him from his family had he managed to dedicate even as much loyalty to people as he had to his three companions. He had not known love strong enough to match what he felt for Bel since the day of his father's death. Distance had diluted his affection for her until he had forgotten how powerful love could seem. Now with her again, it all washed back, and more strongly for the time lost.

Bel snatched the garnet from Arduwyn's hand. 'Let's go.'

The sudden movement and Bel's voice jolted Arduwyn from his thoughts. *Firfan, what kind of monster am I? My best friend is dying, and all I can think about is how much I love his wife.* Guilt tightened Arduwyn's gut. His single swallow of beer went sour in his stomach. 'Mitrian, Garn, Sterrane,' he said, as much for introduction as to gain their attention. 'You stay and get some food. Don't go anywhere else. I'll meet you here.' Rising, he waved Bel toward the door, then followed her into the street.

The cobbles lay, flat and dull in the dusk, and the cooling night breezes blew Bel's long brown hair into Arduwyn's face. The strands smelled pleasantly of cook fire smoke and beer. He caught up to her. Side by side, they walked down Pudar's road in a silence that seemed not the least bit awkward to Arduwyn. Just being with Bel was enough. He let her choose the route, never noticing whether other pedestrians passed. He waited to catch the first whisper of Bel's words or intentions. One part of his mind just wanted to understand, aware that only with knowledge could he hope to salvage a friendship and a love he cherished. But in another portion of his thoughts, he wished they could continue, never speaking, forever in the simple hush of being together. As long as no one spoke, he could pretend everything was all right.

Still Arduwyn and Bel continued walking. The sun dipped lower, plunging the market city into a grayness that left the buildings in encasing rows of shadow. Bel turned a corner. Shortly, the road circled an oval-shaped park with a central stone basin for watering livestock. Bel took a series of shuffling steps that put her ahead of Arduwyn. Suddenly, she whirled, her heels pressed to the basin rim. 'Why did you come back?'

Despite his preparation, the abruptness and hostility of Bel's question caught Arduwyn completely by surprise. 'What?'

'Why did you come back?' Bel rolled her eyes to the heavens, as if beseeching gods rather than addressing Arduwyn. '*Why did you come back to Pudar?*'

'I,' Arduwyn started, knowing the answer was simple, but trying to gather his scrambled wits, wishing he had a clue as to what Bel wanted to hear. 'Kantar sent a message, and . . .'

'Kantar is dead.' Bel met Arduwyn's doelike gaze directly. Her eyes went moist.

Misery tightened Arduwyn's throat, and he found it difficult to breathe. Speaking came even harder. 'I'm sorry,' he managed. The words did not seem like enough, gross understatement at a time when he needed to console. 'Kantar was my closest friend. I loved him, too. You know that.' He came forward to embrace her.

Bel recoiled. Already against the basin rim, her foot mired on stone. She overbalanced backward with a cry of alarm and threw her weight gracelessly forward to counter.

Arduwyn raised his hands in a gesture of peace, waiting until she regained her equilibrium before backing away to give her the space she required. He did not want to make amends by driving her into the trough. 'From his note, I'd thought Kantar had years. I planned to see him before he died. You have to believe that.'

Bel's voice had grown tiny, almost unrecognizable after her previous outspoken bitterness. 'It happened fast. I don't think he ever knew how sick he was.'

'I'm sorry,' Arduwyn repeated.

Strained silence followed his words. Arduwyn had mourned his friend's death too many times to lose his composure now. Instead, he struggled with a thought he tried unsuccessfully to suppress. Somehow, he could not banish a spark of hope and joy, the realization that, without Kantar, Bel could become his. *Bel*. He would never have wished ill luck on Kantar, least of all death, and the realization that he was looking upon his best friend's demise as an opportunity made him sick with guilt.

Arduwyn avoided Bel's gaze, too uncomfortable with his own emotions to deal with hers as well. 'I'm sorry,' he said again. Realizing he had stupidly restated the same platitude for the third time, he winced. 'How are you doing?'

Bel sighed, the sound heavy over the slosh of wind through water. She caught Arduwyn's dark gaze with her own as if daring him to look away. 'Kantar was a good provider while he was well, but there wasn't any extra. I have three children. The eldest girl is only twelve, too young to marry even if she had a dowry. How do you think I'm doing?'

Arduwyn lowered his head, avoiding Bel's eyes, unable to keep from taking the responsibility for her hardships onto himself. *I should have come sooner. She needed me. They both needed me, and I wasn't here.* 'I want to help. Bel, I wasn't being completely honest. I came because of Kantar's note.' He forced himself to meet her gaze again. 'But I also came because I wanted, no, needed, to see you. I love you, Bel.' Again, he moved toward her.

This time, Bel raised a hand to halt Arduwyn. 'Thank you for the money.' She fished the garnet from her apron. 'I don't want you to think I don't appreciate it, but I can't take it under false pretences. If you go with it, I can't take it.'

Arduwyn blinked, uncertain what to make of the statement. He made no move to take the stone. 'I don't understand.'

Bel balanced the garnet on her palm. 'I mean, I can't take your money if you expect me to accept your presence with it.' Despite her firm insistence, she did not extend her hand, as if she unconsciously hoped he would let her keep it.

Bel's rejection stung. Arduwyn bit his lip, fighting tears. 'You hate me, don't you?' Fishing for any way to salvage the situation, he grabbed for the only reason he could find. 'If it's because of what we did before I left, that one night of passion, I'm sorry. It was a mistake. I never meant to hurt you or Kantar and . . .'

'I don't hate you, Arduwyn. I love you.'

Surprise silenced Arduwyn.

'I've already put the mistake to rest.' Bel sat on the basin ledge. 'It was a stupid accident. I was as much to blame as you were. I learned from it; it couldn't have happened twice. Kantar and the children never knew. It's as good as forgotten.'

'Then why?' Arduwyn started. Losing momentum, he tried again. 'I love you. You love me. I can make enough money to support you and the children. What's the problem?'

'The problem is you.' Bel drew her legs to her chest and watched Arduwyn from over the tops of her knees. 'You're a runner.'

'A runner? What do you mean, a runner?'

'After we slept together, I needed someone to talk to. Usually, I could do that with Kantar. I would have told him. If he chose to leave me because of it, well, he deserved better than me. But, for whatever reason, he held you in higher regard than anyone else we knew. I couldn't destroy that friendship.' Bel pursed her lips, looking even more beautiful to Arduwyn. 'The only person I could have talked with was you. But you chose to run instead.'

Arduwyn cringed, and now nothing could keep him from crying. His vision blurred, and a tear rolled down his face. Through a maze of colored pinpoints, he could see Bel had started to weep, too. He took a seat beside her, glad that this time she did not move away. 'I was wrong. I was stupid. I'm sorry, I'm stupid. Can't you ever forgive me?'

'I forgave you a long time ago.' Bel's voice went breathy. 'But I'm twenty-seven years old with three children and a job that feeds us irregularly. I need a husband with a sense of commitment. I need a man who will accept my children as his own, who'll come home every night with enough money to keep us fed and clothed, who can protect us from thieves and keep my bed warm at night. Men like Kantar are hard enough to find. Your presence will make it impossible.'

Arduwyn dared not believe what he was hearing. 'But I can do those things. I love Kantar's children. He was my closest friend. I love you. I've worked before, and, if that isn't enough, I'm a tolerably good hunter. I'm not big nor good with a sword, but I've never known a thief who could outrun an arrow.'

'No!' Bel's fist crashed against the stone. 'It impressed Kantar, the way you made friends so easily yet were so dedicated to the woods you were willing to forgo the simple pleasures most men take for granted. But I see with a woman's eyes things men don't understand. When you wander, you're not really looking for adventure, you're running from responsibility. Always, you believe you're seeking something more, something you think is special out there, maybe over the next hill, something other men can't find. You spend so much time looking, you're blind to the small pleasures that you have. You'll die searching for something that doesn't exist, never having recognized or enjoyed what you had.'

Arduwyn opened his mouth to dispute, but Bel's severe expression told him she had not yet finished.

'And I'll spend every day worrying over whether this is the one when you don't return. Do I have another week? Another month?

The months or even years you stay will be wasted, and I'll have nothing but bitter memories and the knowledge that I'm that much older, that I may have lost a thousand chances to find a stable man. You'll leave hating me, believing I stole your chance at true happiness, your opportunity to make a glorious mark upon the world, mourning time lost from your chase of nameless ghosts and dreams that don't exist.' Bel lapsed into a bout of tears.

Arduwyn drew her to his chest. This time, she did not resist, appreciating the comforting despite its source. His first urge, to deny Bel's accusation, passed quickly. He had never looked at the situation in that light, and he needed a chance to consider her words. One thing seemed clear. *I love Bel so much more than I ever knew.* 'Bel, give me a chance. Please, give me a chance. I love you. I want to be with you. I want to help. I can change. I just want to be with you . . .' Arduwyn trailed off, clutching Bel to him, torn in a thousand directions yet valuing the feel of her warm, soft curves against him.

Bel clung, and they sat together, each mired in thought. Arduwyn's feelings flipped back and forth, hoping the moment would never end, then wishing it had never begun.

Finally, Bel pulled free of his grip. 'You want a chance? I'll give it to you this way. Choose. Me or the forest. You can't have both.'

Arduwyn licked his lips, stalling. He wanted to hold Bel again, to pull her close and tell her everything would be all right. But he knew he had to find peace within himself before he could keep such a promise. To make that vow without dealing with his inner confusion could only be a mistake, opening him to breaking the promise and Bel's heart or trapping himself in an intolerable situation. 'I . . . need time to think.'

Bel relaxed. A smile appeared on her face, and she seemed relieved by his answer. 'I wouldn't have it any other way.'

Mitrian awakened to a menacing growl followed by high-pitched giggling. Startled and confused, she tried to sit up, her rounded abdomen turning her sudden movement into an awkward, flailing roll. She lay on a knitted rug beside a tidy, unlit hearth. Sunlight streamed through the eastern window, blinding her. She threw an arm across her forehead to shield her eyes as wild thumping noises, interspersed with childish screams of delight, rang in her ears. The floor shuddered.

A young, female voice wafted from deeper in the room. 'Hang on, Effer! I'll kill the bear!'

Memory seeped back into Mitrian's sleep-dulled senses. She recalled falling asleep in Garn's arms on the main room floor of Bel's cottage. Now, she lay alone. She twisted toward the noises, her gaze trailing over the door to the outside, across crates pushed away from the center of the room to the single couch. There, Arduwyn sat, staring out the window behind him, one arm curled around a three-year-old girl with frizzled, dark hair. She bounced on his knee excitedly. To the right of the couch, a ladder led up to the loft bedrooms. Beyond it, a doorway opened into the kitchen. Toward the center of the room, Sterrane romped on all fours, a towheaded boy of about six on his back. A girl several years older swatted at the huge man with a broom.

Suddenly, Sterrane wheeled. The boy teetered, giggling furiously, then regained his balance. The eldest girl fled with a shrill noise.

Mitrian smiled at their play. 'Good morning.'

Arduwyn looked over. 'Ah, Mitrian, awake at last. Couldn't imagine how you managed to sleep through the bear hunt, but I'm glad you got your rest.'

When Mitrian and her companions had arrived at Bel's cottage the previous night, the youngsters were asleep in the loft. 'Bel's children, I presume?'

'The bear rider is Effer. The brave woman warrior with the wooden sword is Jani, and the spectator . . .' Arduwyn tightened his grip on the toddler '. . . is Rusha. I believe you know the bear.' He inclined his head to indicate Sterrane.

Jani's tone went singsong. 'Sterrane the bear can't catch me. Sterrane the bear can't catch me.'

Sterrane made a sudden lunge for the girl. She retreated with a shriek, but the bearded man hooked her ankle. Effer tumbled to the floor. Rusha slipped from Arduwyn's lap to her sister's aid. 'Don't leave, Uncle 'dune,' she chided him in a serious tone. 'I come back.'

'All right,' Arduwyn promised.

Mitrian pressed her rumpled clothing with her hands. It seemed strange to watch her traveling companions settle so comfortably into domestic life. Sterrane appeared capable of adapting to any situation. But despite Arduwyn's experiences with cities, the hunter had always seemed far more comfortable in the forest. She remembered his words from the day they met: 'I'd kill myself before I let anyone lock me in a cage.' At the time, she had taken the words literally. Now, she wondered if village boundaries and cottage walls penned him equally as severely. Colbey's lessons had dominated Mitrian's time nearly to the exclusion of all else; yet she had still noticed that it had been Arduwyn who prodded them to keep moving from one town to the next and, if any member of the party was missing, it was always Arduwyn. She found the same restlessness in him that her father displayed when too much time passed between forays, a feeling she knew well herself. More than once, she had caught

Santagithi staring at the creases in his hand, as if he mourned losing something extraordinary, as if every moment he spent on everyday responsibilities and concerns was one forever lost.

Mitrian watched Sterrane romp about the floor, three children hurling themselves at him at once. For a moment, she envied his simplicity, the way he amused himself with whatever situation life gave him whether that meant living alone in a cave, the impermanence of travel, or the stressful, constant hustle of a trading city. Always before, she had been attracted to men like Rache and her father, heroes who lived for the moments of glory, dreading the routine that fell between those peaks. Now, near term and protective of her son and his future, Mitrian worried that Garn might find cities and cottages as confining as Arduwyn did.

Unconsciously, Mitrian's arms looped around her bulging abdomen. Suddenly, she became acutely aware of her husband's absence. 'Where's Garn?'

Rusha ran around Sterrane in a crazy circle, then hurled herself back into Arduwyn's arms. 'Miss me?'

'Terribly,' Arduwyn replied with a straight face. He addressed Mitrian's question. 'Garn walked Bel to work. He was bored, and we thought it would be safer for her. He should be back shortly. Your pack's upstairs, and there's fruit in through there.' He motioned first toward the ladder to the loft then to the entryway to the kitchen. 'Why don't you eat, get washed up, and dressed? Then Sterrane, Garn, and I will have to go out and find ourselves jobs. We'll need some steady income.'

'Why?' Mitrian patted the pouch of gems at her belt. 'I have plenty of money. You're welcome to it.'

Arduwyn hauled Rusha into his lap, his lips pressed into a stern line. 'That's your money, and I think you should keep it for emergencies. I wouldn't feel right using it, and I believe Sterrane would feel the same way. As for Garn, he'll get bored if he's not working.'

A chill shivered up Mitrian's spine as she realized how closely Arduwyn's words fit her previous line of thought.

Sterrane rolled. Children flung themselves out of his path. Jani gave him a sharp poke in the ribs with the broom, and he rushed her.

Ignoring the antics, Mitrian spoke confidentially. 'Garn's not really, um, trained for any trade.'

Arduwyn smiled. The same bold confidence returned that he had displayed while disputing over a deer in the Granite Hills. 'Arduwyn the Job Finder can handle Garn.' His gaze fell on Sterrane, and his grin went crooked. He said nothing more, but Mitrian suspected he

333

would find Sterrane's employment needs more difficult. As glib as Arduwyn sounded, Mitrian knew from Nantel's stories that paying jobs were exceedingly difficult to find. The citizens generally apprenticed to trades. Unskilled labor positions were quickly filled by transients who had lost their money to whores, thieves, or Pudar's gambling parlors.

Mitrian opened her mouth to contradict him, then thought better of it. Arduwyn knew the obstacles he was up against. Undermining his confidence could achieve nothing. She headed into the kitchen to wash and eat.

To Mitrian, the Pudarian market became a wild buzz of colors, noise, and odors. Stands and shops lined the streets, packed so tightly that no finger's breadth of space was wasted. People wound in an endless procession between the stands. At first, the traffic seemed aimless to Mitrian. More than a dozen times her pregnant abdomen jostled into other passersby. Each time, the other turned a hostile look on her. Then, the strangers' gazes naturally fell to her paunch and the sword at her hip, and their expressions changed to haughty disapproval. Apparently, Pudarians thought little of armed women, or pregnant ones roving their market square. Having passed judgment, each stranger would disappear wordlessly back into the crowd.

Gradually, Mitrian mastered moving amid the steady flow of people deeper into the city on the east side and toward the exit on the west. She gawked her way from seemingly endless displays of silks to stands laden with pastries, fruit, or meats, then on to weaponry or household goods. Each time she believed she had discovered every conceivable ware, she found some necessity or novelty she had forgotten. Spices perfumed the air. Remedies with multihued labels promised to cure every ailment from toothache to end-stage consumption. Mitrian's ears ached with the cries of merchants raising their voices to a volume that drowned out their neighbors, all vying, it seemed, for her attention.

Wanting to see it all, Mitrian missed most of the Pudarian bazaar, including the trio of white-robed figures who exchanged knowing glances and glided into the crowd. Dazzled by diamond necklaces, blankets, and rattles shoved toward her amid a rapid-fire sales pitch, she never found her tongue before the items were withdrawn for more interested patrons behind her. She had almost forgotten that she had companions until Garn nudged her.

'Can you move like her?'

Mitrian followed his gaze to a buxom dancer, scantily clad in two strips of gauzy fabric.

Sterrane shook his head. 'Not me. Belly get in way.' He performed a series of awkward, spinning movements that sent Garn and Mitrian into peals of laughter. Oddly, though some passersby stepped around him, no one stopped to stare at the hairy, pot-bellied dancer.

Even Arduwyn seemed unamused. 'Come on,' he said stiffly, waving for them to catch up. Irritation tinged his voice, and Mitrian watched to see what troubled him. She let the crowd split and flow around her as Arduwyn approached a man unloading crates of vials onto a table.

A short exchange followed, the merchant shaking his head throughout it. Arduwyn wandered away, looking more confounded than before.

The sight sobered Mitrian. Arduwyn must be having enough trouble finding employment without his three companions acting like fools on a drunken revelry. Guilt seeped into her at the thought that she was too busy staring at crafts and jewelry to keep Garn and Sterrane from creating an embarrassment. She studied Garn, glad to see he appeared more overwhelmed than defensive and resolved to watch his antics more closely.

As morning trickled into afternoon, exhaustion wore on Mitrian. Her head sagged, and each step seemed an effort of will. Whenever Arduwyn paused to speak with merchants, she found a crate to sit on or a shop wall against which she could lean. It became increasingly difficult to stand. The cries of the merchants merged into a shrill and piercing annoyance. She and Arduwyn had left Garn far behind, riveted to a stand displaying shields and armor. Sterrane continued to look around in silence, stuffed with a variety of exotic foods Arduwyn had chosen and bargained for, the larger man only slightly more subdued than earlier in the morning.

As the sun sank lower in the west, Arduwyn grew more irritable. After what seemed like his fiftieth rejection, he drew up a crate and flopped down next to Mitrian.

'No luck?' Mitrian asked out of politeness. Despite Colbey's conditioning, a full day on her feet while flagrantly pregnant had exhausted her. Her ankles felt as thick as tree trunks.

'Luck has nothing to do with it,' Arduwyn snapped. 'I'm doing something wrong.' His gaze tracked the milling crowd. 'I'm sorry I dragged you along. I didn't know it would take this long.' Despite his words, Arduwyn sounded more aggravated than regretful. He pounded his fist against his leather-covered thigh several times, deeply thoughtful.

'Is there anything I can do?' Mitrian's offer sounded no more sincere than Arduwyn's apology.

'I'm doing something wrong. Something wrong.' Arduwyn's

words sounded more like a chant than shared conversation. 'Something wrong. Merchants. Sales.' A smile raked over his face. 'I've got the answer. Why didn't I think of it before?' His annoyance fled, replaced by the confidence Mitrian had seen in Bel's cottage. 'Mitrian, you're about to watch a master job finder at work.' He leapt to his feet. 'I've decided to work here.' He gestured to an area so choked with patrons that Mitrian could hardly see the stand.

Despite his size, Arduwyn shouldered his way through the throng, with Mitrian trailing curiously after him. He stopped before a table spread with a wide variety of merchandise, from vials of perfume and powders to ornamental letter openers. Two youngsters attended the patrons. Behind them, a middle-aged man dressed in blue silk stood, grim as a statue, with legs widely braced. Clean-shaven, he sported a headful of dark curls. A frown scored his features.

With surprisingly little effort, Arduwyn maneuvered through the crowd to the man in blue. Mitrian pressed to within hearing distance.

Arduwyn used a booming voice, speaking in a swift patter that precluded interruption or pauses for breath. 'Hello. I'm Arduwyn, and I consent to being placed in charge of your sales provided I receive three silver chroams for every ten I sell.'

The merchant jerked his head toward Arduwyn. 'What?'

Arduwyn rubbed at his chin, still rambling. 'Perhaps three seems a bit much, so I'll settle for two provided you have no Béarnides in your company.'

The merchant's frown deepened. His eyes narrowed to slits. 'Who the hell are you? And what business is it of yours if I have Béarnides in my company?'

Arduwyn stepped closer, neatly blocking the merchant's escape. 'A shrewd businessman indeed, sir. But you can't have the best salesman for less than two chroams for ten. And I'm adamant. You mustn't speak my name in front of Béarnides. It seems their most august ruler purchased forged documents from a rogue with my name and general description.'

Mitrian filled her lungs in a deep, shuddering gasp, as if to fulfill Arduwyn's need for breath.

The merchant's cheeks reddened in offense. He stared. 'Why on Ruaidhri's great earth would I hire a thief hunted by the king of Béarn?'

Mitrian wondered the same thing, though, doubtless, Arduwyn had captured the merchant's attention.

'Do you consider selling an item at the highest price you can thieving? I call it good business, don't you?'

'Yes,' the merchant admitted, his normal rhythm sounding abnormally slow in the wake of Arduwyn's rapid-fire speech.

Arduwyn nodded agreeably. 'Any rascal who could sell that Béarnian king false plans and leave Béarn alive must be pretty shrewd, don't you agree?'

'Well, yes, but . . .'

'I know if I were a merchant, I'd grab an opportunity to find a salesman that skilled. Only a fool wouldn't, sir, and you're no fool.'

'I . . .' the merchant started.

'Fine. Two for ten, and I'll start tomorrow.'

'Wait!' The merchant dismissed the suggestion with a brisk wave. 'I don't need . . .'

Arduwyn broke in. 'You're not risking anything. If I don't sell, you needn't pay me. I'll even start now.' He stepped behind the stand before the merchant could protest.

'Wait!' The silk-clad merchant made a grab with a clawed hand that fell short of Arduwyn's shoulder. He shuffled forward, then halted in consideration. Recognition of talent or curiosity held him in quiet suspension. Folding his arms across his chest, he studied Arduwyn at work.

Mitrian watched with the same anticipation.

Arduwyn's face broke into a friendly grin as he approached a man who was fondling a small bag of spice. 'Good day, sir,' the hunter called.

The man nodded stiffly. 'Price?'

'Six copper chroams.'

A skeptical look crossed the merchant's features. He seemed on the verge of laughter.

The patron looked startled. 'That's expensive.'

Arduwyn shrugged. 'Fine ginger. I can't take less.'

The man set down the pouch. He started to turn.

Arduwyn drummed his fingers on the wooden table. 'Hold on. You seem like a good man, and one I could easily grow to like.' Arduwyn leaned forward and cast a sideways glance at the merchant, silently begging forbearance. He finished in a loud whisper. 'I could trade the spice for your dagger.'

The man twisted his lips into a thoughtful grimace. He drew the dagger from its battered leather sheath, examining its worn, nicked blade. His gaze fell to the spice. 'Fine.' He passed it to Arduwyn.

The merchant made an angry noise deep in his throat. He stepped forward to intercede, then stopped again, apparently willing to give Arduwyn the benefit of his doubts. Certainly, the hunter had not yet closed the deal.

Arduwyn clucked excitedly over the knife. 'Exceptional workmanship. The craftsmen here don't have the pride and skill that went into this blade.' Arduwyn let his eyes linger over the steel before looking up at his customer again. 'It served you long and well, didn't it?'

'It was a good dagger.' The man pocketed the spice, but, as Arduwyn grew more enamored with the knife, the customer remained.

'Yes.' Arduwyn's voice went pensive. 'I owned one just like this when I killed my first deer. Why, as old and well-cared for as this appears, I'd guess you had it when you killed your first deer.'

The customer flushed. 'Why, I did in fact. Fifteen years ago, I dressed and skinned my first buck with that very knife.'

'After my first deer, I felt so proud I didn't clean the blood from the blade for a week.'

The patron reached for the dagger. 'In the etching on the blade, I saw a little blood yet.'

'Yes, sir.' Arduwyn tapped the blade on his wrist. 'Priceless memories keep in a knife like this. My first resides on the mantle, a trophy I stare at every night. A good place for memories, don't you think?'

It was a blatant lie. Mitrian knew Arduwyn did not even own a mantle, and she suspected his story about cheating the high king was equally dishonest. The merchant tipped his head, fascinated by Arduwyn's style.

'Friend,' the patron said softly. 'Could I have my dagger back?'

Arduwyn looked shocked. He held the dagger far beyond the man's reach. 'Sorry. You agreed to the trade. It's done.'

The patron breathed a sigh and looked longingly at the knife in Arduwyn's fist. 'A man values few enough things without giving those away.'

'I know what you mean. You can't buy memories in the market.' Arduwyn shook his head. 'I'm sorry, I . . . Wait!' Sudden inspiration showed clearly on Arduwyn's face, the expression an exact duplicate to the one he had formed when he decided how to manipulate the merchant. 'A dagger like this couldn't cost more than fifteen or twenty chroams new. I can't give it to you, but my boss can't get angry if I sell it. As a friend, I'll let you have it for ten.'

'Thank you.' The man reached for his purse, paid, and headed back into the crowd.

Mitrian had never seen a man pass money so eagerly.

Turning, Arduwyn dumped eight gold coins into the merchant's hand. He pocketed the other two.

For several seconds, the two men stood in silence. Mitrian held her breath.

Finally, the merchant pocketed the money. 'It was cinnamon,' he said gruffly. 'Now get back to work.'

'Not so quick.'

The merchant met Arduwyn's sparkling brown eyes with incredulity. 'You've got your two for ten and a job. What more do you want?'

'I've got two friends as good at what they do as I am at what I do.' Arduwyn gestured.

Mitrian followed the movement, noticing for the first time that Sterrane and Garn were headed toward them.

The merchant studied the pair doubtfully. 'Uh, exactly what do they do?'

'They lift things.'

'What?'

'They're strong,' Arduwyn clarified. 'They load and haul merchandise.'

The merchant returned his attention to Arduwyn. 'Is this the last thing you're going to ask from me?'

'Probably not,' Arduwyn admitted. 'But it's the last I can think of just now.'

'Ruaidhri's mercy.' The merchant rolled his eyes heavenward. 'I should just throw you out of here. But you are good.' He sighed. 'Fine. Send your friends to the docks. Have them report to the foreman, Kruger, at dawn, and tell him Brugon suggested he hire them.'

Arduwyn glided to Mitrian's side to give her the news she had already heard. 'I know,' she said before he could speak. 'Where did you learn to sell like that?'

'Practice, observation, experience, trial and error. I discovered that memories can't be bought, but they can be sold.'

'But,' Mitrian pressed, 'how could you possibly know that man would have such an attachment to his knife?'

Arduwyn smiled. Obviously, the explanation went far beyond what he was about to reveal to Mitrian. 'I looked at the age of the man and the age of the sheath. A man grows fond of anything that becomes a part of his life for long, whether or not he knows, wants, or likes the attachment. Had it turned out that he never skinned a deer, I would have found some other sentimental remembrance.'

Mitrian frowned, still skeptical.

'Besides, when we were wandering around, I overheard that same man talking about an upcoming hunt with his friends. He said it had been years since he'd gone traipsing after hoofprints with his father. He hadn't hunted since his father's death.'

Mitrian stared, incredulous. 'But how could you possibly know to listen to that particular man?' She made a stabbing motion with her hand in the direction the buyer had gone. 'How did you know *that* man would just happen to go to the stand where you wanted to work?'

'I saw him headed for the table. Why do you think I *chose* this stand?'

Mitrian laughed. 'But how did you know he'd go to any stand at all?'

'I didn't have to.' Arduwyn glanced into the crowd, picking out a portly pair of women. 'The one on the left just had a fight with her husband. The one with her is her cousin, Zelrina.' He indicated a trio of men. 'The one in the lead tends to spend beyond his means, so his wife allowed him to carry only enough copper to buy fruit and bread. The one closest to us wants a birthday present for his niece.'

'Amazing,' Mitrian said, though she had no proof any of his observations were true. 'You can tell that just by looking?'

'I can tell that because I listened.' Arduwyn kept his gaze on the masses. 'I call it crowd scanning. Whenever I get a free moment, I slip out among the patrons "upstream" from the selling table. I watch to see which people seem interested in certain items, what approaches are working or failing for other salesmen, and overhear what I can from passing conversations. The more you know about a person, the easier he becomes to manipulate. If I happen to find out a woman's name, I can sell her almost anything.'

Mitrian crinkled her nose, finding the method offensive. 'That's ugly.'

'That's sales.' Arduwyn shrugged. 'People expect it. Just see to it you don't fall prey to the same tactics.'

'Hey, Red.' The merchant's voice wafted over the densely mingled hubbub. 'A wise man once reminded me that if you don't sell anything, I don't have to pay you.'

Arduwyn laughed. 'I'll see you at home.' He waved a quick good-bye to Mitrian, then returned to the selling table.

18 Wizard's Work

In the ruins of Myrcidë, the Eastern Wizard, Shadimar, stared at the red falcon perched on his rickety plank and boulder table. Fire from the hearth bathed the room in ruddy light, striking highlights of yellow and silver through the bird's plumage and outlining its crest like a halo. Conjured rain drummed on the rooftops and surrounding meadows, though the courtyards remained dry, safe from his magical downpour. Secodon sat beside the Wizard's chair, his muzzle warm on his master's thigh; but the wolf's loyal presence could not keep Shadimar's thoughts from a Cardinal Wizard's call to war.

It was not within the Eastern Wizard's right to enter Carcophan's Eastland dominion, except while tracking a champion of his own. But Shadimar had not needed to cross the border; his glimpse from the peaks of the Great Frenum Mountains had shown him enough. Carcophan's general, Siderin, had mustered his forces and would reach the Westlands within two months. The time had come for Shadimar to complete his portion of the prophecy by mobilizing Santagithi's army and attending the West's master strategist. *As if Santagithi might need my encouragement to lead men to war.* Through a fold in his slate gray robe, Shadimar clutched at the Pica Stone, the clairsentient sapphire he had collected in payment from Mitrian. *Why would the prophecy waste a Wizard's attention on a general so eager when so much else needs doing?*

After his duty to Santagithi was dispatched, any action by Shadimar paced a delicate line of principle. Winning the Great War hinged upon completing the tasks of the missing Western Wizard, but, as of yet, Shadimar had seen no sign that Tokar had performed any of his prophesied duties. Already, the Eastern Wizard had encroached upon his colleague's province by thrusting the Renshai heritage upon Mitrian. To press further by rallying Pudar or any of the other cities in Tokar's territory would risk Shadimar's Wizards' vows. Yet if the Western Wizard had been destroyed, Shadimar would have to assume his counterpart's duties or risk oblivion for the followers of neutrality as well as destruction of the balance it was his god-meted objective to maintain.

Shadimar balled his left hand into a fist, resting the other palm on Secondon's head. *I have to find out if Tokar lives.* The Eastern Wizard shook his head, knowing the need but not the means. To intrude upon the Western Wizard by sorcery would be a certain violation of his vows, and he had already tried repeatedly to contact his colleague by messenger. *I have to try one more time. What choice do I have?* Gently inching his leg free of Secodon's chin, Shadimar rose and paced to the hearth. From a cubby above the mantle, he retrieved a strip of parchment, a quill, and a short length of twine. Returning to the table, he wrote in the Common trading runes:

'The War is started. Warn the West.'

Shadimar scribbled his signature at the bottom. He stared at the note, unsatisfied. He wanted to question Tokar's intentions, to demand a reply if the Western Wizard could give one, and to convey his urgency and concern. But Shadimar knew a long note would be folly. To say too much would risk offending Tokar or allowing information to fall into the enemy's hands. *How much bolder would Carcophan become if he believed only the weakest of the Wizards could oppose his champion?* Tokar understood his duties and their significance. To know the Great War had begun should be enough. 'Swiftwing.'

The falcon twisted its head, regarding Shadimar through one burning, golden eye. Docilely, it waited. The bird had served as the Wizards' messenger for longer than Shadimar had trained, and the generations of Eastern Wizards' memories passed to him by his mentor's ceremony of passage could not reveal a time when Swiftwing had not attended the cardinal Wizards. Shadimar did not know whether the falcon was eternal or whether the gods replaced it at intervals with a younger specimen. In any case, it was the only bird the Western Wizard could not communicate with any better than his colleagues.

Shadimar rolled the parchment into a packet. Grasping the twine, he bound the message to Swiftwing's scaly leg. 'Take it to the Western Wizard.' He held out an arm, the gray sleeve sagging from his withered flesh. Obediently, the falcon flapped to the Wizard's forearm, and its weight on his limb scarcely disturbed him. The talons dug through fabric but, like all beings and creations of law, they could not pierce the Wizard's skin.

Shadimar entered the long, gray hallway, following it to a statue-filled courtyard. Vines swarmed the walls and monuments. As Secodon padded in behind him, flocks of berry-smeared songbirds exploded from the vines, their wingbeats slapping echoes between the crumbling walls. Shadimar kept his attention trained on Swiftwing. 'If you don't find the Western Wizard, deliver the message to another. Choose a man or woman of consequence.' Shadimar paused, uncertain whether the bird could understand his final command. He knew Swiftwing's comprehension was limited, but he was uncertain of the extent of that limitation. He ended with the traditional send-off, 'Fly, Swiftwing. And beware the arrows of hunters.'

The falcon unfurled wings the color of embers and launched into the sky. Shadimar watched it rise like fire against a darkened sky wound through with lightning from the magical tempest that guarded his ruins. Gradually, the bird faded to black outline and disappeared.

Shadimar dropped his hand to Secondon's head, the thick under-coat dense and soft beneath his touch. No prophecy had divined as many details of Wizards' behaviour as the one about the Great War. The Eastern Wizard knew his lot was to mobilize and advise the West's finest strategist as well as to accompany his army to the battleground. To abandon that duty might undo his efforts to date as well as any gains the Western Wizard might have made. *It's out of my hands now. The balance of mankind's world now rests on a falcon.*

Responsive to his master's mood, Secondon tucked his plumed tail between his legs and loosed a single, short whine.

Seated before the opened gates to Santagithi's citadel, Acting-Captain Jakot spotted the stylus-thin Wizard and his shaggy pet when they were halfway through the village. The guard followed their passage with narrowed eyes, tracking Shadimar's direct route along the cobbled streets and toward his post on the hilltop. Once certain of the elder's destination, Jakot rose, unfolding a tall, intimidatingly strapping frame. He shook sandy bangs from his forehead, rested a hand on his sword hilt, and waited.

As Shadimar started up the hill toward Santagithi's citadel, Jakot discerned the Wizard's fine, white hair and beard, the near-transparent skin that revealed a network of veins, and the wrinkled features that accompanied great age. Still, the old man walked with a steady tread that belied his age, and the creature at his side looked more like a wolf than any dog Jakot had ever seen. The acting-captain did not relax his stance.

At length, Shadimar reached the crest. Man and Wizard stared at one another for several moments until the elder broke the silence. 'Greetings, Jakot. I have important business with Santagithi.'

The personal address caught Jakot by surprise. Barely thirty, he had not yet joined Santagithi's guard force at the time of the Eastern

Wizard's other visit, now fourteen years past. Jakot's gaze dropped to the wolf. Without taking his eyes from the newcomers, he called for his backup. 'Donnerval!'

Several seconds passed.

As the delay lengthened, Jakot's mood slipped from caution to annoyance. Without Rache and Nantel to whip the soldiers and archers into shape, the guards had begun to lapse into an unruly mob. Since Mitrian's kidnapping and Rache's dispatch, Santagithi seemed to have aged a decade. He sank into interminable silences that, if pressed too far, erupted into deadly rages. It had fallen to Jakot to maintain discipline and to hide the depth of his general's depression from his followers. Jakot's dedication to this task had lost him a lover and a number of friends, but he had managed to keep the guards keenly honed. Still, his control alwys teetered on the brink. Anything but a brisk response to his command could not be tolerated.

'Donnerval, front and center! Now!' Jakot's command left no room for question or delay. Though he lacked Rache's mastery, Jakot's sword skills exceeded that of most of his followers, and his size gave him other advantages when the need for threat arose.

Donnerval skidded to attention beside Jakot. His breeks sagged, tied haphazardly. The skirt of his mail shirt lay half-tucked into the waist. Apparently, he had been relieving himself when his captain summoned him.

Jakot bit his lip to keep from smiling. He felt bad for blaming Donnerval's delay on lack of vigilance, yet it pleased him to see how seriously his underling took his command. Jakot softened his tone. 'Take my post. I need to ask Santagithi if he'll see . . .' He trailed off, having never obtained the information, and looked at Shadimar expectantly.

'The Eastern Wizard, Shadimar,' the old man supplied.

Jakot stared, not quite ready to believe a being out of fairy tale had entered the Town of Santagithi, no matter how well Shadimar suited his mental image of the character in the stories his mother used to tell. '. . . The Eastern Wizard, Shadimar,' Jakot finished, holding his incredulity at bay. He turned on his heel, without making judgment, and headed toward the barracks.

Jakot crossed the grassy areas of Santagithi's citadel. Wordlessly passing a trio of off-duty guards, he opened the barracks door and wandered past rows of personal quarters to the strategy room at the end of the hall. He was not disappointed. Its lock was sprung, indicating occupancy. Santagithi had not initiated a foray in the eight months since his daughter had disappeared, and it seemed odd that he would choose his war room for solace. Yet often he did just that. His absences from the house and the dinner table wounded his wife; despite Jakot's cover, Santagithi's disappearance from the guards' daily routines had not gone unnoticed. In the past, Santagithi would occasionally share his concerns with Nantel. With the archer's captain gone, the general confided in no one.

Quietly, Jakot edged open the strategy room door. Santagithi sat with his back to his captain, hunched over a table. Maps lay, neatly stacked, near his left elbow. He was alone.

Concerned that Santagithi might be crying, Jakot cleared his throat to announce his presence. He remained in the doorway.

Santagithi did not move. It was as if he had heard nothing.

'Sir?'

'What is it, Jakot?' Santagithi identified his acting-captain without turning.

Concerned for his leader's sanity, Jakot spoke slowly. 'Sir, you have a visitor. An old man who calls himself Shadimar and claims to be the Eastern Wizard. There's a wolf with him. He says he has important business.'

No reply.

Jakot shuffled uneasily. 'Will you see him?'

Santagithi twisted to face his acting-captain. To Jakot's surprise, the general's gray eyes were dry and clear, marred only by bitterness. They pronounced him fully sane and in control, and his movement revealed the source of his distraction. A chessboard lay on the table-top, the pieces set in stalemate. 'I'll see the Wizard.' He added, as if in afterthought. 'Here.'

'Here, sir?' Jakot bit back his concern, trying not to sound patronizing. 'We could easily set up the audience room for – '

Santagithi broke in forcefully but without hostility. 'Here, Jakot. Safety is of no concern, but secrecy might be. If Shadimar wished to break procedure or harm me, he could have done so already. Bring the Wizard here.'

Jakot backed from the room, too accustomed to trusting Santagithi's judgment to question it even now. Closing the strategy room door, he retraced his steps to the gate where Donnerval stood facing a patient Eastern Wizard.

'Come with me.' Motioning to Donnerval to stay at his post, Jakot led Shadimar back toward the barracks. The wolf padded along behind him.

Several more guards had joined those gathered before the barracks. A card game had begun, and Jakot smelled wine. He smiled tolerantly as they passed. He would have preferred the guards to choose a more productive hobby and a different location, but they had no way of knowing Santagithi would use his strategy room as a

meeting place. Even Rache had not begrudged the off-duty guardsmen an occasional binge.

Jakot held the door for Shadimar and Secodon, followed them
inside, then took the lead again.

Jakot and his charges strode the length of the hallway in a silence
broken only by the tap of the acting-captain's boot soles on stone.
The footfalls of the Wizard and his pet made no sound.

At length, they arrived before the strategy room door. Grasping
the ring, Jakot pulled the unadorned panel open. Santagithi still sat
before the chess table with his back to the door, his head twisted far
enough to watch Wizard, wolf, and guard enter. Shadimar accepted
the seat across from Santagithi, and the wolf settled at his master's
feet. Santagithi waved for Jakot to leave him and the Wizard alone.

Concerned for his leader, Jakot pretended not to see the gesture.
Closing the door, he took a position behind Santagithi where he
could assess the Eastern Wizard's every expression and movement.
Torn between protecting and obeying the general to whom he had
sworn his loyalty, Jakot contemplated the consequences of his
actions. *If Santagithi commands me to leave, will I have the courage
to resist his word? And, if I do, will it undermine his authority in
front of a visiting dignitary?* Sweat broke out on Jakot's forehead as
he contemplated his options.

Luckily, Santagithi saved Jakot the decision. The general settled
into his chair, facing Shadimar, and made no further mention of his
captain's presence.

Though Jakot appreciated the reprieve, he hoped it came of
Santagithi's famous empathy with his men rather than simple apathy.

Shadimar did not dance around his point. 'King Siderin has
mustered his army and is headed for the Westlands. The Great War
has begun.'

Jakot stiffened, not daring to believe a contest steeped in centuries
and generations of legend would begin with an old man nattering
words at an aging general over a chessboard. Carefully, so as not to
draw attention, Jakot shifted to a position where he could clearly
read Santagithi's expression. But, by the time the captain moved, all
sign of the general's initial reaction had disappeared, replaced by the
sagging, weary look that had grown from alarming to familiar in the
last few months.

'Indeed?' Santagithi laced his knuckles at the edge of the game
board. 'Why bring this news to me? You're powerful beyond my
understanding. Why can't you handle the matter yourself?'

The words shocked Jakot. Always before, Santagithi had met
threat with logic and violence, the worse the enemy, the more

complete the attack. To entrust strangers with responsibility for his people went against every tenet the general had upheld.

Surprise creased the Eastern Wizard's face, seeming out of place on his timeless countenance. He followed the expression with a scowl of dissatisfied understanding. Apparently, he had assumed Santagithi would rush into war with the same rash boldness he had in youth and only now realized outside encouragement might become necessary. The Eastern Wizard cared little for the change that had come over Santagithi, and Jakot understood his concern all too well. Impatiently, Shadimar tapped a gnarled finger onto the white king. 'This is you, Santagithi.' Reaching to the opposite side of the board, he indicated the black king. 'This is Siderin.' He sat back. 'This is me.' Shadimar outlined his real person in the chair in Santagithi's strategy room, towering over the tiny figures on the game board.

'Are you saying you manipulate us like toys?'

'No. I'm saying I could. Luckily for humans, my vows forbid it. I can guide. But would you see mankind reduced to mindless figurines manipulated by Wizards and gods? It would take all joy from glory and success, all driving determination from failure. It would leave men without reason or need to live.'

Santagithi changed the subject, dismissing the Wizard's words as beyond the topic. 'But why waste time telling me about the Great War? Why not alert the western cities with armies large enough to handle such a threat?'

The wolf raised his head in distress as his master spoke. 'The cities to your west are the Western Wizard's concern. It's my job to inform the West's prime strategist of the War. Do what you will with the information.' He started to rise.

Santagithi halted the Wizard with a raised hand. 'What does the West need with a withered, old warrior? What sort of strategist would send his finest swordsman away on a fool's errand, stripping him first of the very respect and dignity he would need to succeed?' Santagithi's gaze fell to his knuckles where veins drew bold, blue lines beneath wind-burned skin. 'I've lost my daughter, both my captains, and a piece of my army is in a distant city. My judgment has shriveled with my sword arm. Is that the sort of general the Western armies need?' Santagithi slammed his fist on the table. The force sent chessmen jumping askew. From habit, Santagithi returned each piece to its proper position. 'Prime strategist, indeed.'

Santagithi's self-deprecation pained Jakot. He bit his lip, hoping the Eastern Wizard could say something to break a mood Jakot had tried to chip away at for months without success.

Shadimar remained half-standing, and his voice gained resonance and power. 'You *are* the West's prime strategist. That's fact, not speculation.'

Santagithi opened his mouth to interrupt, but Shadimar shouted him down with a warning. 'Don't question the gods, Santagithi, and don't argue against truth with self-doubt. The only one your reasons could convince is yourself, and you've done too much of that already.' The Wizard took his seat, face flushed with anger. 'There was a time when you made every decision an absolute and stood behind it, when your men followed your word because they would distrust their own decisions and motives before they would question yours. When you revised a course of action, it was not because the decision was wrong, but because circumstances made the change of plan necessary.'

Shadimar leaned across the chessboard. '*Santagithi, your own doubts will destroy you and the Westlands.* Either lose those uncertainties and lead the West to possible victory, or surrender to Siderin and let him shatter everything you've created. Siderin won't just kill your men, he'll torture them and leave them to a slow agony of death. Your women will know the whip and servitude to Easterners, *and that enslavement will prove so harsh, they'll choose to take their own lives.* Santagithi, your wife, Nantel, Rache, and Mitrian will not be spared.'

'Mitrian?' Santagithi went rigid. Guarded hope shone in eyes like ice chips. 'She's alive?'

Joy spiraled through Jakot. He cared for Mitrian, but, mostly he saw the news as a means to break Santagithi's depression.

Santagithi pressed. 'How is she?'

'Changed.'

'Is she well?'

'I don't know.'

Too caught up in his questioning, Santagithi did not seem to realize he had not gotten a satisfactory answer. 'Where is she?'

'I don't know,' the Wizard repeated.

Santagithi frowned. 'You don't know? What do you mean you don't know? Surely you could know these things.'

'Surely,' Shadimar admitted.

Santagithi made a broad gesture to indicate an explanation should be forthcoming.

Shadimar plucked the white queen from its space, moved it randomly across the board, then rested his elbow in the hole where the piece had stood. 'I've not seen her in eight months.'

Jakot cringed. Santagithi guarded his chessboard like a child. While engaged in a game, he knew the location of every piece on the board, and the men had learned never to touch it in his absence unless every piece was carefully set back into the position in which it had been found.

Santagithi glared, but otherwise seemed to take no notice of the Wizard's transgression. 'You know Mitrian's alive?'

Shadimar nodded once. Removing his arm from the board, he sat straighter in his chair.

'You could check on Mitrian anytime, but you haven't done so in the last eight months?' Santagithi's gaze drifted to the displaced queen and froze there.

Noting that Santagithi could no longer see his face, Shadimar spoke as he nodded. 'Correct.'

Irritably, Santagithi replaced the white queen. He met Shadimar's gaze. 'Why not?'

'That's why.' The Eastern Wizard indicated the chess piece that Santagithi had just replaced.

'What?'

'Because,' Shadimar said with a hint of a smile, 'if I watch my people too closely, I'm tempted . . . no . . . obsessed with the need to manipulate them the same way you manipulated that queen. Mitrian specifically asked me not to interfere with her destiny. She wants to make her own mistakes, and I respect that. By not watching her too closely, I remove the temptation.'

'That's crazy!' Enraged, Santagithi toppled all the pieces on the board. Chessmen fell, rattled and rolled, some striking the floor with a shrill splatter of sound. 'Mitrian is a child. She needs direction, guidance . . .'

'She got both of those things,' Shadimar said gently. 'You instilled a sense of morality and also independence. Mitrian wants to make her own life and her own consequences. She has that right.'

'Damn it!' Santagithi shouted, and Jakot could almost feel his general's pain. 'Can't I be a part of that life she's chosen?'

Shadimar's hand fell to his wolf's head. 'Only Mitrian can answer that. She'll almost certainly be among one of the armies at the Great War. You'll see her there, if the West's prime strategist deigns to come.'

'Armies?' Santagithi's voice emerged in a hoarse whisper.

A deep silence fell. Jakot held his breath.

Suddenly, Santagithi whirled to face his acting-captain. 'Jakot, tell those sluggards to burn the damned wine and cards. Send a messenger to King Tenja in Vikerin informing him of the Great War. We'll take Valr Kirin, as promised, and any other men he can spare. Better, tell the Northie bastard to lead his own troops to war. Then I want every guard not on sentry in this room now! And damn it,

Captain, I know you thought you were protecting me, but disobey my command again and I'll have you flogged raw! Now go. Go!'

Surprised by his general's abrupt jolt to normalcy, Jakot scurried from the strategy room. Despite the threat and a coming war, he felt a wild, savage satisfaction he had not known for months.

Just beyond the western boundary of the city of Pudar, wind rocked a line of docked jolly boats into a bobbing dance. Feet braced against the gunwales, Garn hurled crate after crate to the dock, watching as his coworkers struggled in pairs and trios to lug those same boxes to waiting carts. His linen shirt clung, sweat-plastered to the hollows between his muscles and itchy against the tangle of chest hair. Most of the other loaders worked bare-chested, but Garn endured the discomfort of his clothing to obviate the need to explain whip cuts and sword scars to a pack of coarse-mouthed strangers.

Distance muffled the rustle of wind through folded canvas sails and the chime of clamps aginst masts from the ships anchored beyond the docks. Yet their soft, irregularly recurring song lent soothing background to a job Garn had come to enjoy. In the two weeks since he had started, the routine of tossing crates to the docks, sorting cartons by merchant, and bearing them to the carts had become familiar. The work kept his body toned but left his mind free to ramble.

Now Garn watched Sterrane's dark, hairy form toss a crate onto a cart with the same ease as Garn had unloaded it from the jolly boat, though it had taken three others to haul it from the docks to Sterrane's pile. To Garn's right, oars cut water, the paddles streaming a line of droplets that disturbed the surface in widening rings. He grasped another crate. This evening would be his first payday. Excitement awoke in him at the thought. He and Mitrian had used gems from her pouch to buy the cottage next door to Bel's and their necessities for the last two weeks. The idea of supporting his wife and coming child with money earned by his own hand sent a thrill through Garn. The feat of independence allowed him to throw off a few more of the chains that bound him to his past.

Garn tossed the crate to the waiting loaders and turned for the next. There remained two things for him to overcome: a cultural naiveté that made him seem like an outsider, even among his coworkers, and a temper as swift and merciless as lightning. Garn grasped another crate. Social experience, Garn knew, would come with time. The other was not so easy. Since childhood, Garn had learned to react to pain and affronts by killing; Rache had forced that lesson upon him until it had become instinct. Now on the deck, thoughts of Rache drove fiery, irrational rage through Garn. His grip tightened, slivering splinters beneath his fingernails, and the pain fueled his anger further. He heaved the box onto the dock with such violence that it bounced, scudding over the planking. The waiting loaders scurried from its path. Two swore. One shook his fist at Garn, but the green-eyed newcomer had already pivoted for the next crate.

My temper dies the day I gain the control Colbey taught AND USE IT TO DESTROY RACHE. Every week since the elder Renshai's lesson in the forest, Garn had tried to master the riddle of the steel without success. The halves of Colbey's broken horseshoe had become a fixture in Garn's pocket, a constant reminder of his inadequacy and the one Northman captain who still stood between him and freedom. He hefted another crate, prepared to fling it viciously to the dock. Cued by his stance and expression, his coworkers backed away, leaving space for the crate to splinter or ricochet.

Garn hesitated, crate balanced on raised arms, suddenly aware that he was channeling his anger against the wrong target. He calmed himself with thoughts of Mitrian. That the beautiful, vibrant woman of his dreams had become his was the pride of his existence. For the first time he also reveled in the vengeance their coupling had won him. Strangely, knowing the anguish that Mitrian's love for Garn would cause Santagithi seemed nearly enough to balance the years the general had kept Garn enslaved. *The only one who has to die is Rache.* Giving a name and face to the enemy haunting him allowed Garn to funnel his hatred. His manner calmed, and he tossed the crate with appropriate care, to his companions' obvious relief.

Garn continued to think of Mitrian as he worked. He loved her dearly; of that, he was certain. Yet, lately, she was acting unlike the Mitrian he had come to know in the last nine months. One moment, she would be chastising him bitterly for eating the last apple, the next weeping in his arms as apology. The change had distressed him until Bel and Arduwyn reassured him that this behaviour was common in pregnant women and that Mitrian would return to normal after the birth of their child. *Our child. A child who will grow up to be the world's finest swordsman with parents who love him and a free father who earns enough money to buy him the things he wants and needs.*

Thrilled by this new track of thought, Garn doubled his pace, pitching crates in gentle arcs faster than his coworkers could remove them. As dusk colored the sky with layers, each ruffle of baby blue cloud tipped pink as embers, the other loaders left alone or in groups to collect their pay. Garn sprang down and helped Sterrane finish stocking the last of the carts. Even when the last carton was loaded, Garn lingered, enjoying the lap of waves against the dock and the symphony of pulleys against masts. He saw beauty in the sinking rainbow of sunset unmarred by the solid, iron stripes of bars.

Sterrane pulled his shirt over a thickly-padded chest and a back furred with the same black hair that covered his head and face. He nudged Garn. 'Come get pay.'

Though eager for the money that would prove he could pay the midwife and support his family, Garn waved the giant off. He could not explain why he saw something private in the ritual of his first payment, but, for some reason, seeing Sterrane collect the same number of coins would taint the success. 'You go. I'll be along in a moment.'

Sterrane's huge shoulders rose and fell. 'See you home?'

'Yes.' Garn nodded, staring at the sky. 'I'll see you at home.' He listened to Sterrane's shambling footsteps fading into the distance.

Before a grounded oil lantern, the foreman, Kruger, watched Sterrane's approach through slitted eyes. Twelve years at the docks had taught him to read personalities like an expert. Though large to the point of danger, Sterrane's placid manner and telegraphic speech marked him as an imbecile. Likely, the bearlike man could not count. Even if he could, he would certainly fall prey to any of the scams Kruger had adopted both to warn his men not to shirk and to glean some extra income for his family. Eagerly, he awaited the newcomer.

To Kruger's right, his staunch, white gelding stood tethered. It raised its head, snorting, as Sterrane approached, entering the circle of illumination from the foreman's lantern. The big man stopped directly before Kruger and extended his hand. 'Me collect pay,' he said with childish finality and pride.

Kruger flicked coins from his pocket to his hand, then dumped them into Sterrane's beefy palm. He waited while Sterrane counted each coin, flipping them with a finger as he did so. As he came to the last, he met Kruger's gaze with wide eyes nearly as dark as his hair. 'Only ten. Promise twenty.'

'I know, Sterrane. And you have potential, probably more than anyone.' Kruger placed a fatherly hand on Sterrane's massive shoulder. 'I wanted to give you twenty, I honestly did. But you were still learning these last two weeks and, well, you couldn't be expected to jump right in and work as hard as the men who have been here ...'

'Only ten. Promise twenty.' Sterrane pouted, obviously hurt. 'Me do same others.'

Kruger adopted a sincere expression. 'I know it seems that way, Sterrane. I'm sorry. I'd like to give it to you anyway, but I have bosses, too. I have to do as they say, and they say you were still in training. You get half this time. Now that you know what you're doing, you'll certainly get it all next time. You understand, don't you?' He tried to meet Sterrane's gaze.

'Understand.' Sterrane's fist closed over the coins. He dodged the foreman's look, focusing instead on the white gelding that pawed impatiently at the grass beyond the lantern light. 'How much horse worth?'

Unprepared for the question, Kruger jerked his head in the direction of Sterrane's attention. 'You could get one like it for about thirty chroams. Why?'

Fast as a snake, Sterrane caught Kruger's hand, pried it from his own meaty shoulder and dumped the ten coins back into the foreman's palm. 'Here ten. Now horse worth twenty. That mine. I take horse.'

Before Kruger could argue logic or mathematics, Sterrane had mounted and kicked the horse into a gallop toward town.

Swearing, the foreman tightened his fist over the chroams until they bit into his flesh hard enough to leave impressions. *He'll pay for that.* Shaking back sand-colored curls, he regathered his composure. 'Let it go, Kruger,' he mumbled to himself. *Learn a lesson from it. Sterrane's a hard worker and a good one to have on my side. And there's more to that man than I could have guessed. No matter how dim-witted he seems, he's sharp as a knife cut.*

Despite his annoyance, Kruger had to admire the ingenuity of Sterrane's method. The chroams it would take to replace the gelding would be sorely missed, yet the battle was not lost yet. There was one man left to collect his pay, another newcomer. Kruger had debated whether or not to attempt his swindle on Garn; though quiet and naive, there was a tenseness about Garn's manner that made him seem always on the razor-edge of violence. Now Kruger realized he would have to cheat the new man of ten chroams just to break even on his own pay. As Garn's form appeared as a distant shadow emerging from the docks, Kruger readied his argument.

Garn hummed as he headed toward the lantern and the slouching figure silhouetted in its light. Thoughts on his first wages, he did not even notice that the melody running through his mind and throat was one Nantel used to sing while he worked. *Collecting pay.* Garn smiled, his memory filled with guards' chatter about payday dreams. For the married ones, it had involved replenishing food supplies, toys for their children, baubles for their wives, or jokes about money to keep their wife's mother from visiting. The single men invariably anticipated women and a long night at the tavern or a card game. *They justified keeping me caged because they said I'm an animal. Now, I've got a wife any of them would envy and am collecting my pay just like them.* By the time he entered the circle of lantern light, Garn had broken into a broad grin. He held out a hand.

Lean and wiry, Kruger returned the smile. Coins clattered musically as he drew them from his pocket and poured them into Garn's eager palm. Ten chroams gleamed with silver highlights lit violet by the dimming arch of sky.

Garn waited, hand still outstretched for the rest of his wages. When no more came, he met friendly eyes the color of cinnamon. 'That's half,' he reminded.

'I know.' Kruger scuffed his shoe in the grass and made a fluttering gesture of apology. 'I'd really like to pay you twenty, but I can't. The merchants who receive these crates are delinquent in their account. If we don't have money, I can't give you money.' Kruger met Garn's gaze, looking suitably repentant. 'If I had it, I'd give it to you. You understand that?'

Disappointment tightened, viselike, in Garn's chest. 'I understand.' His shoulders drooped as he turned to leave. *Another two weeks dependent on Mitrian's gems. At least I earned a few coins.* He dumped the chroams into his purse.

Behind Garn, Kruger bent for the lantern. Coins jangled, muffled by the lining of his pocket.

Garn whirled, sorrow instantly transformed into fury. He sprang, catching Kruger by his shirt laces before the foreman had come fully erect. The lantern overturned, splashing hot oil across both men's feet. Small fires sputtered through the grass.

'What the hell are you doing?' Kruger regained his balance, cheeks colored scarlet around a long, pinched nose.

Garn's grip tightened. 'You have money.'

'What?'

'You have money. You told me you couldn't pay me, but you have money. I heard it when you moved.'

'That's *my* wages.' Kruger's hands went to Garn's wrists, and he started to pry the larger man's fingers loose with his nails. 'Get your hands off me.'

Garn's hold loosened, but he did not let go.

'Let go. Now! Or you'll never work in this city again.' Kruger's face went purple. 'Do you understand that?'

Thunder beat in Garn's ears. His cheeks felt aflame, and he tried to ground his reason by staring at the trickles of smoke from the dying red pinpoints of grass fires.

'Did you hear me?' Kruger was shouting now. Abruptly, he planted both hands on Garn's chest and shoved violently.

Garn's control snapped. His ears rang with the jeers and cries of spectators and the raging curses of his opponent. His fists clenched spasmodically. He jerked Kruger with a suddenness that sent the foreman lurching toward him. With all the power in his arms, Garn bashed his forehead against Kruger's face. Cartilage cracked and blood ran warm across his cheeks. Stunned by pain and impact, Kruger went limp in Garn's hands. A well-practiced wrench and a twist fractured Kruger's neck. Garn let the body slide from his hands.

Gods. Garn shuffled away, dazed. Blood slicked his arms and face, and the taste of salt on his lips was sickeningly familiar. *The guards were right. I am an animal.* His hatred for Rache trebled in that moment. He slammed his boot into the corpse, watching it roll awkwardly across the grass. *Rache.* He kicked the body again. His mind burned, awash with a collage of whips, chains, blood-smeared pits, and the image of a stern-faced, blond guard with ice blue eyes. Garn stared at the broken body as the last of the fires trickled to smoke. The final edge of sun sank below the horizon, plunging the world into darkness.

Garn turned and fled.

19 Kinesthe

That night, sleep eluded Garn. He lay in his loft bed beside Mitrian, listening to the soft, slow rhythm of her breaths. He kept his lids pinched closed, but darkness could not hold judgment at bay. Repeatedly, Garn relived Kruger's death, seeking answers, and always his mind gave him the same one. Something had driven him from controlled anger to the wild savagery instilled by years in the gladiator pit. To Garn, that something bore the name Rache.

A low growl of hatred escaped Garn's throat. He rolled to his side, awaiting the fuzzy perception preceding sleep. It would not come. Garn listened to the ultra high-pitched ringing that accompanied long, deep silences, his senses almost painfully alert. It was not the killing that bothered Garn; he had been trained since youth to understand the necessity, even to seek joy in the triumph and methods. What goaded Garn to self-hatred and blind fury was killing without intent, by reflex, and the knowledge that he had lost the humanity he had struggled so hard to maintain.

Rache taught me to kill. He whipped his callousness into me until killing has become habit without need for thought. Garn sprang from the bed, no longer able to delude himself that he might find sleep tonight. The loft lay black as pitch, without seam to break the darkness with moonlight. From memory, Garn avoided the chair and clothing chests, pausing only to pull out a cloak and grab one of the three horseshoes balanced across the headboard. Donning the cloak, he stuffed the horseshoe into a pocket and scurried down the ladder.

Sterrane's snores filled the main room, and Garn skirted the dark, sleeping bundle in the corner. Nearer the hearth, a stripe of moonlight from between the curtains revealed Arduwyn's smaller form curled beneath his blanket. Garn assessed the patterns of his companions' air exchange. No doubt, Sterrane had reached the dreaming depths of sleep, but Arduwyn's more delicate breathing revealed he was still awake. Quietly, Garn crept to the outer door. He held the latch, tripping it in silence, then pulled it open. The hinges creaked.

Cringing, Garn glanced at Arduwyn's still form before slipping into the night. He pulled the door closed behind him.

Moonlight spilled over the heavens, lacing the overcast night with silver. Few stars poked through the hazy network of clouds; each pinpoint spark diffused to glare. Chips of quartz and mica glimmered in the road cobbles while cottages stood in dark lines on either side. Behind the cottage, at the bottom of a steep hill, the river that supplied the city with water meandered, a black gash stirred into pearly spray by stone and driftwood. Garn stood, ankle-deep in the tangle of weeds that formed his yard. Locating a familiar rock the size of a large dog, he headed toward it. So many times before in the last two weeks, he had knelt upon that stone, surrounded by horseshoes. The urge to understand the elusive strength of an aging Renshai obsessed him. Yet failure followed failure.

Garn had just reached the stone when Arduwyn's voice wafted from behind him.

'Garn, wait. We need to talk.'

Garn whirled, his back pressed to the shielding bulk of granite. He was more than simply startled; it needled him that he had relaxed his guard enough that a man, even a friend, could come upon him unsuspecting. He crouched against the rock, waiting.

Arduwyn approached, clothed in britches and a hastily wrapped robe. He did not speak again until he reached Garn's side. 'While you were gone this evening, guards came to ask if you and Sterrane had gotten your pay.'

Discomfort clutched Garn. He had told no one about the incident with Kruger, but he guessed Arduwyn's concern would be related.

'We told them you both had,' Arduwyn finished. Though he had asked no question, he seemed to want an answer.

Garn nodded. When Arduwyn did not continue, Garn spoke to reinforce his gesture. 'Kruger paid me.'

Arduwyn intertwined his fingers, resting his hands on the stone. Now fully facing Garn, he abandoned subtlety. 'You killed him, didn't you?'

'Yes,' Garn admitted.

Arduwyn went motionless. Despite the directness of his question, he had apparently not expected Garn to reply so boldly. 'Why?' he finally managed, sounding more curious than chastising.

'He tried to cheat me.'

'And?'

'I killed him.' To Garn's mind, that told as much of the story as Arduwyn needed to know.

Arduwyn leapt to a crevice on the rock. 'I thought you understood. No violence. Couldn't you have talked things through? Better, why didn't you take what he gave you, then come to me? I could have talked the rest of your wages out of him.'

Garn shrugged, unused to having other men handle his problems. 'I didn't think of it.'

'But you thought of killing him.'

Garn shrugged again, finding nothing more to say. He saw no right nor reason in defending murder.

Arduwyn raked a hand through red hair that sleep had plastered into lopsided spikes. 'What now?'

Garn cleared his throat. 'You know better than I do. I suppose I get punished for breaking the law. Right?'

Again, Garn's response seemed to catch Arduwyn completely off his guard. Obviously, the little hunter had prepared arguments that did not fit Garn's compliance. 'After you killed Kruger, did you take those wages he owed you?'

'No.' Garn rested a foot on a rocky outcropping, twisting toward Arduwyn on the stone. 'I just took what he had given me. I was upset.'

'Well, someone did.' Arduwyn's features went lax in thought. 'Apparently, some thief found the body and ransacked it. Luckily, the authorities are assuming the same thug did the killing. Murder for the purpose of robbery.' Arduwyn shook his head. 'The guards have no reason to think one of Kruger's own workers killed him. I don't see why we should tell anyone.' He glanced quickly at Garn for confirmation.

Garn chewed his lip, surprised he had gotten off so easily.

But Arduwyn had not yet finished. 'You may not get caught this time, but I can't in good conscience loose you to kill the next person who annoys you. Do you understand?'

Dread shivered through Garn, and his sinews tightened in defense. Though uncertain of Arduwyn's plans, they sounded suspiciously like captivity. 'What are you saying?'

'You have to learn to control your temper.'

Silence followed while Garn waited for Arduwyn to elaborate. When the hunter said nothing more, Garn spoke tentatively. 'Agreed. I'm working on it.'

Amazement widened Arduwyn's eyes. 'You have a plan?'

Garn nodded, kneading the horseshoe through the fabric of his pocket.

'And you think it'll work?'

'No doubt.' Garn conjured up an image of Rache's broken corpse and could almost feel the wake of calm that would free his mind once the deed was done.

Arduwyn leaned toward Garn. 'What's your idea?'

Garn guarded the thought protectively, aware no one else could understand how one man could shackle another's common sense. 'It's personal, inside myself. It's not something I can share.'

Arduwyn ran his fingers over the cold surface of stone. Some time passed before he answered. 'I think I understand.' He stopped his movement to clamp his fingers onto Garn's shoulder. 'If you decide you need help, I'm here. Just tell me one thing. Will it require us to leave Pudar?' A strained look crossed Arduwyn's face, and his eyes gained a film of pain. Yet a glimmer of hope streaked the dark depths, as if some innate part of him begged the opposite answer.

'We can stay.' Garn watched his friend curiously, wanting to give the reply Arduwyn needed to hear, but uncertain which it might be. 'For a while, at least.' The strangeness of his companion's look encouraged him to question. 'Why?'

Arduwyn straightened his robe, the gesture nervous even to Garn's socially untrained eye. He had never seen the hunter so rattled. 'I'm going to make Bel my wife.'

Garn blinked, the news such a foregone conclusion, he could not believe it was the cause of Arduwyn's concern. Already, most of his pay had gone to support the woman and her children. Since Arduwyn's discussion with Mitrian in the Granite Hills, his pairing with Bel seemed natural and obvious to Garn. 'Good.'

'I'll be going to live in her cottage. I'll take Sterrane with me.'

'Good,' Garn repeated, finding nothing else that needed saying.

His piece spoken, Arduwyn became noticeably more relaxed. 'Counting back days, Mitrian should have had the baby by now. It'll come any day. She ought to rest. Why don't you take over the housework until the baby's born?' He paused, as if expecting protest.

But Garn had been raised with no more than a passing understanding of men's and women's roles, and Arduwyn's underlying intention, to keep Garn out of trouble, slipped right past the ex-gladiator. He nodded agreeably.

'Meanwhile, I'll see if I can find you some work that can either accommodate your temper or, at least, not aggravate it.'

Garn knotted his fingers around the horseshoe in his pocket. He wanted to promise Arduwyn that he would never again kill in anger. But until he unraveled the riddle of steel and Rache lay dead at his hands, he had no reassurances to offer. 'Thank you,' he said at length.

And, for now, that seemed enough.

Three days of housework was enough to convince Garn that being born and raised a townswoman would have driven him to madness.

On the morning of Mitrian's fourth crampy, bed-ridden day, Garn stared at the apron dangling from his fist, aware that from the instant he donned it, he would fall back into the cycle of sweep, clean, carry, and cook. Stalling, he glanced over a living room he knew by heart. Three chairs, a couch, and a low table formed a cheerful circle, all carved and assembled by Sterrane with Garn's help. Mitrian had bought matching, down-filled cushions in the market square for the rigid seats and backs. Currently, horseshoes covered the tabletop from Garn's efforts the previous night.

The sight rekindled Garn's frustration, and his memories of Colbey gave him pause. Early on, Garn had looked for an easy answer to the aging Renshai's display of strength. He had examined the steel for flaws and mentally reconstructed the incident in the farm town's forest down to the minutest detail. He recalled the position of Colbey's hands on the horseshoe, his grip, the tension of each muscle. Garn remembered how the Renshai had asked him to select the horseshoe, and he knew from his thought that no preceding tampering had occurred. Even if it had, how could Colbey have guessed which shoe Garn would choose?

Garn lowered his hand, until the gray linen of the apron touched the floor. Always, he had tried to find the power in his body or hoped the answer would come in a sudden flash of insight. Now he recalled how doomed opponents in the pit had occasionally made a last desperate attack with a strength far exceeding any they had demonstrated until that moment. It was a phenomenon Garn had never discussed, but he had learned to watch for it. And his mind had created a name. He called it 'controlled hysteria' since it came at a time when most men panicked yet it was fully directed and lethal in its danger, a completely mental strength of will. Now, Garn wondered if he could harness that power without the mortal threat.

Absorbed by this new line of thought, Garn drifted toward the horseshoes on the table. His heel tangled in the dangling linen, and he stumbled into a chair. The chair lurched with a screech of scraping wood, then thumped back into position. Catching his balance, Garn profaned his clumsiness.

'Are you all right?' Mitrian's concerned voice wafted from the loft.

'Fine,' Garn shouted back. 'I just tripped. Nothing's broken.' He frowned, meaning his words to refer to the furniture, though it applied equally to the horseshoes that thwarted him. *Work first*, he admonished himself. *Later I'll have plenty of time to channel my thoughts without the guilt of unfinished cleaning hanging over my head.*

'Be careful,' Mitrian returned, a belated warning Garn had heard too often since freedom had exposed him to social conventions. It had always seemed obvious to Garn that, after floundering or falling once, any man would see the wisdom in watching his future steps without friends advising caution.

No reply seemed necessary, but Garn had learned that Mitrian would expect one. 'I will,' he said loudly to end the conversation. Again, he studied the linen apron. An idea seeped into his mind, and his imagination transformed the dingy linen into a hauberk. Skillfully, he lashed the straps taut across his back. Reaching through the doorway into the kitchen, he retrieved the broom, envisioning it as a strange-looking but formidable weapon of war.

With powerful strokes so low the twigs brushed the floor, Garn drove dust from the kitchen to the living room, around the furniture and against the wall. An evil grin of triumph lit his face. Glancing back to ascertain that Mitrian had not descended the ladder from the loft, he kicked loose a familiar floorboard. Three sure strokes disposed of the dirt. Garn replaced the board.

Returning to the kitchen, Garn seized the rope handle of the water bucket. Opening the door to the yard behind the cottage, he slipped out into the morning. His mind conjured the tremor that accompanied unseen danger; years in the pit had taught him well. His imagination added the key. *The bucket. They want the magic bucket.*

Imaginary bolts sailed around Garn as he sprinted for the stream. Dew-moist grass went slick beneath his feet. The added momentum of his downhill run sent him into an uncontrolled skid. Too late, he noticed a knotted, old woman pounding clothes on the bank directly in his path. Garn dropped the bucket and turned his slide into a dive. His body flew over the crone. He crashed into the icy depths of the river, raising a wave that enveloped her.

'Here now!' she screamed. 'Are you daft?'

Garn's only reply was a wake of bubbles. He resurfaced nearly halfway across the stream.

'Are you daft?' She stood with arms clenched to bony hips, her gray hair wetted into strings on her forehead and trailing droplets like tears across her face.

Garn suppressed the urge to laugh. 'Sorry for the soaking.' He could not help adding, 'But isn't the water grand?'

'Idiot!' Obviously, she saw no humor in the situation. 'You've muddied the water. I won't be able to finish till it settles.' She hurled a half-cleaned smock into the dull, brown water at her feet.

Garn swam toward shore with steady strokes. 'See, old woman, you should thank me. I gave you the morning off.'

Both laughed, though not for the same reason. The old woman

made a gesture of disdain. 'At least if you fill your bucket here, you'll drink mud.'

Garn hauled himself from the water, grabbed the bucket and headed upstream. He would only need to walk a few extra steps, ones he would have to retrace with a full bucket.

Ignoring his elderly neighbor's judgmental glare, Garn filled the bucket and headed toward home. As he started up the hill, he heard one last gibe. A faint voice cackled, 'I'd venture you and your missy'd clean house with a sword.'

Garn smiled, aware the woman could have no idea how closely her assessment struck home. Cold, soaked and laden with a full bucket, he struggled up the hill toward home. Dinner would be a lamb stew simmered over a hearth rather than a campfire. A hero who had escaped death as narrowly as Garn imagined he had that morning deserved a few luxuries.

That evening, Garn shoveled spoonfuls of lamb stew into his mouth, proud that its flavor matched the savory richness of the vegetables and gravy Carlithel had served at *The Hungry Lion*. Yet, after a single taste, Mitrian shoved aside her wooden bowl, screwed up her face, and drew her arms to her abdomen.

Garn reached for her across the kitchen table. 'What's wrong?'

Gradually, Mitrian relaxed until the only evidence of her previous pain was her rapid, shallow breaths. 'Cramp. Just another cramp. It won't be long till the baby's born.'

Excitement surged through Garn as a tingle that warmed his chest even as the stew settled in his belly. The pregnancy had dragged on so long, it had become routine. Now, the impending baby rekindled the anticipation Garn had known when Colbey first divulged its presence.

'We haven't given him a name, Garn.' Sweat sparkled on Mitrian's forehead, and she had never seemed more beautiful to Garn.

'How about Garn's son?' he suggested, only partially facetious.

'Fine.' Pain creased Mitrian's features again, and she waited some time before speaking again. 'But he'll need a name of his own, too. Where I come from, we often name children for someone who touched our lives in important ways.'

Garn frowned. Intuition warned him of the possible consequences of opening portions of memory better left sealed. The men Mitrian had cared for were, almost without exception, ones Garn hated. 'We can call him after Colbey.'

Mitrian shook her head. 'Renshai name their children for warriors who reached Valhalla. To call our son after a living Renshai would be insulting.' She anticipated Garn's next question. 'The Renshai believe naming a child after a man who went to Hel dooms that child to a similar fate. Colbey believed all the Renshai who died on Devil's Island were certainly condemned to Hel by the attacking Northmen.'

Garn pondered the significance of the statement. Until Colbey's death, no child could ever bear a true Renshai name. *Or Rache's.* Troubled by the turn of his thoughts, Garn tried to redirect the conversation. He discovered Mitrian racked by another contraction and cringed in sympathy until it passed.

'I'd like,' Mitrian started, and pain made her curt. 'To name our baby for someone I love and miss very much. I'd like to name him for my father.'

The suggestion hit Garn like a stone. Rage seethed within him. His nostrils flared, and his knuckles whitened around his spoon. Seeing the need to control his smoldering temper, he kept his tone flat. 'No.'

Apparently mistaking Garn's calm for tolerance, Mitrian pressed the issue. 'I know he mistreated you. You have a right to feel bitter. But I love . . .'

Fury tightened to a boiling knot in Garn's chest. Driven beyond sanity, he sprang. Mitrian's shriek stopped him halfway across the table. Stunned, Garn skidded to a stop. Realization pounded him, unforgiving as a tempest at sea. He muddled through pooled emotions, the frenzy of anger wound through with the horror of what his wrath could have driven him to do. *I might have hurt Mitrian.* Angry and terrified, he stormed through the back door, his only instinct to find someone or something he could kill.

Evening shadows swallowed Garn as he prowled the silent streets, blindly fighting the beast raging within him. He cut through an alley wedged between an avenue of smiths and a crumbling temple. It was a route seldom traveled, except by beggars, and Garn had learned to use it to avoid the foreign crowds who thronged the market streets in daylight. Now Garn sought solitude, simultaneously needing to destroy and fearing the damage he might inflict on innocents. The empty market with its odd jumble of tables and crates beckoned. Aimlessly, Garn wandered between deserted stands. By the time he discovered the shelter of an immense, overturned crate, the sky had dulled to a blackness the moon scarcely grazed.

Oddly, Mitrian's suggestion had turned Garn's thoughts to his own father, a mountain of muscle and sinew he had barely known. Carad had turned his only son over to Rache to name and raise and train to predator instinct and murder. *Life and death in the pit. That's all my father deserved.* Self-deprecation touched Garn's thoughts. *Perhaps that's all I ever deserved as well.* Tears hot with anger and grief stung his eyes. Huddled in a corner, Garn did not notice he had company until the other spoke.

'Ya go' troubles, sson? I can help. Here.' A scraggly, old man knelt beside Garn, shirtless, barefoot, and dressed in rags. He offered a battered tin cup. The area reeked of urine and wine.

'Go away.' Garn glared. 'I'll kill you.'

'No, you wone.' The old man's words slurred.

Surprised by the other's fearlessness, Garn studied him. Sparse white hair hung to gaunt shoulders, and he watched Garn with yellow-brown irises nearly invisible against jaundiced whites. 'If you were the killin' type, you wouldna warned me. An' killers don' cry.'

'I wasn't crying.'

'Have a drink, sson.'

Garn glowered through moist eyes, but he took the cup and drained it in one gulp. It burned a path to his stomach, the worst wine he had ever tasted. But, afterward, he felt calmer.

Taking back the cup, the old man scrambled to the far end of the crate. Shortly, he returned with two full cups and handed one to Garn. 'Bess stuff inna world, wine is. People say it's evil. When it wears off, you still got problems. Well, I says everyone's got problems, but you got no problems while you drink. People who don' drink gots problems alla time. I drink alla time an' got no problems atall.'

Garn gulped down his wine and laughed. He waited for the old man to refill it, then choked down another cup full. 'Some people would call drinking all the time a problem.'

'Sson,' he said, smiling at Garn's empty cup. 'Some people'd call bein' young an' strong an' fer-tile a problem. Hell, some people'd call bein' a god a problem.' Taking both cups, the stranger scuttled across the crate again.

Garn called after him, 'I don't believe in gods. And what do you have there, a tavern?' The wine soothed, quelling his anger, and he felt happy to the edge of jubilation. Suddenly, his comment struck him as uproariously funny, and he broke into peals of laughter.

The elderly stranger chuckled with him. 'Keg. And you can fill your own now.' Passing Garn's filled cup, he sat, setting his drink between crossed legs. 'Good you don' believe in gods. Not that they're not there,' he added quickly, making an awkward gesture of supplication just in case. 'But man's gotta rely on hisself. You know, believe in what he's doing, even if no one else does.' The man frowned, as if to take stock of his own words.

To Garn, the world seemed to move in slow motion. He found something familiar and important in the old man's statement, but the wine turned it into silly whimsy. He drank another cup only slightly less quickly than before.

Forgetting his decree, the old man accepted Garn's empty cup and wandered back to refill them both. 'I can do anything I want.'

Garn laughed, recalling something dim about horseshoes. 'I don't think that's true.' He accepted the wine but, feeling dizzy, set it aside.

'I could,' insisted the old man. 'Anything I wanted.'

'Could you stop drinking?' Garn grinned wickedly.

The man smiled. 'Why would I want to do a damn fool thing like that?'

Hands jostled Garn. Lights exploded in his head, each accompanied by a flash of pain. The slam and rattle of rising stands and wares whisked into place made Garn's head ache almost as much as the shaking hands. 'Garn! Wake up, you fool.'

The voice annoyed Garn more than anything. He staggered to his feet, made an awkward grab, and caught cloth. Winding his fingers into the fabric, he hoisted a weight that squirmed in his grip. Garn opened his eyes to a bleary, gray dawn. Arduwyn dangled, straining to extricate the front of his cloak from Garn's fingers. Beyond him, Sterrane watched impassively. Merchants and their helpers scurried to place their crates and goods before the morning crowds arrived. There was no sign of the elderly man who had shared his wine.

'Garn, let go. It's Arduwyn.' The hunter twisted free of Garn's hold. Dropping lightly to the ground, Arduwyn scuttled beyond Garn's reach. 'You have a son, Garn. Garn, are you listening?'

Garn's head throbbed, making thought impossible. 'A son,' he repeated dully. 'Mitrian's son?'

'Of course, Mitrian's son. Your son.' Arduwyn directed his next statement at Sterrane. 'Tell Brugon I'll be late. I'm taking Garn home.'

Without reply, Sterrane hurried off to obey.

Garn's stomach clutched. He winced, gathering enough of his wits to question. 'How's Mitrian?'

Arduwyn offered a hand. 'A little mad at you. Otherwise fine.'

Dizziness staggered Garn, and only Arduwyn's dexterous shift of balance spared them both a fall. 'The baby?' Garn asked.

'A beautiful blond boy. Mitrian's been calling him Kinesthe.' Arduwyn pronounced it Kin-es-tay. 'It means strong in . . .' He lowered his voice conspiratorially, to Garn's infinite relief '. . . Renshai.'

Garn tottered.

'This may not be the best time to tell you,' Arduwyn continued, 'but I found you a job I think you'll like. You're now a Pudarian town guard.'

The word 'Renshai' spoken so near to 'guard' bothered Garn, especially in proximity to 'mad' and 'blond.' 'Take me home,' he said.

Arduwyn kept a hold on Garn's arm, leading him through the maze of merchants' stands in a reproachful silence.

Garn followed, glad for the quiet. His head was pounding too hard to listen to anything more Arduwyn might have to say. He let his lids sag closed, though his mind traced the route with a residual alertness that even the aftereffects of wine could not dull. Arduwyn dragged Garn back the way he had come: down the market avenue, through the alley to the street of their cottage.

Arduwyn stopped before the door to Garn's and Mitrian's residence, prodding Garn to the wall. 'Wait here. Let me talk to Mitrian first.'

Garn stumbled, lolling against the mud and stone wall. The granite felt comfortingly cold against his cheek. Before he could reply, Arduwyn had entered. Garn heard the hunter call out a greeting.

'I found Garn, and he's not even hurt much.'

Then the door banged shut, cutting off the rest of the conversation.

Garn closed his eyes. His breathing fell into a deep rhythmical pattern very like sleep. The still, near-stuporous state soothed his aching head.

Shortly, the door creaked open. Garn's eyes flickered open to see Arduwyn gesturing him in with broad sweeps of his arm.

Garn dragged himself inside, aware he should take part in an event of significance, but managing only to momentarily stave off his need for sleep. He approached Mitrian and the carefully wrapped bundle in her arms. 'I love you,' he said, then collapsed on the cottage floor.

20 Ambush

Rache Kallmirsson's huge black stallion crossed the plains and forests north of Iaplege at a steady, tireless lope. The gait combined the speed and ease of a trot with the smoothness of a canter and had been unfamiliar to Rache until the previous week when his appreciative students had presented the stallion to him. Rache's two-sword, mounted method of combat required a horse capable of taking commands from other sources than the reins, and the complete lack of strength or feeling in Rache's feet and calves limited his means of control. Always before, Rache had needed to retrain each horse he rode to his spoken and kneed signals, some with little success. But this time the bond between beast and rider had formed immediately. In one session, he had taught the stallion to respond to shifts in balance, pressure, and voice. Within days, the two had learned one another's patterns well enough to work as a team. It seemed to Rache as if he had only to think of a route and his horse would take it; Rache's cues had become that subtle. It was not Rache's way to name animals, but this horse was special enough to earn, within a week, his loyalty and the name Bein, the Northern term for 'legs.'

Bein's fluid gait had become routine to Rache in the days since he had set out from Iaplege, but his own thoughts were even more so. Repeatedly, he had examined the last year of his life like an artisan seeking flaws in a carpet crafted for a king. A month and a half among outcasts and cripples had taught him much, their lessons different than he had ever imagined. Rache had worried that he would find limping, unbalanced troops plagued by aggressive insecurities and feigning wholeness with a denial easily sparked to violence. Instead, Rache had discovered nearly seven hundred and fifty soldiers, thirty of them women, with varying Western backgrounds and one uniting feature: a feverish, impassioned need to become the best warriors they could despite the odds against them.

Rache had not known anyone with such consistent enthusiasm since Mitrian. Every one of Peusen's soldiers knew his handicap and had come to terms with it. Rache found his knowledge in constant demand, discovered a respect so intense it bordered on embarrassing, and he enjoyed the challenges of revising techniques to fit varying deficiencies without sacrificing defense or ability. The Renshai's way of life had made them masters at healing and therapy. For a handful of men, Rache had designed programs that strengthened wasted limbs to normal. These were his greatest triumphs.

Still, though Rache had found a happy niche, it was not his niche. He would not have traded his time among the soldiers of Iaplege, but his loyalties lay far to the east. Privy to the conversations of others crippled as adults, Rache recognized the mistakes, made by both the victims and their loved ones, that had broken up marriages, alliances, and friendships. He had heard how each of Peusen's soldiers went through a period of internal strife before coming to terms with his illness or injuries. Yet, discovering the normalcy and necessity of such a self-absorbed phase did not appease Rache's conscience for having become intolerant of his friends' support. *I misinterpreted a lot of concern and help as interference and took offense at offhand comments.*

Rache's Renshai upbringing had taught him to channel his life to his sword and the single goal of death in glorious combat. He could let nothing stand in the way of that mission, but Renshai heritage did not preclude enjoying life, its loyalties, friends, family, and pleasures.

Forest loomed ahead. Bein slowed to a walk, calmly picking his way between trunks and over deadfalls while his master remained lost in thought. One at a time, Rache addressed the many specters that haunted him. First, he considered the mother who had sold her soul for him. *The decision to run was hers not mine and made with all the world's best interests in mind. When she died, she was fighting and intact. If Odin chose to send her to Hel, it's not my place to question. But I don't know for certain, and I have reason enough to believe she went to Valhalla, instead.*

Rache lowered his head, laying his mother's memory to rest after seventeen years of dodging grief. Sorrow descended upon him, but it was bittersweet. Renshai celebrated those among them who reached Valhalla, and Rache could not cry for a mother, long dead, who his reminiscence now placed in Valhalla.

Bein tore mouthfuls of leaves from the trees they passed, showering Rache with dew. The captain's consideration turned to Episte's words: 'The Westlands has many villages you could serve with your sword; find one that recognizes the value of your skill, though not its source.' Rache had always considered the allegiance he swore to Santagithi and his town to be inviolate, a tribute to a *torke* who had given his time to the very last hour training Rache as a child. His mind drifted to a day more than a year earlier when he had lain, dizzy and paralyzed, on a pallet of straw. In a flash of bitterness and frenzied frustration, Rache had revealed enough that, had Santagithi questioned, he would have discovered his captain's Renshai heritage. Yet Santagithi had dismissed the words, forgiving Rache's outburst as quickly and easily as the heritage he had unwittingly all but revealed. Rache winced at the memory, hating the cruel epithets that shock and grief had driven him to utter against Santagithi.

Rache thought about the final angry exchange with Santagithi before the captain had ridden off to find Mitrian. *Santagithi was grief-stricken. He probably had no more understanding of what he was shouting than I did after Garn crippled me.* Rache shook his head, wishing he shared Santagithi's instant insights and logic. *I could have put him at ease the same way he did for me. Instead, I let his words hurt me and left him to brood over his mistake.*

Self-directed anger welled up in Rache and, with it, a promise to correct the errors he had made. *I vowed to lead Santagithi's men to war. If he'll have me back, I'll go. But first I have to make one last effort to retrieve Mitrian.*

In Rache's new state of insightful reasoning, many possibilities for Mitrian's actions presented themselves, one more than the others.*I'm forgetting adolescents don't always act like rational adults. Probably, Garn raped her. Perhaps she clung to him because she had no one else or she was more afraid of the town's reaction than of him doing it again.* Rache frowned, finding it difficult to believe any woman could fear punishment more than sexual molestation, but he did not forget that his perspective on gender differed vastly from that of Santagithi's citizens.

I need to find Mitrian and reassure her. Whatever it takes, I'm going to get her home willingly, even if it means claiming Garn's baby as my own. Pain flashed through Rache's chest, but he dismissed it. The idea of raising Garn's child hurt. Years of protecting others from his Renshai heritage had made the thought of calling any child his own revolting. But by accepting Colbey's training, Mitrian had already condemned her infant to being Renshai. *If it'll get Mitrian back, I'll take responsibility, even if it means marrying Mitrian, learning to love Garn's child, or my own banishment. I owe Santagithi that much.*

Rache's decision to head north had come from logic. Alone, Garn would hide in woodlands; the chances of tracking him would be slim. Mitrian was another matter. Pregnant and traveling with friends, she would seek out a city. It made sense that she would choose Pudar, the largest city in the Westlands, the only one about which she had heard detailed stories. For the sake of vengeance,

Rache hoped he would find Garn as well. But for Mitrian's welfare, he prayed that the gladiator had left her long ago.

The forest broke to farmland. From his instructions, Rache knew he was still a full two days from Pudar. He kneed Bein back into a lope, his thoughts turning to the other friend he knew was probably in or near the trading city. Now Rache's anger at Nantel seemed foolish and misplaced. *Nantel's earned my respect forty times over. If he followed me, it could only have been at Santagithi's insistence.* The image of Nantel's coarse, mustached features made him smile. Though never well-liked, the archer captain had won his men's deference honestly, through skill, hard work, fierce loyalty, and infallible common sense. Rache alone had challenged Nantel's rages with sarcasm, and it had allowed him to find a deeply moral, kindly part of the archer that few others saw. Of them all: Mitrian, Santagithi, Emerald, his guards, Rache missed his roommate the most.

Rache patted Bein's glossy neck. It seemed strange that the people he had respected, like Colbey, Nantel, and Santagithi, had always been rebels trying to find a niche in a world of false hopes and illusionary truths, a world that crushed all who did not fit neatly into its narrow vision of humanity. *Soon enough, boy.* Rache wound his fingers through the stallion's inky mane. *Things will come together when I reach Pudar.*

Rache rode onward.

Candles guttered in the antler-shaped, copper brackets that decorated the walls of the taproom in *The Dun Stag Inn*. Smoke swirled through the confines, muting the press of beer-guzzling foreigners to lacy shadows, but their shouted boasts and curses blended to a blustering crescendo that was not so easily ignored.

Alone at a corner table, Nantel sipped his beer, watching the wild horde of revelers with icy detachment. In the past, he had always enjoyed the trading parties he led to Pudar, a change of scenery and a month of business that passed more like holiday. But six months ensconced in the ceaseless whirlwind of the market city had grown tiresome, driving him to a bitterness quelled only with good *Dun Stag* beer and relative isolation. Dazzled by glitter and constant parties, the ten men under Nantel's command had become lethargic, requiring his sharp tongue and temper to drive them to the daily practices that had been simple routine in the Town of Santagithi.

A massive Bruenian jostled Nantel's table, sending his beer into a sloshing dance that soaked the archer's hands. Light flashed golden from hoop earrings. The Bruenian glared, breath fetid with cheese and alcohol, as if daring Nantel to comment on his clumsiness.

For an instant, the archer captain considered the challenge, then, just as quickly dismissed it. A commander in a foreign city should not initiate violence over personal frivolities, and it had never been his way to act in any manner but well-plotted caution. Wiping his hands on his breeks, Nantel let the indiscretion pass uncontested. The Bruenian muttered something dark in the Western tongue that Nantel did not understand, then disappeared back into the crowd.

Nantel smiled, reminded of a less peaceful incident in Santagithi's tavern. Rache had barely reached seventeen, though in his strange, slowly maturing style he looked closer to twelve. While he and Nantel discussed the merits of slashing versus stabbing over bowls of soup and mugs of beer, a loud-mouthed traveler from Pudar had swaggered into the tavern.

Visitors that far east were rare enough, and Nantel had good reason to recall this man's face. The Pudarian had stood tall enough to be imposing but not enough for the ungainly proportions of a giant. Ruggedly handsome with his shrewd, dark eyes, straight nose, and square-cut chin, he seemed the type accustomed to getting whatever he wanted. His gaze had skipped over the wholly male congregation in the tavern, dismissing smiths, hunters, and off-duty guardsmen with a half-smile and a glare of condescension. 'My name is Dilger,' he announced in the common trading tongue with a heavy Western accent. 'I'm from Pudar.' He spoke as if just mentioning the city name placed him leagues above this assembly of ignorant savages.

The rabble stared, conversations forgotten. Rache alone seemed unaware of the newcomer's presence. His explanation to Nantel never faltered. Only the archer's captain sat close enough to catch Rache's gaze slip briefly toward the stranger. Apparently summing the Pudarian's competence with that single glance, Rache dismissed him as harmless.

The Pudarian continued, voice resonant in the near-silence he had inspired. 'I come from the greatest city in the West, and I'm a swordsman of incomparable skill. Perhaps, for enough silver, I might be persuaded to teach you farmers to wield a blade.'

Nantel recalled how the newcomer's words had inflamed him. He leapt to his feet. At the other tables, the men, all too familiar with his rages, cringed at the coming onslaught. 'Listen you arrogant *wisule's* bastard! Who in hell do you think you are?'

Dilger turned to face Nantel directly, a cocksure grin on his chiseled features. 'Ah! My first volunteer.' He sized Nantel up contemptuously. 'You look like you have a lot to learn.'

Nantel's fist had drifted to his sword, but Rache had moved more quickly. Instead of the familiar, wrapped-leather grip, Nantel's fingers closed over the captain's hand.

'Calm down, Nantel.' Rache spooned soup into his mouth with his free hand and whispered, 'The dolt is just flapping his lips.' He raised his voice, addressing Dilger now. 'Please go on. I'm enjoying this immensely.' Dropping his spoon, he leaned forward as if in expectation.

If Dilger recognized Rache's sarcasm, he paid it no heed. 'Good to see your young, at least, recognize talent. I was a student to none other than the great Belzar, the best sword master who ever lived!' He paused, as if accustomed to gasps of awe. But the name meant nothing to Nantel, and he was willing to bet none of his companions had heard it before either. 'Belzar used to fight armies single-handedly. It was he who chased the Golden-Haired Devils back to the North. I am but a shadow of his greatness, but I could still teach you more in a fortnight than you all know together.'

Nantel fumed in silence, wise enough to realize Rache was steering Dilger toward a fall.

'Really?' Rache seemed deeply thoughtful. 'I'm from the North. I've heard of the savage, Golden-Haired Devils. We called them Renshai. But who's this Bell-ringer fellow?'

Snickers fluttered through the common room.

Dilger scowled, closing in on Nantel's and Rache's table. 'Belzar,' he corrected.

Unable to hold his tongue any longer, Nantel joined the exchange. 'Belzar, Bell-ringer. What's the difference?'

Rache cut in, his tone louder, but still composed. 'Look, Dilger, is it?' The Renshai gave the name the musical Northern pronunciation, so it came out sounding more like Deel-ga.

'Dilger.' The Pudarian restored the flat, Western inflection.

Rache did not attempt the name again. 'You've made a mistake. Santagithi's guard force is well-trained in many weapons, especially sword.'

Dilger snorted. 'Farmers and barbarians. You wouldn't know well-trained if you sat in the presence of it . . . obviously.'

'Then, perhaps the great sword master's shadow would consent to fight one of our children.' Nantel indicated Rache with a brisk wave.

Rache's glare was Nantel's only warning. Before he could guess the sword captain's intention, Rache swept his soup into his companion's lap.

Hot liquid splattered Nantel's breeks. He sprang to his feet, swearing.

Apparently taking Nantel's sudden movement as hostility, Dilger drew his sword, the steel a white flash in the candlelight. Abruptly realizing his danger, Nantel pawed for his hilt.

But Rache moved more swiftly. Springing past Dilger's guard, he slapped the sword aside. His hands bashed Dilger's ears in a cuff that sent the Pudarian lurching to one knee. The sword clanged to the floor, its tip slivering wood. Rache slammed his foot down on the blade and kicked it under the table. Retaking his seat, he slid Nantel's soup bowl to his place and continued eating as if nothing had happened.

Fully humiliated, Dilger staggered to his feet. His gaze flickered over every man in the tavern, avoiding direct stares. Having ascertained that no one was going to attack from behind, he approached Rache with infinitely more respect. 'Might I have my sword back ?'

Rache looked up expectantly.

'Please,' Dilger added harshly.

Rache reached beneath the table and came up with the sword without groping. He handed it, hilt first, to its owner. As Dilger's fingers curled about the grip, Rache tugged it back gently, drawing the Pudarian a step toward him. 'Go home to your teacher and apologize for not learning what he tried to teach you.' Rache released his grip.

Suddenly shed of opposing pressure, Dilger caught his balance with an ungainly backstep. Whirling, he rushed from the tavern. Apparently, he had begun his return journey immediately ; Nantel had never seen the man again.

Now in the *Dun Stag*, Nantel grinned at the memory of a guard captain who, after sixteen years of shared quarters, had become closer than either of Nantel's brothers. He could not help but compare methods of command. Nantel's temper flared like dry kindling at the slightest affront. His men had learned to obey his simplest decree to avoid his shouted onslaughts. Yet it took more than a mildly serious indignity to drive him to action. Conversely, Rache had kept his composure far longer, but the line between anger and violence was fine and easily fractured. His men followed his command more from awe than fear of punishment. For a time, Nantel had envied his companion's skill. Later, friendship had displaced jealousy. Nantel learned to accept that each was a competent captain in a different way ; for all his sword skill, Rache had become only an adequate bowman, and the natural competitiveness of allied warriors channeled into harmless pranks.

Homesickness touched Nantel then. He wiped beer from his mustache with the back of his hand, feeling a wash of sadness enhanced by alcohol. Watching Rache shattered physically had pained him, but the emotional deterioration that had resulted from that blow had ached in Nantel like an open wound. No one had worked harder than Nantel to reestablish Rache's familiar confidence, yet he had to wonder if he had pushed too hard. To goad Rache to the best his handicap would allow was one thing. To make him believe an ego and constitution newly built from crystal could take the punishment of his iron will was folly. Nantel knew in a way Santagithi could never understand that Rache should have been allowed to chase Garn alone. Success might finally remove the restless drive to prove he was still a man. Failure would force Rache to understand his limitations, teach him to deal with them or to wither in self-pity. The former would take care of itself; the latter, Nantel hoped he could handle.

Awash in memory, Nantel scarcely noticed the short, round man until he stepped within easy reach. Recognizing Lirtensa, a particularly obnoxious Pudarian guard, Nantel glared.

Oblivious to Nantel's annoyance, Lirtensa snagged the chair beside the archer with his toes and clinched it toward him. He plopped into the seat. 'Nantel, what's the name of that fellow you're looking for?'

Nantel's expression softened despite himself. Months had slid by without sight or news of Mitrian, Garn, or Rache. 'Rache?'

Lirtensa raked a hand through greasy tangles of hair more dirty than brown. His blue eyes seemed locked in a permanent squint. 'Not the Northman. The other one.'

Nantel straightened. 'Garn?'

'Yeah, that's him.'

Nantel's heartbeat quickened. 'What about Garn?'

Lirtensa held out a callused palm rimed with filth, demanding payment.

'Ruaidhri's balls, Lir.' Nantel was in no mood for games. 'You'd better have something important to say or I'll hunt you down, kill you, and take my money back.' He reached into his pocket, retrieved a copper chroam, and dropped it into Lirtensa's hand.

Lirtensa let the coin sit, silently waiting.

With a sigh of annoyance, Nantel plucked a handful of chroams from his pocket, passing the coppers one by one until a stack of half a dozen filled the little man's palm.

Lirtensa closed his hand, and the coppers disappeared into his pocket. 'Late teens, early twenties? Long yellow-brown hair? Burly man with lots of scars.'

The description fit. 'Sounds like Garn. What do you know?'

'He's been a member of Pudar's guard force for three weeks now.'

'What?' The words seemed nonsensical to Nantel. He doubted an animal, even one as wily as Garn, could be trained to the intricacies of guard work. Until now, it had not occurred to him that he and Lirtensa might be discussing different men called Garn. He had never heard the name used by another. Unfamiliar with any conventions of naming, Carad had asked that Rache name his son. Rache had called the gladiator's child 'Galn,' which he said meant 'ferociously crazy' in the Northern tongue. Santagithi's men had found 'Garn' easier to say, so it had stuck, to Rache's amusement. 'Garn' was the Northern term for 'yarn.' Still, Lirtensa's description fit, and it made sense that Garn would try to lose himself in the largest city of the Westlands. The fact that he had lived here at least three weeks without Nantel or his men running into him attested to the wisdom of such a decision. 'That's insane!' Nantel shivered, imagining himself as an unsuspecting Pudarian soldier trusting Garn at his back.

Lirtensa shrugged. 'My silence will cost you a silver.'

Nantel held his tongue while his thoughts clicked into strategy mode. His first idea involved talking to the ruler of Pudar, convincing him of the danger inherent in consigning some of his men's lives to Garn's hand. Surely, King Gasir would see the sense in executing Garn at once. Then Nantel frowned. Unaccustomed to slaves and gladiators, King Gasir might not be able to recognize the danger in his midst but might instead mistake Garn's animal ferocity for courage and see his strength as an asset. 'Gods.' The implications rattled Nantel. *My men and I are the only ones who won't underestimate Garn. We'll have to kill him ourselves and make it look accidental.* Nantel instantly dismissed thoughts of capturing Garn alive. *There's no need, and it can only mean losing men unnecessarily.* Nantel sorted a silver from the chroams and passed it to Lirtensa. 'I'll need to know Garn's schedule and his route home.'

'Two more silver.'

'What?' The payments had begun to wear on Nantel. Camping outside the walls and hunting their own food had saved considerable sums. Still, the men had had to find jobs to support their taste for beer and other luxuries.

'You're asking me to set up one of my fellow guards.' Lirtensa spoke soberly, but Nantel suspected the squint-eyed Pudarian would sell his mother for less.

Nantel paid.

In the lower corner of the cottage's backyard, a tangled copse of blackberries looped in a dense circle that screened Mitrian's sword practices from prying eyes. Simply possessing the sword had marked her as outcast among Pudarian wives, and she saw no need to compound that offense by proving she could use as well as carry it.

For now, the sword dragged, dormant at her hip. Snug in a leather pouch strapped across Mitrian's back, Kinesthe slept while his mother plucked ripened fruit from the vines and dropped them into a bucket at her feet.

Spears of light stabbed at Mitrian through the foliage. She glanced into a sky ruffled with clouds like fish scales, each tinged red by the setting sun. She frowned, hoping to have the blackberry pie finished by the time Garn returned, yet knowing she could barely have the berries picked by then. She lowered her head, ignoring the shroud of dark hair that fell over her face, and quickened her pace.

A deep voice crooned behind her. 'Alone at last, Mitrian Santagithisdatter.'

Starled as much by the reference to her father as the sudden presence of a stranger, Mitrian whirled to face a man as pallid as a corpse. A headband of snow owl feathers blended into the white expanse of his hair and robes. Only his blue eyes seemed to retain any color, and those roved over her in an unwholesome manner.

Recognizing a Leukenyan priest from Arduwyn's quarrel at the Pudarian gates, Mitrian kept her tone icily pointed. 'Go away. I'll have nothing to do with your pagan god.'

'Pagan?' The priest laughed. 'You'll learn soon enough. I've come for the child.' Despite his words, the Leukenyan kept his gaze locked on Mitrian.

Mitrian took an involuntary step back. Briars scratched her neck, and she went still, hoping the leather pack protected Kinesthe better than her thin linen cloak did her back. 'Come for him? For what purpose?' It was a delaying tactic. Mitrian would sooner have turned over her arm than her baby. From the instant of her first glimpse, she had been assessing the Leukenyan's abilities by his movements and stance. Already, she had picked out the line of a curved sword, probably a scimitar, beneath the folds of his cloak. Yet, the stiffness of his gestures suggested he was a mediocre swordsman, at best. Whatever source had revealed her parentage to him had badly misjudged her skill. Other possibilities came to her then. *Perhaps he's deliberately making himself look clumsy to put me off my guard. Or he has half a dozen friends in the yard.*

'Enlightenment,' the albino replied.

Lost in her thoughts and assessments, Mitrian had nearly forgotten she had asked the reason why the priests of Corpa Leukenya wanted her child. Without another word, she plucked Kinesthe from her back and placed him where he would not be crushed or injured if a fight ensued.

Apparently misunderstanding her gesture, the man smiled. He glided toward her.

Protectively, Mitrian stepped between the stranger and her child. Her sword leapt into her fist, and she measured the priest's every action with unhurried deliberateness.

He stiffened, annoyance clearly mingling with surprise. 'Don't make me hurt you.'

In reply, Mitrian crouched.

The Leukenyan priest threw aside a fold in his cloak. The scimitar rasped free of its sheath, its razor edge collecting dusky highlights.

Immediately, Mitrian struck for his wrists. The priest lurched backward, saving his hands. Her blow landed just below his cross-piece, jarring the scimitar from his grasp. Metal thudded to the dirt.

The world seemed to spin. Mitrian's vision fogged with illusion. Suddenly, she was surrounded by a blazing village. Through moonless night, fires lit the scene like day. Children who should have clung, weeping, swung swords. Women who should have cowered fought with the strength, skill, and valor of the finest swordsman.

Mitrian gasped, confused. A rider bore down on her. She blocked his ax, though the force nearly wrenched the sword from her hand. The man's horned helm marked him as a captain of Northmen. He wheeled his mount and charged again. Mitrian ducked beneath his ax, and her sword caught him full in the chest. Her blade sparked against an iron hauberk that spared his life. He tumbled from his horse.

Something seemed wrong about the incident but, hard-pressed by the battle, Mitrian did not take the time to place it. The Northman quickly regained his feet and advanced on Mitrian. She parried his ax, but her double ripostes slapped harmlessly against his hauberk and greaves. Still, the fury of her offensive drove him into a burning hall. Smoke stung her eyes. She tripped over an overturned bench and fell against a wall. The Northman struck for her leg. Mitrian dove over the ax, rolled to her feet, and brought her sword across the unprotected back of his knee. A beam in the ceiling cracked. Flaming thatch fell. Mitrian staggered back raggedly to avoid it, instinctively throwing up an arm in defense.

Suddenly, the demon's vision released Mitrian. Panting, she stared at the priest who sprawled before her, clutching his thigh. Confusion and the uncontrolled ferocity of her assault brought tears to her eyes. She backed away, noticing several small, red stains spreading across the priest's white robes.

'Why?' Mitrian slammed the sword into its sheath and addressed the demon in the gems. 'Why?' she screamed.

The priest stared, wide-eyed. Apparently, declaring her mad, he rolled beyond sword range before clambering to his feet and breaking into a limping, shuffling run toward the city.

Mitrian did not pursue. 'Why?' she pressed the demon again.

He did not answer in words. Instead, the trapped soul of a Hel-bound Renshai gave her a taste of the battle joy her madness gave him. Even without explanation, she knew she had witnessed the demon's last human fight, his final glorious battle among Renshai before infection claimed smoke-seared lungs and he had breathed his last on a sickbed.

The knowledge did not appease Mitrian's need to understand. 'Why now? Why assail me with visions at a time when I most need my wits?'

The demon chose speech. *Because you became a Renshai in eight months, learning skills it will take lifetimes to perfect. One thing only Colbey cannot teach you, the ferocity that comes with Renshai culture, a ruthless love for battle that comes of living among Renshai since birth.*

Mitrian gathered up Kinesthe and returned him to his pouch, never losing the grip on her hilt that allowed her to communicate with the demon. 'I don't need to revere war to become skilled at it. Maybe the new Renshai need to learn temperance as well as technique.'

Modi's blood wrath and mental ferocity were as much factors in the Renshai's success at war as their swordcraft and honor. To remove those things would reduce Renshai to the level of ordinary, capable swordsmen. Like Garn. Colbey's ability does not come from practice alone.

Caught off-guard by the demon's reference to Garn, Mitrian did not gather her arguments clearly. 'So says you.'

The demon lurched in for the closing stroke. *And so says Shadimar. Why else would he have given you the only magic sword on the world of Law to use in the Great War?*

Stranded without retort, Mitrian broke contact, hefted her bucket with a violent tug that sent berries tumbling over the sides, and headed for home.

Garn trotted along the market streets, senses half-tuned to merchants closing their last sales and the pound and rattle of stands coming down for the night. The crowds had dispersed to a last, stubborn trickle as patrons retired to cottages or inns for the evening meal. After a full day of patrolling the upper east side, where most of the foreigners stayed and lived in the rowdy, careless comfort of furlough, Garn felt pleasantly tired. His sword seemed heavy at his hip. Now off-duty, he wore street clothes, carrying the tan linen shirt and britches of his uniform in a sack tied at his belt. Unlike Santagithi, King Gasir made a distinct separation between his town guard and soldiers; the latter wore reinforced leather. In case of war, the town guard would become the elite forces while men who plied other trades most of the year would form the main body of Pudar's army.

Initially, Garn had held trepidations about life as a guard, concerned he might see Rache and Nantel in every leader and a fettering of his freedom in every command. But the duties had come easily, and, with them, a sense of self and well-being. Foreigners came to him for guidance, trusting a town guard rather than the rabble on the streets. The citizenry greeted him with sincere pleasantries, glad of his presence. Though a handful of the guards watched the new man in their midst with mistrust, others instantly accepted their king's decision. Garn found himself with dozens of friends where before he had only three.

A smile creased Garn's face as he turned the corner from the main street into the familiar alleyway. Only one man occupied the area now, an elderly male dressed in filthy rags who leaned against one wall. He looked Garn over as the ex-gladiator entered the alley, studying him with more than casual interest.

The beggar's intensity raised Garn's guard. He slowed, returning the excessive attention in kind.

The beggar seemed not to notice. As Garn came to him, he extended his hand, a jeweled cloak pin clutched between his thumb nd forefinger. 'Please,' he hissed. 'Hold this.'

The request seemed harmless. Accustomed to fast trust and strange requests in his past several weeks since joining the guard force, Garn accepted the trinket, then looked expectantly at the beggar.

The nearly inaudible whisk of wood against fabric sent Garn into a spinning crouch. Five men barred the entrance to the alley. Garn recognized them at once. Though nearly a year had passed, Nantel's homely features were indelibly etched in the ex-gladiator's memory. He knew the other four also, but it was the sight of Nantel and his drawn bow that scattered Garn's thoughts in an explosion of homicidal frenzy.

'Thief!' someone shouted.

Nantel's arrow whistled through the air.

All thought escaped Garn except for hatred and the deep-rooted demand to survive at any cost. Springing backward, he seized the beggar and dragged the old man before him like a shield. The arrow struck home, driving the stranger limply into Garn's arms. There was no time for remorse. Garn had never needed to work as a team, only to survive. Recognizing that distance made him helpless against arrows, Garn dropped the beggar, tore free his sword, and rushed Santagithi's guards with a bull bellow of fury.

Another arrow cleaved air. Garn dodged, but not far enough. The point drew a gash along his arm, flaring pain that only fueled his rage. Nantel's men closed in to protect their leader as Garn fell upon them like a wounded wolf. His sword slashed a red line through one's chest. Unprepared for the complete commitment of Garn to battle, the first fell dead without a return stroke. Another twisted, escaping Garn's savage swipe more from luck than skill.

Nantel tossed aside his useless bow, and it skittered off behind him, clattering on cobble. Drawing his sword, he elbowed for a position among his men.

Garn jabbed a knee into an attacker's groin. The guard doubled over, baring his head to a hilt stroke that shattered his skull. Spots swam before Garn's vision. One step closer to Nantel, he gave himself fully over to battle lust.

Garn's war cry and the chime of steel sent Mitrian into a sprint toward the alleyway before she could think to put Kinesthe in a safe place. At the far side of the alley, she skidded to a halt. Peering down the darkened throughway, she recognized Garn's darkly muscled form. Moonlight flashed from waving steel as Garn staved off a gray blur of attackers. Aware she could do Garn no good by coming up from behind him, she sacrificed time for position and hoped he could hold out a few seconds longer.

Mitrian careened down a parallel roadway, listening for the muffled sounds of combat, frightened that, at any moment, the alley would grow silent as a wave of strangers overwhelmed her husband. She collided with a teenaged boy hard enough to drive him a step backward and her to her knees. Stone sliced the fabric of her underbritches. She struggled to her feet, swearing, forgetting her manners in the heat of the moment. The other dodged from her path, too awed by a sword-bearing, foul-mouthed woman to challenge her.

Every moment wore like an hour upon Mitrian. It seemed like days before she whipped around the corner and momentum hurled her into combat. Spurred by demon blood lust, she drew and cut in one movement. The blade chewed a fatal gash into one man's back before he even realized he was menaced. Mitrian's follow-through severed the tendons behind another's knee. That one spiraled toward her as he fell. Dark eyes met blue. Mitrian recognized Nantel as her blade plunged for his chest. And there was no doubt he had identified her, too.

Nantel tensed to roll even as Mitrian struggled to pull the blow. But Nantel was pinned between a corpse and his companion's legs, and Mitrian had learned her lessons well. The sword scarcely wavered before plunging deep into Nantel's chest.

'Gods!' Mitrian screamed in anguish. She dropped to her knees at Nantel's side. Once free of the sword's haft, blood rage disappeared. She felt empty, a child lost in a foreign city. The one familiar face belonged to her father's archer captain, the eyes rapidly glazing.

Outnumbered, the last of Nantel's men whirled and fled.

Nantel groped blindly for the blade in his flesh. Instinctively, his palm closed over it and he pulled, not noticing that his grip slashed his fingers. Then, apparently at peace, he caught Mitrian's hand in a grip warm and sticky with blood. He spoke, his words nearly lost in a scarlet foam that burbled from his lips. 'He loves you.'

Mitrian's grip tightened, and she closed both hands over Nantel's. She wanted to apologize but granted Nantel's right to speak first, before death claimed him. She wondered who the archer had meant by 'he.' *Garn? My father?*

'How could . . . you . . . betray . . .' Nantel trailed into silence.

At first Mitrian thought he had died. Tears welled, and through a blur, she could see the red stain on Nantel's chest still widening. She had already mentally finished his sentence with 'me,' so his last word caught her unprepared.

'. . . Rac . . . he.' A shudder racked Nantel's body, then he went utterly still.

Mitrian's vision washed to a teary, red glare, and it took her several seconds to realize the source of the color. The gems in the wolf-hilt of her sword had changed from their usual bland yellow to the fiery scarlet of sunset. The demon lay still, silently respectful of Mitrian's need to mourn.

Nantel said nothing more.

21 King Gasir's Court

Grief and guilt held sleep at bay. When exhaustion finally overtook Mitrian, it brought a restless stupor glazed with terror. Something chased Mitrian through her dreams, a creature so terrible she dared not turn to identify it. Instead, she traced its pursuit by its ceaseless cry, 'yulkilafren,' words but not quite words, a message just beyond her ability to grasp. She raced onward. As the substance of nightmare thickened, she could no longer run but was forced to swim through air dense as water. Behind her, the thing drew closer.

'Yulkilafren, yulkilafren, yul-kil-a-fren !' Horrified, Mitrian flailed, desperate to quicken her pace. Painfully slowly, she bounced across the grass on her father's hilltop as the being closed the gap behind her. 'No.'

Suddenly, Nantel appeared before Mitrian. He wore the same joyfully pensive grin she recognized from her first bow lesson, when he had realized he could let Rache lead the archers on the coming foray. Mitrian skidded into his grasp.

In the dream, Nantel's arms tightened around her. She felt the warmth of his presence against her. For an instant, the haunting, relentless 'thing' seemed to disappear. Then Nantel went cold and limp in her embrace. He stared at her with eyes wide as a puppy's and liquid with betrayal.

'No !' Even as Mitrian opened her mouth to deny his murder, Nantel's eyes flared as red as the gems in her sword had done. Blood flowed through her fingers. As Nantel crumpled to the ground, she recognized her sword in his back.

'Yul-kil-a-fren. You-will-kill-a-friend.' As the creature drew up behind her, its cry gained sense.

Mitrian whirled to face a young, blond warrior, the Renshai who had become the demon imprisoned in the Eastern Wizard's topaz. He clutched an exact duplicate of her wolf-hilted sword, its gems the grim scarlet of the blood smeared across her hands.

Startled, Mitrian backed away. Her heel crashed into Nantel's corpse. She overbalanced, twisting to avoid his body, and fell into eternity.

The demon's laughter chased her.

*

Mitrian jerked awake. Her heart slammed in her chest, her breaths came in a shallow pant, and sweat slicked her brow and palms.

Garn's hand closed over one of hers. 'Are you all right?'

'Bad dream.' Mitrian realized her throat felt painfully dry. Her eyes burned, empty of tears. Until now, her sorrow had occupied her thoughts too completely to admit memory of Shadimar's warning. Now, reminded by her subconscious, she realized Nantel was the friend her acceptance of the magical sword had condemned to death.

As her pulse slackened, Mitrian felt fresh tears sting her swollen eyes. She tried to remember Shadimar's other words that night. She recalled only something about fighting in the Great War and restoring a prince to his throne, a prince whom her overly romanticized vision of the world had turned into the brave and dashing husband who would rescue her from the drudgery of becoming a simple townswoman.

Recognizing Mitrian's distress, if not its cause, Garn tried to comfort her. 'I'm sorry about what happened to Nantel.'

Mitrian bit her lip. Thoughts of the archer captain's death had crushed her beneath a sour avalanche of grief. But it was the misery of a trusted friend's blood on her hands that tore her conscience to tatters. The demon's war joy and Colbey's lessons, which had driven the necessity of committed strokes to become instinctive, sickened her. Despair struck like madness, and she turned her anger against the man she loved and his hollow reassurance. 'Damn it, Garn. Don't lie to me.' Her words emerged as a weeping-hoarse roar. 'You hated Nantel. You're glad he's dead.' She lapsed into a wild storm of crying.

'Mitrian.' Garn wrapped an arm around her, pulling her closer. 'I admit I hated Nantel. Given the chance, I'd have killed him long ago.'

Mitrian sobbed, wishing she had anyone else in the world here to soothe her. Garn could never understand.

'But,' he continued, 'I don't have to have liked Nantel to know you did. I have friends, too. I can imagine how I'd feel if I had to kill Arduwyn to save Sterrane. Or the other way.'

No. Mitrian denied the comparison. *You can't possibly imagine.* She felt the grief cut deeper than any she had ever known before. 'I need to talk to someone else. Someone who didn't hate Nantel.' She sprang from the bed, not caring if her words stung, hurting too much to worry about anyone else's pain. She dismissed Sterrane as a confidante, doubting the childlike man had ever taken any life, let alone a friend's. Arduwyn seemed a more likely candidate. His sensitivity to the term 'archer' suggested he had killed before and disliked the memory. At the least, he knew how it felt to betray

Kantar, and his natural empathy might enable him to understand. 'I'm going to see Arduwyn.'

Apparently sensing Mitrian's need for support he could not supply, Garn did not object as she made her way past Kinesthe's crib and down the loft steps. Dressed only in her nightgown, she crossed the floorboards without pausing and exited through the front door.

Night breezes chilled Mitrian's sweat-dampened forehead. The sky lay in darkness except for the wedge of moon and an occasional star that shone through the haze. Barefoot, she trotted across the yard, ignoring the tickle of weeds against her ankles. The chortle of the river formed a sweet duet with the rhythmical shrill of insects. Though soft, Mitrian's knock on the door of Bel's cottage seemed misplaced.

Some time passed without answer. Just as Mitrian raised her fist to tap louder, the door slid open a crack. A single dark eye peered through, at the level of her own. *Arduwyn,* Mitrian guessed by its location. Sterrane would have towered over her, and Bel stood half a head shorter than Mitrian.

Shortly, the door wrenched open and confirmed Mitrian's guess. Dressed in wrinkled breeks and a cloak wrong-side out, Arduwyn stared at her with concern. Sleep had plastered his stiff, red hair onto one side of his head. He would have appeared comical if Mitrian could have found any humor within herself. Briefly, she wondered how Arduwyn had heard her gentle tap from his bed in the loft despite Sterrane's snoring in the main room.

'Can we talk?'

Arduwyn stepped outside, clutching his cloak over his chest with one hand and closing the door with the other. 'What's wrong?' Apparently recognizing the seriousness of Mitrian's problem by her manner, alarm entered his tone. 'Are you all right? Is Garn all right?'

Mitrian wanted to reassure him but did not feel she could do so honestly. Saying nothing more, she led Arduwyn to the river bank where the waters would muffle their exchange. She sat in the grass.

Arduwyn squatted before her. He ran a hand through his hair but managed only to rearrange the untidy spikes around his head. 'Tell me what's wrong.'

'Something happened last night.' Mitrian met his gaze, then wished she had not. His sincere concern made her words that much more difficult to voice.

Arduwyn waited for her to continue.

'Garn and I killed some men in the streets.'

'Oh, no.' Arduwyn closed his eyes, as if that might keep him from hearing the rest of Mitrian's confession.

'That's not the worst,' Mitrian said, her voice wavering as the tears returned.

Arduwyn's lids flared open. He made a pained noise.

'They were soldiers from the town Garn and I came from. They attacked him. I came to help, and, in the process, I killed their captain.' A rush of grief transformed Mitrian's words to a squeak. 'He was a friend. A good friend. Gods, I can't believe I killed Nantel.' She expected Arduwyn to hold her then.

Instead, he caught both of her forearms and shook. 'Captain? What do you mean, captain? That's a military title! Who was this captain? Where does that put him in the chain of command? Damn it, Mitrian. Talk to me.' He jostled her again, frantic.

Mitrian swallowed around a lump forming in her throat, not daring to believe Arduwyn's callousness. 'Captain,' she shouted. 'You know, captain. Archer captain, actually. I don't know. I suppose Nantel was third in command.'

Arduwyn groaned.

Shocked by Arduwyn's attention to trivia while she ached with the burden of killing a friend, Mitrian threw up her hands. 'Who cares about his position? Don't you understand? I killed someone I care for very much.'

Arduwyn released his hold on Mitrian. 'What was this captain doing in Pudar?'

'He comes every year. He trades. Why are you doing this to me? Don't I have enough to worry about?'

'More than you understand, Mitrian.' Arduwyn looked out over the river. 'And I'm as much to blame as anyone. I should have known Garn couldn't handle his temper without my help. Now he's going to die.'

The conversation had taken so many turns, Mitrian could no longer follow it. 'What are you saying?'

Arduwyn seemed to be having enough difficulty ordering his own thoughts. 'Did any of the soldiers escape?'

Mitrian nodded. 'And there's certainly more at their camp, wherever that might be. Nantel never took less than ten men.' The tears dried on her face. 'All the gods damn you, Arduwyn. You can't say Garn's going to die without explaining why.'

Arduwyn breathed a hefty sigh. 'King Gasir's greatest concern is Pudar.'

Anger touched Mitrian as Arduwyn seemed to be going off on another unrelated tangent.

'In his mind, the city and its survival comes first, then its citizens. Lastly, there're the foreigners.'

'All right,' Mitrian grasped the connection slowly. 'But it sounds to me like that should give us the advantage, being citizens.'

'True. If Nantel was some Bruenian rowdy. But a diplomatic captain, a third in command representing another town, falls under city affairs. Politics and diplomacy, city alliances, always come before individuals.'

Tiring of double-speak, Mitrian pushed for a point. 'What does that mean?'

'If this case goes to court, and it almost certainly will, King Gasir will probably give Nantel's men anything they ask for. How likely is it they'll demand Garn's head?'

Terror swept Mitrian's mind of a reply.

Mitrian's silence was enough answer for Arduwyn. 'I thought so.'

'We've got to run away.'

'That's one possibility.' Arduwyn's tone made it clear he thought other courses of action might work better. 'Unfortunately, there's consequences to having the largest city in the Westlands hunting you. Not to mention the town you came from. And, by running, you'd be admitting guilt. If they have to track you down, there's no way you'd get a fair trial.'

'So what do we do?'

Arduwyn shook his head sorrowfully. 'There's no good answer. We could wait and see. Maybe Nantel's men won't press charges. Or we could go to the king first. That would show our intentions are good, at least. We might even manage to win the trial. If you decide to use the course of justice, I'll do what I can. I can't promise I'll find the right words to spare Garn, but I'll do my best.'

None of the options pleased Mitrian. 'There has to be another way. A better way.'

'Confront the problem, run from it, or ignore it.' Arduwyn shrugged. 'What else is there?'

'I don't know,' Mitrian admitted, her grief for Nantel forgotten for the more urgent matter of Garn's life. And possibly her own. She raised her head, meeting Arduwyn's soft stare. 'What should we do?'

'It's not my decision.'

Mitrian felt suddenly, completely alone. 'You're not going to help?'

'I already said I'd help. I'm just not going to make the decision.'

Mitrian rose. 'That's not fair. You're the only one who understands this city, its rules and its power. How come you're willing to throw your opinion around about food and toys and money, then

when it comes to something important, you back out? Thanks a lot
. . .' She emphasized the last word with distinct sarcasm, '. . . *friend.*'
She turned.

'Wait.' Arduwyn seized the hem of Mitrian's sleeping gown.

She whirled back to face him.

'If I talk you into a course of action, and it gets Garn killed, I'm
going to feel like it's my fault.'

Mitrian crouched beside Arduwyn. 'True. But if you don't give
your opinion, we do the wrong thing, and both Garn and I get
killed, you're going to feel worse.'

Arduwyn twined his fingers nervously.

'Right?'

Arduwyn heaved a long sigh. 'Probably right. I think the worst
thing you could do would be to ignore the problem. It happened.
There were witnesses. Running means spending the rest of your lives
watching your backs, hiding, mistrusting anyone who might turn
you in to face a justice you could handle far better now.'

The idea of Kinesthe growing up isolated from people and afraid
of all strangers pained Mitrian. 'You think we should see the king
now?'

'It only seems logical. Ignoring relies on luck, the idea that Nantel's
men will worry more about appearances than justice or revenge.
Running presumes you don't get caught. In either case, if you do get
hauled back to Pudar, you'll have to face the same trial less prepared.
If you and Garn see King Gasir now, before Nantel's men have a
chance to lodge a complaint, it'll be to your credit. At least, the
matter will be settled.'

Mitrian frowned. *Which is worse, having Kinesthe raised as an
outlaw or as an orphan?*

Arduwyn let Mitrian's gown flutter from his grip. 'And we're not
without a case. King Gasir wouldn't have kept Garn among his
guards unless he saw some potential. A good soldier might be worth
some political dissent, especially if the Great War is as imminent as
Colbey seemed to think. We are citizens, and Garn wouldn't have
attacked without provocation. And I'm not a bad talker. I got him
and Sterrane jobs, didn't I?'

A thoughtful pause was spoiled by Arduwyn's chuckle.

Seeing no humor in the situation, Mitrian glared. 'What's so
funny?'

Arduwyn stood, stretching cramps from each short leg. 'Kantar
used to tease me by saying the only thing worse than a salesman is a
lawyer. I wonder what he'd say if he was here now and knew I was
both.'

Arduwyn laughed.

Mitrian did not share her companion's mirth, but the realization that she might also have a trick at her disposal raised her spirits enough for a smile.

By the time Mitrian and Arduwyn gathered their loved ones, explained the situation, and left Kinesthe in Sterrane's care, dawn streaked the sky. Thick, serrated clouds lifted to admit the colored rays of sunrise, and wind howled down the cobbled streets. Mitrian wore her newest dress, Garn his uniform, and both kept their swords strapped to their waists. Only Arduwyn carried no weapons. He walked beside Mitrian, answering her questions optimistically. Yet, between replies, he held his head low, and the fires in his flat, dark eyes seemed more desperate than hopeful.

Mitrian kept her gaze locked on the distant spires of the castle, blind to the regular, business-opening bluster of merchants. Cobbled market streets passed to packed-dirt alleys to near-mazes of thready avenues. As they approached the castle, Mitrian's pulse quickened and her palms went clammy. Repeatedly, she rubbed her hands on her dress.

A crooked branchway brought them directly before King Gasir's keep. Formed of the same carved granite as most of the buildings in town, its four stories towered over the next tallest structure. The spires did not rise from the castle itself, but served as crenellated guard towers at the corners of the rectangular walls enclosing the keep and courtyard. Vines curled and tangled over every wall, interspersed with half-open blue and yellow flowers. Huge windows overlooked the yard. Guards paced the catwalks, their tan uniforms hazy in the weak light of morning.

Arduwyn led Garn and Mitrian to a black, wrought-iron gate where four guards stood at attention. At the sight of Garn, they broke formation. Two opened the gate without awaiting a word or signal from the newcomers. One of the others addressed Garn. 'I'm sorry, Garn.' He sounded sincere. 'We've been ordered to arrest you.'

Arduwyn swore beneath his breath.

Mitrian understood her companion's consternation. Apparently, Nantel's men had arrived first. Though not wholly unexpected, it would give Santagithi's soldiers time to shift the odds in their favor.

Garn nodded, offering no resistance as the guards stripped him of his sword, then led him toward the keep, one on either side.

A thought struck Mitrian, spiraling fear through her. She whispered her concern to Arduwyn. 'You don't think they'll chain or imprison him, do you?'

Arduwyn shrugged his uncertainty, gaze on the guards.

'Kadrak.' Mitrian hoped captivity would not drive Garn to panicked attack. Worried for Garn, it took her several seconds to realize the remaining guards waited for her to identify herself. 'I was there during the fight.' Mitrian avoided details for now as Arduwyn had suggested.

'And I'm Garn's advocate,' the little hunter added.

The taller of the two remaining guards ushered Arduwyn and Mitrian inside. He helped his companion close the gate before leading his charges across the courtyard. By that time, Garn had already disappeared.

The sentry took Mitrian and Arduwyn inside the castle, past the entry hall to a comfortable room with several plush chairs and couches around a low table supporting a bowl of fruit. 'Wait here. We'll come for you when the trial's ready to start. You'll be seated on the bench to the king's right. That means you'll have to pass before the king, and the appropriate social procedures will be expected. Don't get in the way of the guards or you'll have to leave. No weapons allowed in the courtroom.' He held out a hand. 'You'll get them back when you leave.'

Mitrian hesitated. Arduwyn carried no sword, but he fumbled his skinning knife from his breeks and passed it to the guard. Noting her companion's easy surrender, Mitrian handed over her sword, trusting the demon to remain quiescent in the absence of Renshai. The sentry accepted the sword. With a smile of amusement, he tossed back Arduwyn's dagger. 'We can handle the knife. Just keep it in your pocket.'

Arduwyn returned the knife to its proper place.

Emotion entered the sentry's tone. 'Garn's one of us. We stand by our own. Best of luck.'

'Thank you.' Mitrian managed a shaky smile, hoping but doubting the king would prove quite so loyal. However much Gasir might have come to trust Garn in the last three weeks, he certainly had known Nantel for years.

The guard turned on his heel and left the room, closing the door behind him.

Mitrian sat in one of the chairs, sinking so deeply into the cushions she felt lost in folds of plush. Arduwyn plucked an apple from the fruit bowl, munching as he waited. Stomach knotted, Mitrian found the thought of food nauseating, but she did not begrudge Arduwyn his fruit. His reaction to stress always diverged widely from her own.

Shortly, the sentry returned. He gestured Arduwyn and Mitrian out the door, down a corridor, to a door inlaid with carvings of howling wolves. Opening the panel, he waved them through.

Mitrian found herself in the largest room she had ever seen. A man nearly her father's age, with honey-colored curls that swept over his head and into a healthy beard sat on a leather-padded chair on a dais to her right. A semicircle of fourteen guards separated him from the others in the room. Directly in front of Mitrian, six men waited, dressed in the silver and black of Santagithi's guardsmen and surrounded by Pudarian tower guards. She recognized all the prosecutors by name, and her presence did not go unnoticed either. Bartellon caught her gaze, said something softly to the others, and they turned as one to face her. Tense whispers traversed the group. To Mitrian's left, unfamiliar, well-dressed men and women sat on benches.

The sentry led Mitrian and Arduwyn past Nantel's men and over to stand before the king. She curtsied pleasantly as Arduwyn bowed. Then she saw Garn standing alone between two Pudarian guards. Mitrian gave him a reassuring smile before heading to the indicated bench in front of Garn and to King Gasir's right.

The king raised a hand. Gold bracelets slid over muscled forearms and beneath his sleeve. His gesture silenced the room. 'Zaran of Santagithi's Town. You raise the complaint, so you speak first.'

The balding, round-faced guard replied from amidst his companions. He regarded the king directly as he spoke. 'I was walking through town with our leader, Nantel, and four other soldiers. Nantel noticed his cloak pin missing. It's a family heirloom, gold braid twisted into the shape of a swan.' He simulated the figure with his hands. 'I glanced down the alley and saw Garn, here, holding it.' He inclined his head in Garn's direction. 'Now Garn's a known thief in our town, and he's already hunted for being an escaped slave and for viciously disabling and killing some of our guards.' Zaran's gaze skimmed the Pudarian guardsmen, aware his final statement would likely whittle away at Garn's base of support.

Zaran continued. 'Someone yelled, "thief." Garn turned and attacked us. Nantel tried to stop him with an arrow, and Garn saved himself by sacrificing an innocent bystander. Then he charged us. I was the only one who survived.'

Mitrian's hands balled into fists. Zaran's story was lacking key points she wanted to correct, but she knew she would have to wait to be addressed. Though few disputes had been so severe as to require Santagithi's judgment, he did have a courtroom. Mitrian had watched enough cases to have a grasp of procedure.

King Gasir barely stirred. 'Do you have anything else to add, Zaran?'

There were nudges and whispers among Santagithi's men. Zaran spoke up. 'Only, sire, a reminder that Nantel was well-known to you and your people. He was honest, competent, and our leader's confidante and second in command.'

'I thought you said third,' Arduwyn hissed in Mitrian's ear.

Mitrian considered. Rache commanded more men than Nantel, but she could see where Nantel's knowledge of strategy would make him a better leader. If her father had died, she suspected Rache would have turned down the general's position. In reply to Arduwyn, she shrugged, doubting the exact number bore any significance to the case.

King Gasir turned his attention to Garn. 'Would you like to speak in your behalf?'

'Yes, sire.' Garn executed a graceful bow, apparently having learned the proper amenities during his three weeks among the guard force. 'Zaran's story is mostly right.'

Arduwyn grimaced as if in great pain. 'Firfan. The idiot's going to convict himself.'

Arduwyn's lapse spurred fear in Mitrian. Until now, confidence in the hunter's mediating skills had kept her composed. Now, she huddled on the brink of hysteria. 'You told him to just tell the truth,' she shot back.

'I assumed he had a normal survival instinct. Damn it, he needs to tell the story from his own side. He's got legitimate arguments, but they aren't going to sound right from anyone but him.'

'What are you saying?'

The king's glare silenced Mitrian and Arduwyn.

Apparently oblivious to the exchange, Garn amended only one of the omissions and errors in Zaran's description. 'The bystander was a beggar, and he handed me the cloak pin.'

Silence followed as the entire courtroom, including Mitrian, waited for Garn to continue.

After a time, King Gasir cleared his throat. 'Have you nothing more to say, Garn?'

Garn shook his head. 'No, sire.'

Arduwyn knotted his hands in his lap, avoiding Mitrian's stare.

Garn glanced around self-consciously.

'Where is the cloak pin now?' The king addressed no one in particular.

An inappropriately long pause ensued before one of the guards surrounding Garn replied. 'I have it, sire.' He gave Garn an apologetic look. 'We found it in Garn's pocket.'

The king crooked a finger.

The guard who had spoken approached and dropped the trinket into King Gasir's hand. He examined it from all sides before passing it to one of the sentries to his left. 'Is this the missing object?'

The guard carried it to Nantel's soldiers. They gathered around, bobbing their heads and murmuring assent. 'That's it,' Zaran confirmed at length.

King Gasir regarded Santagithi's men and Garn in turn. With a shrug of contrite resignation, he addressed the soldiers. 'What sentence are you seeking?'

Zaran did not falter, despite the harshness of his words. 'Considering the seriousness of the crime, the confessed murder of a visiting diplomat as well as an innocent Pudarian citizen, we believe Garn's execution is not too much to ask.'

Whispers rumbled through King Gasir's courtroom. Sharp pain seared through Mitrian's chest, and she felt suffocated, fighting for each breath. She latched onto Arduwyn's arm so tightly her nails bit into flesh.

Arduwyn gasped in pain, the sound lost in the swell of speculative whispers.

With no trace of emotion in his voice, the King asked, 'Is there anyone in this courtroom who can give evidence that this sentence should not be carried out?'

Mitrian's scream and Arduwyn's calmer, 'I can,' sounded simultaneously. All eyes whipped to the pair on the bench to the king's left.

King Gasir's expression remained unchanging, but his shoulders fell slightly, as if in relief. 'Who would speak first?'

Arduwyn disengaged his arm from Mitrian's fingers.

Flushing, Mitrian released Arduwyn, recognizing blood spots through his sleeve. Shocked by the violence of her grip, she withdrew to let him speak, using the time to gather her control.

Arduwyn stood. 'My name is Arduwyn. I've been a citizen of Pudar for the last five years, making my living honestly as a hunter and selling for merchants in the marketplace. I have a wife and three children.' Having established himself as a stable citizen and therefore worth listening to, Arduwyn continued. 'My objection is not to the punishment; the murder of a diplomat second in line of succession might well demand execution.'

Mitrian seized Arduwyn's leg, not daring to believe what she was hearing.

Arduwyn ignored Mitrian's hold. 'But, for justice to be served, the execution must be granted to Nantel's murderer.'

The background level of noise increased as conjecture about Garn's fate turned to questions about Arduwyn's sanity.

King Gasir leaned forward and to the right, as if to hear Arduwyn better. He looked more interested than perplexed. 'Are you trying to say Garn didn't kill Nantel?'

'Honored sire, did you at any time during the testimony hear either party actually say that Garn killed Nantel?'

The response to this question was a general silence as every person in the room tried to relive the statements. The hunter refreshed their memories. 'Zaran simply claimed he was the only survivor. Garn did not bother to contradict him. No one actually lied. Zaran's motivation confuses me. Garn's, I understand. Wouldn't any good husband spare his wife's life in exchange for his own?' Arduwyn offered a hand to Mitrian. 'This woman killed Nantel. For that, the court has already decided she should be executed.'

Stunned, Mitrian stared at Arduwyn's hand without taking it.

The courtroom erupted in a wave of excited chatter that even the king's raised hands could not stop. It was not until those guards nearest the king bared weapons that the room settled back into a tense near-silence.

King Gasir addressed Zaran. 'Is this true? Did this woman kill Nantel?'

'Yes, sir,' Zaran mumbled, falling back into Santagithi's convention in his discomfort. At a nudge from one of his companions, he corrected his error. 'Sire. But . . .'

The king did not allow Zaran to finish before confronting Garn.

Garn did not speak. He answered by lowering his head in acquiescence.

'So be it.' King Gasir spoke with routine confidence, but the grin Arduwyn hid behind his hand cued Mitrian that there was a game going on beneath the obvious pronouncement. 'Garn's wife killed Nantel. Garn killed a bystander and some of the men under Nantel's command. Those crimes seem nearly equal. I sentence them both to be executed on . . .'

'Wait!' Quillinar, the burliest of Santagithi's guards shouted. His deep bass resonated throughout the court. More fighter than arbitrator, he abandoned formality. 'You can't kill Mitrian.'

His companions made exaggerated nods of agreement.

'Are you saying you'd like to change your sentence?'

'Yes, sire,' Quillinar and Bartellon chorused together.

'On what grounds?'

Bartellon took over the negotiations. 'Sire, if you please. On the grounds that the sentence of a slave can't be applied to a noble lady.

Still condemned to death, along with Garn, Mitrian found the subtleties of the courtroom too difficult for her. 'What's going on?' she whispered to Arduwyn. 'Am I going to die?'

Arduwyn sat in order to discuss the situation in confidence. 'The king was in a bad situation. As it stood, the evidence would have forced him to condemn one of his guards to death in front of the others. Not good for morale or loyalty. I gave him a way out. I guessed from your friendship with Nantel that his fellows wouldn't let you be killed. Apparently, King Gasir trusted my judgment. I think, I *hope*, he's playing along.'

King Gasir's cheeks darkened, and his expression hardened to indignation. 'We have no slaves in Pudar. To us, Garn is a guard and Mitrian a citizen. Their stature is the same, their crimes similar. Therefore, they should be sentenced equally.'

Dangerously angry, Quillinar grabbed for the hilt of a sword that no longer graced his side. 'This is madness.'

One of the huge man's companions seized his arm, restrainingly.

Quillinar turned on his friend with a shove that sent him sprawling into the Pudarian guardsmen, and a hiss that threatened further violence. 'This is a joke! Anyone who would compare a vicious, barbaric gladiator to Santagithi's daughter answers to me.' He leapt into the crowd of guards before the dais.

Steel flashed as swords, spears, and axes formed a protective wall before King Gasir. Quillinar disappeared beneath a huddle of pounding fists and elbows. The circle of tan-clad sentries tightened around Santagithi's guards.

Shortly, the knot of Pudarian guards separated to reveal Quillinar sagging between a pair of men, arms pinioned behind him.

'Take him out until he calms down,' the king instructed. As his guards obeyed, he turned his attention to Mitrian. 'You're Santagithi's daughter?'

Mitrian nodded, too dazed to bother with amenities.

Arduwyn stared, mouth open but uncharacteristically silent.

'Then,' the king continued. 'Why are you letting these soldiers speak for you? You're the highest ranking official present from your town. Do you feel in a position to make a just sentencing?'

The suggestion startled Mitrian. Unlike most of the Westland towns, which were ruled by an aristocracy, Santagithi's Town placed little emphasis on bloodlines. 'Against me and Garn, sire?' Regardless of title, it seemed unrealistic to expect the accused to decide her own penalty impartially.

King Gasir nodded.

'I don't know, sire,' Mitrian said honestly. She glanced at her father's men, watching them fidget in discomfort and frustration. 'But I'll try.' To insist on no penalty would be blatantly unfair, and she knew it would serve Pudar, Nantel's memory, and Santagithi better to at least seem just in her decision.

The room went still as Mitrian considered.

A long time passed. The court and its other occupants seemed to disappear around Mitrian while she reached deep inside her mind for an answer that would appease both sides. Nantel's killing still ached within her. 'I know my father. He would never condemn a man to death for winning a fair fight, no matter the cause. He knows, like most of you here, that the worst punishment a loyal guardsman can suffer is loss of his leader's trust, his position, and his income. Therefore, I would sentence Garn to permanent dismissal from his duties as a Pudarian town guard.' Mitrian's gaze strayed to Garn, who squirmed in helpless distress. 'As to me, I'll never serve Pudar as a soldier.' Mitrian choked out the last words. She knew the ruling was fair and necessary, yet, after years of dreaming about leading legions to war, it hurt to bar herself from one of the few armies that might have considered taking women.

Mitrian looked up. Only then did she notice the twisted expression of discomfort on the king's ruddy features. He hitched long, straight fingers through the curls of his beard. 'To me, that sentencing seems harsh, though I will accept it. If Nantel was nearly as fine a swordsman and captain as I've heard, the man and woman who bested Nantel and his men would make outstanding additions to any army. Santagithi knows the value of a good sword arm. At least, my acceptance of this judgment should demonstrate that Pudar has taken this unfortunate event with the seriousness it merits.'

Santagithi's men said nothing. Four of them scowled. Zaran hid his face in his hands, and Bartellon looked stricken.

King Gasir directed his next question to the guardsmen in black and silver. 'Do you have something more to say?'

'Quillinar, sire?' one reminded.

'Given the circumstances, I won't press any charges for the disruption in my courtroom. He'll be freed when this case is finished.'

'Sire?' Bartellon stepped forward, the repetitive tensing and loosening of the sinews of his upper arms the only clue to his nervousness and diplomatic inexperience. 'Might I speak briefly with Mitrian?'

King Gasir made a lazy gesture toward the bench, but his guards did not move aside.

Bartellon's gaze scurried about the courtroom. Then, accepting that he would not be permitted to talk in private, he called to Mitrian. 'Your father loves you very much. He sent us to bring you home. I don't know why you're protecting Garn, but if it means that much to you, we'll drop the case. Just come home. Please?'

Bartellon fell silent, and every head in the courtroom swung toward Mitrian. She licked her lips, unable to keep her thoughts from rushing into memory: the damp, fresh smell of spring in her town after a frigid winter; walking through woods crisp with autumn leaves of multiple hues while Santagithi told tales of the West and of his soldiers' courage; her mother's soft-spoken gentleness and concern over her only daughter's every discomfort. Her thoughts turned to Rache, his sword skill as constant and elemental as the seasons, his golden grace and beauty so riveting she never tired of watching him. And thoughts of Nantel followed naturally, his gruff exterior hiding a kindness and loyalty Santagithi had recognized long before his men had.

Tears brimmed in Mitrian's eyes. Her gaze found Garn, a shifting blur of tan ringed by tan. She did not need to see him clearly to know what he was. 'Thank you, Bartellon,' she said in a coarse voice she hardly recognized as her own. 'I know my parents love me, and I love them. I love my people. I loved Nantel.' She caught herself before she added Rache. She knew her coupling with Garn would deeply scar Rache, the only man who had encouraged her hopes and dreams to the point of defying her father. To lump Rache's name in with the others would belittle an apology that could only be properly spoken in person, but to add any special messages for Rache would enrage Garn. Wisely, she chose to avoid the subject. 'But Garn is my husband, and the father of my child. I love him, too. Tell my father that Nantel's death was an accident I wish I could undo. But until he and his men learn to treat Garn with the respect he deserves, I can't go home.'

Arduwyn clasped Mitrian's hand, a gesture that seemed as much aimed at stopping her before she further angered Garn as to congratulate her for a case well-handled.

'Adjourned.' King Gasir dismissed Santagithi's men.

As Bartellon and the others filed from the courtroom, Arduwyn faced Mitrian directly. 'Nicely done. Though I could have helped more, quicker, and with less worrying had I known you were a princess. When you said Nantel held the third highest rank, did you place yourself second?'

Mitrian shook her head. 'First, I'm not a princess, just a general's daughter. And, no, I didn't place myself second. Nantel was the captain of archers. Officially, I believe the guard captain, Rache, would be first in succession after my father.'

'Rache?' Arduwyn repeated. A look of shock quickly muted to understanding.

Intrigued, Mitrian wiped away tears, her grief restrained a while longer. 'You've heard of Rache?'

Arduwyn nodded. 'But I'm sworn not to tell.'

Mitrian tightened her grip on Arduwyn. 'If you know something about Rache, you have to tell me. It's more important than you know.'

Arduwyn snorted at the understatement. 'Nothing is more important than not violating the confidence of a Renshai. I'm sorry, Mit. I doubt you're capable of imagining punishments beyond what Colbey could inflict if he ever learned I broke a promise to him.'

Mitrian frowned. 'But why would Colbey . . . ?'

Arduwyn cut in, pressing a finger to Mitrian's lips to silence her. 'Please. You know I can't answer that. Just trust me that Colbey and I have Rache's best interests in mind.'

Stymied, Mitrian nodded reluctantly.

'I'm going to quit my sales job and hunt. I'll take Garn and Sterrane with me. I don't want Garn moping over losing another job, and I think he might find the answer to what's troubling him in the tranquillity of the forest. I always do.' He smiled crookedly. 'If I can't teach Garn to use a bow, Sterrane can bring him on a trap line. Sterrane claims to shoot an accurate crossbow. True or not, maybe Garn could learn that skill instead.'

Mitrian knew Arduwyn would have to exchange a well paying job for a mediocre one. But Sterrane and Garn would bring in more money, so it would even out in the long run. *Besides, although he won't admit it, I think Arduwyn would rather spend the day hunting than selling.* 'Thank you. I appreciate your help.'

The guard who had led Mitrian and Arduwyn into the courtroom now told them to leave.

'Home ?' Mitrian asked Arduwyn as she turned to obey.

'You go. And tell Garn about his new job. I need to talk to my boss, then tend to a personal matter.'

So soon after Arduwyn's references to Rache, the mention of a personal matter bothered Mitrian. But she followed his advice, rising from the bench and heading toward Garn. Now that the trial was over and Garn safe, the grief she had held at bay filled her heart with a weight that no reassurances could lift.

Rache recognized the peaked, black tents of Santagithi's unit through a tear in the foliage of Pudar's forest. Beneath him, Bein veered toward the campsite before Rache realized he had given the command. He smiled. The last few strides of forest and the stretch of sprouting field between him and Pudar's walls would give him time to think of a prank or casual comment with which to greet the roommate he had not seen for nearly a year.

A sound to Rache's left drew his attention to a clump of briars. Quietly, he swerved around the berry- and needle-laden branches. The maneuver brought a man into view. Zaran stood alone in this isolated patch of forest, urinating into the brush.

Rache drew rein. A branch snapped beneath Bein's hoof.

Startled, Zaran glanced up, his hands falling to shield his groin. As he recognized the captain, his mouth rounded, and his brows shot up. 'Rache?' He let his hands slip to his sides. Then, remembering what he was about, he quickly readjusted his clothing.

'Where's Nantel?' Rache asked conversationally. He gazed off toward the camp, but branches and vine loops blocked his view.

Silence.

After some time had passed without an answer, Rache turned back to face the guard. He widened his eyes to indicate a reply was expected.

'Good to have you back.' Zaran's feigned cheerfulness patronized Rache. 'We're headed home. You'll join us, I presume?'

Rache's demeanor went hard as flint. 'Where is Nantel?'

Zaran stared at his boots. 'If you don't mind, Rache, I'd rather talk about it back at the camp.'

Accustomed to instant obedience, Rache found Zaran's delay intolerable. 'I mind.' He sent Bein into a walk that hooked into Zaran's only clear path to camp. 'I'm still your captain, damn it! I asked a question, and I expect a straight answer. Immediately!'

Zaran hesitated.

Provoked to violence, Rache drew his sword, swung with a precision that sent Zaran's cloak pin skittering, then sheathed the blade in the same motion. Catching the brooch in midair, Rache glowered at the errant guard.

Zaran staggered, clutching at his throat as he realized how close he had come to death. Had Rache wanted blood, Zaran would have been dead before he saw the stroke coming.

Rache tossed back the pin. 'Now where's Nantel?'

Recovering, Zaran made an awkward, futile grab for his jewelry. The brooch hit the ground at his feet. 'Nantel's dead, all right? He's dead.'

'Dead?' Rache recoiled, asking the next question from long-ingrained habit. 'In battle?'

'Yes, in battle, you ...' Zaran bit off the insult, still rattled by Rache's attack. 'Does it matter? Nantel's dead.'

'It matters to me.' Rache spoke calmly, aware something of more significance than a soldier's death must be bothering Zaran. The news of Nantel's slaying hit like lead, but Rache would not allow the pain to penetrate until he understood what troubled Zaran. 'I need details. Who killed him?'

Zaran shook his head. 'Please don't make me tell you. Not now.'

'Garn,' Rache guessed.

'Mitrian,' Zaran corrected bitterly.

No other name could have stunned Rache so. 'What?'

'Mitrian killed Nantel.'

'Why?'

'She claimed it was an accident. She was defending Garn. Kadrak's sword, defending a gladiator ? The two of them also "accidentally" killed four of Santagithi's guards. Who taught that girl to fight ?'

'Modi.' It was the first time Rache had used the god's name for emotional rather than physical pain, but it had the same effect. Rage slashed through him, goading him toward berserk, violent action.

'Who ?' Unfamiliar with the name yet apparently tuned to Rache's sudden anger, Zaran backed up several paces. Twigs whipped and snapped against his cloak.

'Garn's not a man or a gladiator or an animal. He's a demon.' Rache's knuckles blanched around the reins. 'He poisons everyone and everything he touches. Me, Mitrian, Nantel, the unity of Santagithi's guard force.' He wheeled Bein.

'Where are you going ?' Zaran shouted.

'To rid the world of a demon,' he called over his shoulder, uncertain whether Zaran had even heard him.

Bein broke into a canter.

Rache had nearly reached the gates of Pudar when a man leading a donkey sidled directly into his path. Bein drew up with a snort and a half-rear that sent Rache lurching against the base of the saddle. Rache regained his balance, swearing viciously.

'Rache ? Is that you, Rache ?'

Startled by a stranger who knew his name, Rache reined Bein to a halt and studied the man. Though small and thin, he met Rache's frost-blue eyes without fear. Gaunt cheeks framed a thin nose, and the stubbly, red hair made an odd contrast. Although the man's features were unfamiliar, Rache recognized Arduwyn by descriptions garnered in Western farm towns.

'I'm Rache,' he admitted. 'Why . . . ?'

Arduwyn interrupted, speaking in rapid-fire Common. 'Thank the gods, it's you. I've been looking for you for months. Literally months. Where have you been ?'

More accustomed to the lazy drawl of Santagithi's Town, Rache found himself several words behind Arduwyn. Some of Peusen's warriors who had come from larger Western cities, like Pudar, spoke with a similar monotonal, crisp speed, though none as hastily as Arduwyn. The rapidity of Arduwyn's delivery made Rache's pause seem interminable. 'What ?' he finally said, his anger dispersing as Arduwyn demanded his complete attention.

Bein snorted, and the donkey crept toward the stallion tentatively.

'You know a Northman named Colbey, I presume ?'

Cold clenched Rache's chest. Forced to confront the probability that his *torke*, the man he respected most in all the world, was ashamed of him, Rache had dismissed the master from his mind. To have it thrown back at him so casually caught him defenseless. The last of his rage trailed away like smoke from a snuffed candle. Carefully, he nodded.

Accepting Rache's gesture as a positive answer, Arduwyn explained. 'Colbey rode south about a month ago. He said to expect you and to send you to him when you came. He didn't seem to think it would take this long. If you hurry, he might still be there.'

Bein and Stubs snuffled loudly at one another's muzzles.

Colbey took precedence over anyone or anything Rache knew. It was all he could do to keep from kicking the black stallion into a gallop randomly southward. 'Where?'

'At the northern base of the Southern mountain range. About halfway between Erythane and the Perionyx River.'

Something about the description struck Rache as odd, but, caught up in the excitement of seeing Colbey, he did not bother to seek the flaw in Arduwyn's statement. Nothing in the world mattered but the chance to reunite with the only other Renshai survivor, a singular opportunity to continue his training with the greatest swordsman who had ever lived.

Bein trumpeted a shrill challenge that sent Stubs into a wild, backward scramble so sudden it unbalanced Arduwyn. He flailed his arms, tripped over Stub's hoof, and crashed, rump first, to the ground.

Tension fled Rache in an explosion of laughter.

Arduwyn leapt gracefully to his feet, glaring at Stubs, his dignity soiled and at least one of the arrows in his back quiver snapped near the base. The feathered end of its shaft rolled to the dirt, vividly revealing Arduwyn's personal colors: one royal blue ring followed by two of gold.

Rache's laughter choked to silence as he recognized a crest he had been trying to trace for months. 'You,' he said accusingly.

Something in Rache's demeanor sent Arduwyn scurrying back. Bein edged forward, keeping the gap between Rache and Arduwyn constant.

Realizing he could never outrun a horse, Arduwyn went still. 'The longer you delay, the less likely you'll find Colbey.'

'Who are you working for?'

'Working for?' Arduwyn blinked twice in succession. 'What are you talking about?'

Rache had tired of games. Patient banter was not his style. Without warning, he whipped one sword from its sheath with his right hand and signaled Bein to the opposite side.

Instinctively, Arduwyn recoiled leftward, his gaze on the blade.

Rache made a lightning quick grab with his left hand, twisting his fingers into the linen front of Arduwyn's shirt. Using the strength of arms trained to serve as arms and legs, he hoisted the little hunter to a seat in front of the saddle. Keeping his arms wrapped around Arduwyn's throat, Rache signaled Bein with his knees. The stallion galloped toward the forest.

As the horse whirled, Rache caught sight of the town guard near the gate, watching gape-mouthed. He dismissed them as harmless. By the time they chose to pursue, they would have no means to judge his direction, and Bein could take them well beyond Pudar's jurisdiction before the guards could find mounts to give chase. Even if they caught him, two town guardsmen would prove little challenge to one annoyed Renshai.

Stubs bleated frantically twice before settling down to graze on the sprouting crops.

Arduwyn did not calm so quickly. 'Firfan! Rache! What the hell are you doing?'

Rache tightened his grip, and Arduwyn fell silent. Bein plunged into the brush, wallowed through a dense tangle of vines, then came to a halt in a clearing just beyond sight of the town walls. Rache raised the sword so it fell clearly into Arduwyn's sight. 'Now talk. Who hired you?'

Arduwyn gurgled something unintelligible to indicate that Rache's arm was uncomfortably tight around his windpipe.

Rache removed his arm from Arduwyn's neck. He twisted the sword so that sunlight flashed from the steel. 'Fine. I won't hold you. But if you decide to jump down, you'd better hope you're faster than me. And my horse.'

Arduwyn rubbed at his neck gratefully. 'I'm not going anywhere. Remember? I was the one who stopped you to talk.'

'Who are you working for that keeps sending me in the wrong direction?' Rache wound his fingers into the extra folds at the back of Arduwyn's shirt. 'Answer quickly and truthfully or, I swear, I'll give you an ear to ear grin via the throat.' He shook the sword once.

'Colbey,' Arduwyn admitted. 'I'm working for Colbey.'

'Why?'

'Because I told him I would, and I've heard Renshai get violent when they think they've been lied to.'

Fully aware of Arduwyn's sarcasm, Rache clarified. 'I meant why as in "why is Colbey avoiding me?"'

'I don't know.'

Rache's grip tensed. The sword rose.

Arduwyn twisted far enough to roll one dark eye in Rache's direction. 'I don't think he knows either. He cares about you and doesn't want to see you come to any harm. That I know. And he seems to have some weird, unexplained fear that if the two of you meet, you'll get hurt.'

The explanation made little sense. Tiring of Arduwyn's lies, Rache lifted the sword until cold steel touched the hunter's throat. He felt Arduwyn go rigid. 'The truth, archer. What's the matter with you city folk? Death doesn't mean anything to you?'

'Please.' Desperation crept into Arduwyn's voice. His hands clutched Rache's wrist. 'I'm telling the truth.'

'There's more.'

'I'm sure,' Arduwyn agreed. 'But Colbey didn't tell me any more. I'm not certain he really understands it himself.'

Rache lowered the sword thoughtfully. 'So Colbey's in Pudar?'

'No.'

'Where is he?'

'I promised Colbey I wouldn't tell you.'

'I can kill you,' Rache reminded.

'Colbey could do worse.'

Rache went silent, stymied. It made little sense for Arduwyn to fear a distant menace more than a Renshai with a sword at his throat. Yet, familiar with Colbey, Rache believed he understood. 'He's not south. I just spent the last month close enough to the location you said Colbey was at that I would have seen him if he was there.'

Arduwyn nodded perceptively. 'I didn't know. That was my mistake.' His stance relaxed slightly as he considered Rache's words, but he did not question why Rache had spent a month in supposedly uninhabited territory.

The words reminded Rache of the actual clue that had tipped him off to Arduwyn's lies. In his excitement, he would have accepted the location Arduwyn had specified if not for the discovery of the crest. And, thoughts of the arrow reminded Rache that he had been seeking the archer to thank him, not threaten him. 'Actually, I hate to admit it, but your mistake was saving my life.'

'Huh?' The sudden shift in manner obviously confused Arduwyn. He strained his neck to an awkward angle that allowed him to partially meet Rache's gaze.

'In the eight months I spent tracking Mitrian, I knew I was being hunted, too. I thought it was just those white assassins and their followers. Things sometimes got fast and confusing during those fights, but I'm a competent enough swordsman to know when someone dies before I cut them. I dug this out of one corpse's chest.' Sheathing his sword, Rache rummaged in his pocket, drawing out the feathered end of a dirt-encrusted piece of arrow. Though faded, Arduwyn's blue and gold crest was unmistakable. 'Thank you.'

Arduwyn kept his tone light, as if fearing to offend with his joke. 'You have an unusual way of showing gratitude. In the future, I'd be happy to accept your thanks from the ground.'

Rache ignored the gibe. 'There were others following me too, a rotating team of scouts from a small army. One of them was even blind. By tracing my progress from sound, he never got close enough for me to spot him. In any case, I spent the last month sorting through the army and trying to match this crest to its owner. I should have guessed you followed me, too. But when I already had an answer, it never occurred to me to look for another.'

Gently, Arduwyn turned around on Bein's withers so that he faced Rache.

Rache tried to put his thoughts back on track. 'Wait, Arduwyn. If Colbey's not in Pudar, and you're working for him, why are you trying to keep me out of the city ?'

Arduwyn hesitated.

'Don't think about that lie too long. I might catch on.' Rache played on an ancient joke that the speed of a man's swordplay was indirectly proportional to the quickness of his wit.

'I'm not making things up.' Arduwyn's brown eyes held Rache's blue ones with a perfect glimmer of sincerity. 'I'm just trying to think of a gentle way of saying this.'

Rache granted Arduwyn time to gather his thoughts.

'All Mitrian saw was a group of men attacking the husband she loves. It wasn't until after she killed Nantel . . .' He trailed off, apparently to see if he was the first to deliver the news to Rache.

Rache nodded to indicate he knew and to encourage Arduwyn to continue.

'. . . that she realized who the attackers were. Now that the trial is finished, she's inconsolable. I never knew Nantel, but if he was as competent and loyal a commander as everyone says, then his death was a bitter loss to the combined forces of the West.' Arduwyn broke off, as if realizing his word choices had become too flowery for the occasion. 'I'm saying the Westlands lost a good warrior for nothing. Absolutely nothing. Mitrian is miserable. Garn and I are upset because she's miserable. And Nantel is dead. No winners, Rache. Just losers.'

Arduwyn's underlying message came through loud and clear. Rache frowned. 'So what are you saying ? I shouldn't enter Pudar because Garn and Mitrian might kill me ? I don't think they could.'

Arduwyn shifted, seeking a comfortable position reversed on Bein's withers. 'I won't argue prowess, except to say that under Colbey's tutelage, Mitrian's sword skill has improved faster than I thought possible. And Garn's been practicing in some more unusual ways. In any case, I don't think there's any way she could come upon you fast enough not to recognize you before she attacked. If she hurt you, it would be with full knowledge of who you are.'

'So much the better. We don't have to worry about a repeat of what happened with Nantel.'

'So much the *worse*,' Arduwyn corrected. 'I thought you liked Mitrian.'

Rache took offense. 'I love Mitrian. She's more sister to me than any blood relative. I want what's best for her.'

'And what's best for her ?'

'Getting her out of the hands of a viciously brutal gladiator and escorting her back home to the people who love her.'

'All right.' Arduwyn accepted the scenario and worked it from the other side. 'So what's best for Mitrian is to watch her beloved husband murdered by her "brother." Then, she and her baby should be dragged to a home where the townsfolk will disdain her for her one focus in life, her sword. And her son will always be a viciously brutal gladiator's brat.'

'No.' Rache delivered what he believed was the coup de grace. 'I've thought of that. I'll claim the boy as my own, if I must. And I'll continue Mitrian's lessons no matter what anyone thinks.'

'And Garn ?'

'Will die, yes.'

'Why does Garn have to die ?'

Arduwyn's question seemed ludicrous to Rache. 'Because he's evil, dangerous, and unpredictable. Why would anyone want him to live ?'

'He's been with Mitrian nearly a year. He's never harmed her. She loves him more now than ever.'

The suggestion pained Rache like fire. 'She only thinks she loves him.'

Arduwyn snorted. 'Loves him, thinks she loves him. What's the difference ?'

'The difference is . . .' Rache could feel rage boiling up inside him again '. . . that when I kill Garn, she'll come to realize she never loved him at all.'

'Or she'll come to realize *you* never loved him at all. I don't think that was ever in doubt.'

'Modi's wrath !' Rache exploded. 'The gladiator crippled me. I'm supposed to love him for that ?'

Arduwyn leaned closer, no longer afraid of Rache's swords despite his building temper. He spoke quickly, so as not to give Rache space to interrupt. 'First . . .' He extended his index finger. 'I'm not asking you to love him, only telling you that Mitrian does. She's already agreed to return home under the condition that her husband is accepted as her husband. I don't think that's much to ask. Second . . .' He drew out his middle finger beside the other. 'It's been nearly a year. Garn's not a gladiator anymore. He's a man. No one is born with a gladiator's personality; that savage temper of his was created. And third . . .' Arduwyn added his ring finger to the previous two. 'You crippled him, too. Or your people did. Someone trained him to meet every crisis with violence and no more thought than a bird needs to fly.' Arduwyn was shaking now. 'Could that someone be the same man who would kidnap a stranger at sword point to thank the man for saving his life?'

Rache caught himself with his hands halfway to Arduwyn's throat. Self-consciously, he turned the gesture toward himself, running his hands through golden hair which had so many times born the crimson stain of blood and triumph-sweetened sweat. A breeze blew the yellow strands back into his face. 'Who told you I trained Garn?' Dropping one hand, he fondled the hilt of his sword, the one love that had never failed nor betrayed him.

'No one had to tell me.' Arduwyn's gaze traced the course of Rache's hand all the way to his sword. 'Anyone who becomes competent forms a strong bond with his teacher. Usually, like Mitrian and Colbey or me and my father, it's a positive bond. For Garn to learn as much as he did of a skill he believes he never wanted to know, he must have had strong ties, indeed. That such closeness went the route of severe hatred rather than love, I'm not surprised.'

Rache's brow furrowed as he assimilated Arduwyn's oddly worded explanation.

'You and Garn are much alike.'

Those words Rache understood, and they infuriated him. 'You have little respect for your own life, archer.'

'Hunter,' Arduwyn corrected. 'And maybe. But I have a lot of respect for your life as well as Garn's and Mitrian's. One thing I know for certain, the only way to get Mitrian back is to accept Garn. If you kill him or even try, she'll want nothing to do with you.'

Unless Garn clearly attacks first. She can't blame me for self-defense. Rache kept that thought to himself. 'So what do you suggest? I enter Pudar bearing gifts for Garn?'

'No.' Arduwyn seemed to read Rache's mind. 'That'll only provoke Garn.' He started to slide from Bein's withers, making his intentions clear enough that Rache could halt him with a command before violence was called for.

Rache said nothing.

Arduwyn landed lightly on the ground, standing near Bein's head. Freed of the extra weight, the black stallion lowered his head to graze. 'Have you ever seen dogs fight?'

Rache nodded.

'Often, if you can get them to meet on neutral territory, they become friends. Pudar is Garn's home. The town you came from is yours. I'd like some time to speak with Garn as freely as I just did with you. Then, I promise, I'll get the two of you together on neutral ground. That place you've been staying near the Southern Mountains will do.'

Rache considered. He had promised not to identify Iaplege as a town of outcasts, but Peusen had not put limits on the number of friends he could meet there. He could not speak for Arduwyn, but Mitrian or Garn could be accepted into the Iaplegian forces based on their pasts and abilities. The thought of riding to war at Garn's side sent a shiver through his body. Accustomed to fighting as an individual and trusting no one, Garn could become as large a danger to his companions as to his enemies. 'You're not lying to me again? Because if I find out you are, you may find I've learned a few tricks from Colbey.'

Arduwyn raised a hand. 'I swear it. I will lead Garn and Mitrian to you within the month.' He broke off with an inappropriate oath. 'What am I doing? I can't lead Garn anywhere. I promised my wife I'd be home every evening.'

It seemed like an odd vow to Rache, but he saw no reason for Arduwyn to make up such a thing. Yet.

'Listen, Rache. I still think this is a good idea. I can't lead them, but I'll see to it that they get to you. I'll talk Sterrane into . . .'

The familiar name jolted Rache. 'Sterrane?' He smiled as pleasant memories rose to the forefront of his consciousness. 'Little Sterrane?'

'Little?' Arduwyn shook his head vigorously. 'I don't think this could possibly be the same Sterrane.'

Rache laughed. 'That was the joke. He was several years younger than me. But, between me aging too damned slowly and him being the size of a small building, we looked like we came from different worlds.' He chuckled again. 'Big, black-haired monster. Looks like he ought to be tripping over his own feet, but the only thing clumsy about him is his speech. Real good with a crossbow.'

'That's him,' Arduwyn admitted. 'How did you know him?'

'He lived in our town for a while by the Eastern Wizard's decree. Where'd you find him?' Another realization sent him into a fresh round of laughter. 'Sterrane is the giant imbecile you've been traveling with?'

'Eastern Wizard ?' Arduwyn looked startled. 'Why would Wizards have an interest in Sterrane ?'

Rache stared. 'You don't know ?'

Arduwyn shook his head.

'When you bring Mitrian and Garn to neutral territory, I'll tell you all about him.' On that note, Rache wheeled Bein and sent him into a canter.

Arduwyn shouted after him. 'Wait ! I told you I can't . . .' The rest was lost beneath the rattle of branches.

Soon, Rache's mount slowed, winding between the trunks, retracing the path by which he had come to Pudar. Wind ruffled Rache's hair like the hand of a lover. Birdsong preceded him through even the densest growth of forest, but Rache concentrated on motivations that went deeper than his surface thoughts could handle. Months ago, no man's words would have been enough to delay his vengeance against Garn. But experience had made him patient, and Arduwyn's words held the same wisdom that Nantel consistently displayed.

Without intention, Rache's thoughts wandered to a future he had evaded as a child. He imagined the sting of the Northern king's whip, the heavy pull of chains, the daily bars to freedom. The more he pondered, the more the vision became real. Gradually, something ancient responded, hot, ugly hatred for the men who kept him. To fight and kill enemies and to die in battle was the glory and life of a soldier. But to fight and kill strangers for an enemy's entertainment and to die in a cage reduced war to slaughter and honor to irony.

For a moment, Rache thought he understood.

22 The Source of Strength

Rain battered the treetops, rolling through gaps in the stiff umbrella of foliage to soak the three hunters below. Chilled to the bone, Garn shook his head hard, flinging water over his companions and leaving his hair nearly as spiky as Arduwyn's. Within moments, the ceaseless drip of rain plastered the mahogany strands flat to his head again.

Despite the drenching, Garn felt dirty. The odor of rancid trap bait and musk pervaded him. Heedless, Arduwyn and Sterrane quartered deer, packing the bundles onto Stubs, whistling and humming as if neither could think of anything more enjoyable in life than standing in the wet, fondling raw meat.

Garn had come to the conclusion that he would never make a good hunter. After years of watching archers huddled like cowards behind drawn crossbows while stronger, more stalwart guards took the risks of training and moving gladiators, Garn held little interest in or respect for the weapon. He enjoyed walking through the woods, savoring his freedom, but the time spent butchering and skinning bored him, and even a caged gladiator knew enough to avoid rain by whatever means at his disposal.

While Sterrane lashed the final bundle of meat into place, Arduwyn took Garn aside. The hunter's sodden leathers clung to his skin, making him look smaller and scrawnier than usual. Water darkened his hair to copper, and droplets wound from the strands. Still, despite his comical appearance and love of the woodlands, he appeared soberly out of his element. 'Garn, there's something we have to discuss that I know you don't want to talk about.'

Now some distance from Sterrane and the donkey, Garn faced Arduwyn. Resting one foot on a stone, he leaned forward to indicate his willingness. It seemed foolish to discuss in the rain what could as easily be discussed in a cottage, but Garn did not question Arduwyn's purpose. Soaked to the skin, he found the rain scarcely bothered him.

Arduwyn kept his gaze on Garn's hands as he spoke. 'That incident with Nantel made me realize just how much danger we're in so long as this feud between you and Mitrian's people continues.'

His eyes flitted to Garn's face then back to his hands. 'Imagine what could have happened if those soldiers had ambushed us out in the woods. With arrows, for example. There's really no way we could defend against that, even now that we know they're hunting you.'

Garn listened patiently but found only concerns without solutions in Arduwyn's words. Discussing Santagithi's people irritated him. The tug of his clinging undergarments and the dribble of rain into his eyes became a more noticeable nuisance. 'So? What's your point?'

'My point.' Arduwyn licked his lips, and Garn recognized the gesture as delay. It seemed ridiculously unlikely they could have felt dry in the downpour. 'We've got to find a way to make peace. We don't need more enemies. As it is, we can't even say Mitrian's a . . .' He mumbled the next word, '. . . Renshai . . .' He resumed his normal tone, '. . . without upsetting everybody in the world. We don't need everybody in the world *plus four hundred soldiers* as enemies.'

Garn still sifted no plans from Arduwyn's words. It was not his way to speculate, so he waited.

Arduwyn scuffed his boot through the mud. 'There's an envoy from Santagithi's Town who wants to see you and is willing to make peace.'

Intrigued, Garn stared. 'An envoy?' Suspicion aroused, he narrowed his eyes to hostile slits. 'You're lying. Santagithi didn't come to Pudar with that bunch of coward-led peons. He's the only one who can speak for the entire town.'

'There might be one other.'

Garn's mind drew a blank. The only high officer he had seen convince large numbers of Santagithi's people of anything had been Nantel. 'Who?'

Arduwyn squirmed. 'You know him, I'm certain. He's got a lot of qualities you have to respect. He's an outstanding fighter. He's got more courage than any single person ought to have. And he cares for Mitrian every bit as much as you do.' He clarified quickly. 'Though with a brother's love.'

Garn felt anger growing warm in the pit of his stomach, but he dared not contemplate its source. 'Who is it?' he demanded, dimly aware speculation might destroy his self-control. 'Arduwyn, who is this so-called envoy?'

'It's Rache.'

'What!' Garn shouted before he realized he had spoken. 'That bastard child of *wisules* is here?'

'He wants to make peace,' Arduwyn reminded hurriedly. 'He realizes you two really aren't that different . . .'

'What do you mean not that different?' Rage crescendoed to an explosion of hatred. 'When did I ever whip slaves? When did I ever force men to fight to the death? When –'

Arduwyn broke in. 'Garn, calm down. Rache understands what you went through. He's sorry –'

Now Garn interrupted. 'This conversation is over!' Garn advanced on Arduwyn, thoughts on the hot seed of anger within him. Unlike the usual superficial wrath of daily conflict or the generalized homicidal frenzy that seized him in the pit, this rage had a deep-seated source that Garn had never before experienced. It came neither from his body nor his mind but from a part of himself he had never learned to consciously use, his soul, perhaps, or a flicker of divine inspiration. Elemental or spiritual, Garn did not know, but he felt suddenly, unequivocally certain he had found the source of Colbey's strength. Caught by this experience, he nearly forgot where he was and the cause of his new emotion.

Arduwyn back-stepped. Fear showed clearly in his eyes. 'Garn. He realizes he made a mistake. Rache –'

If Arduwyn finished his sentence, Garn never knew it. Bitterness shattered his control, pitching him into a flaming agony of hatred and rage. He lunged at Arduwyn, his thoughts feverishly muddled. 'If I ever see Rache, I'm going to kill him.'

Arduwyn sprang backward, but not quickly enough. Garn's sinewy hands ground into his shoulders. The ex-gladiator hefted the smaller man, slamming him into the trunk of an oak.

Arduwyn cried out in pain, surprise, and fear.

Sanity lost, Garn hammered his quarry against the tree again. 'The only time I want to hear that name mentioned is when you tell me where he is.' He battered Arduwyn against the trunk again. 'Where is he?'

Arduwyn gasped. He went limp in Garn's grasp.

Nearby, someone bellowed. Something half again Garn's weight struck him at a full run. Fingers gouged Garn's side. The impact broke his grip on Arduwyn and sent him airborne. Wind knifed beneath his sodden clothing, then he landed in a patch of briars. Branches snapped beneath him, jabbing into his back and rump.

Howling in rage and frustration, Garn leapt to his feet and faced the man who had hit him. Sterrane crouched protectively between Arduwyn and Garn, his rain-plastered hair and beard making him look like a drowned animal.

'Garn, stop it!' Arduwyn hollered. 'If you hate Rache, that's your decision. But don't hurt your friends.'

Friends. Garn's world returned to focus. He stared at Sterrane and Arduwyn blankly, watching long enough to see the red-haired hunter climb painfully to his feet. Guilt descended over him, banishing anger and accompanied by an excitement of a discovery he could not quell. He hated what he knew he had done to Arduwyn, yet his unschooled mind could not conjure the necessary words to express his misgivings. 'I'm sorry,' he said. And though he knew it was not enough, he turned and stomped back toward home alone.

Spring rain pattered on the rooftop of Garn's and Mitrian's cottage in Pudar. In her bed in the loft, Mitrian slept, lulled by the steady rhythm of the droplets. Garn sat on a bench in the main room, ignoring the throb of muscles locked too long in one position and the burning of eyes held open in a stare fixed on Kinesthe in his crib. The infant seemed to be looking back with the same intensity, blue eyes half-opened but unblinking, perhaps in sleep.

'Kinesthe.' The movement cracked Garn's dry lips, reminding him how prolonged his stillness had been. He felt refreshed, as if he had slept, yet he remained fully aware. While Mitrian rested, Garn had explored a depth of person he had never known existed. 'Kinesthe,' he repeated. 'Strength.' There was magic in the name. Spoken now, it filled Garn with a strange elation that bordered on understanding. He rose.

Crossing the room, Garn gathered Kinesthe, snug in his woolen blanket. 'Tonight, we'll find the secret together.'

The infant settled against Garn's chest, innocent, oblivious to the hopes and goals placed upon him by eager parents and an aged Renshai.

Walking to the door, Garn tripped the latch and carried Kinesthe into the dark depths of night. Stars winked down on father and son as they crossed the tangled stretch of weeds, passed the shielding spread of blackberry vines, and sat on the great rock. Garn selected a position where the trees shielded him and Kinesthe from the rain. 'One day, Kinesthe, a man twice my age will come to train you. He'll teach you to fight until no man or woman can best you. Don't forget your father. I can do things even the old man cannot.'

Since Colbey had broken the horseshoe in the woods between the farm towns, Garn had wondered if he had more strength than the elder. Now, when the question went unasked, his mind and body responded together. He did not need to ask; he knew. All that remained was to test that knowledge.

Garn set Kinesthe on the rock beside him. Reaching into his cloak pocket, he retrieved the broken halves of metal he had carried since Colbey's display of strength. If the rain still pounded the leaves or Kinesthe stirred, Garn did not hear them. His mind filled with the self-control he had sought so long to harness. Taking one of the horseshoe pieces into his hands, he shut his eyes, feeling the smooth coolness of the steel in his mind. Nearly an hour passed in what seemed like a moment to Garn. Slowly, the metal warmed to his grasp.

Sweat beaded Garn's brow. His massive muscles pulled. And steel gave. Hurriedly, Garn opened his eyes. The metal had bent, not completely, but noticeably. *I can do it.* Faced with the evidence, Garn's strength erupted in an explosion of will. Throwing himself into the task, he snapped his arms downward.

Without fanfare or sound, the steel broke.

Nothing around Garn had changed, except himself. For the first time, he noticed the simple beauties of the wet leaves and the sweetness of the rain. Suddenly, nothing was impossible. Garn laughed. Kinesthe's eyes seemed to shine like diamonds as Garn hefted him and ran toward home. He skipped across the yard, slipped in the mud, caught his balance, and continued running. He tossed Kinesthe into the air until he cried, then tickled him until he smiled.

Garn burst into his cottage. 'Mitrian! Mitrian!'

The beam of moonlight through the doorway lit red streaks across the floor. 'Mitrian, you have to see this.' He charged up the stairs. 'Mitrian!' Through the darkness, he could see their bed lay empty.

'Mitrian?' Garn pawed the blanket. Seizing the lantern from its bracket, he sparked it with a block of flint against a chest latch. The wick caught, and lantern light spun crazily about the deserted room.

Garn could scarcely catch his breath. The broken quarters of horseshoe fell from his hand, ringing hollowly against the floor-boards. 'Mitrian!' Panic edged his cry. He pounded down the stairs.

The lantern played along the blood-splashed floor.

'Mitrian!' Garn screamed frantically. He sank to the boards. 'Mitrian.'

Kinesthe wailed. Garn hugged the infant more closely, and his gaze fell upon a small pile of crushed, white feathers. The image of the circle of Leukenyan priests surrounding Sterrane came vividly to mind. 'No,' he hissed.

In the wee hours of the morning, Arduwyn startled alert to a frantic hammering on his door that pierced even Sterrane's familiar, raucous snores. Shortly, the snores disappeared, but the pounding continued, undaunted. Bel caught Arduwyn's hand, her fingers fragile and cold in his callused grip. He squeezed once in reassurance, then threw off the covers, careful not to expose Bel at the same time. Pain flashed through his back. Bruises and strains from Garn's wild rage stiffened his gait. He winced, trying not to let Bel see how much his head and neck ached, then headed down the stairs.

As he reached the bottom, he found Sterrane standing with one hand on the knob. The larger man had paused long enough to light a candle in the bracket near the door. Arduwyn watched while Sterrane pulled open the panel and Garn charged through it. He clutched Kinesthe in one arm. The other hand, clenched to a fist, fluttered anxiously. He wore the same rumpled tunic and breeks as the previous day, and his brown hair lay slung in a snarl across one shoulder.

'Garn,' Arduwyn said. It was an identification, not a greeting.

'Mitrian's gone! They've got Mitrian!'

It was impossible to miss the panic in Garn's demeanor, yet Arduwyn was in no mood to soothe nor to draw out the story from a frenzied companion with a history of violence. 'Garn, calm down. Who's got Mitrian?'

In reply, Garn opened his hand. A wash of stained, white feathers floated to the floor.

'Firfan.' Arduwyn watched the feathers fall. 'Leukenyans. Why? How?' Concern for Mitrian displaced all hostility against Garn.

Garn shook his head. 'I don't know. Why would they want Mitrian? There was blood. What if they hurt her?'

Sterrane took the baby from his father's shaky grasp.

Arduwyn snapped to action. 'Sterrane, Garn, pack supplies for a few days' travel. We'll each need a horse. I know you two already have one. See if you can buy another one or two this early.' He passed a generous number of silvers to Garn. 'And don't forget weapons. We're going to Corpa Leukenya.'

Garn whirled and headed out into the night. Sterrane passed Kinesthe to Arduwyn and started on his packing. Aching from a myriad of abrasions and bruises, Arduwyn climbed the stairs to his bedroom in the loft. Setting Kinesthe on the coverlet, he sat at the foot of the bed and gave Bel's ankle an affectionate pinch. 'Mitrian's in trouble . . .' Arduwyn started.

'No.' Though Bel spoke only one word, the coldness in her tone was unmistakable.

Shocked by Bel's nonsensical response, Arduwyn stared. 'What?'

Kinesthe gurgled. Arduwyn poked at the child playfully, and it grabbed his finger.

'I heard what happened downstairs.' Darkness disembodied Bel's voice. 'You promised me you'd be home every night.'

Arduwyn disengaged his finger from the baby. 'And I have been. I love you, Bel. You know that. But Mitrian's life may be at stake. What do you want me to do, abandon her?'

Bel made no reply.

'I thought you liked Mitrian.' Arduwyn knew that while he, Sterrane, and Garn worked, the women often shared chores and shopping. Bel had become attached enough to Kinesthe to start hinting about a new baby of their own.

'I do like Mitrian.' Bel's tone softened, but she did not compromise. 'But I know you. They'll get you out in the forests for a few days, and you'll never come back.'

'That's ridiculous.' The need for haste tore at Arduwyn's sensibilities every bit as much as the necessity of comforting Bel. 'I spend every day in the forest, and I'm still here.' Arduwyn had never revealed the real reason he had chosen to return to hunting. While he did appreciate employment that Sterrane, Garn, and he could perform together, he had actually chosen the pursuit to place him near the gate when Rache reached Pudar. His meeting with the Renshai on the very first day had been sheer coincidence.

'Familiar, close forests,' Bel clarified. 'Once you get out in new territory, even your friends won't be able to drag you home.'

Arduwyn tossed his hands in frustration. Arguing the depth of his love for Bel and his intentions was getting him nowhere. Instead, he tried showing her the reverse side of the situation. 'What do you want me to do? Abandon Mitrian to a temple of priests who probably sacrifice human lives to their bird-god idol? Is that what you'd want me to do if they had taken Rusha or Jani instead of Mitrian?'

Bel sat up, nearly dislodging Kinesthe as she moved. 'Of course not. But why can't Garn and Sterrane rescue Mitrian? They're big and strong.'

Arduwyn caught up the baby and shifted to sit near Bel's head. 'Because Sterrane is . . . well . . . Sterrane. Garn's not stupid, but he's got the social grace of a corpse and he's never had to plan a strategy. He's more apt to respond to his temper than his common sense. He'll get all three of them killed.'

'So you're going to do all the thinking for Garn and Sterrane for the rest of their lives?' Bel accepted Kinesthe from Arduwyn. 'For once, can't you let them solve their own problems?'

Arduwyn recalled Rache's deadly speed and how helpless he had felt in the Renshai's grip. The wrong words might have seen him maimed or dead on the forest floor. Every painful movement reminded him of Garn's unbridled rage at the mere mention of Rache's name. He knew his loyalty to his friends might still become the cause of his own death, yet he dared not discard the closeness, especially not when understanding had cost him dearly in time and misery. 'Bel, if not for Mitrian and Garn, I would never have returned to you. Until I met them, Kantar was the only person who could stand me long enough to call me a friend. He saw something in me that I didn't see myself until Mitrian helped me find it. Without it, I could never have made the commitment to you. I can't abandon her when she's in need.' He took a deep breath, not liking the words he had to say. 'At the least, you know Mitrian and Garn will come back for Kinesthe. I do love you, Bel. I'll leave you plenty of chroams and my promise to return. If that's not enough, I'll understand if you use the time my money buys you to find another man.'

Tears turned the room into a dark smudge. Arduwyn turned away and headed for the stairs, the pain in his limbs insignificant compared with the agony in his heart. Grabbing a change of clothes, he descended the stairs.

A long sword in each fist, Colbey leapt and swayed, whipping the blades in complicated patterns faster than the thoughts that spawned them. Steel flashed firelight across the granite of the Western Wizard's cave in swirling highlights of silver and gold, wound through with the ruddy reflections of dawn. Despite the intensity of maneuvers no other man could perform with such speed or accuracy, Colbey remained aware of all that occurred around him. A rabbit roasted on the campfire. Songbirds twittered from a myriad of holes in and around the Wizard's cave, and a dark spot circled the sky above Colbey's practice.

As the black shape descended, it became discernible as a small hawk. Without missing a beat, Colbey sheathed one sword, using the other to flip the rabbit in the coals. In the same motion, he whisked that blade into its rest as well. Despite an hour of constant sword sweeps and patterns, he was scarcely winded, more concerned with the spiraling, sinking falcon than the single droplet of sweat winding along a strand of hair near his ear. Surely, the bird had not mistaken him for prey, and he doubted any wild hawk would have the audacity to steal food from a man.

Leaning against the cold stone of the cave mouth, Colbey waited, savoring the clarity of mind he had achieved since he had conquered the final voice of madness soon after his arrival at the Wizard's cave. Since then, the prophetic images and the certainty of courses of action had left him, though he had had no opportunity to test whether or not he could still steal thoughts verbatim from strangers' minds. The world had regained the perfect, crystal definition he had known as a child.

The falcon approached, a tiny flame caught in a whirlwind of blue-pink sky. Suddenly, the bird dived, landing between Colbey and the campfire. It flapped red wings and regarded the Renshai with a near-human expression of intelligence. A ridge of silver surrounded its amber eyes and gave them a glare of timeless divinity.

Curious, Colbey watched in silence. In all the time he had spent in the Western Wizard's cave and at the boundary of the Weathered Mountains, he had seen numerous birds. The brush around the cave mouth was choked with thrush, sparrows and gaunt, gray birds of prey. But he had never before seen a hawk so compact nor so completely red.

The falcon cocked its crested head and seemed to study Colbey with matching intensity. Without warning, it flapped to Colbey's forearm. Long, dark toenails gouged the Renshai's naked arm, piercing deeply.

Pain stabbed through Colbey's flesh. Instinctively, he snapped his arm straight.

Unsettled, the falcon tightened its grip for balance, then, as if realizing its mistake, it released, fluttered to a stone near the cave mouth, and waited.

Colbey stared at the bloody punctures and gashes, wondering what sort of idiot falconer had taught his bird to alight on exposed flesh. Concerned this might signal war training, Colbey glared at the bird.

But it stood with its crest low and its feathers ruffled, looking as close to mortified as a falcon could manage.

Taking a rag from his pocket, Colbey clamped pressure against his mauled forearm to stop the bleeding. It hurt, but he had felt far worse in battle, and he had to guess the creature had inflicted injury unintentionally. Surely, anyone wise enough to train a bird to combat would teach it to attack for the eyes first.

The falcon cried out shrilly. It shook scarlet plumage, its neck feathers standing nearly horizontal. Only then, Colbey noticed the message bound to one scaly leg.

Cautiously, Colbey approached, careful to keep his forearms straight and angled downward, discouraging the falcon from perching. The bird watched the Renshai's approach impassively. It did not move as he reached for it, knelt, drew a dagger, and gently slashed the thong from its leg. The strip of parchment tumbled to the dirt. Still studying the falcon's every motion with suspicion, Colbey took the message. He stood.

The falcon waited.

Taking his gaze from the bird, Colbey unrolled the parchment and read in the Common runes:

> 'The War is started. Warn the West.'
> – Shadimar

Beneath the signature, Colbey noted the flourished script symbol he had seen on all of Tokar's correspondence, the mark of a Cardinal Wizard. Colbey crumpled the parchment in his fist. He stared into the sky, cold eyes flashing. 'Thank you, Odin. The Great War has begun at last, and no one can find more joy in it than I.' A lifetime of lightning swordplay, of awakening to the ache of overused muscles and tendons, of timing honed to perfection would find the chance to end as it was meant: in the wild chaos of war. Too long ago, Colbey had realized that his skill would not allow death in single combat. Three to one, six to one, ten to one, the odds did not matter. But in war there was the constant chime of weapons and the savage exchange of battle, blades sweeping in wild, directionless frenzy. Surely, here, in the greatest of all wars, the oldest of the Golden-haired Devils might find his peace at last.

Colbey glanced over at the falcon. It remained in the same position, as if awaiting an answer. It was not Colbey's way to address creatures that could not understand him, but the actions of this falcon seemed to demand that courtesy.

Colbey dropped to his haunches before the bird. 'Don't worry, falcon. The Western Wizard is dead, but I'll deliver your message in his place.'

Apparently satisfied, the red falcon loosed a guttural trill and soared into the sky.

23 Corpa Leukenya

The back of Mitrian's head and her tightly bound wrists and ankles ached with each steady throb of her heart. The stone floor of the cavern on which she lay had warmed to her body heat. Once more, she struggled against the ropes. As before, the knots held, and she managed only to further abrade the skin beneath them. Pain cut through her wrists. Blood ran in a hot and sticky wash across her fingers. The sweat of her exertions stung the wounds. She cried out in frustration and pain, then went still while the agony faded.

Stymied, Mitrian sought clues in the memory of her capture. They had come in her sleep, two Leukenyan priests and four Western followers all chosen, Mitrian guessed, for their size and some experience with weapons. The six men had not caught Mitrian completely unaware. Responding to an unexpected noise, she had met them downstairs in the main chamber. She had even managed to injure one before another caught her with a blow from behind. From that moment she remembered nothing but awakening in this rough-hewn chamber, tied and alone. From the intensity of her headache, it felt as if her attacker had struck her with a block of granite. She was still dressed in her sleeping gown, but her sword was missing.

As the pain waned to a baseline of aches, Mitrian went still, concerned for the fate of her baby. Upon awakening, she had found Garn and Kinesthe missing. Garn commonly wandered outside at night to collect his thoughts, usually with a handful of horseshoes. Mitrian never understood why the latter gave him solace, but when he refused to tell her she had never pressed. If Garn had fought the Leukenyans before her, Mitrian harbored no doubt that the noise would have awakened her sooner. It seemed improbable that the priests had killed or captured Garn and far more likely he had simply strolled off for some time alone. She felt less certain about her baby. *Does Garn have him or the Leukenyans?*

Recalling the albino who had accosted her near the berry vines just before Nantel's death, Mitrian shivered. Until now, the image had become buried and lost in the avalanche of guilt and sorrow that had followed Nantel's slaying. The stress of the trial had chased all thoughts of the encounter from her mind. Now she remembered that the priest had said his people wanted Kinesthe for enlightenment. She had doubted his intentions then. Aware the priests could have killed her rather than take her prisoner, Mitrian realized it had been her they wanted all along.

The door creaked open. Mitrian twisted her head to watch a barefoot albino dressed in the accustomed white robes and feathered headband enter her room and close the door behind him. Silently, he padded across the uneven surface of the floor, stopping beside Mitrian's head. He dropped to a crouch.

Mitrian blinked, meeting eyes as soft and blue as her own.

'Ah, good, you're awake,' he said matter-of-factly. 'I was worried we'd killed you.' Despite his words, his tone did not contain the slightest hint of concern.

'If you want me alive, I suggest you loosen my bindings.' Mitrian tried to hide her fear behind reason. 'If they amputate my wrists and ankles, I'm sure to bleed to death.'

The Leukenyan shrugged off the necessity, his thin, silver hair rising with his shoulders. 'God just likes his sacrifices alive. As far as I know, he doesn't care if they have hands and feet.'

Surprise shocked through Mitrian, verging on panic. No god she had ever heard of demanded men as sacrifices, though Rache had spoken of Odin whose female messengers, the *Valkyries,* accepted the souls of the bravest warriors from battlefields. 'You kidnapped me to sacrifice me to some god?' The suggestion seemed ludicrous. If Pudarian citizens were routinely taken by Leukenyans, Mitrian felt certain she would have heard rumors. She doubted King Gasir would allow such a plague to strike his city without taking vengeance on Corpa Leukenya.

'God,' the priest corrected. 'With a capital "g." The one and only true god. The White God, the All Mighty.' He made a grand gesture of reverence. 'He who stays with His chosen people and stands guard over His altar.' Having corrected Mitrian's error, he addressed her question. 'And no. We took you to lure the Renshai who follows you here. We've left enough of a trail for him to track you. Now we no longer have need for you. If we give you to God, He will bless this endeavor, giving us the strength we need to kill Rache.'

Rache? Perplexed, Mitrian stared. Before, when the priest had called her Santagithi's daughter, Mitrian had marveled at the information he had managed to collect. Now, having heard one link her name to a sword master she had not seen for nearly a year, she realized that, as true as the information was, it was sorely dated. Mitrian considered, recalling that Arduwyn had mentioned something about Rache after the trial. She tried to remember his exact phrasing, but her state of mind at the time had been hazy enough that, combined with her current headache, she could not recall a single word. Hoping to ascertain Kinesthe's safety, she tried a different question. 'I thought it was my baby you wanted, not me.'

'You thought wrong. We have no use for an infant, except, perhaps, as a sacrifice.'

Mitrian shuddered. Still, the priest's ambiguous phrasing suggested they had not captured Kinesthe, and, for that, she was grateful. The ceaseless pounding in her skull made thought nearly impossible. 'Does your god . . .' She caught herself. 'I mean, does God often have you sacrifice people?'

The Leukenyan clasped his hands on his thighs. 'It is not something He asks of us. It is something He appreciates that we do for Him when we can. Usually it's an occasional outcast or a hunter who strayed too far. Rarely, a worshiper becomes gravely ill and begs to become a sacrifice, or one becomes deluded by a false religion and we have to destroy him.' He smiled encouragingly. 'I hear you're a princess.'

'You hear wrong.' Mitrian adopted the priest's speech pattern. 'I'm no one special.'

The priest shrugged.

Mitrian did not press. If the priests accepted outcasts and fatally ill as sacrifices, the position did not require a test of worth. 'What do you want with Rache, anyway?'

The priest made a vague, uninterpretable signal with his head. 'I'm not at liberty to say. In fact, I think I've already told you more than I should. I'm not here to talk, only to see that you don't escape before the ceremony at sundown.'

'Today?' Mitrian had found denying death a simple matter while it remained a distant threat. A date and time gave it an imminence she could not ignore. Terror shivered through her, and the movement chewed the ropes deeper into her wrists.

The albino yawned, apparently bored. 'Why wait?'

'Because.' Mitrian waded through dread and pain to pry logic from her clouded mind. 'Because Rache's not stupid. He'll get you in a compromise position. He'll make you prove you've really got me before he surrenders.' It was a lie. Mitrian knew Rache would act rather than plot. He would hack his way through three-quarters of Corpa Leukenya's citizens before it ever occurred to him to barter, but she also realized he, if anyone, would not be the one who came to rescue her.

The priest smiled. 'Once God has taken our offering, He will see to it we do not fail.'

*

Rage had left Garn an hour back, but his heart still raced at every sound. Urgency thrilled through him, and he would have galloped his steed to its death if not for Arduwyn's logic and Sterrane's restraining hands. Now they stood beneath a canopy of maple and pine that leaked droplets and trickles of rain, Mitrian's trail lost.

'We're wasting time,' Garn growled, fighting the urge to race off without his dawdling companions.

'Garn, please.' Arduwyn spoke through gritted teeth, assailed by his own concern and self-doubt. 'In all the years I've hunted here, I've never seen so many patrols. The Leukenyans are expecting someone, presumably us. You've got a scout. Let me do my job.'

Garn groused, twitching with annoyance. 'What good will it do Mitrian for us to arrive safely after she's dead?'

'What good,' Arduwyn shot back, 'will it do Mitrian for us to die before we reach her?' He tossed his head. 'If the priests wanted to kill her, they could have done so back at the house.' He accepted the reins of his chestnut mare from Sterrane, leaving Sterrane the huge white gelding he had won from the dock foreman. Arduwyn was still amazed no one had accused Sterrane of theft and murder on account of that horse. 'Just follow me.' Arduwyn brushed through the foliage.

Garn and Sterrane followed, the larger man silently, the other grumbling about 'hindrances' and 'thieves in the night.'

Arduwyn winced at the comparative amount of noise Garn made as he moved through the brush. He pitied Sterrane for the time he had spent alone with the ex-slave; it had taken Arduwyn more than a few moments to map the patterns of sentries and watch posts leading to the lone mountain that framed the natural caverns of Corpa Leukenya's temple. In his five years as a Pudarian citizen, Arduwyn had hunted the area thoroughly. In all that time, he had seen Leukenyans only occasionally, rarely armed and never in the clusters and ambush formations he found them in now. *Something's happening. Something big.* The thought chilled him, and the priest's warning glare at the city gates returned, unbidden, to his mind. *Do they still want Sterrane to join them? To kill me for interfering?*

Arduwyn continued from memory, making generous circles around the warded areas, though each loop sparked Garn's protests. The hunter delved into remembrances he would rather have forgotten. Some years ago, in the early days of the cult of Corpa Leukenya, a fellow hunter had returned to Pudar claiming to have found a woman's body, ritually slashed and with rope burns at wrists and ankles. Led to the site of the discovery, the Pudarian authorities had found no trace of the corpse. The Leukenyans had responded politely to questioning, denying knowledge of the incident with a sincerity that had satisfied the king's officials. Soon after, rumors stated that the hunter became so obsessed with the cult he joined it himself. Not long after that, Arduwyn discovered the hunter's body, similarly mutilated.

Arduwyn shivered at the memory. He had thought of packing the hunter's corpse onto Stubs and presenting the evidence directly to the king's men. But to do so would have risked the possibility of being accused of the murder. Relatively new to Pudar then and recently banished from Erythane, Arduwyn doubted his ability to defend himself if such allegations were leveled. Even had he succeeded, he would have had to contend with the vengeance of an entire cult and its followers, a vengeance that might as easily have been taken against Kantar and his family as Arduwyn. To this day, Arduwyn questioned the wisdom and honor of his decision to let the corpse lie.

The sun swept westward, beginning the final downstroke of its daily frown. As the sun sank, the clouds parted, making the day seem endlessly drab, the same damp gray from twilight to dusk. Garn's restlessness transformed into a stinging need for action. Arduwyn's route wasted time and energy, and it had already taken them abreast of and beyond the temple's lone mountain. At length, the hunter snaked toward the jagged rear slope of Corpa Leukenya's peak.

'The entrance is on the other side.' Garn's patience had worn thin.

'I know.' Arduwyn dismounted, scouring the rocks with eyes and hands. Without looking, he pulled his scimitar from the donkey's pack and strapped it to his waist.

Garn and Sterrane clambered down from their steeds as well, helping Arduwyn in a search they did not understand. 'What are we looking for ?' Garn demanded.

'A crack,' Arduwyn called back. 'I found it once when a bear I was hunting seemed to disappear. It ran deep into the mountain, too far for me to risk chasing a predator in the darkness.'

Arduwyn did not need to add that he had no way of knowing if the passage connected with the caverns inside the temple. The possibility seemed unlikely ; if so, he would have expected the crevice to be well-traveled by priests.

Garn groaned. 'Better we'd fought through all their patrols than get lost in a crack that leads nowhere.'

Arduwyn ignored the reproach. He probed more frantically, measuring peaks and angles with his gaze.

Sterrane swore, leaping from a clump of thorny bushes growing beneath an overhang. A dull, brown viper slithered back toward a small cave. Sterrane's ax sliced through air and hacked the snake's head from its body.

'Careful,' Arduwyn said belatedly. He ran to his huge companion's side. 'Are you all right? Did it bite you?'

'It miss.' He smiled happily. 'But I find cave.'

Garn shoved past Sterrane, but Arduwyn moved more quickly. The hunter plunged into the canyon on hands and knees. Garn scuttled after, hearing Sterrane scratch and scramble behind him.

Arduwyn was speaking, but his words disseminated unintelligibly into the darkness. An oath uncharacteristically harsh for Sterrane echoed faintly through the cavern behind Garn. Arduwyn moved with swift precision, and Garn rushed as fast as his cramped position allowed. The floor of the cavern rose and fell, alternately smooth as ice or sharp as shattered glass. Oblivious to rents torn in his clothing and skin, Garn pushed onward. The passage narrowed gradually.

Sterrane's voice wafted clearly to Garn. 'Me stuck. Can't go on.'

Arduwyn responded. 'Sterrane, go back and stay with the horses. If we're not back by morning, get help. If this does lead to the temple, I doubt we'll be able to leave by the same route.'

If it's a route at all. Garn did not waste breath. The rage he had abandoned was returning with each delay. The stone of the walls scraped his jerkin, closing in on Garn until he felt certain he would soon become trapped, wedged between stone. Brutally, he cursed Arduwyn.

Arduwyn stopped suddenly, signaling Garn to be quiet.

Garn obeyed. Only then, could he hear intermittent noises.

Arduwyn crawled forward slowly. The sounds became identifiable as voices wafting from far below them, too muffled to comprehend.

The corridor made a sharp bend. Garn continued until his broad shoulders jammed between the sides. Unable to squeeze past, he swore, retreated, changed his angle of approach, and pressed forward. His jerkin caught on irregularities in the wall. He paused, brought nearly to tears by failure.

Adrenaline heightened Garn's senses enough to decipher most of what was being said below him. A compelling voice droned a story that his audience must have found familiar. Every few lines, they chanted a word or phrase in a powerful unison that indicated great numbers.

'... and God landed on the lone mountain. "Here," He said, "You shall build your temple ..."'

The group chorused. '"Chosen Ones!"'

'"Here beneath the shadow of My wings shall you make a temple of caverns and stone ..."'

Unison: ' "where you shall dwell beneath My protection for eternity." '

Garn stepped back, wriggling out of his leather shirt.

The leader continued, 'This having been done, God inspected the work of His . . .'

'Chosen People !'

'And found it to be good. "I will stay with you so long as your love remains loyal and your faith true," He said. "I will rise against your enemies when the need comes, and, one day, I will take the souls of My faithful from the Yonderworld to a place of ultimate harmony. The souls of the pagans, I shall destroy." '

Garn again attempted to push through the gap. Stone gashed his naked sides, and he felt as if his shoulders might break. Then he slid through into a wider opening. Ahead, Arduwyn crouched before a hole in the floor of the cavern.

The crowd finished as one. 'So saying, God landed on the altar and transformed Himself to stone !'

'Oh, no,' Arduwyn said.

It was the kind of understated expletive most men would use for a minor annoyance, but Arduwyn's tone as he bit off the syllables convinced Garn of a drastic situation. He sprang to the hole and stared over Arduwyn's shoulder.

After the perfect blackness of the tunnel, a vision of gleaming white nearly blinded Garn. Dangerously far below him, a mass of worshipers in white robes and feathers filled the room. Garn twisted his head, pushing Arduwyn down with a hand to gain a better view of the events directly beneath him. Bound hand and foot, Mitrian lay on an altar before an alabaster statue. A fat priest in shimmering garb hovered over her. He clutched Mitrian's jeweled sword in both fists, his hands hovering over her chest.

There was no time for thought. Garn vaulted through the hole. He met resistance as his momentum swept Arduwyn through before him. Mitrian, Arduwyn, and the priest screamed as one. Air surged around Garn, and his wits exploded with the terror of a fall that might prove fatal.

Coincidentally, the sword plummeted from the priest's hand and chimed against the altar block as the fat man clamped his fingers to his face to shut out the sword's demon images.

Garn caught sight of Arduwyn rolling across the platform. Then Garn struck ground feet first, with knees bent. Pain shocked through his legs. He rolled, sword out before he knew he had reached for it.

A bead of sweat wound along the priest's nose. Before it touched his lips, Garn struck the Leukenyan's head from his shoulders.

The gasps of a multitude spun Garn. A sea of white robes, candles, and feathers confronted him. Rage reddened each face. The scene swayed dizzily before Garn. Intoxicated by his own adrenaline, Garn watched them as though through a dream.

Arduwyn hastily cut the cords binding Mitrian.

Garn's sword fell from his fingers, useless against the limitless tide of worshipers surging toward him. Garn glanced right and left but saw no escape. Between him and the Leukenyans stood nothing but the grotesque, ivory statue carved into man-shape with a falcon's head and wings. Its ruby eyes glowed with contempt, as if it dared Garn to challenge a god surrounded by its followers. *I'm going to die.* Garn accepted the penalty, hoping a savage sacrifice might divert the Leukenyans long enough to spare Mitrian and Arduwyn. He retreated inside himself, and there discovered a now familiar strength.

As the cultists surged toward them, Mitrian snatched up her sword and Arduwyn searched the walls for a passage. Far above them, the opening through which they had descended leered, unattainably distant, three times the height of the idol above them.

Garn lunged at the ruby-eyed statue. It towered a full head above him and twice as wide, sneering at the muscular flyspeck with the gall to try to topple a god.

The Leukenyans hesitated, united in shock.

Slick with exertion, Garn knew their surprised outrage would turn to bloodlust the moment it became apparent that the stone rebuffed him easily. Words seared Garn's mind in Colbey's voice: 'If you find no weak spot, create it.' Any man stronger than his task could produce the weaknesses he needed to succeed. Once Garn had heard of a volcano that hurled chunks of stone as large as this for leagues. That power must be his.

A picture of the great explosion formed in his mind, vivid in every detail. Red heat roiled from the pit. Tons of rock flew like pebbles. With a howl, Garn threw his shoulder against the statue, drawing on the power entrenched between body and mind, the strength he had found within his soul. A cracking noise echoed through the cavern temple. The bird-man rocked on its foundation.

Screaming, the Leukenyans retreated. The idol crashed to the floor, shattering itself and dozens of its followers. Chips rattled, skittering across granite.

Breathless, Garn turned to the empty altar. After the roar of the statue's fall, Arduwyn's whisper sounded ridiculous. 'Garn, hurry!'

Despite Arduwyn's haste, the three were in no danger. Garn followed, watching his smaller companion limp between moaning or panicked Leukenyans and fragments of ivory. Mitrian took Garn's arm, and he embraced her with an exuberance that bordered on violence. 'If I can do that to a god, imagine what I can do to a man.'

Mitrian shuddered in his grip.

King Gasir of Pudar studied the lean, aging Northman in his court with a respect usually reserved for other royalty. The silver-flecked golden hair was cropped unusually short, especially for a Northman whose warriors customarily wore their locks in braids. The creases etched in the man's cheeks seemed more from rugged experience than age. The gray eyes never left Gasir's face, and they radiated a stony mercilessness untempered by humanity. His stance was relaxed, yet there was a predatory readiness about him. 'A war,' the king muttered.

'The war, sire,' Colbey said. 'The long awaited confrontation with the East.'

Gasir frowned. *If only I could be certain of this stranger.* Northmen came only occasionally to Pudar and always in close-knit, tribal units. This one had arrived without others of his kind, accompanied by an army of soldiers mustered from the towns between the Weathered Mountains and Pudar. They awaited their leader just outside the open city gates. *By every legend, the Western Wizard would bring news of the Great War.*

Colbey replied as if the king's concern had been spoken aloud. 'The Western Wizard has other business. He sent me in his place.'

Unsettled by Colbey's reference to his thought, King Gasir avoided the Northman's eyes. 'Have your soldiers enter the city. I'll need a few weeks to muster my army and gather allies.'

'Days would be better, sire.' Despite his contradiction, Colbey spoke with the utmost respect. 'I've got scouts out now. From the time they're taking to return, I'd guess the Easterners have come no farther than the Western Plains. Better the battle there, sire, then let them take Béarn's fortifications or siege Pudar.'

'Days, then.' King Gasir felt suddenly old. There had been peace in the Westlands for long enough to make a king careless, but Gasir had resisted laziness. His elite guard force practiced military maneuvers daily; the main body of his army spent eight days of each month training. Raising allies that quickly might prove more difficult, but he had little choice. He hoped Santagithi's returning guards would manage to league with some of the farm towns. Even a swiftly riding messenger might not make the trip to the general's town quickly enough to mobilize Santagithi's troops.

'Sire,' Colbey continued. 'If I may ask about a more personal matter?'

Gasir nodded assent. His usual retinue of guards shifted uneasily.

'A young family came to your city some months ago, Garn, Mitrian, and their unborn child.'

'I know them,' the king admitted, wondering whether Colbey was a friend or foe to this most unusual couple. Swordsmen of their skill would tend to have powerful feuds as well as alliances. 'What of them?'

Colbey glanced casually over the semicircle of guards around their king. 'I don't know your policy on women or foreigners in your ranks, but you could do far worse than Mitrian and Garn and not a lot better.'

Touched by the irony of the situation, King Gasir scratched his chin through his honey-colored beard. 'I currently have no women in my ranks. I would have made an exception for Mitrian, had she not made that impossible.' Briefly, he relayed the encounter in his courtroom.

Colbey remained silent until the tale was told. 'And Rache? Was he involved in that incident as well?'

'Rache?' King Gasir turned the scratch into a repetitive stroking of his beard. He dredged the name from memory. 'Santagithi's legendary Northman sword master?'

'Legendary, sire?' Colbey's pale features knitted. 'Is that how the common man denies hard-won skill these days? In my time, they credited it to lies or magic.' Colbey's words seemed undirected. 'I assure you, sire, Rache is as real as you and I. I wondered if he had a part in the incident?'

'No.' *At least none of the men involved used his name.* King Gasir considered whether he should feel offended by Colbey's reference to the common man. The words did not sting, so he chose to believe Colbey's intentions were harmless.

Again, Colbey appeared to read King Gasir's thoughts. 'If Rache was there, sire, you would know him.' Colbey waved a hand so deeply scarred with calluses that it looked as if his sword had never left his hand since birth. 'If you would like to unite our units, we'll need to meet later for strategy.'

'Here. Over dinner,' King Gasir confirmed. 'Bring any officers you might have.'

Colbey nodded his agreement, turned, and left the courtroom, flanked by a half dozen Pudarian guardsmen.

King Gasir sagged in his chair. He stared after the retreating Northman, sick with an alien certainty that, weaponless or not, Colbey could have killed every man in his courtroom without a thought. The king shook his head, unable to understand why, despite his lethality, the Northman inspired an awe and trust no logic could explain.

24 War to the Death

No moon disturbed the inky depths of the forests south of Pudar. Wind ruffled the treetops, dislodging a rain of moist poplar petals over Mitrian and Arduwyn. The woman sat on a deadfall, the ache of her wrists and ankles accentuating the exhaustion of a full day's travel. *In the wrong direction*, she surmised, and Arduwyn's restless pacing made her all the more certain of her decision to confront him. Unconscious during the ride to Corpa Leukenya, she could not have recognized forest landmarks, even if one tree did appear different to her than another. But it did not require a perfect knowledge of woodlands to realize that they were headed due east rather than north and east.

Even so, Mitrian would have accepted Arduwyn's choice of direction unquestioningly if not for Sterrane's gentle suggestions that they veer north and Arduwyn's obvious discomfort at the mention of changing course. She had never heard the hunter snap at their childlike companion before. Arduwyn's second reprimand to Sterrane had been enough to silence the huge hermit for the last half day of travel.

'You're right,' Arduwyn admitted. 'I'm taking a side trip before returning to Pudar.'

'Why?'

'I promised someone I'd meet him.' Arduwyn stopped at the far edge of his paced route, his back to Mitrian, as if he actually imagined that explanation might placate her.

Mitrian yawned. 'Who? And where?'

Arduwyn answered in the reverse order, his reply soft and garbled beneath the rattle of spring greenery. 'At the edge of the Southern Mountains. And it's . . .' His voice trailed into obscurity.

Mitrian pressed relentlessly. 'It's *who?* Speak up, Ardy. I'm tired, and I can't hear you.'

Arduwyn spun on his heel. 'It's . . .' He raised his voice. Coincidentally, the wind died so that the name emerged louder than he intended '. . . Rache.'

Emotion assaulted Mitrian, a wild mixture she hardly dared to separate. Afraid to be overwhelmed by mistake, she forced a confirmation. 'Rache?'

Arduwyn's reply left no room for doubt. 'Rache the Renshai. Your father's captain.'

Joy rose in a wild crescendo that dwarfed Mitrian's other sentiments. Her heart rate quickened, seeming to flutter in her chest. Leaping to her feet, she caught Arduwyn's hands. 'Rache? You know where Rache is? Gods, Arduwyn. I have to see him.'

Arduwyn's somber expression raised a reality that crushed Mitrian's excitement.

Hurling his hands away from her, she turned. 'Rache? Are you insane, or don't you know? Garn and Rache are bitterest enemies. They'll kill each other.'

'I know,' Arduwyn said softly.

Mitrian whirled, staring. 'And?'

'And?' Arduwyn repeated.

'Are you saying that's what you want?' Incredulity and rage raised Mitrian's voice to a shout.

Arduwyn cringed, reminding Mitrian that their companions, though sleeping, lay not all that far away. 'Of course I don't want them to die. But they have to meet sometime.'

'Why?'

'You heard Colbey. The Great War is imminent. We'll all have to be there.'

'So?'

'You think a Renshai would avoid it? Rache will be there, too.'

Mitrian missed the connection. 'What matter? You're not making sense. In war, they'll be too busy fighting enemies to seek each other out.'

Arduwyn snorted, dismissing Mitrian's argument. 'Do you really believe that, given the choice between decapitating Rache or an Eastern soldier, Garn would choose the stranger? Can you imagine the confusion in the ranks if one warrior turned against a second-in-command on his own side? The potential chaos would be frightening.'

'I'll keep them apart,' Mitrian promised. 'There'll be thousands of other soldiers. Maybe tens of thousands. And I've kept them apart so far.'

'*You've* done it so far?' Now it was Arduwyn who shouted. 'I'll bet you haven't seen Rache since you left home. I've seen him hundreds of times, even talked to him once. He followed us all the way to Pudar, and it's only because of Colbey, me, and a lucky diversion that Rache and Garn haven't met already.'

The news stunned Mitrian. 'I had no idea . . .'

Arduwyn broke in, his voice softer. 'Of course you had no idea. They're both quiet, smart, and quick. In the heat of battle, you'll never be able to keep those men separated. And don't think they won't hunt down one another. You sorely underestimate Garn's hatred if you think that.'

Mitrian recovered swiftly. 'So, what are you saying? Better to let one or both die now? Before the war? I'd rather take my chances on the war killing one before they meet. At least that death would not be in vain.' The tears seemed to come from nowhere. Before Mitrian realized her fear for the two men she loved, her cheeks were wet, her vision a moist blur.

Arduwyn put an arm around Mitrian's shoulder and sat with her on the deadfall. 'Mitrian, in war, anything can happen. Here, I've got some control over the situation. My intention is to see to it both men survive and come to a truce of some sort. Rache, at least, has shown a willingness to try.'

Mitrian looked up, her view of Arduwyn's face marred by multicolored bars of salt water clinging to her lashes. 'Garn?'

Arduwyn dodged the question. 'It has to be done. And I promised Rache. It wouldn't do to break the trust of the one side amenable to compromise.'

Mitrian buried her face in Arduwyn's tunic. And cried.

When the first red streaks of sunlight colored the horizon, Arduwyn, mounted on his chestnut mare, led his companions through warm, damp forests of oak and hickory. He identified mayapple, crocus, and the tracks of animals that Mitrian would have missed without his guidance, all the while telling stories of hunts and myths with such beauty that she almost managed to forget her concerns and the pain of her abraded wrists and ankles for a time.

The forest thinned. Arduwyn drew rein on a trail overgrown with vines and weeds. He pointed to a faded square of gold dye on a tree trunk. '"The Road of the King." Legends say the Eastern Wizard rescued the young prince of Béarn by this route and will return him the same way.' Having imparted that piece of history, he kicked his horse into a slow walk toward the plains.

Recalling Shadimar's reference to her helping to restore the prince of Béarn and glad for the distraction of another of Arduwyn's stories, Mitrian pressed for details. 'Why would a prince need to be rescued?'

Arduwyn swung his head toward Mitrian, clearly surprised. 'I know you lived pretty far east, but you're still from west of the Great Mountains. That means you live in Béarn's realm. All Westerners know Valar's story. Don't they?'

'I don't,' Mitrian admitted.

'Amazing.' Arduwyn shook his head. 'Do your elders teach you anything at all?'

Mitrian opened her mouth to defend her father's historical tales, but before she could speak, Garn broke in.

Resentment chilled his words. 'They teach us how to kill. For fun, they force peaceful men to slaughter one another.' He kicked his mount to a trot.

Dumbfounded by Garn's bitterness, Mitrian stared after him. She had not heard him make reference to his years as a gladiator since their night together in the Granite Hills. Giving Arduwyn a weak grin of apology, she caught up to Garn. 'You're a free man. With a wife who loves you and a child.' Mitrian's words brought home the bitter ache of leaving her infant behind but also the joy she'd felt when she learned for certain that he was safely in Pudar. She knew she would see Kinesthe again soon and that he could not rest in safer arms than Bel's, but those comforts hardly seemed enough. Forced to tend Garn, she pushed concern for her child aside. 'The only chains that bind you now are the ones you've made with hatred.'

Garn did not meet Mitrian's gaze. 'I have one more thing to do before I'm truly free.'

'More?' Mitrian took his arm, trying to guess the task that obsessed Garn. 'You've toppled a god. Surely you could break a horseshoe if that's what ails you.'

Garn raised his head, but he stared through Mitrian. 'I harnessed that strength for a purpose.' Unconsciously, he tensed, and the muscles in his forearms swelled. 'I won't be cheated.'

The distant, feral glow in Garn's eyes frightened Mitrian. 'Garn?'

'I will kill Rache.'

Mitrian's blood seemed to turn to ice. All color drained from her. *How could Garn know where we're going?* It came to her suddenly that Garn was reacting to his own mastery of strength independent of Arduwyn's choice of route. Still, his timing seemed uncanny. Chills racked Mitrian. She huddled deeper into her cloak as despair blossomed into anger. Her grip cinched tight on Garn's flesh. 'Haven't you done enough damage?'

Garn's head snapped toward Mitrian.

'You're free. Nantel is dead. Rache is crippled. You've destroyed two of the few people I've ever loved. Isn't that enough?'

'Destroyed? Not . . .' Garn seemed to have great difficulty speaking the name '. . . Rache. He's not destroyed until he can't fight.' His stare went beyond Mitrian. 'Before I kill him, I'll make certain he never finds Valhalla.' He added carefully, 'And he knows it.'

Garn's words crushed Mitrian into silence. For the first time since

she thought she had come to understand him as a scared teenager
fleeing an oppression that was also the only home he'd ever known,
Mitrian hated Garn. It pained her to admit a mistake. *Perhaps Garn
is every bit the animal the guards described him to be.* The thought
brought warm, fierce tears to her eyes. *Perhaps he only married me
to avenge himself against my father.* Mitrian gritted her teeth, letting
outrage flare until her vision washed red. Then reality slashed
through, belying the direction her thoughts were taking. Garn's love
and tenderness over the past year could not be denied. Her memories
of him remained strong, direct contrast to the side of himself he
chose to show her now. *How can this be the same man?*

Engrossed in thought, Mitrian did not notice when Garn pulled
free of her grip. Her first recognition that Arduwyn had ridden up
beside her was the closeness of his voice when he began his story :

'For many years, the mountain kingdom of Béarn was ruled by a
succession of benevolent kings.'

Mitrian raised her hand, her intention to silence Arduwyn. Then,
hoping but doubting a story could take her mind from the painful
maelstrom of thought that assailed her, she let him continue.

'The land prospered. The Béarnides grew strong and robust.
Eventually, the remainder of the Westlands accepted the Béarnian
ruler as their own.'

Though Arduwyn told the tale with his usual skill, Mitrian heard
it as if from a great distance. They continued riding as he spoke, but
she no longer noticed the beauty around her as they journeyed across
the plains into low mountains. She recalled only a vague story of
twin princes, Valar, who, as eldest, claimed the kingship and
Morhane who usurped the throne by violence and tried to destroy
his brother's line. Arduwyn finished his tale with the legend of a
single survivor of the carnage, a middle child of Valar's seven sons
and seven daughters, a boy rescued by the Eastern Wizard. If the
West won the Great War, the prince, Arduwyn said, would return
to claim his throne.

The forest opened to a lush valley. Uprooted trees and oddly
shaped boulders lay scattered before the entrance. Steep cliffs
stretched toward the sky in two rows, like giant's teeth guarding the
vale. Apparently drawn to the open ease of riding the grassy area,
Garn steered his chestnut straight into the clearing. Arduwyn hesitated, apparently made uneasy by the enclosing mountains. Less
suspicious, Sterrane and Mitrian trailed Garn, and the clop of hooves
behind them cued Mitrian that Arduwyn had swallowed his uneasiness and followed.

Mitrian and her companions had scarcely crossed half the meadow
when a mounted figure glided from a crack in the base of the crags.

Sunlight reflecting from stone glazed him into an unidentifiable, dark shape, and the voice that rumbled between the cliffs was unfamiliar. 'Halt! You're entering private territory. State your business.'

Stunned silent, Mitrian did not think to stop Garn from answering.

The ex-gladiator's violent mood came clearly through his words. 'We're headed home. Just passing by. Get out of our way.' He took the stranger's abrupt appearance in stride, though surely he realized the route home deviated from the one he had taken to get to Corpa Leukenya, if only because he had not met any similar challenges en route.

'Turn around, then.' The man waved a spear, the movement of his arm casting his face momentarily in shadow. Only then, did Mitrian notice one eye socket was empty. 'You may not pass.'

Apparently annoyed by the formality, Garn spurred his mount. 'Try and stop me.'

'Garn, wait . . .' Mitrian started.

The stranger gave a hawklike call as Garn's horse lunged forward. A wall of arrows fell from the cliffs.

Mitrian screamed. Garn drew up. Arduwyn edged to the ex-gladiator's side. 'Be still.' He kept his gaze fixed on rows of drawn bows on the cliffs. 'If they had wanted to kill you, they could have. You can barter better alive than dead.'

A second horseman joined the first, then another and another. Soon a small army grew behind him, lean, hard men with sober faces dressed in armor of rings, scales, or leather. Mitrian's hand slid to her sword. The demon's presence filled her, coiled and questioning. Its excitement combined with her own, heightening her senses until several oddities became clear. Some of the soldiers before her had missing limbs, other had scarred visages that made Nantel seem beautiful. Most looked like normal men, but even those inspired a discomfort that went beyond facing an army of enemies with only three allies.

'Easy, Garn,' Arduwyn whispered, catching the bridle of his companion's horse. 'Anything is preferable to death.'

Garn stared straight ahead. 'I'd welcome death before capture.'

Before the implications of Garn's words touched Mitrian, he kicked his horse savagely. It sprang forward, torn from Arduwyn's grasp.

'No!' Mitrian screamed. The image of Garn filled with arrows made her dizzy with concern, but only one shaft sped for him. It lodged behind the horse's ribs and sank deep.

Garn's mount lurched and tumbled, legs jerking. Garn hurtled. He twisted as he fell, landed on his side and lay still.

Gods. Mitrian caught at her face, staring, afraid of what she might see. Cautious of the archers, she dismounted and knelt at Garn's side. Up close, she watched him struggle for the air the fall had battered from his lungs. The horse kicked in a death frenzy, alone and untended.

No one spoke. Gradually, Garn's breathing eased. As Mitrian's concern ebbed, she dared to wonder why only one archer had fired at Garn. Her mind traced the trajectory of the arrow to its source. *Arduwyn.* Horrified, Mitrian glanced at the flailing horse. The tiny piece of shaft protruding from the wound revealed the edge of a royal blue crest while the arrows of the warning volley all bore double red rings. *How could he!* Mitrian craned her neck toward her trailing companions, latching her gaze onto Arduwyn. 'Traitor,' she snarled. 'You could have killed him.'

Arduwyn lowered his bow and his head. She expected him to rattle something about how the bowmen on the cliffs would certainly have killed Garn if Arduwyn had not felled his headstrong companion first, or to point out that he had, after all, shot the horse and not the man. But Arduwyn wisely chose a regretful silence that allowed Mitrian to turn her attention back to Garn.

Mitrian watched Garn settle into a normal breathing pattern, immobile, as he mentally explored his body for injuries. Against her will, her mind filled with images of the guardhouse warmth and another still figure on a pallet of straw. Suddenly, she felt as protective as a mother bear. Arduwyn's idea of uniting Garn and Rache before the war became the madness of a known betrayer. *Whatever it takes, I'll have to keep one of them from the War.*

Eventually Garn rose, limping back to the party.

Mitrian followed. 'Are you all right?'

'Just bruised,' Garn grumbled. He sounded disappointed, obviously unaware of Arduwyn's treachery.

Mitrian clung close, afraid he would try to rush the soldiers again. Husband and wife paused beside Sterrane's white gelding and faced the strangers again.

Whispers swept the warrior's ranks. Only one was interpretable. The cliffs gathered a voice with a heavy Northern accent and splintered it into echoes. 'Rache, are these the ones you were expecting?'

Garn whirled. Mitrian's heart missed a beat, and the certainty of imminent death swept her before the rhythm corrected itself. She mounted her stocky bay without thought, her eyes locked on the small army blocking the exit from the meadow.

Gradually, the soldiers shifted to admit a hugely muscled black stallion that dwarfed its rider. The row of bowmen on the cliffs blotted the sun enough to display Rache in vivid detail. Mitrian expected the events of the last year to have aged him decades; she knew Garn and she had changed greatly in attitude and appearance. Yet in his ageless, timeless way, Rache looked no different than he had at Mitrian's first sword lesson. Not a single crease marred features that blended the hungry promise of a hero with the innocence of youth. He sat, straight and proud, upon his steed, showing no evidence of his handicap other than the contrast between the slender legs and the brawny arms trained to replace them. Functionally short, wheaten hair framed eyes as blue and chill as sapphire chips. To Mitrian, his beauty was breathtaking. The years seemed to slip away, leaving her a dazzled teen secretly thrilled with the rumors that she and her father's captain were lovers rather than sharing a bond as strong and platonic as siblings.

Mitrian quelled the urge to dismount, run to Rache, and catch him in an embrace, so it completely unbalanced her when Sterrane did exactly that. Her bearlike companion clutched Rache's waist, his head against a leather-clad thigh, his shoulder pressed to the glossy stallion.

Rache laughed, stroking Sterrane's thick, black hair as if the huge man were a puppy. 'He talked you into coming, Sterrane? Inappropriate perhaps, considering the circumstances, but I'm honored.'

Shocked by Rache's familiarity with Sterrane and confused by his words, Mitrian did not notice as Garn sprang to the saddle of Sterrane's white gelding.

Garn's challenge rang over the chatter. 'So, Rache, coward and son of cowards. Still hiding behind drawn bows, I see.'

All eyes whipped to Garn. Rache stiffened at the insult. His hands went instinctively to his hilts, and the stallion sidled away from Sterrane. Still, when Rache spoke, he seemed composed. 'Garn. *Free man.*' Trying too hard, Rache stumbled over the words. 'You can call me savage, violent, a cruel and bitter teacher. You can call me by any swear word you may have learned. But even you know I'm no coward. Whatever else you feel for me, Garn, you can't deny that I never shied from your challenge. Never. In fact, Garn, if I had given you a sharpened weapon when you asked for it in the practice room, you wouldn't be here bothering me now. And I would still walk.'

Mitrian held her breath, glad to see Garn's hatred had not driven him to forget about the archers. Hurling gibes or compliments, at least the two were talking.

Garn granted no quarter. 'I see only what I see now. A swordsman hiding from one man behind rows of bowmen.'

Rache grumbled something unintelligible, but his expression

revealed waning control. He twisted far enough to address a one-handed Northern commander in chain mail.

The other man shouted a foreign command that Mitrian did not understand. The archers on the cliffs lowered their bows, and the soldiers quietly filed back through the pass.

Garn did not waste a second. The gelding charged, matching the speed of Garn's sword as it left its sheath.

But Rache moved more quickly. His stallion lurched around to shield Sterrane from the inevitable battle, and his blades cleared leather while Garn's was only three-quarters free. Draw speed made no difference. By the time the white horse met the black, all three swords cleaved air. Garn's attack crashed against Rache's cross-block with enough force to off-balance the Renshai. Catlike, Rache caught his balance, aided by Bein's equalizing sidestep, but the maneuver sacrificed his offensive. Garn's sword hammered at him again.

This time Rache dodged, apparently not wanting to sample Garn's inhuman strength a second time. Garn's sword swept air, gaining momentum in a whistling circle. Both men attacked at once.

Desperate, Mitrian spurred her mount. The bay leapt for the center of the fray. Mitrian acted half by intent and half by instinct. Of the two, Garn had never needed to learn to pull blows. As a teacher, Rache had learned to react to the unexpected. So Mitrian concentrated on Garn. Her mount shouldered between the other horses, sending the white into a twisted, half-rear while the black stood firm. She saw fear in Garn's eyes as his sword slammed down on hers with a strength that wrenched every tendon in her arms. The demon's screams reverberated through her mind as it knew the certainty of her death on Rache's blade behind her.

But Mitrian felt the breeze of the sword's passage against the side of her head. Rache swore, the redirection of a certain death stroke all but toppling him from the horse. Both men went still.

Even mounted, Garn held the stance of a gladiator, dark and animal-crouched on his snow-colored horse. 'Out of my way. Mitrian, *get out of my way!*'

Mitrian edged her horse to a position where she could see both men clearly. Rache kept his gaze locked on Garn, eyes flashing with anger as bright as the Pica Stone, an alabaster statue on a steed as dark as a demon. Despite her precarious position, Mitrian could not banish the irony. In the past year, the heroes and villains had become as muddled as the colors representing them.

'Quiet, Garn,' she said softly, tears blurring the scene to chess-board patches of black and white.

To her surprise, Garn fell silent.

'Can't you two understand? I love you both so much.' Mitrian saw anger deepen in Garn's eyes and clarified. 'Rache is the only brother I've ever had; Garn my only husband. Please. Try to settle this. For me.'

Garn shook his head, rearranging coarse tangles of hair. His green gaze never left Rache. 'You don't understand. His cruelty took from me not only the life I should have had, but the value of all others. He's mine, Mitrian. And I'm here to collect my debt.'

Garn's words stabbed Mitrian like knives, and she glanced to Rache for aid. But the Renshai sat, grim and silent, on his stallion, sunlight playing through his golden hair.

Many thoughts raced through Mitrian's mind at once. She tried to convince herself that if she moved, the men would not attack. Failing that, she prayed for a miracle. Briefly, her gaze found Arduwyn, but he, too, hung on her words. She jammed her sword into its sheath in angry despair. 'Fine! If my love means nothing to you, go ahead and kill one another. I'm leaving.' She jabbed a hand toward the entrance to the clearing. 'If you come to an agreement, you can find me there. Both of you. If there's only one left, don't bother. I don't want anything to do with anyone who murders my loved ones.' With that, she wheeled the bay and reined her mount toward the entrance, blinded by tears.

The last voice she heard was Arduwyn's. 'Don't move, either of you. You've got plenty of time to fight. Right now, I need to talk to Rache.'

Riding aside with Arduwyn, Rache did not bother to modulate his voice. 'Look, Garn doesn't know how to listen to reason. The sooner this is finished, the sooner I get to my guard post at the armory.' It was a weak lie. He was scheduled to guard the armory. But the mundane soldiers' chore paled in significance, especially since any of Peusen's warriors would gladly take Rache's place. Even in Santagithi's command, Rache had always hated guard duty.

Arduwyn kept his voice low but firm. 'How could you treat Mitrian like that? I thought you cared for her. At the least, I'd have thought you had enough respect for Santagithi to treat his daughter kindly.'

'What are you babbling about?' Rache's forearms lay crossed on his pommel, a hand on each hilt. He could not help watching Garn over Arduwyn's shoulder. 'I'm not the one screaming about debts.' A sudden concern struck him, and his gaze flicked about until he found Sterrane. Unharmed, the huge man leaned against the cliffs, features pouting.

'No,' Arduwyn admitted. 'But you're not making any effort to compromise.'

'As opposed to Garn?' Rache kept his gaze on Sterrane until he made certain his friend had not been injured. Once sure, he returned his attention to Garn.

'Garn's in a different position than you. He respects you. He can't help feeling that way, and it's tearing him apart. For you to stop hating Garn, you only need to forgive him for doing the same thing you would have done in his place. For him to stop hating you requires him to admit that you're his superior. Garn has to prove that he deserves his freedom. He needs to believe he's at your level. The only way he knows to do that is to show he's the better warrior. It's the only thing you've ever competed in before.'

Rache pursed his lips into an annoyed line. Forgiving Garn had proven difficult enough. To consider him an equal went beyond all sense of honor and propriety. *Mitrian loves Garn. She's chosen to marry him.* Memory of the powerful sword stroke that had nearly unhorsed him set him shaking his head in awe. 'Garn's one of the most competent fighters I know. He – '

Arduwyn's sharp gesture cut Rache off. 'Tell Garn that.'

'How?'

'You and Garn need to spend some time alone. When you're finished, there'd better either be two of you or none. Otherwise, the survivor's in for a lonely life.'

Rache was skeptical. 'Would you have us just send everyone else from the clearing?'

'Better the two of you should meet somewhere alone.' A strange smile formed on Arduwyn's face. 'Why not while you're on duty at the armory?'

The suggestion surprised Rache enough to draw his observation from Garn to Arduwyn. 'Wonderful suggestion. Why don't we just meet in a burning barn with me on foot? Armories have weapons in them.'

Arduwyn's tone turned as harshly sarcastic as Rache's. 'That was the definition of armory last I heard. It's one of the few interests you share. I've seen Garn stare at an armorer's wares in the market for ridiculous lengths of time. And weapons, my friend, give the advantage to you.'

Rache's eyes narrowed in consideration.

'I've seen Garn kill without a weapon or even the intention of killing. He's far stronger now than when I first met him. No offense, but if Garn and Colbey faced one another completely unarmed, I'd put my money on Garn.'

Rache frowned at the slight to his mentor.

'But,' Arduwyn continued swiftly, 'if either one had a sword, I'd never doubt Colbey's victory. No matter who started with the weapon, Colbey would wind up with it. Of course, I'm assuming a Northman skilled enough to have become a legend in Pudar has talent approximating Colbey's.'

Rache relaxed enough to loose a sardonic laugh. 'Thank you for the compliment. If gods challenged Colbey, I'd be hard-pressed to pick the winner. But I do take your point. I'm on duty at the armory at sundown. I'll tell General Peusen to give you free passage in the town, assuming you can talk Garn into meeting with me.' He reined his horse about. 'Oh, and please assure Mitrian I care enough about her to do everything in my power to settle this feud in a way that kills neither of us.' Rache spoke with honest sincerity.

Arduwyn met the cold blue gaze. 'I'm certain,' he said carefully, 'you'll do just that.'

Moments before sundown, Rache reined Bein to a halt before the squat flagstone hut hidden beneath a hill that served as armory to the soldiers of Iaplege. He waved off the current sentry. Untying from the saddle the staves that served as his crutches, he lowered them to the ground, letting them lean against the stallion's neck as he gracefully dismounted. The black remained still as Rache peeled off tack and collected his staves. A playful slap on the rump sent the stallion wandering a short distance in search of grass.

Weight balanced on his staves, Rache watched Bein shamble off with a slight smile of pleasure. The horse had served him as no other ever had or, he imagined, could, a lucky find he doubted he could repeat. He hoped, if anything happened to him, the horse would find a master that suited it as well.

Betrayed by his own doubts, Rache's smile wilted to a frown. Dependent on the staves, he could walk with a slow, reasonably natural gait. Over time, he had regained strength and sensation to an area just below his knees, though it had become obvious that time would heal nothing more. With his hands burdened, he could never hope to win a battle against Garn. *Arduwyn promised to talk with Garn, but what could he say now that he couldn't have said during the last two weeks?* Rache staggered back toward Bein's saddle and bridle, thinking it might prove safer to meet Garn mounted.

As if in answer to the thought, hoofbeats rumbled on the pathway to the armory. Garn's white horse whipped around the bend, its rider a wide, dark blur on its back.

The previous sentry detected something odd in Rache's bearing.

Apparently judging the approaching rider a threat, he reached for his sword.

Rache grabbed the other man's arm. 'Relax. I invited him.'

The sentry regarded Rache curiously. With a shrug, he wandered off in the opposite direction as Garn's white gelding drew up before the tying post.

Rache's capable hand curled about his staves. A familiar wariness coiled his sinews. Ignoring Garn's dismount and tie, he hobbled to the door, feeling as awkward and defenseless as a newborn fawn. Mentally, he cursed Arduwyn, wondering how the little hunter had talked him into something so reckless.

Garn drew up beside Rache in the doorway. The ex-gladiator wore his sword at his hip and a face that revealed nothing. The blank pall was a trick Rache had taught Garn to keep him from projecting his intentions to his opponents in the pit. Now the icy lack of expression unnerved Rache. Still, the larger man's weapon remained in its sheath. Garn seemed to have no plans to slice Rache down. Yet.

Rache unlocked the door and pushed it open, balancing on the opposite staff. A movement flashed through his peripheral vision, Garn's sword whisking free. Before Rache could shift his balance, cold steel crashed against his staff. Wood snapped, the pieces skittering across the armory floor. Support abruptly lost, Rache collapsed, rolling on his back to face certain death. His hands flicked instinctively to his sword hilts.

Garn clenched the haft of his longsword in fists gone white with strain. The blade hovered over Rache, positioned for a killing thrust through the throat. Yet it did not fall. Against all of Rache's teachings, Garn had apparently chosen to gloat rather than kill.

The fool. Though his own life was at stake, Rache could not quell the disappointment of seeing a competent student make a fatal error. Carefully, he measured a sudden twist to the nearest table, considered how fast he could draw his own weapons. But cued by Garn's silence, Rache froze. *Killers don't pause, and braggarts don't stand in silence. Whether Garn realizes it or not, he's confused. For once, I need to use my head instead of my sword.*

The sword hung motionless. Garn's features mingled need and uncertainty.

Rache overpowered training and survival instinct with will. 'Are you going to let bitterness destroy all the good you've accomplished?'

Garn's cheeks twitched. His eyes narrowed. 'So this is how it ends? The mighty sword master begs for his life?' The thought seemed to please him.

'Is that what you believe, Garn?' Rache could not keep disgust from his tone. 'You never used to be stupid. To belittle your teacher is to discredit all that he taught you and all that you are. And what honor is there in killing an enemy who is only a coward?' He snorted. 'If you've learned nothing more about self-respect and glory than grounding a cripple with a surprise stroke from behind and slaughtering him without a fight, then perhaps you don't deserve the freedom and love you'll surrender for this so-called honor. I've never known Santagithi nor his daughter to pronounce an idle threat. Is my death really worth losing your wife and child?'

Garn's mouth bunched. His voice became a hiss, poisoned with a malice beyond all reason. 'I hate you and all you've made me into. Your death is worth any price.' Still, he did not complete the killing cut.

Encouraged by Garn's lack of action, if not his words, Rache uncurled his palms from his swords. Cold from the stone floor of the doorway chilled through his tunic. 'If that was so, when Mitrian pushed between us you wouldn't have pulled your blow. You would have hacked through her to get to me.'

Garn said nothing. His gaze never left Rache's eyes.

Doubt about his own diplomatic skills caused Rache's voice to slur. The words came only with difficulty. 'Garn, if you truly believe my death will have some profoundly good effect on your swordsmanship and your life, so be it.' Rache hoped Garn would mistake the somberness of his expression for sincerity. 'My life is worth the sacrifice.' Rache spread his arms, fully opening his defenses to Garn's attack, faking surrender though his eyes measured the distance to the nearest table.

Garn's forearms hardened. The sword raised a finger's breadth, then stopped.

Rache forced himself to remain still, quietly judging the split second timing required to block Garn's death blow.

'Why!' Garn's shout made it clear he had to know. 'Why would you let me do this?'

'Because of a man named Episte. As skilled as Colbey was and is, Episte taught me more. He sacrificed his soul for the time it bought him to train me. He convinced me that any dedicated teacher would do the same for his most skilled student.'

Garn chewed his lip in consideration, the sword still hovering, though his arms must have begun to ache with the strain. Slowly, the implications became clear. 'You're saying I'm your best student?' His surprise radiated clearly.

'Was that ever in doubt?'

Garn stiffened. 'But you betrayed me.' His volume rose with each accusation. 'You chained me. You called me an animal.'

'I never betrayed you.' Rache knew to which incident Garn referred without need for consideration. 'I got you away from the townsfolk in the only way I could without causing a lot of senseless slaughter. And before the trial, I argued to the point of mutiny to keep you free.' Rache saw no reason to deny the truth of Garn's other accusations. 'As to the chains and insults, had I not used them, you would have learned nothing. Without training, your courage would have become only directionless barbarism. You would have died in the pit.'

'And you would have lost money.' Garn spoke with soft rancor.

'No,' Rache replied equally softly. 'You know I never placed bets on the gladiator matches. You know because you learned and remembered every comment you ever heard from or about me. And threw the worst parts of my life back at me every chance you got.'

Garn spoke with the sudden monotony of a phrase that had become habit. 'A man must learn all he can about his enemies.'

Rache let his hands glide naturally back to his sides, scarcely daring to believe his self-sacrifice, though feigned, had earned him the chance to talk. 'But a man should choose his enemies with the same care he chooses friends. I taught you to survive.'

Garn's sword whipped downward.

Rache tensed, but the blade slammed against the floor an arm's length from his body. Steel scraped stone, raising a line of sparks.

'You taught me to kill without remorse!' Garn screamed. 'You rammed your savagery into me until slaughter became a habit I still can't escape.'

'And you believe murdering me will make you less of a killer? One more death will erase all the ones that came before?' Rache struggled to a sitting position on the floor, no longer caring if Garn retaliated. 'I simply taught you how to fight and to survive the violence neither of us could avoid. The savagery was your own, and not necessarily something to be reviled either. Without that audacity you call savagery, you would never have become my finest student.'

Garn's voice dropped to a growl. He had obviously tired of talk. 'You've never been kept like an animal. You can't understand.'

'Can't I?' Rache thrust his left arm upward with a suddenness that sent his sleeve sliding back to his elbow. Over time, the shackle's scar had faded nearly to nothing, yet Rache realized that Garn knew the pattern too well to mistake it.

'You?' Garn did not complete the question.

Rache obviated the need. 'I fought in the pit. Once. Yes. The Northern king tried to keep me as a gladiator rather than a soldier because he was stupid. Santagithi did the same to you because he believed you were too uncontrollable to serve as anything else. Over time, I might have convinced him of his mistake, until your hatred and desire for vengeance proved him right.' Rache paused to let his words settle. 'Bitterness destroyed your chance at freedom once. Are you going to let it do so again? If you slay me and survive, you'll lose your wife and child. And you will be hunted.'

Garn grimaced. 'I'll have no peace until I kill you.'

'The peace you seek doesn't exist.' Rache spread his arms. 'If you won't listen to reason, then kill me and be done with it. I'm sick to death with this feud. If it costs my soul to teach you that nothing good comes of vengefulness and unfaltering resentment, at least you'll learn this lesson well.'

Garn raised his sword.

Rache held his breath, certain this time he had misjudged.

But Garn's weapon sagged in his hand. 'I can't. Not like this. Not without knowing.'

There was no reason to clarify. *Garn can't kill me until he's proven to us both that he's the better warrior.* Rache understood Garn without the need to ask. He fought a smile, his own competitive edge raised by the thought. *And I have to know I'm still better, too.* 'Listen, Garn. We can kill one another any time. Someday, maybe we can get Mitrian to let us have that fight, though chances are it'll prove nothing. No matter who lives, he'll always doubt, always wonder how much of his victory came from skill and how much from luck. Nantel never won a spar against me, yet every time he gained a trick, he challenged me again. And he was never a fraction of the swordsman you are.' Rache studied Garn questioningly, hoping the gladiator had gleaned the unspoken lesson, that competition was healthy and normal, even among friends. 'You might be able to best me.' The confession came hard, but Rache managed to keep the skepticism from leaking into his tone.

Garn frowned, saying nothing.

'For now, as long as we're stuck here, I might as well show you the armory.' Catching the doorjamb, Rache hoisted himself to his feet, then gestured Garn inside.

Garn hesitated, scowling. Then, apparently seeing the wisdom in Rache's words, he entered Iaplege's armory.

Rache gathered his remaining staff and followed.

Weapons, shields, and armor of a myriad of cultures lay in neat groupings on tables spread throughout the room or hung from fasteners on the walls. Iaplege's mixed population combined as many martial crests and styles as it did citizens. Accustomed to the sight, Rache paused to shut the door while the steel captivated Garn the way a shiny coin draws the attention of a raven. Suddenly, Rache might have disappeared while Garn's head jerked and paused, studying the array of weapons. Reverently, he ran a hand down a spike erupting from the iron bell of a horseman's flail. His eyes followed the delicate curve of a glaive before the swords beckoned.

Rache leaned against his staff while Garn admired a great sword nearly as tall as himself. Grasping its hilt in both hands, Garn swung impulsively.

Caught in the blade's path, Rache dropped to the floor. Steel whisked through the air where his head had been.

'Garn! Put it down!' Rache shouted, uncertain whether the attack had been intentional. It seemed unlikely after Garn had sacrificed a far simpler opportunity. And the movement appeared too slow, deliberate, and obvious to fit Garn's style.

Garn answered Rache's unspoken concern by gently lowering the sword.

Rache tried and failed to guess Garn's purpose. The green eyes revealed nothing. 'Surely you know not to swing that large a sword in a small room. A weapon like that isn't made to wield indoors.' Cautiously, braced between tables, he rose.

Garn stared at the blade in wonder. 'Who would wield it indoors or out? What giant could handle this?' Garn used the tone he had reserved for the few instances when Rache's lessons had grown interesting enough for him to put aside hatred for the sake of knowledge.

Surprised but not fooled by the change, Rache replied, 'A man no larger than you used that sword. The Iaplegeans say he came from beyond the ocean and died long ago. I don't know if it's true, but the sword he left is real enough.'

'One sword.' Garn's gaze devoured the many racks and tables. 'How did so small a town acquire so many?'

Rache licked his lips, keeping his attention on Garn's features though they told him little. 'Nearly all the Iaplegeans are warriors wounded in battle. They bring armor and weapons. The ones who die leave them.' Alert to every movement, Rache examined Garn's thick, scarred arms. It struck him how much Garn resembled his gladiator father, yet his motions seemed smoother and more animal-like. 'We also made or bought weapons in preparation for the War.'

Garn's attention became fixed. Rache's gaze followed Garn's. On a table, amidst breastplates and greaves, lay a pair of fighting gauntlets. Approaching it, Garn placed his hand in one lacquered glove, nestling the steel grip against his heavily callused palm.

Rache had laced similar gauntlets so many times, he instinctively drew closer to help. He caught himself, but not soon enough.

'So familiar, eh, Rache?' Garn's eyes burned with the fierce intensity that had meant a bloody death for many adversaries in the pit. He lifted the other gauntlet, and the blades flashed like ghosts in the dim light wafting through cracks in the flagstone.

Rache leaned uneasily against a table, hand resting on one sword hilt. 'I once gave you weapons as a superior. Now let's examine them as equals.' Doubting the words could soothe Garn, Rache kept his guard up. *Things were easing so well. Thor's wife, why did he have to notice those gauntlets?*

Garn clapped the blades together, oblivious to Rache's words. He folded the gauntlets across his chest. Slowly, he swept his right hand across his hip and followed with a punch to the same side. He continued with a series of blocks and strikes. Veins swelled in Garn's arms and neck, but his face remained relaxed. It seemed as if Garn's soul had left his body, and no life looked out from behind his glazed eyes.

Fascinated, Rache watched, assessing him automatically. *The pace is not that of a gladiator. The deliberateness and control were never there before. Nor the power.*

Again, Garn crossed his arms, simulating prayer. Mistrust tightened Rache's hand on his hilt.

Suddenly, Garn drove the blade on his fist deep into the maple column supporting the room. He slipped the gauntlet from his wrist, leaving it impaled in the wood.

'Sif and Modi,' whispered Rache, eyes wide in disbelief. Impressed despite himself, he drifted toward the pole. Confident of the strength he had developed in his upper body, he wrapped one arm around the pole, dropped his staff, and seized the metal frame inside the gauntlet. Bracing himself, he pulled. The blade did not budge.

Shocked, Rache yanked harder with no more success. Obsessed, he threw his weight into the task until his muscles ached and his skin went clammy with sweat. For all his efforts, the blade remained in place.

Abruptly aware of the power of the man at his back, Rache felt fear grip him like a vise. Still clutching the pole for support, he whirled.

Garn's eyes flared green fire. He smirked, patient as a cat with a certain kill.

Rache cursed his incaution. He gripped a table behind him, gaining the stability to retreat.

Garn advanced.

Rache drew his sword.

Garn smiled. His attention fixed on the ceiling. His fingers closed about the handle of the gauntlet, and he drew it from the beam with ease.

Rache gasped, body still taut for battle. His heart pounded in his chest.

Garn laughed. 'Your whips broke me so many times. Just once, Rache. Just once, I wanted you to fear me.'

Rache said nothing.

Garn returned the gauntlets to the table. His manner had changed from hunched to confident, from compliant to regal. For the moment, he was fully in control. And he knew it. 'Colbey taught me some things, too.'

Rache licked his parched lips several times, mouth so dry he thought he would never swallow again. Garn's revelation angered him. As long as he knew another Renshai lived, Colbey had no right to teach any of the maneuvers to outsiders, especially not to Rache's enemies. Gathering his staff, he pointed it at Garn. 'Tell me what he taught you. I have a right to know.'

Garn turned away. 'As much as Colbey saw fit,' he said cryptically. Hefting a scimitar, he swung it.

Rache's tension receded. He laughed without malice. 'I see he didn't teach you any of the sword skills.'

Garn scowled.

'Even I showed you better than that. A scimitar has only one cutting edge. You have to keep that edge forward.' Rache paused, smiling to take the sting from his words. He had never needed to soften his teachings before, but it seemed foolish to antagonize Garn now. 'Strong, clean stroke, though,' he conceded. 'If you were facing an opponent, you'd have bludgeoned him soundly.'

Garn glanced from the scimitar to Rache. 'Perhaps the great Renshai sword master would lower himself to spar with a man who can't tell a sword from a club.'

Rache hesitated, uncertain whether Garn meant spar as a euphemism for fight.

Apparently guessing Rache's concern, Garn clarified. 'Instead of your life, I'll claim only a glass of ale when I win.'

The request seemed in earnest. Rache could not dismiss the curiosity that welled within him. *Crippled and against Garn's newly developed strength, am I still the better swordsman?* Still, he worried that ego might turn the contest into something more deadly. *Neither of us could accept the other's victory. Could we?* He shook his head, his excuse lame. 'I know your repertoire too well. It wouldn't be fair.'

'Afraid?' Garn teased with the same lack of hostility as Nantel once used to goad Rache. 'I'll take that drink as soon as you get off duty. You must have an alehouse.'

Rache balanced on a sword's edge of indecision. He knew their relationship had reached a turning point. Garn's demonstration of inhuman strength and his glimpse of terror in Rache's demeanor seemed to have drained the hatred festering within Garn. Yet Rache knew that a lifetime of whips and oppression could not be forgotten in a day. He studied the ex-gladiator, ignoring the craggy musculature, focusing instead on the emerald eyes. There he found emotions he could not immediately recognize. Directions of thought that came to Garn naturally required Rache to assess and counter-assess in the seconds social propriety granted him to answer the challenge. From Garn's expression, Rache guessed the man had gained a new perspective. No longer a slave glaring at his weapon master, Garn had become a free man in the presence of a competent teacher. Surely, Garn understood the implications of a union in the same manner as Rache often wished he could meet the most skilled enemy warriors over a drink and discuss sword strokes rather than exchanging them. *Garn is Mitrian's husband. Maybe, just maybe, we can turn this malice into tolerance. If we can get through this, we can get through anything.*

'So be it.' Rache grabbed a scimitar from a nearby rack and braced his body against a table. This time, it was interest and hope rather than pride that answered Garn's challenge. And this time, the odds were against Rache. On horseback, Rache knew he could still best Garn. But without mobility, quickness did him little good against Garn's strength.

Garn sprang forward, sword low to drive Rache from the supporting table. Rache parried and riposted. On the defensive, Garn abandoned his strategy. His blade swept at neck level. Rache dove over Garn. As he tumbled, he slapped Garn's back with the flat of his blade.

'That's one !' Rache used another table to pull himself to his feet.

Garn froze, stunned. His lips formed a fierce scowl. Then the ends twitched upward, and he laughed. 'I never dreamed you'd throw yourself onto a stone floor for a mug of ale. Now that I know how seriously you take your drinks, the next match is mine.'

Bracing himself against the table, Rache awaited the next onslaught. Garn rushed him. Rache's scimitar darted out to meet the attack. Dodging aside, Garn struck. Rache parried. Garn disengaged as Rache swept his scimitar overhead. Garn's next blow shattered the table leg. Table and Renshai collapsed amid a shower of decorative shields. Metal belled and rolled across the floor. Pointing the tip of his weapon at Rache's throat, Garn smirked. 'Even,' he said. 'Shall we try one more?'

Rache examined the carnage doubtfully. Cracks wound through the tabletop, its sword-hacked leg splintered. Shields lay in wild disarray against the walls and tables. 'Tables cost more than ale,' Rache said, needing the deciding spar every bit as much as Garn. 'Oh, Hel. I'll need a new foundation, if you please.'

Garn caught Rache's shoulder and escorted him to a table in the middle of the room. A chill shook Rache at the touch of Garn's hand, the same hand that had broken his back and left him crippled.

Oblivious to Rache's distress, Garn retreated. He held the scimitar in both hands and sighted along the unsharpened edge. Engrossed in the charade, Rache circled his blade around his head.

Garn's eyes darted with exaggerated wariness. He danced several paces closer. Then, with a resounding war cry, he charged Rache. Rache flung himself over the wooden table. A row of swords crashed to the floor.

Rache used a corner of the room to gain his feet. Garn leapt onto the table. He raised his scimitar, growling with mock savagery. 'Now, Renshai pig, time for you to die!'

As Garn poised to spring, Rache saw a movement behind the ex-gladiator. The door wrenched open, revealing a troop of Iaplegeans, Mitrian, Arduwyn, and Sterrane among them.

'Garn, no!' Mitrian screamed.

Garn whirled.

Rache lunged forward and tapped Garn's side with his sword.

Garn spun to face Rache, knocking a greave from the tabletop. He pirouetted back to Mitrian. 'Damn you, wench! You lost me a mug of ale.' Garn clambered from the table and helped Rache to stand.

Rache chuckled merrily as he accepted his staff from Garn. 'It was only a spar.' His smile wilted as he noticed the seriousness and size of the troops filing into the armory.

Mitrian glared at Arduwyn. 'A spar?' She took Garn's arm. 'Good thing I came when I did. That spar looked awfully real to me.'

'You came in the third match,' explained Garn. 'I won the second, but the old man got lucky in the first.'

'Lucky,' Rache started, ignoring the more obvious insult, but he broke off as the Iaplegeans pulled weapons and armor from the racks. 'What's going on?'

One of Rache's students answered as he plucked his shield from the spilled chaos on the floor, a confused expression on his face as he stared at the broken table. 'Scouts say the Eastern army will reach the Western Plains in three days. Word is, Pudar's been mobilized, also Western towns as far as the Great Mountains. Even a tribe of Northmen.'

Vikerin, Rache guessed. He tried to find Peusen in the chaos. Soon, the one-handed general would have to face his brother, Valr Kirin, and his own past. Rache only hoped the Northern general's lot went easier and as successfully as his own dealings with Garn. 'Take whatever weapons you can use,' Rache told Garn.

'I have a sword.' Garn drew his weapon. 'That's all I need.'

'Let me see that.' Rache examined the notched edge with disgust. 'You'll need a better weapon than this.' He chose a flawlessly crafted broadsword more suited to Garn's power strokes and handed it to Garn.

Dropping his longsword, Garn accepted the blade.

'Mitrian ?' Rache turned to the woman.

Men continued to funnel into the armory until the room seemed to ring with voices and the clatter of armor and weapons being examined and tested.

Triumphantly, Mitrian turned her blade over to her teacher. Rache admired it with stern respect. 'I commend you. It must have taken days with a very fine stone to hone the edge this sharp without a mark.' Reluctantly, he returned the sword, only then noticing the artistry of its hilt. 'Skilled craftsmanship, too. Who made it ?'

'Listar,' Mitrian answered without emotion. 'The blacksmith's son.' Her words seemed to send her into deep thought. But before Rache could question her, he found himself surrounded by students begging to know which weapon to take to war or to confirm the quality of the ones they had chosen.

Rache fell into the quiet, familiar pattern of instruction. For several moments he tangled with concerns about the newest additions to Iaplege's army. No matter her weapons training, Mitrian had no experience or understanding of real war. Garn might find himself equally unprepared. The pit matches had only taught him to defeat a single opponent; accosted by enemies from all directions, Garn might panic. Sterrane, too, had never fought in a war, and the thought of risking the prince of Béarn rankled. *I may not be the hero of the Great War, but I'll have my hands full of responsibilities. Perhaps my mother truly saw something no one else did.*

Welcoming the fine tremor of excitement that war always inspired, Rache turned his attention back to his students.

Part 3
The Great War

25 Beneath the Banner of the Wolf

Nearly seven hundred and fifty Iaplegian soldiers threaded through the passes of the Southern Weathered Mountains, joined on the second day by three Pudarian scouts. The mismatched band of renegades wore no uniforms nor crests and carried no standard, but they rode and marched with a somber unity that revealed the intensity of their training and their loyalty to their leaders. Though a part of the brigade, Mitrian could not help feeling impressed. Cripples and exiles approached the war with their eyes bright and their heads high.

A gap in the clouds spilled sunlight over chains, links, and scales of bronze and steel. Some of the soldiers wore leather armor, or street garb like Sterrane and Garn. Many carried shields of rich design, while others sported only simple, wooden helmets. Mounted on his black charger, Rache rode near the lead of the cavalry, dressed in a dark leather tunic and breeks that would neither hamper his movements nor foil an enemy sword stroke. He perched with the same regal alertness that Mitrian recognized from her father's forays. Neither time nor repetition dulled the keen edge of excitement that accompanied imminent battle. Several ranks back, Garn conversed casually with one of the Pudarians, a friend from his days as a guard. Arduwyn rode toward the back, among the archers.

Mitrian envied the men's composure. She felt overwhelmed, twitchy, frightened, awed, and excited at once. So many times, she had imagined herself riding at Rache's side, at the lead of a troop of soldiers. Yet the reality of sweat, chafing leather, and blood-sucking insects turned the images to foolish reverie. She could not help glancing at the warriors around her, wondering which ones would survive and which would lie, bloody and mangled, on the Western Plains, mourned briefly, then forgotten for the concerns of the living.

In his rallying speech, General Peusen Raskoggsson had made it clear that, should King Siderin win the war, the dead might have the enviable position. Still, without a glimpse of Siderin's army, the war seemed as distant as the legends Mitrian had heard since infancy. Her mind could not grasp visions of her father's town decimated and overrun by swarthy soldiers, forests striped with the blood of friends and family, her mother, beaten and submissive, a toy in a stranger's bed.

So Mitrian turned her thoughts to closer problems. Garn and Rache seemed to have settled their feud, each now busy with war plans. Yet Mitrian dared not become complacent. *A lifetime of hatred does not disappear in a day.* She thought of Garn, of the coiled rage that always swelled to the forefront at the mere mention of Rache's name, and of how near Garn had come to hurting her when she had suggested calling Kinesthe for Santagithi. Much as she wanted Garn and Rache to be friends, she knew their new relationship was as tenuous as a poorly stitched wound. *And what will happen when my father sees Garn?*

Needing to assess the situation as well as to clear her thoughts, Mitrian rode up beside one of the Pudarian scouts, a slender blond named Glomhar. 'How soon do we reach the main camp?'

The Pudarian flashed a toothy smile. 'This evening, missy.'

'How do things seem there?'

Glomhar looked Mitrian over, apparently uncertain how to respond to her question. 'You mean at the camp?'

Mitrian nodded, specifically wanting information about her father, yet unsure how to ask for it.

'Tense,' Glomhar said. 'They think Siderin's on his way. But last I heard, no one had actually spotted him.' Glomhar glanced around suspiciously, as if revealing a secret. 'He's a demon, you know.'

'I'd heard that.' Mitrian tried to keep her tone serious, though she no longer believed the legend.

'Our generals are in conference about him all the time. I don't envy them the need to plan strategy against a demon.'

I don't envy them the need to plan strategy against anyone. Mitrian tried to imagine making decisions that affected thousands of lives directly and tens of thousands more indirectly, including soldiers' relatives and friends. She concentrated on the opening Glomhar had given her. 'Generals?' She placed emphasis on the plural. 'How many generals do we have?'

'Four at the camp. Plus your man.' Glomhar gestured in the direction of Peusen. Taking one hand from the reins, he counted through the list. 'There's King Gasir of Pudar. He's got the largest army, of course. About four thousand soldiers.' He extended two fingers. 'Then, there's this Northman named Colbey, who came down from the Northern Weathered Mountains. He roused the farm towns and joined them with Pudar. Colbey answers to King Gasir, so I don't know as I'd call him a general. But he does attend the strategy sessions, and he outranks the king's lieutenants.'

Mitrian smiled, pleased but not surprised to know she would soon see Colbey again and that he had swiftly worked his way to a position of command.

Glomhar flicked out a third finger, pinning his smallest digit to his palm with a double-jointed thumb. 'From farther east, there's the master strategist, Santagithi.'

'Master strategist?' Mitrian blurted in surprise.

Glomhar stared, biting off his identification of the final general to address Mitrian's question. 'A talented and experienced leader,' he defended Santagithi. 'Do you think otherwise?'

'No,' Mitrian covered quickly. 'I just never thought a city as large and organized as Pudar would have so much knowledge and respect for the general of a tiny town.'

Glomhar's face puckered into a frown. 'Santagithi may only command six hundred men, but they're competent and eager. And, right now, that's the third largest army we have.'

Glomhar's revelation shocked Mitrian. 'Santagithi's army large? What about the great kingdom of Béarn? Isn't it the largest after Pudar? Even I've heard of the king's knights in Erythane. And what about the Northmen? I thought they loved war.'

Wry amusement colored Glomhar's face. 'There's a single tribe of Northmen here. Vikerians, they call themselves, led by a king named Tenja and his captain, Valr Kirin.' Glomhar slurred title and name together so it sounded like 'Vawlkeerin.' 'There's maybe two hundred fifty of them. Came with Santagithi.'

Mitrian frowned, unable to recall any dealings between her father and Northmen.

Glomhar continued, 'Morhane's ruled Béarn nearly twenty years now. He's as evil as Siderin.' He spat, as if to get the taste of the name from his mouth. 'Some few Erythanians might join Pudar's army, but the king's knights have become little more than Morhane's personal pawns.'

Mitrian did some mental arithmetic. 'We have about five to six thousand men.' The number seemed staggering. 'How can Siderin hope to stand against that?'

Glomhar shook his head. 'Santagithi's guessing the Easterners will outnumber us by half again or double.'

Mitrian's expression wilted to a frown.

'And they're all organized to a single chain of command while our army is piecemeal. There's a lot of potential for clashing personalities on our side, especially with three Northmen among the five generals.' Glomhar shook his head sadly. 'Us Westerners are used to banding together, what with driving off Renshai and preparing for the Easterners and all. But Northmen have enough trouble just getting along with one another.'

Mitrian's scowl deepened. She knew little of war and its varying mentalities, but it seemed obvious that the scout's pessimism could not help morale. Her hand fell to her mount's withers, and she massaged her sword hilt absently.

The demon's presence swelled to sudden life. A fierce storm of violence and desire rushed through Mitrian. Swords glittered through her vision in a silver and red dance of glory. A vast, foreign eagerness seized her, a craving for the dense reek of blood, the battle savagery that overwhelmed thought, fear, and pain, and the artful chime of sword against sword. Death retreated to a distant abstraction, somehow unrelated and unimportant.

Glomhar shied from the strange mask of cruelty that twisted Mitrian's features. Wheeling his horse, he rode off to speak with other soldiers.

Mitrian's fingers slipped from the sword's grip. Instantly, the war lust disappeared, leaving her a troubled but well-trained woman amid a sea of avid warriors. She reached for the haft again, this time tentatively, trying to convey the need for rational conversation.

But the demon's excitement threw her into a maelstrom of ruthless pleasure she could not resist. Her hand tightened around the leather, and she tore the blade from its sheath, oblivious to the abrupt, surprised retreat of those soldiers nearest to her. In her mind, armored men rushed down upon her, grimy swords and axes notched from battle. She met them with a wild net of thrust and parry, a brilliant series of Renshai maneuvers tailored to each attack. Though Mitrian's arm formed each kata, the strategy came from without. The initiation of each cut arose not from her but from the demon in the gems. The honor was his alone.

Suddenly, one attacker ducked through Mitrian's guard. His sword crashed against hers, driving pain through her hands. Torn from her grip, the sword arced through air.

Once freed of the demon's influence, Mitrian recognized Rache in front of her, mounted on his black charger. He snatched her sword from mid-flight, catching it by the hilt. 'What the hell are you doing?' Anger etched his youthfully handsome features.

Mitrian lowered her head, trying to separate reality from demon's images and to regain her composure.

Apparently mistaking her silence for apology, Rache softened. 'I know you don't have any combat experience, but march formation is not the place for practice. You're part of a team now. Except when we're camped and at ease, you need to stay with your unit and obey the orders of your commander. And don't do anything that might distract or harm your companions.' With a curt gesture, he flipped Mitrian's sword, neatly catching the flat of the blade. He offered it back to her.

Hesitantly, Mitrian reached for the hilt. She accepted it into a grip too meek to hold cloth.

Rache released his hold. The sword plummeted to the dirt.

Mitrian watched Rache's gaze follow the route of her sword, saw him stiffen in surprised discomfort. His head jerked up, blue eyes probing, as if uncertain whether to chastise her incaution or seek penance for dishonoring her weapon.

Guessing the cause of Rache's uneasiness, Mitrian placed the blame where it belonged. 'It's my fault. I'm having some trouble getting a feel for the sword.' She sprang from the saddle, studying Rache to delay retrieving her weapon.

'Mitrian, are you certain you want to go to this war?'

Mitrian opened her mouth to protest, but Rache cut her short.

'There's no shame in withdrawing before the enemy arrives. If you feel you aren't ready, I'd rather you stayed behind than endanger the warriors under my command.'

'I'm ready,' Mitrian replied with a blandness that covered building anger. 'I trained under two of the most skilled sword masters in the world.' Though quiet, Mitrian hurled the compliment with the vehemence of an insult. 'Whose teachings are you doubting? Yours or Colbey's?'

Trapped neatly, Rache responded without time for thought. 'Well, neither. I mean . . .'

Mitrian bore in, venting on Rache her annoyance at the demon and her frustration at her inability to control its imagings. 'You mean you doubt my skill.'

'Not your skill,' Rache said quickly. 'Just your experience.'

'Well, how do you expect me to gain experience if I don't go to war?'

Rache sighed, tearing his gaze from Mitrian and her sword to look out over the troops that were now splitting to pass around their conversation. 'Border skirmishes. Forays. When you learn to ride, you don't start with the wildest horse in the stable.'

'I do if it's the only horse in the stable.' Mitrian knelt, as if to pick up her sword. But she stopped with her hand still several fingers' breadth from the hilt. 'Besides, it's not the same thing. The worst a horse could do is kill me. Siderin could torture, enslave, and butcher everyone and everything I ever loved. The West can't afford to leave any soldier behind.' Mitrian dropped modesty to make her point. 'Especially ones with my talent.'

Rache laughed. 'I see self-doubt isn't your weakness.'

'My weakness is this sword.' Mitrian drew determination from Rache's bold presence. 'If you'll let me have a few moments alone, I think I can handle it.'

Mitrian knew that, as a Renshai, Rache had to understand the strange bond between soldier and sword. Though he could not know the scope of her dilemma, he accepted her partial explanation with ease. 'Very well.' He reined his horse about and returned to the main body of the cavalry.

Mitrian sighed heavily. Filling her thoughts with warning, she touched a gem with her finger, trying to send a message rather than receive it. *No images!* She withdrew, feeling the warm wash of violence swell and disappear. Carefully, she brushed a topaz again. *Settle down and just talk* . . . As warmth tingled through her, Mitrian whipped her hand away. A war vision rose, broken as abruptly as the contact. She waited until her thoughts settled back to normal before tapping the gem again . . . *or, I'll leave you in the dirt and take another sword!*

Battle wrath died, replaced by outrage. The demon's presence seethed into Mitrian. *You can't do that! I've waited centuries for this moment! Shadimar gave me to you for a reason.*

Mitrian played her advantage. *A reason I no longer have. You were to help me understand Renshai, to guide me to become one.*

And you still have much to learn.

I have Colbey and Rache to teach me.

Colbey is an old man, Rache a cripple.

And you're a demon.

The soul in the gems did not dispute semantics. *I can't die. Long after the others are gone, I can teach you. And your children.*

Mitrian considered. Many thoughts converged on her at once. She recalled a day in Shadimar's ruins, more dream than reality and less than a year ago, though it seemed more like a decade. Her own bold words, spoken then, now echoed through her mind : 'Let me live my life, not have it displayed like a rich man's feast . . . Right or wrong, I'll believe my life is a consequence of chance and the things I've done.' Now, emboldened by Colbey's training, she addressed the demon. *I appreciate your lessons, but I have no use for your battle lust nor your skill. I deserve the chance to live or die by my own hand. I didn't labor to become Renshai only to have a sword wield me.*

Wield you? I have no wish to wield you. All I want is to hear the savage bell of swordplay, to feel the excitement that turns blood to fire in the veins. I want . . .

'To find Valhalla,' Mitrian finished softly.

Startlement shifted through Mitrian's mind, but the soul in the gems said nothing more.

Mitrian pressed. *That's what you want, isn't it? A chance to die in glory and go to Valhalla. But your chance is gone. Your future is set. You died on a sickbed, and you will go to Hel —*

Stop! His presence lost its cool edge. For the first time, the soul in the gems sounded unsteady.

The Wizard's magic only gained you time to ponder that fate, to make it more frightening. As understanding blossomed, Mitrian bore in ruthlessly. *But you're dead already. All that your overwhelming excitement can accomplish is to damn me to Hel as well.*

No! The demon's presence loomed like a shout, as if he needed to convince himself as well as Mitrian. *That's not it at all. You're Renshai. You're my student. I wouldn't wish Hel on anyone, least of all you. I just want you to fight your finest battle. For yourself. What harm if I live that glory with you?*

Frustration goaded Mitrian to shout, but she settled for a heavy mental focusing. *Live it with me? Or live it for me? There's no joy in someone else's battle. The fever burns hottest when the blood lust in my veins is my own. Without the chance for cowardice, courage has no meaning. Without courage, I can't find Valhalla. Would you damn one of the last Renshai to Hel for a few moments of personal glory?*

You don't understand.

Mitrian rose to a crouch, clutching the hilt between two fingers and letting the blade dangle. *Perhaps not, but neither do you. And I'm going to make myself clear. Here. Now. There's a battle ahead. I'm going to need all my wits about me just to die with dignity and honor. I can't have a sword fogging my mind with its own savagery.* She plowed the tip of the blade into the ground, cutting a sharp line through dirt. *I'm going to war. You're staying here, buried deeply, where no one can accidentally find you and fall prey to your illusions.*

What! The soul in the gems radiated shock, rage, and fear in a tense boil of emotions. Mitrian felt the demon's essence flail through her thoughts, apparently assessing the sincerity of her threat. *You can't do that!*

Mitrian remained calm, shadowing all doubts from her thoughts, though she could not banish them fully. Renshai shunned gimmicks and advantages that did not directly stem from personal skill, including the crudest armor. But her training was still incomplete, and the sword could compensate for that weakness. She kept her thoughts well-hidden: *There's more at stake than just whether I find Valhalla. Can the West afford to leave behind the only magic sword in any world?*

You can't do that! the demon repeated, obviously frustrated by a search that seemed to affirm that Mitrian could and would do precisely what she threatened.

The emanations of demon emotion swayed Mitrian back to her original purpose. *The West can't afford to have one of its best warriors struggling against her own sword.* She allowed this idea to move freely to the surface of her thoughts.

Mitrian, please. A hint of desperation entered the demon's communication. *This is the greatest battle of all time. No Renshai, whole or otherwise, should have to miss it.*

Mitrian released her inner struggle, watching long banks of infantry split around her. Absently, she traced the wolf's muzzle carved into her hilt. *You're the one who forced me to make a decision between us. If I keep you, I lose all chance to fight the way a Renshai should, spurred by my own battle rage and hope. If I leave you, you lose that chance.* She stood, still allowing the sword to hang. Ignoring the curious stares of Peusen's soldiers, she continued her silent conversation. *Since you're already damned to Hel, and I can still reach Valhalla, it only makes sense that, if one of us has to stay behind, it's you.*

You're patronizing me! The cold arrogance returned, and the soul in the gems seemed shocked.

Probably. Spurred by new confidence instilled by experience, Mitrian did not dispute. *But there is only one compromise.*

I can go if I don't allow my battle frenzy to interfere with yours.

Nor with my strategy.

Silence.

Or I'll throw you down and stomp you into the battlefield.

The demon's quiet deepened, now liberally laced with resentment.

Mitrian waited for a reply, patient as a mother. Less so, her bay mare pawed the ground with a white forehoof, showering her boots with dust.

That's the way you want it? The demon seemed distant.

That's the only way we both go to war.

A wordless noise filled Mitrian's consciousness, a strong demon sigh. *Can I suggest Renshai maneuvers?*

Mitrian considered the compromise. *You can suggest anything. There's still much I can learn from you.*

The indignation disappeared, replaced by passive, if grudging, acceptance.

Mitrian stuffed the sword back into its sheath, mounted and kicked her horse toward the cavalry, harboring no delusions. She knew she would fight many more battles, even before the war began.

*

The soldiers from Iaplege arrived on the Western Plains early that evening. Despite their handicaps, they faded into the teeming mass of preparing soldiers, each man too concerned about his own part in the war to worry about his neighbor . . . yet. The air rasped with a ceaseless chorus of steel against whetstone. Hushed conversations blended to a hum that dwarfed the night insects. Tension coiled over the camp like a cougar poised to spring on its prey.

At the farthest edge of the camp, Mitrian caught Garn's arm. 'Wait here. I need to find my father and talk to him about us.'

Garn's arm hardened beneath her touch, but he gave no other sign of rage or unease. His animal-green gaze revealed nothing.

'I know it's hard, but I need you to put your bitterness aside. Whatever evil has passed between the two of you no longer matters. You have a common enemy now.'

Garn spoke with controlled strength. 'Santagithi could never make a slave of me again. Siderin could.' His eyes blazed. 'My son will never know whips and chains. Never.' He looked at Mitrian, but his focus seemed far beyond her. 'I hated only two of the guards. Nantel is dead, and I no longer want to fight Rache.' Wheeling his white gelding, he rode into the press of soldiers.

Awed and pleased by Garn's restraint, Mitrian sent her horse toward the center of the massed warriors. Grass tickled her knees, and the mare's hooves sank into the dull mud beneath it. Her weaving horse did not disturb the sanctity of men praying to their various gods for victory and weighted by thoughts of the consequences of failure. Mitrian recognized many armies by their mail: the steel-studded leather of her father's guards, the Pudarians in smooth black leather or bronze scales, and the glare of plates and rings on officers. Scattered like scars among the war-trained, she saw farmers in ragged homespun, men desperate to defend their land if only with forks, shovels, and fierce determination.

Most of the men bore the brown-eyed, olive-toned features of Westerners, though Mitrian occasionally glimpsed a pale Northman and even a few swarthy Easterners who had abandoned their homes years before and joined the civilizations of the West. She recognized the silver- and black-spiraled pendants of Santagithi's followers and the falcons engraved on Pudarian shields. But the banner bearers waved flags graced with a gray wolf, the new symbol of a unified West.

A voice rose above the din of battle preparations. 'Mitrian?'

Mitrian whirled toward the call.

A man trotted through the crowd toward her. He wore the garb of Santagithi's guards, and blond curls fell to his shoulders. His torso appeared as well-muscled as Rache's and tapered to legs nearly as frail. Hope glimmered in his pale eyes.

Mitrian hesitated, trying to put a name to a visage that no longer seemed familiar. *Listar?* The proud soldier bore little resemblance to the awkward youth who had shared her mother's picnic lunches. *Could this be the blacksmith's peaceful son?*

Before Mitrian could question, shouts knifed the stillness. Santagithi's deep cry rose above the others. Mitrian buried her heels into her horse's ribs, reining it about. The beast twisted, rearing. Warriors scattered, opening a space for its plummeting hooves. Dropping to all fours, the horse broke into a canter, pounding around men and stacked pieces of armor and weaponry.

Shortly, Mitrian rode down upon a ring of enraged men in studded leather. Sterrane stood just outside, one hand clamped tightly to his face. Blood trickled between his fingers.

Horrified, Mitrian rode toward Sterrane.

Closer, Santagithi burst from the gathering crowd of onlookers. He had left his breastplate at his campsite and wore a chain-link shirt. Silver streaked his blond hair, and his cheeks had hollowed, but otherwise he looked exactly as Mitrian remembered. She could not hear his words, but they slapped men aside like physical blows. He gathered Sterrane to his chest.

Shocked, Mitrian slowed her horse to a walk. Before she could make sense of her father's actions, she caught a glimpse of Garn through a gap in the guards. Inside the ring, the ex-gladiator made wary circles, head snapping about to watch the surrounding men. A spear slithered toward him. He beat it aside, then whirled to meet three swords at his back.

'No!' Mitrian plunged toward Garn. The horse's shoulder knocked one guard to his knees, breathless. Others scuttled from her path. 'Leave him alone! Don't hurt Garn! Damn you to Hel, leave my husband alone!'

In the wake of Mitrian's words, a murmur swept the guards, and she found a clear path to Garn's side. As he caught her saddle and swung up behind it, she dared a glance toward Santagithi. Sterrane had disappeared, and Santagithi stood alone, frozen in place. The general's face had gone deathly pale. His lips formed a bloodless line.

'That can't be Mitrian,' one guard wondered aloud, his voice rising clearly over whispered speculation.

The blond youth who had approached Mitrian earlier replied, 'It is. She has the sword I forged for her.'

The guards edged forward, neatly closing the circle. Mitrian's mount trembled into a half rear, all but dumping Garn to the dirt.

'Fools! Stand where you are.' Rache's command boomed over the ensuing confusion.

The soldiers obeyed, though several jerked their heads in Rache's direction; and voices rose to a wild roar. The Renshai's massive black stallion wove through the masses with the grace and ease of a cat. He drew up at Mitrian's side.

'Don't you have enough enemies without creating more?' Though low, Rache's voice dwarfed the myriad conversations erupting between Santagithi's guards. 'Why didn't you just send Siderin a written invitation to your idiocy? He could have heard you pack of yowling curs back in his royal city.'

The voices died to silence. Wind ruffled the soldiers' locks and leather jerkins, but they stood, unmoving.

Mitrian glanced at her father to find him staring at her with an expression so mixed she did not dare to try to decipher it. She smiled, giving him a shy wave, and immediately regretted it. Under the circumstances, the gesture seemed a mockery.

Rache continued, his gaze sweeping every man in the circle. 'Garn is a free man now, unless the Easterners enslave him, along with us, your wives, and your children. Right now, I'd choose his sword arm over all of yours together. At least I know he won't draw enemies to my camp.'

An older guard shouted from the throng. 'With Garn beside you, what need would you have for enemies?'

Rache swiveled his head toward the speaker, fixing an icy stare on the elder. 'I am still your captain, Nito. If the West wasn't in such dire need of soldiers, I'd take you aside and remind you why.'

The chastised guard blanched and quietly retreated into the crowd.

Though he still addressed Nito, Rache glanced over every soldier as he spoke. 'Garn and I can fight our own battles. If I can forgive him, I see no right or reason for any of you to hold a grudge.' Rache's attention jerked suddenly to Santagithi, as if granting his general the privilege he had denied the others. 'At the least, you should offer Garn the respect due the husband of your leader's daughter and the father of your leader's grandson.'

Mitrian watched her father's lips part, then clip closed without any words escaping. Her mare shifted uneasily, snuffling at Rache's horse. The stallion remained still as a statue.

Rache's words drew the guards' attention to Santagithi, where he waited, beside Sterrane, at the fringes of the crowd. The general appeared unsteady, as pale as milk, and Mitrian feared he might collapse. He met her gaze over the heads of his guards.

This time, Mitrian gave him a somber but encouraging nod.

Santagithi cleared his throat. The noise emerged strangely, startling for his previous silence. Color returned to his features. When he spoke, his voice held its usual resonance. 'Jakot will lead the cavalry. Rache, your charge is infantry. I'm placing Mitrian and Garn as subcaptains, directly under your command.' His gaze never left Rache, but he paused, as if to leave his men an opening to challenge the promotion of the armies' newest recruits over its senior members. When no one did, he finished in the same forceful tone. 'Captain, I need to talk with you in private.' He tossed a meaningful glance to Mitrian to indicate he wanted some time alone with her, too, in a less official capacity. 'The rest of you are dismissed.'

Mitrian held her breath. Despite their skill, neither she nor Garn had any command experience. *Why would my father do such a thing? Why would he put his men in danger?*

Rache steered his horse through the muttering, dispersing throng to his leader's side. The two men headed deeper into camp.

Garn placed his hands on Mitrian's hips. She caught his wrists absently, her thoughts fixed on the exchange. She had always known her father to react with logic before emotion, yet she dared not believe her marriage to Garn had left him unaffected. *He wouldn't show it to his soldiers, but he's hurting. And I'm the only one who can comfort him.* As her tension lessened, new thoughts surfaced, and with them an explanation for her father's behavior. *Usually, he would have put Rache in sole command. This way, Rache's still in charge. Promoting Garn and me below him doesn't change that. But my father did defuse a potentially disastrous situation, made it clear to his soldiers that he trusts Garn, and so should they, and showed that he has faith in my judgment and Rache's decisions.* Once confused by Santagithi's decision, now Mitrian admired it. *With one proclamation, he managed to appease everyone. No wonder he's the West's prime strategist.* She pointed over the readying soldiers to a grassy knoll darkened by the growing shadows of evening. 'We'll sleep there. I'll meet you. For now, I have to explain things to my father.'

Garn said nothing, apparently lost in his own thoughts.

Sliding from her saddle, Mitrian headed after Rache and Santagithi.

Garn slept, oblivious to the familiar swish of steel against whetstone and the rhythmical shrill of night insects, higher-pitched than those he had known as a gladiator. These sounds did not awaken him, nor did the chill and darkness that enwrapped him like a blanket. But a softer, lower noise did.

Instantly alert, Garn sprang to his feet, freeing his sword in the same motion. A pale glimmer of metal reflected in the moonlight, a blade whipping toward him. He slashed at it, meeting firm resistance. The ringing crash of steel disappeared amidst the battle preparations, and his sword locked with another. A curly-haired stranger confronted Garn through the block, dressed in Santagithi's silver and black.

'I have no feud with you,' Garn said, though he had killed many men with whom he had no feud. He pressed.

The youth spoke through gritted teeth. 'Mitrian was mine. You stole her. And, for that, *slave*, I'm going to kill you.'

Anger soured Garn's threat. Fury bucked against the same stiff control he used to break horseshoes. 'I don't even know your name. But I do know we're part of the same army.' Garn retreated slightly, then slammed into the block hard enough to throw his antagonist's sword free. He struck a defensive pose. 'One or both of us may die in the coming battle, but we may take Easterners with us. If you still feel we have cause to fight when the war is won, I'll gladly kill you then.'

'You do know my name, Garn.' The youth stepped back, lowering his blade. 'It's Listar. As a child, I watched you slaughter a friend and saw another slip into insanity to escape the pain of that same memory.'

Garn vaguely recalled the blacksmith's son, from the time before survival had become a daily struggle. That childhood taste of freedom had only made his captivity more bitter.

'If you survive the war, I'm the one who'll send you to the pits of Hel.' Whirling on his heel, Listar strode into the darkness.

Garn watched the muscled form disappear into night's darkness. 'You're too late,' he murmured dully. 'I've already been there.'

26 The Flagstone Tomb

Rache's stallion glided like a shadow past sprawled soldiers while Santagithi strode at its side. Neither man spoke, yet the silence between them hung, heavy with potential and need. Rache scarcely steered, letting the horse choose their course, afraid to open his mouth for fear he might offend Santagithi and ruin any chance at reconciliation – if he had not done so already. By announcing Mitrian and Garn's relationship in front of Santagithi's followers, he had backed his general into a tight corner. Santagithi's expression had made it clear that though Nantel's men, whom he'd seen among the troops, had returned with the story of the trial in Pudar they'd not had the courage to give their leader the news of Mitrian's marriage. For Garn's sake, Rache had needed to make an announcement sudden enough to divert the guards' attention; but shocking Santagithi in public had seemed unnecessary to the point of cruelty.

Santagithi stopped at the fringes of the Western camp, near a hill covered with low, twisted herbs whose spice smell perfumed the plains.

Rache drew up Bein, then loosened the reins to allow the horse to graze.

Unbroken, the silence dragged into darkness. Rache studied the crescent of moon, his thoughts shifting to flashing steel, splashed blood, and death screams. This war would provide the chance for so many brave warriors to live or die in glory.

Santagithi placed a hand on Rache's leg.

The Renshai met his gaze, respectfully allowing his general to speak first.

'Rache, I've missed you sorely. And not just for your competence as a weapon master.' Santagithi tapped Rache's calf several times, then squeezed amicably.

'You're everything I would have wanted my son to be.'

Rache stared, uncertain how to respond. Never before had a battlefield served as a place for sentiment. Surely Santagithi would not have wanted his son crippled, but this did not seem the time to raise bitter issues.

'I don't often admit I'm wrong.' Santagithi paused thoughtfully. 'In fact, I don't think I ever have . . .'

Now, Rache grinned, needing to break a mood that was becoming uncomfortably maudlin. 'You don't think you've ever admitted it? Or you don't think you've ever been wrong?'

Santagithi chuckled. 'Either.' Then, his face laspsed back into solemnity. 'I'm sorry, Rache. I made a mistake. In fact, I made several. All of them in the way I treated you. I can't undo them. But I can apologize and hope that's enough.'

'More than enough, sir.' Rache caught Santagithi's wrist in a callused hand, unconsciously gripping it like a sword. 'I never made anything easy for you. I guess neither of your "children" did.'

Santagithi smiled briefly. Now it was his turn to contemplate the moon. 'I had no right to command you to lead my infantry. Do you think Peusen would relieve you of your duties to fight for me again?' His tone grew cautious, and he kept his attention locked on the sky, as if it might hurt him to see Rache's reaction. 'Would you even want him to do that?'

Rache thought of the one-handed Northman's dedication to proving his men's value, gaining respect for them, and returning all his outcast soldiers to their former troops. 'I think Peusen would be thrilled. I suspect that's what he wanted all along.' Rache released Santagithi's hand. 'As for me, well, I guess I can put up with you one more time.' He tried to hide a tight-lipped smile.

Despite the joke, Santagithi remained grave. 'If not for the sword skill you taught her, Mitrian would be dead. I wish things had turned out differently, but if she's happy with . . .' He winced despite his bold words '. . . with Garn, how can I be otherwise? I might as well admit it now. I always hoped you and Mitrian . . .' He let the observation hang.

'No,' Rache said softly, finally becoming serious himself. 'I can't explain it. Not now. But it would have been wrong for me to marry. And wronger still to sire children.'

Santagithi stiffened. 'Rache, there's something I need to tell you about Emerald.'

She's married, Rache guessed. The thought thrilled him. *Loving me was nothing but pain for her. She deserves all the happiness a good and loyal husband can give her.* Sensing Santagithi's discomfort, Rache rescued his general. 'And there are things I need to tell you as well. But first, don't you want to know about your grandson?'

'There really is a child?' Santagithi met Rache's gaze, guarded hope clear on his features. 'A boy? Does he look like Mitrian . . .?' He trailed off, his implication obvious.

'No.'

Santagithi did not look away, but the flicker of disappointment in his eyes did not escape Rache's notice.

'Actually, I hear he's the perfect image of his grandfather.'

A grin crept across Santagithi's lips, arrested suddenly into a stiff grimace. 'Which grandfather ?'

Rache drew out the pause, letting Santagithi sweat for no better reason than cruel amusement. 'You, of course.' He added playfully, 'Unfortunately.'

'Unfortunately ?'

'How would you like to have to follow in the footsteps of a petty, iron-handed, stone-headed leader who never recognized the value of the best captain he ever had.' He smiled broadly to make it clear that he was teasing.

Santagithi's grip went painfully tight on Rache's calf.

Rache laughed. 'I've got little enough feeling in that leg. Are you planning to tear it off ?'

'And beat you to death with it, you Northie bastard.'

'Really ? Well, I'll just wait here until you gather the twelve other generals you'd need to do it.'

'Twelve other . . .' The expression of feigned offense on Santagithi's face would remain, indelibly inscribed on Rache's memory. 'All right. I've obviously spent too many words praising your skill. Now it's time to teach you some respect.' Santagithi's hand whipped from Rache's leg to his own sword hilt, and he whisked the blade free. 'Draw, captain. I'm going to spar you into the mud.'

'Perfect,' Rache said, sarcasm thickening his tone. 'I'm with you sixteen years, and you wait until I'm crippled to test your talents against mine.' As quickly as he spoke the words, Rache cursed himself. *Why did I have to raise the one issue that put a barrier between us?* His hands fell naturally to his swords, then balled to white fists around the hilts.

'Because,' Santagithi said, without missing a cue, 'I'm a damned competent strategist.' He lunged, jabbing for Rache's abdomen with a full commitment.

The general's gibe dispelled the last shred of emotional tension. Rache drew and blocked, catching Santagithi's blade in a double cross. He laughed, twisting to disarm.

But Santagithi spun his sword in the direction of Rache's momentum, drawing it from the block and rescuing his grip. He riposted with an underhand sweep.

Rache parried easily.

A voice rose over the chime of clashing steel. The newcomer spoke the Western trading tongue with a musical Northern accent. 'Excellent strategy, lord. Kill off two of the West's most competent soldiers before the war begins.'

Rache whirled toward the voice without lowering his guard. Santagithi back-stepped and turned.

A brawny Northman waited in the night shadows, his war braids luminescent in the moonlight. Blue eyes sparkled coldly above a familiar, hawklike nose.

'Valr Kirin.' Rache smiled. 'Your brother . . .'

'is here,' Kirin finished abruptly. 'Just as you said he would be, yes. I've spoken with him.' His rudeness seemed uncharacteristic, and it cued Rache that the Slayer had more important matters to relay. 'One of our scouts located Siderin's army.'

Santagithi sheathed his sword. All humor left him. 'Where ?'

'They're camped south of here, on the Western Plains, in a quarry.'

'A quarry ?' Santagithi's brow furrowed, then a tense smile twitched across his features. 'Siderin must have expected to catch us unprepared. Obviously, he chose that camp for discretion, not defense. Probably, he planned on sneaking his army across the barren plains and taking our cities one by one. That mistake will cost him.'

The sound of a footfall drew Rache's attention, though Santagithi and Valr Kirin seemed oblivious. A man as tall and thin as a willow branch wandered into the moonlight, a wolf padding at his heels. *Shadimar ?* Rache stared, incredulous. Despite the significance of the war to himself and the West, he had never expected a Wizard's involvement. *At least not directly.*

Kirin nodded, acknowledging Santagithi's observation. 'King Tenja hopes we can surround them and launch a surprise attack.'

'That may give us the edge we need to win this war.' Santagithi's features puckered in concentration. 'But we're not going to be able to sneak in an army without rousing them. At least not unless we eliminate their scouts and sentries first.'

Rache gave the Wizard an abbreviated gesture of acknowledgement.

The Wizard responded with a slight nod.

Valr Kirin spoke gently, as if in apology. 'We'd hoped you'd have an idea for how to clear the sentries.'

Santagithi considered in silence. 'Damn,' he muttered at length, continuing in a soft monotone that implied he was thinking aloud. 'What we need is a team of assassins, a pair would work. At least one would have to be a mountain man, and both would need to shoot a crossbow with perfect aim.' He addressed Kirin directly. 'Don't we have any Béarnides at all ?'

'Not among the Vikerians, for certain, sir. Peusen probably has a few, but I don't think he'd have any among the archers. Béarn breeds the largest men I've known, and they tend toward huge weapons and strong-arm tactics.'

Santagithi sighed. 'I've got a few soldiers who probably have Béarnian blood, but not one who's seen, let alone climbed, a mountain craggier than the Granite Hills. Any Béarnides in King Gasir's army will probably have the same fault.'

The Eastern Wizard waited quietly, so Rache turned his attention back to his general. 'I can't help with the mountain man problem, but if you're looking for a stealthy, expert marksman, I do have a suggestion.'

Both leaders eyed Rache hopefully.

'Among Iaplege's archers there's a small Erythanian, a redhead called Arduwyn. He tracked me across the entire Western world without my knowledge, then shot down an enemy from a distance I wouldn't have believed possible. I've only ever seen him use long-bow. But Nantel used to say that a good longbowman had to shoot crossbow with both eyes closed just to have a challenge.'

Darkness shrouded Santagithi's expression, but his stance seemed pensive. 'Kirin, see if you can find this Erythanian. Find out if he or anyone else knows a mountain man who can shoot. We'll meet for conference at the usual site as soon as you can gather everyone. We're going to have to work fast.'

Without bothering to acknowledge the command, Valr Kirin rushed off into the darkness.

A thought seeped into Rache's mind, and, though it bothered him, it would not be banished. 'Sir, Arduwyn has a close friend who fits your description perfectly. But I don't think it's going to please you. I know I don't like the idea.'

'Be specific,' Santagithi said, never one to stall for amenities during a strategy session.

'Ster – '

'No!' Santagithi's reply came so quickly, it cut off the second syllable of Rache's suggestion. He lowered his voice. 'I'm not using the heir to Béarn's throne as a common assassin. He shouldn't even be here.'

Rache raised his hands in surrender. 'I'm just saying he fits the description. I'm not suggesting anything.'

'But I am,' the Eastern Wizard said with a quiet certainty that held the authority of a shout. 'If Sterrane is the best warrior for the task, then he should go.'

'That's madness,' Santagithi roared. He hesitated, continuing in a different vein. 'Unless you know he won't get hurt. Is that something you can know or see to?'

Secodon snuffled at Bein's nose, wagging his plumed tail expectantly. Shadimar frowned. 'I affect the future only by guiding men to certain tasks. I learn the effects of my meddling the same way you do, by seeing what happened.'

Santagithi shook his head. 'Sterrane could die. It's not worth the risk.'

The Eastern Wizard approached Santagithi. 'If the West falls, Sterrane will become the king of rubble and as much a slave to Siderin as any peasant. It's in Sterrane's best interests, as well as ours, to use each soldier to his abilities, no matter the cost.'

'Sir.' Rache cleared his throat, trying to make Santagithi's decision easier. 'If Sterrane manages to regain Béarn, he'll need to become a military leader and a diplomat.' Had the mood been less desperate, the idea of childlike Sterrane serving in either role would have sent Rache into a fit of laughter. 'How can he lead men to war when he's never had a chance to see battle?'

Santagithi stared at the moon, pressed by logic as well as time. 'All right,' he said, at length. 'Rache, fetch Sterrane and Arduwyn to the meeting. Quietly, please. It's best no one knows Sterrane's station until after the war.' He added, as if it mattered, 'And I still don't like this.' Turning, he stomped after Valr Kirin.

Rache felt certain only he heard the Eastern Wizard's wry mumble:

'The powers that be have duly noted your concern.'

Rache chuckled beneath his breath. Drawing in Bein's reins, he hurried to obey his general's decree.

In the still youth of evening, three dark horses drifted across the grassy plains. Riding behind Rache, at Sterrane's side, Arduwyn felt as twitchy as a rabbit in the shadow of a hawk. *I can't believe our leaders would put the fate of the Westlands in the hands of an exiled hunter and a sweet but dim-witted hermit.* The idea seemed ludicrous, and responsibility crushed down on Arduwyn until he counted breaths to keep from hyperventilating. He readjusted the crossbow on his shoulder.

Rache reined in his stallion.

Arduwyn and Sterrane pulled up behind him.

'Don't dawdle,' the Renshai cautioned. 'If dawn comes before you finish, you've no chance at all, and our army little more.'

Arduwyn dismounted without comment. He handed his reins to Rache. Sterrane passed the archer four bolts, then slid to the ground beside him, maneuvering his own crossbow into a more comfortable position on his hairy shoulder. The two men walked several paces from Rache before dropping to their bellies. Sterrane waited.

Snakelike, Arduwyn wriggled through the grasses, a dagger clenched in his teeth and the bow and bolts in one hand. Dressed in ebony leather with his arms and legs smeared with soot, he became a lost shadow in night's pitch. Behind him, Sterrane crept more slowly. Swathed in silver wolf pelts, limbs bathed in ash, he lay clearly outlined against the grasses. *But he'll blend well with the flagstone cliffs.* Arduwyn pushed onward.

Archer now, not hunter. Bitterly, Arduwyn reminded himself of his need to kill men. He slithered forward. Though protected by leather, his belly felt raw and his muscles cramped. Cradled in plains grass, he stole a precious moment to stretch.

A movement ahead froze Arduwyn in mid-sprawl. His practiced fingers slid a bolt to the string. He inched toward the sound, vision straining through darkness.

Grass rustled again. Then, abruptly, the sentry became fully visible. He was thin, dressed in ruddy-brown, lacquered leather, with hair black as charcoal. He turned, revealing large irises nearly as dark.

Arduwyn aimed and fired. The bolt embedded in the sentry's right eye, and the Easterner collapsed without a cry.

Regret pressed in on Arduwyn, but he forced it aside. *This is war, and that man is an enemy. In the reverse situation, he would have killed me with no more compunction.* Holding his breath, he crawled to his victim. A touch confirmed that the man lay dead. Several arm's lengths beyond the corpse, cliffs dropped into a quarry. Arduwyn drew to its edge and glanced downward. Moonlight glimmered from quartz veins in the walls, but its depths were an indecipherable pool of darkness.

Arduwyn turned away and crawled along the quarry ledge. Ahead, a twig snapped, and a second sentry appeared. To the archer's chagrin, his hands shook as he reloaded. *Can't let the fact that they're men rattle me. I'm a soldier now.*

In the moment of hesitation, the sentry's gaze found Arduwyn.

Robbed of time for thought, Arduwyn tightened his finger on the trigger. The Easterner recoiled. The bolt plowed through his neck, and he slumped to the ground.

Slick with sweat, Arduwyn slit the quivering throat with his dagger. He wiped blood from his blade on the grass and resignedly returned the dagger to his teeth. It left a warm, salt taste in his mouth. Revolted, he wriggled from the cliffs to where Sterrane waited and gestured at the area he had cleared.

Sterrane nodded, dividing his duty into its simplest denominations. He had never killed a man before. But these Easterners threatened his friends; for that, they must die. He scuttled to the canyon and peered inside as Arduwn had done, seeing the same impenetrable darkness. Grasping a quarry edge, he lowered his feet down the cliff face. One probing toe touched a rock ledge, and he found a firm foothold.

Clinging to the flagstone, Sterrane raised a hand. Arduwyn passed the crossbow to him and retreated. Adherent as a fly to the cliff face, Sterrane scuttled sideways, making each movement of foot or hand with a calm deliberateness that came with years of practice. He knew that on the far side of the sentries, Arduwyn paralleled his course.

Stones bit into Sterrane's fingers and toes. He kept his gaze on the ground above him. Shortly, he discovered the next sentry, facing away from the quarry. Balancing the bow in the crook of his left arm, Sterrane braced the stock against his thigh. He groped along the trigger mechanism. Finding it in place, he nocked a quarrel from his belt quiver.

Sterrane's weight shifted. A stone gave way beneath his left foot. Abruptly thrown off-balance, he hung by one hand while his toes clawed the smooth rock for a hold. Pebbles careened into the quarry, and Sterrane felt his fingers slide. It took an effort of will not to drop the crossbow. Then his foot caught a small ledge, and he carefully pulled himself back into position.

Sterrane raised his head to a pair of the darkest eyes he had ever seen. The guard's mouth parted in a cry of warning. Sterrane's finger tightened reflexively on the trigger. His bolt tore through the sentry's chest.

While Sterrane readjusted his grip, Arduwyn appeared, slicing the sentry from ear to ear. Blood sprayed the archer, and he drew away in revulsion. He tore the quarrel from the dead man, tossed it back to Sterrane, and disappeared into the darkness.

Over time, hunter and heir learned to pace themselves so that they came upon the sentries simultaneously. By the time they had cleared half the quarry cliff, Sterrane's hands and feet felt ravaged. Every step left bloody prints on the mountainside. Each new hold erupted into agony. The pain became so severe, he ceased to notice the stiffness that enveloped his body. But the grimace on Arduwyn's face revealed the torment of kinked muscles. Sterrane believed he heard his small friend curse the gods, himself, everyone in the war on both sides, and even the father who had taught him to shoot.

By the time Sterrane reached the ramp that formed the only exit from the open mine, an ominous glow colored the edge of the sky. He hesitated. The cut stone felt soothing after the crags that had viciously torn skin from his soles and palms. Though sweat had made streaks of gray paste from the ashes on his limbs, the silver pelts matched the flagstone exactly. Without thinking, he shot down the sentry on the ramp.

A grisly figure emerged from the darkness. Sterrane barely recognized Arduwyn, smeared with blood and slime. Saying nothing, the Béarnide killed another scout at the far end of the ramp. He paused, reluctant to return to the sharp cliffs that felt like daggers against his shredded feet. He raised his eyes to a pink-tinged sky. *Dawn.*

Sterrane gripped chunks of flagstone and bit his lip to staunch a scream of pain. More quickly, he scuttled from one sentry to the next, without waiting for Arduwyn or his bolts, caught in a dizzying nightmare of slaughter that filled his eyes with tears.

Soon, rings of color tinged the horizon. Arduwyn whispered, 'Sterrane. It's over.'

Sterrane clambered up the cliff face to where Arduwyn's first, broken victim lay. Catching a thick, furred wrist, the archer helped his companion to level ground. There, they both collapsed, crazed with pain. Sterrane longed for the sleep he knew he would not get.

The gray haze of morning grew around them. Sterrane nudged Arduwyn to his feet. Like ancients, they dragged their complaining bodies to where Rache waited. Now they only needed to race the sun.

In two divisions, from either side of the graded exit, the bowmen of the Western army fanned out along the ledge of the flagstone quarry. Santagithi's swordsmen and those of the other smaller towns milled among the archers, while the larger armies prepared to hold the ramp.

By dawn's pale light, Rache examined the Eastern force below him, a vast sea of warriors awakening from sleep. Excitement touched him, as always, but the ugliness of the coming attack soured his battle joy. Though he had spent most of his years among non-Renshai armies, the thought of soldiers dying by distant, impersonal arrows sickened him. *Even enemies should have the right to die with honor.* Yet he understood the need for strategy, and that, for most of the men, the ends mattered more than the means. So far, the threat of Easterners had kept the Western patchwork of armies united. The common banner, the Eastern Wizard's presence, and trust in Santagithi's abilities as a tactician had kept the leadership cooperative. And the followers of each general or king remained fiercely loyal to his own.

As the sun slid over the horizon, the men in the quarry rose. One shouted an alarm. As the Eastern soldiers rushed to their defense, a rain of Western arrows fell upon them.

Beside Mitrian, Rache stiffened, watching the drama unfold

beneath him in silent dissatisfaction. In the quarry, shields appeared like silver parasols. Helmets hugged black hair. And still another volley of quarrels and arrows found their mark.

'Who's that?' Mitrian jogged Rache's arm and pointed into the depths.

Rache tried to follow Mitrian's gaze into the chaos. Discovering an unusually ornate helmet, he assumed he had found the focus of her attention. 'One of Siderin's lieutenants.' Even as he explained, another figure seized and held his gaze, an immense warrior encased in metal. A steel helmet hid his head and face. Tines ran in a line from his nose to the fur that partially covered its base. He signaled with broad sweeps of his arm. Rache jabbed a finger toward the figure. 'That's got to be Siderin.'

From the cliffs, arrows sped for the Eastern King. Most swung wide. Others bounced from thickly crafted armor. Not one found its mark.

Suddenly, as one, the Eastern soldiers swarmed up the cliffs, avoiding the exit ramp barricaded by Pudarian cavalry. The Western archers retreated, and the swordsmen dismounted and closed. As the Easterners clambered to the hilltops, they met drawn swords. Any head or limb that reached the crest was amputated.

As much as he loved war, Rache cared little for mass murder, so it did not bother him that, mounted, he could not join the fighters on the cliffs. Instead, he drew back, watching his charges, prepared for any Easterners who cut through the first Western ranks. Garn had leapt from his horse and seemed bored with the ease of killing the climbers. Looking dazed, Mitrian sent man after man to his death.

Men had dug this quarry, and men would fill it. Butchered bodies tumbled down upon those Easterners still inside the quarry. Some of the falling corpses dislodged climbers lower on the cliffs, who tumbled to their deaths as well.

As the Easterners massed, they reached the summits in greater numbers. Many fought past the swordsmen, and Rache found himself embroiled in battle as well. His swords flashed through the dawn, like extensions of his arms, and claimed dozens of Eastern lives. Iaplegians and Pudarians hurried to the ledges to help stem the flow, leaving the ramp vulnerable to counterattack.

'Hold the ramp!' Santagithi screamed. Though close, Rache scarcely heard his leader's voice amid the metal and wood harmony of weapons against armor, flesh, and shields.

Then, as if a giant hand had reached into the flagstone quarry and unscrambled the chaos, a pattern shaped in its depths. A semicircle of Eastern archers faced the Pudarian cavalry at the mouth of the

475

ramp. Though rivaled by this new menace, the cavalry stood its ground. Retreat would forfeit the advantage they had gained by surprise and leave an opening for the Easterners' escape.

The Eastern archers fired. The Western ranks held. Men blocked or dodged arrows with shields of bronze or steel. One tumbled from his mount. A horse crumpled and took another down with it.

Now the Pudarian cavalry charged the Eastern archers. But Siderin's cavalry slipped through the ranks of his bowmen. The archers fired a parting round over the heads of the mounted soldiers, then were lost among the infantry behind them.

Rache watched, though the press of Eastern soldiers reaching the summit continued to thicken. With its army spread along the ledges, the Westerners on the ramp were outnumbered four to one. They fought valiantly, but the man-horse barrier across the exit weakened under repeated batterings. A path formed where the Eastern cavalry struck. Slowly, the soldiers of the Pudarian cavalry were driven away, trapped against the sides of the ramp, or killed.

Bodies rolled down the slope, trampled to crimson masses by the feet of horses and men. As the Western cavalry tottered, Siderin rode into the fray, looking every bit the demon legends called him. His silver-spired helmet had no opening for a face, only a notched pair of holes at the eyes that continued, as slits, to the helmet's base. His iron breastplate seemed out of place amid waves of ruddy-brown leather.

As the Easterners shifted toward the ramp, Rache no longer found himself menaced. He watched with concern as King Gasir of Pudar held the ramp with his weakening cavalry. Siderin rode directly for Pudar's king.

An Easterner lunged for Rache.

The Renshai parried easily. His riposte swept a fatal gash through the warrior's throat, and he looked up in time to see Siderin's flail whip toward King Gasir. 'No!' Rache shouted. Even if he had been close enough to be heard, his warning came too late. The spiked, iron ball claimed helmet and head from the Pudarian king. Gasir plummeted from his horse, blood ebbing from his tattered neck. And Siderin's weapon severed the last link in the chain of men on the ramp. Like a river through a broken dam, the Eastern force gained freedom from their flagstone tomb.

'Forward!' Rache commanded. His mount plunged toward the ramp, and he did not look back to see which of his men had followed. He reached the ramp as the last of Siderin's infantry was making its escape. The fragmented Western cavalry strove to reform its barrier. With Rache's reinforcements, they stayed the flow from the quarry, cutting off the last three dozen soldiers from the Eastern ranks. The Renshai recognized Garn among his men.

'Drive them into a pack.' Rache pulled up his horse to change direction. 'Then retreat and let the archers have them.' He bore in, directing warriors with the ease of a dog herding sheep.

As the Easterners bunched, the Western warriors withdrew, one by one. Soon even Rache retreated. But Garn still fought, apparently driven by fervor of battle. And with one of their soldiers engaged, the archers held their fire.

Accustomed to obedience, Rache felt the first stirrings of rage. As Garn cut down another man, Rache drew to his side. 'Pull out!'

Garn continued to fight, his strokes swift and competent, his green eyes blazing.

'Damn it, Garn, I said retreat.'

Oblivious, Garn fought on.

Rache knew he had to draw Garn out quickly. To tolerate insubordination meant to lose the respect of his men, some of whom already seemed hesitant about following a cripple. He understood the need to explain rank and cooperation to Garn, yet speed had to take precedence over diplomacy. Rache seized the bridle of Garn's horse. 'Control yourself, Garn. You're not in the pit!'

Garn recoiled as if whip-struck, and Rache managed to steer them both clear of the Easterners. The archers dropped their volley.

And Garn whirled on his commander. 'I should have killed you when I had the chance.' He hacked for Rache's arm.

Rache jerked back from Garn's bridle, and the blade nicked his fingers, stinging. He drew his own sword and blocked, barely in time to catch Garn's next attack. The force of the blow slammed Rache sideways. Only a simultaneous shift by the Renshai and his stallion kept him in the saddle. 'Garn, stop!'

Enraged, Garn hammered for Rache again. This time the Renshai dodged, not eager to experience Garn's strength again. He returned with a Renshai maneuver that missed Garn's wrist by a hair's breadth. 'Don't be stupid. If I don't kill you, Santagithi's men will.' Rache tried to disengage.

But Garn bore in with a feigned high sweep that reverted to a jab. Rache responded with a parry, intentionally drawing Garn even closer. 'Damn you, Garn. Listen! When this war is finished, you and I *will* fight to the death. Fairly. Your skill against mine. Until then, nothing interferes with my charges' safety or their lives. Including Mitrian's. Do you understand that?'

Garn paused, his strong features flushed, his eyes narrowed to slits.

Rache spoke even more quietly, though his message carried the same note of command. 'The self-control you claim to seek won't come from killing me. It's inside you.' He muttered mostly to himself. 'If you haven't already destroyed it.' Wheeling Bein, Rache rode for the ramp, now addressing his soldiers. 'Men, grab horses where you can. We need to catch our troop.'

Mitrian rode up to Rache at the quarry mouth, and they headed south together. Though she could not have heard the verbal exchange, Garn's antics must have told the story. Rache saw tears in her eyes.

27 Renshai Rage and the God of Wrath

As evening caught up with the Western infantry, Santagithi's horse bunched with anticipation, its sinews as taut as its rider. Though he had led many warriors to glory with impetuous glee, he felt no joy this night. During the raids on barbaric neighbors, he had fought with the same fevered frenzy as his men. But in this war, he understood the need to keep his distance from the line, to direct the strategies that would often need to change at a moment's notice. The Western forces had already lost one of its generals and could not afford another.

Santagithi raised his gaze to a sun ringed with colored haze and reveled in the bittersweet odor of victory. Slowly, he turned his attention to the stately man who rode at his side. King Tenja of Vikerin had the sharp manner of a Northman but lacked Rache's wild exuberance. Rubies and colored beads glittered amid his war braids.

'Fine warriors, your Northmen.'

The fair general nodded. 'And your men as well.'

Amenities brief but completed, Santagithi continued, 'We'd better camp. We left most of our bowmen and many soldiers at the quarry.' *Mitrian among them*, he recalled miserably. Despite Rache's and Shadimar's assurances and his own bold promises, Santagithi despised the thought of his daughter in battle. 'Our cavalry can herd the Easterners toward the ocean while the infantry rests.'

King Tenja nodded. He shouted a few gruff commands in a Northern singsong, and the march slowed to a crawl. A Northman rode forward, presumably to relay the message to Valr Kirin and the cavalry.

Santagithi reined in and dismounted. Men sprawled across the plain, seizing their last chance to sleep before the next battle. Tenja, too, clambered to the ground, and the generals tethered their horses side by side before reclining at the base of a scrub pine. As they discussed strategy, all other concerns fled Santagithi's mind, replaced by the smooth, familiar blend of wisdom and experience.

*

Hours later, blue-black evening framed the rising crescent of moon. A horse threaded through the sleeping camp; and its rider, a Northman, reined to a halt before Tenja and Santagithi. The sky emitted just enough light for Santagithi to recognize the scout's features frozen in fascination.

Alarmed, Santagithi rose. 'You bring news.'

'Yes, sire. From the cavalry ahead.' The scout dismounted and knelt before his king. He stared through Santagithi, his thoughts distant. 'Things are going as ordered. Valr Kirin is riding at the heels of their infantry. They'll have no rest tonight.'

Santagithi returned to his seat, smiling with ruthless calculation. Without sleep, the Eastern army would be in poor condition to fight at the edge of the Southern Sea. 'Any casualties since the quarry?'

The scout chewed his lip, considering a question that should not have required thought. 'No, sire. Not on our side.' His blue eyes gleamed. 'Because a god has come to help us.'

Shocked silent, Santagithi studied the scout through narrowed eyes.

King Tenja settled against the twisted tree trunk. 'A god, Harold? What makes you so certain you've seen a god?'

Harold sat on his folded legs, his hands trembling at his sides. 'He just seemed to appear, mounted on a bay that snorted storm clouds from its nostrils, and right between Siderin's cavalry and infantry. Then he charged toward us, trampling Easterners or reaping soldiers like weeds on his sword. And that sword never stopped. With respect to my liege and commander, Valr Kirin never swung a weapon with such speed or skill.'

Santagithi frowned. Accustomed to his own scouts' direct, factual reports, he found the Northman's embellishments intolerably burdensome. But he could not quell curiosity. The Vikerians were fascinated by and revered Tenja's Nordmirian lieutenant. Any man who could steal a Vikerian's loyalty from Kirin would need to be competent indeed. *But not a god.* Despite the presence of the Eastern Wizard, Santagithi could not believe deities would descend from the heavens. At least, he would not believe it until he saw one with his own eyes.

Harold continued, enthusiasm undiminished by Santagithi's hostile expression. 'As the god broke through Siderin's infantry, two Eastern lieutenants pursued him on horseback, heedlessly stomping their own men. Too far away to come to the god's aid, I thought he was dead. But the god calmly wheeled his mount and charged.' Harold loosed a strained chuckle. 'The bay flew as if winged – right over the lieutenant's horse! Its forehooves struck the Easterner's forehead, throwing him from his mount. Dead. Then the god killed the other lieutenant with his sword and finished by battling and slaying a half-dozen Easterners at once, even before we could come to his aid.' Harold glanced from king to general, apparently seeking some mirror of his own excitement.

King Tenja leaned forward with interest, but his voice remained quietly composed. 'Harold, this god. Can you describe him ?'

The scout bowed his head, turning to the courteous behavior forgotten in the fever pitch of his zeal. 'He looked like Thor, sire. Or Frey, perhaps, sire. His hair glimmered gold and silver, cut short.' He raised his head proudly. 'A Northman, of course, sire. And his sword skill . . .'

King Tenja waved the scout silent before he could launch into another awed oratory on the Northman's competence. The king's hard mouth twitched into a smile of amusement. 'Thank you, Harold. Tell Kirin we're waiting for the archers we left at the quarry. We'll catch the cavalry when we can. Meanwhile, his orders stand.' The king hesitated, glancing to Santagithi to confirm the strategy.

Santagithi nodded absently. Tenja's words had reminded him of Mitrian's, Rache's, and Sterrane's absences, and he strained for the sound of hoofbeats that might signal their return.

'Dismissed.'

The scout paused, seemingly torn between obeying his king and the excitement threatening to overwhelm him. Rising, he mounted his horse. As he kicked it to a canter, he called over his shoulder, 'A god is here, sire ! And I'm glad he's on our side.'

King Tenja stiffened at the scout's defiance, then laughed as he rode from sight.

Santagithi grinned. After Rache and Nantel had left, he had grown accustomed to unquestioned obedience. His men lacked the healthy, if annoying, exuberance trained into Northmen from birth. 'You don't really believe there's a god fighting this war.' He tried to keep his voice flat and nonjudgmental, not wishing to offend the Northern king.

'I think,' Tenja replied carefully, 'that there's a lunatic Northman trying to find Valhalla. He's not one of mine. Otherwise, Harold would have known him by name.' He faced Santagithi directly, brows raised in question.

'I have only one Northman among my ranks. And Rache's still back at the quarry. As far as I know, there are only two other Northmen here, both generals. Surely any commander would know better than to hurl himself into the center of combat.' The sentiment emerged more like a question than a statement.

King Tenja hunched forward, his face a mask of annoyance. 'It's not Kirin's brother. Harold would have mentioned Peusen's missing hand, if only because one of our gods is one-handed. It has to be Colbey.' His musical, Northern pronunciation smoothed it to 'Cull-bay.' His forehead lapsed into creases as he mulled over the name.

'He does fit the description,' Santagithi admitted. 'I don't care much for his methods, but any leader who inspires the men this much should be encouraged.' *I guess.* With King Gasir dead, Santagithi doubted he had the authority to stop Colbey anyway. As general of the largest army, the brazen Northman held the West's highest rank.

The hoofbeats of the stragglers rang like thunder to Santagithi. 'Please forgive me, sire.' Without further explanation or pausing for a reply, he swung aboard his mount, wove through the wary stillness of blood-caked warriors, and met the newcomers as they arrived.

Most of the new arrivals were archers. These Santagithi sorted by troop, then sent to join their cavalry. The archers broke around the general in a harried line, and Santagithi sought familiar faces. He found Sterrane first. His hair and beard wrapped his face in limp strands. Blood slicked his reins, and exhaustion pressed him hard enough that his huge head sagged.

A wave of pity washed over Santagithi. A victim of more worldly men since childhood, Sterrane had many more trials to face after the war was won. The general's discomfort flared to guilt. He, too, had used Sterrane, risking a life far too important to lose. Even Shadimar's support and the realization that the assassination mission had benefited Sterrane at least as much as any leader failed to soothe him.

As Sterrane pulled up before Santagithi, the general clamped a tattered, swollen hand between his own. Sterrane fell against him, unable to gather the strength to speak. 'Forgive me,' Santagithi whispered. 'I asked more of you than I had a right.' Dismounting, he lowered Sterrane to the ground, pulled his own blanket from his horse, and spread the fine cloth on the ground. 'For the rest of the war, you'll remain behind the battle lines. Until this war is won, you'll stay with the generals.'

Another pair of hands helped Santagithi arrange Sterrane on the blanket. The general followed the arms to a scrawny figure in torn, dirty leather. He met Arduwyn's gaze. 'You've earned rest, too. Stay with Sterrane.'

Arduwyn frowned. 'No, sir, I can't. As an archer, I can fight at a distance in safety.' He stroked the bow across his shoulder, but Santagithi's gaze found the scimitar strapped to his belt. 'I'll join the cavalry.'

Though touched by the small man's courage, Santagithi knew Arduwyn would probably come to regret his decision. Still, the general had neither right nor reason to protect the hunter, so he made no protest. He watched the redhead ride into a pack of archers and disappear.

As Arduwyn rode away, Garn and Mitrian pulled up beside Santagithi. Tears filled Santagithi's eyes as he rose and caught his daughter's leg with the same affection as he had touched Rache's. But, where the Renshai's muscles had withered, Mitrian's had become as thick as any soldier's.

Mitrian seized her father's hand, but Santagithi turned his attention on Garn's stony features. No emotion accompanied the confrontation; war and its need for strategy swept away all grudges, and the general felt nothing for his daughter's mate. Still, he could even grant amnesty to Siderin if it meant Mitrian would come home. He cleared his throat, wishing he had the words to atone for years of whips, cages, and forced battles, discarding his own hatred and bitterness for the sake of his daughter's future and happiness. 'Garn, when the war is won, I'd be honored if you and your family returned to my town. You would, of course, be accorded the respect and position that marriage to my daughter demands.'

Santagithi waited, wanting to say much more, yet knowing Garn would respond better to a direct request. To stir any emotion meant reviving deep-seated memories and hatred.

Mitrian, too, watched Garn expectantly.

'I need to think about it,' Garn said, his tone revealing nothing. 'After the war is over and certain matters taken care of.'

Garn's emphasis on the term 'matters' did not escape Santagithi's notice, though it did puzzle him.

No explanation was forthcoming. Catching Mitrian's hand, Garn rode off into the camp with his wife.

Santagithi started to turn to watch them go and was stopped by the sight of Rache's stallion only a short distance away. Surely, the captain had heard Santagithi's proposal to Garn, and the general hoped his attempt to make amends would please Rache.

But the Renshai rode past with a fierce stare. Only a subtle tip of his head showed he even acknowledged his general's presence.

Though dismayed by Rache's curtness, Santagithi dismissed it as battle lust. He made a mental note to tell Rache the news about Emerald as soon as time and Rache's mood allowed it.

Annoyance hammered Rache until rage disrupted his concentration completely. *Endangering the lives of my men, undermining my command in front of my soldiers, attacking an officer in a combat situation.* Any of the charges against Garn spelled treason, an offense punishable by death. *How could I have possibly believed Garn and*

I could settle our differences? Now the suggestion seemed ludicrous. Still, Rache found it impossible to forget the hope on Carad's dying features, the desperate need to have Rache shape his son. Rache fought the memory. *Garn will live to the war's end. I'll see to that. Then, if he still insists on fighting, I'll kill him.*

A horseman drew to Rache's side.

Reluctantly, Rache shifted his attention outward, to a youth in the armor of Santagithi's guards. The features seemed familiar, yet unplaceable, and Rache felt certain he had never trained this soldier.

Sensing Rache's confusion, the youth identified himself. 'It's Listar.'

The name jogged Rache's memory. 'You're the one who forged Mitrian's sword. Beautiful workmanship. Did you craft yours as well?' He held out a hand.

Listar passed his blade to Rache obligingly. 'You know Garn well?'

Rache glared sharply, searching Listar's unscarred face. Convinced the youth had not meant the question as a taunt, he answered stiffly. 'Too well.'

Listar brushed hair from his cheeks with nervous strokes. 'How good is he? With a sword, I mean.'

The words rankled. Rache reined his temper, convinced Listar's cruelty was unintentional. 'Good enough. Why?'

Listar flushed, momentarily at a loss for speech. Then the words tumbled forth. 'He stole Mitrian from me.'

Now more amused than angry, Rache swung figure eights with Listar's sword, testing the balance and finding it respectable. 'Are you certain she was ever yours?' Instantly, he regretted his cavalier attitude. He had nearly forgotten the widespread rumors about Mitrian and himself.

Listar's knuckles blanched about the reins. 'She would have married me.'

Rache saw no need to argue the point.

'When I thought she was dead, I wanted to die, too. That's when I joined the guard force.' Listar slammed a fist on his saddle. 'I will kill Garn.'

Rache suppressed a smile, lowering the sword. His feud with Garn made Listar's seem insignificant. 'Listar.' He tried to keep his tone gentle. 'You've no reason to seek death any longer. If you fought Garn, he would kill you.'

Listar shook with a fury so raw, Rache could feel it. The youth's voice grated. 'Are you challenging the competence of Santagithi's guards?'

Rache checked his own rising rage. 'I *trained* Santagithi's guards.

And I taught Garn to fight before you could lift a hammer. He's a born slayer. As for you, well, you just handed your only sword to a man you scarcely know.'

With a cry of fury, Listar lunged for his weapon.

Rache arched the sword in a graceful circle. The flat crashed harmlessly against Listar's armor, in warning. Then Rache returned the sword without bothering to draw one of his own, confident he could meet any attack Listar might launch. He ran a hand over his knee. 'If Garn could do this to me, imagine what he could do to you.' Wheeling, he rode away, leaving Listar to contemplate his words in a wash of vengeance and humiliation.

At the head of the Eastern cavalry, King Siderin ran a hand through pitch-colored hair matted with sweat. They had ridden through the night and well into the day. Foam dripped from his mount's nostrils, and the mingled odors of horses, men, and blood stung his nose.

An approaching scout waited until his king replaced his helmet, then slowed his mount to Siderin's gait.

Casually, the king unslung his whip, enjoying the subtle intimidation. 'Speak.'

The scout's hands trembled. 'Sire, the men are growing weary.'

Rage boiled through Siderin. His whip snapped air, and the scout's horse danced sideways. The Western army had massed apparently overnight, destroying strategies that had taken years to create. And the Southern Wizard, Carcophan, seemed to have disappeared. 'The men have no reason to sleep. After the war, many will never awaken. Warriors don't tire till the battle is won.'

'Yes, sire.'

'Have we identified the Western force?'

'Sire, they appear to be several loosely bound regiments rather than a single army.' The scout cleared his throat, gaze fixed on the scourge in Siderin's wide-veined fist. 'I believe the Golden-Haired Devils are among them.'

Siderin whirled toward the scout. 'Renshai? More than one?'

The scout shrank away. 'There's a single tribe of Northmen, sire.'

'What makes you think they're Renshai?'

The scout glanced at the sky in silent prayer. 'My liege, one rode through our infantry without taking a single wound. He killed two of our officers.' The scout cowered, though Siderin listened patiently. 'Only one of the Golden-Haired Devils could use a sword as he did.' Despite his words, his voice held no admiration.

Siderin coiled and uncoiled his whip. The sun scattered fiery highlights across his polished helm. His eyes glittered like obsidian chips in a sea of silver. 'What about Rache?'

'No one's seen him yet, eminence. The assassin's been sent, and we've set up several communication chains.'

Siderin considered, absently massaging Carcophan's vial through the leather of his pocket. He had distributed half of the poison to one of his quietest and stealthiest soldiers, with orders to deal with Rache. But Siderin had kept the remainder for himself. He wondered about this new threat. Even compensating for exaggeration, any man who could ride through an army's infantry unscathed would prove a formidable enemy. 'What other news ?' His gaze swept the horizon.

'The enemy is still riding directly behind us. Strangely, though they could catch us, they seem to be keeping a constant distance.'

Siderin's grip tightened. The muscles of his forearm bulged. 'How long have you noticed this ?'

The scout recoiled. 'Since last evening, sire.'

'Fool !' the whip lashed the scout's back.

Through leather, the stroke could feel little worse than a slap, but the scout cringed like a beaten child.

'Have the infantry gather a barricade. Trees if they can find them. Dead horses. Corpses. Whatever they can find. We'll make a stand in the marsh grasses.' He pointed to a distant forest of cattails. 'Go !'

The scout spun his mount to avoid another blow.

'Carcophan be slaughtered !' Siderin bellowed to his last lieutenant, behind him. 'Harrsha, there's salt in the air. They're driving us to the ocean. But it's not over yet ! This war will still be won.'

The leather thong whistled through air, slashing across the rump of Siderin's mount. The beast surged forward. The Eastern cavalry beat at their fatigued horses to follow their king. And the scout rode toward the infantry. Siderin promised victory, Siderin was Sheriva's Chosen One, and Siderin was never wrong.

The Western Plains stretched to a horizon scalloped by dunes, its sand scarred by the passage of myriad hooves and boots. For the sake of his horse, Arduwyn held it to a slow walk, though he fell behind the other archers. He knew the war would not begin until the infantry finished resting and joined them, so he saw no need to hurry. The agony of over-tested sinews had dulled to a throb, accentuated, whenever he moved, by the shooting pain of pulled muscles. The scimitar dragged, like dead weight at his side.

Arduwyn sighted the Western cavalry at midday. They rode in a line wilting due to the weariness of its men. At one end, Jakot led Santagithi's troop, a wave of studded leather that spanned two hundred men. Directly opposite, Peusen rode among his mismatched band of cripples and outcasts, his ranks as tight as the fifty Vikerians beside him. Led by Colbey, about a thousand Pudarians filled the gap between the Vikerians and Santagithi's ranks. Whispers raged through the line, and Arduwyn noticed that men from other Western troops had joined the Pudarians, notably Northmen. Behind the cavalry, the bowmen bunched, trying to match the swordsmen's trained precision with little success.

Colbey. A vague feeling of dread prickled through Arduwyn at the sight of the Renshai, though the two men had long ago made their peace. Silvered hair barely reached the nape of his neck, and the short locks in front feathered away from his eyes. The style clashed with the Vikerians' war braids, though he looked nonetheless a Northman. Surrounded by war-trained horsemen, Colbey appeared small, scarcely taller than Mitrian and half Garn's breadth. His soft cotton shirt and breeks emphasized his slightness, strange beside the armor and shields of his followers. Still, he was their leader. A golden power seemed to radiate from him, and Arduwyn felt certain Colbey was the cause of the Pudarian troops' growth. To the hunter, he seemed like a raging fire, awesome but with the potential for great evil.

Arduwyn picked his way through the cavalry without disturbing it. Though his bow and half-depleted quiver singled him out as an archer, he moved with such grace and quiet caution that no one questioned his presence in the ranks. As he wove between Vikerians and Pudarians, he discovered that the leader of the Northmen, a well-proportioned warrior with a beaklike nose, was also staring at Colbey, bearing an unconcealed expression of rancor. Quick to follow gods and heroes, Northmen were equally quick to find new ones. Arduwyn wondered if the lieutenant resented his followers' natural attraction to Colbey.

Hoping to catch Colbey by surprise, Arduwyn approached deliberately from behind. As he drew near, the Renshai's shoulders stiffened. With the tense caution of a deer who scents a cougar, Colbey turned his head. His gaze flickered over the troop behind him, then zeroed in on Arduwyn. His lips parted in a savage smile, and he crooked a finger to summon the archer.

Unsettled, Arduwyn rode to Colbey.

'I said you'd find a place in the war.'

Bothered by a trace of mockery in Colbey's tone, Arduwyn answered coolly. 'And I never doubted that. We've all found a place.'

'Mitrian and Garn?'

Arduwyn scanned their route, long plains interrupted by a stretch of tidal marsh. A wall of cattails obscured the sand. 'They're with Santagithi's infantry. And the rest of *your* army. King Gasir was killed.'

Colbey said nothing.

Expecting Colbey to ply him with questions, Arduwyn found the silence disturbing. He broke it swiftly. 'Who's he?' He tipped his head toward the Northern lieutenant.

Colbey looked in the indicated direction. 'Kirin? He's Vikerin's commanding officer. A fair swordsman, too, from what I've seen.' Colbey tossed the description lightly, but Arduwyn knew that a 'fair' from Colbey was an extraordinary compliment.

'Rache's with Santagithi's infantry, too.' Arduwyn stared at the ground, watching the shallow imprints his horse's hooves left in the soggy ground before the marsh.

'With Garn and Mitrian?'

'Yes.'

'With Garn?' Colbey stressed again.

'They seem to have come to an agreement.'

Colbey made a thoughtful noise in his throat. Arduwyn would have passed it off as a response to his revelation except that the Renshai's attention became suddenly, fanatically rooted on the marshlands ahead.

'What's wrong?' Arduwyn followed Colbey's gaze to waves of long-stemmed marsh weeds. Nothing seemed amiss.

Colbey reined in his horse. 'Halt!' His gelding's hooves skidded rents into the mud. Behind him, the Pudarian cavalry ground to a stop. The other commanders held their men as well.

Peusen rode to Colbey's side. 'What's the matter?'

'Easterners.' Colbey stroked his beardless chin. 'In the grasses.'

Peusen regarded the forest of cattails with the same skepticism as Arduwyn. 'You've seen them?'

'I feel them.' Colbey continued to stare at the weeds.

A breeze ruffled the tops into a brown wave, then dropped to stillness. Arduwyn frowned, trusting Colbey's instinct enough to believe.

Valr Kirin loosed a scornful snort. 'You feel them? Feel them? This is nonsense.' He kicked his mount forward.

'Wait,' said Peusen.

Outranked by his brother, Kirin drew up. Hostility practically emanated from him.

'We need a bowman,' Colbey said.

Arduwyn glanced over to find Colbey's stare directly on him. Disliking the term and hoping to dispel some of the tension, Arduwyn complained, 'Bowmen shower arrows on an enemy in the hope that one might hit a target. I believe you want an archer.'

'I want you to fire into the weeds.'

Arduwyn fingered one of the few shafts remaining in his quiver. 'Blindly? I stand corrected. You do want a bowman.' Nonetheless, he drew the arrow, nocked it, and loosed it into the cattails. The shaft parted stems, and Arduwyn waited for the scattered rustle of its fall.

The sound did not come. The arrow had struck something and embedded. Yet no cry of pain followed.

Valr Kirin glared.

'Again,' Colbey said.

Arduwyn positioned another arrow. This time, he fired in a gentle arc. The arrow plummeted, met by a broken human scream. *Firfan, there are men in there. How could Colbey know?*

Arduwyn received no answer, nor did he need one. He had spent too much time with Colbey to mistrust the Renshai's instincts.

'Council,' Peusen suggested, and the officers drew together behind the ranks of their men.

Arduwyn followed, reining up a polite distance from the conference that still allowed him to catch most of the strategy.

Peusen's precise, Nordmirian accent rose above the others. 'We have to wait for our infantry. We can't fight Siderin's entire army without them.'

'The marsh grasses are too damned thick.' Jakot's crisp Western dialect seemed out of place amid the Northern generals. 'But if we camp and wait, the Easterners could leave the marsh without us knowing it and head West. While we're preparing for attack, they'd be in our homes making slaves of our families.'

Valr Kirin spoke with calm logic, his bitterness brushed aside for the needs of the war and his men. 'Their army outnumbers our cavalry three to one. If we attack, they'll decimate us and leave before our infantry arrives.'

At an impasse, all looked at Santagithi's captain, as if years of exposure to the West's prime strategist might have imparted even more years of experience.

But Jakot shook his head wordlessly.

Arduwyn raked through his own thoughts, finding no answers. He considered the use of scouts and spies, aware they were probably already deployed.

'Mosquito attacks,' Colbey said.

Eager gazes shifted to the Renshai.

'Our cavalry can drive into the grasses, harass the Easterners, then dodge out. That way we can keep them in place and on the defensive until our infantry arrives and we can launch a full-scale attack.'

'Too risky.' Valr Kirin opposed the plan.

Arduwyn cringed, aware the Northman had undermined what Renshai hold most dear : violent war with unlimited risk.

Colbey's voice gained volume. 'If you fear danger, fellow Northman, then stay home. I'll lead those men brave enough to follow.'

Fury turned Kirin's tone acid. 'I've seen your methods, *lieutenant*.' He emphasized rank, apparently to remind Colbey that the ideas of others in the group took precedence. Apparently, he did not yet know of King Gasir's death. 'They're too perilous for my men. I think we should leave strategy to those with more experience.'

Even from a distance, Arduwyn knew the look Colbey turned on the Northman was savage with contempt. 'I judge my abilities and those of my enemies before I choose strategy. If I die, I'll find Valhalla never having fought a coward. When I lead men, I measure their skills. I would command no one else to do the things I do.' He lowered his voice until Arduwyn strained to hear him. 'And as to experience, I've led men to war since before anyone else in this conference was born.' He turned to Peusen. 'General?'

Valr Kirin gathered his shattered composure, his voice subdued. 'Why not have the bowmen shoot into the marsh? The Easterners' screams will tell us whether they're still in place.'

Even Arduwyn saw the flaw in that plan, and Jakot echoed his concerns exactly. 'And waste their few remaining arrows? No, my friend. Without disrespect, I'd join Colbey's mosquitoes.'

'And I, brother.' Peusen spoke with apology. 'We haven't much time, and I can't think of a better plan. Kirin, keep your troop out. Have your men watch that Siderin's cavalry doesn't work its way behind us. I'll send a message to our infantry. The sooner they arrive, the sooner this business is finished.' He and Colbey rode off to organize their army.

Arduwyn worked his way toward Kirin as the Northerner confronted Jakot. 'You saw the maniac fight. Colbey doesn't know strategy. He's a wanton, chaotic killer.' Valr Kirin's bitterness came through beneath a sincere concern for his men. 'And he can't be much older than I am. Did his mother do battle with him directing from the womb?'

Jakot tried to remain impartial. 'His methods are unorthodox . . .'

A Pudarian captain interrupted. 'He's sixty-five. I asked him.' His gaze followed Colbey admiringly. 'Best damned swordsman I've ever seen.' He kicked his horse to follow his commander.

'Damned, indeed,' Kirin finished. 'One of Hel's own children.'

Colbey's plan went into action with startling quickness. For hours, Arduwyn waited at Valr Kirin's side, watching hordes of Western cavalry plunge blindly into the cattails. Seconds later, most reemerged with bloodied swords. Unlike Peusen and Jakot, Colbey did not hang back to direct his men. Gold-white hair flying, he dodged in and out of the marsh, working with his mount as if linked. The horse swerved effortlessly, responding to commands Arduwyn could not see. Blood splattered Colbey's shirt; it dyed his sword crimson and ran in rivulets down his arms. Arduwyn's sharp eyes discerned rents in Colbey's clothing.

Beside Arduwyn, Valr Kirin scowled. But the furrowed brow and sharp, sad eyes revealed that his concern was for the men rather than his feud with Colbey. Still, he watched the Renshai elder with the same interest as Arduwyn.

Colbey's steed broke from the cattails. It wheeled with an abruptness that nearly required it to fold in on itself. Its hoof skidded through the mud, and it floundered. Colbey howled. He slid halfway down the side of his horse, his sword grazing the ground, his other hand wound in the beast's mane.

Arduwyn gawked as Colbey worked his way back into the saddle. Finding its footing, the horse slowed to a walk. At its rider's urging, it completed the turn and sprang into the weeds. Colbey flung back his head in a spray of blood and sweat. 'Modi!' he screamed. 'Modi!' A scarlet gash opened the back of his shirt in two long flaps.

Arduwyn sucked air through his teeth. 'Colbey!'

Valr Kirin went rigid. His gaze remained where Colbey had disappeared into the marshes. 'Modi,' he repeated, with none of the Renshai's emotion. 'I haven't heard that cry since we rid the world of the devil tribe from Renshai.' His hawklike features drew into a grimace, etching his expression into vengeful lines.

Arduwyn's stomach soured as he realized the direction of Kirin's thoughts, but he shoved concern aside for a more urgent one. Colbey's dive into the cattails seemed to last unusually long. *He's dead for certain this time.* Arduwyn wrung his hands, surprised by rising grief. For all his harshness, Colbey had proven himself a moral and trustworthy ally, one Arduwyn would sorely miss.

Even as Arduwyn recognized his distress, Colbey returned from the weeds, and the pounding march of approaching infantry froze him before he could make another charge. Santagithi's voice cut clearly over the rustle of weeds, the screams, and the war cries. 'Bowmen, let our soldiers out. Then fire a few flights. Spare your arrows. We'll need them later.' He turned to address the other leaders. 'Get the cavalry back. Council!'

Gradually, the cavalry disengaged from the marsh grasses as the infantry joined them on the plain. Arduwyn rode down Colbey on his way to the meeting. 'You're not joining council till I tend that wound.'

Colbey shrugged. 'From the look on your face, I'm guessing it looks worse than it is.' Meticulously, he swept blood from his sword, paying no attention to the gore jelling on his arms.

Both men dismounted. Arduwyn stripped the shirt from Colbey's back, poured water over a gash that extended from shoulder blade to buttocks, and used the rags to hold pressure against it with both hands. Though long and deeply into muscle, the injury had not penetrated to the spine.

'Try this.' Colbey rummaged through his pocket and passed a packet of creamy, black salve. Sinews shifted like knots beneath Arduwyn's palms.

Arduwyn accepted the offering, holding it between his fingers as he continued holding pressure against the wound. 'I think you should be more cautious. A stray arrow or spear could kill even you.'

Colbey swiveled his neck about to make certain no one listened. 'No Renshai should ever get as old as me.'

'No law says Renshai have to die young. It's just a consequence of the way you live. Among a warring tribe, only the most skilled survive. Right now, the West needs skilled men.' Arduwyn worked over the wound with Colbey's salve.

'You have a point,' Colbey conceded. 'But I told you before that if Rache and I ever met, he would die. I know that the same way I knew the Easterners planned to ambush us in the tidal marsh. I can't explain it.' He winced as Arduwyn poked a tender spot. 'With the infantry and cavalry together, avoiding Rache will become impossible. I have to die.'

Arduwyn wanted to dismiss Colbey's fear as superstition, but the Renshai's concern and past experience proved too compelling. 'We need you against Siderin. Now I admit the source of my information is questionable, but I've been told that a Renshai will be the hero of the war and will be the one to fight the Easterner's demon king. I suppose that could mean Rache, but the soldiers' awe of you leads me to believe otherwise.' He fumbled through his effects for bandages, then extracted a clean tunic from amid Colbey's packs and water skins. 'Of course, Sterrane isn't the best reservoir for wisdom and knowledge.' Arduwyn bandaged the wound, knotting cloth around Colbey's torso.

'I think you underestimate Sterrane.'

'Huh?' Arduwyn found the words startlingly incongruous. 'How does one underestimate a twenty-three-year-old child?'

'Oh, I admit he's unsocialized and very naive. He tends to break everything down into its simplest components. But I think that has more to do with his upbringing and philosophy: "Do good and trust others to do the same." ' Colbey donned his tunic and headed toward his mount.

Arduwyn trailed after Colbey, dazed. 'But the man can hardly put two words together.'

Colbey framed a coarse smile. 'Lots of people don't learn foreign languages well. Perhaps if he used his native tongue, he might speak as fluently as you and me.'

'His native tongue?' Arduwyn followed Colbey to his horse. 'What tongue is that? He seems to use Western and Common trade with equal clumsiness.'

'I don't know,' Colbey admitted. 'But I do believe that some higher force wanted me to find Sterrane. The instant he joined us, I lost the urge to travel through the Granite Hills. I don't think that's coincidence.'

Arduwyn dropped the issue for a more important one. 'Wait, there's something else.' He caught Colbey's stirrup. 'Choose the gods you call on with care. Kirin suspects you're Renshai or I'm the worst archer in camp.'

'Archer?' Colbey teased, pulling free. 'I'd say bowman. But, with practice and a full quiver, perhaps you'll hit something.' Laughing, he kicked his mount into a canter.

You bastard. Deftly, Arduwyn nocked an arrow and shot for one of the water skins that bobbed at Colbey's side. The shaft sped true. The bag burst, and a tide of water soaked Colbey's leg.

The Renshai whirled.

For a silent moment, Arduwyn knew terror. 'Sorry,' he said with feigned sheepishness. 'Missed again.'

28 The Eyes of the Dead

Mitrian watched Rache's horse prance from one edge of Santagithi's infantry to the other as he roused the farmers and cattle herders for combat in the tidal march. 'Soon we'll begin a battle far different from the one at the quarry. You won't see the enemy until you're upon him, and you'll have little time to strike. Make sure it's one of Siderin's, then hit fast and hard. You probably won't get a second chance.'

Beside Garn, Mitrian kneaded the hilt of her sword, reassured by Rache's charismatic presence. Garn's stoic silences could only have hurt morale, and she felt as unprepared as any weekend warrior. *When my father made the two of us commanders under Rache, he must have trusted that we would never need to use that authority.*

As if in answer to the thought, a familiar thrill ran along her arm. Mitrian tensed, fighting the demon images that might follow. *Don't do it. Don't you dare.* Surely, to give in to hallucinations now meant death in the marsh grasses. Yet Mitrian could not help seeing the soul in the gems as a safety net, an alternative if fear or inexperience froze her in battle.

I can help you.

No, Mitrian thought. Then, more forcefully, *No! This is my battle, and I'm going to fight it.* Colbey had taught her that the mind controlled itself above all else. The sword would not have her. *You promised. And my threat was not idle. I have enough enemies without struggling against my own weapon as well. One spark of your war wrath and, I swear, you've fought in your last battle.*

I can help you, the demon repeated. Softly, beneath the words came another question, so subtle Mitrian felt uncertain whether it emanated from the demon or her own thoughts. *If you abandon this sword, where would you get another?*

Oblivious to Mitrian's mental conflict, Rache continued, 'Remember, if we lose here, we lose more than our lives. If not checked, those Eastern animals will ride at will through our homelands, and there'll be no hiding. They'll slay our children, disgrace our women, and despoil our land. We've no escape but victory. Even in death, our souls will know the pain of our families. Fight like your world depends on it. It does.'

A cry rose from the masses. 'Death to Siderin !' Others picked up and echoed the words until the dunes seemed to ring with the name of the enemy's king.

Rache rode to Mitrian and Garn, apparently trusting the threat of Siderin's infantry to quell Garn's personal grudge. 'Soldiers will seem to appear from nowhere in the weeds. Always, the men will worry that they've slaughtered an ally instead of an enemy. In front and mounted, we won't have that problem.' His eyes gleamed with excitement. His left hand rested lightly on the hilt of one sword. With the slightest provocation, Mitrian knew he could strike with more speed and venom than a viper.

The bowmen sent their last flight.

As the archers retreated, Rache charged. 'For the West !'

Mitrian's horse plunged into the cattails at his heels. The mare rocked sickeningly, but Mitrian did not dare to see what it had struck. A face graced by a crop of sable hair appeared suddenly. She slashed downward, and the head cracked open. *First blood. Not too bad*. Then weeds wrapped her sword, nearly wrenching it from her sweat-slicked grip.

Swearing, Mitrian wheeled and tore at the hilt. Pain seared her calf with an abruptness that all but unhorsed her. Her sword tore free of its leafy bindings, and she continued its motion in a backhand stroke. The sword crashed against the man who had injured her. He collapsed, lost in the marsh.

A short distance ahead, Rache slashed, battle screaming, through the cattails, swords weaving in arcs of red and silver.

Waves of nausea weakened Mitrian. She kicked her horse. A shriek rose and echoed, a soldier trampled beneath her mare's iron-shod hooves. The horse lurched, tripping over the corpse. Mitrian vomited. A weapon thumped against the side of her horse, sending it skittering sideways. As Mitrian whipped her sword for a strike, the world folded into darkness, then reemerged, glaring in its detail. Colors intensified, a forest of green tipped with brown and broken by flesh tones; scarlet streaks of blood seemed artistically beautiful in comparison. Madness seized her, a wild frenzy of battle that overwhelmed all sense of purpose, except to kill. 'Modi!' she screamed. 'Modi!'

Mitrian swung into the cattails, this time using the give of their tops to bounce and redirect her blow. Steel tore into an Easterner's neck. Scarcely slowed, she surged into a pocket of soldiers. Sweat darkened her jerkin as she hacked her way to Rache's side. The Renshai wall plowed through the marsh, three glimmering swords capering in a crimson dance. Rache swerved to meet an enemy attack, and Mitrian found herself alone again, except for the all-too-real presence of the demon.

A movement in the brush seized Mitrian's heightened attention. Spurred beyond thought, she slammed her blade down on a dark-haired skull. The man staggered back. Gray eyes met Mitrian's from a young face, barely of age. He wore the silver and black leather of Santagithi's civilian volunteers. A look of terror and betrayal crossed his features briefly. Then he crumpled.

Mitrian's blood ran cold, shocked suddenly from the demon's control.

An accident. Mitrian, it happens.

Not to me. Gods, not . . . to . . . me. Mitrian drew her dagger, uncertain what to do with it, knowing only that she wanted to rid herself of the Wizard's magic.

Mitrian, think! You can't disarm yourself in battle.

Frustration flared to hatred. Mitrian knew the demon spoke the truth, yet she could not bear the thought of dealing with its blood lust another moment. *I killed one of my own men! One of my father's soldiers!* Anger drove her to the violence she had just denounced. She slammed the base of her knife down on one of the topaz gems that formed the wolf's eyes.

The Renshai's soul jerked within her mind. *Mitrian. What are you doing?*

Mitrian struck the gem again.

Think. Listen. Panic blazed through the demon. *You're surrounded by enemies!*

A worse enemy attacks me from within. Had she spoken aloud, Mitrian would have hissed. The dagger crashed against the gem once more. A crack wound through the yellow stone.

The demon's scream filled Mitrian's mind, deafening. Its presence seemed to peel away; its voice trickled to a whisper. *So cold. So cold.* Then it was gone.

Mitrian froze, the dagger poised. The sword clenched in her fist seemed unchanged, its edge sharp, its haft a perfect fit in her palm. Yet it seemed as empty and hollow as a corpse. *What have I done?* The knife slipped from her grasp, tumbling into the cattails.

'Mitri, to your left!' Rache's voice shattered Mitrian's daze.

She responded sluggishly, raising the sword as Rache bore in to her defense. His blades rose and fell, hacking down an enemy in the grasses. He pulled up beside her. 'Are you well?'

Mitrian made no reply, nor did Rache seem to expect one. He caught her horse's bridle. 'Come on. We need to keep in front, or we run the risk of crushing our own soldiers.'

Rache's words struck home. Mitrian winced, driving ahead with him. 'Where's Garn?' she managed at length.

'Last I saw, he'd veered off into the Pudarian infantry.'

Mitrian looked up sharply.

'He'll be fine. He's just used to single combat. Can't expect him to understand formations.' Rache spoke gently, incompletely hiding bitterness at having to defend Garn and his fighting style.

Rache drew in suddenly, hacking at a dark head. Almost beneath Bein's hooves, a horse stumbled to its feet, then whipped into a rear.

Bein danced backward. 'Mitrian!' Rache shouted. 'We've struck cavalry.'

Discovered, the Eastern cavalry mounted and raced toward the war in the cattails. Mitrian turned to follow, but Rache seized her arm. 'Let our cavalry have them. If we give chase, we'll be behind or among Siderin's troop. Our own men may attack.' Thoughtful pauses in Rache's speech made Mitrian cautious.

'From the quarry, I got the idea Siderin's army was larger.'

Rache scanned the marsh as his horse ambled forward. 'I was thinking the same thing.' The weeds ended abruptly, and his horse's hoof sank into mud. 'Hoofprints.' He pointed ahead. 'There they go over the dunes!'

Mitrian craned her neck, shielding her eyes from the sun. A few foot soldiers disappeared over the crest of a dune. 'I don't understand.'

Rache pulled a shell horn from his pack and blew a shrill blast. 'We've reached the tidal plain. While our cavalry played their infantry, Siderin waited for the tide to recede. He left us to battle a skeleton force while he escaped across the flats. Probably now they'll ride east or west between the sand dunes.'

Rache reined up on the edge of the plain.

Mitrian smiled, trusting the captain at her side. 'What now?'

Rache stared over the dune. 'I just signaled Santagithi. He should get here soon. For now, we'll follow. See if we can't find out exactly where they're going.' He slapped his mount to a run.

Mitrian followed.

The horses' feet pounded the sand to eddies. At a trot, they careened across the grime to the bottom of the first dune. There, Rache stopped again. 'We need to take a careful look over the dune . . .' He trailed off apologetically.

Confused by Rache's regret, Mitrian hesitated. It came to her suddenly that the person scouting would need to dismount, and she felt a warm flush of guilt. *It's Garn's fault that Rache can't do the spying, yet he's feeling responsible for putting me in danger.* 'I'll do it.' She dismounted before Rache could clarify, trying not to notice his withered legs.

'Careful.'

Dropping to her stomach, Mitrian slithered along the dune face. Sand stung the gash in her calf, reminding her of her new limitations without the demon's instructions. Heart pounding, she peered over the summit.

To the east, between the dunes, Mitrian found a mighty army.

The sun raised snakes of glare from sand speckled with the blood of warriors. Among the archers, Arduwyn assessed Santagithi's plan. Valr Kirin led the joint cavalry eastward to overtake Siderin and block a retreat. Rache and Peusen combined their infantries, preparing to march over the first of the paired dunes and prevent an escape to the west. The Pudarians waited, in Santagithi's command, ready to charge from the north, a wedge to drive Siderin's army toward the ocean. Presumably to avoid Rache, Colbey had chosen to remain in the tidal marsh with a mixed army, directing the slaughter of Siderin's skeleton force.

While the warriors took their positions, the archer captain of Iaplege sent the bowmen to the top of the dune. On the captain's command, arrows rained upon the Easterners. Far closer than at the quarry, the enemy screams tortured Arduwyn. He shot in the second volley. Again arrows plummeted on the forming red chaos. Horrified, Arduwyn missed the third command, blue-gold shaft only halfway nocked when the bowmen fired.

Abruptly, Siderin appeared, hurling a single, guttural syllable. His whip lashed one of his own men.

Arduwyn fired. His arrow glanced from the king's ornate helmet, and a wave of Easterners swarmed up the dune toward them.

The archers whirled in a startled, ill-timed retreat. For a moment, Arduwyn marveled at the power of a general who could command men to charge against hopeless odds. Then he drew his scimitar as men bore down upon him, and the bowman at his side crumpled.

A sword whistled past Arduwyn's ear. Afraid to turn his back, he held his ground. His scimitar met flesh, scratching across a swarthy sword arm. But the man still advanced. As Arduwyn struggled backward, a sword lashed for his face. He dodged aside. His foot slammed down on his fallen neighbor, and he tumbled backward. As he fell, something warm and sticky slid across his cheek. The world spiraled. Legs formed a tangled forest around him.

For several moments, Arduwyn did not realize he had stopped rolling. Through a haze, he felt strong hands heft him. Not bothering to identify his benefactor, he swiped at the viscid mass on his face, trying to clear it from his eye. It colored his fingers black.

'You all right now.' Sterrane's familiar voice floated through Arduwyn's hearing. The large man lowered the archer to the ground.

'Thank Firfan.' Arduwyn rolled his gaze to Sterrane, still half-blinded and feeling weak. 'Help me get this stuff off my face. It's in my eye.'

Sterrane cringed and knelt at Arduwyn's side. Tearing a strip of cloth from his tunic, he wet it from his waterskin and dabbed at Arduwyn's face.

'It could have been worse.' Arduwyn assessed the dull ache of his body. 'No sword wounds, at least that I can feel. A bad headache and a swarm of bruises.' He attempted a joke. 'I wonder if Bel can stand a black and purple husband.' But the gibe fell short, even in his own ears, reminding him of the family he loved but might never see again. *Surely, even Bel can understand my being delayed by the Great War.*

Sterrane washed silently, his dark eyes soft with tears.

Fear clawed Arduwyn. 'Hey, I'm all right. You said so yourself. I'm alive.'

Sterrane made no reply.

'I am alive, aren't I?'

Sterrane nodded. He pulled a dagger from beneath his cloak, cleaning it methodically.

Concerned by Sterrane's strange manner, Arduwyn shrank away. 'What are you doing with that?'

A quaver entered Sterrane's voice. 'Lost eye.'

Arduwyn brushed a hand along his face, not daring to interpret Sterrane's broken sentence. 'Lost you? Lost you what? What do you mean?'

Sterrane shook his head, rearranging the black mane. 'Half gone.' He choked. 'Can't save. Me sorry.' Tears tumbled from his eyes.

Arduwyn slumped to the ground, too weak to think or care.

Still sobbing, Sterrane set to work.

From the crest of the dune, Santagithi watched the wild rampage of war below him, missing nothing. Though he showed no emotion to King Tenja beside him, he felt pleased. His men, from the lowliest shepherd to his captains, battled with the furious intensity necessary to win the war. He had brought no cowards.

Still, over time, sorrow overtook Santagithi. Each death seared like a blade through his own flesh. It meant the loss of a loyal follower, suffering for another widow and her hungry children. The burden would fall upon the survivors. Never before had Santagithi taxed his townsfolk. Instead, he relied on the revenues of traders, war spoils, and the gladiator competitions. For the sake of his daughter's consort, he would put an end to the pit fights. And a long time would pass before he led another foray.

Forcing away thoughts that did not directly affect the war, Santagithi selected warriors from the masses. He found Mitrian at Rache's side, both slashing with a grace that made battle look more like a dance. Mitrian's style mimicked Rache's too closely for coincidence. Yet a stranger might not correctly label master and student. Mitrian's strokes held a smoothness not wholly attributable to her smaller size and sex.

Relieved by her competence as well as her decision to fight near a seasoned veteran, Santagithi let his gaze shift to Garn. Compared to Rache, Garn's strokes seemed ponderously slow. But each powerful blow dealt death to an Easterner.

Santagithi's gaze swept the battle. Near the center, Shadimar sat proudly on his mare, the wolf languid at its flank. The center of a war seemed an odd place for a weaponless old man, yet no one disturbed mage or wolf. Warriors avoided him. When the battle tide brought men near the Eastern Wizard, their swords passed harmlessly by him.

Santagithi continued to stare, until a battle cry at the opposite side of the combat drew his attention. There, Colbey fought with the brazen intensity of a suicide. His thunderous sweeps cleaved a path through the thickest of the battle. Behind him, many warriors echoed his war song, caught up in his killing frenzy. Still, the old Northman's attacks seemed directed, and his gaze kept leaving his opponents to fall longingly upon a figure in the distance. Santagithi searched for Colbey's target.

Near the second sand dune, amid a cluster of Eastern warriors, Siderin gestured boldly. Sun rays scatterd silver highlights from his armor. Suddenly, he broke through the troops and raced over the dune, his cavalry close behind.

'Colbey! After him!' Santagithi spurred his horse down the embankment. Sand showered the infantry below him. Staying at the sparse edge of the battle, he galloped his horse after the fleeing general. As he slashed at Easterners, he hollered orders to his officers. 'Rache! Follow them and to the west. Jakot! Garn! The infantry.' He shot through the war zone, then up and over the second dune and to the east. There, Colbey and his men drove the Eastern cavalry back toward the battle. Siderin's army would not escape in that direction. Surely, the final battle had begun. Between the dunes, Siderin's infantry was doomed. Only his cavalry remained to defeat.

Poised between two battles, Santagithi drew aside. King Tenja pulled up beside him, and two Pudarians, finished with the battle between the dunes, rode toward the beach.

One was speaking. '. . . at least a dozen beyond those reefs, and in formation.'

'Only a dozen,' the other replied as they passed. 'Send Colbey alone.'

As if in answer, the Renshai galloped past, in the direction of the Pudarian's gesture.

Santagithi called to his captain. 'Jakot, get some men over there.' He waved after Colbey.

As Jakot rushed to obey, King Tenja seized Santagithi's arm. 'Will you aid a madman?'

Surprised by Tenja's sudden malice, Santagithi replied evenly, 'Colbey's an ally. The men may think he's a god, but we know no man can defeat an army. It's to our advantage to keep him alive. He inspires the men.'

Disapproval leeched into Tenja's tone. The rubies in his braids glowed the color of the bloodstains on the beach. 'But when one of his brash acts kills him, it'll destroy morale.'

Santagithi pulled free, finding the king's sudden rancor distasteful. 'Then I will see to it that Colbey lives.'

Rache knew that Siderin's infantry between the sand dunes was falling because, over time, the number of Westerners on the shore swelled. With Mitrian at his side, the Renshai raced through enemy troops, meeting all the resistance a meteor encounters as it streaks through the heavens. His swords pranced, claiming lives. And Mitrian was holding her own as well.

As the last warrior directly before them fell, Rache glanced to the right. Through the thinning enemy troop, he saw Siderin's last lieutenant exchanging blows with Listar. The blacksmith's son caught each strike on his sword, scarcely recovering in time for his next block. Outmatched and forced to tend defense, he was unable to return a single attack. 'There!' Rache gestured, spinning to come to Listar's aid.

Mitrian spurred her mount, but the beast responded sluggishly. Listar retreated with a cry. The Easterner's sword glanced off his armor, but the impact unhorsed him.

Harrsha's sword jabbed for Listar but fell on Rache's blade. Mitrian slashed. The Easterner dodged. His riposte crashed against Rache's sword again. Rache slashed with his other weapon, but it slid off a buckler. Both men swung simultaneously.

Mitrian jabbed through Harrsha's guard. The enchanted blade bit into the Easterner's face, driving him from the saddle and tearing Mitrian's sword from her grip.

Rache smiled at the irony, Siderin's last officer claimed by a woman. He watched Listar rise, the Renshai tending Mitrian's defense while she retrieved her weapon. With only a nod to the youth, Rache waved Mitrian toward the Southern Sea. 'Come on.'

Westerners pummeled the weakened Eastern army into the ocean. Rache and Mitrian joined the throng at the water's edge. The horses stepped high, uneasy with the waves tossing against their knees. Though the majority of the Easterners on the beach had come from the cavalry, an unusual number now fought on foot. Rache noticed this peculiarity, but he did not pause to ponder. Instead, he herded Easterners deeper into the ocean. The surf roiled with human flesh, dyeing the sea wine red. The impending end of a long battle crazed both armies. Spurred by undeniable victory, the Westerners met the desperate frenzy of Easterners fighting for their lives.

Rache chose a trio of leather-clad men, one mounted. His sword lashed for a swarthy head. As he raised his arm for a killing blow, a metallic flash broke through the waters. The Easterner's face twisted in shock. His head bobbed beneath the surface. It reappeared almost instantly, tattered shreds where his legs had been.

Sharks! 'To shore!' Rache wheeled.

All along the beach, men screamed. The Westerners retreated, and, instantly, the heat of combat changed. Faced with the choice of battling men or sharks, Rache's two opponents charged the Renshai. Rache killed the one on foot with a single strike. The other rode by, bolting across the sand toward the distant dunes.

'No!' Rache slapped the flat of his blade across Bein's rump. The stallion hurtled after the Easterner like a wild, black arrow seeking its target. Rache leaned to the glistening neck as he narrowed the gap. Sand flung up by the Easterner's horse's hooves stung Rache's face. Above the roar of wind in his ears, he could hear the soldier screaming words in his guttural language. He thought he heard his own name more than once, but dismissed it as impossible.

The dunes heaved back into sight. The coarse tail of the Easterner's mount whipped Rache's hand, and the Renshai raised his sword. Still at a gallop, both beasts plunged up the sandy slope, splattering grit to the beach below. A sudden, horrible thought jolted Rache as they topped the crest. *We're moving too fast.* Concerned for Bein, he reined, but too late. As one, the horses sailed through the air. In soft sand, they landed half ton bodies on ankles no thicker than a man's.

A crack sounded, aching through Rache's ears. Bein lurched, then went down. Rache flew over his horse's neck. He landed on a broken corpse, skidded to the sand, then rolled from training. *Bein. Gods,*

Bein. You served me so well. What have I done? Grief warred with guilt, numbing the battle joy that had filled him moments before. Only bruised, but nearly helpless without his mount, Rache scanned the valley for his opponent. Bein lay on his side in the sand, neck twining like a serpent. Nearby, the Easterner's mount kicked, a mad thing in pain. Its rider crouched, his dark eyes locked on Rache. A smile crossed the swarthy features, and he lurched to his feet, sword in hand. Again, he shouted something unrecognizable that seemed to include Rache's name. This time, his voice echoed between the dunes.

Using one sword as a staff, Rache pulled to his knees. Then, driving the blade into the sand, he inched to his feet, supported by the tripod of metal and withered legs.

The Easterner studied Rache's clumsiness with a chuckle of triumphant amusement. Brandishing his weapon, he closed the distance between them.

Rache breathed a prayer. 'Mistress Sif, mighty shield maiden, mother of battle and goddess of my people. Just this once let me stand.' His hand trembled on the hilt of a sword he had raised so many times in her name.

The Easterner charged.

Rache edged the tip from the ground. Immediately, he unbalanced forward, but the little strength remaining in his legs held. Rache stood, gritting his teeth, unable to thrill to the frenzied cadence his heart beat against his ribs. He'd never feared death, only that it might not find him worthy.

The Easterner howled a challenge. Rache was silent. The ensuing second passed like an hour while Rache assessed his rushing opponent, calculating abilities and disabilities in an instant.

The Easterner's blade plunged for Rache's head. Rache blocked with an upstroke and returned the strike. His blade cleaved the Easterner's neck. He collapsed, blood spraying the sand then dropping to a steady wash.

For a moment, Rache basked in triumph. Then an almost inaudible rustle from behind compelled him to turn. Slowed by his crippled legs, he had scarcely moved when agony tore into his side. A blade's impact hurled him violently to a clear stretch of sand. His own sword tumbled from his grip. 'Modi! Modi! Mo-deeee!' The cry tore from his throat before he could suppress it, slamming him with a fresh, hot dose of battle madness. He estimated damage as he hunted for its source. His attempt to spin had not stopped the blow, but it had diminished the damage. If he could staunch the bleeding, he might still live. Yet the wound seared in a way no cut had before.

Pain blurred thought and vision. A warrior in ruddy leather raised his sword for a killing blow.

Rache's head buzzed, too heavy to hold. A glimmer of metal caught his eye. He forced his hand toward his sword through sand scarlet with his own blood. Every vein in his side felt on fire, and his left hand was going numb.

The Easterner's blade plunged. Rache caught his hilt and slashed upward with all the power he could muster. His strike met flesh. The Easterner's sword dropped harmlessly to the sand, and he fell, whirling in uneven arcs before Rache's hazed sight.

Rache knew he had to bind the gash in his side, yet his limbs would not obey him. He felt his consciousness waver. 'At least I took him with me.' Pain spasmed through him, driving him into a twitching seizure. Then agony dissolved to an inner peace.

Though nearly deafened by death screams, Colbey heard Rache's call. The anguish and sincerity in the voice slammed battle wrath through him; he sliced a path through the Easterners. And though he believed it would doom Rache, he could no more ignore the pleas than his own survival instincts. A Renshai needed him. And Colbey would be there for him. Without heed to his followers, he left them to their scattered battles and rode for the dunes.

Colbey passed Garn on his way, embroiled in single combat with a bearded horseman. Colbey cut the Easterner down with an overhand stroke, then gestured to Garn to join him without explanation. The ex-gladiator followed.

When Rache's scream did not recur, Colbey detoured toward the dunes to gather Santagithi and Sterrane. The two men perched on the sand, apart from the killing, overseeing their warriors. Arduwyn sat nearby, clutching his knees to his chest. A crudely-wrapped bandage encircled his head, covering one eye. Colbey drew up.

'This way.' He gestured. 'Rache needs us.' Without waiting to see if they followed, he spurred his horse down the slope and into the valley between the dunes.

Shortly, he found Mitrian's horse grazing on sparse clumps of plain grasses. She knelt on brown-stained sand, surrounded by corpses and looking nearly as pale as the head she cradled. Behind Colbey, Santagithi and the others went still, leaving a silence complete except for the gentle trickle of Rache's blood on the sand and the distant sounds of battle.

Dismounting, Colbey pushed past the others and caught Rache's head. Breath stirred limp strands of hair around his face. In an instant, Colbey surveyed the wound, estimated the loss of blood, and found Rache far paler and stiller than the sum of his injuries.

Poisoned. Rage boiled through him. *Cheaters and cowards. What an ugly, dishonorable way to kill . . . and to die.* Afraid to lose the last thread of Rache's life, he knelt and slapped the white cheeks with enough force to redden the skin.

Mitrian recoiled in horror. Sterrane's growl warned Colbey that he did not approve.

Rache's eyes opened to slits. 'Rac-kee.' He slurred out his own name.

Colbey smiled, certain Rache had mistaken him for his own namesake in Valhalla. 'It's Colbey.'

Rache's eyes twitched, framed by wrinkles. '*Torke.* So, it's true. I'm not the last Renshai.'

Colbey nodded, though he doubted Rache could see the gesture. 'No. But one of the finest.' He saw potential in every sinew of Rache's honed body. But the last hope for the Renshai to continue with even a splash of its warrior blood lay a finger's breadth from death.

Santagithi replied with words. 'Rache, you're not even the last of your line. That's what I was trying to tell you. Emerald bore you a son.'

Rache choked. His handsome features contorted into a harrowing mass of lines. 'I should be damned to Hel for bringing a child into this.' His muscles tensed spasmodically, wrenching water from glazing eyes.

Colbey moved aside. His approval was all Rache needed from him but others still had to make their peace. And now Colbey had other ideas to occupy his mind, two boys who would need Renshai training.

Sterrane moved in, wiping Rache's eyes with pawlike hands, and Mitrian kissed his forehead lightly.

Surrounded by friends, Rache chose to address his enemy. 'Garn.'

Hesitantly, Garn approached.

Though feeble, Rache's words could not be mistaken. 'Carad entrusted his son to me. Treat my son better than I did . . . his . . .' Rache's eyes closed.

Garn reached forward uncertainly, clasping a hand to Rache's shoulder.

Colbey knew that touch was the last thing Rache felt in life. Looking up, he found himself staring at a woman who appeared at Rache's side. Thick yellow hair fell about her seamless silver armor, and a golden halo threw the rest of the world into shadow.

'Gods!' Colbey staggered backward. *A Valkyrie!* He threw a defensive hand before his eyes, terrified for the first time in his life. Only brave warriors slain in battle could see such a sight, yet Colbey felt very much alive. And the odd stares of his companions made it clear only he could see the image.

The *Valkyrie* faded, leaving Colbey to adjust his eyes to the gloom of normal day.

'Colbey, what's wrong?' Santagithi took the elder Renshai's arm.

Colbey shook his head, lacking the desire or courage to describe what he had seen. Quickly, he reassembled his wits and outwardly returned to his normal, unperturbable manner. 'When a child of our people was born at a time when we had no heroes in Valhalla to name as guardian, we gave them a *kjaelnavnir*. If, after one year, there's still no guardian, the *kjaelnavnir* became the child's real name. We called those children *uvakt*, the unguarded. Many of them died in glory, and their names became part of our culture. But it was considered a severe handicap, a likely curse to Hel.' He studied Mitrian. She sat with her head low, stroking Rache's hair ceaselessly, as if her touch might restore his life. 'Your child is still young.'

Quiet gathered. Mitrian seemed not to have heard.

Garn cleared his throat. 'My son named for Rache?'

Mitrian looked up.

Garn stared into Colbey's rigidly intense face. 'I think,' Garn said slowly, 'I think that . . .' He considered a long moment. 'I think I might like that.'

Colbey swung around to confront Santagithi. 'I have two boys and your daughter to train. May I teach them in your town, or must my people return to exile?'

Santagithi's gaze met Colbey's, then turned aside. 'Renshai,' he said. 'My only daughter.' He glanced at Mitrian, then his gaze fell to Rache. 'And my only son.' He shook his head in sorrow. 'Of course, you're welcome to stay in my town and under my protection. But the decision as to whether Garn and his family return with you is their own.'

Garn's lips crushed together, then flowed into a tense smile. With Colbey as an ally, surely he had nothing to fear from the prejudice of Santagithi's men. 'I've considered your offer, Santagithi. If Mitrian wants to go home, I'll come with her.'

Though strained, Santagithi's answering smile was sincere.

29 The Legend of Béarn

Steel crashed, now too scattered to drown the break of the surf. Colbey picked his route carefully among the maimed and dead. The ugliness touched even the cruel Deathseeker from Renshi. Few shared his respect for death, nor his hatred for dishonorable or needless casualties. As a youth, he had fought for glory and life. Later, he had fought for glory and death. Now, faced with the burden of reforming a nation, he fought for glory and life again.

Removed from the combat, Colbey watched the final battles amid the scarlet spindrift of the shore. Near the dunes, a cluster of farmers sat in uncomfortable silence, unable to discuss a tragedy they had never been trained to fight. Colbey knew the war would affect them in a way no warrior could understand. Years later, they would startle from sleep, bask in the guilt of having survived what their neighbors had not, perhaps panic at the sight of a sword or fly into violent rages. Their plight awakened pity, an emotion that did not come often or easily. Recalling the conquests of his people, he raised his sword in a vow to Sif: 'The Renshai will remain the finest swordsmen in the world, but never again will we ravage lands at peace without cause.'

The ocean roared against the beach. Two dozen riderless horses stampeded in a herd across the sand. Chestnuts, blacks, and bays kicked up their heels as they ran, led by a solid buckskin, its dark mane flying, stark contrast to its golden hide.

Even with his thoughts distant, Colbey recognized the stocky lead horse. *Siderin's horse.* Suspicion sparked, he spurred his mount. Quickly, the long-legged bay narrowed the distance between itself and the weary herd.

Within twenty strides, Colbey drew up beside a gaunt chestnut. As his horse adjusted its pace to match the herd, Colbey measured the pack with his gaze, knowing horses nearly as well as swords. Reaching out, he seized the chestnut's mane and slithered to its back. From there, he sprang to a more centrally located gray. He was rewarded by a glint of steel at the middle of the pack. An armored form crouched on a sable horse, shielded by the running herd.

Carefully, Colbey leapt to a chestnut beside the black. 'Very clever, Siderin.'

The general sat up suddenly. Demon's eyes shone from a human face darkened in the shadow of his helmet. 'Renshai,' he whispered. 'Carcophan was wrong.' His hand whipped from his pocket, and he smashed a vial over the spines of his horseman's flail. Clear liquid oozed over the head.

Poison. Colbey remained still, trusting his speed and training, letting his enemy make the first strike.

'And prophecies can be thwarted.' The metal ball thrashed for Colbey.

Quicker than sight, Colbey drew. The chain enwrapped the blade. The links ruptured on its razor edge, and the weapon's head flew free.

Siderin swore, tearing at his sword. Still chain-wrapped, Colbey's blade crashed against the general's breastplate. Siderin lurched, then caught his balance as his sword whipped free.

Blade locked on blade. With his left hand, Siderin pulled a dagger and lunged. Colbey blocked with his free arm. The king's wrist struck Colbey's. Something on the blade splashed Colbey's hand, burning like acid. *More poison*, he thought, rubbing it off on his clothes before it could work real damage. 'You have the morals of a swamp rat.'

Siderin laughed, a sound like rasping steel. 'This from a Renshai.' His sword and dagger plunged. Colbey parried both, hating the general as he never had any opponent before. Reeling, he returned the strike. His blade struck sparks from a mailed shoulder. Smoothly, he reversed the stroke, slamming aside Siderin's sword. The dagger nicked Colbey's sleeve and ripped through the flesh of his mount.

The beast screamed, lurching. Though forced to tend his balance, Colbey wove defensive patterns with his blade. The horse stumbled. Unable to take his gaze from Siderin's weapons, Colbey leapt blindly. Even as he moved, the horse collapsed beneath him.

Leather scraped Colbey's legs. A stirrup cracked painfully against his shin, then he was mounted awkwardly in front of a saddle. Siderin's sword jabbed. The dagger raced upward.

Can't die of poison. Colbey swung to block the dagger first. His blade tore the knife from the king's grasp, then met the sword a finger's breadth from his throat. His riposte blazed for Siderin.

Suddenly, the Easterner stiffened. Surprise flashed through his eyes. Colbey's sword lashed through a cleft in the armor, hurling Siderin from his mount.

Catching the reins, Colbey flicked into the saddle and yanked until his horse fell to the back of the herd. It tossed its head, trying to regain its control and stay with the herd. Colbey hauled on one rein, forcing it into a tight arc until it had no choice but to stop. As its herd mates thundered away, Colbey steered it to Siderin's body at a walk.

Dismounting, Colbey examined the remains. Hooves had shredded Siderin. One had dented the masterwork of iron that the king had used as a helmet. Colbey hefted it, surprised by its weight. 'The steel lives on, Siderin, but you're dead. Just as well. What glory could there be in watching venom win the battle for you? What skill does it take to let your armor fend blows? I fear a day may come when men wear steel shells like turtles, and the contest is won by the man strong enough to raise his arms and his sword. What joy . . . ?' the sight of a bloody feather protruding from Siderin's neck cut short Colbey's self-indulgent speech. Some unseen archer had stolen Colbey's victory, just before the killing blow.

Gingerly, Colbey eased the arrow from the general's flesh. It broke off in his hand, a painted shaft with three rings: two gold and the last royal blue.

Colbey threw back his head, enraged. 'Arduwyn! You bastard child of a weasel! When I catch you, you'll freeze in Hell!' Colbey scanned the dunes, hands balled to fists.

But the red-haired archer had wisely chosen to disappear. Colbey saw nothing but the bodies of the dead.

Garn perched on a dune, staring at a beach that the setting sun striped red and white. Corpses littered the sand, twisted gory lumps that little resembled the anxious warriors who had begun the war. An injured soldier moaned, his steady complaint pierced by an occasional clang of distant steel as the final, scattered battles played out their course. But, for Garn, the war was over. And other things had concluded as well.

Rache is dead. The thought failed to soothe, though it brought no sorrow either. The Easterners and their poison had robbed Garn of the chance to prove himself the better swordsman. Still, he did not begrudge Rache the death in battle he had sought for so many years.

Few religious tenets made sense to Garn, least of all the obsessive care Colbey and Mitrian had taken to see that Rache's body went to pyre with all its parts intact. Clearly, if there was some sort of post-death paradise, whether the Northmen's Valhalla or the Westerner's Yonderworld, a man's body remained behind, along with its flaws. *If a soul has no visible form, how can it fit a man's body exactly? If the gods are so damned powerful, why couldn't they give him a new leg? And, why would a one-armed soldier have any more difficulty in Valhalla than here?*

Garn shrugged, tossing the questions into the same, unanswered part of his mind that wondered why, if the gods were real, they tolerated so many violently strong and varying opinions about them. He questioned why Sheriva didn't use his mighty fist to smash the Western army. If the Northerners' Odin had created the world, how could the Westerners' Ruaidhri or the Easterners' Sheriva have done the deed? And why would Ruaidhri allow a faithful follower like King Gasir to die while the atheist Garn lived on? Garn had heard priests of varying religions defend inequality by saying that men could not comprehend the vast wisdom and reasons of the gods. And the ex-gladiator dared to question why anyone would waste his time trying. Or worshiping.

It made as much sense to Garn to believe that the ground and sky simply were, that the world itself, and the people in it, made their own consequences. In fact, it made more sense because it did not imply the presence of deities who, despite supposedly infinite wisdom, ignored stupidities and injustices plainly obvious even to Garn. Yet though Garn disdained the gods, all of whom had ignored his prayers for freedom in his days as a gladiator, he respected Mitrian's and Colbey's faith and the intensity of their belief. They seemed reasonably pleased by the manner of Rache's death. *So how,* Garn wondered, *could I be otherwise?*

Still, Rache's life had meant more to Mitrian than it ever had to Rache. Since his death, she had become a crazed stranger. One moment, Garn found her on the verge of tears. But, when he tried to hold and comfort her, she pounded his chest with her fists in a blind fury of rage, blubbering something about how she should honor instead of mourn a brave warrior slain in battle. If Mitrian knew joy for Rache's demise, Garn hoped he would never see her grief-stricken; and if what she displayed was sorrow, frustration and guilt had riddled it with violence. She seemed to need solitude to sort her feelings. So, despite or because of the fact that he loved her, Garn left Mitrian to her own company.

Garn buried his chin in his hands and studied the crimson and black of the ocean, wondering if its colors reflected the dusk or the blood of so many slain in its waters. As he stared, death struck soundlessly, the breeze of steel slicing air his only warning. Garn recoiled. A blade scratched down his arm, tearing his tunic, then embedded in the dune.

Garn sprang to his feet, pawing for his sword. Had he moved any more slowly, the stroke would have opened him from head to abdomen.

The other wrenched his blade free in a spray of sand.

Garn crouched, drawing his weapon, expecting to meet swarthy features and flinty eyes. But the man he faced was no Easterner. Blond curls hugged his head in sweat-damp ringlets, and his pale eyes looked as wild as any gladiator's. *Listar.*

The blacksmith's son rushed Garn.

Side-stepping, Garn deflected with a broad sweep. Listar's surprise attack enraged Garn, yet he fought for the self-control he had promised himself would accompany Rache's death. The wound in his arm ached. 'Listar, don't be stupid. Mitrian has always made her own decisions. Even if you killed me, she would never have you.'

'You've done something to her.' Listar lunged, cutting high. 'You tricked her into becoming someone else.'

Garn battered Listar's flailing sword to the ground and pinned it beneath his own. He glared into Listar's flushed face. 'There was a time when I would have killed you before I could think to do anything else.' Garn felt his restraint slipping and bolstered it with remembrance of the animal savagery he wanted to escape. 'If you really care for Mitrian, talk to her. Trust the choices she makes and her reasons. If she really wants you instead of me, I won't fight you.' The words came easily. Garn never doubted Mitrian's love or loyalty.

With a condescending toss of his bronze hair, Garn freed Listar's blade, turned his back, and strode along the dune. It was the ultimate insult, demonstrating contempt for Listar's skill by making the threat of a weapon at his back seem trivial. Garn had seen the blacksmith's son in action, and did not doubt his own ability to counter any attack. Still, he was no fool. Ears attuned to any noise from behind, he basked in the warm glow of triumph, not over Listar, but over his own barbaric instincts. Rache had proven right about so many things, especially those issues that pertained to war and sword training. But when he claimed Garn's self-control would not come as a result of his death, Rache had made a mistake. Since the Renshai had spoken his final words, Garn had not lost his calm composure over mind and body. Despite his outrage, he had left the impudent youth alive on the dune.

The sound of shuffling feet behind Garn interrupted his thoughts. A sword whistled through the night air. Dropping to one knee, Garn whirled and slashed. His sword tore open studded leather and flesh.

Screaming, Listar collapsed, leaking entrails to the splattered sand. As Garn raised his sword for a killing stroke, a line of blood wound along the blade.

'Garn ?' Mitrian's call sounded close.

Garn froze. Listar's screams became frenzied, and he writhed like an injured snake.

'Garn ?' Alarm entered Mitrian's tone. She appeared over the dune's crest at a run.

Guiltily, Garn sheathed his sword, stepping in front of Listar as if to hide the twitching, shrieking man.

Mitrian skidded to a stop, staring at the figure behind Garn. Her sword dangled from her hand. Slowly, she walked forward, as if drawn. Her face revealed no emotion.

Garn fingered the tear in his sleeve, not knowing what to say. The scene told its own story.

Listar's screams fell to sobbing moans. Blood trickled from his lips. 'I . . . just wanted what was mine. You belong to . . . to me. Not some slave's bastard.'

Rage boiled in the pit of Garn's stomach. He lowered his head, starting the sequence of mental exercises that he used to empty his mind before attempting to break a horseshoe. A sword stroke now would only hasten the inevitable. To all intents and purposes, Listar was already dead.

Mitrian's cheeks flared. The hand on her sword hilt lost all the color her cheeks had gained. 'I never wanted to hurt you.' Emotion robbed her tone of the sincerity she obviously felt and intended.

Garn recognized the rage that had ebbed and flowed through Mitrian since Rache's death, and he recoiled from it.

Mitrian's sword whipped upward, then claimed the life of its crafter so quickly that Listar's expression never changed.

Garn watched helplessly as Mitrian slumped to the ground. The hilt fell from her grip, and she wept like a child, curled on the sand.

Kneeling, Garn took Mitrian in his arms. 'It's all right,' he whispered. 'I killed him. You just dealt the mercy stroke . . .' He continued to talk, though he knew his comforting fell on deaf ears. She might never admit it, even to herself, but Garn knew her tears were less for Listar than for Rache. Renshai tradition did not allow her to weep for one who had earned Valhalla, but it said nothing of mourning a foolish youth who had forced her hand against him.

Garn hugged Mitrian closer, felt her arms tighten about him, and knew his presence meant far more to her than his words.

Night inked the sky, and campfires dotted the beach like candles in a tomb. Warriors broke into groups to talk or sleep, while others combed the beach for injured companions.

Colbey rode alone across the beach, plagued by many thoughts. His joy for Rache's undeniable entrance into Valhalla was tempered by his fear and awe at having seen the dead man's escort. In his decades of battle, Colbey had watched hundreds of Northmen ride bravely to a valorous death that surely earned them their places in heaven, yet never before had he seen a *Valkyrie*. The image would not leave his mind; indelibly burned into his memory he could picture Odin's battle maiden in all her splendid detail. *I've seen a Valkyrie. What does that mean?* Colbey continued his slow, silent ride. The only stories he had heard of visualized *Valkyries* came from men recovered from the brink of death. And, always, these soldiers knew the choosers of the slain had come for them. At no time did Colbey doubt the *Valkyrie* had appeared for Rache.

Finding no answer, Colbey discarded the concern, attributing it to the same unearthly madness that had convinced him Rache would die if they were reunited, that he would wander through the Granite Hills until Sterrane joined his traveling companions, and that he should spend some time in the Western Wizard's cave. He had believed the insanity banished from his mind, its final spark destroyed. He knew it had left aftereffects; thought-reading had allowed him to discover Siderin's army in the cattails. But the sight of a *Valkyrie* had taken him totally by surprise.

The sigh of breakers grew louder as Colbey wound past most of the camps to a sparser area of beach. A single fire winked through the night, its flame unnaturally steady.

Drawn by curiosity, Colbey dismounted and approached. As he drew nearer, he found an old man sitting before the fire, alone except for a bay mare with its head bowed in sleep and a wolf curled at his feet. A sapphire filled the elder's cupped palm, a gem Colbey recognized with a single glance.

The Pica. Surprise flickered through Colbey and deepened to anger. He strode into the circle of firelight.

The wolf crouched, growling. A light momentarily appeared in the old man's eyes. the glow from flames and sapphire mingled green highlights on wrinkled cheeks.

'The Pica Stone,' Colbey said in accusation.

'Indeed.' The elder did not seem to recognize the hostility in Colbey's voice, though the wolf's growls deepened.

'It belongs to my people.' Colbey bit each syllable short.

The Wizard nodded, his gaunt, robed frame like a ghost against the dark expanse of sky and sand. 'At one time, yes. After yours took it from mine by force.'

Colbey hesitated. The Pica Stone had been in Renshai hands since his childhood, lost during the battle that saw the destruction of Devil's Island. But he still recalled the war against the wizards of Myrcidë in which the Renshai had first obtained the Pica, a bloody battle against a valiant defense. 'I had thought the Myrcidians all dead.'

'And I had thought the same of the Renshai. Until I discovered Rache. Then Mitrian.' The Wizard snapped his fingers, and Secodon padded to his side. The wolf's frame remained taut, its hackles raised and its yellow eyes on Colbey. 'What I can't understand, Golden Prince of Demons, is why not even the sources of magic knew of your existence.'

Colbey frowned, disliking the title the Wizard chose enough to let the reference to magic go unchallenged. 'I'm no demon. No more than Siderin was. And neither were my people, so I am no prince among demons.'

'Truth is less significant to a title than the effect it inspires. To the people of the West, you will become the Golden Prince of Demons. To the Wizards, Colbey, you always have been.'

Colbey frowned, only vaguely familiar with the prophecy. 'You know my name well enough to feel free with nicknames. But I don't know yours at all. That hardly seems fair.'

'Shadimar. The Eastern Wizard.' He pointed to the wolf. 'This is Secodon.'

'Of course.' Colbey nodded sagely as the last pieces fit into place. 'You're the one with the falcon who doesn't know a glove from bare flesh. You sent the message. In many ways, you won the war, though your bird did its best to ruin my sword arm before the battle started.'

Shadimar smiled, amused, but he did not address the issue of the falcon. 'No. Warriors like you won the war. But how did you come upon my message? I sent it to the Western Wizard.'

'I'm afraid Tokar is dead.' Colbey studied Shadimar, waiting for a reaction that might disclose the Wizard's motives.

'How?'

'I don't know,' Colbey admitted. Though present at the end, he did not understand the events that had taken the lives of Tokar and his apprentice. The most superficial memory still shocked pain through Colbey; though diluted by time and distance, it still seemed as excruciating as a real injury. Quickly, he changed the subject. 'What did you mean when you said the sources of magic didn't know of my existence?'

Shadimar rose. The firelight emphasized lines of uncertainty in his ancient features. 'You saw Tokar's corpse?'

'Yes.'

'And Haim?' The Wizard clarified. 'His apprentice.'

'Dead also.'

Shadimar tensed. His expression mingled concern with fear, and both looked eerily foreign on a face like wind-battered stone.

Secodon bared his teeth, still positioned between Colbey and Shadimar.

'The sources of magic,' Colbey prodded. 'Why would they want me? And if they wanted to know I existed, what would stop them?'

Shadimar relaxed slightly as the conversation shifted from the

Western Wizard to Colbey. Secodon uncoiled with his master. 'What need would anyone have for the prophesied hero of the Great War.' Though phrased like a question, his words were undoubtedly statement and answer. 'Their side wanted you dead, our side alive. Surely, the Southern Wizard consorted with demons to find the last Renshai, yet, by Siderin's actions, he only worried about Rache.'

Colbey considered. 'He missed Mitrian as well.'

Shadimar clutched the Pica Stone in both hands, his long fingers surrounding the sapphire like a web. 'Easily explained. He may have ignored her. Early Wizards named the Golden Prince of Demons a man. And Carcophan probably only asked about full-blooded Renshai to sort out the children of conquerors, those conceived of Renshai without the heritage ties.'

Colbey kept his attention split between the Wizard and the wolf. Though more relaxed, Secodon seemed prepared to spring, and there was still the matter of the Pica Stone to settle. 'Neither of those things that made Mitrian unacceptable would have ruled me out.'

'Exactly.' Shadimar hesitated. 'Unless . . .' he trailed off thoughtfully.

Colbey went on the defensive. 'I admit, none of my couplings has ever produced a child, but I'm still certainly a man.'

For the first time since the mention of the Western Wizard, Shadimar grinned. 'Your gender was never in doubt, Colbey. But perhaps your parentage – '

Colbey broke in, more insulted by the slight to his history than his sex. 'My father, Calistin the Bold, died in my first battle. My mother, Ranilda Battlemad, never saw her third decade. Both were born of Renshai, and died in the glory of Renshai.'

Though Colbey's words proved nothing, Shadimar did not press. 'Then there's another reason, one we'll have plenty of time to discuss after I return from Béarn.'

Colbey caught the reference at once. 'You're going to take the Western Wizard's place in helping return Béarn's throne to its rightful heir.'

With gentle reverence, Shadimar passed the Pica from hand to hand as he spoke. 'The prophecies say a Wizard will accompany the prince.'

'And a Renshai. Tokar said that would be me.'

'Tokar was wrong.'

The pronouncement startled Colbey into silence, yet he found a certain comfort in it. The knowledge of two young boys awaiting Renshai training fully absorbed him. He wanted to attend to them as quickly as possible. But he also held a devout devotion to the gods. Odin had created the Wizards. Therefore, their prophecies had to take precedence over mortal proceedings, no matter how significant to the Renshai.

'Mitrian will accompany the king.' Shadimar started to pocket the Pica Stone.

Quicker than thought, Colbey lunged forward and caught the Wizard's arm. 'I can't suffer the idea of the Pica in a stranger's hands.'

Secodon advanced, stiff-legged.

Shadimar stilled the wolf with a gesture. 'Your sword and skill can't hurt me. Surely you don't want to die over a pretty rock.'

Colbey did not draw a weapon, amused by the Wizard's reaction. 'There was a time when I would have taken your words as a challenge, one I might even win. But, for now, the Renshai need allies more than battles. If we both claim the Pica Stone for our people, then our peoples must become one and you my brother. You may keep the Pica.'

Shadimar stared, surprise looking as alien on his features as fear. 'You are unique among Renshai.' He relaxed again, and the wolf whined. 'I'll join this union and consider it an honor.'

They gripped hands briefly. The Wizard's fingers felt thin and weak as paper in Colbey's firm hold.

Releasing the bond, Shadimar strode to his horse and mounted gingerly. 'I need to find Mitrian and her friends. I presume they're with Santagithi?'

'Probably.' Colbey swung into his own saddle.

Both horses walked the silent sands together. The full moon drew a glittering line through the breakers. A bond of brotherhood between Northmen was a link stronger than blood, and Colbey wondered idly what his vow might entail.

The campfire light danced across the drawn features of Mitrian and her companions. She sat with Garn, Sterrane, Arduwyn, and Santagithi, sharing a meal of roasted sea bird, shot and prepared by the archer. Grief felt like a lead weight in her stomach, and the food only made her queasy, but the presence of friends allowed her to force down a few morsels.

On Mitrian's knee, Garn's hand stilled suddenly. Mitrian looked up to see Garn, Sterrane, and Arduwyn staring toward the beach. Only then, she heard the faint slap of hoofbeats. She watched as Colbey and Shadimar appeared from the darkness together, flanked by the Wizard's wolf.

Both men dismounted at the camp. Colbey joined the lopsided circle. Shadimar crouched at Sterrane's side. He spoke softly, using words Mitrian did not understand in a deep mellow language she did not recognize.

Without raising his gaze from the fire, Sterrane uttered two hostile syllables. He lifted a huge hand to wave the Eastern Wizard away.

The exchange shocked Mitrian. The association seemed so unlikely as to be impossible. Yet Sterrane used the same disrespectful manner and tone as a teenager with a parent.

Undaunted, Shadimar spoke again. Arduwyn's eyes widened. Apparently, the archer knew the tongue and found the words disturbing.

Suddenly, Sterrane leaped to his feet. 'No!' he shouted in the trading language. 'Not ready.' His face twisted into the pout of a petulant child.

Shadimar continued talking, a thin shadow dwarfed by Sterrane's huge bulk.

Mitrian caught Arduwyn's sleeve. 'What are they talking about?' she whispered. 'And what language are they speaking?'

'Béarnese. And nothing much.' Arduwyn's sarcasm came through clearly. 'Just about how Sterrane's the rightful heir to Béarn and has to claim his throne now.'

Mitrian snorted, not appreciating the humor. 'Be serious for once. This could be important. That's a Cardinal Wizard.'

'And that's a king.' Arduwyn gestured toward Sterrane, then groaned. 'Firfan's bow, I called the high king an imbecile.' He clamped his hands to his head, fingering the bandage. 'Twice, at least.'

Mitrian estimated it was more like a dozen times, but Arduwyn's pronouncement bothered her too much to quibble now. 'Be serious.'

'He's not kidding, Mitrian.' Santagithi joined the hissed conversation. 'When I found out, I offered my army to reclaim his throne, but Shadimar insisted on the need for stealth. He said Sterrane would only have a few companions, one a Renshai. Naturally I assumed Rache . . .'

The flow of words continued past Mitrian, unheard. *Sterrane a king. King Sterrane. Sterrane, ruler of Béarn.* No matter how she considered it, the words slurred to nonsense. Her mind could not grasp her gentle, bearlike companion as royalty. Then her mind settled on a more familiar concept. *A Renshai will help reseat the king.* 'Not Rache. Me. With Garn and Arduwyn.' Horror clutched at her. *Another delay. When will I see Kinesthe . . .* she amended, *'Rache' again?* The urgency of war and her sorrow for Rache had allowed her to drive aside thoughts of the infant she loved. Now they crushed down upon her, painful in their reality. *But Sterrane has done so much for us. How can I abandon him in his time of need?*

Santagithi lowered his head, obviously hating the thought of being separated from the daughter he had just regained. Arduwyn fidgeted, looking equally distraught.

'No Arduwyn,' Sterrane said. 'Not need archer, and Bel need Arduwyn.' He looked directly at the redhead now. 'Send for you and Bel after win. All live in Béarn.'

Arduwyn's remaining eye flitted over the haggard faces of his companions. He stared longest at Mitrian, as if to gauge her judgment on the fairness of Sterrane's decision. His dark eye seemed hollow, almost pleading.

Santagithi intervened. 'We'll detour through Pudar. That'll give Arduwyn an escort and us a way to get my grandson. Colbey can train the boys until you return.' He glanced at Mitrian. 'Surely you trust your son in my charge? And Colbey's?'

Mitrian nodded, pleased to see Garn do the same, though with far less vigor. 'I have to go.' She sidled a look at Shadimar to make certain she spoke truth.

'It's in the prophecies,' the Wizard said. 'I can't force you. You already know that. But I will do all I can to convince you to go. Without you, Sterrane stands little chance of doing anything more than dying at his uncle's hands. Even with you, he may fail. You all may die.'

Mitrian drew on the courage Rache and Colbey had taught her to embrace. Soon enough, she would see Kinesthe/Rache again. If not, he could have no better teacher than Colbey nor a more fair and loving parent than Santagithi. 'I'm going, and I agree with Sterrane. Arduwyn should go back to Pudar.'

Arduwyn bowed humbly before addressing Sterrane. 'I wish you all the luck Firfan gives the shafts of his archers, my liege.'

Sterrane swept Arduwyn into an embrace. He wept huge, moist tears befitting a king.

Epilogue

King Tenja of Vikerin watched his horse's hooves dimple the sand, suffering from an exhaustion more mental than physical.

Beside him, Valr Kirin fidgeted, apparently wanting to talk, yet uncertain of exactly what to say. Tenja waited while the lieutenant cleared his throat and bowed with the respect a king deserves. 'Sire, that man, Colbey. I think he's Renshai.'

Tenja nodded without raising his head. He turned his thoughts inward, releasing an ancient memory. Again, he saw himself as a child, one of three boys brave enough to enter the crypts at Kor N'rual. There they had read the prophecy of the Great War and its Renshai hero.

Kirin's hawklike face framed a scowl. His eyes flashed innocent vengeance. 'We have to kill him, sire.'

King Tenja marveled at how easily Valr Kirin described a hopeless task. With his army exhausted and Colbey under the guardianship of Santagithi, this was not the place or time to challenge the Golden Prince of Demons. 'One battle at a time, Kirin,' he said. 'One battle at a time.'

Appendix

People

Northmen

Alvis (AHL-vee): VIKERIAN. Adviser to King Tenja.

Arvo Ranulfsson (AR-voe-RAN-oolf-son): GJAR. A tinsmith.

Calistin the bold (Ka-LEES-tin): RENSHAI. Colbey's father.

Colbey (KULL-bay): RENSHAI. The Sword master.

Eldir (EL-deer): VIKERIAN. King Tenja's bodyguard.

Episte (Ep-PISS-teh): RENSHAI. Elderly spy in Nordmir.

Harold (HAHR-uld): VIKERIAN. A scout.

Kallmir (KAWL-meer): RENSHAI. Rache's father.

Menglir (MEN-gleer): RENSHAI. One of the two founders of the Western Renshai. See also Sjare.

Peusen Raskogsson (Pyoo-SEN Rass-KOG-son): NORDMIRIAN. One-armed general of Iaplege.

Rache (RACK-ee): RENSHAI. Santagithi's guard captain.

Ranilda Battlemad (Ran-HEEL-da): RENSHAI. Colbey's mother.

Riodhr (REE-odd): VIKERIAN. A low level officer.

Sigurd (SEE-gerd): A soldier in the war against Renshai.

Sjare (See–YAR-eh): RENSHAI. Founded the Western Renshai with Menglir.

Tenja (TEN-ya): VIKERIAN. King of Vikerin.

Thorwald (THOR-walld): DVAULIRIAN. A peasant.

Valr Kirin (Vawl-KEER-in): NORDMIRIAN. Lieutenant to the high king in Nordmir. Peusen's brother.

Westerners

Ancar (AN-kar): one of Santagithi's archers.

Arduwyn (AR-dwin): ERYTHANIAN. A hunter.

Bartellon (Bar-TELL-in): one of Santagithi's guards.

Bel (BELL): PUDARIAN. Kantar's wife.

Belzar (BELL-zar): PUDARIAN. Legendary swordsman.

Bromdun (BROMM-dun): one of Santagithi's guards.

Brugon (BREW-gun): PUDARIAN. A merchant.

Buirane (BYOOR-ain): BÉARNIAN. A previous king. Father to the twins Valar and Morhane.

Carad (Ka-ROD): a competent gladiator; Garn's father.

Carlithel (KAR-lith-ell): PUDARIAN. Proprietor of *The Hungry Lion*.

Davrin (DAV-vrin): MIXED WESTERN. A bard.

Dilger (DILL-jer): PUDARIAN. A braggart.

Donnerval (DON-ner-vull): one of Santagithi's guards.

Effer (EFF-er): Bel's middle child. A son.

Emerald: Rache's girlfriend.

Garn: Carad's son. A gladiator.

Gasir (GAH-zeer): PUDARIAN King of Pudar.

Haim (Haym): PUDARIAN. Tokar's apprentice.

Halnor (HAL-nor): one of Santagithi's guards.

Helvor (HELL-vor): Halnor's son.

Jakot (Jah-KOE): one of Santagithi's lower officers.

Jani (JAN-ee): Bel's oldest child. A girl.

Kantar (KAN-tar): ERYTHANIAN. Arduwyn's best friend. Bel's husband.

Kinesthe (Kin-ESS-teh): Mitrian's son.

Kruger (KROO-ger): PUDARIAN. A dock foreman.

Lirtensa (Leer-TEN-sa): PUDARIAN. A dishonest guard.

Listar (LISS-star): Santagithi's blacksmith's son.

Lonriya (Lon-REE-ya): Mar Lon's great grandmother. Created the lonriset.

Mar Lon (MAR-LONN): Davrin's son. A bard.

Martinel (Mar-tin-ELL): an ancestor of Mar Lon.

Mitrian (MIH-tree-in): Santagithi's daughter.

Monsamer (MON-sa-mer): one of Santagithi's guards.

Morhane (MORE-hayn): BÉARNIAN. King of Béarn. Valar's younger twin.

Mukesh (Myu-KESH): a merchant's son in Santagithi's Town.

Nantel (Nan-TELL): Santagithi's archer captain.

Nito (NEE-toe): one of Santagithi's guards.

Quantar (QUAN-tar): one of Santagithi's guards.

Quillinar (QUILL-ih-nar): one of Santagithi's guards.

Rusha (RUSH-a): Bel's youngest child. A girl.

Santagithi (San-TAG-ih-thigh): the Westland's best strategist. Leader of the Town of Santagithi.

Sterrane (Stir-RAIN): BÉARNIAN. A hermit in the Granite Hills.

Valar (VAY-lar): Morhane's twin. Murdered for the throne.

Zaran (ZAHR-in): one of Santagithi's guards.

Easterners

Abrith (A-brayth): a young peasant.

Harrsha (HAR-sha): one of Siderin's first lieutenants.

Narisen (NAIR-eh-son): Siderin's other first lieutenant.

Siderin (SID-er-in): King of the Eastlands.

Trinthka (TRANTH-ka): a peasant.

Tyrle (Tie-AR-lay): an elderly peasant.

Animals

Bein (BAYN): Rache's black stallion.

Raven: a horse in Nordmir owned by the Northern king.

Secodon (SEK-o-don): Shadimar's wolf.

Stubs: Arduwyn's donkey.

Swiftwing: a falcon. The Cardinal Wizards' messenger.

Gods & Wizards

Northern

Aegir (AY-jeer): Northern god of the sea.

Baldur (BALL-der): Northern god of beauty and gentleness.

Frey (FRAY): Northern god of rain, sunshine, and fortune.

Freya (FRAY-a): Frey's sister. Northern goddess of battle.

Frigg (FRIGG): Odin's wife. Northern goddess of fate.

Hati (HAH-tee): the wolf who swallows the moon at the *Ragnarok*.

Hel: Northern goddess of the cold underrealm for those who do not die in valorous combat.

Heimdall (HIME-dahl): Northern god of vigilance and father of mankind.

Loki (LOH-kee): Northern god of fire and guile.

Magni (MAG-nee): Thor's and Sif's son. Northern god of might.

Mana-garmr (MAH-nah Garm): Northern wolf destined to extinguish the sun with the blood of men at the *Ragnarok*.

Modi (MOE-dee): Thor's and Sif's son. Northern god of blood wrath.

Odin (OH-din): Northern leader of the pantheon. Father of the gods.

Sif (SIFF): Thor's wife. Northern goddess of fertility and fidelity.

Skol (SKOEWL): Northern wolf who will swallow the sun at the *Ragnarok*.

Syn (SIN): Northern goddess of justice and innocence.

Thor (THOR): Northern god of storms, farmers, and law.

Trilless (Trill-ESS): Northern Wizard. Champion of goodness and the Northlands.

Tyr (TEER): Northern one-handed god of war and faith.

Western

Aphrikelle (Ah-fri-KELL): Western goddess of spring.

Cathan (KAY-than): Western goddess of war, specifically hand to hand combat. Twin to Kadrak.

Dakoi (Dah-KOY): Western god of death.

The Faceless god: Western god of winter.

Firfan (FEER-fan): Western god of archers and hunters.

Itu (EE-too): Western goddess of knowledge and truth.

Kadrak (KAD-drak): Western god of war. Twin to Cathan.

Ruaidhri (Roo-AY-dree): Western leader of the pantheon.

Shadimar (SHAD-ih-mar): Eastern Wizard. Champion of neutrality and the Westlands.

Suman (SOO-mon): Western god of farmers and peasants.

Tokar (TOE-kar): Western Wizard. Champion of neutrality and the Westlands.

Weese (WEESSS): Western god of winds.

Yvesen (IV-e-sen): Western god of steel and women.

Zera'im (ZAIR-a-eem): Western god of honor.

Eastern

Carcophan (KAR-ka-fan): Southern Wizard. Champion of evil and the Eastlands.

God: the only name for the bird/man god of the Leukenyans. Created by Siderin.

Sheriva (Sha-REE-vah): omnipotent, only god of the Eastlands.

Foreign words

aristiri (ah-riss-TEER-ee): TRADING. a breed of singing hawks.

bein (bayn): NORTHERN. 'legs'.

chroams (krohms): WESTERN. specific coinage of copper, silver, or gold.

corpa (KOR-pa): WESTERN. 'brotherhood, town' lit. 'body'.

demon (DEE-mun): ANCIENT TONGUE. a creature of magic.

Einherjar (INE-herr-yar): NORTHERN. 'the dead warriors in Valhalla'.

Forsvarir (fours-var-EER): RENSHAI. a specific disarming maneuver.

galn (gahln): NORTHERN. 'ferociously crazy'.

garn (garn): NORTHERN. 'yarn'.

Gerlinr (Gerr-LEEN): RENSHAI. a specific aesthetic and difficult sword maneuver.

Harval (Harr-VALL): ANCIENT TONGUE. 'the gray blade'.

kenya (KEN-ya): WESTERN. 'bird'.

kjaelnavnir (kyahl-NAHV-neer): RENSHAI. temporary name for a child until a hero's name becomes available.

kinesthe (Kin-ESS-teh): NORTHERN. 'strength'.

leuk (Luke): WESTERN. 'white'.

lonriset (LON-ri-set): WESTERN. a ten-stringed musical instrument.

magni (MAG-nee): NORTHERN. 'might'.

modi (MOE-dee): NORTHERN. 'wrath'.

Morshock (MORE-shock): ANCIENT TONGUE. 'sword of darkness'.

mynten (MIN-tin): NORTHERN. a specific type of coin.

Ristoril (RIS-tor-ril): ANCIENT TONGUE. 'sword of tranquility'.

svergelse (swerr-GELL-seh): RENSHAI. 'sword figures practiced alone; katas'.

torke (TOR-keh): RENSHAI. 'teacher, sword instructor'.

uvakt (oo-VAKT): RENSHAI. 'the unguarded' A term for children whose *kjaelnavnir* becomes a permanent name.

Valhalla (VAWL-holl-a): NORTHERN. 'Hall of the Slain'. The walled 'heaven' for brave warriors slain in battle.

valr (VAWL): NORTHERN. 'slayer'.

Valkyrie (VAWL-kerr-ee): NORTHERN. 'Chooser of the Slain'.

wisule (WISS-ool): TRADING. a foul-smelling, disease-carrying breed of rodents which has many offspring because the adults will abandon them when threatened.

Places

Northlands

The area north of the Weathered Mountains and west of the Great Frenum Range. The Northmen live in eighteen tribes, each with its own town surrounded by forest and farmland. The boundaries change, and the map is correct for the year 11,240.

Asci (ASS-kee): home to the Ascai. Patron god: Aegir.

Blathe (BLAYTH-eh): home to the Blathe. Patron god: Aegir.

Drymir (DRY-meer): home to the Drymirians. Patron: Frey.

Devil's Island: an island in the Amirannak. A home to the Renshai after their exile.

Dvaulir (Dwah-LEER): home to the Dvaulirians. Patron: Thor.

Erd (URD): home to the Erdai. Patron goddess: Freya.

Farbutiri (Far-byu-TEER-ee): home to the Farbui. Patron: Aegir.

Gilshnir (GEELSH-neer): home to the Gilshni. Patron: Tyr.

Gjar (GYAR): home to the Gjar. Patron: Heimdall.

Kor N'rual (KOR en-ROOL): sacred crypts near Nordmir.

Nordmir (NORD-meer): the Northland's high kingdom. Home to the Nordmirians. Patron: Odin.

Othkin (OTH-keen): home to the Othi. Patron: Aegir & Frigg.

Renshi (Ren-SHEE): original home of the Renshai, now a part of Thortire. Patron: Sif & Modi.

Shamir (Sha-MEER): home of the Shamirians. Patron: Freya.

Skrytil (SKRY-teel): home of the Skrytila. Patron: Thor.

Svelbni (SWELL-nee): home of the Svelbnai. Patron: Baldur.

Talmir (TAHL-meer): home of the Talmirians. Patron: Frey.

Thortire (Thor-TEER-eh): home of the Thortirians. Patron: Thor.

Varli (VAR-lee): home of the Varlians. Patron: Frey & Freya.

Vikerin (Vee-KAIR-in): home of the Vikerians. Patron: Thor.

Westlands

The Westlands are bounded by the Great Frenum Mountains to the east, the Weathered Mountains to the north, and the sea to the west and south. In general, the cities become larger and more civilized as the land sweeps westward. The central area is packed with tiny farm towns dwarfed by lush farm fields that, over time, have nearly coalesced. The easternmost portions of the Westlands are forested, with sparse towns and rare barbarian tribes. To the south lies an uninhabited tidal plain.

Ahktar (AHK-tar): one of the largest central farm towns.

Auer (OUR): a small town in the eastern section.

Béarn (Bay-ARN): the high kingdom. A mountain city.

Bellenet Fields (Bell-e-NAY): a tourney field in Erythane.

Bruen (Broo-EN): a medium-sized city near Pudar.

Corpa Bickat (KORE-pa Bi-KAY): a large city.

Corpa Leukenya (KORE-pa Loo-KEN-ya): home of the cult of the white bird, created by Siderin

Corpa Schaull (KORE-pa Shawl): a medium-sized city; one of the 'Twin Cities' (see Frist).

Erythane (AIR-eh-thane): a large city closely allied with Béarn. Famous for its knights.

The Fields of Wrath: legendary home to the Western Renshai.

Frist (FRIST): a medium-sized city; one of the 'Twin Cities' (see Corpa Schaull).

Granite Hills: a small, low range of mountains.

Great Frenum Mountains (FREN-um): towering, impassable mountains that divide the Eastlands from the Westlands and Northlands.

Greentree: a tiny farm town.

Iaplege (EE-a-pleej): a secret gathering place of cripples, criminals, and outcasts.

Loven (Low-VENN): a medium-sized city.

Myrcidë (Meer-si-DAY): a town of legendary wizards, now in ruins.

Porvada (Poor-VAH-da): a medium-sized city.

Pudar (Poo-DAR): the largest city of the West; the great trade center.

The Road of Kings: the legendary route by which the Eastern Wizard is believed to have rescued the high king's heir after a bloody coup.

Town of Santagithi: a medium-sized town, relatively young.
Shidrin (SHIH-drin): a farm town.
Sholton-Or (SHOLE-tin OR): a Western farm town.
Strinia (STRINN-ee-a): a small, barbarian settlement.
Western Plains: a barren salt flat.
Wolf Point: a rock formation in the forest surrounding Erythane.
Wynix (Why-NIX): a farm town.

Eastlands

The area east of the Great Frenum Mountains. It is a vast,
  overpopulated wasteland filled with crowded cities and eroded
  fields. Little forest remains.
LaZar the Decadent (LA-zar): a poor, dirty city.
Rock of Peace: a stone near the road from Rozmath to Stalmize
  where the bard, Mar Lon, preached peace.
Rozmath (ROZZ-mith): a medium-sized city.
Stalmize (STAHL-meez): the Eastern high kingdom.

Bodies of Water

Amirannak Sea (A-MEER-an-nak): the Northernmost ocean.
Brunn River (BRUN): a muddy river in the Northlands.
Conus River (KONE-uss): a shared river of the Eastlands and
  Westlands.
Icy River: a cold, Northern river.
Jewel River: one of the rivers that flows to Trader's Lake.
Perionyx River (Peh-ree-ON-ix): a Western river.
Southern Sea: the southernmost ocean.
Trader's Lake: a harbor for trading boats in Pudar.
Trader's River: the main route for overwater trade.

Objects

Cardinal Wizards: a system of balance created by Odin in the
  beginning of time consisting of four, near immortal opposing
  guardians of evil, neutrality, and goodness who are tightly
  constrained by Odin's laws.
The Pica Stone (PIE-ka): a clairsentient sapphire. One of the rare
  items with magical power.

The Seven Tasks of Wizardry: a series of tasks designed by the gods to test the power and worth of the Cardinal Wizards' chosen successors.

Swords of Power: three magical swords crafted by the Cardinal Wizards and kept on the plain of magic except in the hands of a Wizard's champion. It is prophesied that the world will end if all three are brought into the world at once.

Lines of the Cardinal Wizards

Western

Reign	Name	Sex	Apprenticeship	Notes
0–747	Rudiger	male	—	
747–1167	Montroy	male	695–747	
1167–1498	Jaela	female	1122–1167	
1498–2013	Melandry	female	1460–1498	
2013–2632	Dorn	male	1977–2013	
2632–2933	Tellyn	male	2599–2632	
2933–3759	Dane	male	2880–2933	
3759–4741	Annika	female	3705–3759	
4741–5085	Niejal	male	4691–4741	*
5085–5633	Bael	male	5020–5085	
5633–6236	Renata	female	5602–5633	
6236–6535	Caulin	male	6178–6236	
6535–7455	Sonjia	female	6500–6535	
7455–7926	Sudyar	male	7406–7455	**
7926–8426	Shelvyan	male	7878–7926	
8426–8814	Natalia	female	8380–8426	
8814–9522	Rebah	female	8771–8814	
9522–10,194	Muir	female	9476–9522	
10,194–10,556	Vikeltrin	male	10,146–10,194	
10,556–11,225	Tokar	male	10,500–10,556	

* insane
** no contact with other wizards

Eastern

Reign	Name	Sex	Apprenticeship	Notes
0–636	Kadira	female	—	
636–934	Rhynnel	female	601–636	
934–1299	Raf	male	897–934	
1299–2086	Aklir	male	1258–1299	
2086–2988	Trinn	female	2057–2086	
2988–3319	Gherhan	male	2940–2988	*
3319–3768	Benghta	female	3317–3319	
3768–4278	Shorfin	male	3742–3768	
4278–4937	Annber	female	4246–4278	
4937–5439	Mikay	male	4900–4937	
5439–5818	Takian	male	5400–5439	
5818–6298	Seguin	male	5788–5818	
6298–6657	Resa	female	6265–6298	
6657–7221	Elcott	male	6612–6657	
7221–7665	L'effrich	female	7180–7221	
7665–7971	Dandriny	female	7640–7665	
7971–8289	Mylynn	male	7941–7971	
8289–9083	Ascof	male	8243–8289	**
9098–9426	Pinahar	male	—	
9426–9734	Jalona	female	9389–9426	
9734–10,221	Zibetha	female	9700–9734	
10,221–10,737	Drero	male	10,187–10,221	
10,737–11,126	Donnell	male	10,700–10,737	
11,126–	Shadimar	male	11,100–11,126	

* killed by demon
** killed by demon

Northern

Reign	Name	Sex	Apprenticeship	Notes
0–790	Tertrilla	female	—	
790–1276	Mendir	male	743–790	
1276–1897	Reeguar	male	1217–1276	
1897–2739	Ranulf	male	1848–1897	
2739–3138	Chane	male	2688–2739	
3138–3614	Sigrid	female	3087–3138	
3614–4128	Quisiria	female	3570–3614	
4128–4792	Brill	male	4083–4128	
4792–5289	Xansiki	female	4751–4792	
5289–5854	Johirild	male	5254–5289	
5854–6531	Disa	female	5813–5854	
6531–7249	Tagrin	male	6492–6531	
7249–7747	Elthor	male	7202–7249	
7747–8369	Frina	female	7700–7747	
8369–8954	Yllen	female	8312–8369	
8954–9628	Alengrid	female	8922–8954	
9628–10,244	Sval	male	9590–9628	
10,244–10,803	Giddrin	male	10,210–10,244	
10,803–	Trilless	female	10,762–10,803	

Southern

Reign	Name	Sex	Apprenticeship	Notes
0–810	Havlar	male	—	
810–1306	Kaffrint	male	767–810	
1306–1821	Pelchrin	male	1270–1306	
1821–2798	Schatza	female	1762–1821	
2798–3510	Ocrell	male	2750–2798	
3510–4012	Laurn	male	3461–3510	
4012–4690	Quart	male	3954–4012	*
4690–5189	Ufi	male	4687–4690	
5189–5925	Achorfin	female	5130–5189	
5925–6617	Mir	female	5872–5925	
6617–7217	Nalexia	male	6574–6617	
7217–7793	Buchellin	male	7177–7217	
7793–8508	Amta	male	7747–7793	
8508–8991	Kaleira	female	8450–8508	
8991–9614	Zittich	male	8940–8991	
9614–10,284	Pladnor	male	9565–9614	
10,284–11,002	Bontu	male	10,220–10,284	
11,002–	Carcophan	male	10,968–11,002	

* killed by Ristoril